Introduction
to the Dover Edition

It is generally recognized that Joseph Sheridan LeFanu (1814-1873) was the greatest of Victorian ghost story writers. A metaphysician in an unmetaphysical age, he wrote many stories like "The Watcher," "Green Tea," "Carmilla" and "The Haunted Baronet" that are unique in their narrative skill, emotional power, and profundity. His best work is as living today as it was when first written, and it is not merely chance that "Carmilla," the best of all vampire stories, has moved into the sister arts of the motion picture and experimental opera.

LeFanu's supernatural work is wide in range, certainly the most varied of his century. He wrote stories on folkloristic themes, in which the fairy lore of his Ireland was transformed into stories of quaint menace and sometimes rough humor; he also wrote sombre fate-stories, tales of supernatural vengeance for past injuries. In his work are to be found stories of material horror and diabolic visions, and there are also strangely involuted tales in which the universe is a vast living machine that parallels the human mind, with plants and birds and swamps as materialized symbols. Best of all are his highly personal stories of tortuous psychologies, of remarkable guilts and their hypostatization, of strange states of consciousness and unconsciousness, where the boundaries of the fanciful and the real swirl away into a mist of pain and terror.

In external circumstance there is little to reveal the strange inner life
that must have permeated the organism known as Joseph Sheridan
LeFanu. Born in Dublin in 1814, the son of the Rev. Dean Philip
LeFanu, he was descended from Huguenot refugees and the gifted
Sheridan family, Richard Brinsley Sheridan being his great-uncle.
Reared in the brilliant last-gasp of Anglo-Irish culture, mostly around
Dublin and Limerick, he attended Trinity College, and after a brief interest in the law (in which he paralleled Dickens and Wilkie Collins) he
entered journalism. He was a successful businessman, editing and
publishing several newspapers and periodicals; the most important was
the *Dublin University Magazine*, which under his management became a
journal of international reputation. His life was uneventful, and it is
curious to note that none of the great cultural cataclysms that beset
Ireland during his lifetime—the great famine, the emigration, the
political upheavals—is reflected in his fiction. Politically he considered
himself an Irishman, and his sympathies were with Irish nationalism,
but within the English system.

Just as his stories often have many layers of meaning and have
changed in tone over the years, his personality seems to have been very
complex. On the one hand he was remembered as a very pleasant, witty
man, with a puckish sense of humor that manifested itself occasionally
in practical jokes. Less obvious to his contemporaries, on the other
hand, were the worlds of blackness that his inner mind inhabited. In his
later years he became practically a recluse, pondering spiritual
problems, fascinated by the thought of Swedenborg (though not a convert), writing his fiction in the dark hours of the morning, stimulated by
green tea. He died in 1873, presumably of a heart attack. According to
the often-repeated anecdote, he had been suffering from a repetitive
nightmare: a strange high house towered dizzily above him, about to
collapse on him. When his body was examined by the physician who
attended him, the physician remarked that the house had finally
collapsed. His own house, however, now 80 Meryon Square, Dublin,
once a center of Dublin brilliance, still stands, with a blue marker com-
memorating LeFanu. I came upon it by accident not too long ago.

II

LeFanu was a fairly prolific writer, with fourteen novels, some of
them of considerable length; many short stories; articles; reviews;
poems; political journalism; and miscellaneous editorial work. His
exact production is not certain, since, in accordance with the custom of
the day, much of his work was published anonymously as ephemeral
journalism. Many of his novels and short stories, in addition to book
publication, appeared in major English periodicals such as *Belgravia*,
London Society, *Temple Bar*, and Dickens's *All the Year Round*.

With this present collection and its predecessor, *Best Ghost Stories of*

J.S. LeFanu, all LeFanu's ghost stories are now in print. These include all the supernatural stories from the fabulously rare *Ghost Stories and Tales of Mystery* (1851), the major *In a Glass Darkly* (1872), the posthumous *Purcell Papers* (1880), and the many stories that appeared in contemporary periodicals or were imbedded as gems in his longer, more prosaic novels.

Several of the ghostly stories here are among LeFanu's better work. They were omitted from the previous volume partly for reasons of space, partly because they recapitulated themes that LeFanu had used in other stories. Other stories, however, show LeFanu not as the Invisible Prince, as he was called in his lifetime, but as an immature writer with a humorous touch, or as a reworker of the folklore of his native land. While these last are not the great LeFanu, they are still inimitable in their own way, still superior to most of the work of his contemporaries, so far did he tower above them in this area.

"The Drunkard's Dream" (*Dublin University Magazine*, 1838) and "The Vision of Tom Chuff" (*All the Year Round*, 1870) fall together as variants on a basic theme that seems to have interested LeFanu, since he reworked it several times: a physical confrontation with Evil, sometimes Hell, sometimes the Devil. It isolates Evil as a peculiar experience that can befall man, something that comes from outside, yet is matched from inside, perhaps like ground and sky lightning. But man must open the doors to it. More sophisticated, more elaborate versions of this idea, of course, are to be found in LeFanu's "Green Tea" and "The Watcher."

The element of folklore enters strongly in several of the other stories. "Stories of Lough Guir" (*All the Year Round*, 1870) is based on folktales that LeFanu heard as a young man from the lips of one of the most noted storytellers of his day, a Miss Anne Baily of Lough Guir in Limerick. While the point is overlooked at times, since LeFanu made little direct use of folklore in his major fiction, he did have an interest in collecting folktales. He is known to have assisted Samuel Carter Hall and his wife Anna Maria in their compilation of fictionalized Irish folk stories.

Original, though based on folklore, is "The Ghost and the Bone-Setter" (*Dublin University Magazine*, 1838), which is probably LeFanu's first published fiction. Its humor is less unexpected when one remembers that LeFanu wrote a fair amount of humorous verse. Of similar origin—a fine retelling of a common Irish folktale—is "The Child That Went with the Fairies" (*All the Year Round*, 1870). Many of the other versions of this story go on to reveal the way that the child was ultimately rescued. It is to LeFanu's credit that he left it a mystery. "Laura Silver Bell" (*Belgravia Annual*, 1872) maintains the same theme, but with a more individual treatment. It is one of many stories that LeFanu localized in the North of England, around the mythical Golden Friars.

"Ghost Stories of Chapelizod" (*Dublin University Magazine*, 1851) is connected with LeFanu's later novel, *The House by the Churchyard* (1863). Both are set in a then rural suburb of Dublin, in the early eighteenth century, when it was a garrison town for the Royal Irish Artillery. Whether the wicked Captain Devereux of the ghost story is the Captain Devereux of *The House by the Churchyard*, however, is very doubtful, since the soldier in the novel is an honorable man. LeFanu simply had a penchant for reusing certain names which he liked: Marston, Devereux, Cresseron, Mardyke, and others.

Two of LeFanu's most chilling tales are "Wicked Captain Walshawe, of Wauling" (*Dublin University Magazine*, 1869) and "Dickon the Devil" (*London Society*, 1872). The first conveys suggestions of the horrific wake in Maturin's *Melmoth the Wanderer*; the second is more conventionally conceived, but is masterfully told.

The remaining ghost story in this collection, "The Mysterious Lodger" (*Dublin University Magazine*, 1850), is problematic. It was printed anonymously, was never reprinted in any of the later LeFanu collections, and (to the best of my knowledge) was never claimed by LeFanu. It is very unlike anything else that LeFanu wrote in subject matter, presentation, values, and style. At this point it might be well to make a small digression and explain how the canon of LeFanu's fiction has been achieved. LeFanu seems to have kept very detailed working ledgers of his writings, but these were lost after his death, and since most of his shorter fiction was published anonymously, his canon has had to be established by indirect means. This was done mostly by one man, the noted ghost-story writer and scholar Montague Rhodes James, who spent much time working through files of Victorian periodicals trying to identify LeFanu's contributions by means of names, settings, motives, and cross references. His work was continued by S. M. Ellis. In the collection of LeFanu's stories entitled *Madam Crowl's Ghost* (1923) edited by James, James was the first to attribute "The Mysterious Lodger" to LeFanu: "I find the following stories which are undoubtedly by LeFanu, though they do not bear his name." James was followed in this attribution by S. M. Ellis and Nelson Browne. My own belief is that this is all a mistake, and that LeFanu did not write "The Mysterious Lodger." But in deference to the men who have really established LeFanu studies, I am including it in this collection. They may be right. In any case, it is an unusual story, and my expression of doubt may evoke some proof of its authorship.

III

From LeFanu's ghost stories to his tales of mystery is an easy transition; he apparently did not feel a strong line of demarcation between the two forms. His ghost stories often have elements of crime and mystery in them, and his mystery stories often contain elements of supernaturalism. In *The Wyvern Mystery* (1869), for example, which is LeFanu's version of *Jane Eyre*, a supernatural black veil falls from a certain doorway, sending up clouds of unreal dust, presaging evil to come —even though the remainder of the story is matter-of-fact. Complete independent ghost stories sometimes occur within the novels, such as the fine "Madam Crowl's Ghost" in "A Strange Adventure in the Life of Miss Laura Mildmay" (1871) or the ghost stories of the Tyled House in *The House by the Churchyard* (1863). Fate, even divine destiny, too, may play a part in the murder mysteries. The doom of Mark Wylder in *Wylder's Hand* (1864) is foretold by a mysterious Oriental ring; omens and an ancient prophecy foretell the extinction of the house of Shadwell in *A Lost Name* (1868), and Laura Challys Gray in *Haunted Lives* (1868) is, in a way, a supernatural instrument of vengeance.

Much of LeFanu's output consisted of mystery fiction. A tally reveals the mildly surprising result that his mystery fiction outweighs his supernatural fiction, in wordage, perhaps four or five to one. Among his long novels that are unquestionably Victorian mystery and detection stories are *The House by the Churchyard* (1863), *Wylder's Hand* (1864), *Uncle Silas* (1864), *Guy Deverell* (1865), *The Tenants of Malory* (1867), *A Lost Name* (1868), *Haunted Lives* (1868), and *Checkmate* (1871). "The Evil Guest" (1851, in *Ghost Stories and Tales of Mystery*) and "A Strange Adventure in the Life of Miss Laura Mildmay" (in *Chronicles of Golden Friars*, 1871) are shorter mystery novels. By stretching definitions a little, *The Cock and Anchor* (1845), *The Wyvern Mystery* (1869), and *The Rose and the Key* (1871) may also be included, since there are mysterious things going on in the background.

The element of quality, unfortunately, is not always present in LeFanu's novels, and a modern reader may suspect that LeFanu deliberately slanted his novels toward the mass market, rather than (as in the case with his best supernatural fiction) writing the story as he wanted it well. Yet not all these novels should be forgotten. *Uncle Silas* is preeminent, the best Victorian mystery novel, a novel that is pointed in direction, incredibly sustained in mood through every scene and setting, thrilling, and thought-provoking. As for the other novels, opinions change with the times.

With earlier readers, *The House by the Churchyard*, *Checkmate*, and *Wylder's Hand* were favorites. Modern readers, however, may not always treasure the same characteristics as did the Victorians and Edwardians. *The House by the Churchyard* has remarkable comic episodes involving the Royal Irish garrison at Chapelizod, and a thrilling scene as the renegade surgeon Black Dillon performs a trepanation that may unlock the silence of a dying man, and is certain to cause several deaths. But the novel as a whole is episodic, unconvincing, and confusing, and the reader may lose himself in a welter of minor Dickensian characters who have little to do with the story. *Checkmate* and *Wylder's Hand* are murder mysteries, but they are also lengthy society novels that bow to Victorian fictional conventions too much. They are overlong, rambling, and in places simply boring.

Much more to the modern taste are *Haunted Lives* and *A Lost Name*, which LeFanu's contemporaries seem to have regarded with indifference, and the Edwardians did not like. It is my guess that these will be the novels most appreciated in the near future. They are strong and sparse in story, economical in episode and character, saturated with a mood of inevitability, brilliantly written, and fascinating in their symbolic abstraction: the reader at times feels himself involved in cosmic processes of good and evil. *A Lost Name*, once a slow beginning is passed, offers remarkable dialogue. *Haunted Lives* is an incredibly sustained ambiguity: although the modern reader soon recognizes that one of the characters is in masquerade, and that there is no mystery in this aspect of the novel, he must admire the skill with which LeFanu flaunts the ambiguity, instead of concealing it. Both these novels have fewer market tricks than the other novels. Unfortunately, they were never reissued in cheap reprints, and are practically unobtainable.

LeFanu's shorter mysteries, on the whole, are more satisfying than the novels, although here a special aspect of his working habits calls for comment. This is his practice of using the same material over and over: sometimes as a short story, then as a short novel, then as a long novel. Whether he did this for the sake of utilizing the baked meats, or whether he felt that he could retell the story better is not known, but the end is that the reader is likely to notice similarities from one story to another, though these are seldom strong enough to destroy one's anticipation.

"A Chapter in the History of a Tyrone Family" first appeared in the *Dublin University Magazine* in 1839, and it has often been cited as a source for *Jane Eyre*. Thirty years later LeFanu used the same basic situation in expanded form as *The Wyvern Mystery*, although he would seem consciously to have moved his novel in different directions from that taken by *Jane Eyre*. The sequences with the malign blind Dutchwoman, Bertha Velderkaust, are among the strongest LeFanu ever wrote, but LeFanu, after sustaining the mystery of the horror-bride for a time, discards it and moves on to a subtler, more potent form of evil. If the reader does not mind a leisurely novel with a contrived ending that is a sop to sentimentality, he may be pleased to read *The Wyvern Mystery*. It has many strengths.

"Passage in the Secret History of an Irish Countess" was first published in the *Dublin University Magazine* in 1838; it was reprinted, with slight alterations, under the title "The Murdered Cousin" in *Ghost Stories and Tales of Mystery* (1851), which latter text has been followed in this collection. An odd touch in LeFanu's revision is that he brought the names of the characters in line with Godwin's *Caleb Williams*, which is the first important detective novel. "The Murdered Cousin" marks LeFanu's first use of a theme that occurs many times in his work: the hidden persecutor, the embodiment of evil, masquerading as virtue. Uncle Silas, Longcluse of *Checkmate*, Alfred Dacre of *Haunted Lives*, Paul Dangerfield of *The House by the Churchyard*, Lady Vernon of *The Rose and the Key* all share this Gothic aspect, with which LeFanu usually associates pallor.

The reader should also note LeFanu's use of a sealed-room situation which avoids the puerilities of the secret passages and similar devices often found in the earlier Gothic and Romantic literature. While proclaiming first occasions is dangerous, this story seems to present the first seriously thought-out, conscious sealed-room situation in modern mystery fiction. LeFanu retained the mechanism when he expanded "The Murdered Cousin" into *Uncle Silas*.

LeFanu also made use of an isolated-room mystery (it is not rigorous enough to be a sealed room) in the tri-story "Some Account of the Latter Days of the Hon. Richard Marston of Dunoran" (*Dublin University Magazine*, 1848), "The Evil Guest" (*Ghost Stories and Tales of Mystery*, 1851), and *A Lost Name* (1868). What seemed to be a sealed exit turns out to have been accessible, permitting the true murderer to enter. Within this tri-story LeFanu retained the basic situation, but made many changes in detail. When he adapted "Richard Marston" to "The Evil Guest," he cut it somewhat, abandoned one of the subplots, and in general tightened up the story. He also shifted the setting from eighteenth-century Ireland to eighteenth-century England. For *A Lost Name* the setting was changed to Victorian England, and a different cast of characters provided. The novel version offers one of LeFanu's greatest achievements, the half-mad maunderings of the pseudo-murderer Carmel Sherlock.

The last of LeFanu's important tales of mystery is "The Room in the Dragon Volant" (*London Society*, 1872), which is easily one of the best mystery-adventure stories of the nineteenth century. In this story LeFanu invaded the territory of Wilkie Collins quite successfully, creating an exotic background, an involved plot with many fine touches, and strong, vital characters (as opposed to the muted personalities of the fiction that is more peculiarly his own).

"The Room in the Dragon Volant," with its subtle misdirections and reversible web, is such a successful work that I regret that LeFanu did not live to work more in this vein. While no one would want to be without *In a Glass Darkly* and *Uncle Silas* and several of the supernatural stories, most of us would be happy to exchange *All in the Dark* and *Willing to Die* for another "Room in the Dragon Volant."

But this is an if of history that did not occur, and we must remain grateful to LeFanu for the best ghost stories of the Victorian period, the best mystery novel, and a host of smaller greatnesses.

— E. F. BLEILER

New York, 1973

Contents

THE ROOM IN
THE DRAGON VOLANT

PROLOGUE

The curious case which I am about to place before you, is referred to, very pointedly, and more than once, in the extraordinary Essay upon the drugs of the Dark and the Middle Ages, from the pen of Doctor Hesselius.

This Essay he entitles *Mortis Imago*, and he, therein, discusses the *Vinum letiferum*, the *Beatifica*, the *Somnus Angelorum*, the *Hypnus Sagarum*, the *Aqua Thessalliae*, and about twenty other infusions and distillations, well known to the sages of eight hundred years ago, and two of which are still, he alleges, known to the fraternity of thieves, and, among them, as police-office inquiries sometimes disclose to this day, in practical use.

The Essay, *Mortis Imago*, will occupy as nearly as I can, at present, calculate, two volumes, the ninth and tenth, of the collected papers of Doctor Martin Hesselius.

This Essay, I may remark, in conclusion, is very curiously enriched by citations, in great abundance, from mediaeval verse and prose romance, some of the most valuable of which, strange to say, are Egyptian.

I have selected this particular statement from among many cases equally striking, but hardly, I think, so effective as mere narratives, in this irregular form of publication, it is simply as a story that I present it.

CHAPTER I

On the Road

In the eventful year, 1815, I was exactly three-and-twenty, and had just succeeded to a very large sum in consols, and other securities. The first fall of Napoleon had thrown the continent open to English excursionists, anxious, let us suppose, to improve their minds by foreign travel; and I—the slight check of the "hundred days" removed, by the genius of Wellington, on the field of Waterloo—was now added to the philosophic throng.

I was posting up to Paris from Bruxelles, following, I presume, the route that the allied army had pursued but a few weeks before—more carriages than you could believe were pursuing the same line. You could not look back or forward, without seeing into far perspective the clouds of dust which marked the line of the long series of vehicles. We were, perpetually, passing relays of return-horses, on their way, jaded and dusty, to the inns from which they had been taken. They were arduous times for those patient public servants. The whole world seemed posting up to Paris.

I ought to have noted it more particularly, but my head was so full of Paris and the future, that I passed the intervening scenery with little patience and less attention; I think, however, that it was about four miles to the frontier side of a rather picturesque little town, the name of which, as of many more important places through which I posted in my hurried journey, I forget, and about two hours before sunset, that we came up with a carriage in distress.

It was not quite an upset. But the two leaders were lying flat. The booted postillions had got down, and two servants who seemed very much at sea in such matters, were by way of assisting them. A pretty little bonnet and head were popped out of the window of the carriage in distress. Its *tournure*, and that of the shoulders that also appeared for a moment, was captivating: I resolved to play the part of a good Samaritan; stopped my chaise, jumped out, and with my servant lent a very willing hand in the emergency. Alas! the lady with the pretty bonnet wore a very thick, black veil. I could see nothing but the pattern of the Bruxelles lace, as she drew back.

A lean old gentleman, almost at the same time, stuck his head out of the window. An invalid he seemed, for although the day was hot, he wore a black muffler which came up to his ears and nose, quite covering the lower part of his face, an arrangement which he disturbed by pulling it down for a moment, and poured forth a torrent of French thanks, as he uncovered his black wig, and gesticulated with grateful animation.

One of my very few accomplishments besides boxing, which was cultivated by all Englishmen at that time, was French; and I replied, I hope and believe, grammatically. Many bows being exchanged, the old gentleman's head went in again, and the demure, pretty little bonnet once more appeared.

The lady must have heard me speak to my servant, for she framed her little speech in such pretty, broken English, and in a voice so sweet, that I more than ever cursed the black veil that baulked my romantic curiosity.

The arms that were emblazoned on the panel were peculiar; I remember especially, one device, it was the figure of a stork, painted in carmine, upon what the heralds call a "field or." The bird was standing upon one leg, and in the other claw held a stone. This is, I believe, the emblem of vigilance. Its oddity struck me, and remained impressed upon my memory. There were supporters besides, but I forget what they were.

The courtly manners of these people, the style of their servants, the elegance of their travelling carriage, and the supporters to their arms, satisfied me that they were noble.

The lady, you may be sure, was not the less interesting on that account. What a fascination a title exercises upon the imagination! I do not mean on that of snobs or moral flunkies. Superiority of rank is a powerful and genuine influence in love. The idea of superior refinement is associated with it. The careless notice of the squire tells more upon the heart of the pretty milkmaid, than years of honest Dobbin's manly devotion, and so on and up. It is an unjust world!

But in this case there was something more. I was conscious of being good looking. I really believe I was; and there could be no mistake about my being nearly six feet high. Why need this lady have thanked me? Had not her husband, for such I assumed him to be, thanked me quite enough, and for both? I was instinctively aware that the lady was looking on me with no unwilling eyes; and, through her veil, I felt the power of her gaze.

She was now rolling away, with a train of dust behind her wheels, in the golden sunlight, and a wise young gentleman followed her with ardent eyes, and sighed profoundly as the distance increased.

I told the postillions on no account to pass the carriage, but to keep it steadily in view, and to pull up at whatever posting-house it should stop at. We were soon in the little town, and the carriage we followed drew up at the Belle Etoile, a comfortable old inn. They got out of the carriage and entered the house.

At a leisurely pace we followed. I got down, and mounted the steps listlessly, like a man quite apathetic and careless.

Audacious as I was, I did not care to inquire in what room I should find them. I peeped into the apartment to my right, and then into that on my left. *My* people were not there.

I ascended the stairs. A drawing-room door stood open. I entered with the most innocent air in the world. It was a spacious room, and, beside myself, contained but one living figure—a very pretty and lady-like one. There was the very bonnet with which I had fallen in love. The lady stood with her back towards me. I could not tell whether the envious veil was raised; she was reading a letter.

I stood for a minute in fixed attention, gazing upon her, in the vague hope that she might turn about, and give me an opportunity of seeing her features. She did not; but with a step or two she placed herself before a little cabriole-table, which stood against the wall, from which rose a tall mirror, in a tarnished frame.

I might, indeed, have mistaken it for a picture; for it now reflected a half-length portrait of a singularly beautiful woman.

She was looking down upon a letter which she held in her slender fingers, and in which she seemed absorbed.

The face was oval, melancholy, sweet. It had in it, nevertheless, a faint and undefinably sensual quality also. Nothing could exceed the delicacy of its features, or the brilliancy of its tints. The eyes, indeed, were lowered, so that I could not see their colour; nothing but their long lashes, and delicate eyebrows. She continued reading. She must have been deeply interested; I never saw a living form so motionless—I gazed on a tinted statue.

Being at that time blessed with long and keen vision, I saw this beautiful face with perfect distinctness. I saw even the blue veins that traced their wanderings on the whiteness of her full throat.

I ought to have retreated as noiselessly as I came in, before my presence was detected. But I was too much interested to move from the spot, for a few moments longer; and while they were passing, she raised her eyes. Those eyes were large, and of that hue which modern poets term "violet."

These splendid melancholy eyes were turned upon me from the glass with a haughty stare, and hastily the lady lowered her black veil, and turned about.

I fancied that she hoped I had not seen her. I was watching every look and movement, the minutest, with an attention as intense as if an ordeal involving my life depended on them.

CHAPTER II

The Inn-Yard of the Belle Etoile

The face was, indeed, one to fall in love with at first sight. Those sentiments that take such sudden possession of young men were now dominating my curiosity. My audacity faltered before her; and I felt that my presence in this room was probably an impertinence. This point she quickly settled, for the same very sweet voice I had heard before, now said coldly, and this time in French, "Monsieur cannot be aware that this apartment is not public."

I bowed very low, faltered some apologies, and backed to the door.

I suppose I looked penitent and embarrassed. I certainly felt so; for the lady said, by way it seemed of softening matters, "I am happy, however, to have an opportunity of again thanking Monsieur for the assistance, so prompt and effectual, which he had the goodness to render us to-day."

It was more the altered tone in which it was spoken, than the speech itself that encouraged me. It was also true that she need not have recognised me; and even if she had, she certainly was not obliged to thank me over again.

All this was indescribably flattering, and all the more so that it followed so quickly on her slight reproof.

The tone in which she spoke had become low and timid, and I observed that she turned her head quickly towards a second door of the room, I fancied that the gentleman in the black wig, a jealous husband, perhaps, might reappear through it. Almost at the same moment, a voice at once reedy and nasal, was heard snarling some directions to a servant, and evidently approaching. It was the voice that had thanked me so profusely, from the carriage windows, about an hour before.

"Monsieur will have the goodness to retire," said the lady, in a tone that resembled entreaty, at the same time gently waving her hand towards the door through which I had entered. Bowing again very low, I stepped back, and closed the door.

I ran down the stairs, very much elated. I saw the host of the Belle Etoile which, as I said, was the sign and designation of my inn.

I described the apartment I had just quitted, said I liked it, and asked whether I could have it.

He was extremely troubled, but that apartment and the two adjoining rooms were engaged—

"By whom?"

"People of distinction."

"But who are they? They must have names, or titles."

"Undoubtedly, Monsieur, but such a stream is rolling into Paris, that we have ceased to inquire the names or titles of our guests—we designate them simply by the rooms they occupy."

"What stay do they make?"

"Even that, Monsieur, I cannot answer. It does not interest us. Our rooms, while this continues, can never be, for a moment, disengaged."

"I should have liked those rooms so much! Is one of them a sleeping apartment?"

"Yes, sir, and Monsieur will observe that people do not usually engage bedrooms, unless they mean to stay the night."

"Well, I can, I suppose, have some rooms, any, I don't care in what part of the house?"

"Certainly, Monsieur can have two apartments. They are the last at present disengaged."

I took them instantly.

It was plain these people meant to make a stay here; at least they would not go till morning. I began to feel that I was all but engaged in an adventure.

I took possession of my rooms, and looked out of the window, which I found commanded the inn-yard. Many horses were being liberated from the traces, hot and weary, and others fresh from the stables, being put to. A great many vehicles—some private carriages, others, like mine, of that public class, which is equivalent to our old English post-chaise, were standing on the pavement, waiting their turn for relays. Fussy servants were to-ing and fro-ing, and idle ones lounging or laughing, and the scene, on the whole, was animated and amusing.

Among these objects, I thought I recognised the travelling carriage, and one of the servants of the "persons of distinction" about whom I was, just then, so profoundly interested.

I therefore ran down the stairs, made my way to the back door; and so, behold me, in a moment, upon the uneven pavement, among all these sights and sounds which in such a place attend upon a period of extraordinary crush and traffic.

By this time the sun was near its setting, and threw its golden beams on the red brick chimneys of the offices, and made the two barrels, that figured as pigeon-houses, on the tops of poles, look as if they were on fire. Everything in this light becomes picturesque; and things interest us which, in the sober grey of morning, are dull enough.

After a little search, I lighted upon the very carriage, of which I was in quest. A servant was locking one of the doors, for it was made with the security of lock and key. I paused near, looking at the panel of the door.

"A very pretty device that red stork!" I observed, pointing to the shield on the door, "and no doubt indicates a distinguished family?"

The servant looked at me, for a moment, as he placed the little key in his pocket, and said with a slightly sarcastic bow and smile, "Monsieur is at liberty to conjecture."

Nothing daunted, I forthwith administered that laxative which, on occasion, acts so happily upon the tongue—I mean a "tip."

The servant looked at the Napoleon in his hand, and then, in my face, with a sincere expression of surprise.

"Monsieur is very generous!"

"Not worth mentioning—who are the lady and gentleman who came here, in this carriage, and whom, you may remember, I and my servant assisted to-day in an emergency, when their horses had come to the ground?"

"They are the Count, and the young lady we call the Countess—but I know not, she may be his daughter."

"Can you tell me where they live?"

"Upon my honour, Monsieur, I am unable—I know not."

"Not know where your master lives! Surely you know something more about him than his name?"

"Nothing worth relating, Monsieur; in fact, I was hired in Bruxelles, on the very day they started. Monsieur Picard, my fellow-servant, Monsieur the Comte's gentleman, he has been years in his service and knows everything; but he never speaks except to communicate an order. From him I have learned nothing. We are going to Paris, however, and there I shall speedily pick up all about them. At present I am as ignorant of all that as Monsieur himself."

"And where is Monsieur Picard?"

"He has gone to the cutler's to get his razors set. But I do not think he will tell anything."

This was a poor harvest for my golden sowing. The man, I think, spoke truth, and would honestly have betrayed the secrets of the family, if he had possessed any. I took my leave politely; and mounting the stairs, again I found myself once more in my room.

Forthwith I summoned my servant. Though I had brought him with me from England, he was a native of France—a useful fellow, sharp, bustling, and, of course, quite familiar with the ways and tricks of his countrymen.

"St. Clair, shut the door; come here. I can't rest till I have made out something about those people of rank who have got the apartments under mine. Here are fifteen francs; make out the servants we assisted to-day; have them to a *petit souper*, and come back and tell me their entire history. I have, this moment, seen one of them who knows nothing, and has communicated it. The other, whose name I forget, is the unknown nobleman's valet, and knows everything. Him you must pump. It is, of course, the venerable peer, and not the young lady who accompanies him, that interests me—you understand? Begone! fly! and return with all the details I sigh for, and every circumstance that can possibly interest me."

It was a commission which admirably suited the tastes and spirits of my worthy St. Clair, to whom, you will have observed, I had accustomed myself to talk with the peculiar familiarity which the old French comedy establishes between master and valet.

I am sure he laughed at me in secret; but nothing could be more polite and deferential.

With several wise looks, nods and shrugs, he withdrew; and looking down from my window, I saw him, with incredible quickness, enter the yard, where I soon lost sight of him among the carriages.

CHAPTER III

Death and Love Together Mated

When the day drags, when a man is solitary, and in a fever of impatience and suspense; when the minute-hand of his watch travels as slowly as the hour-hand used to do, and the hour-hand has lost all appreciable motion; when he yawns, and beats the devil's tattoo, and flattens his handsome nose against the window, and whistles tunes he hates, and, in short, does not know what to do with himself, it is deeply to be regretted that he cannot make a solemn dinner of three courses more than once in a day. The laws of matter, to which we are slaves, deny us that resource.

But in the times I speak of, supper was still a substantial meal, and its hour was approaching. This was consolatory. Three-quarters of an hour, however, still interposed. How was I to dispose of that interval?

I had two or three idle books, it is true, as travelling-companions; but there are many moods in which one cannot read. My novel lay with my rug and walking-stick on the sofa, and I did not care if the heroine and the hero were both drowned together in the water-barrel that I saw in the inn-yard under my window.

I took a turn or two up and down my room, and sighed, looking at myself in the glass, adjusted my great white "choker," folded and tied after Brummel, the immortal "Beau," put on a buff waistcoat and my blue swallow-tailed coat with gilt buttons; I deluged my pocket handkerchief with eau-de-Cologne (we had not then the variety of bouquets with which the genius of perfumery has since blessed us); I arranged my hair, on which I piqued myself, and which I loved to groom in those days. That dark-brown *chevelure*, with a natural curl, is now represented by a few dozen perfectly white hairs, and its place—a smooth, bald, pink head—knows it no more. But let us forget these mortifications. It was then rich, thick, and dark-brown. I was making a very careful toilet. I took my unexceptionable hat from its case, and placed it lightly on my wise head, as nearly as memory and practice enabled me to do so, at that very slight inclination which the immortal person I have mentioned was wont to give to his. A pair of light French gloves and a rather club-like knotted walking-stick, such as just then came into vogue, for a year or two again in England, in the phraseology of Sir Walter Scott's romances, "completed my equipment."

All this attention to effect, preparatory to a mere lounge in the yard, or on the steps of the Belle Etoile, was a simple act of devotion to the wonderful eyes which I had that evening beheld for the first time, and never, never could forget! In plain terms, it was all done in the vague, very vague hope that those eyes might behold the unexceptionable get-up of a melancholy slave, and retain the image, not altogether without secret approbation.

As I completed my preparations the light failed me; the last level streak of sunlight disappeared, and a fading twilight only remained. I sighed in unison with the pensive hour, and threw open the window, intending to look out for a moment before going downstairs. I perceived instantly that the window underneath mine was also open, for I heard two voices in conversation, although I could not distinguish what they were saying.

The male voice was peculiar; it was, as I told you, reedy and nasal. I knew it, of course, instantly. The answering voice spoke in those sweet tones which I recognised only too easily. The dialogue was only for a minute; the repulsive male voice laughed, I fancied, with a kind of devilish satire, and retired from the window, so that I almost ceased to hear it.

The other voice remained nearer the window, but not so near as at first.

It was not an altercation; there was evidently nothing the least exciting in the colloquy. What would I not have given that it had been a quarrel—a violent one—and I the redresser of wrongs, and the defender of insulted beauty! Alas! so far as I could pronounce upon the character of the tones I heard, they might be as tranquil a pair as any in existence. In a moment more the lady began to sing an odd little *chanson*. I need not remind you how much farther the voice is heard *singing* than speaking. I could distinguish the words. The voice was of that exquisitely sweet kind which is called, I believe, a semi-contralto; it had something pathetic, and something, I fancied, a little mocking in its tones. I venture a clumsy, but adequate translation of the words:

> "Death and Love, together mated,
>   Watch and wait in ambuscade;
> At early morn, or else belated,
>   They meet and mark the man or maid.
>
> "Burning sigh, or breath that freezes,
>   Numbs or maddens man or maid;
> Death or Love the victim seizes,
>   Breathing from their ambuscade."

"Enough, Madame!" said the old voice, with sudden severity. "We do not desire, I believe, to amuse the grooms and hostlers in the yard with our music."

The lady's voice laughed gaily.

"You desire to quarrel, Madame!" And the old man, I presume, shut down the window. Down it went, at all events, with a rattle that might easily have broken the glass.

Of all thin partitions, glass is the most effectual excluder of sound. I heard no more, not even the subdued hum of the colloquy.

What a charming voice this Countess had! How it melted, swelled, and trembled! How it moved, and even agitated me! What a pity that a hoarse old jackdaw should have power to crow down such a Philomel! "Alas! what a life it is!" I moralized, wisely. "That beautiful Countess, with the patience of an angel and the beauty of a Venus and the accomplishments of all the Muses, a slave! She knows perfectly who occupies the apartments over hers; she heard me raise my window. One may conjecture pretty well for whom that music was intended—ay, old gentleman, and for whom you suspected it to be intended."

In a very agreeable flutter I left my room, and descending the stairs, passed the Count's door very much at my leisure. There was just a chance that the beautiful songstress might emerge. I dropped my stick on the lobby, near their door, and you may be sure it took me some little time to pick it up! Fortune, nevertheless, did not favour me. I could not stay on the lobby all night picking up my stick, so I went down to the hall.

I consulted the clock, and found that there remained but a quarter of an hour to the moment of supper.

Every one was roughing it now, every inn in confusion; people might do at such a juncture what they never did before. Was it just possible that, for once, the Count and Countess would take their chairs at the table-d'hôte?

CHAPTER IV

Monsieur Droqville

Full of this exciting hope, I sauntered out, upon the steps of the Belle Etoile. It was now night, and a pleasant moonlight over everything. I had entered more into my romance since my arrival, and this poetic light heightened the sentiment. What a drama, if she turned out to be the Count's daughter, and in love with me! What a delightful—*tragedy*, if she turned out to be the Count's wife!

In this luxurious mood, I was accosted by a tall and very elegantly-made gentleman, who appeared to be about fifty. His air was courtly and graceful, and there was in his whole manner and appearance something so distinguished, that it was impossible not to suspect him of being a person of rank.

He had been standing upon the steps, looking out, like me, upon the moonlight effects that transformed, as it were, the objects and buildings in the little street. He accosted me, I say, with the politeness, at once easy and lofty, of a French nobleman of the old school. He asked me if I were not Mr. Beckett? I assented; and he immediately introduced himself as the Marquis d'Harmonville (this information he gave me in a

low tone), and asked leave to present me with a letter from Lord R——,
who knew my father slightly, and had once done me, also, a trifling
kindness.

This English peer, I may mention, stood very high in the political
world, and was named as the most probable successor to the distinguished post of English Minister at Paris.

I received it with a low bow, and read:

"*My Dear Beckett,*
    "I beg to introduce my very dear friend, the Marquis d'Harmonville,
who will explain to you the nature of the services it may be in your
power to render him and us."

He went on to speak of the Marquis as a man whose great wealth,
whose intimate relations with the old families, and whose legitimate influence with the court rendered him the fittest possible person for those
friendly offices which, at the desire of his own sovereign, and of our
government, he has so obligingly undertaken.

It added a great deal to my perplexity, when I read further—

"By-the-bye, Walton was here yesterday, and told me that your seat
was likely to be attacked; something, he says, is unquestionably going
on at Domwell. You know there is an awkwardness in my meddling
ever so cautiously. But I advise, if it is not very officious, your making
Haxton look after it, and report immediately. I fear it is serious. I ought
to have mentioned that, for reasons that you will see, when you have
talked with him for five minutes, the Marquis—with the concurrence of
all our friends—drops his title, for a few weeks, and is at present plain
Monsieur Droqville.

"I am this moment going to town, and can say no more.

                                            "Yours faithfully,
                                                "R——."

I was utterly puzzled. I could scarcely boast of Lord ——'s acquaintance. I knew no one named Haxton, and, except my hatter, no
one called Walton; and this peer wrote as if we were intimate friends! I
looked at the back of the letter, and the mystery was solved. And now,
to my consternation—for I was plain Richard Beckett—I read—

                "To George Stanhope Beckett, Esq., M.P."

I looked with consternation in the face of the Marquis.

"What apology can I offer to Monsieur the Mar—to Monsieur Droqville? It is true my name is Beckett—it is true I am known, though very
slightly to Lord R——; but the letter was not intended for me. My

name is Richard Beckett—this is to Mr. Stanhope Beckett, the member for Shillingsworth. What can I say, or do, in this unfortunate situation? I can only give you my honour as a gentleman, that, for me, the letter, which I now return, shall remain as unviolated a secret as before I opened it. I am so shocked and grieved that such a mistake should have occurred!''

I dare say my honest vexation and good faith were pretty legibly written in my countenance; for the look of gloomy embarrassment which had for a moment settled on the face of the Marquis, brightened; he smiled, kindly, and extended his hand.

"I have not the least doubt that Monsieur Beckett will respect my little secret. As a mistake was destined to occur, I have reason to thank my good stars that it should have been with a gentleman of honour. Monsieur Beckett will permit me, I hope, to place his name among those of my friends?''

I thanked the Marquis very much for his kind expressions. He went on to say—

"If, Monsieur, I can persuade you to visit me at Claironville, in Normandy, where I hope to see, on the 15th of August, a great many friends, whose acquaintance it might interest you to make, I shall be too happy.''

I thanked him, of course, very gratefully for his hospitality. He continued:

"I cannot, for the present, see my friends, for reasons which you may surmise, at my house in Paris. But Monsieur will be so good as to let me know the hotel he means to stay at in Paris; and he will find that although the Marquis d'Harmonville is not in town, that Monsieur Droqville will not lose sight of him.''

With many acknowledgments I gave him the information he desired.

"And in the meantime,'' he continued, "if you think of any way in which Monsieur Droqville can be of use to you, our communication shall not be interrupted, and I shall so manage matters that you can easily let me know.''

I was very much flattered. The Marquis had, as we say, taken a fancy to me. Such likings at first sight often ripen into lasting friendships. To be sure it was just possible that the Marquis might think it prudent to keep the involuntary depository of a political secret, even so vague a one, in good humour.

Very graciously the Marquis took his leave, going up the stairs of the Belle Etoile.

I remained upon the steps, for a minute lost in speculation upon this new theme of interest. But the wonderful eyes, the thrilling voice, the exquisite figure of the beautiful lady who had taken possession of my imagination, quickly reasserted their influence. I was again gazing at the sympathetic moon, and descending the steps, I loitered along the pavements among strange objects, and houses that were antique and picturesque, in a dreamy state, thinking.

In a little while, I turned into the inn-yard again. There had come a lull. Instead of the noisy place it was, an hour or two before, the yard was perfectly still and empty, except for the carriages that stood here and there. Perhaps there was a servants' table-d'hôte just then. I was rather pleased to find solitude; and undisturbed I found out my lady-love's carriage, in the moonlight. I mused, I walked round it; I was as utterly foolish and maudlin as very young men, in my situation, usually are. The blinds were down, the doors, I suppose, locked. The brilliant moonlight revealed everything, and cast sharp, black shadows of wheel, and bar, and spring, on the pavement. I stood before the escutcheon painted on the door, which I had examined in the daylight. I wondered how often her eyes had rested on the same object. I pondered in a charming dream. A harsh, loud voice over my shoulder, said suddenly,

"A red stork—good! The stork is a bird of prey; it is vigilant, greedy and catches gudgeons. Red, too!—blood red! Ha! ha! the symbol is appropriate."

I had turned about, and beheld the palest face I ever saw. It was broad, ugly, and malignant. The figure was that of a French officer, in undress, and was six feet high. Across the nose and eyebrow there was a deep scar, which made the repulsive face grimmer.

The officer elevated his chin and his eyebrows, with a scoffing chuckle, and said—"I have shot a stork, with a rifle bullet, when he thought himself safe in the clouds, for mere sport!" (He shrugged, and laughed malignantly.) "See, Monsieur; when a man like me—a man of energy, you understand, a man with all his wits about him, a man who has made the tour of Europe under canvas, and, *parbleu!* often without it —resolves to discover a secret, expose a crime, catch a thief, spit a robber on the point of his sword, it is odd if he does not succeed. Ha! ha! ha! Adieu, Monsieur!"

He turned with an angry whisk on his heel and swaggered with long strides out of the gate.

CHAPTER V

Supper at the Belle Etoile

The French army were in a rather savage temper, just then. The English, especially, had but scant courtesy to expect at their hands. It was plain, however, that the cadaverous gentleman who had just apostrophized the heraldry of the Count's carriage with such mysterious acrimony, had not intended any of his malevolence for me. He was stung by some old recollection, and had marched off, seething with fury.

I had received one of those unacknowledged shocks which startle us, when, fancying ourselves perfectly alone, we discover on a sudden, that our antics have been watched by a spectator, almost at our elbow. In this case, the effect was enhanced by the extreme repulsiveness of the face, and, I may add, its proximity, for, as I think, it almost touched mine. The enigmatical harangue of this person, so full of hatred and implied denunciation, was still in my ears. Here at all events was new matter for the industrious fancy of a lover to work upon.

It was time now to go to the table-d'hôte. Who could tell what lights the gossip of the supper-table might throw upon the subject that interested me so powerfully!

I stepped into the room, my eyes searching the little assembly, about thirty people, for the persons who specially interested me.

It was not easy to induce people, so hurried and overworked as those of the Belle Etoile just now, to send meals up to one's private apartments, in the midst of this unparalleled confusion; and, therefore, many people who did not like it, might find themselves reduced to the alternative of supping at the table-d'hôte, or starving.

The Count was not there, nor his beautiful companion; but the Marquis d'Harmonville, whom I hardly expected to see in so public a place, signed, with a significant smile, to a vacant chair beside himself. I secured it, and he seemed pleased, and almost immediately entered into conversation with me.

"This is, probably, your first visit to France?" he said.

I told him it was, and he said:

"You must not think me very curious and impertinent; but Paris is about the most dangerous capital a high-spirited and generous young gentleman could visit without a Mentor. If you have not an experienced friend as a companion during your visit——" He paused.

I told him I was not so provided, but that I had my wits about me; that I had seen a good deal of life in England, and that, I fancied, human nature was pretty much the same in all parts of the world. The Marquis shook his head, smiling.

"You will find very marked differences, notwithstanding," he said. "Peculiarities of intellect and peculiarities of character, undoubtedly, do pervade different nations; and this results, among the criminal classes, in a style of villainy no less peculiar. In Paris, the class who live by their wits, is three or four times as great as in London; and they live much better; some of them even splendidly. They are more ingenious than the London rogues; they have more animation, and invention, and the dramatic faculty, in which your countrymen are deficient, is everywhere. These invaluable attributes place them upon a totally different level. They can affect the manners and enjoy the luxuries of people of distinction. They live, many of them, by play."

"So do many of our London rogues."

"Yes, but in a totally different way. They are the *habitués* of certain gaming-tables, billiard-rooms, and other places, including your races, where high play goes on; and by superior knowledge of chances, by masking their play, by means of confederates, by means of bribery, and

other artifices, varying with the subject of their imposture, they rob the
unwary. But here it is more elaborately done, and with a really exquisite *finesse*. There are people whose manners, style, conversation, are
unexceptionable, living in handsome houses in the best situations, with
everything about them in the most refined taste, and exquisitely luxurious, who impose even upon the Parisian bourgeois, who believe them
to be, in good faith, people of rank and fashion, because their habits are
expensive and refined, and their houses are frequented by foreigners of
distinction, and, to a degree, by foolish young Frenchmen of rank. At
all these houses play goes on. The ostensible host and hostess seldom
join in it; they provide it simply to plunder their guests, by means of
their accomplices, and thus wealthy strangers are inveigled and
robbed."

"But I have heard of a young Englishman, a son of Lord Rooksbury,
who broke two Parisian gaming-tables only last year."

"I see," he said, laughing, "you are come here to do likewise. I,
myself, at about your age, undertook the same spirited enterprise. I
raised no less a sum than five hundred thousand francs to begin with; I
expected to carry all before me by the simple expedient of going on
doubling my stakes. I had heard of it, and I fancied that the sharpers,
who kept the table, knew nothing of the matter. I found, however, that
they not only knew all about it, but had provided against the possibility
of any such experiments; and I was pulled up before I had well begun,
by a rule which forbids the doubling of an original stake more than four
times, consecutively."

"And is that rule in force still?" I inquired, chap-fallen.

He laughed and shrugged, "Of course it is, my young friend. People
who live by an art, always understand it better than an amateur. I see
you had formed the same plan, and no doubt came provided."

I confessed I had prepared for conquest upon a still grander scale. I
had arrived with a purse of thirty thousand pounds sterling.

"Any acquaintance of my very dear friend, Lord R——, interests
me; and, besides my regard for him, I am charmed with you; so you
will pardon all my, perhaps, too officious questions and advice."

I thanked him most earnestly for his valuable counsel, and begged
that he would have the goodness to give me all the advice in his power.

"Then if you take my advice," said he, "you will leave your money in
the bank where it lies. Never risk a Napoleon in a gaming-house. The
night I went to break the bank, I lost between seven and eight thousand
pounds sterling of your English money; and my next adventure, I had
obtained an introduction to one of those elegant gaming-houses which
affect to be the private mansions of persons of distinction, and was
saved from ruin by a gentleman, whom, ever since, I have regarded with
increasing respect and friendship. It oddly happens he is in this house
at this moment. I recognized his servant, and made him a visit in his
apartments here, and found him the same brave, kind, honourable man
I always knew him. But that he is living so entirely out of the world,

now, I should have made a point of introducing you. Fifteen years ago he would have been the man of all others to consult. The gentleman I speak of is the Comte de St. Alyre. He represents a very old family. He is the very soul of honour, and the most sensible man in the world, except in one particular."

"And that particular?" I hesitated. I was now deeply interested.

"Is that he has married a charming creature, at least five-and-forty years younger than himself, and is, of course, although I believe absolutely without cause, horribly jealous."

"And the lady?"

"The Countess is, I believe, in every way worthy of so good a man," he answered, a little drily.

"I think I heard her sing this evening."

"Yes, I daresay; she is very accomplished." After a few moments' silence he continued.

"I must not lose sight of you, for I should be sorry, when next you meet my friend Lord R——, that you had to tell him you had been pigeoned in Paris. A rich Englishman as you are, with so large a sum at his Paris bankers, young, gay, generous, a thousand ghouls and harpies will be contending who shall be first to seize and devour you."

At this moment I received something like a jerk from the elbow of the gentleman at my right. It was an accidental jog, as he turned in his seat.

"On the honour of a soldier, there is no man's flesh in this company heals so fast as mine."

The tone in which this was spoken was harsh and stentorian, and almost made me bounce. I looked round and recognised the officer, whose large white face had half scared me in the inn-yard, wiping his mouth furiously, and then with a gulp of Macon, he went on—

"*No* one! It's not blood; it is ichor! it's miracle! Set aside stature, thew, bone, and muscle—set aside courage, and by all the angels of death, I'd fight a lion naked and dash his teeth down his jaws with my fist, and flog him to death with his own tail! Set aside, I say, all those attributes, which I am allowed to possess, and I am worth six men in any campaign, for that one quality of healing as I do—rip me up; punch me through, tear me to tatters with bomb-shells, and nature has me whole again, while your tailor would fine-draw an old-coat. *Parbleu!* gentlemen, if you saw me naked, you would laugh? Look at my hand, a sabre-cut across the palm, to the bone, to save my head, taken up with three stitches, and five days afterwards I was playing ball with an English general, a prisoner in Madrid, against the wall of the convent of the Santa Maria de la Castita! At Arcola, by the great devil himself! that was an action. Every man there, gentlemen, swallowed as much smoke in five minutes as would smother you all, in this room! I received, at the same moment, two musket balls in the thighs, a grape shot through the calf of my leg, a lance through my left shoulder, a piece of a shrapnel in the left deltoid, a bayonet through the cartilage of my right ribs, a sabre-cut that carried away a pound of flesh from my chest, and the better part of a congreve rocket on my forehead. Pretty well, ha, ha! and all while you'd say *bah!* and in eight days and a half I was making a forced march, without shoes, and only one gaiter, the life and soul of my company, and as sound as a roach!"

"Bravo! Bravissimo! Per Bacco! un galant uomo!" exclaimed, in a martial ecstasy, a fat little Italian, who manufactured toothpicks and wicker cradles on the island of Notre Dame; "your exploits shall resound through Europe! and the history of those wars should be written in your blood!"

"Never mind! a trifle!" exclaimed the soldier. "At Ligny, the other day, where we smashed the Prussians into ten hundred thousand milliards of atoms, a bit of a shell cut me across the leg and opened an artery. It was spouting as high as the chimney, and in half a minute I had lost enough to fill a pitcher. I must have expired in another minute, if I had not whipped off my sash like a flash of lightning, tied it round my leg above the wound, whipped a bayonet out of the back of a dead Prussian, and passing it under, made a tourniquet of it with a couple of twists, and so stayed the hemorrhage, and saved my life. But, *sacré bleu!* gentlemen, I lost so much blood, I have been as pale as the bottom of a plate ever since. No matter. A trifle. Blood well spent, gentlemen." He applied himself now to his bottle of *vin ordinaire*.

The Marquis had closed his eyes, and looked resigned and disgusted, while all this was going on.

"*Garçon*," said the officer, for the first time speaking in a low tone over the back of his chair to the waiter; "who came in that travelling carriage, dark yellow and black, that stands in the middle of the yard, with arms and supporters emblazoned on the door, and a red stork, as red as my facings?"

The waiter could not say.

The eye of the eccentric officer, who had suddenly grown grim and serious, and seemed to have abandoned the general conversation to other people, lighted, as it were, accidentally, on me.

"Pardon me, Monsieur," he said. "Did I not see you examining the panel of that carriage at the same time that I did so, this evening? Can you tell me who arrived in it?"

"I rather think the Count and Countess de St. Alyre."

"And are they here, in the Belle Etoile?" he asked.

"They have got apartments upstairs," I answered.

He started up, and half pushed his chair from the table. He quickly sat down again, and I could hear him *sacré*-ing and muttering to himself, and grinning and scowling. I could not tell whether he was alarmed or furious.

I turned to say a word or two to the Marquis, but he was gone. Several other people had dropped out also, and the supper party soon broke up.

Two or three substantial pieces of wood smouldered on the hearth, for the night had turned out chilly. I sat down by the fire in a great arm-chair, of carved oak, with a marvellously high back, that looked as old as the days of Henry IV.

"*Garçon*," said I, "do you happen to know who that officer is?"

"That is Colonel Gaillarde, Monsieur."

"Has he been often here?"

"Once before, Monsieur, for a week; it is a year since."

"He is the palest man I ever saw."

"That is true, Monsieur; he has been often taken for a *revenant*."

"Can you give me a bottle of really good Burgundy?"

"The best in France, Monsieur."

"Place it, and a glass by my side, on this table, if you please. I may sit here for half an hour?"

"Certainly, Monsieur."

I was very comfortable, the wine excellent, and my thoughts glowing and serene. "Beautiful Countess! Beautiful Countess! shall we ever be better acquainted."

CHAPTER VI

The Naked Sword

A man who has been posting all day long, and changing the air he breathes every half-hour, who is well pleased with himself, and has nothing on earth to trouble him, and who sits alone by a fire in a comfortable chair after having eaten a hearty supper, may be pardoned if he takes an accidental nap.

I had filled my fourth glass when I fell asleep. My head, I daresay, hung uncomfortably; and it is admitted, that a variety of French dishes is not the most favourable precursor to pleasant dreams.

I had a dream as I took mine ease in mine inn on this occasion. I fancied myself in a huge cathedral, without light except from four tapers that stood at the corners of a raised platform hung with black, on which lay, draped also in black, what seemed to me the dead body of the Countess de St. Alyre. The place seemed empty, it was cold, and I could see only (in the halo of the candles) a little way round.

The little I saw bore the character of Gothic gloom, and helped my fancy to shape and furnish the black void that yawned all round me. I heard a sound like the slow tread of two persons walking up the flagged aisle. A faint echo told of the vastness of the place. An awful sense of expectation was upon me, and I was horribly frightened when the body that lay on the catafalque said (without stirring), in a whisper that froze me, "They come to place me in the grave alive; save me."

I found that I could neither speak nor move. I was horribly frightened.

The two people who approached now emerged from the darkness.

One, the Count de St. Alyre, glided to the head of the figure and placed his long thin hands under it. The white-faced Colonel, with the scar across his face, and a look of infernal triumph, placed his hands under her feet, and they began to raise her.

With an indescribable effort I broke the spell that bound me, and started to my feet with a gasp.

I was wide awake, but the broad, wicked face of Colonel Gaillarde was staring, white as death, at me, from the other side of the hearth.

"Where is she?" I shuddered.

"That depends on who she is, Monsieur," replied the Colonel curtly.

"Good heavens!" I gasped, looking about me.

The Colonel, who was eyeing me sarcastically, had had his *demi-tasse* of *café noir*, and now drank his *tasse*, diffusing a pleasant perfume of brandy.

"I fell asleep and was dreaming," I said, lest any strong language, founded on the *rôle* he played in my dream, should have escaped me. "I did not know for some moments where I was."

"You are the young gentleman who has the apartments over the Count and Countess de St. Alyre?" he said, winking one eye, close in meditation, and glaring at me with the other.

"I believe so—yes," I answered.

"Well, younker, take care you have not worse dreams than that some night," he said, enigmatically, and wagged his head with a chuckle. "Worse dreams," he repeated.

"What does Monsieur the Colonel mean?" I inquired.

"I am trying to find that out myself," said the Colonel; "and I think I shall. When *I* get the first inch of the thread fast between my finger and thumb, it goes hard but I follow it up, bit by bit, little by little, tracing it this way and that, and up and down, and round about, until the whole clue is wound up on my thumb, and the end, and its secret, fast in my fingers. Ingenious! Crafty as five foxes! wide awake as a weasel! *Parbleu!* if I had descended to that occupation I should have made my fortune as a spy. Good wine here?" he glanced interrogatively at my bottle.

"Very good," said I, "Will Monsieur the Colonel try a glass?"

He took the largest he could find, and filled it, raised it with a bow, and drank it slowly. "Ah! ah! Bah! That is not it," he exclaimed, with some disgust, filling it again. "You ought to have told *me* to order your Burgundy, and they would not have brought you that stuff."

I got away from this man as soon as I civilly could, and, putting on my hat, I walked out with no other company than my sturdy walking stick. I visited the inn-yard, and looked up to the windows of the Countess's apartments. They were closed, however, and I had not even the unsubstantial consolation of contemplating the light in which that beautiful lady was at that moment writing, or reading, or sitting and thinking of—any one you please.

I bore this serious privation as well as I could, and took a little

saunter through the town. I shan't bore you with moonlight effects, nor
with the maunderings of a man who has fallen in love at first sight with
a beautiful face. My ramble, it is enough to say, occupied about half an
hour, and, returning by a slight *détour*, I found myself in a little square,
with about two high gabled houses on each side, and a rude stone
statue, worn by centuries of rain, on a pedestal in the centre of the pavement. Looking at this statue was a slight and rather tall man, whom I
instantly recognised as the Marquis d'Harmonville; he knew me almost
as quickly. He walked a step towards me, shrugged and laughed:

"You are surprised to find Monsieur Droqville staring at that old
stone figure by moonlight. Anything to pass the time. You, I see, suffer
from *ennui*, as I do. These little provincial towns! Heavens! what an
effort it is to live in them! If I could regret having formed in early life a
friendship that does me honour, I think its condemning me to sojourn
in such a place would make me do so. You go on towards Paris, I suppose, in the morning?"

"I have ordered horses."

"As for me I await a letter, or an arrival, either would emancipate
me; but I can't say how soon either event will happen."

"Can I be of any use in this matter?" I began.

"None, Monsieur, I thank you a thousand times. No, this is a piece in
which every *rôle* is already cast. I am but an amateur, and induced, solely by friendship, to take a part."

So he talked on, for a time, as we walked slowly towards the Belle
Etoile, and then came a silence, which I broke by asking him if he knew
anything of Colonel Gaillarde.

"Oh! yes, to be sure. He is a little mad; he has had some bad injuries
of the head. He used to plague the people in the War Office to death.
He has always some delusion. They contrived some employment for
him—not regimental, of course—but in this campaign Napoleon, who
could spare nobody, placed him in command of a regiment. He was
always a desperate fighter, and such men were more than ever needed."

There is, or was, a second inn, in this town, called l'Ecu de France.
At its door the Marquis stopped, bade me a mysterious good night, and
disappeared.

As I walked slowly towards my inn, I met, in the shadow of a row of
poplars, the *garçon* who had brought me my Burgundy a little time ago.
I was thinking of Colonel Gaillarde, and I stopped the little waiter as he
passed me.

"You said, I think, that Colonel Gaillarde was at the Belle Etoile for
a week at one time."

"Yes, Monsieur."

"Is he perfectly in his right mind?"

The waiter stared. "Perfectly, Monsieur."

"Has he been suspected at any time of being out of his mind?"

"Never, Monsieur; he is a little noisy, but a very shrewd man."

"What is a fellow to think?" I muttered, as I walked on.

I was soon within sight of the lights of the Belle Etoile. A carriage, with four horses, stood in the moonlight at the door, and a furious altercation was going on in the hall, in which the yell of Colonel Gaillarde outtopped all other sounds.

Most young men like, at least, to witness a row. But, intuitively, I felt that this would interest me in a very special manner. I had only fifty yards to run, when I found myself in the hall of the old inn. The principal actor in this strange drama was, indeed, the Colonel, who stood facing the old Count de St. Alyre, who, in his travelling costume, with his black silk scarf covering the lower part of his face, confronted him; he had evidently been intercepted in an endeavour to reach his carriage. A little in the rear of the Count stood the Countess, also in travelling costume, with her thick black veil down, and holding in her delicate fingers a white rose. You can't conceive a more diabolical effigy of hate and fury than the Colonel; the knotted veins stood out on his forehead, his eyes were leaping from their sockets, he was grinding his teeth, and froth was on his lips. His sword was drawn, in his hand, and he accompanied his yelling denunciations with stamps upon the floor and flourishes of his weapon in the air.

The host of the Belle Etoile was talking to the Colonel in soothing terms utterly thrown away. Two waiters, pale with fear, stared uselessly from behind. The Colonel screamed, and thundered, and whirled his sword. "I was not sure of your red birds of prey; I could not believe you would have the audacity to travel on high roads, and to stop at honest inns, and lie under the same roof with honest men. You! you! both—vampires, wolves, ghouls. Summon the *gendarmes*, I say. By St. Peter and all the devils, if either of you try to get out of that door I'll take your heads off."

For a moment I had stood aghast. Here was a situation! I walked up to the lady; she laid her hand wildly upon my arm. "Oh! Monsieur," she whispered, in great agitation, "that dreadful madman! What are we to do? He won't let us pass; he will kill my husband."

"Fear nothing, Madame," I answered, with romantic devotion, and stepping between the Count and Gaillarde, as he shrieked his invective, "Hold your tongue, and clear the way, you ruffian, you bully, you coward!" I roared.

A faint cry escaped the lady, which more than repaid the risk I ran, as the sword of the frantic soldier, after a moment's astonished pause, flashed in the air to cut me down.

CHAPTER VII

The White Rose

I was too quick for Colonel Gaillarde. As he raised his sword, reckless of all consequences but my condign punishment, and quite resolved to cleave me to the teeth, I struck him across the side of his head, with my heavy stick; and while he staggered back, I struck him another blow, nearly in the same place, that felled him to the floor, where he lay as if dead.

I did not care one of his own regimental buttons, whether he was dead or not; I was, at that moment, carried away by such a tumult of delightful and diabolical emotions!

I broke his sword under my foot, and flung the pieces across the street. The old Count de St. Alyre skipped nimbly without looking to the right or left, or thanking anybody, over the floor, out of the door, down the steps, and into his carriage. Instantly I was at the side of the beautiful Countess, thus left to shift for herself; I offered her my arm, which she took, and I led her to her carriage. She entered, and I shut the door. All this without a word.

I was about to ask if there were any commands with which she would honour me—my hand was laid upon the lower edge of the window, which was open.

The lady's hand was laid upon mine timidly and excitedly. Her lips almost touched my cheek as she whispered hurriedly.

"I may never see you more, and, oh! that I could forget you. Go—farewell—for God's sake, go!"

I pressed her hand for a moment. She withdrew it, but tremblingly pressed into mine the rose which she had held in her fingers during the agitating scene she had just passed through.

All this took place while the Count was commanding, entreating, cursing his servants, tipsy, and out of the way during the crisis, my conscience afterwards insinuated, by my clever contrivance. They now mounted to their places with the agility of alarm. The postillions' whips cracked, the horses scrambled into a trot, and away rolled the carriage, with its precious freightage, along the quaint main street, in the moonlight, towards Paris.

I stood on the pavement, till it was quite lost to eye and ear in the distance.

With a deep sigh, I then turned, my white rose folded in my handkerchief—the little parting *gage*—the

"Favour secret, sweet, and precious,"

which no mortal eye but hers and mine had seen conveyed to me.

The care of the host of the Belle Etoile, and his assistants, had raised the wounded hero of a hundred fights partly against the wall, and propped him at each side with portmanteaus and pillows, and poured a glass of brandy, which was duly placed to his account, into his big mouth, where, for the first time, such a Godsend remained unswallowed.

A bald-headed little military surgeon of sixty, with spectacles, who had cut off eighty-seven legs and arms to his own share, after the battle of Eylau, having retired with his sword and his saw, his laurels and his sticking-plaster to this, his native town, was called in, and rather thought the gallant Colonel's skull was fractured, at all events there was concussion of the seat of thought, and quite enough work for his remarkable self-healing powers, to occupy him for a fortnight.

I began to grow a little uneasy. A disagreeable surprise, if my excursion, in which I was to break banks and hearts, and, as you see, heads, should end upon the gallows or the guillotine. I was not clear, in those times of political oscillation, which was the established apparatus.

The Colonel was conveyed, snorting apoplectically to his room.

I saw my host in the apartment in which we had supped. Wherever you employ a force of any sort, to carry a point of real importance, reject all nice calculations of economy. Better to be a thousand per cent over the mark, than the smallest fraction of a unit under it. I instinctively felt this.

I ordered a bottle of my landlord's very best wine; made him partake with me, in the proportion of two glasses to one; and then told him that he must not decline a trifling *souvenir* from a guest who had been so charmed with all he had seen of the renowned Belle Etoile. Thus saying, I placed five-and-thirty Napoleons in his hand. At touch of which his countenance, by no means encouraging before, grew sunny, his manners thawed, and it was plain, as he dropped the coins hastily into his pocket, that benevolent relations had been established between us.

I immediately placed the Colonel's broken head upon the *tapis*. We both agreed that if I had not given him that rather smart tap of my walking-cane, he would have beheaded half the inmates of the Belle Etoile. There was not a waiter in the house who would not verify that statement on oath.

The reader may suppose that I had other motives, beside the desire to escape the tedious inquisition of the law, for desiring to recommence my journey to Paris with the least possible delay. Judge what was my horror then to learn, that for love or money, horses were nowhere to be had that night. The last pair in the town had been obtained from the Ecu de France, by a gentleman who dined and supped at the Belle Etoile, and was obliged to proceed to Paris that night.

Who was that gentleman? Had he actually gone? Could he possibly be induced to wait till morning?

The gentleman was now upstairs getting his things together, and his name was Monsieur Droqville.

I ran upstairs. I found my servant St. Clair in my room. At sight of him, for a moment, my thoughts were turned into a different channel.

"Well, St. Clair, tell me this moment who the lady is?" I demanded.

"The lady is the daughter or wife, it matters not which, of the Count de St. Alyre—the old gentleman who was so near being sliced like a cucumber to-night, I am informed, by the sword of the general whom Monsieur, by a turn of fortune, has put to bed of an apoplexy."

"Hold your tongue, fool! The man's beastly drunk—he's sulking—he could talk if he liked—who cares? Pack up my things. Which are Monsieur Droqville's apartments?"

He knew, of course; he always knew everything.

Half an hour later Monsieur Droqville and I were travelling towards Paris, in my carriage, and with his horses. I ventured to ask the Marquis d'Harmonville, in a little while, whether the lady, who accompanied the Count, was certainly the Countess. "Has he not a daughter?"

"Yes; I believe a very beautiful and charming young lady—I cannot say—it may have been she, his daughter by an earlier marriage. I saw only the Count himself to-day."

The Marquis was growing a little sleepy and, in a little while, he actually fell asleep in his corner. I dozed and nodded; but the Marquis slept like a top. He awoke only for a minute or two at the next posting-house, where he had fortunately secured horses by sending on his man, he told me.

"You will excuse my being so dull a companion," he said, "but till to-night I have had but two hours' sleep, for more than sixty hours. I shall have a cup of coffee here; I have had my nap. Permit me to recommend you to do likewise. Their coffee is really excellent." He ordered two cups of *café noir*, and waited, with his head from the window. "We will keep the cups," he said, as he received them from the waiter, "and the tray. Thank you."

There was a little delay as he paid for these things; and then he took in the little tray, and handed me a cup of coffee.

I declined the tray; so he placed it on his own knees, to act as a miniature table.

"I can't endure being waited for and hurried," he said, "I like to sip my coffee at leisure."

I agreed. It really *was* the very perfection of coffee.

"I, like Monsieur le Marquis, have slept very little for the last two or three nights; and find it difficult to keep awake. This coffee will do wonders for me; it refreshes one so."

Before we had half done, the carriage was again in motion.

For a time our coffee made us chatty, and our conversation was animated.

The Marquis was extremely good-natured, as well as clever, and gave me a brilliant and amusing account of Parisian life, schemes, and dangers, all put so as to furnish me with practical warnings of the most valuable kind.

In spite of the amusing and curious stories which the Marquis related, with so much point and colour, I felt myself again becoming gradually drowsy and dreamy.

Perceiving this, no doubt, the Marquis good-naturedly suffered our conversation to subside into silence. The window next him was open. He threw his cup out of it; and did the same kind office for mine, and finally the little tray flew after, and I heard it clank on the road; a valuable waif, no doubt, for some early wayfarer in wooden shoes. I leaned back in my corner; I had my beloved *souvenir*—my white rose—close to my heart, folded, now, in white paper. It inspired all manner of romantic dreams. I began to grow more and more sleepy. But actual slumber did not come. I was still viewing, with my half-closed eyes, from my corner, diagonally, the interior of the carriage. I wished for sleep; but the barrier between waking and sleeping seemed absolutely insurmountable; and instead, I entered into a state of novel and indescribable indolence.

The Marquis lifted his despatch-box from the floor, placed it on his knees, unlocked it, and took out what proved to be a lamp, which he hung with two hooks, attached to it, to the window opposite to him. He lighted it with a match, put on his spectacles, and taking out a bundle of letters, began to read them carefully.

We were making way very slowly. My impatience had hitherto employed four horses from stage to stage. We were in this emergency, only too happy to have secured two. But the difference in pace was depressing.

I grew tired of the monotony of seeing the spectacled Marquis reading, folding, and docketing, letter after letter. I wished to shut out the image which wearied me, but something prevented my being able to shut my eyes. I tried again and again; but, positively, I had lost the power of closing them.

I would have rubbed my eyes, but I could not stir my hand, my will no longer acted on my body—I found that I could not move one joint or muscle, no more than I could, by an effort of my will, have turned the carriage about.

Up to this I had experienced no sense of horror. Whatever it was, simple nightmare was not the cause. I was awfully frightened! Was I in a fit?

It was horrible to see my good-natured companion pursue his occupation so serenely, when he might have dissipated my horrors by a single shake.

I made a stupendous exertion to call out but in vain; I repeated the effort again and again, with no result.

My companion now tied up his letters, and looked out of the window,

humming an air from an opera. He drew back his head, and said, turning to me—

"Yes, I see the lights; we shall be there in two or three minutes."

He looked more closely at me, and with a kind smile, and a little
shrug, he said, "Poor child! how fatigued he must have been—how
profoundly he sleeps! when the carriage stops he will waken."

He then replaced his letters in the despatch-box, locked it, put his
spectacles in his pocket, and again looked out of the window.

We had entered a little town. I suppose it was past two o'clock by this
time. The carriage drew up, I saw an inn-door open, and a light issuing
from it.

"Here we are!" said my companion, turning gaily to me. But I did
not awake.

"Yes, how tired he must have been!" he exclaimed, after he had
waited for an answer.

My servant was at the carriage door, and opened it.

"Your master sleeps soundly, he is so fatigued! It would be cruel to
disturb him. You and I will go in, while they change the horses, and
take some refreshment, and choose something that Monsieur Beckett
will like to take in the carriage, for when he awakes by-and-by, he will, I
am sure, be hungry."

He trimmed his lamp, poured in some oil; and taking care not to disturb me, with another kind smile, and another word of caution to my
servant, he got out, and I heard him talking to St. Clair, as they entered
the inn-door, and I was left in my corner, in the carriage, in the same
state.

CHAPTER VIII

A Three Minutes' Visit

I have suffered extreme and protracted bodily pain, at different periods
of my life, but anything like that misery, thank God, I never endured
before or since. I earnestly hope it may not resemble any type of death,
to which we are liable. I was, indeed, a spirit in prison; and unspeakable was my dumb and unmoving agony.

The power of thought remained clear and active. Dull terror filled my
mind. How would this end? Was it actual death?

You will understand that my faculty of observing was unimpaired. I
could hear and see anything as distinctly as ever I did in my life. It was
simply that my will had, as it were, lost its hold of my body.

I told you that the Marquis d'Harmonville had not extinguished his
carriage lamp on going into this village inn. I was listening intently,
longing for his return, which might result, by some lucky accident, in
awakening me from my catalepsy.

Without any sound of steps approaching, to announce an arrival, the carriage-door suddenly opened, and a total stranger got in silently and shut the door.

The lamp gave about as strong a light as a wax-candle, so I could see the intruder perfectly. He was a young man, with a dark grey, loose surtout, made with a sort of hood, which was pulled over his head. I thought, as he moved, that I saw the gold band of a military undress cap under it; and I certainly saw the lace and buttons of a uniform, on the cuffs of the coat that were visible under the wide sleeves of his outside wrapper.

This young man had thick moustaches, and an imperial, and I observed that he had a red scar running upward from his lip across his cheek.

He entered, shut the door softly, and sat down beside me. It was all done in a moment; leaning toward me, and shading his eyes with his gloved hand, he examined my face closely, for a few seconds.

This man had come as noiselessly as a ghost; and everything he did was accomplished with the rapidity and decision, that indicated a well defined and pre-arranged plan. His designs were evidently sinister. I thought he was going to rob, and, perhaps, murder me. I lay, nevertheless, like a corpse under his hands. He inserted his hand in my breast-pocket, from which he took my precious white rose and all the letters it contained, among which was a paper of some consequence to me.

My letters he glanced at. They were plainly not what he wanted. My precious rose, too, he laid aside with them. It was evidently about the paper I have mentioned, that he was concerned; for the moment he opened it, he began with a pencil, in a small pocket-book, to make rapid notes of its contents.

This man seemed to glide through his work with a noiseless and cool celerity which argued, I thought, the training of the police-department.

He re-arranged the papers, possibly in the very order in which he had found them, replaced them in my breast-pocket, and was gone.

His visit, I think, did not quite last three minutes. Very soon after his disappearance, I heard the voice of the Marquis once more. He got in, and I saw him look at me, and smile, half envying me, I fancied, my sound repose. If he had but known all!

He resumed his reading and docketing, by the light of the little lamp which had just subserved the purposes of a spy.

We were now out of the town, pursuing our journey at the same moderate pace. We had left the scene of my police visit, as I should have termed it, now two leagues behind us, when I suddenly felt a strange throbbing in one ear, and a sensation as if air passed through it into my throat. It seemed as if a bubble of air, formed deep in my ear, swelled, and burst there. The indescribable tension of my brain seemed all at once to give way; there was an odd humming in my head, and a sort of vibration through every nerve of my body, such as I have experienced in a limb that has been, in popular phraseology, asleep. I uttered a cry and half rose from my seat, and then fell back trembling, and with a sense of mortal faintness.

The Marquis stared at me, took my hand, and earnestly asked if I was ill. I could answer only with a deep groan.

Gradually the process of restoration was completed; and I was able, though very faintly, to tell him how very ill I had been; and then to describe the violation of my letters, during the time of his absence from the carriage.

"Good heaven!" he exclaimed, "the miscreant did not get at my despatch-box?"

I satisfied him, so far as I had observed, on that point. He placed the box on the seat beside him, and opened and examined its contents very minutely.

"Yes, undisturbed; all safe, thank heaven!" he murmured. "There are half a dozen letters here, that I would not have some people read, for a great deal."

He now asked with a very kind anxiety all about the illness I complained of. When he had heard me, he said—

"A friend of mine once had an attack as like yours as possible. It was on board ship, and followed a state of high excitement. He was a brave man like you; and was called on to exert both his strength and his courage suddenly. An hour or two after, fatigue overpowered him, and he appeared to fall into a sound sleep. He really sank into a state which he afterwards described so, that I think it must have been precisely the same affection as yours."

"I am happy to think that my attack was not unique. Did he ever experience a return of it?"

"I knew him for years after, and never heard of any such thing. What strikes me is a parallel in the predisposing causes of each attack. Your unexpected, and gallant, hand-to-hand encounter, at such desperate odds, with an experienced swordsman, like that insane colonel of dragoons, your fatigue, and, finally, your composing yourself, as my other friend did, to sleep.

"I wish," he resumed, "one could make out who that *coquin* was, who examined your letters. It is not worth turning back, however, because we should learn nothing. Those people always manage so adroitly. I am satisfied, however, that he must have been an agent of the police. A rogue of any other kind would have robbed you."

I talked very little, being ill and exhausted, but the Marquis talked on agreeably.

"We grow so intimate," said he, at last, "that I must remind you that I am not, for the present, the Marquis d'Harmonville, but only Monsieur Droqville; nevertheless, when we get to Paris, although I cannot see you often, I may be of use. I shall ask you to name to me the hotel at which you mean to put up; because the Marquis being, as you are aware, on his travels, the Hôtel d'Harmonville is, for the present, tenanted only by two or three old servants, who must not even see Monsieur Droqville. That gentleman will, nevertheless, contrive to get you access to the box of Monsieur le Marquis, at the Opera; as well, possibly, as to other places more difficult; and so soon as the diplomatic office of the Marquis d'Harmonville is ended, and he at liberty to declare himself, he will not excuse his friend, Monsieur Beckett, from fulfilling his promise to visit him this autumn at the Château d'Harmonville."

You may be sure I thanked the Marquis.

The nearer we got to Paris, the more I valued his protection. The countenance of a great man on the spot, just then, taking so kind an interest in the stranger whom he had, as it were, blundered upon, might make my visit ever so many degrees more delightful than I had anticipated.

Nothing could be more gracious than the manner and looks of the Marquis; and, as I still thanked him, the carriage suddenly stopped in front of the place where a relay of horses awaited us, and where, as it turned out, we were to part.

CHAPTER IX

Gossip and Counsel

My eventful journey was over, at last. I sat in my hotel window looking out upon brilliant Paris, which had, in a moment, recovered all its gaiety, and more than its accustomed bustle. Every one has read of the kind of excitement that followed the catastrophe of Napoleon, and the second restoration of the Bourbons. I need not, therefore, even if, at this distance, I could, recall and describe my experiences and impressions of the peculiar aspect of Paris, in those strange times. It was, to be sure, my first visit. But, often as I have seen it since, I don't think I ever saw that delightful capital in a state, pleasurably, so excited and exciting.

I had been two days in Paris, and had seen all sorts of sights, and experienced none of that rudeness and insolence of which others complained, from the exasperated officers of the defeated French army.

I must say this, also. My romance had taken complete possession of me; and the chance of seeing the object of my dream, gave a secret and delightful interest to my rambles and drives in the streets and environs, and my visits to the galleries and other sights of the metropolis.

I had neither seen nor heard of Count or Countess, nor had the Marquis d'Harmonville made any sign. I had quite recovered from the strange indisposition under which I had suffered during my night journey.

It was now evening, and I was beginning to fear that my patrician acquaintance had quite forgotten me, when the waiter presented me the card of "Monsieur Droqville"; and, with no small elation and hurry, I desired him to show the gentleman up.

In came the Marquis d'Harmonville, kind and gracious as ever.

"I am a night-bird at present," said he, so soon as we had exchanged the little speeches which are usual. "I keep in the shade, during the daytime, and even now I hardly ventured to come in a close carriage. The friends for whom I have undertaken a rather critical service, have so ordained it. They think all is lost, if I am known to be in Paris. First let me present you with these orders for my box. I am so vexed that I cannot command it oftener during the next fortnight; during my absence, I had directed my secretary to give it for any night to the first of my friends who might apply, and the result is, that I find next to nothing left at my disposal."

I thanked him very much.

"And now, a word, in my office of Mentor. You have not come here, of course, without introductions?"

I produced half a dozen letters, the addresses of which he looked at.

"Don't mind these letters," he said. "I will introduce you. I will take you myself from house to house. One friend at your side is worth many letters. Make no intimacies, no acquaintances, until then. You young men like best to exhaust the public amusements of a great city, before embarrassing yourself with the engagements of society. Go to all these. It will occupy you, day and night, for at least three weeks. When this is over, I shall be at liberty, and will myself introduce you to the brilliant but comparatively quiet routine of society. Place yourself in my hands; and in Paris remember, when once in society, you are always there."

I thanked him very much, and promised to follow his counsels implicitly.

He seemed pleased, and said—

"I shall now tell you some of the places you ought to go to. Take your map, and write letters or numbers upon the points I will indicate, and we will make out a little list. All the places that I shall mention to you are worth seeing."

In this methodical way, and with a great deal of amusing and scandalous anecdote, he furnished me with a catalogue and a guide, which, to a seeker of novelty and pleasure, was invaluable.

"In a fortnight, perhaps in a week," he said, "I shall be at leisure to be of real use to you. In the meantime, be on your guard. You must not play; you will be robbed if you do. Remember, you are surrounded, here, by plausible swindlers and villains of all kinds, who subsist by devouring strangers. Trust no one but those you know."

I thanked him again, and promised to profit by his advice. But my heart was too full of the beautiful lady of the Belle Etoile, to allow our interview to close without an effort to learn something about her. I therefore asked for the Count and Countess de St. Alyre, whom I had had the good fortune to extricate from an extremely unpleasant row in the hall of the inn.

Alas! he had not seen them since. He did not know where they were staying. They had a fine old house only a few leagues from Paris; but he thought it probable that they would remain, for a few days at least, in the city, as preparations would, no doubt, be necessary, after so long an absence, for their reception at home.

"How long have they been away?"

"About eight months, I think."

"They are poor, I think you said?"

"What *you* would consider poor. But, Monsieur, the Count has an income which affords them the comforts, and even the elegancies of life, living as they do, in a very quiet and retired way, in this cheap country."

"Then they are very happy?"

"One would say they *ought* to be happy."

"And what prevents?"

"He is jealous."

"But his wife—she gives him no cause?"

"I am afraid she does."

"How, Monsieur?"

"I always thought she was a little too—a *great deal* too——"

"Too *what*, Monsieur?"

"Too handsome. But although she has remarkably fine eyes, exquisite features, and the most delicate complexion in the world, I believe that she is a woman of probity. You have never seen her?"

"There was a lady, muffled up in a cloak, with a very thick veil on, the other night, in the hall of the Belle Etoile, when I broke that fellow's head who was bullying the old Count. But her veil was so thick I could not see a feature through it." My answer was diplomatic, you observe. "She may have been the Count's daughter. Do they quarrel?"

"Who, he and his wife?"

"Yes."

"A little."

"Oh! and what do they quarrel about?"

"It is a long story; about the lady's diamonds. They are valuable—they are worth, La Perelleuse says, about a million of francs. The Count wishes them sold and turned into revenue, which he offers to settle as she pleases. The Countess, whose they are, resists, and for a reason which, I rather think, she can't disclose to him."

"And pray what is that?" I asked, my curiosity a good deal piqued.

"She is thinking, I conjecture, how well she will look in them when she marries her second husband."

"Oh?—yes, to be sure. But the Count de St. Alyre is a good man?"

"Admirable, and extremely intelligent."

"I should wish so much to be presented to the Count: you tell me he's so——"

"So agreeably married. But they are living quite out of the world. He takes her now and then to the Opera, or to a public entertainment; but that is all."

"And he must remember so much of the old *régime*, and so many of the scenes of the revolution!"

"Yes, the very man for a philosopher, like you! And he falls asleep after dinner; and his wife doesn't. But, seriously, he has retired from the gay and the great world, and has grown apathetic; and so has his wife; and nothing seems to interest her now, not even—her husband!"

The Marquis stood up to take his leave.

"Don't risk your money," said he. "You will soon have an opportunity of laying out some of it to great advantage. Several collections of really good pictures, belonging to persons who have mixed themselves up in this Bonapartist restoration, must come within a few weeks to the hammer. You can do wonders when these sales commence. There will be startling bargains! Reserve yourself for them. I shall let you know all about it. By-the-bye," he said, stopping short as he approached the door, "I was so near forgetting. There is to be, next week, the very thing you would enjoy so much, because you see so little of it in England—I mean a *bal masqué*, conducted, it is said, with more than usual splendour. It takes place at Versailles—all the world will be there; there is such a rush for cards! But I think I may promise you one. Good night! Adieu!"

CHAPTER X

The Black Veil

Speaking the language fluently and with unlimited money, there was nothing to prevent my enjoying all that was enjoyable in the French capital. You may easily suppose how two days were passed. At the end of that time, and at about the same hour, Monsieur Droqville called again.

Courtly, good-natured, gay, as usual, he told me that the masquerade ball was fixed for the next Wednesday, and that he had applied for a card for me.

How awfully unlucky. I was so afraid I should not be able to go.

He stared at me for a moment with a suspicious and menacing look which I did not understand, in silence, and then inquired, rather sharply,

"And will Monsieur Beckett be good enough to say, why not?"

I was a little surprised, but answered the simple truth: I had made an engagement for that evening with two or three English friends, and did not see how I could.

"Just so! You English, wherever you are, always look out for your English boors, your beer and '*bifstek*'; and when you come here, instead of trying to learn something of the people you visit, and pretend to study, you are guzzling, and swearing, and smoking with one another, and no wiser or more polished at the end of your travels than if you had been all the time carousing in a booth at Greenwich."

He laughed sarcastically, and looked as if he could have poisoned me.

"There it is," said he, throwing the card on the table. "Take it or leave it, just as you please. I suppose I shall have my trouble for my pains; but it is not usual when a man, such as I, takes trouble, asks a favour, and secures a privilege for an acquaintance, to treat him so."

This was astonishingly impertinent!

I was shocked, offended, penitent. I had possibly committed unwittingly a breach of good-breeding, according to French ideas, which almost justified the brusque severity of the Marquis's undignified rebuke.

In a confusion, therefore, of many feelings, I hastened to make my apologies, and to propitiate the chance friend who had showed me so much disinterested kindness.

I told him that I would, at any cost, break through the engagement in which I had unluckily entangled myself; that I had spoken with too little reflection, and that I certainly had not thanked him at all in proportion to his kindness and to my real estimate of it.

"Pray say not a word more; my vexation was entirely on your account; and I expressed it, I am only too conscious, in terms a great deal too strong, which, I am sure, your good nature will pardon. Those who know me a little better are aware that I sometimes say a good deal more than I intend; and am always sorry when I do. Monsieur Beckett will forget that his old friend, Monsieur Droqville, has lost his temper in his cause, for a moment, and—we are as good friends as before."

He smiled like the Monsieur Droqville of the Belle Etoile, and extended his hand, which I took very respectfully and cordially.

Our momentary quarrel had left us only better friends.

The Marquis then told me I had better secure a bed in some hotel at Versailles, as a rush would be made to take them; and advised my going down next morning for the purpose.

I ordered horses accordingly for eleven o'clock; and, after à little more conversation, the Marquis d'Harmonville bid me good night, and ran down the stairs with his handkerchief to his mouth and nose, and, as I saw from my window, jumped into his close carriage again and drove away.

Next day I was at Versailles. As I approached the door of the Hôtel de France, it was plain that I was not a moment too soon, if, indeed, I were not already too late.

A crowd of carriages were drawn up about the entrance, so that I had no chance of approaching except by dismounting and pushing my way among the horses. The hall was full of servants and gentlemen screaming to the proprietor, who, in a state of polite distraction, was assuring them, one and all, that there was not a room or a closet disengaged in his entire house.

I slipped out again, leaving the hall to those who were shouting, expostulating, wheedling, in the delusion that the host might, if he pleased, manage something for them. I jumped into my carriage and drove, at my horses' best pace, to the Hôtel du Réservoir. The blockade about this door was as complete as the other. The result was the same. It was very provoking, but what was to be done? My postillion had, a little officiously, while I was in the hall talking with the hotel authorities, got his horses, bit by bit, as other carriages moved away, to the very steps of the inn door.

This arrangement was very convenient so far as getting in again was concerned. But, this accomplished, how were we to get on? There were carriages in front, and carriages behind, and no less than four rows of carriages, of all sorts, outside.

I had at this time remarkably long and clear sight, and if I had been impatient before, guess what my feelings were when I saw an open carriage pass the narrow strip of roadway left open at the other side, a barouche in which I was certain I recognised the veiled Countess and her husband. This carriage had been brought to a walk by a cart which occupied the whole breadth of the narrow way, and was moving with the customary tardiness of such vehicles.

I should have done more wisely if I had jumped down on the *trottoir*, and run round the block of carriages in front of the barouche. But, unfortunately, I was more of a Murat than a Moltke, and preferred a direct charge upon my object to relying on *tactique*. I dashed across the back seat of a carriage which was next mine, I don't know how; tumbled through a sort of gig, in which an old gentleman and a dog were dozing; stepped with an incoherent apology over the side of an open carriage, in which were four gentlemen engaged in hot dispute; tripped at the far side in getting out, and fell flat across the backs of a pair of horses, who instantly began plunging and threw me head foremost in the dust.

To those who observed my reckless charge without being in the secret of my object I must have appeared demented. Fortunately, the interesting barouche had passed before the catastrophe, and covered as I was with dust, and my hat blocked, you may be sure I did not care to present myself before the object of my Quixotic devotion.

I stood for a while amid a storm of *sacré*-ing, tempered disagreeably with laughter; and in the midst of these, while endeavouring to beat the dust from my clothes with my handkerchief, I heard a voice with which I was acquainted call, "Monsieur Beckett."

I looked and saw the Marquis peeping from a carriage-window. It was a welcome sight. In a moment I was at his carriage side.

"You may as well leave Versailles," he said; "you have learned, no doubt, that there is not a bed to hire in either of the hotels; and I can add that there is not a room to let in the whole town. But I have managed something for you that will answer just as well. Tell your servant to follow us, and get in here and sit beside me."

Fortunately an opening in the closely-packed carriages had just occurred, and mine was approaching.

I directed the servant to follow us; and the Marquis having said a word to his driver, we were immediately in motion.

"I will bring you to a comfortable place, the very existence of which is known to but few Parisians, where, knowing how things were here, I secured a room for you. It is only a mile away, and an old comfortable inn, called Le Dragon Volant. It was fortunate for you that my tiresome business called me to this place so early."

I think we had driven about a mile and a half to the farther side of the palace when we found ourselves upon a narrow old road, with the woods of Versailles on one side, and much older trees, of a size seldom seen in France, on the other.

We pulled up before an antique and solid inn, built of Caen stone, in a fashion richer and more florid than was ever usual in such houses, and which indicated that it was originally designed for the private mansion of some person of wealth, and probably, as the wall bore many carved shields and supporters, of distinction also. A kind of porch, less ancient than the rest, projected hospitably with a wide and florid arch, over which, cut in high relief in stone, and painted and gilded, was the sign of the inn. This was the Flying Dragon, with wings of brilliant red and gold, expanded, and its tail, pale green and gold, twisted and knotted into ever so many rings, and ending in a burnished point barbed like the dart of death.

"I shan't go in—but you will find it a comfortable place; at all events better than nothing. I would go in with you, but my incognito forbids. You will, I daresay, be all the better pleased to learn that the inn is haunted—I should have been, in my young days, I know. But don't allude to that awful fact in hearing of your host, for I believe it is a sore subject. Adieu. If you want to enjoy yourself at the ball take my advice, and go in a domino. I think I shall look in; and certainly, if I do, in the same costume. How shall we recognize one another? Let me see, something held in the fingers—a flower won't do, so many people will have flowers. Suppose you get a red cross a couple of inches long— you're an Englishman—stitched or pinned on the breast of your domino, and I a white one? Yes, that will do very well; and whatever room you go into keep near the door till we meet. I shall look for you at all the doors I pass; and you, in the same way, for me; and we *must* find each other soon. So that is understood. I can't enjoy a thing of that kind with any but a young person; a man of my age requires the contagion of young spirits and the companionship of someone who enjoys everything spontaneously. Farewell; we meet to-night."

By this time I was standing *on* the road; I shut the carriage-door; bid him good-bye; and away he drove.

CHAPTER XI

The Dragon Volant

I took one look about me.

The building was picturesque; the trees made it more so. The antique and sequestered character of the scene, contrasted strangely with the glare and bustle of the Parisian life, to which my eye and ear had become accustomed.

Then I examined the gorgeous old sign for a minute of two. Next I surveyed the exterior of the house more carefully. It was large and solid, and squared more with my ideas of an ancient English hostelry, such as the Canterbury pilgrims might have put up at, than a French house of entertainment. Except, indeed, for a round turret, that rose at the left flank of the house, and terminated in the extinguisher-shaped roof that suggests a French château.

I entered and announced myself as Monsieur Beckett, for whom a room had been taken. I was received with all the consideration due to an English milord, with, of course, an unfathomable purse.

My host conducted me to my apartment. It was a large room, a little sombre, panelled with dark wainscoting, and furnished in a stately and sombre style, long out of date. There was a wide hearth, and a heavy mantelpiece, carved with shields, in which I might, had I been curious enough, have discovered a correspondence with the heraldry on the outer walls. There was something interesting, melancholy, and even depressing in all this. I went to the stone-shafted window, and looked out upon a small park, with a thick wood, forming the background of a chateau, which presented a cluster of such conical-topped turrets as I have just now mentioned.

The wood and château were melancholy objects. They showed signs of neglect, and almost of decay; and the gloom of fallen grandeur, and a certain air of desertion hung oppressively over the scene.

I asked my host the name of the château.

"That, Monsieur, is the Château de la Carque," he answered.

"It is a pity it is so neglected," I observed. "I should say, perhaps, a pity that its proprietor is not more wealthy?"

"Perhaps so, Monsieur."

"*Perhaps?*"—I repeated, and looked at him. "Then I suppose he is not very popular."

"Neither one thing nor the other, Monsieur," he answered; "I meant only that we could not tell what use he might make of riches."

"And who is he?" I inquired.

"The Count de St. Alyre."

"Oh! The Count! You are quite sure?" I asked, very eagerly.

It was now the innkeeper's turn to look at me.

"*Quite* sure, Monsieur, the Count de St. Alyre."

"Do you see much of him in this part of the world?"

"Not a great deal, Monsieur; he is often absent for a considerable time."

"And is he poor?" I inquired.

"I pay rent to him for this house. It is not much; but I find he cannot wait long for it," he replied, smiling satirically.

"From what I have heard, however, I should think he cannot be very poor?" I continued.

"They say, Monsieur, he plays. I know not. He certainly is not rich. About seven months ago, a relation of his died in a distant place. His body was sent to the Count's house here, and by him buried in Père la Chaise, as the poor gentleman had desired. The Count was in profound affliction; although he got a handsome legacy, they say, by that death. But money never seems to do him good for any time."

"He is old, I believe?"

"Old? we call him the 'Wandering Jew,' except, indeed, that he has not always the five *sous* in his pocket. Yet, Monsieur, his courage does not fail him. He has taken a young and handsome wife."

"And she?" I urged—

"Is the Countess de St. Alyre."

"Yes; but I fancy we may say something more? She has attributes?"

"Three, Monsieur, three, at least most amiable."

"Ah! And what are they?"

"Youth, beauty, and—diamonds."

I laughed. The sly old gentleman was foiling my curiosity.

"I see, my friend," said I, "you are reluctant——"

"To quarrel with the Count," he concluded. "True. You see, Monsieur, he could vex me in two or three ways; so could I him. But, on the whole, it is better each to mind his business, and to maintain peaceful relations; you understand."

It was, therefore, no use trying, at least for the present. Perhaps he had nothing to relate. Should I think differently, by-and-by, I could try the effect of a few Napoleons. Possibly he meant to extract them.

The host of the Dragon Volant was an elderly man, thin, bronzed, intelligent, and with an air of decision, perfectly military. I learned afterwards that he had served under Napoleon in his early Italian campaigns.

"One question, I think you may answer," I said, "without risking a quarrel. Is the Count at home?"

"He has many homes, I conjecture," said the host evasively. "But—

but I think I may say, Monsieur, that he is, I believe, at present staying at the Château de la Carque."

I looked out of the window, more interested than ever, across the undulating grounds to the château, with its gloomy background of foliage.

"I saw him to-day, in his carriage at Versailles," I said.

"Very natural."

"Then his carriage and horses and servants are at the château?"

"The carriage he puts up here, Monsieur, and the servants are hired for the occasion. There is but one who sleeps at the château. Such a life must be terrifying for Madame the Countess," he replied.

"The old screw!" I thought. "By this torture, he hopes to extract her diamonds. What a life! What fiends to contend with—jealousy and extortion!"

The knight having made this speech to himself, cast his eyes once more upon the enchanter's castle, and heaved a gentle sigh—a sigh of longing, of resolution, and of love.

What a fool I was! and yet, in the sight of angels, are we any wiser as we grow older? It seems to me, only, that our illusions change as we go on; but, still, we are madmen all the same.

"Well, St. Clair," said I, as my servant entered, and began to arrange my things. "You have got a bed?"

"In the cock-loft, Monsieur, among the spiders, and, *par ma foi!* the cats and the owls. But we agree very well. *Vive la bagatelle!*"

"I had no idea it was so full."

"Chiefly the servants, Monsieur, of those persons who were fortunate enough to get apartments at Versailles."

"And what do you think of the Dragon Volant?"

"The Dragon Volant! Monsieur; the old fiery dragon! The devil himself, if all is true! On the faith of a Christian, Monsieur, they say that diabolical miracles have taken place in this house."

"What do you mean? *Revenants?*"

"Not at all, sir; I wish it was no worse. *Revenants?* No! People who have *never* returned—who vanished, before the eyes of half a dozen men, all looking at them."

"What do you mean, St. Clair? Let us hear the story, or miracle, or whatever it is."

"It is only this, Monsieur, that an ex-master-of-the-horse of the late king, who lost his head—Monsieur will have the goodness to recollect, in the revolution—being permitted by the Emperor to return to France, lived here in this hotel, for a month, and at the end of that time vanished, visibly, as I told you, before the faces of half a dozen credible witnesses! The other was a Russian nobleman, six feet high and upwards, who, standing in the centre of the room, downstairs, describing to seven gentlemen of unquestionable veracity, the last moments of Peter the Great, and having a glass of *eau de vie* in his left hand, and his *tasse de café*, nearly finished, in his right, in like manner vanished. His boots were found on the floor where he had been standing; and the gentleman at his right, found, to his astonishment, his cup of coffee in his fingers, and the gentleman at his left, his glass of *eau de vie*——"

"Which he swallowed in his confusion," I suggested.

"Which was preserved for three years among the curious articles of this house, and was broken by the *curé* while conversing with Mademoiselle Fidone in the housekeeper's room; but of the Russian nobleman himself, nothing more was ever seen or heard! *Parbleu!* when *we* go out of the Dragon Volant, I hope it may be by the door. I heard all this, Monsieur, from the postillion who drove us."

"Then it *must* be true!" said I, jocularly: but I was beginning to feel the gloom of the view, and of the chamber in which I stood; there had stolen over me, I know not how, a presentiment of evil; and my joke was with an effort, and my spirit flagged.

CHAPTER XII

The Magician

No more brilliant spectacle than this masked ball could be imagined. Among other *salons* and galleries, thrown open, was the enormous perspective of the "Grande Galerie des Glaces," lighted up on that occasion with no less than four thousand wax candles, reflected and repeated by all the mirrors, so that the effect was almost dazzling. The grand suite of *salons* was thronged with masques, in every conceivable costume. There was not a single room deserted. Every place was animated with music, voices, brilliant colours, flashing jewels, the hilarity of extemporized comedy, and all the spirited incidents of a cleverly sustained masquerade. I had never seen before anything, in the least, comparable to this magnificent *fête*. I moved along, indolently, in my domino and mask, loitering, now and then, to enjoy a clever dialogue, a farcical song, or an amusing monologue, but, at the same time, keeping by eyes about me, lest my friend in the black domino, with the little white cross on his breast, should pass me by.

I had delayed and looked about me, specially, at every door I passed, as the Marquis and I had agreed; but he had not yet appeared.

While I was thus employed, in the very luxury of lazy amusement, I saw a gilded sedan chair, or, rather, a Chinese palanquin, exhibiting the fantastic exuberance of "Celestial" decoration, borne forward on gilded poles by four richly-dressed Chinese; one with a wand in his hand marched in front, and another behind; and a slight and solemn man, with a long black beard, a tall fez, such as a dervish is represented as wearing, walked close to its side. A strangely-embroidered robe fell over his shoulders, covered with hieroglyphic symbols; the embroidery was in black and gold, upon a variegated ground of brilliant colours. The robe was bound about his waist with a broad belt of gold, with cabalistic devices traced on it, in dark red and black; red stockings, and shoes embroidered with gold, and pointed and curved upward at the toes, in Oriental fashion, appeared below the skirt of the robe. The man's face was dark, fixed, and solemn, and his eyebrows black, and enormously heavy—he carried a singular-looking book under his arm, a wand of polished black wood in his other hand, and walked with his chin sunk on his breast, and his eyes fixed upon the floor. The man in front waved his wand right and left to clear the way for the advancing palanquin, the curtains of which were closed; and there was something so singular, strange, and solemn about the whole thing, that I felt at once interested.

I was very well pleased when I saw the bearers set down their burthen within a few yards of the spot on which I stood.

The bearers and the men with the gilded wands forthwith clapped their hands, and in silence danced round the palanquin a curious and half frantic dance, which was yet, as to figures and postures, perfectly methodical. This was soon accompanied by a clapping of hands and a ha-ha-ing, rhythmically delivered.

While the dance was going on a hand was lightly laid on my arm, and, looking round, a black domino with a white cross stood beside me.

"I am so glad I have found you," said the Marquis; "and at this moment. This is the best group in the rooms. *You* must speak to the wizard. About an hour ago I lighted upon them, in another *salon*, and consulted the oracle, by putting questions. I never was more amazed. Although his answers were a little disguised it was soon perfectly plain that he knew every detail about the business, which no one on earth had heard of but himself, and two or three other men, about the most cautious persons in France. I shall never forget that shock. I saw other people who consulted him, evidently as much surprised, and more frightened than I. I came with the Count St. Alyre and the Countess."

He nodded towards a thin figure, also in a domino. It was the Count.

"Come," he said to me, "I'll introduce you."

I followed, you may suppose, readily enough.

The Marquis presented me, with a very prettily-turned allusion to my fortunate intervention in his favour at the Belle Etoile; and the Count overwhelmed me with polite speeches, and ended by saying, what pleased me better still:

"The Countess is near us, in the next *salon* but one, chatting with her old friend the Duchesse d'Argensaque; I shall go for her in a few minutes; and when I bring her here, she shall make your acquaintance; and thank you, also, for your assistance, rendered with so much courage when we were so very disagreeably interrupted."

"You must, positively, speak with the magician," said the Marquis to the Count de St. Alyre, "you will be so much amused. *I* did so; and, I assure you, I could not have anticipated such answers! I don't know what to believe."

"Really! Then, by all means, let us try," he replied.

We three approached, together, the side of the palanquin, at which the black-bearded magician stood.

A young man, in a Spanish dress, who, with a friend at his side, had just conferred with the conjuror, was saying, as he passed us by:

"Ingenious mystification! Who is that in the palanquin? He seems to know everybody!"

The Count, in his mask and domino, moved along, stiffly, with us, towards the palanquin. A clear circle was maintained by the Chinese attendants, and the spectators crowded round in a ring.

One of these men—he who with a gilded wand had preceded the procession—advanced, extending his empty hand, palm upward.

"Money?" inquired the Count.

"Gold," replied the usher.

The Count placed a piece of money in his hand; and I and the Marquis were each called on in turn to do likewise as we entered the circle. We paid accordingly.

The conjuror stood beside the palanquin, its silk curtain in his hand; his chin sunk, with its long, jet-black beard, on his chest; the outer hand grasping the black wand, on which he leaned; his eyes were lowered, as before, to the ground; his face looked absolutely lifeless. Indeed, I never saw face or figure so moveless, except in death.

The first question the Count put, was:

"Am I married, or unmarried?"

The conjuror drew back the curtain quickly, and placed his ear towards a richly-dressed Chinese, who sat in the litter; withdrew his head, and closed the curtain again; and then answered:

"Yes."

The same preliminary was observed each time, so that the man with the black wand presented himself, not as a prophet, but as a medium; and answered, as it seemed, in the words of a greater than himself.

Two or three questions followed, the answers to which seemed to amuse the Marquis very much; but the point of which I could not see, for I knew next to nothing of the Count's peculiarities and adventures.

"Does my wife love me?" asked he, playfully.

"As well as you deserve."

"Whom do I love best in the world?"

"Self."

"Oh! That I fancy is pretty much the case with every one. But, putting myself out of the question, do I love anything on earth better than my wife?"

"Her diamonds."

"Oh!" said the Count.

The Marquis, I could see, laughed.

"Is it true," said the Count, changing the conversation peremptorily, "that there has been a battle in Naples?"

"No; in France."

"Indeed," said the Count, satirically, with a glance round. "And may I inquire between what powers, and on what particular quarrel?"

"Between the Count and Countess de St. Alyre, and about a document they subscribed on the 25th July, 1811."

The Marquis afterwards told me that this was the date of their marriage settlement.

The Count stood stock-still for a minute or so; and one could fancy that they saw his face flushing through his mask.

Nobody, but we two, knew that the inquirer was the Count de St. Alyre.

I thought he was puzzled to find a subject for his next question; and perhaps, repented having entangled himself in such a colloquy. If so, he was relieved; for the Marquis, touching his arm, whispered:

"Look to your right, and see who is coming."

I looked in the direction indicated by the Marquis, and I saw a gaunt figure stalking towards us. It was not a masque. The face was broad, scarred, and white. In a word, it was the ugly face of Colonel Gaillarde, in the costume of a corporal of the Imperial Guard, with his left arm so adjusted as to look like a stump, leaving the lower part of the coat-sleeve empty, and pinned up to the breast. There were strips of very real sticking-plaster across his eyebrows and temple, where my stick had left its mark, to score, hereafter, among the more honourable scars of war.

CHAPTER XIII

The Oracle Tells Me Wonders

I forgot for a moment how impervious my mask and domino were to the hard stare of the old campaigner, and was preparing for an animated scuffle. It was only for a moment, of course; but the Count cautiously drew a little back as the gasconading corporal, in blue uniform, white vest, and white gaiters—for my friend Gaillarde was as loud and swaggering in his assumed character as in his real one of a colonel of dragoons—drew near. He had already twice all but got himself turned out of doors for vaunting the exploits of Napoleon le Grand, in terrific mock-heroics, and had very nearly come to hand-grips with a Prussian hussar. In fact, he would have been involved in several sanguinary rows already, had not his discretion reminded him that the object of his coming there at all, namely, to arrange a meeting with an affluent widow, on whom he believed he had made a tender impression, would not have been promoted by his premature removal from the festive scene, of which he was an ornament, in charge of a couple of gendarmes.

"Money! Gold! Bah! What money can a wounded soldier like your humble servant have amassed, with but his sword-hand left, which, being necessarily occupied, places not a finger at his command with which to scrape together the spoils of a routed enemy?"

"No gold from him," said the magician. "His scars frank him."

"Bravo, Monsieur le prophète! Bravissimo! Here I am. Shall I begin, *mon sorcier,* without further loss of time, to question you?"

Without waiting for an answer, he commenced, in stentorian tones. After half a dozen questions and answers, he asked:

"Whom do I pursue at present?"

"Two persons."

"Ha! Two? Well, who are they?"

"An Englishman, whom, if you catch, he will kill you; and a French widow, whom if you find, she will spit in your face."

"Monsieur le magicien calls a spade a spade, and knows that his cloth protects him. No matter! Why do I pursue them?"

"The widow has inflicted a wound on your heart, and the Englishman a wound on your head. They are each separately too strong for you; take care your pursuit does not unite them."

"Bah! How could that be?"

"The Englishman protects ladies. He has got that fact into your head. The widow, if she sees, will marry him. It takes some time, she will reflect, to become a colonel, and the Englishman is unquestionably young."

"I will cut his cock's-comb for him," he ejaculated with an oath and a grin; and in a softer tone he asked, "Where is she?"

"Near enough to be offended if you fail."

"So she ought, by my faith. You are right, Monsieur le prophète! A hundred thousand thanks! Farewell!" And staring about him, and stretching his lank neck as high as he could, he strode away with his scars, and white waistcoat and gaiters, and his bearskin shako.

I had been trying to see the person who sat in the palanquin. I had only once an opportunity of a tolerably steady peep. What I saw was singular. The oracle was dressed, as I have said, very richly, in the Chinese fashion. He was a figure altogether on a larger scale than the interpreter, who stood outside. The features seemed to me large and heavy, and the head was carried with a downward inclination! the eyes were closed, and the chin rested on the breast of his embroidered pelisse. The face seemed fixed, and the very image of apathy. Its character and *pose* seemed an exaggerated repetition of the immobility of the figure who communicated with the noisy outer world. This face looked blood-red; but that was caused, I concluded, by the light entering through the red silk curtains. All this struck me almost at a glance; I had not many seconds in which to make my observation. The ground was now clear, and the Marquis said, "Go forward, my friend."

I did so. When I reached the magician, as we called the man with the black wand, I glanced over my shoulder to see whether the Count was near.

No, he was some yards behind; and he and the Marquis, whose curiosity seemed to be, by this time, satisfied, were now conversing generally upon some subject of course quite different.

I was relieved, for the sage seemed to blurt out secrets in an unexpected way; and some of mine might not have amused the Count.

I thought for a moment. I wished to test the prophet. A Church-of-England man was a *rara avis* in Paris.

"What is my religion?" I asked.

"A beautiful heresy," answered the oracle instantly.

"A heresy?—and pray how is it named?"

"Love."

"Oh! Then I suppose I am a polytheist, and love a great many?"

"One."

"But, seriously," I asked, intending to turn the course of our colloquy a little out of an embarrassing channel, "have I ever learned any words of devotion by heart?"

"Yes."

"Can you repeat them?"

"Approach."

I did, and lowered my ear.

The man with the black wand closed the curtains, and whispered, slowly and distinctly, these words, which, I need scarcely tell you, I instantly recognised:

I may never see you more; and, oh! that I could forget you! go—farewell—for God's sake, go!

I started as I heard them. They were, you know, the last words whispered to me by the Countess.

Good Heaven! How miraculous! Words heard, most assuredly, by no ear on earth but my own and the lady's who uttered them, till now!

I looked at the impassive face of the spokesman with the wand. There was no trace of meaning, or even of a consciousness that the words he had uttered could possibly interest me.

"What do I most long for?" I asked, scarcely knowing what I said.

"Paradise."

"And what prevents my reaching it?"

"A black veil."

Stronger and stronger! The answers seemed to me to indicate the minutest acquaintance with every detail of my little romance, of which not even the Marquis knew anything! And I, the questioner, masked and robed so that my own brother could not have known me!

"You said I loved someone. Am I loved in return?" I asked.

"Try."

I was speaking lower than before, and stood near the dark man with the beard, to prevent the necessity of his speaking in a loud key.

"Does any one love me?" I repeated.

"Secretly," was the answer.

"Much or little?" I inquired.

"Too well."

"How long will that love last?"

"Till the rose casts its leaves."

The rose—another allusion!

"Then—darkness!" I sighed. "But till then I live in light."

"The light of violet eyes."

Love, if not a religion, as the oracle had just pronounced it, is, at least, a superstition. How it exalts the imagination! How it enervates the reason! How credulous it makes us!

All this which, in the case of another, I should have laughed at, most powerfully affected me in my own. It inflamed my ardour, and half crazed my brain, and even influenced my conduct.

The spokesman of this wonderful trick—if trick it were—now waved me backward with his wand, and as I withdrew, my eyes still fixed upon the group, by this time encircled with an aura of mystery in my fancy; backward toward the ring of spectators, I saw him raise his hand suddenly, with a gesture of command, as a signal to the usher who carried the golden wand in front.

The usher struck his wand on the ground, and, in a shrill voice, proclaimed: "The great Confu is silent for an hour."

Instantly the bearers pulled down a sort of blind of bamboo, which descended with a sharp clatter, and secured it at the bottom; and then the man in the tall fez, with the black beard and wand, began a sort of dervish dance. In this the men with the gold wands joined, and finally, in an outer ring, the bearers, the palanquin being the centre of the circles described by these solemn dancers, whose pace, little by little, quickened, whose gestures grew sudden, strange, frantic, as the motion became swifter and swifter, until at length the whirl became so rapid that the dancers seemed to fly by with the speed of a mill-wheel, and amid a general clapping of hands, and universal wonder, these strange performers mingled with the crowd, and the exhibition, for the time at least, ended.

The Marquis d'Harmonville was standing not far away, looking on the ground, as one could judge by his attitude and musing. I approached, and he said:

"The Count has just gone away to look for his wife. It is a pity she was not here to consult the prophet; it would have been amusing, I daresay, to see how the Count bore it. Suppose we follow him. I have asked him to introduce you."

With a beating heart, I accompanied the Marquis d'Harmonville.

CHAPTER XIV

Mademoiselle de la Vallière

We wandered through the *salons*, the Marquis and I. It was no easy matter to find a friend in rooms so crowded.

"Stay here," said the Marquis, "I have thought of a way of finding him. Besides, his jealousy may have warned him that there is no particular advantage to be gained by presenting you to his wife, I had better go and reason with him; as you seem to wish an introduction so very much."

This occurred in the room that is now called the "Salon d'Apollon." The paintings remained in my memory, and my adventure of that evening was destined to occur there.

I sat down upon a sofa; and looked about me. Three or four persons beside myself were seated on this roomy piece of gilded furniture. They were chatting all very gaily; all—except the person who sat next me, and she was a lady. Hardly two feet interposed between us. The lady sat apparently in a reverie. Nothing could be more graceful. She wore the costume perpetuated in Collignan's full-length portrait of Mademoiselle de la Vallière. It is, as you know, not only rich, but elegant. Her hair was powdered, but one could perceive that it was naturally a dark brown. One pretty little foot appeared, and could anything be more exquisite than her hand?

It was extremely provoking that this lady wore her mask, and did not, as many did, hold it for a time in her hand.

I was convinced that she was pretty. Availing myself of the privilege of a masquerade, a microcosm in which it is impossible, except by voice and allusion, to distinguish friend from foe, I spoke—

"It is not easy, Mademoiselle, to deceive me," I began.

"So much the better for Monsieur," answered the mask, quietly.

"I mean," I said, determined to tell my fib, "that beauty is a gift more difficult to conceal than Mademoiselle supposes."

"Yet Monsieur has succeeded very well," she said in the same sweet and careless tones.

"I see the costume of this, the beautiful Mademoiselle de la Vallière, upon a form that surpasses her own; I raise my eyes, and I behold a mask, and yet I recognise the lady; beauty is like that precious stone in the *Arabian Nights*, which emits, no matter how concealed, a light that betrays it."

"I know the story," said the young lady. "The light betrayed it, not in the sun, but in darkness. Is there so little light in these rooms, Monsieur, that a poor glow-worm can show so brightly? I thought we were in a luminous atmosphere, wherever a certain countess moved?"

Here was an awkward speech! How was I to answer? This lady might be, as they say some ladies are, a lover of mischief, or an intimate of the Countess de St. Alyre. Cautiously, therefore, I inquired,

"What countess?"

"If you know me, you must know that she is my dearest friend. Is she not beautiful?"

"How can I answer, there are so many countesses."

"Every one who knows me, knows who my best beloved friend is. You don't know me?"

"That is cruel. I can scarcely believe I am mistaken."

"With whom were you walking, just now?" she asked.

"A gentleman, a friend," I answered.

"I saw him, of course, a friend; but I think I know him, and should like to be certain. Is he not a certain marquis?"

Here was another question that was extremely awkward.

"There are so many people here, and one may walk, at one time, with one, and at another with a different one, that——"

"That an unscrupulous person has no difficulty in evading a simple question like mine. Know then, once for all, that nothing disgusts a person of spirit so much as suspicion. You, Monsieur, are a gentleman of discretion. I shall respect you accordingly."

"Mademoiselle would despise me, were I to violate a confidence."

"But you don't deceive me. You imitate your friend's diplomacy. I hate diplomacy. It means fraud and cowardice. Don't you think I know him? The gentleman with the cross of white ribbon on his breast. I know the Marquis d'Harmonville perfectly. You see to what good purpose your ingenuity has been expended."

"To that conjecture I can answer neither yes nor no."

"You need not. But what was your motive in mortifying a lady?"

"It is the last thing on earth I should do."

"You affected to know me, and you don't; through caprice or listlessness or curiosity you wished to converse, not with a lady, but with a costume. You admired, and you pretend to mistake me for another. But who is quite perfect? Is truth any longer to be found on earth?"

"Mademoiselle has formed a mistaken opinion of me."

"And you also of me; you find me less foolish than you supposed. I know perfectly whom you intend amusing with compliments and melancholy declamation, and whom, with that amiable purpose, you have been seeking."

"Tell me whom you mean," I entreated.

"Upon one condition."

"What is that?"

"That you will confess if I name the lady."

"You describe my object unfairly," I objected. "I can't admit that I proposed speaking to any lady in the tone you describe."

"Well, I shan't insist on that; only if I name the lady, you will promise to admit that I am right."

"*Must* I promise?"

"Certainly not, there is no compulsion; but your promise is the only condition on which I will speak to you again."

I hesitated for a moment; but how could she possibly tell? The Countess would scarcely have admitted this little romance to anyone; and the mask in the la Vallière costume could not possibly know who the masked domino beside her was.

"I consent," I said, "I promise."

"You must promise on the honour of a gentleman."

"Well, I do; on the honour of a gentleman."

"Then this lady is the Countess de St. Alyre." I was speakably surprised; I was disconcerted; but I remembered my promise, and said—

"The Countess de St. Alyre *is*, unquestionably, the lady to whom I hoped for an introduction to-night; but I beg to assure you also on the honour of a gentleman, that she has not the faintest imaginable suspicion that I was seeking such an honour, nor, in all probability, does she remember that such a person as I exists. I had the honour to render her and the Count a trifling service, too trifling, I fear, to have earned more than an hour's recollection."

"The world is not so ungrateful as you suppose; or if it be, there are, nevertheless, a few hearts that redeem it. I can answer for the Countess de St. Alyre, she never forgets a kindness. She does not show all she feels; for she is unhappy, and cannot."

"Unhappy! I feared, indeed, that might be. But for all the rest that you are good enough to suppose, it is but a flattering dream."

"I told you that I am the Countess's friend, and being so I must know something of her character; also, there are confidences between us, and I may know more than you think, of those trifling services of which you suppose the recollection is so transitory."

I was becoming more and more interested. I was as wicked as other young men, and the heinousness of such a pursuit was as nothing, now that self-love and all the passions that mingle in such a romance, were roused. The image of the beautiful Countess had now again quite superseded the pretty counterpart of La Vallière, who was before me. I would have given a great deal to hear, in solemn earnest, that she did remember the champion who, for her sake, had thrown himself before the sabre of an enraged dragoon, with only a cudgel in his hand, and conquered.

"You say the Countess is unhappy," said I. "What causes her unhappiness?"

"Many things. Her husband is old, jealous and tyrannical. Is not that enough? Even when relieved from his society, she is lonely."

"But you are her friend?" I suggested.

"And you think one friend enough?" she answered; "she has one alone, to whom she can open her heart."

"Is there room for another friend?"

"Try."

"How can I find a way?"

"She will aid you."

"How?"

She answered by a question. "Have you secured rooms in either of the hotels of Versailles?"

"No, I could not. I am lodged in the Dragon Volant, which stands at the verge of the grounds of the Château de la Carque."

"That is better still. I need not ask if you have courage for an adventure. I need not ask if you are a man of honour. A lady may trust herself to you, and fear nothing. There are few men to whom the interview, such as I-shall arrange, could be granted with safety. You shall meet her at two o'clock this morning in the Park of the Château de la Carque. What room do you occupy in the Dragon Volant?"

I was amazed at the audacity and decision of this girl. Was she, as we say in England, hoaxing me?

"I can describe that accurately," said I. "As I look from the rear of the house, in which my apartment is, I am at the extreme right, next the angle; and one pair of stairs up, from the hall."

"Very well; you must have observed, if you looked into the park, two or three clumps of chestnut and lime-trees, growing so close together as to form a small grove. You must return to your hotel, change your dress, and, preserving a scrupulous secrecy, as to why or where you go, leave the Dragon Volant, and climb the park-wall, unseen; you will easily recognise the grove I have mentioned; there you will meet the Countess, who will grant you an audience of a few minutes, who will expect the most scrupulous reserve on your part, and who will explain to you, in a few words, a great deal which *I* could not so well tell you here."

I cannot describe the feeling with which I heard these words. I was astounded. Doubt succeeded. I could not believe these agitating words.

"Mademoiselle will believe that if I only dared assure myself that so great a happiness and honour were really intended for me, my gratitude would be as lasting as my life. But how dare I believe that Mademoiselle does not speak, rather from her own sympathy or goodness, than from a certainty that the Countess de St. Alyre would concede so great an honour?"

"Monsieur believes either that I am not, as I pretend to be, in the secret which he hitherto supposed to be shared by no one but the Countess and himself, or else that I am cruelly mystifying him. That I am in her confidence, I swear by all that is dear in a whispered farewell. By the last companion of this flower!" and she took for a moment in her fingers the nodding head of a white rosebud that was nestled in her bouquet. "By my own good star, and hers—or shall I call it our 'belle étoile? Have I said enough?"

"Enough?" I repeated, "more than enough—a thousand thanks."

"And being thus in her confidence, I am clearly her friend; and being a friend would it be friendly to use her dear name so; and all for sake of practising a vulgar trick upon you—a stranger?"

"Mademoiselle will forgive me. Remember how very precious is the hope of seeing, and speaking to the Countess. Is it wonderful, then, that I should falter in my belief? You have convinced me, however, and will forgive my hesitation."

"You will be at the place I have described, then, at two o'clock?"

"Assuredly," I answered.

"And Monsieur, I know, will not fail, through fear. No, he need not assure me; his courage is already proved."

"No danger, in such a case, will be unwelcome to me."

"Had you not better go now, Monsieur, and rejoin your friend?"

"I promised to wait here for my friend's return. The Count de St. Alyre said that he intended to introduce me to the Countess."

"And Monsieur is so simple as to believe him?"

"Why should I not?"

"Because he is jealous and cunning. You will see. He will never introduce you to his wife. He will come here and say he cannot find her, and promise another time."

"I think I see him approaching, with my friend. No—there is no lady with him."

"I told you so. You will wait a long time for that happiness, if it is never to reach you except through his hands. In the meantime, you had better not let him see you so near me. He will suspect that we have been talking of his wife; and that will whet his jealousy and his vigilance."

I thanked my unknown friend in the mask, and withdrawing a few steps, came, by a little "circumbendibus," upon the flank of the Count.

I smiled under my mask, as he assured me that the Duchesse de la Roqueme had changed her place, and taken the Countess with her; but he hoped, at some very early time, to have an opportunity of enabling her to make my acquaintance.

I avoided the Marquis d'Harmonville, who was following the Count. I was afraid he might propose accompanying me home, and had no wish to be forced to make an explanation.

I lost myself quickly, therefore, in the crowd, and moved, as rapidly as it would allow me, towards the Galerie des Glaces, which lay in the direction opposite to that in which I saw the Count and my friend the Marquis moving.

CHAPTER XV

Strange Story of the Dragon Volant

These fêtes were earlier in those days, and in France, than our modern balls are in London. I consulted my watch. It was a little past twelve.

It was a still and sultry night; the magnificent suite of rooms, vast as some of them were, could not be kept at a temperature less than oppressive, especially to people with masks on. In some places the crowd was inconvenient, and the profusion of lights added to the heat. I removed my mask, therefore, as I saw some other people do, who were as careless of mystery as I. I had hardly done so, and began to breathe more comfortably, when I heard a friendly English voice call me by my name. It was Tom Whistlewick, of the —th Dragoons. He had unmasked, with a very flushed face, as I did. He was one of those Waterloo heroes, new from the mint of glory, whom, as a body, all the world, ex-cept France, revered; and the only thing I knew against him, was a habit of allaying his thirst, which was excessive, at balls, *fêtes*, musical parties, and all gatherings, where it was to be had, with champagne; and, as he introduced me to his friend, Monsieur Carmaignac, I observed that he spoke a little thick. Monsieur Carmaignac was little, lean, and as straight as a ramrod. He was bald, took snuff, and wore spectacles; and, as I soon learned, held an official position.

Tom was facetious, sly, and rather difficult to understand, in his present pleasant mood. He was elevating his eyebrows and screwing his lips oddly, and fanning himself vaguely with his mask.

After some agreeable conversation, I was glad to observe that he preferred silence, and was satisfied with the *rôle* of listener, as I and Monsieur Carmaignac chatted; and he seated himself, with extraor-dinary caution and indecision, upon a bench, beside us, and seemed very soon to find a difficulty in keeping his eyes open.

"I heard you mention," said the French gentleman, "that you had engaged an apartment in the Dragon Volant, about half a league from this. When I was in a different police department, about four years ago, two very strange cases were connected with that house. One was of a wealthy *émigré*, permitted to return to France, by the Em—by Napoleon. He vanished. The other—equally strange—was the case of a Russian of rank and wealth. He disappeared just as mysteriously."

"My servant," I said, "gave me a confused account of some oc-currences, and, as well as I recollect he described the same persons—I mean a returned French nobleman, and a Russian gentleman. But he made the whole story so marvellous—I mean in the supernatural sense —that, I confess, I did not believe a word of it."

"No, there was nothing supernatural; but a great deal inexplicable," said the French gentleman. "Of course there may be theories; but the thing was never explained, nor, so far as I know, was a ray of light ever thrown upon it."

"Pray let me hear the story," I said. "I think I have a claim, as it affects my quarters. You don't suspect the people of the house?"

"Oh! it has changed hands since then. But there seemed to be a fatality about a particular room."

"Could you describe that room?"

"Certainly. It is a spacious, panelled bedroom, up one pair of stairs, in the back of the house, and at the extreme right, as you look from its windows."

"Ho! Really? Why, then, I have got the very room!" I said, begin-ning to be more interested—perhaps the least bit in the world, dis-agreeably. "Did the people die, or were they actually spirited away?"

"No, they did not die—they disappeared very oddly. I'll tell you the particulars—I happen to know them exactly, because I made an official visit, on the first occasion, to the house, to collect evidence; and although I did not go down there, upon the second, the papers came before me, and I dictated the official letter despatched to the relations of the people who had disappeared; they had applied to the government to investigate the affair. We had letters from the same relations more than two years later, from which we learned that the missing men had never turned up."

He took a pinch of snuff, and looked steadily at me.

"Never! I shall relate all that happened, so far as we could discover. The French noble, who was the Chevalier Chateau Blassemare, unlike most *émigrés*, had taken the matter in time, sold a large portion of his property before the revolution had proceeded so far as to render that next to impossible, and retired with a large sum. He brought with him about half a million of francs, the greater part of which he invested in the French funds; a much larger sum remained in Austrian land and securities. You will observe then that this gentleman was rich, and there was no allegation of his having lost money, or being, in any way, embarrassed. You see?"

I assented.

"This gentleman's habits were not expensive in proportion to his means. He had suitable lodgings in Paris; and for a time, society, the theatres, and other reasonable amusements, engrossed him. He did not play. He was a middle-aged man, affecting youth, with the vanities which are usual in such persons; but, for the rest, he was a gentle and polite person, who disturbed nobody—a person, you see, not likely to provoke an enmity."

"Certainly not," I agreed.

"Early in the summer of 1811, he got an order permitting him to copy a picture in one of these *salons*, and came down here, to Versailles, for the purpose. His work was getting on slowly. After a time he left his hotel, here, and went, by way of change, to the Dragon Volant: there he took, by special choice, the bedroom which has fallen to you by chance. From this time, it appeared, he painted little; and seldom visited his apartments in Paris. One night he saw the host of the Dragon Volant, and told him that he was going into Paris, to remain for a day or two, on very particular business; that his servant would accompany him, but that he would retain his apartments at the Dragon Volant, and return in a few days. He left some clothes there, but packed a portmanteau, took his dressing-case, and the rest, and, with his servant behind his carriage, drove into Paris. You observe all this, Monsieur?"

"Most attentively," I answered.

"Well, Monsieur, as soon as they were approaching his lodgings, he stopped the carriage on a sudden, told his servant that he had changed his mind; that he would sleep elsewhere that night, that he had very particular business in the north of France, not far from Rouen, that he would set out before daylight on his journey, and return in a fortnight. He called a *fiacre*, took in his hand a leather bag which, the servant said, was just large enough to hold a few shirts and a coat, but that it was enormously heavy, as he could testify, for he held it in his hand, while his master took out his purse to count thirty-six Napoleons, for which the servant was to account when he should return. He then sent him on, in the carriage; and he, with the bag I have mentioned, got into the *fiacre*. Up to that, you see, the narrative is quite clear."

"Perfectly," I agreed.

"Now comes the mystery," said Monsieur Carmaignac. "After that, the Count Chateau Blassemare was never more seen, so far as we can make out, by acquaintance or friend. We learned that the day before the Count's stockbroker had, by his direction, sold all his stock in the French funds, and handed him the cash it realised. The reason he gave him for this measure tallied with what he said to his servant. He told him that he was going to the north of France to settle some claims, and did not know exactly how much might be required. The bag, which had puzzled the servant by its weight, contained, no doubt, a large sum in gold. Will Monsieur try my snuff?"

He politely tendered his open snuff-box, of which I partook, experimentally.

"A reward was offered," he continued, "when the inquiry was instituted, for any information tending to throw a light upon the mystery, which might be afforded by the driver of the *fiacre* 'employed on the night of' (so-and-so), 'at about the hour of half-past ten, by a gentleman, with a black-leather travelling-bag in his hand, who descended from a private carriage, and gave his servant some money, which he counted twice over.' About a hundred and fifty drivers applied, but not one of them was the right man. We did, however, elicit a curious and unexpected piece of evidence in quite another quarter. What a racket that plaguey harlequin makes with his sword!"

"Intolerable!" I chimed in.

The harlequin was soon gone, and he resumed.

"The evidence I speak of, came from a boy, about twelve years old, who knew the appearance of the Count perfectly, having been often employed by him as a messenger. He stated that about half-past twelve o'clock, on the same night—upon which you are to observe, there was a brilliant moon—he was sent, his mother having been suddenly taken ill, for the *sage femme* who lived within a stone's throw of the Dragon Volant. His father's house, from which he started, was a mile away, or more, from that inn, in order to reach which he had to pass round the park of the Château de la Carque, at the site most remote from the point to which he was going. It passes the old churchyard of St. Aubin, which is separated from the road only by a very low fence, and two or three enormous old trees. The boy was a little nervous as he approached this ancient cemetery; and, under the bright moonlight, he saw a man whom he distinctly recognised as the Count, whom they designated by a soubriquet which means 'the man of smiles.' He was looking rueful enough now, and was seated on the side of a tombstone, on which he had laid a pistol, while he was ramming home the charge of another.

"The boy got cautiously by, on tiptoe, with his eyes all the time on the Count Château Blassemare, or the man he mistook for him; his dress was not what he usually wore, but the witness swore that he could not be mistaken as to his identity. He said his face looked grave and stern; but though he did not smile, it was the same face he knew so well. Nothing would make him swerve from that. If that were he, it was the last time he was seen. He has never been heard of since. Nothing could be heard of him in the neighbourhood of Rouen. There has been no evidence of his death; and there is no sign that he is living."

"That certainly is a most singular case," I replied; and was about to ask a question or two, when Tom Whistlewick who, without my observing it, had been taking a ramble, returned, a great deal more awake, and a great deal less tipsy.

"I say, Carmaignac, it is getting late, and I must go; I really must, for the reason I told you—and, Beckett, we must soon meet again."

"I regret very much, Monsieur, my not being able at present to relate to you the other case, that of another tenant of the very same room—a case more mysterious and sinister than the last—and which occurred in the autumn of the same year."

"Will you both do a very good-natured thing, and come and dine with me at the Dragon Volant to-morrow?"

So, as we pursued our way along the Galerie des Glaces, I extracted their promise.

"By Jove!" said Whistlewick, when this was done; "look at that pagoda, or sedan chair, or whatever it is, just where those fellows set it down, and not one of them near it! I can't imagine how they tell fortunes so devilish well. Jack Nuffles—I met him here to-night—says they are gipsies—where are they, I wonder? I'll go over and have a peep at the prophet."

I saw him plucking at the blinds, which were constructed something on the principle of Venetian blinds; the red curtains were inside; but they did not yield, and he could only peep under one that did not come quite down.

When he rejoined us, he related: "I could scarcely see the old fellow, it's so dark. He is covered with gold and red, and has an embroidered hat on like a mandarin's; he's fast asleep; and, by Jove, he smells like a pole-cat! It's worth going over only to have it to say. Fiew! pooh! oh! It *is* a perfume. Faugh!"

Not caring to accept this tempting invitation, we got along slowly towards the door. I bid them good night, reminding them of their promise. And so found my way at last to my carriage; and was soon rolling slowly towards the Dragon Volant, on the loneliest of roads, under old trees, and the soft moonlight.

What a number of things had happened within the last two hours! what a variety of strange and vivid pictures were crowded together in that brief space! What an adventure was before me!

The silent, moonlighted, solitary road, how it contrasted with the many-eddied whirl of pleasure from whose roar and music, lights, diamonds and colours, I had just extricated myself.

The sight of lonely Nature at such an hour, acts like a sudden sedative. The madness and guilt of my pursuit struck me with a momentary compunction and horror. I wished I had never entered the labyrinth which was leading me, I knew not whither. It was too late to think of that now; but the bitter was already stealing into my cup; and vague anticipations lay, for a few minutes, heavy on my heart. It would not have taken much to make me disclose my unmanly state of mind to my lively friend, Alfred Ogle, nor even to the milder ridicule of the agreeable Tom Whistlewick.

CHAPTER XVI

The Parc of the Château de la Carque

There was no danger of the Dragon Volant's closing its doors on that occasion till three or four in the morning. There were quartered there many servants of great people, whose masters would not leave the ball till the last moment, and who could not return to their corners in the Dragon Volant, till their last services had been rendered.

I knew, therefore, I should have ample time for my mysterious excursion without exciting curiosity by being shut out.

And now we pulled up under the canopy of boughs, before the sign of the Dragon Volant, and the light that shone from its hall-door.

I dismissed my carriage, ran up the broad staircase, mask in hand, with my domino fluttering about me, and entered the large bedroom. The black wainscoting and stately furniture, with the dark curtains of the very tall bed, made the night there more sombre.

An oblique patch of moonlight was thrown upon the floor from the window to which I hastened. I looked out upon the landscape slumbering in those silvery beams. There stood the outline of the Château de la Carque, its chimneys, and many turrets with their extinguisher-shaped roofs black against the soft grey sky. There, also, more in the foreground, about midway between the window where I stood, and the chateau, but a little to the left, I traced the tufted masses of the grove which the lady in the mask had appointed as the trysting-place, where I and the beautiful Countess were to meet that night.

I took "the bearings" of this gloomy bit of wood, whose foliage glimmered softly at top in the light of the moon.

You may guess with what a strange interest and swelling of the heart I gazed on the unknown scene of my coming adventure.

But time was flying, and the hour already near. I threw my robe upon a sofa; I groped out a pair of boots, which I substituted for those thin heelless shoes, in those days called "pumps," without which a gentleman could not attend an evening party. I put on my hat, and lastly, I took a pair of loaded pistols which I had been advised were satisfactory companions in the then unsettled state of French society: swarms of disbanded soldiers, some of them alleged to be desperate characters, being everywhere to be met with. These preparations made, I confess I took a looking-glass to the window to see how I looked in the moonlight; and being satisfied, I replaced it, and ran downstairs.

In the hall I called for my servant.

"St. Clair," said I, "I mean to take a little moonlight ramble, only ten minutes or so. You must not go to bed until I return. If the night is very beautiful, I may possibly extend my ramble a little."

So down the steps I lounged, looking first over my right, and then over my left shoulder, like a man uncertain which direction to take, and I sauntered up the road, gazing now at the moon, and now at the thin white clouds in the opposite direction, whistling, all the time, an air which I had picked up at one of the theatres.

When I had got a couple of hundred yards away from the Dragon Volant, my minstrelsy totally ceased; and I turned about, and glanced sharply down the road that looked as white as hoar-frost under the moon, and saw the gable of the old inn, and a window, partly concealed by the foliage, with a dusky light shining from it.

No sound of footsteps was stirring; no sign of human figure in sight. I consulted my watch, which the light was sufficiently strong to enable me to do. It now wanted but eight minutes of the appointed hour. A thick mantle of ivy at this point covered the wall and rose in a clustering head at top.

It afforded me facilities for scaling the wall, and a partial screen for my operations, if any eye should chance to be looking that way. And now it was done. I was in the park of the Château de la Carque, as nefarious a poacher as ever trespassed on the grounds of unsuspicious lord!

Before me rose the appointed grove, which looked as black as a clump of gigantic hearse-plumes. It seemed to tower higher and higher at every step; and cast a broader and blacker shadow towards my feet. On I marched, and was glad when I plunged into the shadow which concealed me. Now I was among the grand old lime and chestnut trees —my heart beat fast with expectation.

This grove opened, a little, near the middle; and in the space thus cleared, there stood with a surrounding flight of steps, a small Greek temple or shrine, with a statue in the centre. It was built of white marble with fluted Corinthian columns, and the crevices were tufted with grass; moss had shown itself on pedestal and cornice, and signs of long neglect and decay were apparent in its discoloured and weather-worn marble. A few feet in front of the steps a fountain, fed from the great ponds at the other side of the chateau, was making a constant tinkle and plashing in a wide marble basin, and the jet of water glimmered like a shower of diamonds in the broken moonlight. The very neglect and half-ruinous state of all this made it only the prettier, as well as sadder. I was too intently watching for the arrival of the lady, in the direction of the château, to study these things; but the half-noted effect of them was romantic, and suggested somehow the grotto and the fountain, and the apparition of Egeria.

As I watched a voice spoke to me, a little behind my left shoulder. I turned, almost with a start, and the masque, in the costume of Mademoiselle de la Vallière, stood there.

"The Countess will be here presently," she said. The lady stood upon the open space, and the moonlight fell unbroken upon her. Nothing could be more becoming; her figure looked more graceful and elegant than ever. "In the meantime I shall tell you some peculiarities of her situation. She is unhappy; miserable in an ill-assorted marriage, with a jealous tyrant who now would constrain her to sell her diamonds, which are——"

"Worth thirty thousand pounds sterling. I heard all that from a friend. Can I aid the Countess in her unequal struggle? Say but how, and the greater the danger or the sacrifice, the happier will it make me. *Can* I aid her?"

"If you despise a danger—which, yet, is not a danger; if you despise, as she does, the tyrannical canons of the world; and, if you are chivalrous enough to devote yourself to a lady's cause, with no reward but her poor gratitude; if you can do these things you can aid her, and earn a foremost place, not in her gratitude only, but in her friendship."

At those words the lady in the mask turned away, and seemed to weep.

I vowed myself the willing slave of the Countess. "But," I added, "you told me she would soon be here."

"That is, if nothing unforeseen should happen; but with the eye of the Count de St. Alyre in the house, and open, it is seldom safe to stir."

"Does she wish to see me?" I asked, with a tender hesitation.

"First, say have you really thought of *her*, more than once, since the adventure of the Belle Etoile."

"She never leaves my thoughts; day and night her beautiful eyes haunt me; her sweet voice is always in my ear."

"Mine is said to resemble hers," said the mask.

"So it does," I answered. "But it is only a resemblance."

"Oh! then mine is better?"

"Pardon me, Mademoiselle, I did not say *that*. Yours is a sweet voice, but I fancy a little higher."

"A little shriller, you would say," answered the de la Valliere, I fancied a good deal vexed.

"No, not shriller: your voice is not shrill, it is beautifully sweet; but not so pathetically sweet as hers."

"That is prejudice, Monsieur; it is not true."

I bowed; I could not contradict a lady.

"I see, Monsieur, you laugh at me; you think me vain, because I claim in some points to be equal to the Countess de St. Alyre. I challenge you to say, my hand, at least, is less beautiful than hers." As she thus spoke, she drew her glove off, and extended her hand, back upward, in the moonlight.

The lady seemed really nettled. It was undignified and irritating; for in this uninteresting competition the precious moments were flying, and my interview leading apparently to nothing.

"You will admit, then, that my hand is as beautiful as hers?"

"I cannot admit it, Mademoiselle," said I, with the honesty of irritation. "I will not enter into comparisons, but the Countess de St. Alyre is, in all respects, the most beautiful lady I ever beheld."

The masque laughed coldly, and then, more and more softly, said, with a sigh, "I will prove all I say." And as she spoke she removed the mask: and the Countess de St. Alyre, smiling, confused, bashful, more beautiful than ever, stood before me!

"Good Heavens!" I exclaimed. "How monstrously stupid I have been. And it was to Madame la Comtesse that I spoke for so long in the *salon*!" I gazed on her in silence. And with a low sweet laugh of good nature she extended her hand. I took it, and carried it to my lips.

"No, you must not do that," she said, quietly, "we are not old enough friends yet. I find, although you were mistaken, that you do remember the Countess of the Belle Etoile, and that you are a champion true and fearless. Had you yielded to the claims just now pressed upon you by the rivalry of Mademoiselle de la Vallière, in her mask, the Countess de St. Alyre should never have trusted or seen you more. I now am sure that you are true, as well as brave. You now know that I have not forgotten you; and, also, that if you would risk your life for me, I, too, would brave some danger, rather than lose my friend for ever. I have but a few moments more. Will you come here again to-morrow night, at a quarter past eleven? I will be here at that moment; you must exercise the most scrupulous care to prevent suspicion that you have come here, Monsieur. *You owe that to me.*"

She spoke these last words with the most solemn entreaty.

I vowed again and again, that I would die rather than permit the least rashness to endanger the secret which made all the interest and value of my life.

She was looking, I thought, more and more beautiful every moment. My enthusiasm expanded in proportion.

"You must come to-morrow night by a different route," she said; "and if you come again, we can change it once more. At the other side of the château there is a little churchyard, with a ruined chapel. The neighbours are afraid to pass it by night. The road is deserted there, and a stile opens a way into these grounds. Cross it and you can find a covert of thickets, to within fifty steps of this spot."

I promised, of course, to observe her instructions implicitly.

"I have lived for more than a year in an agony of irresolution. I have decided at last. I have lived a melancholy life; a lonelier life than is passed in the cloister. I have had no one to confide in; no one to advise me; no one to save me from the horrors of my existence. I have found a brave and prompt friend at last. Shall I ever forget the heroic tableau of the hall of the Belle Etoile? Have you—have you really kept the rose I gave you, as we parted? Yes—you swear it. You need not; I trust you. Richard, how often have I in solitude repeated your name, learned from my servant. Richard, my hero! Oh! Richard! Oh, my king! I love you."

I would have folded her to my heart—thrown myself at her feet. But this beautiful and—shall I say it—inconsistent woman repelled me.

"No, we must not waste our moments in extravagances. Understand my case. There is no such thing as indifference in the married state. Not to love one's husband," she continued, "is to hate him. The Count, ridiculous in all else, is formidable in his jealousy. In mercy, then, to me, observe caution. Affect to all you speak to, the most complete ignorance of all the people in the Château de la Carque; and, if any one in your presence mentions the Count or Countess de St. Alyre, be sure you say you never saw either. I shall have more to say to you to-morrow night. I have reasons that I cannot now explain, for all I do, and all I postpone. Farewell. Go! Leave me."

She waved me back, peremptorily. I echoed her "farewell," and obeyed.

This interview had not lasted, I think, more than ten minutes. I scaled the park-wall again, and reached the Dragon Volant before its doors were closed.

I lay awake in my bed, in a fever of elation. I saw, till the dawn broke, and chased the vision, the beautiful Countess de St. Alyre, always in the dark, before me.

CHAPTER XVII

The Tenant of the Palanquin

The Marquis called on me next day. My late breakfast was still upon the table.

He had come, he said, to ask a favour. An accident had happened to his carriage in the crowd on leaving the ball, and he begged, if I were going into Paris, a seat in mine—I was going in, and was extremely glad of his company. He came with me to my hotel; we went up to my rooms. I was surprised to see a man seated in an easy chair, with his back towards us, reading a newspaper. He rose. It was the Count de St. Alyre, his gold spectacles on his nose; his black wig, in oily curls, lying close to his narrow head, and showing, like carved ebony over a repulsive visage of boxwood. His black muffler had been pulled down. His right arm was in a sling. I don't know whether there was anything unusual in his countenance that day, or whether it was but the effect of prejudice arising from all I had heard in my mysterious interview in his park, but I thought his countenance was more strikingly forbidding than I had seen it before.

I was not callous enough in the ways of sin to meet this man, injured at least in intent, thus suddenly, without a momentary disturbance.

He smiled.

"I called, Monsieur Beckett, in the hope of finding you here," he croaked, "and I meditated, I fear, taking a great liberty, but my friend the Marquis d'Harmonville, on whom I have perhaps some claim, will perhaps give me the assistance I require so much."

"With great pleasure," said the Marquis, "but not till after six o'clock. I must go this moment to a meeting of three or four people, whom I cannot disappoint, and I know, perfectly, we cannot break up earlier."

"What am I to do?" exclaimed the Count. "An hour would have done it all. Was ever *contretemps* so unlucky!"

"I'll give you an hour, with pleasure," said I.

"How very good of you, Monsieur, I hardly dare to hope it. The business, for so gay and charming a man as Monsieur Beckett, is a little *funeste*. Pray read this note which reached me this morning."

It certainly was not cheerful. It was a note stating that the body of his, the Count's cousin, Monsieur de St. Amand, who had died at his house, the Château Clery, had been, in accordance with his written directions, sent for burial at Père la Chaise, and, with the permission of the Count de St. Alyre, would reach his house (the Château de la Carque), at about ten o'clock on the night following, to be conveyed thence in a hearse, with any member of the family who might wish to attend the obsequies.

"I did not see the poor gentleman twice in my life," said the Count, "but this office, as he has no other kinsman, disagreeable as it is, I could scarcely decline, and so I want to attend at the office to have the book signed, and the order entered. But here is another misery. By ill luck, I have sprained my thumb, and can't sign my name for a week to come. However, one name answers as well as another. Yours as well as mine. And as you are so good as to come with me, all will go right."

Away we drove. The Count gave me a memorandum of the Christian and surnames of the deceased, his age, the complaint he died of, and the usual particulars; also a note of the exact position in which a grave, the dimensions of which were described, of the ordinary simple kind, was to be dug, between two vaults belonging to the family of St. Amand. The funeral, it was stated, would arrive at half-past one o'clock a.m. (the next night but one); and he handed me the money, with extra fees, for a burial by night. It was a good deal; and I asked him, as he entrusted the whole affair to me, in whose name I should take the receipt.

"Not in mine, my good friend. They wanted me to become an executor, which I, yesterday, wrote to decline; and I am informed that if the receipt were in my name it would constitute me an executor in the eye of the law, and fix me in that position. Take it, pray, if you have no objection, in your own name."

This, accordingly, I did.

"You will see, by-and-by, why I am obliged to mention all these particulars."

The Count, meanwhile, was leaning back in the carriage, with his black silk muffler up to his nose, and his hat shading his eyes, while he dozed in his corner; in which state I found him on my return.

Paris had lost its charm for me. I hurried through the little business I had to do, longed once more for my quiet room in the Dragon Volant, the melancholy woods of the Château de la Carque, and the tumultuous and thrilling influence of proximity to the object of my wild but wicked romance.

I was delayed some time by my stockbroker. I had a very large sum, as I told you, at my banker's, uninvested. I cared very little for a few days' interest—very little for the entire sum, compared with the image that occupied my thoughts, and beckoned me with a white arm, through the dark, towards the spreading lime-trees and chestnuts of the Château de la Carque. But I had fixed this day to meet him, and was relieved when he told me that I had better let it lie in my banker's hands for a few days longer, as the funds would certainly fall immediately. This accident, too, was not without its immediate bearing on my subsequent adventures.

When I reached the Dragon Volant, I found, in my sitting-room, a good deal to my chagrin, my two guests, whom I had quite forgotten. I inwardly cursed my own stupidity for having embarrassed myself with their agreeable society. It could not be helped now, however, and a word to the waiters put all things in train for dinner.

Tom Whistlewick was in great force; and he commenced almost immediately with a very odd story.

He told me that not only Versailles, but all Paris, was in a ferment, in consequence of a revolting, and all but sacrilegious, practical joke, played off on the night before.

The pagoda, as he persisted in calling the palanquin, had been left standing on the spot where we last saw it. Neither conjuror, nor usher, nor bearers had ever returned. When the ball closed, and the company at length retired, the servants who attended to put out the lights, and secure the doors, found it still there.

It was determined, however, to let it stand where it was until next morning, by which time, it was conjectured, its owners would send messengers to remove it.

None arrived. The servants were then ordered to take it away; and its extraordinary weight, for the first time, reminded them of its forgotten human occupant. Its door was forced; and, judge what was their disgust, when they discovered, not a living man, but a corpse! Three or four days must have passed since the death of the burly man in the Chinese tunic and painted cap. Some people thought it was a trick designed to insult the Allies, in whose honour the ball was got up. Others were of opinion that it was nothing worse than a daring and cynical jocularity which, shocking as it was, might yet be forgiven to the high spirits and irrepressible buffoonery of youth. Others, again, fewer in number, and mystically given, insisted that the corpse was *bona fide* necessary to the exhibition, and that the disclosures and allusions which had astonished so many people were distinctly due to necromancy.

"The matter, however, is now in the hands of the police," observed Monsieur Carmaignac, "and they are not the body they were two or three months ago, if the offenders against propriety and public feeling are not traced, and convicted, unless, indeed, they have been a great deal more cunning than such fools generally are."

I was thinking within myself how utterly inexplicable was my colloquy with the conjuror, so cavalierly dismissed by Monsieur Carmaignac as a "fool"; and the more I thought, the more marvellous it seemed.

"It certainly was an original joke, though not a very clear one," said Whistlewick.

"Not even original," said Carmaignac. "Very nearly the same thing was done, a hundred years ago or more, at a state ball in Paris; and the rascals who played the trick were never found out."

In this Monsieur Carmaignac, as I afterwards discovered, spoke truly; for, among my books of French anecdote and memoirs, the very incident is marked, by my own hand.

While we were thus talking, the waiter told us that dinner was served; and we withdrew accordingly; my guests more than making amends for my comparative taciturnity.

CHAPTER XVIII

The Churchyard

Our dinner was really good, so were the wines; better, perhaps, at this out-of-the-way inn, than at some of the more pretentious hotels in Paris. The moral effect of a really good dinner is immense—we all felt it. The serenity and good nature that follow are more solid and comfortable than the tumultuous benevolences of Bacchus.

My friends were happy, therefore, and very chatty; which latter relieved me of the trouble of talking, and prompted them to entertain me and one another incessantly with agreeable stories and conversation, of which, until suddenly a subject emerged, which interested me powerfully, I confess, so much were my thoughts engaged elsewhere, I heard next to nothing.

"Yes," said Carmaignac, continuing a conversation which had escaped me, "there was another case, beside that Russian nobleman, odder still. I remembered it this morning, but cannot recall the name. He was a tenant of the very same room. By-the-by, Monsieur, might it not be as well," he added, turning to me, with a laugh, half joke whole earnest, as they say, "if you were to get into another apartment, now that the house is no longer crowded? that is, if you mean to make any stay here."

"A thousand thanks! no. I'm thinking of changing my hotel; and I can run into town so easily at night; and though I stay here, for this night, at least, I don't expect to vanish like those others. But you say there is another adventure, of the same kind, connected with the same room. Do let us hear it. But take some wine first."

The story he told was curious.

"It happened," said Carmaignac, "as well as I recollect, before either of the other cases. A French gentleman—I wish I could remember his name—the son of a merchant, came to this inn (the Dragon Volant), and was put by the landlord into the same room of which we have been speaking. *Your* apartment, Monsieur. He was by no means young—past forty—and very far from good looking. The people here said that he was the ugliest man, and the most good-natured, that ever lived. He played on the fiddle, sang, and wrote poetry. His habits were odd and desultory. He would sometimes sit all day in his room writing, singing, and fiddling, and go out at night for a walk. An eccentric man! He was by no means a millionaire, but he had a *modicum bonum*, you understand —a trifle more than half a million francs. He consulted his stockbroker about investing this money in foreign stocks, and drew the entire sum from his banker. You now have the situation of affairs when the catastrophe occurred."

"Pray fill your glass," I said.

"Dutch courage, Monsieur, to face the catastrophe!" said Whistlewick, filling his own.

"Now, that was the last that ever was heard of his money," resumed Carmaignac. "You shall hear about himself. The night after this financial operation, he was seized with a poetic frenzy; he sent for the then landlord of this house, and told him that he long meditated an epic, and meant to commence that night, and that he was on no account to be disturbed until nine o'clock in the morning. He had two pairs of wax candles, a little cold supper on a side-table, his desk open, paper enough upon it to contain the entire Henriade, and a proportionate store of pens and ink.

Seated at this desk he was seen by the waiter who brought him a cup of coffee at nine o'clock, at which time the intruder said he was writing fast enough to set fire to the paper—that was his phrase; he did not look up, he appeared too much engrossed. But, when the waiter came back, half an hour afterwards, the door was locked; and the poet, from within, answered, that he must not be disturbed.

Away went the *garçon*; and next morning at nine o'clock knocked at his door, and receiving no answer, looked through the key-hole; the lights were still burning, the window-shutters were closed as he had left them; he renewed his knocking, knocked louder, no answer came. He reported this continued and alarming silence to the innkeeper, who, finding that his guest had not left his key in the lock, succeeded in finding another that opened it. The candles were just giving up the ghost in their sockets, but there was light enough to ascertain that the tenant of the room was gone! The bed had not been disturbed; the window-shutter was barred. He must have let himself out, and, locking the door on the outside, put the key in his pocket, and so made his way out of the house. Here, however, was another difficulty, the Dragon Volant shut its doors and made all fast at twelve o'clock; after that hour no one could leave the house, except by obtaining the key and letting himself out, and of necessity leaving the door unsecured, or else by collusion and aid of some person in the house.

Now it happened that, some time after the doors were secured, at half-past twelve, a servant who had not been apprized of his order to be left undisturbed, seeing a light shine through the key-hole, knocked at the door to inquire whether the poet wanted anything. He was very little obliged to his disturber, and dismissed him with a renewed charge that he was not to be interrupted again during the night. This incident established the fact that he was in the house after the doors had been locked and barred. The inn-keeper himself kept the keys, and swore that he found them hung on the wall above his head, in his bed, in their usual place, in the morning; and that nobody could have taken them away without awakening him. That was all we could discover. The Count de St. Alyre, to whom this house belongs, was very active and very much chagrined. But nothing was discovered."

"And nothing heard since of the epic poet?" I asked.

"Nothing—not the slightest clue—he never turned up again. I suppose he is dead; if he is not, he must have got into some devilish bad scrape, of which we have heard nothing, that compelled him to abscond with all the secrecy and expedition in his power. All that we know for certain is that, having occupied the room in which you sleep, he vanished, nobody every knew how, and never was heard of since."

"You have now mentioned three cases," I said, "and all from the same room."

"Three. Yes, all equally unintelligible. When men are murdered, the great and immediate difficulty the assassins encounter is how to conceal the body. It is very hard to believe that three persons should have been consecutively murdered, in the same room, and their bodies so effectually disposed of that no trace of them was ever discovered."

From this we passed to other topics, and the grave Monsieur Carmaignac amused us with a perfectly prodigious collection of scandalous anecdote, which his opportunities in the police department had enabled him to accumulate.

My guests happily had engagements in Paris, and left me about ten.

I went up to my room, and looked out upon the grounds of the Château de la Carque. The moonlight was broken by clouds, and the view of the park in this desultory light, acquired a melancholy and fantastic character.

The strange anecdotes recounted of the room in which I stood, by Monsieur Carmaignac, returned vaguely upon my mind, drowning in sudden shadows the gaiety of the more frivolous stories with which he had followed them. I looked round me on the room that lay in ominous gloom, with an almost disagreeable sensation. I took my pistols now with an undefined apprehension that they might be really needed before my return to-night. This feeling, be it understood, in nowise chilled my ardour. Never had my enthusiasm mounted higher. My adventure absorbed and carried me away; but it added a strange and stern excitement to the expedition.

I loitered for a time in my room. I had ascertained the exact point at which the little churchyard lay. It was about a mile away; I did not wish to reach it earlier than necessary.

I stole quietly out, and sauntered along the road to my left, and thence entered a narrower track, still to my left, which, skirting the park-wall, and describing a circuitous route, all the way, under grand old trees, passes the ancient cemetery. That cemetery is embowered in trees, and occupies little more than half an acre of ground, to the left of the road, interposing between it and the park of the Château de la Carque.

Here, at this haunted spot, I paused and listened. The place was utterly silent. A thick cloud had darkened the moon, so that I could distinguish little more than the outlines of near objects, and that vaguely enough; and sometimes, as it were, floating in black fog, the white surface of a tombstone emerged.

Among the forms that met my eye against the iron-grey of the horizon, were some of those shrubs or trees that grow like our junipers, some six feet high, in form like a miniature poplar, with the darker foliage of the yew. I do not know the name of the plant, but I have often seen it in such funereal places.

Knowing that I was a little too early, I sat down upon the edge of a tombstone to wait, as, for aught I knew, the beautiful Countess might have wise reasons for not caring that I should enter the grounds of the château earlier than she had appointed. In the listless state induced by waiting, I sat there, with my eyes on the object straight before me, which chanced to be that faint black outline I have described. It was right before me, about half a dozen steps away.

The moon now began to escape from under the skirt of the cloud that had hid her face for so long; and, as the light gradually improved, the tree on which I had been lazily staring began to take a new shape. It was no longer a tree, but a man standing motionless. Brighter and brighter grew the moonlight, clearer and clearer the image became, and at last stood out perfectly distinctly. It was Colonel Gaillarde.

Luckily, he was not looking towards me. I could only see him in profile; but there was no mistaking the white moustache, the *farouche* visage, and the gaunt six-foot stature. There he was, his shoulder towards me, listening and watching, plainly, for some signal or person expected, straight in front of him.

If he were, by chance, to turn his eyes in my direction, I knew that I must reckon upon an instantaneous renewal of the combat only commenced in the hall of the Belle Etoile. In any case, could malignant fortune have posted, at this place and hour, a more dangerous watcher? What ecstasy to him, by a single discovery, to hit me so hard, and blast the Countess de St. Alyre, whom he seemed to hate.

He raised his arm; he whistled softly; I heard an answering whistle as low; and, to my relief, the Colonel advanced in the direction of this sound, widening the distance between us at every step; and immediately I heard talking, but in a low and cautious key.

I recognised, I thought, even so, the peculiar voice of Gaillarde.

I stole softly forward in the direction in which those sounds were audible. In doing so, I had, of course, to use the extremest caution.

I thought I saw a hat above a jagged piece of ruined wall, and then a second—yes, I saw two hats conversing; the voices came from under them. They moved off, not in the direction of the park, but of the road, and I lay along the grass, peeping over a grave, as a skirmisher might, observing the enemy. One after the other, the figures emerged full into view as they mounted the stile at the road-side. The Colonel, who was last, stood on the wall for awhile, looking about him, and then jumped down on the road. I heard their steps and talk as they moved away together, with their backs towards me, in the direction which led them farther and farther from the Dragon Volant.

I waited until these sounds were quite lost in distance before I entered the park. I followed the instructions I had received from the Countess de St. Alyre, and made my way among brushwood and thickets to the point nearest the ruinous temple, and crossed the short intervening space of open ground rapidly.

I was now once more under the gigantic boughs of the old lime and chestnut trees; softly, and with a heart throbbing fast, I approached the little structure.

The moon was now shining steadily, pouring down its radiance on the soft foliage, and here and there mottling the verdure under my feet.

I reached the steps; I was among its worn marble shafts. She was not there, nor in the inner sanctuary, the arched windows of which were screened almost entirely by masses of ivy. The lady had not yet arrived.

CHAPTER XIX

The Key

I stood now upon the steps, watching and listening. In a minute or two I heard the crackle of withered sticks trod upon, and, looking in the direction, I saw a figure approaching among the trees, wrapped in a mantle.

I advanced eagerly. It was the Countess. She did not speak, but gave me her hand, and I led her to the scene of our last interview. She repressed the ardour of my impassioned greeting with a gentle but peremptory firmness. She removed her hood, shook back her beautiful hair, and, gazing on me with sad and glowing eyes, sighed deeply. Some awful thought seemed to weigh upon her.

"Richard, I must speak plainly. The crisis of my life has come. I am sure you would defend me. I think you pity me; perhaps you even love me."

At these words I became eloquent, as young madmen in my plight do. She silenced me, however, with the same melancholy firmness.

"Listen, dear friend, and then say whether you can aid me. How madly I am trusting you; and yet my heart tells me how wisely! To meet you here as I do—what insanity it seems! How poorly you must think of me! But when you know all, you will judge me fairly. Without your aid I cannot accomplish my purpose. That purpose unaccomplished, I must die. I am chained to a man whom I despise—whom I abhor. I have resolved to fly. I have jewels, principally diamonds, for which I am offered thirty thousand pounds of your English money. They are my separate property by my marriage settlement; I will take them with me. You are a judge, no doubt, of jewels. I was counting mine when the hour came, and brought this in my hand to show you. Look."

"It is magnificent!" I exclaimed, as a collar of diamonds twinkled and flashed in the moonlight, suspended from her pretty fingers. I thought, even at that tragic moment, that she prolonged the show, with a feminine delight in these brilliant toys.

"Yes," she said, "I shall part with them all. I will turn them into money, and break, for ever, the unnatural and wicked bonds that tied me, in the name of a sacrament, to a tyrant. A man young, handsome, generous, brave as you, can hardly be rich. Richard, you say you love me; you shall share all this with me. We will fly together to Switzerland; we will evade pursuit; my powerful friends will intervene and arrange a separation; and I shall, at length, be happy and reward my hero."

You may suppose the style, florid and vehement, in which I poured forth my gratitude, vowed the devotion of my life, and placed myself absolutely at her disposal.

"To-morrow night," she said, "my husband will attend the remains of his cousin, Monsieur de St. Amand, to Père la Chaise. The hearse, he says, will leave this at half-past nine. You must be here, where we stand, at nine o'clock."

I promised punctual obedience.

"I will not meet you here; but you see a red light in the window of the tower at that angle of the château?"

I assented.

"I placed it there, that, to-morrow night, when it comes, you may recognise it. So soon as that rose-coloured light appears at that window, it will be a signal to you that the funeral has left the château, and that you may approach safely. Come, then, to that window; I will open it, and admit you. Five minutes after a travelling-carriage, with four horses, shall stand ready in the *porte-cochère*. I will place my diamonds in your hands; and so soon as we enter the carriage, our flight commences. We shall have at least five hours' start; and with energy, stratagem, and resource, I fear nothing. Are you ready to undertake all this for my sake?"

Again I vowed myself her slave.

"My only difficulty," she said, "is how we shall quickly enough convert my diamonds into money; I dare not remove them while my husband is in the house."

Here was the opportunity I wished for. I now told her that I had in my banker's hands no less a sum than thirty thousand pounds, with which, in the shape of gold and notes, I should come furnished, and thus the risk and loss of disposing of her diamonds in too much haste would be avoided.

"Good heaven!" she exclaimed, with a kind of disappointment. "You are rich, then? and I have lost the felicity of making my generous friend more happy. Be it so! since so it must be. Let us contribute, each, in equal shares, to our common fund. Bring you, your money; I, my jewels. There is a happiness to me even in mingling my resources with yours."

On this there followed a romantic colloquy, all poetry and passion, such as I should, in vain, endeavour to reproduce.

Then came a very special instruction.

"I have come provided, too, with a key, the use of which I must explain."

It was a double key—a long, slender stem, with a key at each end— one about the size which opens an ordinary room door; the other, as small, almost, as the key of a dressing-case.

"You cannot employ too much caution to-morrow night. An interruption would murder all my hopes. I have learned that you occupy the haunted room in the Dragon Volant. It is the very room I would have wished you in. I will tell you why—there is a story of a man who, having shut himself up in that room one night, disappeared before morning. The truth is, he wanted, I believe, to escape from creditors; and the host of the Dragon Volant, at that time, being a rogue, aided him in absconding. My husband investigated the matter, and discovered how his escape was made. It was by means of this key. Here is a memorandum and a plan describing how they are to be applied. I have taken them from the Count's escritoire. And now, once more I must leave to your ingenuity how to mystify the people at the Dragon Volant. Be sure you try the keys first, to see that the locks turn freely. I will have my jewels ready. You, whatever we divide, had better bring your money, because it may be many months before you can revisit Paris, or disclose our place of residence to any one; and our passports—arrange all that; in what names, and whither, you please. And now, dear Richard" (she leaned her arm fondly on my shoulder, and looked with ineffable passion in my eyes, with her other hand clasped in mine), "my very life is in your hands; I have staked all on your fidelity."

As she spoke the last word, she, on a sudden, grew deadly pale, and gasped, "Good God! who is here?"

At the same moment she receded through the door in the marble screen, close to which she stood, and behind which was a small roofless chamber, as small as the shrine, the window of which was darkened by a clustering mass of ivy so dense that hardly a gleam of light came through the leaves.

I stood upon the threshold which she had just crossed, looking in the direction in which she had thrown that one terrified glance. No wonder she was frightened. Quite close upon us, not twenty yards away, and approaching at a quick step, very distinctly lighted by the moon, Colonel Gaillarde and his companion were coming. The shadow of the cornice and a piece of wall were upon me. Unconscious of this, I was expecting the moment when, with one of his frantic yells, he should spring forward to assail me.

I made a step backward, drew one of my pistols from my pocket, and cocked it. It was obvious he had not seen me.

I stood, with my finger on the trigger, determined to shoot him dead if he should attempt to enter the place where the Countess was. It would, no doubt, have been a murder; but, in my mind, I had no question or qualm about it. When once we engage in secret and guilty practices we are nearer other and greater crimes than we at all suspect.

"There's the statue," said the Colonel, in his brief discordant tones. "That's the figure."

"Alluded to in the stanzas?" inquired his companion.

"The very thing. We shall see more next time. Forward, Monsieur; let us march."

And, much to my relief, the gallant Colonel turned on his heel, and marched through the trees, with his back towards the château, striding over the grass, as I quickly saw, to the park-wall, which they crossed not far from the gables of the Dragon Volant.

I found the Countess trembling in no affected, but a very real terror. She would not hear of my accompanying her towards the château. But I told her that I would prevent the return of the mad Colonel; and upon that point, at least, that she need fear nothing. She quickly recovered, again bid me a fond and lingering good night, and left me, gazing after her, with the key in my hand, and such a phantasmagoria floating in my brain as amounted very nearly to madness.

There was I, ready to brave all dangers, all right and reason, plunge into murder itself, on the first summons, and entangle myself in consequences inextricable and horrible (what cared I?) for a woman of whom I knew nothing, but that she was beautiful and reckless!

I have often thanked heaven for its mercy in conducting me through the labyrinths in which I had all but lost myself.

CHAPTER XX

A High-Cauld Cap

I was now upon the road, within two or three hundred yards of the Dragon Volant. I had undertaken an adventure with a vengeance! And by way of prelude, there not improbably awaited me, at my inn, another encounter, perhaps, this time, not so lucky, with the grotesque sabreur.

I was glad I had my pistols. I certainly was bound by no law to allow a ruffian to cut me down, unresisting.

Stooping boughs from the old park, gigantic poplars on the other side, and the moonlight over all, made the narrow road to the inn-door picturesque.

I could not think very clearly just now; events were succeeding one another so rapidly, and I, involved in the action of a drama so extravagant and guilty, hardly knew myself or believed my own story, as I slowly paced towards the still open door of the Flying Dragon.

No sign of the Colonel, visible or audible, was there. In the hall I inquired. No gentleman had arrived at the inn for the last half-hour. I looked into the public room. It was deserted. The clock struck twelve, and I heard the servant barring the great door. I took my candle. The lights in this rural hostelry were by this time out, and the house had the air of one that had settled to slumber for many hours. The cold moonlight streamed in at the window on the landing, as I ascended the broad staircase; and I paused for a moment to look over the wooded grounds to the turreted château, to me, so full of interest. I bethought me, however, that prying eyes might read a meaning in this midnight

gazing, and possibly the Count himself might, in his jealous mood, surmise a signal in this unwonted light in the stair-window of the Dragon
Volant.

On opening my room door, with a little start, I met an extremely old
woman with the longest face I ever saw; she had what used to be termed
a high-cauld cap on, the white border of which contrasted with her
brown and yellow skin, and made her wrinkled face more ugly. She
raised her curved shoulders, and looked up in my face, with eyes unnaturally black and bright.

"I have lighted a little wood, Monsieur, because the night is chill."

I thanked her, but she did not go. She stood with her candle in her
tremulous fingers.

"Excuse an old woman, Monsieur," she said; "but what on earth can
a young English *milord*, with all Paris at his feet, find to amuse him in
the Dragon Volant?"

Had I been at the age of fairy tales, and in daily intercourse with the
delightful Countess d'Aulnois, I should have seen in this withered apparition, the *genius loci*, the malignant fairy, at the stamp of whose foot,
the ill-fated tenants of this very room had, from time to time, vanished.
I was past that, however; but the old woman's dark eyes were fixed on
mine, with a steady meaning that plainly told me that my secret was
known. I was embarrassed and alarmed; I never thought of asking her
what business that was of hers.

"These old eyes saw you in the park of the château to-night."

"*I!*" I began, with all the scornful surprise I could affect.

"It avails nothing, Monsieur; I know why you stay here; and I tell
you to begone. Leave this house to-morrow morning, and never come
again."

She lifted her disengaged hand, as she looked at me with intense
horror in her eyes.

"There is nothing on earth—I don't know what you mean," I
answered; "and why should you care about me?"

"I don't care about you, Monsieur—I care about the honour of an
ancient family, whom I served in their happier days, when to be noble,
was to be honoured. But my words are thrown away, Monsieur; you
are insolent. I will keep my secret, and you, yours; that is all. You will
soon find it hard enough to divulge it."

The old woman went slowly from the room and shut the door, before
I had made up my mind to say anything. I was standing where she had
left me, nearly five minutes later. The jealousy of Monsieur the Count, I
assumed, appears to this old creature about the most terrible thing in
creation. Whatever contempt I might entertain for the dangers which
this old lady so darkly intimated, it was by no means pleasant, you may
suppose, that a secret so dangerous should be so much as suspected by
a stranger, and that stranger a partisan of the Count de St. Alyre.

Ought I not, at all risks, to apprize the Countess, who had trusted me
so generously, or, as she said herself, so madly, of the fact that our

secret was, at least, suspected by another? But was there not greater danger in attempting to communicate? What did the beldame mean by saying, "Keep your secret, and I'll keep mine"?

I had a thousand distracting questions before me. My progress seemed like a journey through the Spessart, where at every step some new goblin or monster starts from the ground or steps from behind a tree.

Peremptorily I dismissed these harassing and frightful doubts. I secured my door, sat myself down at my table, and with a candle at each side, placed before me the piece of vellum which contained the drawings and notes on which I was to rely for full instructions as to how to use the key.

When I had studied this for awhile, I made my investigation. The angle of the room at the right side of the window was cut off by an oblique turn in the wainscot. I examined this carefully, and, on pressure, a small bit of the frame of the woodwork slid aside, and disclosed a keyhole. On removing my finger, it shot back to its place again, with a spring. So far I had interpreted my instructions successfully. A similar search, next the door, and directly under this, was rewarded by a like discovery. The small end of the key fitted this, as it had the upper keyhole; and now, with two or three hard jerks at the key, a door in the panel opened, showing a strip of the bare wall, and a narrow, arched doorway, piercing the thickness of the wall; and within which I saw a screw-staircase of stone.

Candle in hand I stepped in. I do not know whether the quality of air, long undisturbed, is peculiar; to me it has always seemed so, and the damp smell of the old masonry hung in this atmosphere. My candle faintly lighted the bare stone wall that enclosed the stair, the foot of which I could not see. Down I went, and a few turns brought me to the stone floor. Here was another door, of the simple, old, oak kind, deep sunk in the thickness of the wall. The large end of the key fitted this. The lock was stiff; I set the candle down upon the stair, and applied both hands; it turned with difficulty, and as it revolved, uttered a shriek that alarmed me for my secret.

For some minutes I did not move. In a little time, however, I took courage, and opened the door. The night-air floating in, puffed out the candle. There was a thicket of holly and underwood, as dense as a jungle, close about the door. I should have been in pitch-darkness, were it not that through the topmost leaves, there twinkled, here and there, a glimmer of moonshine.

Softly, lest anyone should have opened his window, at the sound of the rusty bolt, I struggled through this, till I gained a view of the open grounds. Here I found that the brushwood spread a good way up the park, uniting with the wood that approached the little temple I have described.

A general could not have chosen a more effectually-covered approach

from the Dragon Volant to the trysting-place where hitherto I had conferred with the idol of my lawless adoration.

Looking back upon the old inn, I discovered that the stair I had
descended, was enclosed in one of those slender turrets that decorate
such buildings. It was placed at that angle which corresponded with the
part of the panelling of my room indicated in the plan I had been studying.

Thoroughly satisfied with my experiment, I made my way back to
the door, with some little difficulty, re-mounted to my room, locked my
secret door again; kissed the mysterious key that her hand had pressed
that night, and placed it under my pillow, upon which, very soon after,
my giddy head was laid, not, for some time, to sleep soundly.

CHAPTER XXI

I See Three Men in a Mirror

I awoke very early next morning, and was too excited to sleep again. As
soon as I could, without exciting remark, I saw my host. I told him that
I was going into town that night, and thence to——, where I had to see
some people on business, and requested him to mention my being there
to any friend who might call. That I expected to be back in about a
week, and that in the meantime my servant, St. Clair, would keep the
key of my room, and look after my things.

Having prepared this mystification for my landlord, I drove into
Paris, and there transacted the financial part of the affair. The problem
was to reduce my balance, nearly thirty thousand pounds, to a shape in
which it would be not only easily portable, but available, wherever I
might go, without involving correspondence, or any other incident
which would disclose my place of residence, for the time being. All
these points were as nearly provided for as they could be. I need not
trouble you about my arrangements for passports. It is enough to say
that the point I selected for our flight was, in the spirit of romance, one
of the most beautiful and sequestered nooks in Switzerland.

Luggage, I should start with none. The first considerable town we
reached next morning, would supply an extemporised wardrobe. It was
now two o'clock; *only* two! How on earth was I to dispose of the
remainder of the day?

I had not yet seen the cathedral of Notre Dame; and thither I drove. I
spent an hour or more there; and then to the Conciergerie, the Palais de
Justice, and the beautiful Sainte Chapelle. Still there remained some
time to get rid of, and I strolled into the narrow streets adjoining the
cathedral. I recollect seeing, in one of them, an old house with a mural
inscription stating that it had been the residence of Canon Fulbert, the

uncle of Abelard's Eloise. I don't know whether these curious old streets, in which I observed fragments of ancient Gothic churches fitted up as warehouses, are still extant. I lighted, among other dingy and eccentric shops, upon one that seemed that of a broker of all sorts of old decorations, armour, china, furniture. I entered the shop; it was dark, dusty, and low. The proprietor was busy scouring a piece of inlaid armour, and allowed me to poke about his shop, and examine the curious things accumulated there, just as I pleased. Gradually I made my way to the farther end of it, where there was but one window with many panes, each with a bull's-eye in it, and in the dirtiest possible state. When I reached this window, I turned about, and in a recess, standing at right angles with the side wall of the shop, was a large mirror in an old-fashioned dingy frame. Reflected in this I saw, what in old houses I have heard termed an "alcove," in which, among lumber, and various dusty articles hanging on the wall, there stood a table, at which three persons were seated, as it seemed to me, in earnest conversation. Two of these persons I instantly recognised; one was Colonel Gaillarde, the other was the Marquis d'Harmonville. The third, who was fiddling with a pen, was a lean, pale man, pitted with the smallpox, with lank black hair, and about as mean-looking a person as I had ever seen in my life. The Marquis looked up, and his glance was instantaneously followed by his two companions. For a moment I hesitated what to do. But it was plain that I was not recognised, as indeed I could hardly have been, the light from the window being behind me, and the portion of the shop immediately before me, being very dark indeed.

Perceiving this, I had presence of mind to affect being entirely engrossed by the objects before me, and strolled slowly down the shop again. I paused for a moment to hear whether I was followed, and was relieved when I heard no step. You may be sure I did not waste more time in that shop, where I had just made a discovery so curious and so unexpected.

It was no business of mine to inquire what brought Colonel Gaillarde and the Marquis together, in so shabby, and even dirty a place, or who the mean person, biting the feather end of his pen, might be. Such employments as the Marquis had accepted sometimes make strange bed-fellows.

I was glad to get away, and just as the sun set, I had reached the steps of the Dragon Volant, and dismissed the vehicle in which I arrived, carrying in my hand a strong box, of marvellously small dimensions considering all it contained, strapped in a leather cover, which disguised its real character.

When I got to my room, I summoned St. Clair. I told him nearly the same story, I had already told my host. I gave him fifty pounds, with orders to expend whatever was necessary on himself, and in payment for my rooms till my return. I then ate a slight and hasty dinner. My eyes were often upon the solemn old clock over the chimney-piece, which was my sole accomplice in keeping tryst in this iniquitous venture. The sky favoured my design, and darkened all things with a sea of clouds.

The innkeeper met me in the hall, to ask whether I should want a vehicle to Paris? I was prepared for this question, and instantly answered that I meant to walk to Versailles, and take a carriage there. I called St. Clair.

"Go," said I, "and drink a bottle of wine with your friends. I shall call you if I should want anything; in the meantime, here is the key of my room; I shall be writing some notes, so don't allow anyone to disturb me, for at least half an hour. At the end of that time you will probably find that I have left this for Versailles; and should you not find me in my room, you may take that for granted; and you may take charge of everything, and lock the door, you understand?"

St. Clair took his leave, wishing me all happiness and no doubt promising himself some little amusement with my money. With my candle in my hand, I hastened upstairs. It wanted now but five minutes to the appointed time. I do not think there is anything of the coward in my nature; but I confess, as the crisis approached, I felt something of the suspense and awe of a soldier going into action. Would I have receded? Not for all this earth could offer.

I bolted my door, put on my greatcoat, and placed my pistols, one in each pocket. I now applied my key to the secret locks; drew the wainscot-door a little open, took my strong box under my arm, extinguished my candle, unbolted my door, listened at it for a few moments to be sure that no one was approaching, and then crossed the floor of my room swiftly, entered the secret door, and closed the spring lock after me. I was upon the screw-stair in total darkness, the key in my fingers. Thus far the undertaking was successful.

CHAPTER XXII

Rapture

Down the screw-stair I went in utter darkness; and having reached the stone floor, I discerned the door and groped out the keyhole. With more caution, and less noise than upon the night before, I opened the door, and stepped out into the thick brushwood. It was almost as dark in this jungle.

Having secured the door, I slowly pushed my way through the bushes, which soon became less dense. Then, with more ease, but still under thick cover, I pursued in the track of the wood, keeping near its edge.

At length, in the darkened air, about fifty yards away, the shafts of the marble temple rose like phantoms before me, seen through the trunks of the old trees. Everything favoured my enterprise. I had effectually mystified my servant and the people of the Dragon Volant, and so dark was the night, that even had I alarmed the suspicions of all the tenants of the inn, I might safely defy their united curiosity, though posted at every window of the house.

Through the trunks, over the roots of the old trees, I reached the appointed place of observation. I laid my treasure, in its leathern case, in the embrasure, and leaning my arms upon it, looked steadily in the direction of the château. The outline of the building was scarcely discernible, blending dimly, as it did, with the sky. No light in any window was visible. I was plainly to wait; but for how long?

Leaning on my box of treasure, gazing towards the massive shadow that represented the château, in the midst of my ardent and elated longings, there came upon me an odd thought, which you will think might well have struck me long before. It seemed on a sudden, as it came, that the darkness deepened, and a chill stole into the air around me.

Suppose I were to disappear finally, like those other men whose stories I had listened to! Had I not been at all the pains that mortal could, to obliterate every trace of my real proceedings, and to mislead every one to whom I spoke as to the direction in which I had gone?

This icy, snake-like thought stole through my mind, and was gone.

It was with me the full-blooded season of youth, conscious strength, rashness, passion, pursuit, the adventure! Here were a pair of double-barrelled pistols, four lives in my hands? What could possibly happen? The Count—except for the sake of my dulcinea, what was it to me whether the old coward whom I had seen, in an ague of terror before the brawling Colonel, interposed or not? I was assuming the worst that could happen. But with an ally so clever and courageous as my beautiful Countess, could any such misadventure befall? Bah! I laughed at all such fancies.

As I thus communed with myself, the signal light sprang up. The rose-coloured light, *couleur de rose*, emblem of sanguine hope, and the dawn of a happy day.

Clear, soft, and steady, glowed the light from the window. The stone shafts showed black against it. Murmuring words of passionate love as I gazed upon the signal, I grasped my strong box under my arm, and with rapid strides approached the Château de la Carque. No sign of light or life, no human voice, no tread of foot, no bark of dog, indicated a chance of interruption. A blind was down; and as I came close to the tall window, I found that half a dozen steps led up to it and that a large lattice, answering for a door, lay open.

A shadow from within fell upon the blind; it was drawn aside, and as I ascended the steps, a soft voice murmured—"Richard, dearest Richard, come, oh! come! how I have longed for this moment!"

Never did she look so beautiful. My love rose to passionate enthusiasm. I only wished there were some real danger in the adventure worthy of such a creature. When the first tumultuous greeting was over, she made me sit beside her on a sofa. There we talked for a minute or two. She told me that the Count had gone, and was by that time more than a mile on his way, with the funeral, to Père la Chaise. Here were her diamonds. She exhibited, hastily, an open casket containing a profusion of the largest brilliants.

"What is this?" she asked.

"A box containing money to the amount of thirty thousand pounds," I answered.

"What! all that money?" she exclaimed.

"Every *sou*."

"Was it not unnecessary to bring so much, seeing all these?" she said, touching the diamonds. "It would have been kind of you, to allow me to provide for both for a time, at least. It would have made me happier even than I am."

"Dearest, generous angel!" Such was my extravagant declamation. "You forget that it may be necessary, for a long time, to observe silence as to where we are, and impossible to communicate safely with any one."

"You have then here this great sum—are you certain; have you counted it?"

"Yes, certainly; I received it to-day," I answered, perhaps showing a little surprise in my face. "I counted it, of course, on drawing it from my bankers."

"It makes me feel a little nervous, travelling with so much money; but these jewels make as great a danger; *that* can add but little to it. Place them side by side; you shall take off your greatcoat when we are ready to go, and with it manage to conceal these boxes. I should not like the drivers to suspect that we were conveying such a treasure. I must ask you now to close the curtains of that window, and bar the shutters."

I had hardly done this when a knock was heard at the room-door.

"I know who this is," she said, in a whisper to me.

I saw that she was not alarmed. She went softly to the door, and a whispered conversation for a minute followed.

"My trusty maid, who is coming with us. She says we cannot safely go sooner than ten minutes. She is bringing some coffee to the next room."

She opened the door and looked in.

"I must tell her not to take too much luggage. She is so odd! Don't follow—stay where you are—it is better that she should not see you."

She left the room with a gesture of caution.

A change had come over the manner of this beautiful woman. For the last few minutes a shadow had been stealing over her, an air of abstraction, a look bordering on suspicion. Why was she pale? Why had there come that dark look in her eyes? Why had her very voice become changed? Had anything gone suddenly wrong? Did some danger threaten?

This doubt, however, speedily quieted itself. If there had been anything of the kind, she would, of course, have told me. It was only natural that, as the crisis approached, she should become more and more nervous. She did not return quite so soon as I had expected. To a man in my situation absolute quietude is next to impossible. I moved restlessly about the room. It was a small one. There was a door at the other end. I opened it, rashly enough. I listened, it was perfectly silent. I was in an excited, eager state, and every faculty engrossed about what was coming, and in so far detached from the immediate present. I can't account, in any other way, for my having done so many foolish things that night, for I was, naturally, by no means deficient in cunning. About the most stupid of those was, that instead of immediately closing that door, which I never ought to have opened, I actually took a candle and walked into the room.

There I made, quite unexpectedly, a rather startling discovery.

CHAPTER XXIII

A Cup of Coffee

The room was carpetless. On the floor were a quantity of shavings and some score of bricks. Beyond these, on a narrow table, lay an object, which I could hardly believe I saw aright.

I approached and drew from it a sheet which had very slightly disguised its shape. There was no mistake about it. It was a coffin; and on the lid was a plate, with the inscription in French:

PIERRE DE LA ROCHE ST. AMAND.
AGÉ DE XXIII ANS.

I drew back with a double shock. So, then, the funeral after all had not yet left! Here lay the body. I had been deceived. This, no doubt, accounted for the embarrassment so manifest in the Countess's manner. She would have done more wisely had she told me the true state of the case.

I drew back from this melancholy room, and closed the door. Her distrust of me was the worst rashness she could have committed. There is nothing more dangerous than misapplied caution. In entire ignorance of the fact I had entered the room, and there I might have lighted upon some of the very persons it was our special anxiety that I should avoid.

These reflections were interrupted, almost as soon as begun, by the return of the Countess de St. Alyre. I saw at a glance that she detected in my face some evidence of what had happened, for she threw a hasty look towards the door.

"Have you seen anything—anything to disturb you, dear Richard? Have you been out of this room?"

I answered promptly, "Yes," and told her frankly what had happened.

"Well, I did not like to make you more uneasy than necessary. Besides, it is disgusting and horrible. The body *is* there; but the Count had departed a quarter of an hour before I lighted the coloured lamp, and prepared to receive you. The body did not arrive till eight or ten minutes after he had set out. He was afraid lest the people at Père la Chaise should suppose that the funeral was postponed. He knew that the remains of poor Pierre would certainly reach this to-night although an unexpected delay has occurred; and there are reasons why he wishes the funeral completed before to-morrow. The hearse with the body must leave this house in ten minutes. So soon as it is gone, we shall be free to set out upon our wild and happy journey. The horses are to the carriage in the *porte-cochère*. As for this *funeste* horror (she shuddered very prettily), let us think of it no more."

She bolted the door of communication, and when she turned, it was with such a pretty penitence in her face and attitude, that I was ready to throw myself at her feet.

"It is the last time," she said, in a sweet sad little pleading, "I shall ever practice a deception on my brave and beautiful Richard—my hero? Am I forgiven?"

Here was another scene of passionate effusion, and lovers' raptures and declamations, but only murmured, lest the ears of listeners should be busy.

At length, on a sudden, she raised her hand, as if to prevent my stirring, her eyes fixed on me, and her ear towards the door of the room in which the coffin was placed, and remained breathless in that attitude for a few moments. Then, with a little nod towards me, she moved on tip-toe to the door, and listened, extending her hand backward as if to warn me against advancing; and, after a little time, she returned still on tip-toe, and whispered to me, "They are removing the coffin—come with me."

I accompanied her into the room from which her maid, as she told me, had spoken to her. Coffee and some old china cups, which appeared to me quite beautiful, stood on a silver tray; and some liqueur glasses with a flask, which turned out to be noyeau, on a salver beside it.

"I shall attend you. I'm to be your servant here; I am to have my own way; I shall not think myself forgiven by my darling if he refuses to indulge me in anything."

She filled a cup with coffee, and handed it to me with her left hand, her right arm she fondly passed over my shoulder, and with her fingers through my curls caressingly, she whispered, "Take this, I shall take some just now."

It was excellent; and when I had done she handed me the liqueur, which I also drank.

"Come back, dearest, to the next room," she said. "By this time those terrible people must have gone away, and we shall be safer there, for the present, than here."

"You shall direct, and I obey; you shall command me, not only now, but always, and in all things, my beautiful queen!" I murmured.

My heroics were unconsciously, I daresay, founded upon my ideal of the French school of lovemaking. I am, even now, ashamed as I recall the bombast to which I treated the Countess de St. Alyre.

"There, you shall have another miniature glass—a fairy glass—of noyeau," she said, gaily. In this volatile creature, the funereal gloom of the moment before, and the suspense of an adventure on which all her future was staked, disappeared in a moment. She ran and returned with another tiny glass, which, with an eloquent or tender little speech, I placed to my lips and sipped.

I kissed her hand, I kissed her lips, I gazed in her beautiful eyes, and kissed her again unresisting.

"You call me Richard, by what name am I to call my beautiful divinity?" I asked.

"You call me Eugenie, it is my name. Let us be quite real; that is, if you love as entirely as I do."

"Eugenie!" I exclaimed, and broke into a new rapture upon the name.

It ended by my telling her how impatient I was to set out upon our journey; and, as I spoke, suddenly an odd sensation overcame me. It was not in the slightest degree like faintness. I can find no phrase to describe it, but a sudden constraint of the brain; it was as if the membrane, in which it lies, if there be such a thing, contracted, and became inflexible.

"Dear Richard! what is the matter?" she exclaimed, with terror in her looks. "Good Heavens! are you ill? I conjure you, sit down; sit in this chair." She almost forced me into one; I was in no condition to offer the least resistance. I recognised but too truly the sensations that supervened. I was lying back in the chair in which I sat without the power, by this time, of uttering a syllable, of closing my eyelids, of moving my eyes, of stirring a muscle. I had in a few seconds glided into precisely the state in which I had passed so many appalling hours when approaching Paris, in my night-drive with the Marquis d'Harmonville.

Great and loud was the lady's agony. She seemed to have lost all sense of fear. She called me by my name, shook me by the shoulder, raised my arm and let it fall, all the time imploring of me, in distracting sentences, to make the slightest sign of life, and vowing that if I did not, she would make away with herself.

These ejaculations, after a minute or two, suddenly subsided. The lady was perfectly silent and cool. In a very business-like way she took a candle and stood before me, pale indeed, very pale, but with an expression only of intense scrutiny with a dash of horror in it. She moved the candle before my eyes slowly, evidently watching the effect. She then set it down, and rang a hand-bell two or three times sharply. She placed the two cases (I mean hers containing the jewels and my strong box) side by side on the table; and I saw her carefully lock the door that gave access to the room in which I had just now sipped my coffee.

CHAPTER XXIV

Hope

She had scarcely set down my heavy box, which she seemed to have considerable difficulty in raising on the table, when the door of the room in which I had seen the coffin, opened, and a sinister and unexpected apparition entered.

It was the Count de St. Alyre, who had been, as I have told you, reported to me to be, for some considerable time, on his way to Père la Chaise. He stood before me for a moment, with the frame of the doorway and a background of darkness enclosing him, like a portrait. His slight, mean figure was draped in the deepest mourning. He had a pair of black gloves in his hand, and his hat with crape round it.

When he was not speaking his face showed signs of agitation; his mouth was puckering and working. He looked damnably wicked and frightened.

"Well, my dear Eugenie? Well, child—eh? Well, it all goes admirably?"

"Yes," she answered, in a low, hard tone. "But you and Planard should not have left that door open."

This she said sternly. "He went in there and looked about wherever he liked; it was fortunate he did not move aside the lid of the coffin."

"Planard should have seen to that," said the Count, sharply. "*Ma foi!* I can't be everywhere!" He advanced half a dozen short quick steps into the room towards me, and placed his glasses to his eyes.

"Monsieur Beckett," he cried sharply, two or three times, "Hi! don't you know me?"

He approached and peered more closely in my face; raised my hand and shook it, calling me again, then let it drop, and said—"It has set in admirably, my pretty *mignonne*. When did it commence?"

The Countess came and stood beside him, and looked at me steadily for some seconds.

You can't conceive the effect of the silent gaze of those two pairs of evil eyes.

The lady glanced to where, I recollected, the mantelpiece stood, and upon it a clock, the regular click of which I sharply heard.

"Four—five—six minutes and a half," she said slowly, in a cold hard way.

"Brava! Bravissima! my beautiful queen! my little Venus! my Joan of Arc! my heroine! my paragon of women!"

He was gloating on me with an odious curiosity, smiling, as he groped backwards with his thin brown fingers to find the lady's hand; but she, not (I dare say) caring for his caresses, drew back a little.

"Come, *ma chère*, let us count these things. What is it? Pocket-book? Or—or—*what?*"

"It is *that!*" said the lady, pointing with a look of disgust to the box, which lay in its leather case on the table.

"Oh! Let us see—let us count—let us see," he said, as he was unbuckling the straps with his tremulous fingers. "We must count them—we must see to it. I have pencil and pocket-book—but—where's the key? See this cursed lock! My ——! What is it? Where's the key?"

He was standing before the Countess, shuffling his feet, with his hands extended and all his fingers quivering.

"I have not got it; how could I? It is in his pocket, of course," said the lady.

In another instant the fingers of the old miscreant were in my pockets: he plucked out everything they contained, and some keys among the rest.

I lay in precisely the state in which I had been during my drive with the Marquis to Paris. This wretch I knew was about to rob me. The whole drama, and the Countess's *rôle* in it, I could not yet comprehend. I could not be sure—so much more presence of mind and histrionic resource have women than fall to the lot of our clumsy sex—whether the return of the Count was not, in truth a surprise to her; and this scrutiny of the contents of my strong box, an extempore undertaking of the Count's. But it was clearing more and more every moment: and I was destined, very soon, to comprehend minutely my appalling situation.

I had not the power of turning my eyes this way or that, the smallest fraction of a hair's breadth. But let any one, placed as I was at the end of a room, ascertain for himself by experiment how wide is the field of sight, without the slightest alteration in the line of vision, he will find that it takes in the entire breadth of a large room, and that up to a very short distance before him; and imperfectly, by a refraction, I believe, in the eye itself, to a point very near indeed. Next to nothing that passed in the room, therefore, was hidden from me.

The old man had, by this time, found the key. The leather case was open. The box cramped around with iron, was next unlocked. He turned out its contents upon the table.

"Rouleaux of a hundred Napoleons each. One, two, three. Yes, quick. Write down a thousand Napoleons. One, two; yes, right. Another thousand, *write!*" And so, on and on till the gold was rapidly counted. Then came the notes.

"Ten thousand francs. *Write.* Ten thousand francs again: is it written? Another ten thousand francs: is it down? Smaller notes would have been better. They should have been smaller. These are horribly embarrassing. Bolt that door again; Planard would become unreasonable if he knew the amount. Why did you not tell him to get it in smaller notes? No matter now—go on—it can't be helped—*write*—another ten thousand francs—another—another." And so on, till my treasure was counted out, before my face, while I saw and heard all that passed with the sharpest distinctness, and my mental perceptions were horribly vivid. But in all other respects I was dead.

He had replaced in the box every note and rouleau as he counted it, and now having ascertained the sum total, he locked it, replaced it, very methodically, in its cover, opened a buffet in the wainscoting, and, having placed the Countess' jewel-case and my strong box in it, he locked it; and immediately on completing these arrangements he began to complain, with fresh acrimony and maledictions, of Planard's delay.

He unbolted the door, looked in the dark room beyond, and listened. He closed the door again, and returned. The old man was in a fever of suspense.

"I have kept ten thousand francs for Planard," said the Count, touching his waistcoat pocket.

"Will that satisfy him?" asked the lady.

"Why—curse him!" screamed the Count. "Has he no conscience? I'll swear to him it's half the entire thing."

He and the lady again came and looked at me anxiously for a while, in silence; and then the old Count began to grumble again about Planard, and to compare his watch with the clock. The lady seemed less impatient; she sat no longer looking at me, but across the room, so that her profile was towards me—and strangely changed, dark and witch-like it looked. My last hope died as I beheld that jaded face from which the mask had dropped. I was certain that they intended to crown their robbery by murder. Why did they not despatch me at once? What object could there be in postponing the catastrophe which would expedite their own safety? I cannot recall, even to myself, adequately the horrors unutterable that I underwent. You must suppose a real nightmare—I mean a nightmare in which the objects and the danger are real, and the spell of corporal death appears to be protractable at the pleasure of the persons who preside at your unearthly torments. I could have no doubt as to the cause of the state in which I was.

In this agony, to which I could not give the slightest expression, I saw the door of the room where the coffin had been, open slowly, and the Marquis d'Harmonville entered the room.

CHAPTER XXV

Despair

A moment's hope, hope violent and fluctuating, hope that was nearly torture, and then came a dialogue, and with it the terrors of despair.

"Thank heaven, Planard, you have come at last," said the Count, taking him, with both hands, by the arm and clinging to it, and drawing him towards me. "See, look at him. It has all gone sweetly, sweetly, sweetly up to this. Shall I hold the candle for you?"

My friend d'Harmonville, Planard, whatever he was, came to me, pulling off his gloves, which he popped into his pocket.

"The candle, a little this way," he said, and stooping over me he looked earnestly in my face. He touched my forehead, drew his hand across it, and then looked in my eyes for a time.

"Well, doctor, what do you think?" whispered the Count.

"How much did you give him?" said the Marquis, thus suddenly stunted down to a doctor.

"Seventy drops," said the lady.

"In the hot coffee?"

"Yes; sixty in a hot cup of coffee and ten in the liqueur."

Her voice, low and hard, seemed to me to tremble a little. It takes a long course of guilt to subjugate nature completely, and prevent those exterior signs of agitation that outlive all good.

The doctor, however, was treating me as coolly as he might a subject which he was about to place on the dissecting-table for a lecture.

He looked into my eyes again for a while, took my wrist, and applied his fingers to the pulse.

"That action suspended," he said to himself.

Then again he placed something that, for the moment I saw it, looked like a piece of gold-beater's leaf, to my lips, holding his head so far that his own breathing could not affect it.

"Yes," he said in soliloquy, very low.

Then he plucked my shirt-breast open and applied the stethoscope, shifted it from point to point, listened with his ear to its end, as if for a very far off sound, raised his head, and said, in like manner, softly to himself, "All appreciable action of the lungs has subsided."

Then turning from the sound, as I conjectured, he said:

"Seventy drops, allowing ten for waste, ought to hold him fast for six hours and a half—that is ample. The experiment I tried in the carriage was only thirty drops, and showed a highly sensitive brain. It would not do to kill him, you know. You are certain you did not exceed *seventy*?"

"Perfectly," said the lady.

"If he were to die the evaporation would be arrested, and foreign matter, some of it poisonous, would be found in the stomach, don't you see? If you are doubtful, it would be well to use the stomach-pump."

"Dearest Eugenie, be frank, be frank, do be frank," urged the Count.

"I am *not* doubtful, I am *certain*," she answered.

"How long ago, exactly? I told you to observe the time."

"I did; the minute-hand was exactly there, under the point of that Cupid's foot."

"It will last, then, probably for seven hours. He will recover then; the evaporation will be complete, and not one particle of the fluid will remain in the stomach."

It was reassuring, at all events, to hear that there was no intention to murder me. No one who has not tried it knows the terror of the approach of death, when the mind is clear, the instincts of life unimpaired, and no excitement to disturb the appreciation of that entirely new horror.

The nature and purpose of this tenderness was very, very peculiar, and as yet I had not a suspicion of it.

"You leave France, I suppose?" said the ex-Marquis.

"Yes, certainly, to-morrow," answered the Count.

"And where do you mean to go?"

"That I have not yet settled," he answered quickly.

"You won't tell a friend, eh?"

"I can't till I know. This has turned out an unprofitable affair."

"We shall settle that by-and-by."

"It is time we should get him lying down, eh?" said the Count, indicating me with one finger.

"Yes, we must proceed rapidly now. Are his night-shirt and nightcap—you understand—here?"

"All ready," said the Count.

"Now, Madame," said the doctor, turning to the lady, and making her, in spite of the emergency, a bow, "it is time you should retire."

The lady passed into the room, in which I had taken my cup of treacherous coffee, and I saw her no more.

The Count took a candle, and passed through the door at the farther end of the room, returning with a roll of linen in his hand. He bolted first one door, then the other.

They now, in silence, proceeded to undress me rapidly. They were not many minutes in accomplishing this.

What the doctor had termed my night-shirt, a long garment which reached below my feet, was now on, and a cap, that resembled a female nightcap more than anything I had ever seen upon a male head, was fitted upon mine, and tied under my chin.

And now, I thought, I shall be laid in a bed, to recover how I can, and, in the meantime, the conspirators will have escaped with their booty, and pursuit be in vain.

This was my best hope at the time; but it was soon clear that their plans were very different.

The Count and Planard now went, together, into the room that lay straight before me. I heard them talking low, and a sound of shuffling feet; then a long rumble; it suddenly stopped; it recommenced; it continued; side by side they came in at the door, their backs towards me. They were dragging something along the floor that made a continued boom and rumble, but they interposed between me and it, so that I could not see it until they had dragged it almost beside me; and then, merciful heaven! I saw it plainly enough. It was the coffin I had seen in the next room. It lay now flat on the floor, its edge against the chair in which I sat. Planard removed the lid. The coffin was empty.

CHAPTER XXVI

Catastrophe

"Those seem to be good horses, and we change on the way," said Planard. "You give the men a Napoleon or two; we must do it within three hours and a quarter. Now, come; I'll lift him, upright, so as to place his feet in their proper berth, and you must keep them together, and draw the white shirt well down over them."

In another moment I was placed, as he described, sustained in Planard's arms, standing at the foot of the coffin, and so lowered backward, gradually, till I lay my length in it. Then the man, whom he called Planard, stretched my arms by my sides, and carefully arranged the frills at my breast, and the folds of the shroud, and after that, taking his stand at the foot of the coffin, made a survey which seemed to satisfy him.

The Count, who was very methodical, took my clothes, which had just been removed, folded them rapidly together and locked them up, as I afterwards heard, in one of the three presses which opened by doors in the panel.

I now understood their frightful plan. This coffin had been prepared for *me*; the funeral of St. Amand was a sham to mislead inquiry; I had myself given the order at Père la Chaise, signed it, and paid the fees for the interment of the fictitious Pierre de St. Amand, whose place I was to take, to lie in his coffin, with his name on the plate above my breast, and with a ton of clay packed down upon me; to waken from this catalepsy, after I had been for hours in the grave, there to perish by a death, the most horrible that imagination can conceive.

If, hereafter, by any caprice of curiosity or suspicion, the coffin should be exhumed, and the body it enclosed examined, no chemistry could detect a trace of poison, nor the most cautious examination the slightest mark of violence.

I had myself been at the utmost pains to mystify inquiry, should my disappearance excite surmises, and had even written to my few correspondents in England to tell them that they were not to look for a letter from me for three weeks at least.

In the moment of my guilty elation death had caught me, and there was no escape. I tried to pray to God in my unearthly panic, but only thoughts of terror, judgment, and eternal anguish, crossed the distraction of my immediate doom.

I must not try to recall what is indeed indescribable—the multiform horrors of my own thoughts. I will relate, simply, what befell, every detail of which remains sharp in my memory as if cut in steel.

"The undertaker's men are in the hall," said the Count.

"They must not come till this is fixed," answered Planard. "Be good enough to take hold of the lower part while I take this end." I was not left long to conjecture what was coming, for in a few seconds more something slid across, a few inches above my face, and entirely excluded the light, and muffled sound, so that nothing that was not very distinct reached my ears henceforward; but very distinctly came the working of a turnscrew, and the crunching home of screws in succession. Than these vulgar sounds, no doom spoken in thunder could have been more tremendous.

The rest I must relate, not as it then reached my ears, which was too imperfectly and interruptedly to supply a connected narrative, but as it was afterwards told me by other people.

The coffin-lid being screwed down, the two gentlemen arranged the room, and adjusted the coffin so that it lay perfectly straight along the boards, the Count being specially anxious that there should be no appearance of hurry or disorder in the room, which might have suggested remark and conjecture.

When this was done, Doctor Planard said he would go to the hall to summon the men who were to carry the coffin out and place it in the hearse. The Count pulled on his black gloves, and held his white handkerchief in his hand, a very impressive chief-mourner. He stood a little behind the head of the coffin, awaiting the arrival of the persons who accompanied Planard, and whose fast steps he soon heard approaching.

Planard came first. He entered the room through the apartment in which the coffin had been originally placed. His manner was changed; there was something of a swagger in it.

"Monsieur le Comte," he said, as he strode through the door, followed by half a dozen persons. "I am sorry to have to announce to you a most unseasonable interruption. Here is Monsieur Carmaignac, a gentleman holding an office in the police department, who says that information to the effect that large quantities of smuggled English and other goods have been distributed in this neighbourhood, and that a portion of them is concealed in your house. I have ventured to assure him, of my own knowledge, that nothing can be more false than that information, and that you would be only too happy to throw open for his inspection, at a moment's notice, every room, closet, and cupboard in your house."

"Most assuredly," exclaimed the Count, with a stout voice, but a very white face. "Thank you, my good friend, for having anticipated me. I will place my house and keys at his disposal, for the purpose of his scrutiny, so soon as he is good enough to inform me, of what specific contraband goods he comes in search."

"The Count de St. Alyre will pardon me," answered Carmaignac, a little dryly. "I am forbidden by my instructions to make that disclosure; and that I *am* instructed to make a general search, this warrant will sufficiently apprise Monsieur le Comte."

"Monsieur Carmaignac, may I hope," interposed Planard, "that you will permit the Count de St. Alyre to attend the funeral of his kinsman, who lies here, as you see—" (he pointed to the plate upon the coffin)— "and to convey whom to Père la Chaise, a hearse waits at this moment at the door."

"That, I regret to say, I cannot permit. My instructions are precise; but the delay, I trust, will be but trifling. Monsieur le Comte will not suppose for a moment that I suspect him; but we have a duty to perform, and I must act as if I did. When I am ordered to search, I search; things are sometimes hid in such *bizarre* places. I can't say, for instance, what that coffin may contain."

"The body of my kinsman, Monsieur Pierre de St. Amand," answered the Count, loftily.

"Oh! then you've seen him?"

"Seen him? Often, too often!" The Count was evidently a good deal moved.

"I mean the body?"

The Count stole a quick glance at Planard.

"N—no, Monsieur—that is, I mean only for a moment." Another quick glance at Planard.

"But quite long enough, I fancy, to recognise him?" insinuated that gentleman.

"Of course—of course; instantly—perfectly. What! Pierre de St. Amand? Not know him at a glance? No, no, poor fellow, I know him too well for that."

"The things I am in search of," said Monsieur Carmaignac, "would fit in a narrow compass—servants are so ingenious sometimes. Let us raise the lid."

"Pardon me, Monsieur," said the Count, peremptorily, advancing to the side of the coffin, and extending his arm across it. "I cannot permit that indignity—that desecration."

"There shall be none, sir,—simply the raising of the lid; you shall remain in the room. If it should prove as we all hope, you shall have the pleasure of one other look, really the last, upon your beloved kinsman."

"But, sir, I can't."

"But, Monsieur, I must."

"But, besides, the thing, the turnscrew, broke when the last screw was turned; and I give you my sacred honour there is nothing but the body in this coffin."

"Of course Monsieur le Comte believes all that; but he does not know so well as I the legerdemain in use among servants, who are accustomed to smuggling. Here, Philippe, you must take off the lid of that coffin."

The Count protested; but Philippe—a man with a bald head, and a smirched face, looking like a working blacksmith—placed on the floor a leather bag of tools, from which, having looked at the coffin, and picked with his nail at the screw-heads, he selected a turnscrew, and, with a few deft twirls at each of the screws, they stood up like little rows of mushrooms, and the lid was raised. I saw the light, of which I thought I had seen my last, once more; but the axis of vision remained fixed. As I was reduced to the cataleptic state in a position nearly perpendicular, I continued looking straight before me, and thus my gaze was now fixed upon the ceiling. I saw the face of Carmaignac leaning over me with a curious frown. It seemed to me that there was no recognition in his eyes. Oh, heaven! that I could have uttered were it but one cry! I saw the dark, mean mask of the little Count staring down at me from the other side; the face of the pseudo-Marquis also peering at me, but not so full in the line of vision; there were other faces also.

"I see, I see," said Carmaignac, withdrawing. "Nothing of the kind there."

"You will be good enough to direct your man to re-adjust the lid of the coffin, and to fix the screws," said the Count, taking courage; "and —and—really the funeral *must* proceed. It is not fair to the people who have but moderate fees for night-work, to keep them hour after hour beyond the time."

"Count de St. Alyre, you shall go in a very few minutes. I will direct, just now, all about the coffin."

The Count looked toward the door, and there saw a gendarme; and two or three more grave and stalwart specimens of the same force were also in the room. The Count was very uncomfortably excited; it was growing insupportable.

"As this gentleman makes a difficulty about my attending the obsequies of my kinsman, I will ask you, Planard, to accompany the funeral in my stead."

"In a few minutes," answered the incorrigible Carmaignac. "I must first trouble you for the key that opens that press."

He pointed direct at the press, in which the clothes had just been locked up.

"I—I have no objection," said the Count—"none, of course; only they have not been used for an age. I'll direct some one to look for the key."

"If you have not got it about you, it is quite unnecessary. Philippe, try your skeleton-keys with that press. I want it opened. Whose clothes are these?" inquired Carmaignac when, the press having been opened, he took out the suit that had been placed there scarcely two minutes since.

"I can't say," answered the Count. "I know nothing of the contents of that press. A roguish servant, named Lablais, whom I dismissed about a year ago, had the key. I have not seen it open for ten years or more. The clothes are probably his.

"Here are visiting cards, see, and here a marked pocket-handkerchief —'R. B.' upon it. He must have stolen them from a person named Beckett—R. Beckett. 'Mr. Beckett, Berkeley Square,' the card says; and, my faith! here's a watch and a bunch of seals; one of them with the initials 'R. B.' upon it. That servant, Lablais, must have been a consummate rogue!"

"So he was; you are right, sir."

"It strikes me that he possibly stole these clothes," continued Carmaignac, "from the man in the coffin, who, in that case, would be Monsieur Beckett, and not Monsieur de St. Amand. For, wonderful to relate, Monsieur, the watch is still going! That man in the coffin, I believe, is not dead, but simply drugged. And for having robbed and intended to murder him, I arrest you, Nicolas de la Marque, Count de St. Alyre."

In another moment the old villain was a prisoner. I heard his discordant voice break quaveringly into sudden vehemence and volubility; now croaking—now shrieking, as he oscillated between protests, threats, and impious appeals to the God who will "judge the secrets of men!" And thus lying and raving, he was removed from the room, and placed in the same coach with his beautiful and abandoned accomplice, already arrested; and, with two *gendarmes* sitting beside them, they were immediately driving at a rapid pace towards the Conciergerie.

There were now added to the general chorus two voices, very different in quality; one was that of the gasconading Colonel Gaillarde, who had with difficulty been kept in the background up to this; the other was that of my jolly friend Whistlewick, who had come to identify me.

I shall tell you, just now, how this project against my property and life, so ingenious and monstrous, was exploded. I must first say a word about myself. I was placed in a hot bath, under the direction of Planard, as consummate a villain as any of the gang, but now thoroughly in the interests of the prosecution. Thence I was laid in a warm bed, the window of the room being open. These simple measures restored me in about three hours; I should otherwise, probably, have continued under the spell for nearly seven.

The practices of these nefarious conspirators had been carried on with consummate skill and secrecy. Their dupes were led, as I was, to be themselves auxiliary to the mystery which made their own destruction both safe and certain.

A search was, of course, instituted. Graves were opened in Père la Chaise. The bodies exhumed had lain there too long, and were too much decomposed to be recognised. One only was identified. The notice for the burial, in this particular case, had been signed, the order given, and the fees paid, by Gabriel Gaillarde, who was known to the official clerk, who had to transact with him this little funereal business. The very trick, that had been arranged for me, had been successfully practised in his case. The person for whom the grave had been ordered, was purely fictitious; and Gabriel Gaillarde himself filled the coffin, on the cover of which that false name was inscribed as well as upon a tomb-stone over the grave. Possibly, the same honour, under my pseudonym, may have been intended for me.

The identification was curious. This Gabriel Gaillarde had had a bad fall from a run-away horse, about five years before his mysterious disappearance. He had lost an eye and some teeth, in this accident, besides sustaining a fracture of the right leg, immediately above the ankle. He had kept the injuries to his face as profound a secret as he could. The result was, that the glass eye which had done duty for the one he had lost, remained in the socket, slightly displaced, of course, but recognisable by the "artist" who had supplied it.

More pointedly recognisable were the teeth, peculiar in workmanship, which one of the ablest dentists in Paris had himself adapted to the chasms, the cast of which, owing to peculiarities in the accident, he happened to have preserved. This cast precisely fitted the gold plate found in the mouth of the skull. The mark, also, above the ankle, in the bone, where it had re-united, corresponded exactly with the place where the fracture had knit in the limb of Gabriel Gaillarde.

The Colonel, his younger brother, had been furious about the disappearance of Gabriel, and still more so about that of his money, which he had long regarded as his proper keepsake, whenever death should remove his brother from the vexations of living. He had suspected for a long time, for certain adroitly discovered reasons, that the Count de St. Alyre and the beautiful lady, his companion, countess, or whatever else she was, had pigeoned him. To this suspicion were added some others of a still darker kind; but in their first shape, rather the exaggerated reflections of his fury, ready to believe anything, than well-defined conjectures.

At length an accident had placed the Colonel very nearly upon the right scent; a chance, possibly lucky for himself, had apprized the scoundrel Planard that the conspirators—himself among the number— were in danger. The result was that he made terms for himself, became an informer, and concerted with the police this visit made to the Château de la Carque, at the critical moment when every measure had been completed that was necessary to construct a perfect case against his guilty accomplices.

I need not describe the minute industry or forethought with which the police collected all the details necessary to support the case. They had brought an able physician, who, even had Planard failed, would have supplied the necessary medical evidence.

My trip to Paris, you will believe, had not turned out quite so agreeably as I had anticipated. I was the principal witness for the prosecution in this *cause célèbre*, with all the *agréments* that attend that enviable position. Having had an escape, as my friend Whistlewick said, "with a squeak" for my life, I innocently fancied that I should have been an object of considerable interest to Parisian society; but, a good deal to my mortification, I discovered that I was the object for a good-natured but contemptuous merriment. I was a *balourd*, a *benêt*, *un âne*, and figured even in caricatures. I became a sort of public character, a dignity,

"Unto which I was not born,"

and from which I fled as soon as I conveniently could, without even paying my friend the Marquis d'Harmonville a visit at his hospitable château.

The Marquis escaped scot-free. His accomplice, the Count, was executed. The fair Eugenie, under extenuating circumstances—consisting, so far as I could discover of her good looks—got off for six years' imprisonment.

Colonel Gaillarde recovered some of his brother's money, out of the not very affluent estate of the Count and *soi-disant* Countess. This, and the execution of the Count, put him in high good humour. So far from insisting on a hostile meeting, he shook me very graciously by the hand, told me that he looked upon the wound on his head, inflicted by the knob of my stick, as having been received in an honourable, though irregular duel, in which he had no disadvantage of unfairness to complain of.

I think I have only two additional details to mention. The bricks discovered in the room with the coffin, had been packed in it, in straw, to supply the weight of a dead body, and to prevent the suspicions and contradictions that might have been excited by the arrival of an empty coffin at the château.

Secondly, the Countess's magnificent brilliants were examined by a lapidary, and pronounced to be worth about five pounds to a tragedy-queen, who happened to be in want of a suite of paste.

The Countess had figured some years before as one of the cleverest actresses on the minor stage of Paris, where she had been picked up by the Count and used as his principal accomplice.

She it was who, admirably disguised, had rifled my papers in the carriage on my memorable night-journey to Paris. She also had figured as the interpreting magician of the palanquin at the ball at Versailles. So far as I was affected by that elaborate mystification it was intended to re-animate my interest, which, they feared, might flag in the beautiful Countess. It had its design and action upon other intended victims also; but of them there is, at present, no need to speak. The introduction of a real corpse—procured from a person who supplied the Parisian anatomists—involved no real danger, while it heightened the mystery and kept the prophet alive in the gossip of the town and in the thoughts of the noodles with whom he had conferred.

I divided the remainder of the summer and autumn between Switzerland and Italy.

As the well-worn phrase goes, I was a sadder if not a wiser man. A great deal of the horrible impression left upon my mind was due, of course, to the mere action of nerves and brain. But serious feelings of another and deeper kind remained. My after life was ultimately formed by the shock I had then received. Those impressions led me—but not till after many years—to happier though not less serious thoughts; and I have deep reason to be thankful to the all-merciful Ruler of events, for an early and terrible lesson in the ways of sin.

LAURA SILVER BELL

In the five Northumbrian counties you will scarcely find so bleak, ugly, and yet, in a savage way, so picturesque a moor as Dardale Moss. The moor itself spreads north, south, east, and west, a great undulating sea of black peat and heath.

What we may term its shores are wooded wildly with birch, hazel, and dwarf-oak. No towering mountains surround it, but here and there you have a rocky knoll rising among the trees, and many a wooded promontory of the same pretty, because utterly wild, forest, running out into its dark level.

Habitations are thinly scattered in this barren territory, and a full mile away from the meanest was the stone cottage of Mother Carke.

Let not my southern reader who associates ideas of comfort with the term "cottage" mistake. This thing is built of shingle, with low walls. Its thatch is hollow; the peat-smoke curls stingily from its stunted chimney. It is worthy of its savage surroundings.

The primitive neighbours remark that no rowan-tree grows near, nor holly, nor bracken, and no horseshoe is nailed on the door.

Not far from the birches and hazels that straggle about the rude wall of the little enclosure, on the contrary, they say, you may discover the broom and the rag-wort, in which witches mysteriously delight. But this is perhaps a scandal.

Mall Carke was for many a year the *sage femme* of this wild domain. She has renounced practice, however, for some years; and now, under the rose, she dabbles, it is thought, in the black art, in which she has always been secretly skilled, tells fortunes, practises charms, and in popular esteem is little better than a witch.

Mother Carke has been away to the town of Willarden, to sell knit stockings, and is returning to her rude dwelling by Dardale Moss. To her right, as far away as the eye can reach, the moor stretches. The narrow track she has followed here tops a gentle upland, and at her left a sort of jungle of dwarf-oak and brushwood approaches its edge. The sun is sinking blood-red in the west. His disk has touched the broad black level of the moor, and his parting beams glare athwart the gaunt figure of the old beldame, as she strides homeward stick in hand, and bring into relief the folds of her mantle, which gleam like the draperies of a bronze image in the light of a fire. For a few moments this light floods the air—tree, gorse, rock, and bracken glare; and then it is out, and gray twilight over everything.

All is still and sombre. At this hour the simple traffic of the thinly-peopled country is over, and nothing can be more solitary.

From this jungle, nevertheless, through which the mists of evening are already creeping, she sees a gigantic man approaching her.

In that poor and primitive country robbery is a crime unknown. She, therefore, has no fears for her pound of tea, and pint of gin, and sixteen shillings in silver which she is bringing home in her pocket. But there is something that would have frighted another woman about this man.

He is gaunt, sombre, bony, dirty, and dressed in a black suit which a beggar would hardly care to pick out of the dust.

This ill-looking man nodded to her as he stepped on the road.

"I don't know you," she said.

He nodded again.

"I never sid ye neyawheere," she exclaimed sternly.

"Fine evening, Mother Carke," he says, and holds his snuff-box toward her.

She widened the distance between them by a step or so, and said again sternly and pale,

"I hev nowt to say to thee, whoe'er thou beest."

"You know Laura Silver Bell?"

"That's a byneyam; the lass's neyam is Laura Lew," she answered, looking straight before her.

"One name's as good as another for one that was never christened, mother."

"How know ye that?" she asked grimly; for it is a received opinion in that part of the world that the fairies have power over those who have never been baptised.

The stranger turned on her a malignant smile.

"There is a young lord in love with her," the stranger says, "and I'm that lord. Have her at your house to-morrow night at eight o'clock, and you must stick cross pins through the candle, as you have done for many a one before, to bring her lover thither by ten, and her fortune's made. And take this for your trouble."

He extended his long finger and thumb toward her, with a guinea temptingly displayed.

"I have nowt to do wi' thee. I nivver sid thee afoore. Git thee awa'! I earned nea goold o' thee, and I'll tak' nane. Awa' wi' thee, or I'll find ane that will mak' thee!"

The old woman had stopped, and was quivering in every limb as she thus spoke.

He looked very angry. Sulkily he turned away at her words, and strode slowly toward the wood from which he had come; and as he approached it, he seemed to her to grow taller and taller, and stalked into it as high as a tree.

"I conceited there would come something o't", she said to herself. "Farmer Lew must git it done nesht Sunda'. The a'ad awpy!"

Old Farmer Lew was one of that sect who insist that baptism shall be but once administered, and not until the Christian candidate had attained to adult years. The girl had indeed for some time been of an age not only, according to this theory, to be baptised, but if need be to be married.

Her story was a sad little romance. A lady some seventeen years before had come down and paid Farmer Lew for two rooms in his house. She told him that her husband would follow her in a fortnight, and that he was in the mean time delayed by business in Liverpool.

In ten days after her arrival her baby was born, Mall Carke acting as *sage femme* on the occasion; and on the evening of that day the poor young mother died. No husband came; no wedding-ring, they said, was on her finger. About fifty pounds was found in her desk, which Farmer Lew, who was a kind old fellow and had lost his two children, put in bank for the little girl, and resolved to keep her until a rightful owner should step forward to claim her.

They found half-a-dozen love-letters signed "Francis," and calling the dead woman "Laura."

So Farmer Lew called the little girl Laura; and her *sobriquet* of "Silver Bell" was derived from a tiny silver bell, once gilt, which was found among her poor mother's little treasures after her death, and which the child wore on a ribbon round her neck.

Thus, being very pretty and merry, she grew up as a North-country farmer's daughter; and the old man, as she needed more looking after, grew older and less able to take care of her; so she was, in fact, very nearly her own mistress, and did pretty much in all things as she liked.

Old Mall Carke, by some caprice for which no one could account, cherished an affection for the girl, who saw her often, and paid her many a small fee in exchange for the secret indications of the future.

It was too late when Mother Carke reached her home to look for a visit from Laura Silver Bell that day.

About three o'clock next afternoon, Mother Carke was sitting knitting, with her glasses on, outside her door on the stone bench, when she saw the pretty girl mount lightly to the top of the stile at her left under the birch, against the silver stem of which she leaned her slender hand, and called,

"Mall, Mall! Mother Carke, are ye alane all by yersel'?"

"Ay, Laura lass, we can be clooas enoo, if ye want a word wi' me," says the old woman, rising, with a mysterious nod, and beckoning her stiffly with her long fingers.

The girl was, assuredly, pretty enough for a "lord" to fall in love with. Only look at her. A profusion of brown rippling hair, parted low in the middle of her forehead, almost touched her eyebrows, and made the pretty oval of her face, by the breadth of that rich line, more marked. What a pretty little nose! what scarlet lips, and large, dark, long-fringed eyes!

Her face is transparently tinged with those clear Murillo tints which appear in deeper dyes on her wrists and the backs of her hands. These are the beautiful gipsy-tints with which the sun dyes young skins so richly.

The old woman eyes all this, and her pretty figure, so round and slender, and her shapely little feet, cased in the thick shoes that can't hide their comely proportions, as she stands on the top of the stile. But it is with a dark and saturnine aspect.

"Come, lass, what stand ye for atoppa t' wall, whar folk may chance to see thee? I hev a thing to tell thee, lass."

She beckoned her again.

"An' I hev a thing to tell *thee*, Mall."

"Come hidder," said the old woman peremptorily.

"But ye munna gie me the creepin's" (make me tremble). "I winna look again into the glass o' water, mind ye."

The old woman smiled grimly, and changed her tone.

"Now, hunny, git tha down, and let ma see thy canny feyace," and she beckoned her again.

Laura Silver Bell did get down, and stepped lightly toward the door of the old woman's dwelling.

"Tak this," said the girl, unfolding a piece of bacon from her apron, "and I hev a silver sixpence to gie thee, when I'm gaen away heyam."

They entered the dark kitchen of the cottage, and the old woman stood by the door, lest their conference should be lighted on by surprise.

"Afoore ye begin," said Mother Carke (I soften her patois), "I mun tell ye there's ill folk watchin' ye. What's auld Farmer Lew about, he doesna get t' sir" (the clergyman) "to baptise thee? If he lets Sunda' next pass, I'm afeared ye'll never be sprinkled nor signed wi' cross, while there's a sky aboon us."

"Agoy!" exclaims the girl, "who's lookin' after me?"

"A big black fella, as high as the kipples, came out o' the wood near Deadman's Grike, just after the sun gaed down yester e'en; I knew weel what he was, for his feet ne'er touched the road while he made as if he walked beside me. And he wanted to gie me snuff first, and I wouldna hev that; and then he offered me a gowden guinea, but I was no sic awpy, and to bring you here to-night, and cross the candle wi' pins, to call your lover in. And he said he's a great lord, and in luve wi' thee."

"And you refused him?"

"Well for thee I did, lass," says Mother Carke.

"Why, it's every word true!" cries the girl vehemently, starting to her feet, for she had seated herself on the great oak chest.

"True, lass? Come, say what ye mean," demanded Mall Carke, with a dark and searching gaze.

"Last night I was coming heyam from the wake, wi' auld farmer Dykes and his wife and his daughter Nell, and when we came to the stile, I bid them good-night, and we parted."

"And ye came by the path alone in the night-time, did ye?" exclaimed old Mall Carke sternly.

"I wasna afeared, I don't know why; the path heyam leads down by the wa'as o' auld Hawarth Castle."

"I knaa it weel, and a dowly path it is; ye'll keep indoors o' nights for a while, or ye'll rue it. What saw ye?"

"No freetin, mother; nowt I was feared on."

"Ye heard a voice callin' yer neyame?"

"I heard nowt that was dow, but the hullyhoo in the auld castle wa's," answered the pretty girl. "I heard nor sid nowt that's dow, but mickle that's conny and gladsome. I heard singin' and laughin' a long way off, I consaited; and I stopped a bit to listen. Then I walked on a step or two, and there, sure enough in the Pie-Mag field, under the castle wa's, not twenty steps away, I sid a grand company; silks and satins, and men wi' velvet coats, wi' gowd-lace striped over them, and ladies wi' necklaces that would dazzle ye, and fans as big as griddles; and powdered footmen, like what the shirra hed behind his coach, only these was ten times as grand."

"It was full moon last night," said the old woman.

"Sa bright 'twould blind ye to look at it," said the girl.

"Never an ill sight but the deaul finds a light," quoth the old woman. 'There's a rinnin brook thar—you were at this side, and they at that; did they try to mak ye cross over?"

"Agoy! didn't they? Nowt but civility and kindness, though. But ye mun let me tell it my own way. They was talkin' and laughin', and eatin', and drinkin' out o' long glasses and goud cups, seated on the grass, and music was playin'; and I keekin' behind a bush at all the grand doin's; and up they gits to dance; and says a tall fella I didna see afoore, 'Ye mun step across, and dance wi' a young lord that's faan in luv wi' thee, and that's mysel',' and sure enow I keeked at him under my lashes and a conny lad he is, to my teyaste, though he be dressed in black, wi' sword and sash, velvet twice as fine as they sells in the shop at Gouden Friars; and keekin' at me again fra the corners o' his een. And the same fella telt me he was mad in luv wi' me, and his fadder was there, and his sister, and they came all the way from Catstean Castle to see me that night; and that's t' other side o' Gouden Friars."

"Come, lass, yer no mafflin; tell me true. What was he like? Was his feyace grimed wi' sut? a tall fella wi' wide shouthers, and lukt like an ill-thing, wi' black clothes amaist in rags?"

"His feyace was long, but weel-faured, and darker nor a gipsy; and his clothes were black and grand, and made o' velvet, and he said he was the young lord himsel'; and he lukt like it."

"That will be the same fella I sid at Deadman's Grike," said Mall Carke, with an anxious frown.

"Hoot, mudder! how cud that be?" cried the lass, with a toss of her pretty head and a smile of scorn. But the fortune-teller made no answer, and the girl went on with her story.

"When they began to dance," continued Laura Silver Bell, "he urged me again, but I wudna step o'er; 'twas partly pride, coz I wasna dressed fine enough, and partly contrairiness, or something, but gaa I wudna, not a fut. No but I more nor half wished it a' the time."

"Weel for thee thou dudstna cross the brook."

"Hoity-toity, why not?"

"Keep at heyame after nightfall, and don't ye be walking by yersel' by daylight or any light lang lonesome ways, till after ye're baptised," said Mall Carke.

"I'm like to be married first."

"Tak care *that* marriage won't hang i' the bell-ropes," said Mother Carke.

"Leave me alane for that. The young lord said he was maist daft wi' luv o' me. He wanted to gie me a conny ring wi' a beautiful stone in it. But, drat it, I was sic an awpy I wudna tak it, and he a young lord!"

"Lord, indeed! are ye daft or dreamin'? Those fine folk, what were they? I'll tell ye. Dobies and fairies; and if ye don't du as yer bid, they'll tak ye, and ye'll never git out o' their hands again while grass grows," said the old woman grimly.

"Od wite it!" replies the girl impatiently, "who's daft or dreamin' noo? I'd a bin dead wi' fear, if 'twas any such thing. It cudna be; all was sa luvesome, and bonny, and shaply."

"Weel, and what do ye want o' me, lass?" asked the old woman sharply.

"I want to know—here's t' sixpence—what I sud du," said the young lass. " 'Twud be a pity to lose such a marrow, hey?"

"Say yer prayers, lass; *I* can't help ye," says the old woman darkly. "If ye gaa wi' *the* people, ye'll never come back. Ye munna talk wi' them, nor eat wi' them, nor drink wi' them, nor tak a pin's-worth by way o' gift fra them—mark weel what I say—or ye're *lost!*"

The girl looked down, plainly much vexed.

The old woman stared at her with a mysterious frown steadily, for a few seconds.

"Tell me, lass, and tell me true, are ye in luve wi' that lad?"

"What for sud I?" said the girl with a careless toss of her head, and blushing up to her very temples.

"I see how it is," said the old woman, with a groan, and repeated the words, sadly thinking; and walked out of the door a step or two, and looked jealously round. "The lass is witched, the lass is witched!"

"Did ye see him since?" asked Mother Carke, returning.

The girl was still embarrassed; and now she spoke in a lower tone, and seemed subdued.

"I thought I sid him as I came here, walkin' beside me among the trees; but I consait it was only the trees themsels that lukt like rinnin' one behind another, as I walked on."

"I can tell thee nowt, lass, but what I telt ye afoore," answered the old woman peremptorily. "Get ye heyame, and don't delay on the way; and say yer prayers as ye gaa; and let none but good thoughts come nigh ye; and put nayer foot autside the door-steyan again till ye gaa to be christened; and get that done a Sunda' next."

And with this charge, given with grizzly earnestness, she saw her over the stile, and stood upon it watching her retreat, until the trees quite hid her and her path from view.

The sky grew cloudy and thunderous, and the air darkened rapidly, as the girl, a little frightened by Mall Carke's view of the case, walked homeward by the lonely path among the trees.

A black cat, which had walked close by her—for these creatures sometimes take a ramble in search of their prey among the woods and thickets—crept from under the hollow of an oak, and was again with her. It seemed to her to grow bigger and bigger as the darkness deepened, and its green eyes glared as large as halfpennies in her affrighted vision as the thunder came booming along the heights from the Willarden-road.

She tried to drive it away; but it growled and hissed awfully, and set up its back as if it would spring at her, and finally it skipped up into a tree, where they grew thickest at each side of her path, and accompanied her, high over head, hopping from bough to bough as if meditating a pounce upon her shoulders. Her fancy being full of strange thoughts, she was frightened, and she fancied that it was haunting her steps, and destined to undergo some hideous transformation, the moment she ceased to guard her path with prayers.

She was frightened for a while after she got home. The dark looks of Mother Carke were always before her eyes, and a secret dread prevented her passing the threshold of her home again that night.

Next day it was different. She had got rid of the awe with which Mother Carke had inspired her. She could not get the tall dark-featured lord, in the black velvet dress, out of her head. He had "taken her fancy"; she was growing to love him. She could think of nothing else.

Bessie Hennock, a neighbour's daughter, came to see her that day, and proposed a walk toward the ruins of Hawarth Castle, to gather "blaebirries." So off the two girls went together.

In the thicket, along the slopes near the ivied walls of Hawarth Castle, the companions began to fill their baskets. Hours passed. The sun was sinking near the west, and Laura Silver Bell had not come home.

Over the hatch of the farm-house door the maids leant ever and anon with outstretched necks, watching for a sign of the girl's return, and wondering, as the shadows lengthened, what had become of her.

At last, just as the rosy sunset gilding began to overspread the landscape, Bessie Hennock, weeping into her apron, made her appearance without her companion.

Her account of their adventures was curious.

I will relate the substance of it more connectedly than her agitation would allow her to give it, and without the disguise of the rude Northumbrian dialect.

The girl said, that, as they got along together among the brambles that grow beside the brook that bounds the Pie-Mag field, she on a sudden saw a very tall big-boned man, with an ill-favoured smirched face, and dressed in worn and rusty black, standing at the other side of a little stream. She was frightened; and while looking at this dirty, wicked, starved figure, Laura Silver Bell touched her, gazing at the same tall scarecrow, but with a countenance full of confusion and even rapture. She was peeping through the bush behind which she stood, and with a sigh she said:

"Is na that a conny lad? Agoy! See his bonny velvet clothes, his sword and sash; that's a lord, I can tell ye; and weel I know who he follows, who he luves, and who he'll wed."

Bessie Hennock thought her companion daft.

"See how luvesome he luks!" whispered Laura.

Bessie looked again, and saw him gazing at her companion with a malignant smile, and at the same time he beckoned her to approach.

"Darrat ta! gaa not near him! he'll wring thy neck!" gasped Bessie in great fear, as she saw Laura step forward with a look of beautiful bashfulness and joy.

She took the hand he stretched across the stream, more for love of the hand than any need of help, and in a moment was across and by his side, and his long arm about her waist.

"Fares te weel, Bessie, I'm gain my ways," she called, leaning her head to his shoulder; "and tell gud Fadder Lew I'm gain my ways to be happy, and may be, at lang last, I'll see him again."

And with a farewell wave of her hand, she went away with her dismal partner; and Laura Silver Bell was never more seen at home, or among the "coppies" and "wickwoods," the bonny fields and bosky hollows, by Dardale Moss.

Bessie Hennock followed them for a time.

She crossed the brook, and though they seemed to move slowly enough, she was obliged to run to keep them in view; and she all the time cried to her continually, "Come back, come back, bonnie Laurie!" until, getting over a bank, she was met by a white-faced old man, and so frightened was she, that she thought she fainted outright. At all events, she did not come to herself until the birds were singing their vespers in the amber light of sunset, and the day was over.

No trace of the direction of the girl's flight was ever discovered. Weeks and months passed, and more than a year.

At the end of that time, one of Mall Carke's goats died, as she suspected, by the envious practices of a rival witch who lived at the far end of Dardale Moss.

All alone in her stone cabin the old woman had prepared her charm to ascertain the author of her misfortune.

The heart of the dead animal, stuck all over with pins, was burnt in the fire; the windows, doors, and every other aperture of the house being first carefully stopped. After the heart, thus prepared with suitable incantations, is consumed in the fire, the first person who comes to the door or passes by it is the offending magician.

Mother Carke completed these lonely rites at dead of night. It was a dark night, with the glimmer of the stars only, and a melancholy night-wind was soughing through the scattered woods that spread around.

After a long and dead silence, there came a heavy thump at the door, and a deep voice called her by name.

She was startled, for she expected no man's voice; and peeping from the window, she saw, in the dim light, a coach and four horses, with gold-laced footmen, and coachman in wig and cocked hat, turned out as if for a state occasion.

She unbarred the door; and a tall gentleman, dressed in black, waiting at the threshold, entreated her, as the only *sage femme* within reach, to come in the coach and attend Lady Lairdale, who was about to give birth to a baby, promising her handsome payment.

Lady Lairdale! She had never heard of her.

"How far away is it?"

"Twelve miles on the old road to Golden Friars."

Her avarice is roused, and she steps into the coach. The footman claps-to the door; the glass jingles with the sound of a laugh. The tall dark-faced gentleman in black is seated opposite; they are driving at a furious pace; they have turned out of the road into a narrower one, dark with thicker and loftier forest than she was accustomed to. She grows anxious; for she knows every road and by-path in the country round, and she has never seen this one.

He encourages her. The moon has risen above the edge of the horizon, and she sees a noble old castle. Its summit of tower, watch-tower and battlement, glimmers faintly in the moonlight. This is their destination.

She feels on a sudden all but overpowered by sleep; but although she nods, she is quite conscious of the continued motion, which has become even rougher.

She makes an effort, and rouses herself. What has become of the coach, the castle, the servants? Nothing but the strange forest remains the same.

She is jolting along on a rude hurdle, seated on rushes, and a tall, big-boned man, in rags, sits in front, kicking with his heel the ill-favoured beast that pulls them along, every bone of which sticks out, and holding the halter which serves for reins. They stop at the door of a miserable building of loose stone, with a thatch so sunk and rotten, that the roof-tree and couples protrude in crooked corners, like the bones of the wretched horse, with enormous head and ears, that dragged them to the door.

The long gaunt man gets down, his sinister face grimed like his hands.

It was the same grimy giant who had accosted her on the lonely road near Deadman's Grike. But she feels that she "must go through with it" now, and she follows him into the house.

Two rushlights were burning in the large and miserable room, and on a coarse ragged bed lay a woman groaning piteously.

"That's Lady Lairdale," says the gaunt dark man, who then began to stride up and down the room rolling his head, stamping furiously, and thumping one hand on the palm of the other, and talking and laughing in the corners, where there was no one visible to hear or to answer.

Old Mall Carke recognized in the faded half-starved creature who lay on the bed, as dark now and grimy as the man, and looking as if she had never in her life washed hands or face, the once blithe and pretty Laura Lew.

The hideous being who was her mate continued in the same odd fluctuations of fury, grief, and merriment; and whenever she uttered a groan, he parodied it with another, as Mother Carke thought, in saturnine derision.

At length he strode into another room, and banged the door after him.

In due time the poor woman's pains were over, and a daughter was born.

Such an imp! with long pointed ears, flat nose, and enormous restless eyes and mouth. It instantly began to yell and talk in some unknown language, at the noise of which the father looked into the room, and told the *sage femme* that she should not go unrewarded.

The sick woman seized the moment of his absence to say in the ear of Mall Carke:

"If ye had not been at ill work tonight, he could not hev fetched ye. Tak no more now than your rightful fee, or he'll keep ye here."

At this moment he returned with a bag of gold and silver coins, which he emptied on the table, and told her to help herself.

She took four shillings, which was her primitive fee, neither more nor less; and all his urgency could not prevail with her to take a farthing more. He looked so terrible at her refusal, that she rushed out of the house.

He ran after her.

"You'll take your money with you," he roared, snatching up the bag, still half full, and flung it after her.

It lighted on her shoulder; and partly from the blow, partly from terror, she fell to the ground; and when she came to herself, it was morning, and she was lying across her own door-stone.

It is said that she never more told fortune or practised spell. And though all that happened sixty years ago and more, Laura Silver Bell, wise folk think, is still living, and will so continue till the day of doom among the fairies.

WICKED CAPTAIN WALSHAWE,
OF WAULING

CHAPTER I.

Peg O'Neill Pays the Captain's Debts

A very odd thing happened to my uncle, Mr. Watson, of Haddlestone; and to enable you to understand it, I must begin at the beginning.

In the year 1822, Mr. James Walshawe, more commonly known as Captain Walshawe, died at the age of eighty-one years. The Captain in his early days, and so long as health and strength permitted, was a scamp of the active, intriguing sort; and spent his days and nights in sowing his wild oats, of which he seemed to have an inexhaustible stock. The harvest of this tillage was plentifully interspersed with thorns, nettles, and thistles, which stung the husbandman unpleasantly, and did not enrich him.

Captain Walshawe was very well known in the neighborhood of Wauling, and very generally avoided there. A "captain" by courtesy, for he had never reached that rank in the army list. He had quitted the service in 1766, at the age of twenty-five; immediately previous to which period his debts had grown so troublesome, that he was induced to extricate himself by running away with and marrying an heiress.

Though not so wealthy quite as he had imagined, she proved a very comfortable investment for what remained of his shattered affections; and he lived and enjoyed himself very much in his old way, upon her income, getting into no end of scrapes and scandals, and a good deal of debt and money trouble.

When he married his wife, he was quartered in Ireland, at Clonmel, where was a nunnery, in which, as pensioner, resided Miss O'Neill, or as she was called in the country, Peg O'Neill—the heiress of whom I have spoken.

Her situation was the only ingredient of romance in the affair, for the young lady was decidedly plain, though good-humoured looking, with that style of features which is termed *potato*; and in figure she was a little too plump, and rather short. But she was impressible; and the handsome young English Lieutenant was too much for her monastic tendencies, and she eloped.

In England there are traditions of Irish fortune-hunters, and in Ireland of English. The fact is, it was the vagrant class of each country that chiefly visited the other in old times; and a handsome vagabond, whether at home or abroad, I suppose, made the most of his face, which was also his fortune.

At all events, he carried off the fair one from the sanctuary; and for some sufficient reason, I suppose, they took up their abode at Wauling, in Lancashire.

Here the gallant captain amused himself after his fashion, sometimes running up, of course on business, to London. I believe few wives have ever cried more in a given time than did that poor, dumpy, potato-faced heiress, who got over the nunnery garden wall, and jumped into the handsome Captain's arms, for love.

He spent her income, frightened her out of her wits with oaths and threats, and broke her heart.

Latterly she shut herself up pretty nearly altogether in her room. She had an old, rather grim, Irish servant-woman in attendance upon her. This domestic was tall, lean, and religious, and the Captain knew instinctively she hated him; and he hated her in return, often threatened to put her out of the house, and sometimes even to kick her out of the window. And whenever a wet day confined him to the house, or the stable, and he grew tired of smoking, he would begin to swear and curse at her for a *diddled* old mischief-maker, that could never be easy, and was always troubling the house with her cursed stories, and so forth.

But years passed away, and old Molly Doyle remained still in her original position. Perhaps he thought that there must be somebody there, and that he was not, after all, very likely to change for the better.

CHAPTER II

The Blessed Candle

He tolerated another intrusion, too, and thought himself a paragon of patience and easy good nature for so doing. A Roman Catholic clergyman, in a long black frock, with a low standing collar, and a little white muslin fillet round his neck—tall, sallow, with blue chin, and dark steady eyes—used to glide up and down the stairs, and through the passages; and the Captain sometimes met him in one place and sometimes in another. But by a caprice incident to such tempers he treated this cleric exceptionally, and even with a surly sort of courtesy, though he grumbled about his visits behind his back.

I do not know that he had a great deal of moral courage, and the ecclesiastic looked severe and self-possessed; and somehow he thought he had no good opinion of him, and if a natural occasion were offered, might say extremely unpleasant things, and hard to be answered.

Well the time came at last, when poor Peg O'Neill—in an evil hour Mrs. James Walshawe—must cry, and quake, and pray her last. The doctor came from Penlynden, and was just as vague as usual, but more gloomy, and for about a week came and went oftener. The cleric in the long black frock was also daily there. And at last came that last sacrament in the gates of death, when the sinner is traversing those dread steps that never can be retraced; when the face is turned for ever from life, and we see a receding shape, and hear a voice already irrevocably in the land of spirits.

So the poor lady died; and some people said the Captain "felt it very much." I don't think he did. But he was not very well just then, and looked the part of mourner and penitent to admiration—being seedy and sick. He drank a great deal of brandy and water that night, and called in Farmer Dobbs, for want of better company, to drink with him; and told him all his grievances, and how happy he and "the poor lady up-stairs" might have been, had it not been for liars, and pick-thanks, and tale-bearers, and the like, who came between them—meaning Molly Doyle—whom, as he waxed eloquent over his liquor, he came at last to curse and rail at by name, with more than his accustomed freedom. And he described his own natural character and amiability in such moving terms, that he wept maudlin tears of sensibility over his theme; and when Dobbs was gone, drank some more grog, and took to railing and cursing again by himself; and then mounted the stairs unsteadily, to see "what the devil Doyle and the other——old witches were about in poor Peg's room."

When he pushed open the door, he found some half-dozen crones, chiefly Irish, from the neighbouring town of Hackleton, sitting over tea and snuff, etc., with candles lighted round the corpse, which was arrayed in a strangely cut robe of brown serge. She had secretly belonged to some order—I think the Carmelite, but I am not certain—and wore the habit in her coffin.

"What the d——are you doing with my wife?" cried the Captain, rather thickly. "How dare you dress her up in this——trumpery, you—you cheating old witch; and what's that candle doing in her hand?"

I think he was a little startled, for the spectacle was grisly enough. The dead lady was arrayed in this strange brown robe, and in her rigid fingers, as in a socket, with the large wooden beads and cross wound round it, burned a wax candle, shedding its white light over the sharp features of the corpse. Moll Doyle was not to be put down by the Captain, whom she hated, and accordingly, in her phrase, "he got as good as he gave." And the Captain's wrath waxed fiercer, and he chucked the wax taper from the dead hand, and was on the point of flinging it at the old serving-woman's head.

"The holy candle, you sinner!" cried she.

"I've a mind to make you eat it, you beast," cried the Captain.

But I think he had not known before what it was, for he subsided a little sulkily, and he stuffed his hand with the candle (quite extinct by this time) into his pocket, and said he—

"You know devilish well you had no business going on with y-y-your d—— *witch*-craft about my poor wife, without my leave—you do—and you'll please take off that d——brown pinafore, and get her decently into her coffin, and I'll pitch your devil's waxlight into the sink."

And the Captain stalked out of the room.

"An' now her poor sowl's in prison, you wretch, be the mains o' ye; an' may yer own be shut into the wick o' that same candle, till it's burned out, ye savage."

"I'd have you ducked for a witch, for two-pence," roared the Captain up the staircase, with his hand on the banisters, standing on the lobby. But the door of the chamber of death clapped angrily, and he went down to the parlour, where he examined the holy candle for a while, with a tipsy gravity, and then with something of that reverential feeling for the symbolic, which is not uncommon in rakes and scamps, he thoughtfully locked it up in a press, where were accumulated all sorts of obsolete rubbish—soiled packs of cards, disused tobacco pipes, broken powder flasks, his military sword, and a dusky bundle of the "Flash Songster," and other questionable literature.

He did not trouble the dead lady's room any more. Being a volatile man it is probable that more cheerful plans and occupations began to entertain his fancy.

CHAPTER III

My Uncle Watson Visits Wauling

So the poor lady was buried decently, and Captain Walshawe reigned alone for many years at Wauling. He was too shrewd and too experienced by this time to run violently down the steep hill that leads to ruin. So there was a method in his madness; and after a widowed career of more than forty years, he, too, died at last with some guineas in his purse.

Forty years and upwards is a great *edax rerum*, and a wonderful chemical power. It acted forcibly upon the gay Captain Walshawe. Gout supervened, and was no more conducive to temper than to enjoyment, and made his elegant hands lumpy at all the small joints, and turned them slowly into crippled claws. He grew stout when his exercise was interfered with, and ultimately almost corpulent. He suffered from what Mr. Holloway calls "bad legs," and was wheeled about in a great leathern-backed chair, and his infirmities went on accumulating with his years.

I am sorry to say, I never heard that he repented, or turned his thoughts seriously to the future. On the contrary, his talk grew fouler, and his fun ran upon his favourite sins, and his temper waxed more truculent. But he did not sink into dotage. Considering his bodily infirmities, his energies and his malignities, which were many and active, were marvellously little abated by time. So he went on to the close. When his temper was stirred, he cursed and swore in a way that made decent people tremble. It was a word and a blow with him; the latter, luckily, not very sure now. But he would seize his crutch and make a swoop or a pound at the offender, or shy his medicine-bottle, or his tumbler, at his head.

It was a peculiarity of Captain Walshawe, that he, by this time, hated nearly everybody. My uncle, Mr. Watson, of Haddlestone, was cousin to the Captain, and his heir-at-law. But my uncle had lent him money on mortgage of his estates, and there had been a treaty to sell, and terms and a price were agreed upon, in "articles" which the lawyers said were still in force.

I think the ill-conditioned Captain bore him a grudge for being richer than he, and would have liked to do him an ill turn. But it did not lie in his way; at least while he was living.

My uncle Watson was a Methodist, and what they call a "class-leader"; and, on the whole, a very good man. He was now near fifty—grave, as beseemed his profession—somewhat dry—and a little severe, perhaps—but a just man.

A letter from the Penlynden doctor reached him at Haddlestone, announcing the death of the wicked old Captain; and suggesting his attendance at the funeral, and the expediency of his being on the spot to look after things at Wauling. The reasonableness of this striking my good uncle, he made his journey to the old house in Lancashire incontinently, and reached it in time for the funeral.

My uncle, whose traditions of the Captain were derived from his mother, who remembered him in his slim, handsome youth—in shorts, cocked-hat and lace, was amazed at the bulk of the coffin which contained his mortal remains; but the lid being already screwed down, he did not see the face of the bloated old sinner.

CHAPTER IV

In the Parlour

What I relate, I had from the lips of my uncle, who was a truthful man, and not prone to fancies.

The day turning out awfully rainy and tempestuous, he persuaded the doctor and the attorney to remain for the night at Wauling.

There was no will—the attorney was sure of that; for the Captain's enmities were perpetually shifting, and he could never quite make up his mind, as to how best to give effect to a malignity whose direction was constantly being modified. He had had instructions for drawing a will a dozen times over. But the process had always been arrested by the intending testator.

Search being made, no will was found. The papers, indeed, were all right, with one important exception: the leases were nowhere to be seen. There were special circumstances connected with several of the principal tenancies on the estate—unnecessary here to detail—which rendered the loss of these documents one of very serious moment, and even of very obvious danger.

My uncle, therefore, searched strenuously. The attorney was at his elbow, and the doctor helped with a suggestion now and then. The old serving-man seemed an honest deaf creature, and really knew nothing.

My uncle Watson was very much perturbed. He fancied—but this possibly was only fancy—that he had detected for a moment a queer look in the attorney's face; and from that instant it became fixed in his mind that he knew all about the leases. Mr. Watson expounded that evening in the parlour to the doctor, the attorney, and the deaf servant. Ananias and Sapphira figured in the foreground; and the awful nature of fraud and theft, of tampering in anywise with the plain rule of honesty in matters pertaining to estates, etc., were pointedly dwelt upon; and then came a long and strenuous prayer, in which he entreated with fervour and aplomb that the hard heart of the sinner who had abstracted the leases might be softened or broken in such a way as to lead to their restitution; or that, if he continued reserved and contumacious, it might at least be the will of Heaven to bring him to public justice and the documents to light. The fact is, that he was praying all this time at the attorney.

When these religious exercises were over, the visitors retired to their rooms, and my Uncle Watson wrote two or three pressing letters by the fire. When his task was done, it had grown late; the candles were flaring in their sockets, and all in bed, and, I suppose, asleep, but he.

The fire was nearly out, he chilly, and the flame of the candles throbbing strangely in their sockets, shed alternate glare and shadow round the old wainscoted room and its quaint furniture. Outside were all the wild thunder and piping of the storm; and the rattling of distant windows sounded through the passages, and down the stairs, like angry people astir in the house.

My Uncle Watson belonged to a sect who by no means rejected the supernatural, and whose founder, on the contrary, has sanctioned ghosts in the most emphatic way. He was glad therefore to remember, that in prosecuting his search that day, he had seen some six inches of wax candle in the press in the parlour; for he had no fancy to be overtaken by darkness in his present situation. He had no time to lose; and taking the bunch of keys—of which he was now master—he soon fitted the lock, and secured the candle—a treasure in his circumstances; and lighting it, he stuffed it into the socket of one of the expiring candles, and extinguishing the other, he looked round the room in the steady light reassured. At the same moment, an unusual violent gust of the storm blew a handful of gravel against the parlour window, with a sharp rattle that startled him in the midst of the roar and hubbub; and the flame of the candle itself was agitated by the air.

CHAPTER V

The Bed-Chamber

My uncle walked up to bed, guarding his candle with his hand, for the lobby windows were rattling furiously, and he disliked the idea of being left in the dark more than ever.

His bedroom was comfortable, though old-fashioned. He shut and bolted the door. There was a tall looking-glass opposite the foot of his four-poster, on the dressing-table between the windows. He tried to make the curtains meet, but they would not draw; and like many a gentleman in a like perplexity, he did not possess a pin, nor was there one in the huge pincushion beneath the glass.

He turned the face of the mirror away therefore, so that its back was presented to the bed, pulled the curtains together, and placed a chair against them, to prevent their falling open again. There was a good fire, and a reinforcement of round coal and wood inside the fender. So he piled it up to ensure a cheerful blaze through the night, and placing a little black mahogany table, with the legs of a satyr, beside the bed, and his candle upon it, he got between the sheets, and laid his red nightcapped head upon his pillow, and disposed himself to sleep.

The first thing that made him uncomfortable was a sound at the foot of his bed, quite distinct in a momentary lull of the storm. It was only the gentle rustle and rush of the curtains, which fell open again; and as his eyes opened, he saw them resuming their perpendicular dependence, and sat up in his bed almost expecting to see something uncanny in the aperture.

There was nothing, however, but the dressing-table, and other dark furniture, and the window-curtains faintly undulating in the violence of the storm. He did not care to get up, therefore—the fire being bright and cheery—to replace the curtains by a chair, in the position in which he had left them, anticipating possibly a new recurrence of the relapse which had startled him from his incipient doze.

So he got to sleep in a little while again, but he was disturbed by a sound, as he fancied, at the table on which stood the candle. He could not say what it was, only that he wakened with a start, and lying so in some amaze, he did distinctly hear a sound which startled him a good deal, though there was nothing necessarily supernatural in it. He described it as resembling what would occur if you fancied a thinnish table-leaf, with a convex warp in it, depressed the reverse way, and suddenly with a spring recovering its natural convexity. It was a loud, sudden thump, which made the heavy candlestick jump, and there was an end, except that my uncle did not get again into a doze for ten minutes at least.

The next time he awoke, it was in that odd, serene way that sometimes occurs. We open our eyes, we know not why, quite placidly, and are on the instant wide awake. He had had a nap of some duration this time, for his candle-flame was fluttering and flaring, *in articulo*, in the silver socket. But the fire was still bright and cheery; so he popped the extinguisher on the socket, and almost at the same time there came a tap at his door, and a sort of crescendo "hush-sh-sh!" Once more my uncle was sitting up, scared and perturbed, in his bed. He recollected, however, that he had bolted his door; and such inveterate materialists are we in the midst of our spiritualism, that this reassured him, and he breathed a deep sigh, and began to grow tranquil. But after a rest of a minute or two, there came a louder and sharper knock at his door; so that instinctively he called out, "Who's there?" in a loud, stern key. There was no sort of response, however. The nervous effect of the start subsided; and I think my uncle must have remembered how constantly, especially on a stormy night, these creaks or cracks which simulate all manner of goblin noises, make themselves naturally audible.

CHAPTER VI

The Extinguisher Is Lifted

After a while, then, he lay down with his back turned toward that side of the bed at which was the door, and his face toward the table on which stood the massive old candlestick, capped with its extinguisher, and in that position he closed his eyes. But sleep would not revisit them. All kinds of queer fancies began to trouble him—some of them I remember.

He felt the point of a finger, he averred, pressed most distinctly on the tip of his great toe, as if a living hand were between his sheets, and making a sort of signal of attention or silence. Then again he felt something as large as a rat make a sudden bounce in the middle of his bolster, just under his head. Then a voice said "Oh!" very gently, close at the back of his head. All these things he felt certain of, and yet investigation led to nothing. He felt odd little cramps stealing now and then about him; and then, on a sudden, the middle finger of his right hand was plucked backwards, with a light playful jerk that frightened him awfully.

Meanwhile the storm kept singing, and howling, and ha-ha-hooing hoarsely among the limbs of the old trees and the chimney-pots; and my Uncle Watson, although he prayed and meditated as was his wont when he lay awake, felt his heart throb excitedly, and sometimes thought he was beset with evil spirits, and at others that he was in the early stage of a fever.

He resolutely kept his eyes closed, however, and, like St. Paul's shipwrecked companions, wished for the day. At last another little doze seems to have stolen upon his senses, for he awoke quietly and completely as before—opening his eyes all at once, and seeing everything as if he had not slept for a moment.

The fire was still blazing redly—nothing uncertain in the light—the massive silver candlestick, topped with its tall extinguisher, stood on the centre of the black mahogany table as before; and, looking by what seemed a sort of accident to the apex of this, he beheld something which made him quite misdoubt the evidence of his eyes.

He saw the extinguisher lifted by a tiny hand, from beneath, and a small human face, no bigger than a thumb-nail, with nicely proportioned features, peep from beneath it. In this Lilliputian countenance was such a ghastly consternation as horrified my uncle unspeakably. Out came a little foot then and there, and a pair of wee legs, in short silk stockings and buckled shoes, then the rest of the figure; and, with the arms holding about the socket, the little legs stretched and stretched, hanging about the stem of the candlestick till the feet reached the base, and so down the satyr-like leg of the table, till they reached the floor, extending elastically, and strangely enlarging in all proportions as they approached the ground, where the feet and buckles were those of a well-shaped, full grown man, and the figure tapering upward until it dwindled to its original fairy dimensions at the top, like an object seen in some strangely curved mirror.

Standing upon the floor he expanded, my amazed uncle could not tell how, into his proper proportions; and stood pretty nearly in profile at the bedside, a handsome and elegantly shaped young man, in a bygone military costume, with a small laced, three-cocked hat and plume on his head, but looking like a man going to be hanged—in unspeakable despair.

He stepped lightly to the hearth, and turned for a few seconds very dejectedly with his back toward the bed and the mantel-piece, and he saw the hilt of his rapier glittering in the firelight; and then walking across the room he placed himself at the dressing-table, visible through the divided curtains at the foot of the bed. The fire was blazing still so brightly that my uncle saw him as distinctly as if half a dozen candles were burning.

CHAPTER VII

The Visitation Culminates

The looking-glass was an old-fashioned piece of furniture, and had a drawer beneath it. My uncle had searched it carefully for the papers in the daytime; but the silent figure pulled the drawer quite out, pressed a spring at the side, disclosing a false receptable behind it, and from this he drew a parcel of papers tied together with pink tape.

All this time my uncle was staring at him in a horrified state, neither winking nor breathing, and the apparition had not once given the smallest intimation of consciousness that a living person was in the same room. But now, for the first time, it turned its livid stare full upon my uncle with a hateful smile of significance, lifting up the little parcel of papers between his slender finger and thumb. Then he made a long, cunning wink at him, and seemed to blow out one of his cheeks in a burlesque grimace, which, but for the horrific circumstances, would have been ludicrous. My uncle could not tell whether this was really an intentional distortion or only one of those horrid ripples and deflections which were constantly disturbing the proportions of the figure, as if it were seen through some unequal and perverting medium.

The figure now approached the bed, seeming to grow exhausted and malignant as it did so. My uncle's terror nearly culminated at this point, for he believed it was drawing near him with an evil purpose. But it was not so; for the soldier, over whom twenty years seemed to have passed in his brief transit to the dressing-table and back again, threw himself into a great high-backed arm-chair of stuffed leather at the far side of the fire, and placed his heels on the fender. His feet and legs seemed indistinctly to swell, and swathings showed themselves round them, and they grew into something enormous, and the upper figure swayed and shaped itself into corresponding proportions, a great mass of corpulence, with a cadaverous and malignant face, and the furrows of a great old age, and colourless glassy eyes; and with these changes, which came indefinitely but rapidly as those of a sunset cloud, the fine regimentals faded away, and a loose, gray, woollen drapery, somehow, was there in its stead; and all seemed to be stained and rotten, for swarms of worms seemed creeping in and out, while the figure grew paler and paler, till my uncle, who liked his pipe, and employed the simile naturally, said the whole effigy grew to the colour of tobacco ashes, and the clusters of worms into little wriggling knots of sparks such as we see running over the residuum of a burnt sheet of paper. And so with the strong draught caused by the fire, and the current of air from the window, which was rattling in the storm, the feet seemed to be drawn into the fire-place, and the whole figure, light as ashes, floated away with them, and disappeared with a whisk up the capacious old chimney.

It seemed to my uncle that the fire suddenly darkened and the air grew icy cold, and there came an awful roar and riot of tempest, which shook the old house from top to base, and sounded like the yelling of a blood-thirsty mob on receiving a new and long-expected victim.

Good Uncle Watson used to say, "I have been in many situations of fear and danger in the course of my life, but never did I pray with so much agony before or since; for then, as now, it was clear beyond a cavil that I had actually beheld the phantom of an evil spirit."

CONCLUSION

Now there are two curious circumstances to be observed in this relation of my uncle's, who was, as I have said, a perfectly veracious man.

First—The wax candle which he took from the press in the parlour and burnt at his bedside on that horrible night was unquestionably, according to the testimony of the old deaf servant, who had been fifty years at Wauling, that identical piece of "holy candle" which had stood in the fingers of the poor lady's corpse, and concerning which the old Irish crone, long since dead, had delivered the curious curse I have mentioned against the Captain.

Secondly—Behind the drawer under the looking-glass, he did actually discover a second but secret drawer, in which were concealed the identical papers which he had suspected the attorney of having made away with. There were circumstances, too, afterwards disclosed which convinced my uncle that the old man had deposited them there preparatory to burning them, which he had nearly made up his mind to do.

Now, a very remarkable ingredient in this tale of my Uncle Watson was this, that so far as my father, who had never seen Captain Walshawe in the course of his life, could gather, the phantom had exhibited a horrible and grotesque, but unmistakeable resemblance to that defunct scamp in the various stages of his long life.

Wauling was sold in the year 1837, and the old house shortly after pulled down, and a new one built nearer to the river. I often wonder whether it was rumoured to be haunted, and, if so, what stories were current about it. It was a commodious and stanch old house, and withal rather handsome; and its demolition was certainly suspicious.

GHOST STORIES
OF CHAPELIZOD

Take my word for it, there is no such thing as an ancient village, especially if it has seen better days, unillustrated by its legends of terror. You might as well expect to find a decayed cheese without mites, or an old house without rats, as an antique and dilapidated town without an authentic population of goblins. Now, although this class of inhabitants are in nowise amenable to the police authorities, yet, as their demeanor directly affects the comforts of her Majesty's subjects, I cannot but regard it as a grave omission that the public have hitherto been left without any statistical returns of their numbers, activity, etc., etc. And I am persuaded that a Commission to inquire into and report upon the numerical strength, habits, haunts, etc., etc., of supernatural agents resident in Ireland, would be a great deal more innocent and entertaining than half the Commissions for which the country pays, and at least as instructive. This I say, more from a sense of duty, and to deliver my mind of a grave truth, than with any hope of seeing the suggestion adopted. But, I am sure, my readers will deplore with me that the comprehensive powers of belief, and apparently illimitable leisure, possessed by parliamentary commissions of inquiry, should never have been applied to the subject I have named, and that the collection of that species of information should be confided to the gratuitous and desultory labours of individuals, who, like myself, have other occupations to attend to. This, however, by the way.

Among the village outposts of Dublin, Chapelizod once held a considerable, if not a foremost rank. Without mentioning its connexion with the history of the great Kilmainham Preceptory of the Knights of

St. John, it will be enough to remind the reader of its ancient and celebrated Castle, not one vestige of which now remains, and of the fact that it was for, we believe, some centuries, the summer residence of the Viceroys of Ireland. The circumstance of its being up, we believe, to the period at which that corps was disbanded, the head-quarters of the Royal Irish Artillery, gave it also a consequence of an humbler, but not less substantial kind. With these advantages in its favour, it is not wonderful that the town exhibited at one time an air of substantial and semi-aristocratic prosperity unknown to Irish villages in modern times.

A broad street, with a well-paved foot-path, and houses as lofty as were at that time to be found in the fashionable streets of Dublin; a goodly stone-fronted barrack; an ancient church, vaulted beneath, and with a tower clothed from its summit to its base with the richest ivy; an humble Roman Catholic chapel; a steep bridge spanning the Liffey, and a great old mill at the near end of it, were the principal features of the town. These, or at least most of them, remain still, but the greater part in a very changed and forlorn condition. Some of them indeed are superseded, though not obliterated by modern erections, such as the bridge, the chapel, and the church in part; the rest forsaken by the order who originally raised them, and delivered up to poverty, and in some cases to absolute decay.

The village lies in the lap of the rich and wooded valley of the Liffey, and is overlooked by the high grounds of the beautiful Phoenix Park on the one side, and by the ridge of the Palmerstown hills on the other. Its situation, therefore, is eminently picturesque; and factory-fronts and chimneys notwithstanding, it has, I think, even in its decay, a sort of melancholy picturesqueness of its own. Be that as it may, I mean to relate two or three stories of that sort which may be read with very good effect by a blazing fire on a shrewd winter's night, and are all directly connected with the altered and somewhat melancholy little town I have named. The first I shall relate concerns

The Village Bully

About thirty years ago there lived in the town of Chapelizod an ill-conditioned fellow of herculean strength, well known throughout the neighbourhood by the title of Bully Larkin. In addition to his remarkable physical superiority, this fellow had acquired a degree of skill as a pugilist which alone would have made him formidable. As it was, he was the autocrat of the village, and carried not the sceptre in vain. Conscious of his superiority, and perfectly secure of impunity, he lorded it over his fellows in a spirit of cowardly and brutal insolence, which made him hated even more profoundly than he was feared.

Upon more than one occasion he had deliberately forced quarrels upon men whom he had singled out for the exhibition of his savage prowess; and in every encounter his over-matched antagonist had received an amount of "punishment" which edified and appalled the spectators, and in some instances left ineffaceable scars and lasting injuries after it.

Bully Larkin's pluck had never been fairly tried. For, owing to his prodigious superiority in weight, strength, and skill, his victories had always been certain and easy; and in proportion to the facility with which he uniformly smashed an antagonist, his pugnacity and insolence were inflamed. He thus became an odious nuisance in the neighbourhood, and the terror of every mother who had a son, and of every wife who had a husband who possessed a spirit to resent insult, or the smallest confidence in his own pugilistic capabilities.

Now it happened that there was a young fellow named Ned Moran—better known by the soubriquet of "Long Ned," from his slender, lathy proportions—at that time living in the town. He was, in truth, a mere lad, nineteen years of age, and fully twelve years younger than the stalwart bully. This, however, as the reader will see, secured for him no exemption from the dastardly provocations of the ill-conditioned pugilist. Long Ned, in an evil hour, had thrown eyes of affection upon a certain buxom damsel, who, notwithstanding Bully Larkin's amorous rivalry, inclined to reciprocate them.

I need not say how easily the spark of jealousy, once kindled, is blown into a flame, and how naturally, in a coarse and ungoverned nature, it explodes in acts of violence and outrage.

"The bully" watched his opportunity, and contrived to provoke Ned Moran, while drinking in a public-house with a party of friends, into an altercation, in the course of which he failed not to put such insults upon his rival as manhood could not tolerate. Long Ned, though a simple, good-natured sort of fellow, was by no means deficient in spirit, and retorted in a tone of defiance which edified the more timid, and gave his opponent the opportunity he secretly coveted.

Bully Larkin challenged the heroic youth, whose pretty face he had privately consigned to the mangling and bloody discipline he was himself so capable of administering. The quarrel, which he had himself contrived to get up, to a certain degree covered the ill blood and malignant premeditation which inspired his proceedings, and Long Ned, being full of generous ire and whiskey punch, accepted the gauge of battle on the instant. The whole party, accompanied by a mob of idle men and boys, and in short by all who could snatch a moment from the calls of business, proceeded in slow procession through the old gate into the Phoenix Park, and mounting the hill over-looking the town, selected near its summit a level spot on which to decide the quarrel.

The combatants stripped, and a child might have seen in the contrast presented by the slight, lank form and limbs of the lad, and the muscular and massive build of his veteran antagonist, how desperate was the chance of poor Ned Moran.

"Seconds" and "bottle-holders"—selected of course for their love of the game—were appointed, and "the fight" commenced.

I will not shock my readers with a description of the cool-blooded butchery that followed. The result of the combat was what anybody might have predicted. At the eleventh round, poor Ned refused to "give in"; the brawny pugilist, unhurt, in good wind, and pale with concentrated and as yet unslaked revenge, had the gratification of seeing his opponent seated upon his second's knee, unable to hold up his head, his left arm disabled; his face a bloody, swollen, and shapeless mass; his breast scarred and bloody, and his whole body panting and quivering with rage and exhaustion.

"Give in, Ned, my boy," cried more than one of the bystanders.

"Never, never," shrieked he, with a voice hoarse and choking.

Time being "up," his second placed him on his feet again. Blinded with his own blood, panting and staggering, he presented but a helpless mark for the blows of his stalwart opponent. It was plain that a touch would have been sufficient to throw him to the earth. But Larkin had no notion of letting him off so easily. He closed with him without striking a blow (the effect of which, prematurely dealt, would have been to bring him at once to the ground, and so put an end to the combat), and getting his battered and almost senseless head under his arm, fast in that peculiar "fix" known to the fancy pleasantly by the name of "chancery," he held him firmly, while with monotonous and brutal strokes he beat his fist, as it seemed, almost into his face. A cry of "shame" broke from the crowd, for it was plain that the beaten man was now insensible, and supported only by the herculean arm of the bully. The round and the fight ended by his hurling him upon the ground, falling upon him at the same time with his knee upon his chest.

The bully rose, wiping the perspiration from his white face with his blood-stained hands, but Ned lay stretched and motionless upon the grass. It was impossible to get him upon his legs for another round. So he was carried down, just as he was, to the pond which then lay close to the old Park gate, and his head and body were washed beside it. Contrary to the belief of all he was not dead. He was carried home, and after some months to a certain extent recovered. But he never held up his head again, and before the year was over he had died of consumption. Nobody could doubt how the disease had been induced, but there was no actual proof to connect the cause and effect, and the ruffian Larkin escaped the vengeance of the law. A strange retribution, however, awaited him.

After the death of Long Ned, he became less quarrelsome than before, but more sullen and reserved. Some said "he took it to heart," and others, that his conscience was not at ease about it. Be this as it may, however, his health did not suffer by reason of his presumed agitations, nor was his worldly prosperity marred by the blasting curses with which poor Moran's enraged mother pursued him; on the contrary, he had rather risen in the world, and obtained regular and well-remunerated employment from the Chief Secretary's gardener, at the other side of the Park. He still lived in Chapelizod, whither, on the close of his day's work, he used to return across the Fifteen Acres.

It was about three years after the catastrophe we have mentioned, and late in the autumn, when, one night, contrary to his habit, he did not appear at the house where he lodged, neither had he been seen anywhere, during the evening, in the village. His hours of return had been so very regular, that his absence excited considerable surprise, though, of course, no actual alarm; and, at the usual hour, the house was closed for the night, and the absent lodger consigned to the mercy of the elements, and the care of his presiding star. Early in the morning, however, he was found lying in a state of utter helplessness upon the slope immediately overlooking the Chapelizod gate. He had been smitten with a paralytic stroke: his right side was dead; and it was many weeks before he had recovered his speech sufficiently to make himself at all understood.

He then made the following relation:—He had been detained, it appeared, later than usual, and darkness had closed before he commenced his homeward walk across the Park. It was a moonlit night, but masses of ragged clouds were slowly drifting across the heavens. He had not encountered a human figure, and no sounds but the softened rush of the wind sweeping through bushes and hollows met his ear. These wild and monotonous sounds, and the utter solitude which surrounded him, did not, however, excite any of those uneasy sensations which are ascribed to superstition, although he said he did feel depressed, or, in his own phraseology, "lonesome." Just as he crossed the brow of the hill which shelters the town of Chapelizod, the moon shone out for some moments with unclouded lustre, and his eye, which happened to wander by the shadowy enclosures which lay at the foot of the slope, was arrested by the sight of a human figure climbing, with all the haste of one pursued, over the church-yard wall, and running up the steep ascent directly towards him. Stories of "resurrectionists" crossed his recollection, as he observed this suspicious-looking figure. But he began, momentarily, to be aware with a sort of fearful instinct which he could not explain, that the running figure was directing his steps, with a sinister purpose, towards himself.

The form was that of a man with a loose coat about him, which, as he ran, he disengaged, and as well as Larkin could see, for the moon was again wading in clouds, threw from him. The figure thus advanced until within some two score yards of him, it arrested its speed, and approached with a loose, swaggering gait. The moon again shone out bright and clear, and, gracious God! what was the spectacle before him? He saw as distinctly as if he had been presented there in the flesh, Ned Moran, himself, stripped naked from the waist upward, as if for pugilistic combat, and drawing towards him in silence. Larkin would have shouted, prayed, cursed, fled across the Park, but he was absolutely powerless; the apparition stopped within a few steps, and leered on him with a ghastly mimicry of the defiant stare with which pugilists strive to cow one another before combat. For a time, which he could not so much as conjecture, he was held in the fascination of that unearthly gaze, and at last the thing, whatever it was, on a sudden swaggered close up to him with extended palms. With an impulse of horror, Larkin put out his hand to keep the figure off, and their palms touched—at least, so he believed—for a thrill of unspeakable agony, running through his arm, pervaded his entire frame, and he fell senseless to the earth.

Though Larkin lived for many years after, his punishment was terrible. He was incurably maimed; and being unable to work, he was forced, for existence, to beg alms of those who had once feared and flattered him. He suffered, too, increasingly, under his own horrible interpretation of the preternatural encounter which was the beginning of all his miseries. It was vain to endeavour to shake his faith in the reality of the apparition, and equally vain, as some compassionately did, to try to persuade him that the greeting with which his vision closed was intended, while inflicting a temporary trial, to signify a compensating reconciliation.

"No, no," he used to say, "all won't do. I know the meaning of it well enough; it is a challenge to meet him in the other world—in Hell, where I am going—that's what it means, and nothing else."

And so, miserable and refusing comfort, he lived on for some years, and then died, and was buried in the same narrow churchyard which contains the remains of his victim.

I need hardly say, how absolute was the faith of the honest inhabitants, at the time when I heard the story, in the reality of the preternatural summons which, through the portals of terror, sickness, and misery, had summoned Bully Larkin to his long, last home, and that, too, upon the very ground on which he had signalised the guiltiest triumph of his violent and vindictive career.

I recollect another story of the preternatural sort, which made no small sensation, some five-and-thirty years ago, among the good gossips of the town; and, with your leave, courteous reader, I shall relate it.

The Sexton's Adventure

Those who remember Chapelizod a quarter of a century ago, or more, may possibly recollect the parish sexton. Bob Martin was held much in awe by truant boys who sauntered into the churchyard on Sundays, to read the tomb-stones, or play leap frog over them, or climb the ivy in search of bats or sparrows' nests, or peep into the mysterious aperture under the eastern window, which opened a dim perspective of descending steps losing themselves among profounder darkness, where lidless coffins gaped horribly among tattered velvet, bones, and dust, which time and mortality had strewn there. Of such horribly curious, and otherwise enterprising juveniles, Bob was, of course, the special scourge and terror. But terrible as was the official aspect of the sexton, and repugnant as his lank form, clothed in rusty, sable vesture, his small, frosty visage, suspicious grey eyes, and rusty, brown scratch-wig, might appear to all notions of genial frailty; it was yet true, that Bob Martin's severe morality sometimes nodded, and that Bacchus did not always solicit him in vain.

Bob had a curious mind, a memory well stored with "merry tales," and tales of terror. His profession familiarized him with graves and goblins, and his tastes with weddings, wassail, and sly frolics of all sorts. And as his personal recollections ran back nearly three score years into the perspective of the village history, his fund of local anecdote was copious, accurate, and edifying.

As his ecclesiastical revenues were by no means considerable, he was not unfrequently obliged, for the indulgence of his tastes, to arts which were, at the best, undignified.

He frequently invited himself when his entertainers had forgotten to do so; he dropped in accidentally upon small drinking parties of his acquaintance in public houses, and entertained them with stories, queer or terrible, from his inexhaustible reservoir, never scrupling to accept an acknowledgment in the shape of hot whiskey-punch, or whatever else was going.

There was at that time a certain atrabilious publican, called Philip Slaney, established in a shop nearly opposite the old turnpike. This man was not, when left to himself, immoderately given to drinking; but being naturally of a saturnine complexion, and his spirits constantly requiring a fillip, he acquired a prodigious liking for Bob Martin's company. The sexton's society, in fact, gradually became the solace of his existence, and he seemed to lose his constitutional melancholy in the fascination of his sly jokes and marvellous stories.

This intimacy did not redound to the prosperity or reputation of the convivial allies. Bob Martin drank a good deal more punch than was good for his health, or consistent with the character of an ecclesiastical functionary. Philip Slaney, too, was drawn into similar indulgences, for it was hard to resist the genial seductions of his gifted companion; and as he was obliged to pay for both, his purse was believed to have suffered even more than his head and liver.

Be this as it may, Bob Martin had the credit of having made a drunkard of "black Phil Slaney"—for by this cognomen was he distinguished; and Phil Slaney had also the reputation of having made the sexton, if possible, a "bigger blieggard" than ever. Under these circumstances, the accounts of the concern opposite the turnpike became somewhat entangled; and it came to pass one drowsy summer morning, the weather being at once sultry and cloudy, that Phil Slaney went into a small back parlour, where he kept his books, and which commanded, through its dirty window-panes, a full view of a dead wall, and having bolted the door, he took a loaded pistol, and clapping the muzzle in his mouth, blew the upper part of his skull through the ceiling.

This horrid catastrophe shocked Bob Martin extremely; and partly on this account, and partly because having been, on several late occasions, found at night in a state of abstraction, bordering on insensibility, upon the high road, he had been threatened with dismissal; and, as some said, partly also because of the difficulty of finding anybody to "treat" him as poor Phil Slaney used to do, he for a time forswore alcohol in all its combinations, and became an eminent example of temperance and sobriety.

Bob observed his good resolutions, greatly to the comfort of his wife, and the edification of the neighbourhood, with tolerable punctuality. He was seldom tipsy, and never drunk, and was greeted by the better part of society with all the honours of the prodigal son.

Now it happened, about a year after the grisly event we have mentioned, that the curate having received, by the post, due notice of a funeral to be consummated in the churchyard of Chapelizod, with certain instructions respecting the site of the grave, despatched a summons for Bob Martin, with a view to communicate to that functionary these official details.

It was a lowering autumn night: piles of lurid thunder-clouds, slowly rising from the earth, had loaded the sky with a solemn and boding canopy of storm. The growl of the distant thunder was heard afar off upon the dull, still air, and all nature seemed, as it were, hushed and cowering under the oppressive influence of the approaching tempest.

It was past nine o'clock when Bob, putting on his official coat of seedy black, prepared to attend his professional superior.

"Bobby, darlin'," said his wife, before she delivered the hat she held in her hand to his keeping, "sure you won't, Bobby, darlin'—you won't—you know what."

"I *don't* know what," he retorted, smartly, grasping at his hat.

"You won't be throwing up the little finger, Bobby, acushla?" she said, evading his grasp.

"Arrah, why would I, woman? there, give me my hat, will you?"

"But won't you promise me, Bobby darlin'—won't you, alanna?"

"Ay, ay, to be sure I will—why not?—there, give me my hat, and let me go."

"Ay, but you're not promisin', Bobby, mavourneen; you're not promisin' all the time."

"Well, divil carry me if I drink a drop till I come back again," said the sexton, angrily; "will that do you? And *now* will you give me my hat?"

"Here it is, darlin'," she said, "and God send you safe back."

And with this parting blessing she closed the door upon his retreating figure, for it was now quite dark, and resumed her knitting till his return, very much relieved; for she thought he had of late been oftener tipsy than was consistent with his thorough reformation, and feared the allurements of the half dozen "publics" which he had at that time to pass on his way to the other end of the town.

They were still open, and exhaled a delicious reek of whiskey, as Bob glided wistfully by them; but he stuck his hands in his pockets and looked the other way, whistling resolutely, and filling his mind with the image of the curate and anticipations of his coming fee. Thus he steered his morality safely through these rocks of offence, and reached the curate's lodging in safety.

He had, however, an unexpected sick call to attend, and was not at home, so that Bob Martin had to sit in the hall and amuse himself with the devil's tattoo until his return. This, unfortunately, was very long delayed, and it must have been fully twelve o'clock when Bob Martin set out upon his homeward way. By this time the storm had gathered to a pitchy darkness, the bellowing thunder was heard among the rocks and hollows of the Dublin mountains, and the pale, blue lightning shone upon the staring fronts of the houses.

By this time, too, every door was closed; but as Bob trudged homeward, his eye mechanically sought the public-house which had once belonged to Phil Slaney. A faint light was making its way through the shutters and the glass panes over the door-way, which made a sort of dull, foggy halo about the front of the house.

As Bob's eyes had become accustomed to the obscurity by this time, the light in question was quite sufficient to enable him to see a man in a sort of loose riding-coat seated upon a bench which, at that time, was fixed under the window of the house. He wore his hat very much over his eyes, and was smoking a long pipe. The outline of a glass and a quart bottle were also dimly traceable beside him; and a large horse saddled, but faintly discernible, was patiently awaiting his master's leisure.

There was something odd, no doubt, in the appearance of a traveller refreshing himself at such an hour in the open street; but the sexton accounted for it easily by supposing that, on the closing of the house for the night, he had taken what remained of his refection to the place where he was now discussing it al fresco.

At another time Bob might have saluted the stranger as he passed with a friendly "good night"; but, somehow, he was out of humour and in no genial mood, and was about passing without any courtesy of the sort, when the stranger, without taking the pipe from his mouth, raised the bottle, and with it beckoned him familiarly, while, with a sort of lurch of the head and shoulders, and at the same time shifting his seat to the end of the bench, he pantomimically invited him to share his seat and his cheer. There was a divine fragrance of whiskey about the spot, and Bob half relented; but he remembered his promise just as he began to waver, and said:

"No, I thank you, sir, I can't stop to-night."

The stranger beckoned with vehement welcome, and pointed to the vacant space on the seat beside him.

"I thank you for your polite offer," said Bob, "but it's what I'm too late as it is, and haven't time to spare, so I wish you a good night."

The traveller jingled the glass against the neck of the bottle, as if to intimate that he might at least swallow a dram without losing time. Bob was mentally quite of the same opinion; but, though his mouth watered, he remembered his promise, and shaking his head with incorruptible resolution, walked on.

The stranger, pipe in mouth, rose from his bench, the bottle in one hand, and the glass in the other, and followed at the sexton's heels, his dusky horse keeping close in his wake.

There was something suspicious and unaccountable in this importunity.

Bob quickened his pace, but the stranger followed close. The sexton began to feel queer, and turned about. His pursuer was behind, and still inviting him with impatient gestures to taste his liquor.

"I told you before," said Bob, who was both angry and frightened, "that I would not taste it, and that's enough. I don't want to have anything to say to you or your bottle; and in God's name," he added, more vehemently, observing that he was approaching still closer, "fall back and don't be tormenting me this way."

These words, as it seemed, incensed the stranger, for he shook the bottle with violent menace at Bob Martin; but, notwithstanding this gesture of defiance, he suffered the distance between them to increase. Bob, however, beheld him dogging him still in the distance, for his pipe shed a wonderful red glow, which duskily illuminated his entire figure like the lurid atmosphere of a meteor.

"I wish the devil had his own, my boy," muttered the excited sexton, "and I know well enough where you'd be."

The next time he looked over his shoulder, to his dismay he observed the importunate stranger as close as ever upon his track.

"Confound you," cried the man of skulls and shovels, almost beside himself with rage and horror, "what is it you want of me?"

The stranger appeared more confident, and kept wagging his head and extending both glass and bottle toward him as he drew near, and Bob Martin heard the horse snorting as it followed in the dark.

"Keep it to yourself, whatever it is, for there is neither grace nor luck about you," cried Bob Martin, freezing with terror; "leave me alone, will you."

And he fumbled in vain among the seething confusion of his ideas for a prayer or an exorcism. He quickened his pace almost to a run; he was now close to his own door, under the impending bank by the river side.

"Let me in, let me in, for God's sake; Molly, open the door," he cried, as he ran to the threshold, and leant his back against the plank. His pursuer confronted him upon the road; the pipe was no longer in his mouth, but the dusky red glow still lingered round him. He uttered some inarticulate cavernous sounds, which were wolfish and indescribable, while he seemed employed in pouring out a glass from the bottle.

The sexton kicked with all his force against the door, and cried at the same time with a despairing voice.

"In the name of God Almighty, once for all, leave me alone."

His pursuer furiously flung the contents of the bottle at Bob Martin; but instead of fluid it issued out in a stream of flame, which expanded and whirled round them, and for a moment they were both enveloped in a faint blaze; at the same instant a sudden gust whisked off the stranger's hat, and the sexton beheld that his skull was roofless. For an instant he beheld the gaping aperture, black and shattered, and then he fell senseless into his own doorway, which his affrighted wife had just unbarred.

I need hardly give my reader the key to this most intelligible and authentic narrative. The traveller was acknowledged by all to have been the spectre of the suicide, called up by the Evil One to tempt the convivial sexton into a violation of his promise, sealed, as it was, by an imprecation. Had he succeeded, no doubt the dusky steed, which Bob had seen saddled in attendance, was destined to have carried back a double burden to the place from whence he came.

As an attestation of the reality of this visitation, the old thorn tree which overhung the doorway was found in the morning to have been blasted with the infernal fires which had issued from the bottle, just as if a thunder-bolt had scorched it.

The moral of the above tale is upon the surface, apparent, and, so to speak, *self-acting*—a circumstance which happily obviates the necessity of our discussing it together. Taking our leave, therefore, of honest Bob Martin, who now sleeps soundly in the same solemn dormitory where, in his day, he made so many beds for others, I come to a legend of the Royal Irish Artillery, whose headquarters were for so long a time in the town of Chapelizod. I don't mean to say that I cannot tell a great many more stories, equally authentic and marvellous, touching this old town; but as I may possibly have to perform a like office for other localities, and as Anthony Poplar is known, like Atropos, to carry a shears, wherewith to snip across all "yarns" which exceed reasonable bounds, I consider it, on the whole, safer to despatch the traditions of Chapelizod with one tale more.

Let me, however, first give it a name; for an author can no more despatch a tale without a title, than an apothecary can deliver his physic without a label. We shall, therefore, call it—

The Spectre Lovers

There lived some fifteen years since in a small and ruinous house, little better than a hovel, an old woman who was reported to have considerably exceeded her eightieth year, and who rejoiced in the name of Alice, or popularly, Ally Moran. Her society was not much courted, for she was neither rich, nor, as the reader may suppose, beautiful. In addition to a lean cur and a cat she had one human companion, her grandson, Peter Brien, whom, with laudable good nature, she had supported from the period of his orphanage down to that of my story, which finds him in his twentieth year. Peter was a good-natured slob of a fellow, much more addicted to wrestling, dancing, and love-making, than to hard work, and fonder of whiskey-punch than good advice. His grandmother had a high opinion of his accomplishments, which indeed was but natural, and also of his genius, for Peter had of late years begun to apply his mind to politics; and as it was plain that he had a mortal hatred of honest labour, his grandmother predicted, like a true fortune-teller, that he was born to marry an heiress, and Peter himself (who had no mind to forego his freedom even on such terms) that he was destined to find a pot of gold. Upon one point both agreed, that being unfitted by the peculiar bias of his genius for work, he was to acquire the immense fortune to which his merits entitled him by means of a pure run of good luck. This solution of Peter's future had the double effect of reconciling both himself and his grandmother to his idle courses, and also of maintaining that even flow of hilarious spirits which made him everywhere welcome, and which was in truth the natural result of his consciousness of approaching affluence.

It happened one night that Peter had enjoyed himself to a very late hour with two or three choice spirits near Palmerstown. They had talked politics and love, sung songs, and told stories, and, above all, had swallowed, in the chastened disguise of punch, at least a pint of good whiskey, every man.

It was considerably past one o'clock when Peter bid his companions goodbye, with a sigh and a hiccough, and lighting his pipe set forth on his solitary homeward way.

The bridge of Chapelizod was pretty nearly the midway point of his night march, and from one cause or another his progress was rather slow, and it was past two o'clock by the time he found himself leaning over its old battlements, and looking up the river, over whose winding current and wooded banks the soft moonlight was falling.

The cold breeze that blew lightly down the stream was grateful to him. It cooled his throbbing head, and he drank it in at his hot lips. The scene, too, had, without his being well sensible of it, a secret fascination. The village was sunk in the profoundest slumber, not a mortal stirring, not a sound afloat, a soft haze covered it all, and the fairy moonlight hovered over the entire landscape.

In a state between rumination and rapture, Peter continued to lean over the battlements of the old bridge, and as he did so he saw, or fancied he saw, emerging one after another along the river bank in the little gardens and enclosures in the rear of the street of Chapelizod, the queerest little white-washed huts and cabins he had ever seen there before. They had not been there that evening when he passed the bridge on the way to his merry tryst. But the most remarkable thing about it was the odd way in which these quaint little cabins showed themselves. First he saw one or two of them just with the corner of his eye, and when he looked full at them, strange to say, they faded away and disappeared. Then another and another came in view, but all in the same coy way, just appearing and gone again before he could well fix his gaze upon them; in a little while, however, they began to bear a fuller gaze, and he found, as it seemed to himself, that he was able by an effort of attention to fix the vision for a longer and a longer time, and when they waxed faint and nearly vanished, he had the power of recalling them into light and substance, until at last their vacillating indistinctness became less and less, and they assumed a permanent place in the moonlit landscape.

"Be the hokey," said Peter, lost in amazement, and dropping his pipe into the river unconsciously, "them is the quarist bits iv mud cabins I ever seen, growing up like musharoons in the dew of an evening, and poppin' up here and down again there, and up again in another place, like so many white rabbits in a warren; and there they stand at last as firm and fast as if they were there from the Deluge; bedad it's enough to make a man a'most believe in the fairies."

This latter was a large concession from Peter, who was a bit of a freethinker, and spoke contemptuously in his ordinary conversation of that class of agencies.

Having treated himself to a long last stare at these mysterious fabrics, Peter prepared to pursue his homeward way; having crossed the bridge and passed the mill, he arrived at the corner of the main-street of the little town, and casting a careless look up the Dublin road, his eye was arrested by a most unexpected spectacle.

This was no other than a column of foot soldiers, marching with perfect regularity towards the village, and headed by an officer on horseback. They were at the far side of the turnpike, which was closed; but much to his perplexity he perceived that they marched on through it without appearing to sustain the least check from that barrier.

On they came at a slow march; and what was most singular in the matter was, that they were drawing several cannons along with them; some held ropes, others spoked the wheels, and others again marched in front of the guns and behind them, with muskets shouldered, giving a stately character of parade and regularity to this, as it seemed to Peter, most unmilitary procedure.

It was owing either to some temporary defect in Peter's vision, or to some illusion attendant upon mist and moonlight, or perhaps to some other cause, that the whole procession had a certain waving and vapoury character which perplexed and tasked his eyes not a little. It was like the pictured pageant of a phantasmagoria reflected upon smoke. It was as if every breath disturbed it; sometimes it was blurred, sometimes obliterated; now here, now there. Sometimes, while the upper part was quite distinct, the legs of the column would nearly fade away or vanish outright, and then again they would come out into clear relief, marching on with measured tread, while the cocked hats and shoulders grew, as it were, transparent, and all but disappeared.

Notwithstanding these strange optical fluctuations, however, the column continued steadily to advance. Peter crossed the street from the corner near the old bridge, running on tip-toe, and with his body stooped to avoid observation, and took up a position upon the raised footpath in the shadow of the houses, where, as the soldiers kept the middle of the road, he calculated that he might, himself undetected, see them distinctly enough as they passed.

"What the div——, what on airth," he muttered, checking the irreligious ejaculation with which he was about to start, for certain queer misgivings were hovering about his heart, notwithstanding the factitious courage of the whiskey bottle. "What on airth is the manin' of all this? is it the French that's landed at last to give us a hand and help us in airnest to this blessed repale? If it is not them, I simply ask who the div——, I mane who on airth are they, for such sogers as them I never seen before in my born days?"

By this time the foremost of them were quite near, and truth to say they were the queerest soldiers he had ever seen in the course of his life. They wore long gaiters and leather breeches, three-cornered hats, bound with silver lace, long blue coats, with scarlet facings and linings, which latter were shewn by a fastening which held together the two opposite corners of the skirt behind; and in front the breasts were in like manner connected at a single point, where and below which they sloped back, disclosing a long-flapped waistcoat of snowy whiteness; they had very large, long cross-belts, and wore enormous pouches of white leather hung extraordinarily low, and on each of which a little silver star was glittering. But what struck him as most grotesque and outlandish in their costume was their extraordinary display of shirt-frill in front, and of ruffle about their wrists, and the strange manner in which their hair was frizzled out and powdered under their hats, and clubbed up into great rolls behind. But one of the party was mounted. He rode a tall white horse, with high action and arching neck; he had a snow-white feather in his three-cornered hat, and his coat was shimmering all over with a profusion of silver lace. From these circumstances Peter concluded that he must be the commander of the detachment, and examined him as he passed attentively. He was a slight, tall man, whose legs did not half fill his leather breeches, and he appeared to be at the wrong side of sixty. He had a shrunken, weather-beaten, mulberry-coloured face, carried a large black patch over one eye, and turned neither to the right nor to the left, but rode on at the head of his men, with a grim, military inflexibility.

The countenances of these soldiers, officers as well as men, seemed all full of trouble, and, so to speak, scared and wild. He watched in vain for a single contented or comely face. They had, one and all, a melancholy and hang-dog look; and as they passed by, Peter fancied that the air grew cold and thrilling.

He had seated himself upon a stone bench, from which, staring with all his might, he gazed upon the grotesque and noiseless procession as it filed by him. Noiseless it was; he could neither hear the jingle of accoutrements, the tread of feet, nor the rumble of the wheels; and when the old colonel turned his horse a little, and made as though he were giving the word of command, and a trumpeter, with a swollen blue nose and white feather fringe round his hat, who was walking beside him, turned about and put his bugle to his lips, still Peter heard nothing, although it was plain the sound had reached the soldiers, for they instantly changed their front to three abreast.

"Botheration!" muttered Peter, "is it deaf I'm growing?"

But that could not be, for he heard the sighing of the breeze and the rush of the neighbouring Liffey plain enough.

"Well," said he, in the same cautious key, "by the piper, this bangs Banagher fairly! It's either the Frinch army that's in it, come to take the town iv Chapelizod by surprise, an' makin' no noise for feard iv wakenin' the inhabitants; or else it's—it's—what it's—somethin' else. But, tundher-an-ouns, what's gone wid Fitzpatrick's shop across the way?"

The brown, dingy stone building at the opposite side of the street looked newer and cleaner than he had been used to see it; the front door of it stood open, and a sentry, in the same grotesque uniform, with shouldered musket, was pacing noiselessly to and fro before it. At the angle of this building, in like manner, a wide gate (of which Peter had no recollection whatever) stood open, before which, also, a similar sentry was gliding, and into this gateway the whole column gradually passed, and Peter finally lost sight of it.

"I'm not asleep; I'm not dhramin'," said he, rubbing his eyes, and stamping slightly on the pavement, to assure himself that he was wide awake. "It is a quare business, whatever it is; an' it's not alone that, but everything about town looks strange to me. There's Tresham's house new painted, bedad, an' them flowers in the windies! An' Delany's house, too, that had not a whole pane of glass in it this morning, and scarce a slate on the roof of it! It is not possible it's what it's dhrunk I am. Sure there's the big tree, and not a leaf of it changed since I passed, and the stars overhead, all right. I don't think it is in my eyes it is."

And so looking about him, and every moment finding or fancying new food for wonder, he walked along the pavement, intending, without further delay, to make his way home.

But his adventures for the night were not concluded. He had nearly reached the angle of the short land that leads up to the church, when for the first time he perceived that an officer, in the uniform he had just seen, was walking before, only a few yards in advance of him.

The officer was walking along at an easy, swinging gait, and carried his sword under his arm, and was looking down on the pavement with an air of reverie.

In the very fact that he seemed unconscious of Peter's presence, and disposed to keep his reflections to himself, there was something reassuring. Besides, the reader must please to remember that our hero had a *quantum sufficit* of good punch before his adventure commenced, and was thus fortified against those qualms and terrors under which, in a more reasonable state of mind, he might not impossibly have sunk.

The idea of the French invasion revived in full power in Peter's fuddled imagination, as he pursued the nonchalant swagger of the officer.

"Be the powers iv Moll Kelly, I'll ax him what it is," said Peter, with a sudden accession of rashness. "He may tell me or not, as he plases, but he can't be offinded, anyhow."

With this reflection having inspired himself, Peter cleared his voice and began—

"Captain!" said he, "I ax your pardon, captain, an' maybe you'd be so condescindin' to my ignorance as to tell me, if it's plasin' to yer honour, whether your honour is not a Frinchman, if it's plasin' to you."

This he asked, not thinking that, had it been as he suspected, not one word of his question in all probability would have been intelligible to the person he addressed. He was, however, understood, for the officer answered him in English, at the same time slackening his pace and moving a little to the side of the pathway, as if to invite his interrogator to take his place beside him.

"No; I am an Irishman," he answered.

"I humbly thank your honour," said Peter, drawing nearer—for the affability and the nativity of the officer encouraged him—"but maybe your honour is in the *sarvice* of the King of France?"

"I serve the same King as you do," he answered, with a sorrowful significance which Peter did not comprehend at the time; and, interrogating in turn, he asked, "But what calls you forth at this hour of the day?"

"The *day*, your honour!—the night, you mane."

"It was always our way to turn night into day, and we keep to it still," remarked the soldier. "But, no matter, come up here to my house; I have a job for you, if you wish to earn some money easily. I live here."

As he said this, he beckoned authoritatively to Peter, who followed almost mechanically at his heels, and they turned up a little lane near the old Roman Catholic chapel, at the end of which stood, in Peter's time, the ruins of a tall, stone-built house.

Like everything else in the town, it had suffered a metamorphosis. The stained and ragged walls were now erect, perfect, and covered with pebble-dash; window-panes glittered coldly in every window; the green hall-door had a bright brass knocker on it. Peter did not know whether to believe his previous or his present impressions; seeing is believing, and Peter could not dispute the reality of the scene. All the records of his memory seemed but the images of a tipsy dream. In a trance of astonishment and perplexity, therefore, he submitted himself to the chances of his adventure.

The door opened, the officer beckoned with a melancholy air of authority to Peter, and entered. Our hero followed him into a sort of hall, which was very dark, but he was guided by the steps of the soldier, and, in silence, they ascended the stairs. The moonlight, which shone in at the lobbies, showed an old, dark wainscoting, and a heavy, oak banister. They passed by closed doors at different landing-places, but all was dark and silent as, indeed, became that late hour of the night.

Now they ascended to the topmost floor. The captain paused for a minute at the nearest door, and, with a heavy groan, pushing it open, entered the room. Peter remained at the threshold. A slight female form in a sort of loose, white robe, and with a great deal of dark hair hanging loosely about her, was standing in the middle of the floor, with her back towards them.

The soldier stopped short before he reached her, and said, in a voice of great anguish, "Still the same, sweet bird—sweet bird! still the same." Whereupon, she turned suddenly, and threw her arms about the neck of the officer, with a gesture of fondness and despair, and her frame was agitated as if by a burst of sobs. He held her close to his breast in silence; and honest Peter felt a strange terror creep over him, as he witnessed these mysterious sorrows and endearments.

"To-night, to-night—and then ten years more—ten long years—another ten years."

The officer and the lady seemed to speak these words together; her voice mingled with his in a musical and fearful wail, like a distant summer wind, in the dead hour of night, wandering through ruins. Then he heard the officer say, alone, in a voice of anguish—

"Upon me be it all, for ever, sweet birdie, upon me."

And again they seemed to mourn together in the same soft and desolate wail, like sounds of grief heard from a great distance.

Peter was thrilled with horror, but he was also under a strange fascination; and an intense and dreadful curiosity held him fast.

The moon was shining obliquely into the room, and through the window Peter saw the familiar slopes of the Park, sleeping mistily under its shimmer. He could also see the furniture of the room with tolerable distinctness—the old balloon-backed chairs, a four-post bed in a sort of recess, and a rack against the wall, from which hung some military clothes and accoutrements; and the sight of all these homely objects reassured him somewhat, and he could not help feeling unspeakably curious to see the face of the girl whose long hair was streaming over the officer's epaulet.

Peter, accordingly, coughed, at first slightly, and afterward more loudly, to recall her from her reverie of grief; and, apparently, he succeeded; for she turned round, as did her companion, and both, standing hand in hand, gazed upon him fixedly. He thought he had never seen such large, strange eyes in all his life; and their gaze seemed to chill the very air around him, and arrest the pulses of his heart. An eternity of misery and remorse was in the shadowy faces that looked upon him.

If Peter had taken less whisky by a single thimbleful, it is probable that he would have lost heart altogether before these figures, which seemed every moment to assume a more marked and fearful, though hardly definable, contrast to ordinary human shapes.

"What is it you want with me?" he stammered.

"To bring my lost treasure to the churchyard," replied the lady, in a silvery voice of more than mortal desolation.

The word "treasure" revived the resolution of Peter, although a cold sweat was covering him, and his hair was bristling with horror; he believed, however, that he was on the brink of fortune, if he could but command nerve to brave the interview to its close.

"And where," he gasped, "is it hid—where will I find it?"

They both pointed to the sill of the window, through which the moon was shining at the far end of the room, and the soldier said—

"Under that stone."

Peter drew a long breath, and wiped the cold dew from his face, preparatory to passing to the window, where he expected to secure the reward of his protracted terrors. But looking steadfastly at the window, he saw the faint image of a new-born child sitting upon the sill in the moonlight, with its little arms stretched toward him, and a smile so heavenly as he never beheld before.

At sight of this, strange to say, his heart entirely failed him, he looked on the figures that stood near, and beheld them gazing on the infantine form with a smile so guilty and distorted, that he felt as if he were entering alive among the scenery of hell, and shuddering, he cried in an irrepressible agony of horror—

"I'll have nothing to say with you, and nothing to do with you; I don't know what yez are or what yez want iv me, but let me go this minute, every one of yez, in the name of God."

With these words there came a strange rumbling and sighing about Peter's ears; he lost sight of everything, and felt that peculiar and not unpleasant sensation of falling softly, that sometimes supervenes in sleep, ending in a dull shock. After that he had neither dream nor consciousness till he wakened, chill and stiff, stretched between two piles of old rubbish, among the black and roofless walls of the ruined house.

We need hardly mention that the village had put on its wonted air of neglect and decay, or that Peter looked around him in vain for traces of those novelties which had so puzzled and distracted him upon the previous night.

"Ay, ay," said his grandmother, removing her pipe, as he ended his description of the view from the bridge, "sure enough I remember myself, when I was a slip of a girl, these little white cabins among the gardens by the river side. The artillery sogers that was married, or had not room in the barracks, used to be in them, but they're all gone long ago.

"The Lord be merciful to us!" she resumed, when he had described the military procession, "It's often I seen the regiment marchin' into the town, jist as you saw it last night, acushla. Oh, voch, but it makes my heart sore to think iv them days; they were pleasant times, sure enough; but is not it terrible, avick, to think it's what it was the ghost of the rigiment you seen? The Lord betune us an' harm, for it was nothing else, as sure as I'm sittin' here."

When he mentioned the peculiar physiognomy and figure of the old officer who rode at the head of the regiment—

"*That*," said the old crone, dogmatically, "was ould Colonel Grimshaw, the Lord presarve us! he's buried in the churchyard iv Chapelizod, and well I remember him, when I was a young thing, an' a cross ould floggin' fellow he was wid the men, an' a devil's boy among the girls—rest his soul!"

"Amen!" said Peter; "it's often I read his tomb-stone myself; but he's a long time dead."

"Sure, I tell you he died when I was no more nor a slip iv a girl—the Lord betune us and harm!"

"I'm afeard it is what I'm not long for this world myself, afther seeing such a sight as that," said Peter, fearfully.

"Nonsinse, avourneen," retorted his grandmother, indignantly, though she had herself misgivings on the subject; "sure there was Phil Doolan, the ferryman, that seen black Ann Scanlan in his own boat, and what harm ever kem of it?"

Peter proceeded with his narrative, but when he came to the description of the house, in which his adventure had had so sinister a conclusion, the old woman was at fault.

"I know the house and the ould walls well, an' I can remember the time there was a roof on it, and the doors an' windows in it, but it had a bad name about being haunted, but by who, or for what, I forget intirely."

"Did you ever hear was there goold or silver there?" he inquired.

"No, no, avick, don't be thinking about the likes; take a fool's advice, and never go next to near them ugly black walls again the longest day you have to live; an' I'd take my davy, it's what it's the same word the priest himself id be afther sayin' to you if you wor to ax his raverence consarnin' it, for it's plain to be seen it was nothing good you seen there, and there's neither luck nor grace about it."

Peter's adventure made no little noise in the neighbourhood, as the reader may well suppose; and a few evenings after it, being on an errand to old Major Vandeleur, who lived in a snug old-fashioned house, close by the river, under a perfect bower of ancient trees, he was called on to relate the story in the parlour.

The Major was, as I have said, an old man; he was small, lean, and upright, with a mahogany complexion, and a wooden inflexibility of face; he was a man, besides, of few words, and if *he* was old, it follows plainly that his mother was older still. Nobody could guess or tell *how* old, but it was admitted that her own generation had long passed away, and that she had not a competitor left. She had French blood in her veins, and although she did not retain her charms quite so well as Ninon de l'Enclos, she was in full possession of all her mental activity, and talked quite enough for herself and the Major.

"So, Peter," she said, "you have seen the dear, old Royal Irish again in the streets of Chapelizod. Make him a tumbler of punch, Frank; and Peter, sit down, and while you take it let us have the story."

Peter accordingly, seated near the door, with a tumbler of the nectarian stimulant steaming beside him, proceeded with marvellous courage, considering they had no light but the uncertain glare of the fire, to relate with minute particularity his awful adventure. The old lady listened at first with a smile of goodnatured incredulity; her cross-examination touching the drinking-bout at Palmerstown had been teazing, but as the narrative proceeded she became attentive, and at length absorbed, and once or twice she uttered ejaculations of pity or awe. When it was over, the old lady looked with a somewhat sad and stern abstraction on the table, patting her cat assiduously meanwhile, and then suddenly looking upon her son, the Major, she said—

"Frank, as sure as I live he has seen the wicked Captain Devereux."

The Major uttered an inarticulate expression of wonder.

"The house was precisely that he has described. I have told you the story often, as I heard it from your dear grandmother, about the poor young lady he ruined, and the dreadful suspicion about the little baby. *She*, poor thing, died in that house heart-broken, and you know he was shot shortly after in a duel."

This was the only light that Peter ever received respecting his adventure. It was supposed, however, that he still clung to the hope that treasure of some sort was hidden about the old house, for he was often seen lurking about its walls, and at last his fate overtook him, poor fellow, in the pursuit; for climbing near the summit one day, his holding gave way, and he fell upon the hard uneven ground, fracturing a leg and a rib, and after a short interval died, and he, like the other heroes of these true tales, lies buried in the little churchyard of Chapelizod.

THE CHILD THAT
WENT WITH THE FAIRIES

Eastward of the old city of Limerick, about ten Irish miles under the range of mountains known as the Slieveelim hills, famous as having afforded Sarsfield a shelter among their rocks and hollows, when he crossed them in his gallant descent upon the cannon and ammunition of King William, on its way to the beleaguering army, there runs a very old and narrow road. It connects the Limerick road to Tipperary with the old road from Limerick to Dublin, and runs by bog and pasture, hill and hollow, straw-thatched village, and roofless castle, not far from twenty miles.

Skirting the healthy mountains of which I have spoken, at one part it becomes singularly lonely. For more than three Irish miles it traverses a deserted country. A wide, black bog, level as a lake, skirted with copse, spreads at the left, as you journey northward, and the long and irregular line of mountain rises at the right, clothed in heath, broken with lines of grey rock that resemble the bold and irregular outlines of fortifications, and riven with many a gully, expanding here and there into rocky and wooded glens, which open as they approach the road.

A scanty pasturage, on which browsed a few scattered sheep or kine, skirts this solitary road for some miles, and under shelter of a hillock, and of two or three great ash-trees, stood, not many years ago, the little thatched cabin of a widow named Mary Ryan.

Poor was this widow in a land of poverty. The thatch had acquired the grey tint and sunken outlines, that show how the alternations of rain and sun have told upon that perishable shelter.

But whatever other dangers threatened, there was one well provided against by the care of other times. Round the cabin stood half a dozen mountain ashes, as the rowans, inimical to witches, are there called. On the worn planks of the door were nailed two horse-shoes, and over the lintel and spreading along the thatch, grew, luxuriant, patches of that ancient cure for many maladies, and prophylactic against the machinations of the evil one, the house-leek. Descending into the doorway, in the *chiaroscuro* of the interior, when your eye grew sufficiently accustomed to that dim light, you might discover, hanging at the head of the widow's wooden-roofed bed, her beads and a phial of holy water.

Here certainly were defences and bulwarks against the intrusion of that unearthly and evil power, of whose vicinity this solitary family were constantly reminded by the outline of Lisnavoura, that lonely hill-haunt of the "Good people," as the fairies are called euphemistically, whose strangely dome-like summit rose not half a mile away, looking like an outwork of the long line of mountain that sweeps by it.

It was at the fall of the leaf, and an autumnal sunset threw the lengthening shadow of haunted Lisnavoura, close in front of the solitary little cabin, over the undulating slopes and sides of Slieveelim. The birds were singing among the branches in the thinning leaves of the melancholy ash-trees that grew at the roadside in front of the door. The widow's three younger children were playing on the road, and their voices mingled with the evening song of the birds. Their elder sister, Nell, was "within in the house," as their phrase is, seeing after the boiling of the potatoes for supper.

Their mother had gone down to the bog, to carry up a hamper of turf on her back. It is, or was at least, a charitable custom—and if not dis-used, long may it continue—for the wealthier people when cutting their turf and stacking it in the bog, to make a smaller stack for the behoof of the poor, who were welcome to take from it so long as it lasted, and thus the potato pót was kept boiling, and hearth warm that would have been cold enough but for that good-natured bounty, through wintry months.

Moll Ryan trudged up the steep "bohereen" whose banks were overgrown with thorn and brambles, and stooping under her burden, re-entered her door, where her dark-haired daughter Nell met her with a welcome, and relieved her of her hamper.

Moll Ryan looked round with a sigh of relief, and drying her forehead, uttered the Munster ejaculation:

"Eiah, wisha! It's tired I am with it, God bless it. And where's the craythurs, Nell?"

"Playin' out on the road, mother; didn't ye see them and you comin' up?"

"No; there was no one before me on the road," she said, uneasily; "not a soul, Nell; and why didn't ye keep an eye on them?"

"Well, they're in the haggard, playin' there, or round by the back o' the house. Will I call them in?"

"Do so, good girl, in the name o' God. The hens is comin' home, see, and the sun was just down over Knockdoulah, an' I comin' up."

So out ran tall, dark-haired Nell, and standing on the road, looked up and down it; but not a sign of her two little brothers, Con and Bill, or her little sister, Peg, could she see. She called them; but no answer came from the little haggard, fenced with straggling bushes. She listened, but the sound of their voices was missing. Over the stile, and behind the house she ran—but there all was silent and deserted.

She looked down toward the bog, as far as she could see; but they did not appear. Again she listened—but in vain. At first she had felt angry, but now a different feeling overcame her, and she grew pale. With an undefined boding she looked toward the heathy boss of Lisnavoura, now darkening into the deepest purple against the flaming sky of sunset.

Again she listened with a sinking heart, and heard nothing but the farewell twitter and whistle of the birds in the bushes around. How many stories had she listened to by the winter hearth, of children stolen by the fairies, at nightfall, in lonely places! With this fear she knew her mother was haunted.

No one in the country round gathered her little flock about her so early as this frightened widow, and no door "in the seven parishes" was barred so early.

Sufficiently fearful, as all young people in that part of the world are of such dreaded and subtle agents, Nell was even more than usually afraid of them, for her terrors were infected and redoubled by her mother's. She was looking towards Lisnavoura in a trance of fear, and crossed herself again and again, and whispered prayer after prayer. She was interrupted by her mother's voice on the road calling her loudly. She answered, and ran round to the front of the cabin, where she found her standing.

"And where in the world's the craythurs—did ye see sight o' them anywhere?" cried Mrs. Ryan, as the girl came over the stile.

"Arrah! mother, 'tis only what they're run down the road a bit. We'll see them this minute coming back. It's like goats they are, climbin' here and runnin' there; an' if I had them here, in my hand, maybe I wouldn't give them a hiding all round."

"May the Lord forgive you, Nell! the childhers gone. They're took, and not a soul near us, and Father Tom three miles away! And what'll I do, or who's to help us this night? Oh, wirristhru, wirristhru! The craythurs is gone!"

"Whisht, mother, be aisy: don't ye see them comin' up?"

And then she shouted in menacing accents, waving her arm, and beckoning the children, who were seen approaching on the road, which some little way off made a slight dip, which had concealed them. They were approaching from the westward, and from the direction of the dreaded hill of Lisnavoura.

But there were only two of the children, and one of them, the little girl, was crying. Their mother and sister hurried forward to meet them, more alarmed than ever.

"Where is Billy—where is he?" cried the mother, nearly breathless, so soon as she was within hearing.

"He's gone—they took him away; but they said he'll come back again," answered little Con, with the dark brown hair.

"He's gone away with the grand ladies," blubbered the little girl.

"What ladies—where? Oh, Leum, asthora! My darlin', are you gone away at last? Where is he? Who took him? What ladies are you talkin' about? What way did he go?" she cried in distraction.

"I couldn't see where he went, mother; 'twas like as if he was going to Lisnavoura."

With a wild exclamation the distracted woman ran on towards the hill alone, clapping her hands, and crying aloud the name of her lost child.

Scared and horrified, Nell, not daring to follow, gazed after her, and burst into tears; and the other children raised high their lamentations in shrill rivalry.

Twilight was deepening. It was long past the time when they were usually barred securely within their habitation. Nell led the younger children into the cabin, and made them sit down by the turf fire, while she stood in the open door, watching in great fear for the return of her mother.

After a long while they did see their mother return. She came in and sat down by the fire, and cried as if her heart would break.

"Will I bar the doore, mother?" asked Nell.

"Ay, do—didn't I lose enough, this night, without lavin' the doore open, for more o' yez to go; but first take an' sprinkle a dust o' the holy waters over ye, acuishla, and bring it here till I throw a taste iv it over myself and the craythurs; an' I wondher, Nell, you'd forget to do the like yourself, lettin' the craythurs out so near nightfall. Come here and sit on my knees, asthora, come to me, mavourneen, and hould me fast, in the name o' God, and I'll hould you fast that none can take yez from me, and tell me all about it, and what it was—the Lord between us and harm—an' how it happened, and who was in it."

And the door being barred, the two children, sometimes speaking together, often interrupting one another, often interrupted by their mother, managed to tell this strange story, which I had better relate connectedly and in my own language.

The Widow Ryan's three children were playing, as I have said, upon the narrow old road in front of her door. Little Bill or Leum, about five years old, with golden hair and large blue eyes, was a very pretty boy, with all the clear tints of healthy childhood, and that gaze of earnest simplicity which belongs not to town children of the same age. His little sister Peg, about a year older, and his brother Con, a little more than a year elder than she, made up the little group.

Under the great old ash-trees, whose last leaves were falling at their feet, in the light of an October sunset, they were playing with the hilarity and eagerness of rustic children, clamouring together, and their faces were turned toward the west and storied hill of Lisnavoura.

Suddenly a startling voice with a screech called to them from behind, ordering them to get out of the way, and turning, they saw a sight, such as they never beheld before. It was a carriage drawn by four horses that were pawing and snorting, in impatience, as if just pulled up. The children were almost under their feet, and scrambled to the side of the road next their own door.

This carriage and all its appointments were old-fashioned and gorgeous, and presented to the children, who had never seen anything finer than a turf car, and once, an old chaise that passed that way from Killaloe, a spectacle perfectly dazzling.

Here was antique splendour. The harness and trappings were scarlet, and blazing with gold. The horses were huge, and snow white, with great manes, that as they tossed and shook them in the air, seemed to stream and float sometimes longer and sometimes shorter, like so much smoke—their tails were long, and tied up in bows of broad scarlet and gold ribbon. The coach itself was glowing with colours, gilded and emblazoned. There were footmen in gay liveries, and three-cocked hats, like the coachman's; but he had a great wig, like a judge's, and their hair was frizzed out and powdered, and a long thick "pigtail," with a bow to it, hung down the back of each.

All these servants were diminutive, and ludicrously out of proportion with the enormous horses of the equipage, and had sharp, sallow features, and small, restless fiery eyes, and faces of cunning and malice that chilled the children. The little coachman was scowling and showing his white fangs under his cocked hat, and his little blazing beads of eyes were quivering with fury in their sockets as he whirled his whip round and round over their heads, till the lash of it looked like a streak of fire in the evening sun, and sounded like the cry of a legion of "fillapoueeks" in the air.

"Stop the princess on the highway!" cried the coachman, in a piercing treble.

"Stop the princess on the highway!" piped each footman in turn, scowling over his shoulder down on the children, and grinding his keen teeth.

The children were so frightened they could only gape and turn white in their panic. But a very sweet voice from the open window of the carriage reassured them, and arrested the attack of the lackeys.

A beautiful and "very grand-looking" lady was smiling from it on them, and they all felt pleased in the strange light of that smile.

"The boy with the golden hair, I think," said the lady, bending her large and wonderfully clear eyes on little Leum.

The upper sides of the carriage were chiefly of glass, so that the children could see another woman inside, whom they did not like so well.

This was a black woman, with a wonderfully long neck, hung round with many strings of large variously-coloured beads, and on her head was a sort of turban of silk striped with all the colours of the rainbow, and fixed in it was a golden star.

This black woman had a face as thin almost as a death's-head, with high cheekbones, and great goggle eyes, the whites of which, as well as her wide range of teeth, showed in brilliant contrast with her skin, as she looked over the beautiful lady's shoulder, and whispered something in her ear.

"Yes; the boy with the golden hair, I think," repeated the lady.

And her voice sounded sweet as a silver bell in the children's ears, and her smile beguiled them like the light of an enchanted lamp, as she leaned from the window with a look of ineffable fondness on the golden-haired boy, with the large blue eyes; insomuch that little Billy, looking up, smiled in return with a wondering fondness, and when she stooped down, and stretched her jewelled arms towards him, he stretched his little hands up, and how they touched the other children did not know; but, saying, "Come and give me a kiss, my darling," she raised him, and he seemed to ascend in her small fingers as lightly as a feather, and she held him in her lap and covered him with kisses.

Nothing daunted, the other children would have been only too happy to change places with their favoured little brother. There was only one thing that was unpleasant, and a little frightened them, and that was the black woman, who stood and stretched forward, in the carriage as before. She gathered a rich silk and gold handkerchief that was in her fingers up to her lips, and seemed to thrust ever so much of it, fold after fold, into her capacious mouth, as they thought to smother her laughter, with which she seemed convulsed, for she was shaking and quivering, as it seemed, with suppressed merriment; but her eyes, which remained uncovered, looked angrier than they had ever seen eyes look before.

But the lady was so beautiful they looked on her instead, and she continued to caress and kiss the little boy on her knee; and smiling at the other children she held up a large russet apple in her fingers, and the carriage began to move slowly on, and with a nod inviting them to take the fruit, she dropped it on the road from the window; it rolled some way beside the wheels, they following, and then she dropped another, and then another, and so on. And the same thing happened to all; for just as either of the children who ran beside had caught the rolling apple, somehow it slipt into a hole or ran into a ditch, and looking up they saw the lady drop another from the window, and so the chase was taken up and continued till they got, hardly knowing how far they had gone, to the old cross-road that leads to Owney. It seemed that there the horses' hoofs and carriage wheels rolled up a wonderful dust, which being caught in one of those eddies that whirl the dust up into a column, on the calmest day, enveloped the children for a moment, and passed whirling on towards Lisnavoura, the carriage, as they fancied, driving in the centre of it; but suddenly it subsided, the straws and leaves floated to the ground, the dust dissipated itself, but the white horses and the lackeys, the gilded carriage, the lady and their little golden-haired brother were gone.

At the same moment suddenly the upper rim of the clear setting sun disappeared behind the hill of Knockdoula, and it was twilight. Each child felt the transition like a shock—and the sight of the rounded summit of Lisnavoura, now closely overhanging them, struck them with a new fear.

They screamed their brother's name after him, but their cries were lost in the vacant air. At the same time they thought they heard a hollow voice say, close to them, "Go home."

Looking round and seeing no one, they were scared, and hand in hand—the little girl crying wildly, and the boy white as ashes, from fear, they trotted homeward, at their best speed, to tell, as we have seen, their strange story.

Molly Ryan never more saw her darling. But something of the lost little boy was seen by his former playmates.

Sometimes when their mother was away earning a trifle at hay-making, and Nelly washing the potatoes for their dinner, or "beatling" clothes in the little stream that flows in the hollow close by, they saw the pretty face of little Billy peeping in archly at the door, and smiling silently at them, and as they ran to embrace him, with cries of delight, he drew back, still smiling archly, and when they got out into the open day, he was gone, and they could see no trace of him anywhere.

This happened often, with slight variations in the circumstances of the visit. Sometimes he would peep for a longer time, sometimes for a shorter time, sometimes his little hand would come in, and, with bended finger, beckon them to follow; but always he was smiling with the same arch look and wary silence—and always he was gone when they reached the door. Gradually these visits grew less and less frequent, and in about eight months they ceased altogether, and little Billy, irretrievably lost, took rank in their memories with the dead.

One wintry morning, nearly a year and a half after his disappearance, their mother having set out for Limerick soon after cock-crow, to sell some fowls at the market, the little girl, lying by the side of her elder sister, who was fast asleep, just at the grey of the morning heard the latch lifted softly, and saw little Billy enter and close the door gently after him. There was light enough to see that he was barefoot and ragged, and looked pale and famished. He went straight to the fire, and cowered over the turf embers, and rubbed his hands slowly, and seemed to shiver as he gathered the smouldering turf together.

The little girl clutched her sister in terror and whispered, "Waken, Nelly, waken; here's Billy come back!"

Nelly slept soundly on, but the little boy, whose hands were extended close over the coals, turned and looked toward the bed, it seemed to her, in fear, and she saw the glare of the embers reflected on his thin cheek as he turned toward her. He rose and went, on tiptoe, quickly to the door, in silence, and let himself out as softly as he had come in.

After that, the little boy was never seen any more by any one of his kindred.

"Fairy doctors," as the dealers in the preternatural, who in such cases were called in, are termed, did all that in them lay—but in vain. Father Tom came down, and tried what holier rites could do, but equally without result. So little Billy was dead to mother, brother, and sisters; but no grave received him. Others whom affection cherished, lay in holy ground, in the old church-yard of Abington, with headstone to mark the spot over which the survivor might kneel and say a kind prayer for the peace of the departed soul. But there was no landmark to show where little Billy was hidden from their loving eyes, unless it was in the old hill of Lisnavoura, that cast its long shadow at sunset before the cabin-door; or that, white and filmy in the moonlight, in later years, would occupy his brother's gaze as he returned from fair or market, and draw from him a sigh and a prayer for the little brother he had lost so long ago, and was never to see again.

STORIES OF LOUGH GUIR

When the present writer was a boy of twelve or thirteen, he first made the acquaintance of Miss Anne Baily, of Lough Guir, in the county of Limerick. She and her sister were the last representatives at that place, of an extremely good old name in the county. They were both what is termed "old maids," and at that time past sixty. But never were old ladies more hospitable, lively, and kind, especially to young people. They were both remarkably agreeable and clever. Like all old county ladies of their time, they were great genealogists, and could recount the origin, generations, and intermarriages, of every county family of note.

These ladies were visited at their house at Lough Guir by Mr. Crofton Croker; and are, I think, mentioned, by name, in the second series of his fairy legends; the series in which (probably communicated by Miss Anne Baily), he recounts some of the picturesque traditions of those beautiful lakes—lakes, I should no longer say, for the smaller and prettier has since been drained, and gave up from its depths some long lost and very interesting relics.

In their drawing-room stood a curious relic of another sort: old enough, too, though belonging to a much more modern period. It was the ancient stirrup cup of the hospitable house of Lough Guir. Crofton Croker has preserved a sketch of this curious glass. I have often had it in my hand. It had a short stem; and the cup part, having the bottom rounded, rose cylindrically, and, being of a capacity to contain a whole bottle of claret, and almost as narrow as an old-fashioned ale glass, was tall to a degree that filled me with wonder. As it obliged the rider to extend his arm as he raised the glass, it must have tried a tipsy man, sitting in the saddle, pretty severely. The wonder was that the marvellous tall glass had come down to our times without a crack.

There was another glass worthy of remark in the same drawing-room. It was gigantic, and shaped conically, like one of those old-fashioned jelly glasses which used to be seen upon the shelves of confectioners. It was engraved round the rim with the words, "The glorious, pious, and immortal memory"; and on grand occasions, was filled to the brim, and after the manner of a loving cup, made the circuit of the Whig guests, who owed all to the hero whose memory its legend invoked.

It was now but the transparent phantom of those solemn convivialities of a generation, who lived, as it were, within hearing of the cannon and shoutings of those stirring times. When I saw it, this glass had long retired from politics and carousals, and stood peacefully on a little table in the drawing-room, where ladies' hands replenished it with fair water, and crowned it daily with flowers from the garden.

Miss Anne Baily's conversation ran oftener than her sister's upon the legendary and supernatural; she told her stories with the sympathy, the colour, and the mysterious air which contribute so powerfully to effect, and never wearied of answering questions about the old castle, and amusing her young audience with fascinating little glimpses of old adventure and bygone days. My memory retains the picture of my early friend very distinctly. A slim straight figure, above the middle height; a general likeness to the full-length portrait of that delightful Countess d'Aulnois, to whom we all owe our earliest and most brilliant glimpses of fairy-land; something of her gravely-pleasant countenance, plain, but refined and ladylike, with that kindly mystery in her side-long glance and uplifted finger, which indicated the approaching climax of a tale of wonder.

Lough Guir is a kind of centre of the operations of the Munster fairies. When a child is stolen by the "good people," Lough Guir is conjectured to be the place of its unearthly transmutation from the human to the fairy state. And beneath its waters lie enchanted, the grand old castle of the Desmonds, the great earl himself, his beautiful young countess, and all the retinue that surrounded him in the years of his splendour, and at the moment of his catastrophe.

Here, too, are historic associations. The huge square tower that rises at one side of the stable-yard close to the old house, to a height that amazed my young eyes, though robbed of its battlements and one story, was a stronghold of the last rebellious Earl of Desmond, and is specially mentioned in that delightful old folio, the *Hibernia Pacata*, as having, with its Irish garrison on the battlements, defied the army of the lord deputy, then marching by upon the summits of the overhanging hills. The house, built under shelter of this stronghold of the once proud and turbulent Desmonds, is old, but snug, with a multitude of small low rooms, such as I have seen in houses of the same age in Shropshire and the neighbouring English counties.

The hills that overhang the lakes appeared to me, in my young days (and I have not seen them since), to be clothed with a short soft verdure, of a hue so dark and vivid as I had never seen before.

In one of the lakes is a small island, rocky and wooded, which is believed by the peasantry to represent the top of the highest tower of the castle which sank, under a spell, to the bottom. In certain states of the atmosphere, I have heard educated people say, when in a boat you have reached a certain distance, the island appears to rise some feet from the water, its rocks assume the appearance of masonry, and the whole circuit presents very much the effect of the battlements of a castle rising above the surface of the lake.

This was Miss Anne Baily's story of the submersion of this lost castle:

The Magician Earl

It is well known that the great Earl of Desmond, though history pretends to dispose of him differently, lives to this hour enchanted in his castle, with all his household, at the bottom of the lake.

There was not, in his day, in all the world, so accomplished a magician as he. His fairest castle stood upon an island in the lake, and to this he brought his young and beautiful bride, whom he loved but too well; for she prevailed upon his folly to risk all to gratify her imperious caprice.

They had not been long in this beautiful castle, when she one day presented herself in the chamber in which her husband studied his forbidden art, and there implored him to exhibit before her some of the wonders of his evil science. He resisted long; but her entreaties, tears, and wheedlings were at length too much for him and he consented.

But before beginning those astonishing transformations with which he was about to amaze her, he explained to her the awful conditions and dangers of the experiment.

Alone in this vast apartment, the walls of which were lapped, far below, by the lake whose dark waters lay waiting to swallow them, she must witness a certain series of frightful phenomena, which once commenced, he could neither abridge nor mitigate; and if throughout their ghastly succession she spoke one word, or uttered one exclamation, the castle and all that it contained would in one instant subside to the bottom of the lake, there to remain, under the servitude of a strong spell, for ages.

The dauntless curiosity of the lady having prevailed, and the oaken door of the study being locked and barred, the fatal experiments commenced.

Muttering a spell, as he stood before her, feathers sprouted thickly over him, his face became contracted and hooked, a cadaverous smell filled the air, and, with heavy winnowing wings, a gigantic vulture rose in his stead, and swept round and round the room, as if on the point of pouncing upon her.

The lady commanded herself through this trial, and instantly another began.

The bird alighted near the door, and in less than a minute changed, she saw not how, into a horribly deformed and dwarfish hag: who, with yellow skin hanging about her face and enormous eyes, swung herself on crutches toward the lady, her mouth foaming with fury, and her grimaces and contortions becoming more and more hideous every moment, till she rolled with a yell on the floor, in a horrible convulsion, at the lady's feet, and then changed into a huge serpent, with crest erect, and quivering tongue. Suddenly, as it seemed on the point of darting at her, she saw her husband in its stead, standing pale before her, and, with his finger on his lip, enforcing the continued necessity of silence. He then placed himself at his length on the floor, and began to stretch himself out and out, longer and longer, until his head nearly reached to one end of the vast room, and his feet to the other.

This horror overcame her. The ill-starred lady uttered a wild scream, whereupon the castle and all that was within it, sank in a moment to the bottom of the lake.

But, once in every seven years, by night, the Earl of Desmond and his retinue emerge, and cross the lake, in shadowy cavalcade. His white horse is shod with silver. On that one night, the earl may ride till daybreak, and it behoves him to make good use of his time; for, until the silver shoes of his steed be worn through, the spell that holds him and his beneath the lake, will retain its power.

When I (Miss Anne Baily) was a child, there was still living a man named Teigue O'Neill, who had a strange story to tell.

He was a smith, and his forge stood on the brow of the hill, overlooking the lake, on a lonely part of the road to Cahir Conlish. One bright moonlight night, he was working very late, and quite alone. The clink of his hammer, and the wavering glow reflected through the open door on the bushes at the other side of the narrow road, were the only tokens that told of life and vigil for miles around.

In one of the pauses of his work, he heard the ring of many hoofs ascending the steep road that passed his forge, and, standing in this doorway, he was just in time to see a gentleman, on a white horse, who was dressed in a fashion the like of which the smith had never seen before. This man was accompanied and followed by a mounted retinue, as strangely dressed as he.

They seemed, by the clang and clatter that announced their approach, to be riding up the hill at a hard hurry-scurry gallop; but the pace abated as they drew near, and the rider of the white horse who, from his grave and lordly air, he assumed to be a man of rank, and accustomed to command, drew bridle and came to a halt before the smith's door.

He did not speak, and all his train were silent, but he beckoned to the smith, and pointed down to one of his horse's hoofs.

Teigue stooped and raised it, and held it just long enough to see that it was shod with a silver shoe; which, in one place, he said, was worn as thin as a shilling. Instantaneously, his situation was made apparent to him by this sign, and he recoiled with a terrified prayer. The lordly rider, with a look of pain and fury, struck at him suddenly, with something that whistled in the air like a whip; and an icy streak seemed to traverse his body as if he had been cut through with a leaf of steel. But he was without scathe or scar, as he afterwards found. At the same moment he saw the whole cavalcade break into a gallop and disappear down the hill, with a momentary hurtling in the air, like the flight of a volley of cannon shot.

Here had been the earl himself. He had tried one of his accustomed stratagems to lead the smith to speak to him. For it is well known that either for the purpose of abridging or of mitigating his period of enchantment, he seeks to lead people to accost him. But what, in the event of his succeeding, would befall the person whom he had thus ensnared, no one knows.

Moll Rial's Adventure

When Miss Anne Baily was a child, Moll Rial was an old woman. She had lived all her days with the Bailys of Lough Guir; in and about whose house, as was the Irish custom of those days, were a troop of bare-footed country girls, scullery maids, or laundresses, or employed about the poultry yard, or running of errands.

Among these was Moll Rial, then a stout good-humoured lass, with little to think of, and nothing to fret about. She was once washing clothes by the process known universally in Munster as beetling. The washer stands up to her ankles in water, in which she has immersed the clothes, which she lays in that state on a great flat stone, and smacks with lusty strokes of an instrument which bears a rude resemblance to a cricket bat, only shorter, broader, and light enough to be wielded freely with one hand. Thus, they smack the dripping clothes, turning them over and over, sousing them in the water, and replacing them on the same stone, to undergo a repetition of the process, until they are thoroughly washed.

Moll Rial was plying her "beetle" at the margin of the lake, close under the old house and castle. It was between eight and nine o'clock on a fine summer morning, everything looked bright and beautiful. Though quite alone, and though she could not see even the windows of the house (hidden from her view by the irregular ascent and some interposing bushes), her loneliness was not depressing.

Standing up from her work, she saw a gentleman walking slowly down the slope toward her. He was a "grand-looking" gentleman, arrayed in a flowered silk dressing-gown, with a cap of velvet on his head; and as he stepped toward her, in his slippered feet, he showed a very handsome leg. He was smiling graciously as he approached, and drawing a ring from his finger with an air of gracious meaning, which seemed to imply that he wished to make her a present, he raised it in his fingers with a pleased look, and placed it on the flat stones beside the clothes she had been beetling so industriously.

He drew back a little, and continued to look at her with an encouraging smile, which seemed to say: "You have earned your reward; you must not be afraid to take it."

The girl fancied that this was some gentleman who had arrived, as often happened in those hospitable and haphazard times, late and unexpectedly the night before, and who was now taking a little indolent ramble before breakfast.

Moll Rial was a little shy, and more so at having been discovered by so grand a gentleman with her petticoats gathered a little high about her bare shins. She looked down, therefore, upon the water at her feet, and then she saw a ripple of blood, and then another, ring after ring, coming and going to and from her feet. She cried out the sacred name in horror, and, lifting her eyes, the courtly gentleman was gone, but the blood-rings about her feet spread with the speed of light over the surface of the lake, which for a moment glowed like one vast estuary of blood.

Here was the earl once again, and Moll Rial declared that if it had not been for that frightful transformation of the water she would have spoken to him next minute, and would thus have passed under a spell, perhaps as direful as his own.

The Banshee

So old a Munster family as the Bailys, of Lough Guir, could not fail to have their attendant banshee. Everyone attached to the family knew this well, and could cite evidences of that unearthly distinction. I heard Miss Baily relate the only experience she had personally had of that wild spiritual sympathy.

She said that, being then young, she and Miss Susan undertook a long attendance upon the sick bed of their sister, Miss Kitty, whom I have heard remembered among her contemporaries as the merriest and most entertaining of human beings. This light-hearted young lady was dying of consumption. The sad duties of such attendance being divided among many sisters, as there then were, the night watches devolved upon the two ladies I have named: I think, as being the eldest.

It is not improbable that these long and melancholy vigils, lowering the spirits and exciting the nervous system, prepared them for illusions. At all events, one night at dead of night, Miss Baily and her sister, sitting in the dying lady's room, heard such sweet and melancholy music as they had never heard before. It seemed to them like distant cathedral music. The room of the dying girl had its windows toward the yard, and the old castle stood near, and full in sight. The music was not in the house, but seemed to come from the yard, or beyond it. Miss Anne Baily took a candle, and went down the back stairs. She opened the back door, and, standing there, heard the same faint but solemn harmony, and could not tell whether it most resembled the distant music of instruments, or a choir of voices. It seemed to come through the windows of the old castle, high in the air. But when she approached the tower, the music, she thought, came from above the house, at the other side of the yard; and thus perplexed, and at last frightened, she returned.

This aerial music both she and her sister, Miss Susan Baily, avowed that they distinctly heard, and for a long time. Of the fact she was clear, and she spoke of it with great awe.

The Governess's Dream

This lady, one morning, with a grave countenance that indicated something weighty upon her mind, told her pupils that she had, on the night before, had a very remarkable dream.

The first room you enter in the old castle, having reached the foot of the spiral stone stair, is a large hall, dim and lofty, having only a small window or two, set high in deep recesses in the wall. When I saw the castle many years ago, a portion of this capacious chamber was used as a store for the turf laid in to last the year.

Her dream placed her, alone, in this room, and there entered a grave-looking man, having something very remarkable in his countenance: which impressed her, as a fine portrait sometimes will, with a haunting sense of character and individuality.

In his hand this man carried a wand, about the length of an ordinary walking cane. He told her to observe and remember its length, and to mark well the measurements he was about to make, the result of which she was to communicate to Mr. Baily of Lough Guir.

From a certain point in the wall, with this wand, he measured along the floor, at right angles with the wall, a certain number of its lengths, which he counted aloud; and then, in the same way, from the adjoining wall he measured a certain number of its lengths, which he also counted distinctly. He then told her that at the point where these two lines met, at a depth of a certain number of feet which he also told her, treasure lay buried. And so the dream broke up, and her remarkable visitant vanished.

She took the girls with her to the old castle, where, having cut a switch to the length represented to her in her dream, she measured the distances, and ascertained, as she supposed, the point on the floor beneath which the treasure lay. The same day she related her dream to Mr. Baily. But he treated it laughingly, and took no step in consequence.

Some time after this, she again saw, in a dream, the. same remarkable-looking man, who repeated his message, and appeared displeased. But the dream was treated by Mr. Baily as before.

The same dream occurred again, and the children became so clamorous to have the castle floor explored, with pick and shovel, at the point indicated by the thrice-seen messenger, that at length Mr. Baily consented, and the floor was opened, and a trench was sunk at the spot which the governess had pointed out.

Miss Anne Baily, and nearly all the members of the family, her father included, were present at this operation. As the workmen approached the depth described in the vision, the interest and suspense of all increased; and when the iron implements met the solid resistance of a broad flagstone, which returned a cavernous sound to the stroke, the excitement of all present rose to its acme.

With some difficulty the flag was raised, and a chamber of stone work, large enough to receive a moderately-sized crock or pit, was disclosed. Alas! it was empty. But in the earth at the bottom of it, Miss Baily said, she herself saw, as every other bystander plainly did, the circular impression of a vessel: which had stood there, as the mark seemed to indicate, for a very long time.

Both the Miss Bailys were strong in their belief hereafterwards, that the treasure which they were convinced had actually been deposited there, had been removed by some more trusting and active listener than their father had proved.

This same governess remained with them to the time of her death, which occurred some years later, under the following circumstances as extraordinary as her dream.

The Earl's Hall

The good governess had a particular liking for the old castle, and when lessons were over, would take her book or her work into a large room in the ancient building, called the Earl's Hall. Here she caused a table and chair to be placed for her use, and in the chiaroscuro would so sit at her favourite occupations, with just a little ray of subdued light, admitted through one of the glassless windows above her, and falling upon her table.

The Earl's Hall is entered by a narrow-arched door, opening close to the winding stair. It is a very large and gloomy room, pretty nearly square, with a lofty vaulted ceiling, and a stone floor. Being situated high in the castle, the walls of which are immensely thick, and the windows very small and few, the silence that reigns here is like that of a subterranean cavern. You hear nothing in this solitude, except perhaps twice in a day, the twitter of a swallow in one of the small windows high in the wall.

This good lady having one day retired to her accustomed solitude, was missed from the house at her wonted hour of return. This in a country house, such as Irish houses were in those days, excited little surprise, and no harm. But when the dinner hour came, which was then, in country houses, five o'clock, and the governess had not appeared, some of her young friends, it being not yet winter, and sufficient light remaining to guide them through the gloom of the dim ascent and passages, mounted the old stone stair to the level of the Earl's Hall, gaily calling to her as they approached.

There was no answer. On the stone floor, outside the door of the Earl's Hall, to their horror, they found her lying insensible. By the usual means she was restored to consciousness; but she continued very ill, and was conveyed to the house, where she took to her bed.

It was there and then that she related what had occurred to her. She had placed herself, as usual, at her little work table, and had been either working or reading—I forget which—for some time, and felt in her usual health and serene spirits. Raising her eyes, and looking towards the door, she saw a horrible-looking little man enter. He was dressed in red, was very short, had a singularly dark face, and a most atrocious countenance. Having walked some steps into the room, with his eyes fixed on her, he stopped, and beckoning to her to follow, moved back toward the door. About half way, again he stopped once more and turned. She was so terrified that she sat staring at the apparition without moving or speaking. Seeing that she had not obeyed him, his face became more frightful and menacing, and as it underwent this change, he raised his hand and stamped on the floor. Gesture, look, and all, expressed diabolical fury. Through sheer extremity of terror she did rise, and, as he turned again, followed him a step or two in the direction of the door. He again stopped, and with the same mute menace, compelled her again to follow him.

She reached the narrow stone doorway of the Earl's Hall, through which he had passed; from the threshold she saw him standing a little way off, with his eyes still fixed on her. Again he signed to her, and began to move along the short passage that leads to the winding stair. But instead of following him further, she fell on the floor in a fit.

The poor lady was thoroughly persuaded that she was not long to survive this vision, and her foreboding proved true. From her bed she never rose. Fever and delirium supervened in a few days and she died. Of course it is possible that fever, already approaching, had touched her brain when she was visited by the phantom, and that it had no external existence.

THE VISION OF TOM CHUFF

At the edge of melancholy Catstean Moor, in the north of England, with half-a-dozen ancient poplar-trees with rugged and hoary stems around, one smashed across the middle by a flash of lightning thirty summers before, and all by their great height dwarfing the abode near which they stand, there squats a rude stone house, with a thick chimney, a kitchen and bedroom on the ground-floor, and a loft, accessible by a ladder, under the shingle roof, divided into two rooms.

Its owner was a man of ill repute. Tom Chuff was his name. A shock-headed, broad-shouldered, powerful man, though somewhat short, with lowering brows and a sullen eye. He was a poacher, and hardly made an ostensible pretence of earning his bread by any honest industry. He was a drunkard. He beat his wife, and led his children a life of terror and lamentation, when he was at home. It was a blessing to his frightened little family when he absented himself, as he sometimes did, for a week or more together.

On the night I speak of he knocked at the door with his cudgel at about eight o'clock. It was winter, and the night was very dark. Had the summons been that of a bogie from the moor, the inmates of this small house could hardly have heard it with greater terror.

His wife unbarred the door in fear and haste. Her hunchbacked sister stood by the hearth, staring toward the threshold. The children cowered behind.

Tom Chuff entered with his cudgel in his hand, without speaking, and threw himself into a chair opposite the fire. He had been away two or three days. He looked haggard, and his eyes were bloodshot. They knew he had been drinking.

Tom raked and knocked the peat fire with his stick, and thrust his feet close to it. He signed towards the little dresser, and nodded to his wife, and she knew he wanted a cup, which in silence she gave him. He pulled a bottle of gin from his coat-pocket, and nearly filling the teacup, drank off the dram at a few gulps.

He usually refreshed himself with two or three drams of this kind before beating the inmates of his house. His three little children, cowering in a corner, eyed him from under a table, as Jack did the ogre in the nursery tale. His wife, Nell, standing behind a chair, which she was ready to snatch up to meet the blow of the cudgel, which might be levelled at her at any moment, never took her eyes off him; and hunchbacked Mary showed the whites of a large pair of eyes, similarly employed, as she stood against the oaken press, her dark face hardly distinguishable in the distance from the brown panel behind it.

Tom Chuff was at his third dram, and had not yet spoken a word since his entrance, and the suspense was growing dreadful, when, on a sudden, he leaned back in his rude seat, the cudgel slipped from his hand, a change and a death-like pallor came over his face.

For a while they all stared on; such was their fear of him, they dared not speak or move, lest it should prove to have been but a doze, and Tom should wake up and proceed forthwith to gratify his temper and exercise his cudgel.

In a very little time, however, things began to look so odd, that they ventured, his wife and Mary, to exchange glances full of doubt and wonder. He hung so much over the side of the chair, that if it had not been one of cyclopean clumsiness and weight, he would have borne it to the floor. A leaden tint was darkening the pallor of his face. They were becoming alarmed, and finally braving everything his wife timidly said, "Tom!" and then more sharply repeated it, and finally cried the appellative loudly, and again and again, with the terrified accompaniment, "He's dying—he's dying!" her voice rising to a scream, as she found that neither it nor her plucks and shakings of him by the shoulder had the slightest effect in recalling him from his torpor.

And now from sheer terror of a new kind the children added their shrilly piping to the talk and cries of their seniors; and if anything could have called Tom up from his lethargy, it might have been the piercing chorus that made the rude chamber of the poacher's habitation ring again. But Tom continued unmoved, deaf, and stirless.

His wife sent Mary down to the village, hardly a quarter of a mile away, to implore of the doctor, for whose family she did duty as laundress, to come down and look at her husband, who seemed to be dying.

The doctor, who was a good-natured fellow, arrived. With his hat still on, he looked at Tom, examined him, and when he found that the emetic he had brought with him, on conjecture from Mary's description, did not act, and that his lancet brought no blood, and that he felt a pulseless wrist, he shook his head, and inwardly thought:

"What the plague is the woman crying for? Could she have desired a greater blessing for her children and herself than the very thing that has happened?"

Tom, in fact, seemed quite gone. At his lips no breath was perceptible. The doctor could discover no pulse. His hands and feet were cold, and the chill was stealing up into his body.

The doctor, after a stay of twenty minutes, had buttoned up his great-coat again and pulled down his hat, and told Mrs. Chuff that there was no use in his remaining any longer, when, all of a sudden, a little rill of blood began to trickle from the lancet-cut in Tom Chuff's temple.

"That's very odd," said the doctor. "Let us wait a little."

I must describe now the sensations which Tom Chuff had experienced.

With his elbows on his knees, and his chin upon his hands, he was staring into the embers, with his gin beside him, when suddenly a swimming came in his head, he lost sight of the fire, and a sound like one stroke of a loud church bell smote his brain.

Then he heard a confused humming, and the leaden weight of his head held him backward as he sank in his chair, and consciousness quite forsook him.

When he came to himself he felt chilled, and was leaning against a huge leafless tree. The night was moonless, and when he looked up he thought he had never seen stars so large and bright, or sky so black. The stars, too, seemed to blink down with longer intervals of darkness, and fiercer and more dazzling emergence, and something, he vaguely thought, of the character of silent menace and fury.

He had a confused recollection of having come there, or rather of having been carried along, as if on men's shoulders, with a sort of rushing motion. But it was utterly indistinct; the imperfect recollection simply of a sensation. He had seen or heard nothing on his way.

He looked round. There was not a sign of a living creature near. And he began with a sense of awe to recognise the place.

The tree against which he had been leaning was one of the noble old beeches that surround at irregular intervals the churchyard of Shackleton, which spreads its green and wavy lap on the edge of the Moor of Catstean, at the opposite side of which stands the rude cottage in which he had just lost consciousness. It was six miles or more across the moor to his habitation, and the black expanse lay before him, disappearing dismally in the darkness. So that, looking straight before him, sky and land blended together in an undistinguishable and awful blank.

There was a silence quite unnatural over the place. The distant murmur of the brook, which he knew so well, was dead; not a whisper in the leaves about him; the air, earth, everything about and above was indescribably still; and he experienced that quaking of the heart that seems to portend the approach of something awful. He would have set out upon his return across the moor, had he not an undefined presentiment that he was waylaid by something he dared not pass.

The old grey church and tower of Shackleton stood like a shadow in the rear. His eye had grown accustomed to the obscurity, and he could just trace its outline. There were no comforting associations in his mind connected with it; nothing but menace and misgiving. His early training in his lawless calling was connected with this very spot. Here his father used to meet two other poachers, and bring his son, then but a boy, with him.

Under the church porch, towards morning, they used to divide the game they had taken, and take account of the sales they had made on the previous day, and make partition of the money, and drink their gin. It was here he had taken his early lessons in drinking, cursing, and lawlessness. His father's grave was hardly eight steps from the spot where he stood. In his present state of awful dejection, no scene on earth could have so helped to heighten his fear.

There was one object close by which added to his gloom. About a yard away, in rear of the tree, behind himself, and extending to his left, was an open grave, the mould and rubbish piled on the other side. At the head of this grave stood the beech-tree; its columnar stem rose like a huge monumental pillar. He knew every line and crease on its smooth surface. The initial letters of his own name, cut in its bark long ago, had spread out and wrinkled like the grotesque capitals of a fanciful engraver, and now with a sinister significance overlooked the open grave, as if answering his mental question, "Who for is t' grave cut?"

He felt still a little stunned, and there was a faint tremor in his joints that disinclined him to exert himself; and, further, he had a vague apprehension that take what direction he might, there was danger around him worse than that of staying where he was.

On a sudden the stars began to blink more fiercely, a faint wild light overspread for a minute the bleak landscape, and he saw approaching from the moor a figure at a kind of swinging trot, with now and then a zig-zag hop or two, such as men accustomed to cross such places make, to avoid the patches of slob or quag that meet them here and there. This figure resembled his father's, and like him, whistled through his finger by way of signal as he approached; but the whistle sounded not now shrilly and sharp, as in old times, but immensely far away, and seemed to sing strangely through Tom's head. From habit or from fear, in answer to the signal, Tom whistled as he used to do five-and-twenty years ago and more, although he was already chilled with an unearthly fear.

Like his father, too, the figure held up the bag that was in his left hand as he drew near, when it was his custom to call out to him what was in it. It did not reassure the watcher, you may be certain, when a shout unnaturally faint reached him, as the phantom dangled the bag in the air, and he heard with a faint distinctness the words, "Tom Chuff's soul!"

Scarcely fifty yards away from the low churchyard fence at which Tom was standing, there was a wider chasm in the peat, which there threw up a growth of reeds and bulrushes, among which, as the old poacher used to do on a sudden alarm, the approaching figure suddenly cast itself down.

From the same patch of tall reeds and rushes emerged instantaneously what he at first mistook for the same figure creeping on all-fours, but what he soon perceived to be an enormous black dog with a rough coat like a bear's, which at first sniffed about, and then started towards him in what seemed to be a sportive amble, bouncing this way and that, but as it drew near it displayed a pair of fearful eyes that glowed like live coals, and emitted from the monstrous expanse of its jaws a terrifying growl.

This beast seemed on the point of seizing him, and Tom recoiled in panic and fell into the open grave behind him. The edge which he caught as he tumbled gave way, and down he went, expecting almost at the same instant to reach the bottom. But never was such a fall! Bottomless seemed the abyss! Down, down, down, with immeasurable and still increasing speed, through utter darkness, with hair streaming straight upward, breathless, he shot with a rush of air against him, the force of which whirled up his very arms, second after second, minute after minute, through the chasm downward he flew, the icy perspiration of horror covering his body, and suddenly, as he expected to be dashed into annihilation, his descent was in an instant arrested with a tremendous shock, which, however, did not deprive him of consciousness even for a moment.

He looked about him. The place resembled a smoke-stained cavern or catacomb, the roof of which, except for a ribbed arch here and there faintly visible, was lost in darkness. From several rude passages, like the galleries of a gigantic mine, which opened from this centre chamber, was very dimly emitted a dull glow as of charcoal, which was the only light by which he could imperfectly discern the objects immediately about him.

What seemed like a projecting piece of the rock, at the corner of one of these murky entrances, moved on a sudden, and proved to be a human figure, that beckoned to him. He approached, and saw his father. He could barely recognise him, he was so monstrously altered.

"I've been looking for you, Tom. Welcome home, lad; come along to your place."

Tom's heart sank as he heard these words, which were spoken in a hollow and, he thought, derisive voice that made him tremble. But he could not help accompanying the wicked spirit, who led him into a place, in passing which he heard, as it were from within the rock, dreadful cries and appeals for mercy.

"What is this?" said he.

"Never mind."

"Who are they?"

"New-comers, like yourself, lad," answered his father apathetically. "They give over that work in time, finding it is no use."

"What shall I do?" said Tom, in an agony.

"It's all one."

"But what shall I do?" reiterated Tom, quivering in every joint and nerve.

"Grin and bear it, I suppose."

"For God's sake, if ever you cared for me, as I am your own child, let me out of this!"

"There's no way out."

"If there's a way in there's a way out, and for Heaven's sake let me out of this."

But the dreadful figure made no further answer, and glided backwards by his shoulder to the rear; and others appeared in view, each with a faint red halo round it, staring on him with frightful eyes, images, all in hideous variety, of eternal fury or derision. He was growing mad, it seemed, under the stare of so many eyes, increasing in number and drawing closer every moment, and at the same time myriads and myriads of voices were calling him by his name, some far away, some near, some from one point, some from another, some from behind, close to his ears. These cries were increased in rapidity and multitude, and mingled with laughter, with flitting blasphemies, with broken insults and mockeries, succeeded and obliterated by others, before he could half catch their meaning.

All this time, in proportion to the rapidity and urgency of these dreadful sights and sounds, the epilepsy of terror was creeping up to his brain, and with a long and dreadful scream he lost consciousness.

When he recovered his senses, he found himself in a small stone chamber, vaulted above, and with a ponderous door. A single point of light in the wall, with a strange brilliancy illuminated this cell.

Seated opposite to him was a venerable man with a snowy beard of immense length; an image of awful purity and severity. He was dressed in a coarse robe, with three large keys suspended from his girdle. He might have filled one's idea of an ancient porter of a city gate; such spiritual cities, I should say, as John Bunyan loved to describe.

This old man's eyes were brilliant and awful, and fixed on him as they were, Tom Chuff felt himself helplessly in his power. At length he spoke:

"The command is given to let you forth for one trial more. But if you are found again drinking with the drunken, and beating your fellow-servants, you shall return through the door by which you came, and go out no more."

With these words the old man took him by the wrist and led him through the first door, and then unlocking one that stood in the cavern outside, he struck Tom Chuff sharply on the shoulder, and the door shut behind him with a sound that boomed peal after peal of thunder near and far away, and all round and above, till it rolled off gradually into silence. It was totally dark, but there was a fanning of fresh cool air that overpowered him. He felt that he was in the upper world again.

In a few minutes he began to hear voices which he knew, and first a faint point of light appeared before his eyes, and gradually he saw the flame of the candle, and, after that, the familiar faces of his wife and children, and he heard them faintly when they spoke to him, although he was as yet unable to answer.

He also saw the doctor, like an isolated figure in the dark, and heard him say:

"There, now, you have him back. He'll do, I think."

His first words, when he could speak and saw clearly all about him, and felt the blood on his neck and shirt, were:

"Wife, forgie me. I'm a changed man. Send for't sir."

Which last phrase means, "Send for the clergyman."

When the vicar came and entered the little bedroom where the scared poacher, whose soul had died within him, was lying, still sick and weak, in his bed, and with a spirit that was prostrate with terror, Tom Chuff feebly beckoned the rest from the room, and, the door being closed, the good parson heard the strange confession, and with equal amazement the man's earnest and agitated vows of amendment, and his helpless appeals to him for support and counsel.

These, of course, were kindly met; and the visits of the rector, for some time, were frequent.

One day, when he took Tom Chuff's hand on bidding him good-bye, the sick man held it still, and said:

"Ye'r vicar o' Shackleton, sir, and if I sud dee, ye'll promise me a'e thing, as I a promised ye a many. I a said I'll never gie wife, nor barn, nor folk o' no sort, skelp nor sizzup more, and ye'll know o' me no more among the sipers. Nor never will Tom draw trigger, nor set a snare again, but in an honest way, and after that ye'll no make it a bootless bene for me, but bein', as I say, vicar o' Shackleton, and able to do as ye list, ye'll no let them bury me within twenty good yerd-wands measure o' the a'd beech trees that's round the churchyard of Shackleton."

"I see; you would have your grave, when your time really comes, a good way from the place where lay the grave you dreamed of."

"That's jest it. I'd lie at the bottom o' a marl-pit liefer! And I'd be laid in anither churchyard just to be shut o' my fear o' that, but that a' my kinsfolk is buried beyond in Shackleton, and ye'll gie me yer promise, and no break yer word."

"I do promise, certainly. I'm not likely to outlive you; but, if I should, and still be vicar of Shackleton, you shall be buried somewhere as near the middle of the churchyard as we can find space."

"That'll do."

And so content they parted.

The effect of the vision upon Tom Chuff was powerful, and promised to be lasting. With a sore effort he exchanged his life of desultory adventure and comparative idleness for one of regular industry. He gave up drinking; he was as kind as an originally surly nature would allow to his wife and family; he went to church; in fine weather they crossed the moor to Shackleton Church; the vicar said he came there to look at the scenery of his vision, and to fortify his good resolutions by the reminder.

Impressions upon the imagination, however, are but transitory, and a bad man acting under fear is not a free agent; his real character does not appear. But as the images of the imagination fade, and the action of fear abates, the essential qualities of the man reassert themselves.

So, after a time, Tom Chuff began to grow weary of his new life; he grew lazy, and people began to say that he was catching hares, and pursuing his old contraband way of life, under the rose.

He came home one hard night, with signs of the bottle in his thick speech and violent temper. Next day he was sorry, or frightened, at all events repentant, and for a week or more something of the old horror returned, and he was once more on his good behaviour. But in a little time came a relapse, and another repentance, and then a relapse again, and gradually the return of old habits and the flooding in of all his old way of life, with more violence and gloom, in proportion as the man was alarmed and exasperated by the remembrance of his despised, but terrible, warning.

With the old life returned the misery of the cottage. The smiles, which had begun to appear with the unwonted sunshine, were seen no more. Instead, returned to his poor wife's face the old pale and heartbroken look. The cottage lost its neat and cheerful air, and the melancholy of neglect was visible. Sometimes at night were overheard, by a chance passer-by, cries and sobs from that ill-omened dwelling. Tom Chuff was now often drunk, and not very often at home, except when he came in to sweep away his poor wife's earnings.

Tom had long lost sight of the honest old parson. There was shame mixed with his degradation. He had grace enough left when he saw the thin figure of "t' sir" walking along the road to turn out of his way and avoid meeting him. The clergyman shook his head, and sometimes groaned, when his name was mentioned. His horror and regret were more for the poor wife than for the relapsed sinner, for her case was pitiable indeed.

Her brother, Jack Everton, coming over from Hexley, having heard stories of all this, determined to beat Tom, for his ill-treatment of his sister, within an inch of his life. Luckily, perhaps, for all concerned, Tom happened to be away upon one of his long excursions, and poor Nell besought her brother, in extremity of terror, not to interpose between them. So he took his leave and went home muttering and sulky.

Now it happened a few months later that Nelly Chuff fell sick. She had been ailing, as heartbroken people do, for a good while. But now the end had come.

There was a coroner's inquest when she died, for the doctor had doubts as to whether a blow had not, at least, hastened her death. Nothing certain, however, came of the inquiry. Tom Chuff had left his home more than two days before his wife's death. He was absent upon his lawless business still when the coroner had held his quest.

Jack Everton came over from Hexley to attend the dismal obsequies of his sister. He was more incensed than ever with the wicked husband, who, one way or other, had hastened Nelly's death. The inquest had closed early in the day. The husband had not appeared.

An occasional companion—perhaps I ought to say accomplice—of Chuff's happened to turn up. He had left him on the borders of Westmoreland, and said he would probably be home next day. But Everton affected not to believe it. Perhaps it was to Tom Chuff, he suggested, a secret satisfaction to crown the history of his bad married life with the scandal of his absence from the funeral of his neglected and abused wife.

Everton had taken on himself the direction of the melancholy preparations. He had ordered a grave to be opened for his sister beside her mother's, in Shackleton churchyard, at the other side of the moor. For the purpose, as I have said, of marking the callous neglect of her husband, he determined that the funeral should take place that night. His brother Dick had accompanied him, and they and his sister, with Mary and the children, and a couple of the neighbours, formed the humble cortège.

Jack Everton said he would wait behind, on the chance of Tom Chuff coming in time, that he might tell him what had happened, and make him cross the moor with him to meet the funeral. His real object, I think, was to inflict upon the villain the drubbing he had so long wished to give him. Anyhow, he was resolved, by crossing the moor, to reach the churchyard in time to anticipate the arrival of the funeral, and to have a few.words with the vicar, clerk, and sexton, all old friends of his, for the parish of Shackleton was the place of his birth and early recollections.

But Tom Chuff did not appear at his house that night. In surly mood, and without a shilling in his pocket, he was making his way homeward. His bottle of gin, his last investment, half emptied, with its neck protruding, as usual on such returns, was in his coat-pocket.

His way home lay across the moor of Catstean, and the point at which he best knew the passage was from the churchyard of Shackleton. He vaulted the low wall that forms its boundary, and strode across the graves, and over many a flat, half-buried tombstone, toward the side of the churchyard next Catstean Moor.

The old church of Shackleton and its tower rose, close at his right, like a black shadow against the sky. It was a moonless night, but clear. By this time he had reached the low boundary wall, at the other side, that overlooks the wide expanse of Catstean Moor. He stood by one of the huge old beech-trees, and leaned his back to its smooth trunk. Had he ever seen the sky look so black, and the stars shine out and blink so vividly? There was a deathlike silence over the scene, like the hush that precedes thunder in sultry weather. The expanse before him was lost in utter blackness. A strange quaking unnerved his heart. It was the sky and scenery of his vision! The same horror and misgiving. The same invincible fear of venturing from the spot where he stood. He would have prayed if he dared. His sinking heart demanded a restorative of some sort, and he grasped the bottle in his coat-pocket. Turning to his left, as he did so, he saw the piled-up mould of an open grave that gaped with its head close to the base of the great tree against which he was leaning.

He stood aghast. His dream was returning and slowly enveloping him. Everything he saw was weaving itself into the texture of his vision. The chill of horror stole over him.

A faint whistle came shrill and clear over the moor, and he saw a figure approaching at a swinging trot, with a zig-zag course, hopping now here and now there, as men do over a surface where one has need to choose their steps. Through the jungle of reeds and bulrushes in the foreground this figure advanced; and with the same unaccountable impulse that had coerced him in his dream, he answered the whistle of the advancing figure.

On that signal it directed its course straight toward him. It mounted the low wall, and, standing there, looked into the graveyard.

"Who med answer?" challenged the new-comer from his post of observation.

"Me," answered Tom.

"Who are you?" repeated the man upon the wall.

"Tom Chuff; and who's this grave cut for?" He answered in a savage tone, to cover the secret shudder of his panic.

"I'll tell you that, ye villain!" answered the stranger, descending from the wall, "I a' looked for you far and near, and waited long, and now you're found at last."

Not knowing what to make of the figure that advanced upon him, Tom Chuff recoiled, stumbled, and fell backward into the open grave. He caught at the sides as he fell, but without retarding his fall.

An hour later, when lights came with the coffin, the corpse of Tom Chuff was found at the bottom of the grave. He had fallen direct upon his head, and his neck was broken. His death must have been simultaneous with his fall. Thus far his dream was accomplished.

It was his brother-in-law who had crossed the moor and approached the churchyard of Shackleton, exactly in the line which the image of his father had seemed to take in his strange vision. Fortunately for Jack Everton, the sexton and clerk of Shackleton church were, unseen by him, crossing the churchyard toward the grave of Nelly Chuff, just as Tom the poacher stumbled and fell. Suspicion of direct violence would otherwise have inevitably attached to the exasperated brother. As it was, the catastrophe was followed by no legal consequences.

The good vicar kept his word, and the grave of Tom Chuff is still pointed out by the old inhabitants of Shackleton pretty nearly in the centre of the churchyard. This conscientious compliance with the entreaty of the panic-stricken man as to the place of his sepulture gave a horrible and mocking emphasis to the strange combination by which fate had defeated his precaution, and fixed the place of his death.

The story was for many a year, and we believe still is, told round many a cottage hearth, and though it appeals to what many would term superstition, it yet sounded, in the ears of a rude and simple audience, a thrilling, and let us hope, not altogether fruitless homily.

THE DRUNKARD'S DREAM

*Being a Fourth Extract fron the Legacy
of the Late F. Purcell,
P. P. of Drumcoolagh*

"All this *he* told with some confusion and
Dismay, the usual consequence of dreams
Of the unpleasant kind, with none at hand
To expound their vain and visionary gleams.
I've known some odd ones which seemed really planned
Prophetically, as that which one deems
'A strange coincidence,' to use a phrase
By which such things are settled now-a-days. "

BYRON.

Dreams—What age, or what country of the world has not felt and acknowledged the mystery of their origin and end? I have thought not a little upon the subject, seeing it is one which has been often forced upon my attention, and sometimes strangely enough; and yet I have never arrived at any thing which at all appeared a satisfactory conclusion. It does appear that a mental phenomenon so extraordinary cannot be wholly without its use. We know, indeed, that in the olden times it has been made the organ of communication between the Deity and his creatures; and when, as I have seen, a dream produces upon a mind, to all appearance hopelessly reprobate and depraved, an effect so powerful and so lasting as to break down the inveterate habits, and to reform the life of an abandoned sinner. We see in the result, in the reformation of morals, which appeared incorrigible in the reclamation of a human soul which seemed to be irretrievably lost, something more than could be produced by a mere chimaera of the slumbering fancy, something more than could arise from the capricious images of a terrified imagination; but once prevented, we behold in all these things, in the tremendous and mysterious results, the operation of the hand of God. And while Reason rejects as absurd the superstition which will read a prophecy in every dream, she may, without violence to herself, recognize, even in the wildest and most incongruous of the wanderings of a slumbering intellect, the evidences and the fragments of a language which may be spoken, which *has* been spoken to terrify, to warn, and to command. We have reason to believe too, by the promptness of action, which in the age of the prophets, followed all intimations of this kind, and by the strength of conviction and strange permanence of the effects resulting from certain dreams in latter times, which effects ourselves may have witnessed, that when this medium of communication has been employed by the Deity, the evidences of his presence have been unequivocal. My thoughts were directed to this subject, in a manner to leave a lasting impression upon my mind, by the events which I shall now relate, the statement of which, however extraordinary, is nevertheless *accurately correct*.

About the year 17—having been appointed to the living of C——h, I rented a small house in the town, which bears the same name: one morning, in the month of November, I was awakened before my usual time, by my servant, who bustled into my bed-room for the purpose of announcing a sick call. As the Catholic Church holds her last rites to be totally indispensable to the safety of the departing sinner, no conscientious clergyman can afford a moment's unnecessary delay, and in little more than five minutes I stood ready cloaked and booted for the road in the small front parlour, in which the messenger, who was to act as my guide, awaited my coming. I found a poor little girl crying piteously near the door, and after some slight difficulty I ascertained that her father was either dead, or just dying.

"And what may be your father's name, my poor child?" said I. She held down her head, as if ashamed. I repeated the question, and the wretched little creature burst into floods of tears, still more bitter than she had shed before. At length, almost provoked by conduct which appeared to me so unreasonable, I began to lose patience, spite of the pity which I could not help feeling towards her, and I said rather harshly, "If you will not tell me the name of the person to whom you would lead me, your silence can arise from no good motive, and I might be justified in refusing to go with you at all."

"Oh! don't say that, don't say that," cried she. "Oh! sir, it was that I was afeard of when I would not tell you—I was afeard when you heard his name you would not come with me; but it is no use hidin' it now— it's Pat Connell, the carpenter, your honour."

She looked in my face with the most earnest anxiety, as if her very existence depended upon what she should read there; but I relieved her at once. The name, indeed, was most unpleasantly familiar to me; but, however fruitless my visits and advice might have been at another time, the present was too fearful an occasion to suffer my doubts of their utility as my reluctance to re-attempting what appeared a hopeless task to weigh even against the lightest chance, that a consciousness of his imminent danger might produce in him a more docile and tractable disposition. Accordingly I told the child to lead the way, and followed her in silence. She hurried rapidly through the long narrow street which forms the great thoroughfare of the town. The darkness of the hour, rendered still deeper by the close approach of the old fashioned houses, which lowered in tall obscurity on either side of the way; the damp dreary chill which renders the advance of morning peculiarly cheerless, combined with the object of my walk, to visit the death-bed of a presumptuous sinner, to endeavour, almost against my own conviction, to infuse a hope into the heart of a dying reprobate—a drunkard, but too probably perishing under the consequences of some mad fit of intoxication; all these circumstances united served to enhance the gloom and solemnity of my feelings, as I silently followed my little guide, who with quick steps traversed the uneven pavement of the main street. After a walk of about five minutes she turned off into a narrow lane, of that obscure and comfortless class which are to be found in almost all small old fashioned towns, chill without ventilation, reeking with all manner of offensive effluviae, dingy, smoky, sickly and pent-up buildings, frequently not only in a wretched but in a dangerous condition.

"Your father has changed his abode since I last visited him, and, I am afraid, much for the worse," said I.

"Indeed he has, sir, but we must not complain," replied she; "we have to thank God that we have lodging and food, though it's poor enough, it is, your honour."

Poor child! thought I, how many an older head might learn wisdom from thee—how many a luxurious philosopher, who is skilled to preach but not to suffer, might not thy patient words put to the blush! The manner and language of this child were alike above her years and station; and, indeed, in all cases in which the cares and sorrows of life have anticipated their usual date, and have fallen, as they sometimes do, with melancholy prematurity to the lot of childhood, I have observed the result to have proved uniformly the same. A young mind, to which joy and indulgence have been strangers, and to which suffering and self-denial have been familiarised from the first, acquires a solidity and an elevation which no other discipline could have bestowed, and which, in the present case, communicated a striking but mournful peculiarity to the manners, even to the voice of the child. We paused before a narrow, crazy door, which she opened by means of a latch, and we forthwith began to ascend the steep and broken stairs, which led upwards to the sick man's room. As we mounted flight after flight towards the garret floor, I heard more and more distinctly the hurried talking of many voices. I could also distinguish the low sobbing of a female. On arriving upon the uppermost lobby, these sounds became fully audible.

"This way, your honor," said my little conductress, at the same time pushing open a door of patched and half rotten plank, she admitted me into the squalid chamber of death and misery. But one candle, held in the fingers of a scared and haggard-looking child, was burning in the room, and that so dim that all was twilight or darkness except within its immediate influence. The general obscurity, however, served to throw into prominent and startling relief the death-bed and its occupant. The light was nearly approximated to, and fell with horrible clearness upon, the blue and swollen features of the drunkard. I did not think it possible that a human countenance could look so terrific. The lips were black and drawn apart—the teeth were firmly set—the eyes a little unclosed, and nothing but the whites appearing—every feature was fixed and livid, and the whole face wore a ghastly and rigid expression of despairing terror such as I never saw equalled; his hands were crossed upon his breast, and firmly clenched, while, as if to add to the corpse-like effect of the whole, some white cloths, dipped in water, were wound about the forehead and temples. As soon as I could remove my eyes from this horrible spectacle, I observed my friend Dr. D——, one of the most humane of a humane profession, standing by the bed-side. He had been attempting, but unsuccessfully, to bleed the patient, and had now applied his finger to the pulse.

"Is there any hope?" I inquired in a whisper.

A shake of the head was the reply. There was a pause while he continued to hold the wrist; but he waited in vain for the throb of life, it was not there, and when he let go the hand it fell stiffly back into its former position upon the other.

"The man is dead," said the physician, as he turned from the bed where the terrible figure lay.

Dead! thought I, scarcely venturing to look upon the tremendous and revolting spectacle—dead! without an hour for repentance, even a moment for reflection—dead! without the rites which even the best should have. Is there a hope for him? The glaring eyeball, the grinning mouth, the distorted brow—that unutterable look in which a painter would have sought to embody the fixed despair of the nethermost hell—these were my answer.

The poor wife sat at a little distance, crying as if her heart would break—the younger children clustered round the bed, looking, with wondering curiosity, upon the form of death, never seen before. When the first tumult of uncontrollable sorrow had passed away, availing myself of the solemnity and impressiveness of the scene, I desired the heart-stricken family to accompany me in prayer, and all knelt down, while I solemnly and fervently repeated some of those prayers which appeared most applicable to the occasion. I employed myself thus in a manner which, I trusted, was not unprofitable, at least to the living, for about ten minutes, and having accomplished my task, I was the first to arise. I looked upon the poor, sobbing, helpless creatures who knelt so humbly around me, and my heart bled for them. With a natural transition, I turned my eyes from them to the bed in which the body lay, and, great God! what was the revulsion, the horror which I experienced on seeing the corpse-like, terrific thing seated half upright before me—the white cloths, which had been wound about the head, had now partly slipped from their position, and were hanging in grotesque festoons about the face and shoulders, while the distorted eyes leered from amid them—

"A sight to dream of, not to tell."

I stood actually rivetted to the spot. The figure nodded its head and lifted its arm, I thought with a menacing gesture. A thousand confused and horrible thoughts at once rushed upon my mind. I had often read that the body of a presumptuous sinner, who, during life, had been the willing creature of every satanic impulse, after the human tenant had deserted it, had been known to become the horrible sport of demoniac possession. I was roused from the stupefaction of terror in which I stood, by the piercing scream of the mother, who now, for the first time, perceived the change which had taken place. She rushed towards the bed, but, stunned by the shock and overcome by the conflict of violent emotions, before she reached it, she fell prostrate upon the floor. I am perfectly convinced that had I not been startled from the torpidity of horror in which I was bound, by some powerful and arousing stimulant, I should have gazed upon this unearthly apparition until I had fairly lost my senses. As it was, however, the spell was broken, superstition gave way to reason: the man whom all believed to have been actually dead, was living! Dr. D—— was instantly standing by the bedside, and, upon examination, he found that a sudden and copious flow of blood had taken place from the wound which the lancet had left, and this, no doubt, had effected his sudden and almost preternatural restoration to an existence from which all thought he had been for ever removed. The man was still speechless, but he seemed to understand the physician when he forbid his repeating the painful and fruitless attempts which he made to articulate, and he at once resigned himself quietly into his hands.

I left the patient with leeches upon his temples, and bleeding freely—apparently with little of the drowsiness which accompanies apoplexy; indeed, Dr. D—— told me that he had never before witnessed a seizure which seemed to combine the symptoms of so many kinds, and yet which belonged to none of the recognized classes; it certainly was not apoplexy, catalepsy, nor *delirium tremens*, and yet it seemed, in some degree, to partake of the properties of all—it was strange, but stranger things are coming.

During two or three days Dr. D—— would not allow his patient to converse in a manner which could excite or exhaust him, with any one;

he suffered him merely, as briefly as possible, to express his immediate wants, and it was not until the fourth day after my early visit, the particulars of which I have just detailed, that it was thought expedient that I should see him, and then only because it appeared that his extreme importunity and impatience were likely to retard his recovery more than the mere exhaustion attendant upon a short conversation could possibly do; perhaps, too, my friend entertained some hope that if by holy confession his patient's bosom were eased of the perilous stuff, which no doubt, oppressed it, his recovery would be more assured and rapid. It was, then, as I have said, upon the fourth day after my first professional call, that I found myself once more in the dreary chamber of want and sickness. The man was in bed, and appeared low and restless. On my entering the room he raised himself in the bed, and muttered twice or thrice—"Thank God! thank God." I signed to those of his family who stood by, to leave the room, and took a chair beside the bed. So soon as we were alone, he said, rather doggedly—"There's no use now in telling me of the sinfulness of bad ways—I know it all—I know where they lead to—I seen everything about it with my own eyesight, as plain as I see you." He rolled himself in the bed, as if to hide his face in the clothes, and then suddenly raising himself, he exclaimed with startling vehemence—"Look, sir, there is no use in mincing the matter; I'm blasted with the fires of hell; I have been in hell; what do you think of that?—in hell—I'm lost for ever—I have not a chance—I am damned already—damned—damned——." The end of this sentence he actually shouted; his vehemence was perfectly terrific; he threw himself back, and laughed, and sobbed hysterically. I poured some water into a tea-cup, and gave it to him. After he had swallowed it, I told him if he had anything to communicate, to do so as briefly as he could, and in a manner as little agitating to himself as possible; threatening at the same time, though I had no intention of doing so, to leave him at once, in case he again gave way to such passionate excitement. "It's only foolishness," he continued, "for me to try to thank you for coming to such a villain as myself at all; it's no use for me to wish good to you, or to bless you; for such as me has no blessings to give." I told him that I had but done my duty, and urged him to proceed to the matter which weighed upon his mind; he then spoke nearly as follows: —I came in drunk on Friday night last, and got to my bed here, I don't remember how; sometime in the night, it seemed to me, I wakened, and feeling unasy in myself, I got up out of the bed. I wanted the fresh air, but I would not make a noise to open the window, for fear I'd waken the crathurs. It was very dark, and throublesome to find the door; but at last I did get it, and I groped my way out, and went down as asy as I could. I felt quite sober, and I counted the steps one after another, as I was going down, that I might not stumble at the bottom. When I came to the first landing-place, God be about us always! the floor of it sunk under me, and I went down, down, down, till the senses almost left me.

I do not know how long I was falling, but it seemed to me a great while. When I came rightly to myself at last, I was sitting at a great table, near the top of it; and I could not see the end of it, if it had any, it was so far off; and there was men beyond reckoning, sitting down, all along by it, at each side, as far as I could see at all. I did not know at first was it in the open air; but there was a close smothering feel in it, that was not natural, and there was a kind of light that my eyesight never saw before, red and unsteady, and I did not see for a long time where it was coming from, until I looked straight up, and then I seen that it came from great balls of blood-coloured fire, that were rolling high over head with a sort of rushing, trembling sound, and I perceived that they shone on the ribs of a great roof of rock that was arched overhead instead of the sky. When I seen this, scarce knowing what I did, I got up, and I said, 'I have no right to be here; I must go,' and the man that was sitting at my left hand, only smiled, and said, 'sit down again, you can *never* leave this place,' and his voice was weaker than any child's voice I ever heerd, and when he was done speaking he smiled again. Then I spoke out very loud and bold, and I said—'in the name of God, let me out of this bad place.' And there was a great man, that I did not see before, sitting at the end of the table that I was near, and he was taller than twelve men, and his face was very proud and terrible to look at, and he stood up and stretched out his hand before him, and when he stood up, all that was there, great and small, bowed down with a sighing sound, and a dread came on my heart, and he looked at me, and I could not speak. I felt I was his own, to do what he liked with, for I knew at once who he was, and he said, 'if you promise to return, you may depart for a season'; and the voice he spoke with was terrible and mournful, and the echoes of it went rolling and swelling down the endless cave, and mixing with the trembling of the fire overhead; so that, when he sate down, there was a sound after him, all through the place like the roaring of a furnace, and I said, with all the strength I had, 'I promise to come back; in God's name let me go,' and with that I lost the sight and the hearing of all that was there, and when my senses came to me again, I was sitting in the bed with the blood all over me, and you and the rest praying around the room." Here he paused and wiped away the chill drops of horror which hung upon his forehead.

I remained silent for some moments. The vision which he had just described struck my imagination not a little, for this was long before Vathek and the "Hall of Iblis" had delighted the world; and the description which he gave had, as I received it, all the attractions of novelty beside the impressiveness which always belongs to the narration of an *eye-witness*, whether in the body or in the spirit, of the scenes which he describes. There was something, too, in the stern horror with which the man related these things, and in the incongruity of his description, with the vulgarly received notions of the great place of punishment, and of its presiding spirit, which struck my mind with awe, almost with fear. At length he said, with an expression of horrible, imploring earnestness, which I shall never forget—"Well, sir, is there any hope; is there any chance at all? or, is my soul pledged and promised away for ever? is it gone out of my power? must I go back to the place?"

In answering him I had no easy task to perform; for however clear might be my internal conviction of the groundlessness of his fears, and however strong my scepticism respecting the reality of what he had described, I nevertheless felt that his impression to the contrary, and his humility and terror resulting from it, might be made available as no mean engines in the work of his conversion from profligacy, and of his restoration to decent habits, and to religious feeling. I therefore told him that he was to regard his dream rather in the light of a warning than in that of a prophecy; that our salvation depended not upon the word or deed of a moment, but upon the habits of a life; that, in fine, if he at once discarded his idle companions and evil habits, and firmly adhered to a sober, industrious, and religious course of life, the powers of darkness might claim his soul in vain, for that there were higher and firmer pledges than human tongue could utter, which promised salvation to him who should repent and lead a new life.

I left him much comforted, and with a promise to return upon the next day. I did so, and found him much more cheerful, and without any remains of the dogged sullenness which I suppose had arisen from his despair. His promises of amendment were given in that tone of deliberate earnestness, which belongs to deep and solemn determination; and it was with no small delight that I observed, after repeated visits, that his good resolutions, so far from failing, did but gather strength by time; and when I saw that man shake off the idle and debauched companions, whose society had for years formed alike his amusement and his ruin, and revive his long discarded habits of industry and sobriety, I said within myself, there is something more in all this than the operation of an idle dream. One day, sometime after his perfect restoration to health, I was surprised on ascending the stairs, for the purpose of visiting this man, to find him busily employed in nailing down some planks upon the landing place, through which, at the commencement of his mysterious vision, it seemed to him that he had sunk. I perceived at once that he was strengthening the floor with a view to securing himself against such a catastrophe, and could scarcely forbear a smile as I bid "God bless his work."

He perceived my thoughts, I suppose, for he immediately said,

"I can never pass over that floor without trembling. I'd leave this house if I could, but I can't find another lodging in the town so cheap, and I'll not take a better till I've paid off all my debts, please God; but I could not be asy in my mind till I made it as safe as I could. You'll hardly believe me, your honor, that while I'm working, maybe a mile away, my heart is in a flutter the whole way back, with the bare thoughts of the two little steps I have to walk upon this bit of a floor. So it's no wonder, sir, I'd thry to make it sound and firm with any idle timber I have."

I applauded his resolution to pay off his debts, and the steadiness with which he pursued his plans of conscientious economy, and passed on.

Many months elapsed, and still there appeared no alteration in his resolutions of amendment. He was a good workman, and with his better habits he recovered his former extensive and profitable employment. Every thing seemed to promise comfort and respectability. I have little more to add, and that shall be told quickly. I had one evening met Pat Connell, as he returned from his work, and as usual, after a mutual, and on his side respectful salutation, I spoke a few words of encouragement and approval. I left him industrious, active, healthy—when next I saw him, not three days after, he was a corpse. The circumstances which marked the event of his death were somewhat strange—I might say fearful. The unfortunate man had accidentally met an early friend, just returned, after a long absence, and in a moment of excitement, forgetting everything in the warmth of his joy, he yielded to his urgent invitation to accompany him into a public house, which lay close by the spot where the encounter had taken place. Connell, however, previously to entering the room, had announced his determination to take nothing more than the strictest temperance would warrant. But oh! who can describe the inveterate tenacity with which a drunkard's habits cling to him through life. He may repent—he may reform—he may look with actual abhorrence upon his past profligacy; but amid all this reformation and compunction, who can tell the moment in which the base and ruinous propensity may not recur, triumphing over resolution, remorse, shame, everything, and prostrating its victim once more in all that is destructive and revolting in that fatal vice.

The wretched man left the place in a state of utter intoxication. He was brought home nearly insensible, and placed in his bed, where he lay in the deep calm lethargy of drunkenness. The younger part of the family retired to rest much after their usual hour; but the poor wife remained up sitting by the fire, too much grieved and shocked at the recurrence of what she had so little expected, to settle to rest; fatigue, however, at length overcame her, and she sunk gradually into an uneasy slumber. She could not tell how long she had remained in this state, when she awakened, and immediately on opening her eyes, she perceived by the faint red light of the smouldering turf embers, two persons, one of whom she recognized as her husband noiselessly gliding out of the room.

"Pat, darling, where are you going?" said she. There was no answer —the door closed after them; but in a moment she was startled and terrified by a loud and heavy crash, as if some ponderous body had been hurled down the stair. Much alarmed, she started up, and going to the head of the staircase, she called repeatedly upon her husband, but in vain. She returned to the room, and with the assistance of her daughter, whom I had occasion to mention before, she succeeded in finding and lighting a candle, with which she hurried again to the head of the staircase. At the bottom lay what seemed to be a bundle of clothes, heaped together, motionless, lifeless—it was her husband. In going down the stairs, for what purpose can never now be known, he had fallen helplessly and violently to the bottom, and coming head foremost, the spine at the neck had been dislocated by the shock, and instant death must have ensued. The body lay upon that landing-place to which his dream had referred. It is scarcely worth endeavouring to clear up a single point in a narrative where all is mystery; yet I could not help suspecting that the second figure which had been seen in the room by Connell's wife on the night of his death, might have been no other than his own shadow. I suggested this solution of the difficulty; but she told me that the unknown person had been considerably in advance of the other, and on reaching the door, had turned back as if to communicate something to his companion—it was then a mystery. Was the dream verified?—whither had the disembodied spirit sped?—who can say? We know not. But I left the house of death that day in a state of horror which I could not describe. It seemed to me that I was scarce awake. I heard and saw everything as if under the spell of a nightmare. The coincidence was terrible.

DICKON THE DEVIL

About thirty years ago I was selected by two rich old maids to visit a property in that part of Lancashire which lies near the famous forest of Pendle, with which Mr. Ainsworth's "Lancashire Witches" has made us so pleasantly familiar. My business was to make partition of a small property, including a house and demesne, to which they had a long time before succeeded as co-heiresses.

The last forty miles of my journey I was obliged to post, chiefly by cross-roads, little known, and less frequented, and presenting scenery often extremely interesting and pretty. The picturesqueness of the landscape was enhanced by the season, the beginning of September, at which I was travelling.

I had never been in this part of the world before; I am told it is now a great deal less wild, and, consequently, less beautiful.

At the inn where I had stopped for a relay of horses and some dinner—for it was then past five o'clock—I found the host, a hale old fellow of five-and-sixty, as he told me, a man of easy and garrulous benevolence, willing to accommodate his guests with any amount of talk, which the slightest tap sufficed to set flowing, on any subject you pleased.

I was curious to learn something about Barwyke, which was the name of the demesne and house I was going to. As there was no inn within some miles of it, I had written to the steward to put me up there, the best way he could, for a night.

The host of the "Three Nuns," which was the sign under which he entertained wayfarers, had not a great deal to tell. It was twenty years, or more, since old Squire Bowes died, and no one had lived in the Hall ever since, except the gardener and his wife.

"Tom Wyndsour will be as old a man as myself; but he's a bit taller, and not so much in flesh, quite," said the fat innkeeper.

"But there were stories about the house," I repeated, "that they said, prevented tenants from coming into it?"

"Old wives' tales; many years ago, that will be, sir; I forget 'em; I forget 'em all. Oh yes, there always will be, when a house is left so; foolish folk will always be talkin'; but I hadn't heard a word about it this twenty year."

It was vain trying to pump him; the old landlord of the "Three Nuns," for some reason, did not choose to tell tales of Barwyke Hall, if he really did, as I suspected, remember them.

I paid my reckoning, and resumed my journey, well pleased with the good cheer of that old-world inn, but a little disappointed.

We had been driving for more than an hour, when we began to cross a wild common; and I knew that, this passed, a quarter of an hour would bring me to the door of Barwyke Hall.

The peat and furze were pretty soon left behind; we were again in the wooded scenery that I enjoyed so much, so entirely natural and pretty, and so little disturbed by traffic of any kind. I was looking from the chaise-window, and soon detected the object of which, for some time, my eye had been in search. Barwyke Hall was a large, quaint house, of that cage-work fashion known as "black-and-white," in which the bars and angles of an oak framework contrast, black as ebony, with the white plaster that overspreads the masonry built into its interstices. This steep-roofed Elizabethan house stood in the midst of park-like grounds of no great extent, but rendered imposing by the noble stature of the old trees that now cast their lengthening shadows eastward over the sward, from the declining sun.

The park-wall was grey with age, and in many places laden with ivy. In deep grey shadow, that contrasted with the dim fires of evening reflected on the foliage above it, in a gentle hollow, stretched a lake that looked cold and black, and seemed, as it were, to skulk from observation with a guilty knowledge.

I had forgot that there was a lake at Barwyke; but the moment this caught my eye, like the cold polish of a snake in the shadow, my instinct seemed to recognize something dangerous, and I knew that the lake was connected, I could not remember how, with the story I had heard of this place in my boyhood.

I drove up a grass-grown avenue, under the boughs of these noble trees, whose foliage, dyed in autumnal red and yellow, returned the beams of the western sun gorgeously.

We drew up at the door. I got out, and had a good look at the front of the house; it was a large and melancholy mansion, with signs of long neglect upon it; great wooden shutters, in the old fashion, were barred, outside, across the windows; grass, and even nettles, were growing thick on the courtyard, and a thin moss streaked the timber beams; the plaster was discoloured by time and weather, and bore great russet and yellow stains. The gloom was increased by several grand old trees that crowded close about the house.

I mounted the steps, and looked round; the dark lake lay near me now, a little to the left. It was not large; it may have covered some ten or twelve acres; but it added to the melancholy of the scene. Near the centre of it was a small island, with two old ash trees, leaning toward each other, their pensive images reflected in the stirless water. The only cheery influence in this scene of antiquity, solitude, and neglect was that the house and landscape were warmed with the ruddy western beams. I knocked, and my summons resounded hollow and ungenial in my ear; and the bell, from far away, returned a deep-mouthed and surly ring, as if it resented being roused from a score years' slumber.

A light-limbed, jolly-looking old fellow, in a barracan jacket and gaiters, with a smile of welcome, and a very sharp, red nose, that seemed to promise good cheer, opened the door with a promptitude that indicated a hospitable expectation of my arrival.

There was but little light in the hall, and that little lost itself in darkness in the background. It was very spacious and lofty, with a gallery running round it, which, when the door was open, was visible at two or three points. Almost in the dark my new acquaintance led me across this wide hall into the room destined for my reception. It was spacious, and wainscoted up to the ceiling. The furniture of this capacious chamber was old-fashioned and clumsy. There were curtains still to the windows, and a piece of Turkey carpet lay upon the floor; those windows were two in number, looking out, through the trunks of the trees close to the house, upon the lake. It needed all the fire, and all the pleasant associations of my entertainer's red nose, to light up this melancholy chamber. A door at its farther end admitted to the room that was prepared for my sleeping apartment. It was wainscoted, like the other. It had a four-post bed, with heavy tapestry curtains, and in other respects was furnished in the same old-world and ponderous style as the other room. Its window, like those of that apartment, looked out upon the lake.

Sombre and sad as these rooms were, they were yet scrupulously clean. I had nothing to complain of; but the effect was rather dispiriting. Having given some directions about supper—a pleasant incident to look forward to—and made a rapid toilet, I called on my friend with the gaiters and red nose (Tom Wyndsour) whose occupation was that of a "bailiff," or under-steward, of the property, to accompany me, as we had still an hour or so of sun and twilight, in a walk over the grounds.

It was a sweet autumn evening, and my guide, a hardy old fellow, strode at a pace that tasked me to keep up with.

Among clumps of trees at the northern boundary of the demesne we lighted upon the little antique parish church. I was looking down upon it, from an eminence, and the park-wall interposed; but a little way down was a stile affording access to the road, and by this we approached the iron gate of the churchyard. I saw the church door open; the sexton was replacing his pick, shovel, and spade, with which he had just been digging a grave in the churchyard, in their little repository under the stone stair of the tower. He was a polite, shrewd little hunchback, who was very happy to show me over the church. Among the monuments was one that interested me; it was erected to commemorate the very Squire Bowes from whom my two old maids had inherited the house and estate of Barwyke. It spoke of him in terms of grandiloquent eulogy, and informed the Christian reader that he had died, in the bosom of the Church of England, at the age of seventy-one.

I read this inscription by the parting beams of the setting sun, which disappeared behind the horizon just as we passed out from under the porch.

"Twenty years since the Squire died," said I, reflecting as I loitered still in the churchyard.

"Ay, sir; 'twill be twenty year the ninth o' last month."

"And a very good old gentleman?"

"Good-natured enough, and an easy gentleman he was, sir; I don't think while he lived he ever hurt a fly," acquiesced Tom Wyndsour. "It ain't always easy sayin' what's in 'em though, and what they may take or turn to afterwards; and some o' them sort, I think, goes mad."

"You don't think he was out of his mind?" I asked.

"He? La! no; not he, sir; a bit lazy, mayhap, like other old fellows; but a knew devilish well what he was about."

Tom Wyndsour's account was a little enigmatical; but, like old Squire Bowes, I was "a bit lazy" that evening, and asked no more questions about him.

We got over the stile upon the narrow road that skirts the churchyard. It is overhung by elms more than a hundred years old, and in the twilight, which now prevailed, was growing very dark. As side-by-side we walked along this road, hemmed in by two loose stone-like walls, something running towards us in a zig-zag line passed us at a wild pace, with a sound like a frightened laugh or a shudder, and I saw, as it passed, that it was a human figure. I may confess now, that I was a little startled. The dress of this figure was, in part, white: I know I mistook it at first for a white horse coming down the road at a gallop. Tom Wyndsour turned about and looked after the retreating figure.

"He'll be on his travels to-night," he said, in a low tone. "Easy served with a bed, *that* lad be; six foot o' dry peat or heath, or a nook in a dry ditch. That lad hasn't slept once in a house this twenty year, and never will while grass grows."

"Is he mad?" I asked.

"Something that way, sir; he's an idiot, an awpy; we call him 'Dickon the devil,' because the devil's almost the only word that's ever in his mouth."

It struck me that this idiot was in some way connected with the story of old Squire Bowes.

"Queer things are told of him, I dare say?" I suggested.

"More or less, sir; more or less. Queer stories, some."

"Twenty years since he slept in a house? That's about the time the Squire died," I continued.

"So it will be, sir; and not very long after."

"You must tell me all about that, Tom, to-night, when I can hear it comfortably, after supper."

Tom did not seem to like my invitation; and looking straight before him as we trudged on, he said,

"You see, sir, the house has been quiet, and nout's been troubling folk inside the walls or out, all round the woods of Barwyke, this ten year, or more; and my old woman, down there, is clear against talking about such matters, and thinks it best—and so do I—to let sleepin' dogs be."

He dropped his voice towards the close of the sentence, and nodded significantly.

We soon reached a point where he unlocked a wicket in the park wall, by which we entered the grounds of Barwyke once more.

The twilight deepening over the landscape, the huge and solemn trees, and the distant outline of the haunted house, exercised a sombre influence on me, which, together with the fatigue of a day of travel, and the brisk walk we had had, disinclined me to interrupt the silence in which my companion now indulged.

A certain air of comparative comfort, on our arrival, in great measure dissipated the gloom that was stealing over me. Although it was by no means a cold night, I was very glad to see some wood blazing in the grate; and a pair of candles aiding the light of the fire, made the room look cheerful. A small table, with a very white cloth, and preparations for supper, was also a very agreeable object.

I should have liked very well, under these influences, to have listened to Tom Wyndsour's story; but after supper I grew too sleepy to attempt to lead him to the subject; and after yawning for a time, I found there was no use in contending against my drowsiness, so I betook myself to my bedroom, and by ten o'clock was fast asleep.

What interruption I experienced that night I shall tell you presently. It was not much, but it was very odd.

By next night I had completed my work at Barwyke. From early morning till then I was so incessantly occupied and hard-worked, that I had not time to think over the singular occurrence to which I have just referred. Behold me, however, at length once more seated at my little supper-table, having ended a comfortable meal. It had been a sultry day, and I had thrown one of the large windows up as high as it would go. I was sitting near it, with my brandy and water at my elbow, looking out into the dark. There was no moon, and the trees that are grouped about the house make the darkness round it supernaturally profound on such nights.

"Tom," said I, so soon as the jug of hot punch I had supplied him with began to exercise its genial and communicative influence; "you must tell me who beside your wife and you and myself slept in the house last night."

Tom, sitting near the door, set down his tumbler, and looked at me askance, while you might count seven, without speaking a word.

"Who else slept in the house?" he repeated, very deliberately. "Not a living soul, sir"; and he looked hard at me, still evidently expecting something more.

"That *is* very odd," I said returning his stare, and feeling really a little odd. "You are sure *you* were not in my room last night?"

"Not till I came to call you, sir, this morning; *I* can make oath of that."

"Well," said I, "there was some one there, *I* can make oath of that. I was so tired I could not make up my mind to get up; but I was waked by a sound that I thought was some one flinging down the two tin boxes in which my papers were locked up violently on the floor. I heard a slow step on the ground, and there was light in the room, although I remembered having put out my candle. I thought it must have been you, who had come in for my clothes, and upset the boxes by accident. Whoever it was, he went out and the light with him. I was about to settle again, when, the curtain being a little open at the foot of the bed, I saw a light on the wall opposite; such as a candle from outside would cast if the door were very cautiously opening. I started up in the bed, drew the side curtain, and saw that the door *was* opening, and admitting light from outside. It is close, you know, to the head of the bed. A hand was holding on the edge of the door and pushing it open; not a bit like yours; a very singular hand. Let me look at yours."

He extended it for my inspection.

"Oh no; there's nothing wrong with your hand. This was differently shaped; fatter; and the middle finger was stunted, and shorter than the rest, looking as if it had once been broken, and the nail was crooked like a claw. I called out 'Who's there?' and the light and the hand were withdrawn, and I saw and heard no more of my visitor."

"So sure as you're a living man, that was him!" exclaimed Tom Wyndsour, his very nose growing pale, and his eyes almost starting out of his head.

"Who?" I asked.

"Old Squire Bowes; 'twas *his* hand you saw; the Lord a' mercy on us!" answered Tom. "The broken finger, and the nail bent like a hoop. Well for you, sir, he didn't come back when you called, that time. You came here about them Miss Dymock's business, and he never meant they should have a foot o' ground in Barwyke; and he was making a will to give it away quite different, when death took him short. He never was uncivil to no one; but he couldn't abide them ladies. My mind misgave me when I heard 'twas about their business you were coming; and now you see how it is; he'll be at his old tricks again!"

With some pressure and a little more punch, I induced Tom Wyndsour to explain his mysterious allusions by recounting the occurrences which followed the old Squire's death.

"Squire Bowes of Barwyke died without making a will, as you know," said Tom. "And all the folk round were sorry; that is to say, sir, as sorry as folk will be for an old man that has seen a long tale of years, and has no right to grumble that death has knocked an hour too soon at his door. The Squire was well liked; he was never in a passion, or said a hard word; and he would not hurt a fly; and that made what happened after his decease the more surprising.

"The first thing these ladies did, when they got the property, was to buy stock for the park.

"It was not wise, in any case, to graze the land on their own account. But they little knew all they had to contend with.

"Before long something went wrong with the cattle; first one, and then another, took sick and died, and so on, till the loss began to grow heavy. Then, queer stories, little by little, began to be told. It was said, first by one, then by another, that Squire Bowes was seen, about evening time, walking, just as he used to do when he was alive, among the old trees, leaning on his stick; and, sometimes when he came up with the cattle, he would stop and lay his hand kindly like on the back of one of them; and that one was sure to fall sick next day, and die soon after.

"No one ever met him in the park, or in the woods, or ever saw him, except a good distance off. But they knew his gait and his figure well, and the clothes he used to wear; and they could tell the beast he laid his hand on by its colour—white, dun, or black; and that beast was sure to sicken and die. The neighbours grew shy of taking the path over the park; and no one liked to walk in the woods, or come inside the bounds of Barwyke: and the cattle went on sickening and dying as before.

"At that time there was one Thomas Pyke; he had been a groom to the old Squire; and he was in care of the place, and was the only one that used to sleep in the house.

"Tom was vexed, hearing these stories; which he did not believe the half on 'em; and more especial as he could not get man or boy to herd the cattle; all being afeared. So he wrote to Matlock in Derbyshire, for his brother, Richard Pyke, a clever lad, and one that knew nout o' the story of the old Squire walking.

"Dick came; and the cattle was better; folk said they could still see the old Squire, sometimes, walking, as before, in openings of the wood, with his stick in his hand; but he was shy of coming nigh the cattle, whatever his reason might be, since Dickon Pyke came; and he used to stand a long bit off, looking at them, with no more stir in him than a trunk o' one of the old trees, for an hour at a time, till the shape melted away, little by little, like the smoke of a fire that burns out.

"Tom Pyke and his brother Dickon, being the only living souls in the house, lay in the big bed in the servants' room, the house being fast barred and locked, one night in November.

"Tom was lying next the wall, and he told me, as wide awake as ever he was at noonday. His brother Dickon lay outside, and was sound asleep.

"Well, as Tom lay thinking, with his eyes turned toward the door, it opens slowly, and who should come in but old Squire Bowes, his face lookin' as dead as he was in his coffin.

"Tom's very breath left his body; he could not take his eyes off him; and he felt the hair rising up on his head.

"The Squire came to the side of the bed, and put his arms under Dickon, and lifted the boy—in a dead sleep all the time—and carried him out so, at the door.

"Such was the appearance, to Tom Pyke's eyes, and he was ready to swear to it, anywhere.

"When this happened, the light, wherever it came from, all on a sudden went out, and Tom could not see his own hand before him.

"More dead than alive, he lay till daylight.

"Sure enough his brother Dickon was gone. No sign of him could he discover about the house; and with some trouble he got a couple of the neighbours to help him to search the woods and grounds. Not a sign of him anywhere.

"At last one of them thought of the island in the lake; the little boat was moored to the old post at the water's edge. In they got, though with small hope of finding him there. Find him, nevertheless, they did, sitting under the big ash tree, quite out of his wits; and to all their questions he answered nothing but one cry—'Bowes, the devil! See him; see him; Bowes, the devil!' An idiot they found him; and so he will be till God sets all things right. No one could ever get him to sleep under roof-tree more. He wanders from house to house while daylight lasts; and no one cares to lock the harmless creature in the workhouse. And folk would rather not meet him after nightfall, for they think where he is there may be worse things near."

A silence followed Tom's story. He and I were alone in that large room; I was sitting near the open window, looking into the dark night air. I fancied I saw something white move across it; and I heard a sound like low talking that swelled into a discordant shriek—"Hoo-oo-oo! Bowes, the devil! Over your shoulder. Hoo-oo-oo! ha! ha! ha!" I started up, and saw, by the light of the candle with which Tom strode to the window, the wild eyes and blighted face of the idiot, as, with a sudden change of mood, he drew off, whispering and tittering to himself, and holding up his long fingers, and looking at the tips like a "hand of glory."

Tom pulled down the window. The story and its epilogue were over. I confess I was rather glad when I heard the sound of the horses' hoofs on the court-yard, a few minutes later; and still gladder when, having bidden Tom a kind farewell, I had left the neglected house of Barwyke a mile behind me.

THE GHOST
AND THE BONE-SETTER

In looking over the papers of my late valued and respected friend, Francis Purcell, who for nearly fifty years discharged the arduous duties of a parish priest in the south of Ireland, I met with the following document. It is one of many such, for he was a curious and industrious collector of old local traditions—a commodity in which the quarter where he resided mightily abounded. The collection and arrangement of such legends was, as long as I can remember him, his *hobby*; but I had never learned that his love of the marvellous and whimsical had carried him so far as to prompt him to commit the results of his enquiries to writing, until, in the character of *residuary legatee*, his will put me in possession of all his manuscript papers. To such as may think the composing of such productions as these inconsistent with the character and habits of a country priest, it is necessary to observe, that there did exist a race of priests—those of the old school, a race now nearly extinct—whose habits were from many causes more refined, and whose tastes more literary than are those of the alumni of Maynooth.

It is perhaps necessary to add that the superstition illustrated by the following story, namely, that the corpse last buried is obliged, during his juniority of interment, to supply his brother tenants of the churchyard in which he lies, with fresh water to allay the burning thirst of purgatory, is prevalent throughout the south of Ireland. The writer can vouch for a case in which a respectable and wealthy farmer, on the borders of Tipperary, in tenderness to the corns of his departed helpmate, enclosed in her coffin two pair of brogues, a light and a heavy, the one for dry, the other for sloppy weather; seeking thus to mitigate the fatigues of her inevitable perambulations in procuring water, and administering it to the thirsty souls of purgatory. Fierce and desperate conflicts have ensued in the case of two funeral parties approaching the same churchyard together, each endeavouring to secure to his own dead priority of sepulture, and a consequent immunity from the tax levied upon the pedestrian powers of the last comer. An instance not long since occurred, in which one of two such parties, through fear of losing to their deceased friend this inestimable advantage, made their way to the churchyard by a *short cut*, and in violation of one of their strongest prejudices, actually threw the coffin over the wall, lest time should be lost in making their entrance through the gate. Innumerable instances of the same kind might be quoted, all tending to shew how strongly, among the peasantry of the south, this superstition is entertained. However, I shall not detain the reader further, by any prefatory remarks, but shall proceed to lay before him the following:—

Extract from the Ms. Papers of the Late Rev. Francis Purcell, of Drumcoolagh

"I tell the following particulars, as nearly as I can recollect them, in the words of the narrator. It may be necessary to observe that he was what is termed a *well-spoken* man, having for a considerable time instructed the ingenious youth of his native parish in such of the liberal arts and sciences as he found it convenient to profess—a circumstance which may account for the occurrence of several big words, in the course of this narrative, more distinguished for euphonious effect, than for correctness of application. I proceed then, without further preface, to lay before you the wonderful adventures of Terry Neil."

"Why, thin, 'tis a quare story, an' as thrue as you're sittin' there; and I'd make bould to say there isn't a boy in the seven parishes could tell it better nor crickther than myself, for 'twas my father himself it happened to, an' many's the time I heerd it out iv his own mouth; an' I can say, an' I'm proud av that same, my father's word was as incredible as any squire's oath in the counthry; and so signs an' if a poor man got into any unlucky throuble, he was the boy id go into the court an' prove; but that dosen't signify—he was as honest and as sober a man, barrin' he was a little bit too partial to the glass, as you'd find in a day's walk; an' there wasn't the likes of him in the counthry round for nate labourin' an' *baan* diggin'; and he was mighty handy entirely for carpenther's work, and mendin' ould spudethrees, an' the likes i' that. An' so he tuck up with bone-setting, as was most nathural, for none of them could come up to him in mendin' the leg iv a stool or a table; an' sure, there never was a bone-setter got so much custom—man an' child, young an' ould—there never was such breakin' and mendin' of bones known in the memory of man. Well, Terry Neil, for that was my father's name, began to feel his heart growin' light and his purse heavy; an' he took a bit iv a farm in Squire Phalim's ground, just undher the ould castle, an' a pleasant little spot it was; an' day an' mornin', poor crathurs not able to put a foot to the ground, with broken arms and broken legs, id be comin' ramblin' in from all quarters to have their bones spliced up. Well, yer honour, all this was as well as well could be; but it was customary when Sir Phelim id go any where out iv the coun-try, for some iv the tinants to sit up to watch in the ould castle, just for a kind of a compliment to the ould family—an' a mighty unpleasant com-pliment it was for the tinants, for there wasn't a man of them but knew there was some thing quare about the ould castle. The neighbours had it, that the squire's ould grandfather, as good a gintleman, God be with him, as I heer'd as ever stood in shoe leather, used to keep walkin' about in the middle iv the night, ever sinst he bursted a blood vessel pullin' out a cork out iv a bottle, as you or I might be doin', and will too, plase God; but that dosen't signify. So, as I was sayin', the ould squire used to come down out of the frame, where his picthur was hung up, and to brake the bottles and glasses, God be marciful to us all, an' dhrink all he could come at—an' small blame to him for that same; and then if any of the family id be comin' in, he id be up again in his place, looking as quite an' innocent as if he didn't know any thing about it—the mischievous ould chap.

"Well, your honour, as I was sayin', one time the family up at the castle was stayin' in Dublin for a week or two; and so as usual, some of the tenants had to sit up in the castle, and the third night it kem to my father's turn. 'Oh, tare an ouns,' says he unto himself, 'an' must I sit up all night, and that ould vagabond of a sperit, glory be to God,' says he, 'serenading through the house, an' doin' all sorts iv mischief.' However, there was no gettin' aff, and so he put a bould face on it, an' he went up at night-fall with a bottle of pottieen, and another of holy wather.

"It was rainin' smart enough, an' the evenin' was darksome and gloomy, when my father got in, and the holy wather he sprinkled on himself, it wasn't long till he had to swallee a cup iv the pottieen, to keep the cowld out iv his heart. It was the ould steward, Lawrence Con-nor, that opened the door—and he an' my father wor always very great. So when he seen who it was, an' my father tould him how it was his turn to watch in the castle, he offered to sit up along with him; and you may be sure my father wasn't sorry for that same. So says Larry,

" 'We'll have a bit iv fire in the parlour,' says he.

" 'An' why not in the hall?' says my father, for he knew that the squire's picthur was hung in the parlour.

" 'No fire can be lit in the hall,' says Lawrence, 'for there's an ould jackdaw's nest in the chimney.'

" 'Oh thin,' says my father, 'let us stop in the kitchen, for it's very umproper for the likes iv me to be sittin' in the parlour,' says he.

" 'Oh, Terry, that can't be,' says Lawrence; 'if we keep up the ould custom at all, we may as well keep it up properly,' says he.

" 'Divil sweep the ould custom,' says my father—to himself, do ye mind, for he didn't like to let Lawrence see that he was more afeard himself.

" 'Oh, very well,' says he. 'I'm agreeable, Lawrence,' says he; and so down they both went to the kitchen, until the fire id be lit in the parlour —an' that same wasn't long doin'.

"Well, your honour, they soon wint up again, an' sat down mighty comfortable by the parlour fire, and they beginn'd to talk, an' to smoke, an' to dhrink a small taste iv the pottieen; and, moreover, they had a good rousing fire of bogwood and turf, to warm their shins over.

"Well, sir, as I was sayin' they kep convarsin' and smokin' together most agreeable, until Lawrence beginn'd to get sleepy, as was but nathural for him, for he was an ould sarvint man, and was used to a great dale iv sleep.

" 'Sure it's impossible,' says my father, 'it's gettin' sleepy you are?'

" 'Oh, divil a taste,' says Larry, 'I'm only shuttin' my eyes,' says he, 'to keep out the parfume of the tibacky smoke, that's makin' them wather,' says he. 'So don't you mind other people's business,' says he stiff enough (for he had a mighty high stomach av his own, rest his sowl), 'and go on,' says he, 'with your story, for I'm listenin',' says he, shuttin' down his eyes.

"Well, when my father seen spakin' was no use, he went on with his story.—By the same token, it was the story of Jim Soolivan and his ould goat he was tellin'—an' a pleasant story it is—an' there was so much divarsion in it, that it was enough to waken a dormouse, let alone to pervint a Christian goin' asleep. But, faix, the way my father tould it, I believe there never was the likes heerd sinst nor before for he bawled out every word av it, as if the life was fairly leavin' him thrying to keep ould Larry awake; but, faix, it was no use, for the hoorsness came an him, an' before he kem to the end of his story, Larry O'Connor beginned to snore like a bagpipes.

" 'Oh, blur an' agres,' says my father, 'isn't this a hard case,' says he, 'that ould villain, lettin' on to be my friend, and to go asleep this way, an' us both in the very room with a sperit,' says he. 'The crass o' Christ about us,' says he; and with that he was goin' to shake Lawrence to waken him, but he just remimbered if he roused him, that he'd surely go off to his bed, an lave him completely alone, an' that id be by far worse.

" 'Oh thin,' says my father, 'I'll not disturb the poor boy. It id be neither friendly nor good-nathured,' says he, 'to tormint him while he is asleep,' says he; 'only I wish I was the same way myself,' says he.

"An' with that he beginned to walk up an' down, an' sayin' his prayers, until he worked himself into a sweat, savin' your presence. But it was all no good; so he dhrunk about a pint of sperits, to compose his mind.

" 'Oh,' says he, 'I wish to the Lord I was as asy in my mind as Larry there. Maybe,' says he, 'if I thried I could go asleep'; an' with that he pulled a big arm-chair close beside Lawrence, an' settled himself in it as well as he could.

"But there was one quare thing I forgot to tell you. He couldn't help, in spite av himself, lookin' now an' thin at the picthur, an' he immediately observed that the eyes av it was follyin' him about, an' starin' at him, an' winkin' at him, wherever he wint. 'Oh,' says he, when he seen that, 'it's a poor chance I have,' says he; 'an' bad luck was with me the day I kem into this unforthunate place,' says he; 'but any way there's no use in bein' freckened now,' says he; 'for if I am to die, I may as well parspire undaunted,' says he.

"Well, your honour, he thried to keep himself quite an' asy, an' he thought two or three times he might have wint asleep, but for the way the storm was groanin' and creekin' through the great heavy branches outside, an' whistlin' through the ould chimneys iv the castle. Well, afther one great roarin' blast iv the wind, you'd think the walls iv the castle was just goin' to fall, quite an' clane, with the shakin' iv it. All av a suddint the storm stopt, as silent an' as quite as if it was a July evenin'. Well, your honour, it wasn't stopped blowin' for three minnites, before he thought he hard a sort iv a noise over the chimneypiece; an' with that my father just opened his eyes the smallest taste in life, an' sure enough he seen the ould squire gettin' out iv the picthur, for all the world as if he was throwin' aff his ridin' coat, until he stept out clane an' complate, out av the chimly-piece, an' thrun himself down an the floor. Well, the slieveen ould chap—an' my father thought it was the dirtiest turn iv all—before he beginned to do anything out iv the way, he stopped, for a while, to listen wor they both asleep; an' as soon as he thought all was quite, he put out his hand, and tuck hould iv the whiskey bottle, an' dhrank at laste a pint iv it. Well, your honour, when he tuck his turn out iv it, he settled it back mighty cute intirely, in the very same spot it was in before. An' he beginn'd to walk up an' down the room, lookin' as sober an' as solid as if he never done the likes at all. An' whinever he went apast my father, he thought he felt a great scent of brimstone, an' it was that that freckened him entirely; for he knew it was brimstone that was burned in hell, savin' your presence. At any rate, he often heer'd it from Father Murphy, an' he had a right to know what belonged to it—he's dead since, God rest him. Well, your honour, my father was asy enough until the sperit kem past him; so close, God be marciful to us all, that the smell iv the sulphur tuck the breath clane out iv him; an' with that he tuck such a fit iv coughin', that it al-a-most shuck him out iv the chair he was sittin' in.

" 'Ho, ho!' says the squire, stoppin' short about two steps aff, and turnin' round facin' my father, 'is it you that's in it?—an' how's all with you, Terry Neil?'

" 'At your honour's sarvice,' says my father (as well as the fright id let him, for he was more dead than alive), 'an' it's proud I am to see your honour to-night,' says he.

" 'Terence,' says the squire, 'you're a respectable man (an' it was thrue for him), an industhrious, sober man, an' an example of inebriety to the whole parish,' says he.

" 'Thank your honour,' says my father, gettin' courage, 'you were always a civil spoken gintleman, God rest your honour.'

" 'Rest my honour,' says the sperit (fairly gettin' red in the face with the madness), 'Rest my honour?' says he. 'Why, you ignorant spalpeen,' says he, 'you mane, niggarly ignoramush,' says he, 'where did you lave your manners?' says he. 'If I *am* dead, it's no fault iv mine,' says he; 'an' it's not to be thrun in my teeth at every hand's turn, by the likes iv you,' says he, stampin' his foot an the flure, that you'd think the boords id smash undher him.

" 'Oh,' says my father, 'I'm only a foolish, ignorant, poor man,' says he.

" 'You're nothing else,' says the squire; 'but any way,' says he, 'it's not to be listenin' to your gosther, nor convarsin' with the likes iv you, that I came *up*—down I mane,' says he—(an' as little as the mistake was, my father tuck notice iv it). 'Listen to me now, Terence Neil,' says he, 'I was always a good masther to Pathrick Neil, your grandfather,' says he.

" 'Tis thrue for your honour,' says my father.

" 'And, moreover, I think I was always a sober, riglar gintleman,' says the squire.

" 'That's your name, sure enough,' says my father (though it was a big lie for him, but he could not help it).

" 'Well,' says the sperit, 'although I was as sober as most men—at laste as most gintlemen'—says he; 'an' though I was at different pariods a most extempory Christian, and most charitable and inhuman to the poor,' says he; 'for all that I'm not as asy where I am now,' says he, 'as I had a right to expect,' says he.

" 'An' more's the pity,' says my father; 'maybe your honour id wish to have a word with Father Murphy?'

" 'Hould your tongue, you misherable bliggard,' says the squire; 'it's not iv my sowl I'm thinkin'—an' I wondher you'd have the impitence to talk to a gintleman consarnin' his sowl;—and when I want *that* fixed,' says he, slappin' his thigh, 'I'll go to them that knows what belongs to the likes,' says he. 'It's not my sowl,' says he, sittin' down opposite my father; 'it's not my sowl that's annoyin' me most—I'm unasy on my right leg,' says he, 'that I bruck at Glenvarloch cover the day I killed black Barney.'

" (My father found out afther, it was a favourite horse that fell undher him, afther leapin' the big fince that runs along by the glen.)

" 'I hope,' says my father, 'your honour's not unasy about the killin' iv him?

" 'Hould your tongue, ye fool,' said the squire, 'an' I'll tell you why I'm anasy an my leg,' says he. 'In the place, where I spend most iv my time,' says he, 'except the little leisure I have for lookin' about me here,' says he, 'I have to walk a great dale more than I was ever used to,' says he, 'and by far more than is good for me either,' says he; 'for I must tell you,' says he, 'the people where I am is ancommonly fond iv could wather, for there is nothin' betther to be had; an', moreover, the weather is hotter than is altogether plisint,' says he; 'and I'm appinted,' says he, 'to assist in carryin' the wather, an' gets a mighty poor share iv it myself,' says he, 'an' a mighty throublesome, warin' job it is, I can tell you,' says he; 'for they're all iv them surprisingly dhry, an' dhrinks it as fast as my legs can carry it,' says he; 'but what kills me intirely,' says he, 'is the wakeness in my leg,' says he, 'an' I want you to give it a pull or two to bring it to shape,' says he, 'and that's the long an' the short iv it,' says he.

" 'Oh, plase your honour,' says my father (for he didn't like to handle the sperit at all), 'I wouldn't have the impitence to do the likes to your honour,' says he; 'it's only to poor crathurs like myself I'd do it to,' says he.

" 'None iv your blarney,' says the squire, 'here's my leg,' says he, cockin' it up to him, 'pull it for the bare life,' says he; 'an' if you don't, by the immortial powers I'll not lave a bone in your carcish I'll not powdher,' says he.

" 'When my father heerd that, he seen there was no use in purtendin', so he tuck hould iv the leg, an' he kept pullin' an' pullin', till the sweat, God bless us, beginned to pour down his face.''

" 'Pull, you divil', says the squire.

" 'At your sarvice, your honour,' says my father.

" 'Pull harder,' says the squire.

"My father pulled like the divil.

" 'I'll take a little sup,' says the squire, rachin' over his hand to the bottle, 'to keep up my courage,' says he, lettin' an to be very wake in himself intirely. But, as cute as he was, he was out here, for he tuck the wrong one. 'Here's to your good health, Terence,' says he, 'an' now pull like the very divil,' 'an' with that he lifted the bottle of holy wather, but it was hardly to his mouth, whin he let a screech out, you'd think the room id fairly split with it, an' made one chuck that sent the leg clane aff his body in my father's hands; down wint the squire over the table, an' bang wint my father half way across the room on his back, upon the flure. Whin he kem to himself the cheerful mornin' sun was shinin' through the windy shutthers, an' he was lying flat an his back, with the leg iv one of the great ould chairs pulled clane out iv the socket an' tight in his hand, pintin' up to the ceilin', an' ould Larry fast asleep, an' snorin' as loud as ever. My father wint that mornin' to Father Murphy, an' from that to the day of his death, he never neglected confission nor mass, an' what he tould was betther believed that he spake av it but seldom. An', as for the squire, that is the sperit, whether it was that he did not like his liquor, or by rason iv the loss iv his leg, he was never known to walk again.''

A CHAPTER IN THE HISTORY
OF A TYRONE FAMILY

Being a Tenth Extract from the Legacy
of the Late Francis Purcell,
P. P. of Drumcoolagh

INTRODUCTION.   In the following narrative, I have endeavoured‚to give as nearly as possible the *"ipsissima verba"* of the valued friend from whom I received it, conscious that any aberration from *her* mode of telling the tale of her own life, would at once impair its accuracy and its effect. Would that, with her words, I could also bring before you her animated gesture, her expressive countenance, the solemn and thrilling air and accent with which she related the dark passages in her strange story; and, above all, that I could communicate the impressive consciousness that the narrator had seen with her own eyes, and personally acted in the scenes which she described; these accompaniments, taken with the additional circumstance, that she who told the tale was one far too deeply and sadly impressed with religious principle, to misrepresent or fabricate what she repeated as fact, gave to the tale a depth of interest which the events recorded could hardly, themselves, have produced. I became acquainted with the lady from whose lips I heard this narrative, nearly twenty years since, and the story struck my fancy so much, that I committed it to paper while it was still fresh in my mind, and should its perusal afford you entertainment for a listless half hour, my labour shall not have been bestowed in vain. I find that I have taken the story down as she told it, in the first person, and, perhaps, this is as it should be. She began as follows.

My maiden name was Richardson,* the designation of a family of some distinction in the county of Tyrone. I was the younger of two daughters, and we were the only children. There was a difference in our ages of nearly six years, so that I did not, in my childhood, enjoy that close companionship which sisterhood, in other circumstances, necessarily involves; and while I was still a child, my sister was married. The person upon whom she bestowed her hand, was a Mr. Carew, a gentleman of property and consideration in the north of England. I remember well the eventful day of the wedding; the thronging carriages, the noisy menials, the loud laughter, the merry faces, and the gay dresses. Such sights were then new to me, and harmonized ill with the sorrowful feelings with with I regarded the event which was to separate me, as it turned out, for ever, from a sister whose tenderness alone had hitherto more than supplied all that I wanted in my mother's affection. The day soon arrived which was to remove the happy couple from Ashtown-house. The carriage stood at the hall-door, and my poor sister kissed me again, and again, telling me that I should see her soon. The carriage drove away, and I gazed after it until my eyes filled with tears, and, returning slowly to my chamber, I wept more bitterly, and so, to speak more desolately, than ever I had done before. My father had never seemed to love, or to take an interest in me. He had desired a son, and I think he never thoroughly forgave me my unfortunate sex. My having come into the world at all as his child, he regarded as a kind of fraudulent intrusion, and, as his antipathy to me had its origin in an imperfection of mine, too radical for removal, I never even hoped to stand high in his good graces. My mother was, I dare say, as fond of me as she was of any one; but she was a woman of a masculine and a worldly cast of mind. She had no tenderness or sympathy for the weaknesses, or even for the affections of woman's nature, and her demeanour towards me was peremptory, and often even harsh. It is not to be supposed, then, that I found in the society of my parents much to supply the loss of my sister. About a year after her marriage, we received letters from Mr. Carew, containing accounts of my sister's health, which, though not actually alarming, were calculated to make us seriously uneasy. The symptoms most dwelt upon, were loss of appetite and cough. The letters concluded by intimating that he would avail himself of my father and mother's repeated invitation to spend some time at Ashtown, particularly as the physician who had been consulted as to my sister's health had strongly advised a removal to her native air. There were added repeated assurances that nothing serious was apprehended, as it was supposed that a deranged state of the liver was the only source of the symptoms which seemed to intimate con-

*I have carefully altered the names as they appear in the original MSS., for the reader will see that some of the circumstances recorded are not of a kind to reflect honour upon those involved in them; and, as many are still living, in every way honoured and honourable, who stand in close relation to the principal actors in this drama, the reader will see the necessity of the course which we have adopted.

sumption. In accordance with this announcement, my sister and Mr. Carew arrived in Dublin, where one of my father's carriages awaited them, in readiness to start upon whatever day or hour they might choose for their departure. It was arranged that Mr. Carew was, as soon as the day upon which they were to leave Dublin was definitely fixed, to write to my father, who intended that the two last stages should be performed by his own horses, upon whose speed and safety far more reliance might be placed than upon those of the ordinary *post-horses*, which were, at that time, almost without exception, of the very worst order. The journey, one of about ninety miles, was to be divided; the larger portion to be reserved for the second day. On Sunday, a letter reached us, stating that the party would leave Dublin on Monday, and, in due course, reach Ashtown upon Tuesday evening. Tuesday came: the evening closed in, and yet no carriage appeared; darkness came on, and still no sign of our expected visitors. Hour after hour passed away, and it was now past twelve; the night was remarkably calm, scarce a breath stirring, so that any sound, such as that produced by the rapid movement of a vehicle, would have been audible at a considerable distance. For some such sound I was feverishly listening. It was, however, my father's rule to close the house at nightfall, and the window-shutters being fastened, I was unable to reconnoitre the avenue as I would have wished. It was nearly one o'clock, and we began almost to despair of seeing them upon that night, when I thought I distinguished the sound of wheels, but so remote and faint as to make me at first very uncertain. The noise approached; it become louder and clearer; it stopped for a moment. I now heard the shrill screaking of the rusty iron, as the avenue gate revolved on its hinges; again came the sound of wheels in rapid motion.

"It is they," said I, starting up. "the carriage is in the avenue." We all stood for a few moments, breathlessly listening. On thundered the vehicle with the speed of a whirlwind; crack went the whip, and clatter went the wheels, as it rattled over the uneven pavement of the court; a general and furious barking from all the dogs about the house, hailed its arrival. We hurried to the hall in time to hear the steps let down with the sharp clanging noise peculiar to the operation, and the hum of voices exerted in the bustle of arrival. The hall-door was now thrown open, and we all stepped forth to greet our visitors. The court was perfectly empty; the moon was shining broadly and brightly upon all around; nothing was to be seen but the tall trees with their long spectral shadows, now wet with the dews of midnight. We stood gazing from right to left, as if suddenly awakened from a dream; the dogs walked suspiciously, growling and snuffing about the court, and by totally and suddenly ceasing their former loud barking, as also by carrying their tails between their legs, expressing the predominance of fear. We looked one upon the other in perplexity and dismay, and I think I never beheld more pale faces assembled. By my father's direction, we looked about to find anything which might indicate or account for the noise which we had heard; but no such thing was to be seen—even the mire which lay upon the avenue was undisturbed. We returned to the house, more panic struck than I can describe. On the next day, we learned by a messenger, who had ridden hard the greater part of the night, that my sister was dead. On Sunday evening, she had retired to bed rather unwell, and, on Monday, her indisposition declared itself unequivocally to be malignant fever. She became hourly worse, and, on Tuesday night, a little after midnight, she expired.* I mention this circumstance, because it was one upon which a thousand wild and fantastical reports were founded, though one would have thought that the truth scarcely required to be improved upon; and again, because it produced a strong and lasting effect upon my spirits, and indeed, I am inclined to think, upon my character. I was, for several years after this occurrence, long after the violence of my grief subsided, so wretchedly low-spirited and nervous, that I could scarcely be said to live, and during this time, habits of indecision, arising out of a listless acquiescence in the will of others, a fear of encountering even the slightest opposition, and a disposition to shrink from what are commonly called amusements, grew upon me so strongly, that I have scarcely even yet, altogether overcome them. We saw nothing more of Mr. Carew. He returned to England as soon as the melancholy rites attendant upon the event which I have just mentioned were performed; and not being altogether inconsolable, he married again within two years; after which, owing to the remoteness of our relative situations, and other circumstances, we gradually lost sight of him. I was now an only child; and, as my elder sister had died without issue, it was evident that, in the ordinary course of things, my

---

*The residuary legatee of the late Francis Purcell, who has the honour of selecting such of his lamented old friend's manuscripts as may appear fit for publication, in order that the lore which they contain may reach the world before scepticism and utility have robbed our species of the precious gift of credulity, and scornfully kicked before them, or trampled into annihilation, those harmless fragments of picturesque superstition, which it is our object to preserve, has been subjected to the charge of dealing too largely in the marvellous; and it has been half insinuated that such is his love for *diablerie*, that he is content to wander a mile out of his way, in order to meet a fiend or a goblin, and thus to sacrifice all regard for truth and accuracy to the idle hope of affrighting the imagination, and thus pandering to the bad taste of his reader. He begs leave, then, to take this opportunity of asserting his perfect innocence of all the crimes laid to his charge, and to assure his reader that he never *pandered to his bad taste*, nor went one inch out of his way to introduce witch, fairy, devil, ghost, or any other of the grim fraternity of the redoubted Raw-head and bloody-bones. His province, touching these tales, has been attended with no difficulty and little responsibility; indeed, he is accountable for nothing more than an alteration in the names of persons mentioned therein, when such a step seemed necessary, and for an occasional note, whenever he conceived it possible, innocently, to edge in a word. These tales have been *written down*, as the heading of each announces, by the Rev. Francis Purcell, P. P. of Drumcoolagh; and in all the instances, which are many, in which the present writer has had an opportunity of comparing the manuscript of his departed friend with the actual traditions which are current amongst the families whose fortunes they pretend to illustrate, he has uniformly found that whatever of supernatural occurred in the story, so far from having been exaggerated by him, had been rather softened down, and, wherever it could be attempted, accounted for.

father's property, which was altogether in his power, would go to me, and the consequence was, that before I was fourteen, Ashtown-house was besieged by a host of suitors; however, whether it was that *I* was too young, or that none of the aspirants to my hand stood sufficiently high in rank or wealth, I was suffered by both parents to do exactly as I pleased; and well was it for me, as I afterwards found that fortune, or, rather Providence, had so ordained it, that I had not suffered my affections to become in any degree engaged, for my mother would never have suffered any *silly fancy* of mine, as she was in the habit of styling an attachment, to stand in the way of her ambitious views; views which she was determined to carry into effect, in defiance of every obstacle, and in order to accomplish which, she would not have hesitated to sacrifice anything so unreasonable and contemptible as a girlish passion.

When I reached the age of sixteen, my mother's plans began to develope themselves, and, at her suggestion, we moved to Dublin to sojourn for the winter, in order that no time might be lost in disposing of me to the best advantage. I had been too long accustomed to consider myself as of no importance whatever, to believe for a moment that I was in reality the cause of all the bustle and preparation which surrounded me, and being thus relieved from the pain which a consciousness of my real situation would have inflicted, I journeyed towards the capital with a feeling of total indifference.

My father's wealth and connection had established him in the best society, and, consequently, upon our arrival in the metropolis, we commanded whatever enjoyment or advantages its gaieties afforded. The tumult and novelty of the scenes in which I was involved did not fail considerably to amuse me, and my mind gradually recovered its tone, which was naturally cheerful. It was almost immediately known and reported that I was an heiress, and of course my attractions were pretty generally acknowledged. Among the many gentlemen whom it was my fortune to please, one, ere long, established himself in my mother's good graces, to the exclusion of all less important aspirants. However, I had not understood, or even remarked his attentions, nor, in the slightest degree, suspected his or my mother's plans respecting me, when I was made aware of them rather abruptly by my mother herself. We had attended a splendid ball, given by Lord M——, at his residence in Stephen's-green, and I was, with the assistance of my waiting-maid, employed in rapidly divesting myself of the rich ornaments which, in profuseness and value, could scarcely have found their equals in any private family in Ireland. I had thrown myself into a lounging chair beside the fire, listless and exhausted, after the fatigues of the evening, when I was aroused from the reverie into which I had fallen, by the sound of footsteps approaching my chamber, and my mother entered.

"Fanny, my dear," said she, in her softest tone. "I wish to say a word or two with you before I go to rest. You are not fatigued, love, I hope?"

"No, no, madam, I thank you," said I, rising at the same time from my seat with the formal respect so little practised now.

"Sit down, my dear," said she, placing herself upon a chair beside me; "I must chat with you for a quarter of an hour or so. Saunders (to the maid), you may leave the room; do not close the room door, but shut that of the lobby."

This precaution against curious ears having been taken as directed, my mother proceeded.

"You have observed, I should suppose, my dearest Fanny; indeed, you *must* have observed, Lord Glenfallen's marked attentions to you?"

"I assure you, madam," I began.

"Well, well, that is all right," interrupted my mother; "of course you must be modest upon the matter; but listen to me for a few moments, my love, and I will prove to your satisfaction that your modesty is quite unnecessary in this case. You have done better than we could have hoped, at least, so very soon. Lord Glenfallen is in love with you. I give you joy of your conquest," and saying this, my mother kissed my forehead.

"In love with me!" I exclaimed, in unfeigned astonishment.

"Yes, in love with you," repeated my mother; "devotedly, distractedly in love with you. Why, my dear, what is there wonderful in it; look in the glass, and look at these," she continued, pointing with a smile to the jewels which I had just removed from my person, and which now lay a glittering heap upon the table.

"May there not," said I, hesitating between confusion and real alarm; "is it not possible that some mistake may be at the bottom of all this?"

"Mistake! dearest; none," said my mother. "None, none in the world; judge for yourself; read this, my love," and she placed in my hand a letter, addressed to herself, the seal of which was broken. I read it through with no small surprise. After some very fine complimentary flourishes upon my beauty and perfections, as, also, upon the antiquity and high reputation of our family, it went on to make a formal proposal of marriage, to be communicated or not to me at present, as my mother should deem expedient; and the letter wound up by a request that the writer might be permitted, upon our return to Ashtown-house, which was soon to take place, as the spring was now tolerably advanced, to visit us for a few days, in case his suit was approved.

"Well, well, my dear," said my mother, impatiently; "do you know who Lord Glenfallen is?"

"I do, madam," said I rather timidly, for I dreaded an altercation with my mother.

"Well, dear, and what frightens you?" continued she; "are you afraid of a title? What has he done to alarm you? he is neither old nor ugly."

I was silent, though I might have said, "He is neither young nor handsome."

"My dear Fanny," continued my mother, "in sober seriousness you have been most fortunate in engaging the affections of a nobleman such as Lord Glenfallen, young and wealthy, with first-rate, yes, acknowledged *first-rate* abilities and of a family whose influence is not exceeded by that of any in Ireland—of course you see the offer in the same light that I do—indeed I think you *must.*"

This was uttered in no very dubious tone. I was so much astonished by the suddenness of the whole communication that I literally did not know what to say.

"You are not in love?" said my mother, turning sharply, and fixing her dark eyes upon me, with severe scrutiny.

"No, madam," said I, promptly; horrified, as what young lady would not have been, at such a query.

"I am glad to hear it," said my mother, dryly. "Once, nearly twenty years ago, a friend of mine consulted me how he should deal with a daughter who had made what they call a love match, beggared herself, and disgraced her family; and I said, without hesitation, take no care of her, but cast her off; such punishment I awarded for an offence committed against the reputation of a family not my own; and what I advised respecting the child of another, with full as small compunction I would *do* with mine. I cannot conceive anything more unreasonable or intolerable than that the fortune and the character of a family should be marred by the idle caprices of a girl."

She spoke this with great severity, and paused as if she expected some observation from me. I, however, said nothing.

"But I need not explain to you, my dear Fanny," she continued, "my views upon this subject; you have always known them well, and I have never yet had reason to believe you likely, voluntarily, to offend me, or to abuse or neglect any of those advantages which reason and duty tell you should be improved—come hither, my dear, kiss me, and do not look so frightened. Well, now, about this letter, you need not answer it yet; of course you must be allowed time to make up your mind; in the mean time I will write to his lordship to give him my permission to visit us at Ashtown—good night, my love."

And thus ended one of the most disagreeable, not to say astounding, conversations I had ever had; it would not be easy to describe exactly what were my feelings towards Lord Glenfallen; whatever might have been my mother's suspicions, my heart was perfectly disengaged; and hitherto, although I had not been made in the slightest degree acquainted with his real views, I had liked him very much, as an agreeable, well informed man, whom I was always glad to meet in society; he had served in the navy in early life, and the polish which his manners received in his after intercourse with courts and cities had not served to obliterate that frankness of *manner* which belongs proverbially to the sailor. Whether this apparent candour went deeper than the outward bearing I was yet to learn; however there was no doubt that as far as I had seen of Lord Glenfallen, he was, though perhaps not so young as might have been desired in a lover, a singularly pleasing man, and whatever feeling unfavourable to him had found its way into my mind, arose altogether from the dread, not an unreasonable one, that constraint might be practised upon my inclinations. I reflected, however, that Lord Glenfallen was a wealthy man, and one highly thought of; and although I could never expect to love him in the romantic sense of the term, yet I had no doubt but that, all things considered, I might be more happy with him than I could hope to be at home. When next I met him it was with no small embarrassment, his tact and good breeding, however, soon reassured me, and effectually prevented my awkwardness being remarked upon; and I had the satisfaction of leaving Dublin for the country with the full conviction that nobody, not even those most intimate with me, even suspected the fact of Lord Glenfallen's having made me a formal proposal. This was to me a very serious subject of self gratulation, for, besides my instinctive dread of becoming the topic of the speculations of gossip, I felt that if the situation which I occupied in relation to him were made publicly known, I should stand committed in a manner which would scarcely leave me the power of retraction. The period at which Lord Glenfallen had arranged to visit Ashtown-house was now fast approaching, and it became my mother's wish to form me thoroughly to her will, and to obtain my consent to the proposed marriage before his arrival, so that all things might proceed smoothly without apparent opposition or objection upon my part; whatever objections, therefore, I had entertained were to be subdued; whatever disposition to resistance I had exhibited or had been supposed to feel, were to be completely eradicated before he made his appearance, and my mother addressed herself to the task with a decision and energy against which even the barriers, which her imagination had created, could hardly have stood. If she had, however, expected any determined opposition from me, she was agreeably disappointed; my heart was perfectly free, and all my feelings of liking and preference were in favour of Lord Glenfallen, and I well knew that in case I refused to dispose of myself as I was desired, my mother had alike the power and the will to render my existence as utterly miserable as any, even the most ill-assorted marriage could possibly have done. You will remember, my good friend, that I was very young and very completely under the controul of my parents, both of whom, my mother particularly, were unscrupulously determined in matters of this kind, and willing, when voluntary obedience on the part of those within their power was withheld, to compel a forced acquiescence by an unsparing use of all the engines of the most stern and rigorous domestic discipline. All these combined, not unnaturally, induced me to resolve upon yielding at once, and without useless opposition, to what appeared almost to be my fate. The appointed time was come, and my now accepted suitor arrived; he was in high spirits, and, if possible, more entertaining than ever. I was not, however, quite in the mood to enjoy his sprightliness; but whatever I wanted in gaiety was amply made up in the triumphant and gracious good humour of my mother, whose smiles of benevolence and exultation were showered around as bountifully as the summer sunshine. I will not weary you with unnecessary prolixity. Let it suffice to say, that I was married to Lord Glenfallen with all the attendant pomp and circumstance of wealth, rank, and grandeur. According to the usage of the times, now humanely reformed, the ceremony was made until long past midnight, the season of wild, uproarious, and promiscuous feasting and revelry. Of all this I have a painfully vivid recollection, and particularly of the little annoyances inflicted upon me by the dull and coarse jokes of the wits and wags who abound in all such places, and upon all such occasions. I was not sorry, when, after a few days, Lord Glenfallen's carriage appeared at the door to convey us both from Ashtown; for any change would have been a relief from the irksomeness of ceremonial and formality which the visits received in honour of my newly acquired titles hourly entailed upon me. It was arranged that we were to proceed to Cahergillagh, one of the Glenfallen estates, lying, however, in a southern county, so that a tedious journey (then owing to the impracticability of the roads,) of three days intervened. I set forth with my noble companion, followed by the regrets of some, and by the envy of many, though God knows I little deserved the latter; the three days of travel were now almost spent, when passing the brow of a wild heathy hill, the domain of Cahergillagh opened suddenly upon our view. It formed a striking and a beautiful scene. A lake of considerable extent stretching away towards the west, and reflecting from its broad, smooth waters, the rich glow of the setting sun, was overhung by steep hills, covered by a rich mantle of velvet sward, broken here and there by the grey front of some old rock, and exhibiting on their shelving sides, their slopes and hollows, every variety of light and shade; a thick wood of dwarf oak, birch, and hazel skirted these hills, and clothed the shores of the lake, running out in rich luxuriance upon every promontory, and spreading upward considerably upon the side of the hills.

"There lies the enchanted castle," said Lord Glenfallen, pointing towards a considerable level space intervening between two of the picturesque hills, which rose dimly around the lake. This little plain was chiefly occupied by the same low, wild wood which covered the other parts of the domain; but towards the centre a mass of taller and statelier forest trees stood darkly grouped together, and among them stood an ancient square tower, with many buildings of an humbler character, forming together the manor-house, or, as it was more usually called, the court of Cahergillagh. As we approached the level upon which the mansion stood, the winding road gave us many glimpses of the time-worn castle and its surrounding buildings; and seen as it was through the long vistas of the fine old trees, and with the rich glow of evening upon it, I have seldom beheld an object more picturesquely striking. I was glad to perceive, too, that here and there the blue curling smoke ascended from stacks of chimneys now hidden by the rich, dark ivy, which, in a great measure, covered the building; other indications of comfort made themselves manifest as we approached; and indeed, though the place was evidently one of considerable antiquity, it had nothing whatever of the gloom of decay about it.

"You must not, my love," said Lord Glenfallen, "imagine this place worse than it is. I have no taste for antiquity, at least I should not choose a house to reside in because it is old. Indeed I do not recollect that I was even so romantic as to overcome my aversion to rats and rheumatism, those faithful attendants upon your noble relics of feudalism; and I much prefer a snug, modern, unmysterious bedroom, with well-aired sheets, to the waving tapestry, mildewed cushions, and all the other interesting appliances of romance; however, though I cannot promise you all the discomfort generally pertaining to an old castle, you will find legends and ghostly lore enough to claim your respect; and if old Martha be still to the fore, as I trust she is, you will soon have a supernatural and appropriate anecdote for every closet and corner of the mansion; but here we are—so, without more ado, welcome to Cahergillagh."

We now entered the hall of the castle, and while the domestics were employed in conveying our trunks and other luggage which we had brought with us for immediate use to the apartments which Lord Glenfallen had selected for himself and me, I went with him into a spacious sitting room, wainscoted with finely polished black oak, and hung round with the portraits of various of the worthies of the Glenfallen family. This room looked out upon an extensive level covered with the softest green sward, and irregularly bounded by the wild wood I have before mentioned, through the leafy arcade formed by whose boughs and trunks the level beams of the setting sun were pouring; in the distance, a group of dairy maids were plying their task, which they accompanied throughout with snatches of Irish songs which, mellowed by the distance, floated not unpleasingly to the ear; and beside them sat or lay, with all the grave importance of conscious protection, six or seven large dogs of various kinds; farther in the distance, and through the cloisters of the arching wood, two or three ragged urchins were employed in driving such stray kine as had wandered farther than the rest to join their fellows. As I looked upon this scene which I have described, a feeling of tranquillity and happiness came upon me, which I have never experienced in so strong a degree; and so strange to me was the sensation that my eyes filled with tears. Lord Glenfallen mistook the cause of my emotion, and taking me kindly and tenderly by the hand he said, "Do not suppose, my love, that it is my intention to *settle* here, whenever you desire to leave this, you have only to let me know your wish and it shall be complied with, so I must entreat of you not to suffer any circumstances which I can controul to give you one moment's uneasiness; but here is old Martha, you must be introduced to her, one of the heirlooms of our family."

A hale, good-humoured, erect, old woman was Martha, and an agreeable contrast to the grim, decrepit hag, which my fancy had conjured up, as the depository of all the horrible tales in which I doubted not this old place was most fruitful. She welcomed me and her master with a profusion of gratulations, alternately kissing our hands and apologising for the liberty, until at length Lord Glenfallen put an end to this somewhat fatiguing ceremonial, by requesting her to conduct me to my chamber if it were prepared for my reception. I followed Martha up an old-fashioned, oak stair-case into a long, dim passage at the end of which lay the door which communicated with the apartments which had been selected for our use; here the old woman stopped, and respectfully requested me to proceed. I accordingly opened the door and was about to enter, when something like a mass of black tapestry as it appeared disturbed by my sudden approach, fell from above the door, so as completely to screen the aperture; the startling unexpectedness of the occurrence, and the rustling noise which the drapery made in its descent, caused me involuntarily to step two or three paces backwards, I turned, smiling and half ashamed to the old servant, and said, "You see what a coward I am." The woman looked puzzled, and without saying any more, I was about to draw aside the curtain and enter the room, when upon turning to do so, I was surprised to find that nothing whatever interposed to obstruct the passage. I went into the room, followed by the servant woman, and was amazed to find that it, like the one below, was wainscoted, and that nothing like drapery was to be found near the door.

"Where is it," said I; "what has become of it?"

"What does your ladyship wish to know?" said the old woman.

"Where is the black curtain that fell across the door, when I attempted first to come to my chamber," answered I.

"The cross of Christ about us," said the old woman, turning suddenly pale.

"What is the matter, my good friend," said I; "you seem frightened."

"Oh, no, no, your ladyship," said the old woman, endeavouring to conceal her agitation; but in vain, for tottering towards a chair, she sunk into it, looking so deadly pale and horror-struck that I thought every moment she would faint.

"Merciful God, keep us from harm and danger," muttered she at length.

"What can have terrified you so," said I, beginning to fear that she had seen something more than had met my eye, "you appear ill, my poor woman."

"Nothing, nothing, my lady," said she, rising; "I beg your ladyship's pardon for making so bold; may the great God defend us from misfortune."

"Martha," said I, "something *has* frightened you very much, and I insist on knowing what it is; your keeping me in the dark upon the subject will make me much more uneasy than any thing you could tell me; I desire you, therefore, to let me know what agitates you; I command you to tell me."

"Your ladyship said you saw a black curtain falling across the door when you were coming into the room," said the old woman.

"I did," said I; "but though the whole thing appears somewhat strange I cannot see any thing in the matter to agitate you so excessively.

"It's for no good you saw that, my lady," said the crone; "something terrible is coming; it's a sign, my lady—a sign that never fails."

"Explain, explain what you mean, my good woman," said I, in spite of myself, catching more than I could account for, of her superstitious terror.

"Whenever something—something *bad* is going to happen to the Glenfallen family, some one that belongs to them sees a black handkerchief or curtain just waved or falling before their faces; I saw it myself," continued she, lowering her voice, "when I was only a little girl, and I'll never forget it; I often heard of it before, though I never saw it till then, nor since, praised be God; but I was going into Lady Jane's room to waken her in the morning; and sure enough when I got first to the bed and began to draw the curtain, something dark was waved across the division, but only for a moment; and when I saw rightly into the bed, there was she lying cold and dead, God be merciful to me; so, my lady, there is small blame to me to be daunted when any one of the family sees it, for it's many's the story I heard of it, though I saw it but once."

I was not of a superstitious turn of mind; yet I could not resist a feeling of awe very nearly allied to the fear which my companion had so unreservedly expressed; and when you consider my situation, the loneliness, antiquity, and gloom of the place, you will allow that the weakness was not without excuse. In spite of old Martha's boding predictions, however, time flowed on in an unruffled course; one little incident, however, though trifling in itself, I must relate as it serves to make what follows more intelligible. Upon the day after my arrival, Lord Glenfallen of course desired to make me acquainted with the house and domain; and accordingly we set forth upon our ramble; when returning, he became for some time silent and moody, a state so unusual with him as considerably to excite my surprise, I endeavoured by observations and questions to arouse him—but in vain; at length as we approached the house, he said, as if speaking to himself, " 'twere madness—madness—madness," repeating the word bitterly—"sure and speedy ruin." There was here a long pause; and at length turning sharply towards me in a tone very unlike that in which he had hitherto addressed me, he said, "Do you think it possible that a woman can keep a secret?"

"I am sure," said I, "that women are very much belied upon the score of talkativeness, and that I may answer your question with the same directness with which you put it; I reply that I *do* think a woman can keep a secret."

"But I do not," said he, drily.

We walked on in silence for a time; I was much astonished at his unwonted abruptness; I had almost said rudeness. After a considerable pause he seemed to recollect himself, and with an effort resuming his sprightly manner, he said, "well, well, the next thing to keeping a secret well is, not to desire to possess one—talkativeness and curiosity generally go together; now I shall make test of you in the first place, respecting the latter of these qualities. I shall be your *Bluebeard*—tush, why do I trifle thus; listen to me, my dear Fanny, I speak now in solemn earnest; what I desire is, intimately, inseparably, connected with your happiness and honour as well as my own; and your compliance with my request will not be difficult; it will impose upon you a very trifling restraint during your sojourn here, which certain events which have occurred since our arrival, have determined me shall not be a long one. You must promise me, upon your sacred honour, that you will visit *only* that part of the castle which can be reached from the front entrance, leaving the back entrance and the part of the building commanded immediately by it, to the menials, as also the small garden whose high wall you see yonder; and never at any time seek to pry or peep into them, nor to open the door which communicates from the front part of the house through the corridor with the back. I do not urge this in jest or in caprice, but from a solemn conviction that danger and misery will be the certain consequences of your not observing what I prescribe. I cannot explain myself further at present—promise me, then, these things as you hope for peace here and for mercy hereafter."

I did make the promise as desired, and he appeared relieved; his manner recovered all its gaiety and elasticity, but the recollection of the strange scene which I have just described dwelt painfully upon my mind. More than a month passed away without any occurrence worth recording; but I was not destined to leave Cahergillagh without further adventure; one day intending to enjoy the pleasant sunshine in a ramble through the woods, I ran up to my room to procure my bonnet and shawl; upon entering the chamber, I was surprised and somewhat startled to find it occupied; beside the fireplace and nearly opposite the door, seated in a large, old-fashioned elbow-chair, was placed the figure of a lady; she appeared to be nearer fifty than forty, and was dressed suitably to her age, in a handsome suit of flowered silk; she had a profusion of trinkets and jewellery about her person, and many rings upon her fingers; but although very rich, her dress was not gaudy or in ill taste; but what was remarkable in the lady was, that although her features were handsome, and upon the whole pleasing, the pupil of each eye was dimmed with the whiteness of cataract, and she was evidently stone blind. I was for some seconds so surprised at this unaccountable apparition, that I could not find words to address her.

"Madam," said I, "there must be some mistake here—this is my bed-chamber."

"Marry come up," said the lady, sharply; "*your* chamber! Where is Lord Glenfallen?"

"He is below, madam," replied I; "and I am convinced he will be not a little surprised to find you here."

"I do not think he will," said she; "with your good leave, talk of what you know something about; tell him I want him; why does the minx dilly dally so?"

In spite of the awe which this grim lady inspired, there was something in her air of confident superiority which, when I considered our relative situations, was not a little irritating.

"Do you know, madam, to whom you speak?" said I.

"I neither know nor care," said she; "but I presume that you are some one about the house, so, again, I desire you, if you wish to continue here, to bring your master hither forthwith."

"I must tell you madam," said I, "that I am Lady Glenfallen."

"What's that?" said the stranger, rapidly.

"I say, madam," I repeated, approaching her, that I might be more distinctly heard, "that I am Lady Glenfallen."

"It's a lie, you trull," cried she, in an accent which made me start, and, at the same time, springing forward, she seized me in her grasp and shook me violently, repeating, "it's a lie, it's a lie," with a rapidity and vehemence which swelled every vein of her face; the violence of her action, and the fury which convulsed her face, effectually terrified me, and disengaging myself from her grasp, I screamed as loud as I could for help; the blind woman continued to pour out a torrent of abuse upon me, foaming at the mouth with rage, and impotently shaking her clenched fists towards me. I heard Lord Glenfallen's step upon the stairs, and I instantly ran out; as I past him I perceived that he was deadly pale, and just caught the words, "I hope that demon has not hurt you?" I made some answer, I forget what, and he entered the chamber, the door of which he locked upon the inside; what passed within I know not; but I heard the voices of the two speakers raised in loud and angry altercation. I thought I heard the shrill accents of the woman repeat the words, "let her look to herself"; but I could not be quite sure. This short sentence, however, was, to my alarmed imagination, pregnant with fearful meaning; the storm at length subsided, though not until after a conference of more than two long hours. Lord Glenfallen then returned, pale and agitated, "That unfortunate woman," said he, "is out of her mind; I dare say she treated you to some of her ravings, but you need not dread any further interruption from her, I have brought her so far to reason. She did not hurt you, I trust."

"No, no," said I; "but she terrified me beyond measure." "Well," said he, "she is likely to behave better for the future, and I dare swear that neither you nor she would desire after what has passed to meet again."

This occurrence, so startling and unpleasant, so involved in mystery, and giving rise to so many painful surmises, afforded me no very agreeable food for rumination. All attempts on my part to arrive at the truth were baffled; Lord Glenfallen evaded all my enquiries, and at length peremptorily forbid any further allusion .to the matter. I was thus obliged to rest satisfied with what I had actually seen, and to trust to time to resolve the perplexities in which the whole transaction had involved me. Lord Glenfallen's temper and spirits gradually underwent a complete and most painful change; he became silent and abstracted, his manner to me was abrupt and often harsh, some grievous anxiety seemed ever present to his mind; and under its influence his spirits sunk and his temper became soured. I soon perceived that his gaiety was rather that which the stir and excitement of society produces, than the result of a healthy habit of mind; and every day confirmed me in the opinion, that the considerate good nature which I had so much admired in him was little more than a mere manner; and to my infinite grief and surprise, the gay, kind, open-hearted nobleman who had for months followed and flattered me, was rapidly assuming the form of a gloomy, morose, and singularly selfish man; this was a bitter discovery, and I strove to conceal it from myself as long as I could, but the truth was not to be denied, and I was forced to believe that Lord Glenfallen no longer loved me, and that he was at little pains to conceal the alteration in his sentiments. One morning after breakfast, Lord Glenfallen had been for some time walking silently up and down the room, buried in his moody reflections, when pausing suddenly, and turning towards me, he exclaimed,

"I have it, I have it; we must go abroad and stay there, too, and if that does not answer, why—why we must try some more effectual expedient. Lady Glenfallen, I have become involved in heavy embarrassments; a wife you know must share the fortunes of her husband, for better for worse, but I will waive my right if you prefer remaining here —here at Cahergillagh; for I would not have you seen elsewhere without the state to which your rank entitled you; besides it would break your poor mother's heart," he added, with sneering gravity, "so make up your mind—Cahergillagh or France, I will start if possible in a week, so determine between this and then."

He left the room and in a few moments I saw him ride past the window, followed by a mounted servant; he had directed a domestic to inform me that he should not be back until the next day. I was in very great doubt as to what course of conduct I should pursue, as to accompanying him in the continental tour so suddenly determined upon, I felt that it would be a hazard too great to encounter; for at Cahergillagh I had always the consciousness to sustain me, that if his temper at any time led him into violent or unwarrantable treatment of me, I had a remedy within reach, in the protection and support of my own family, from all useful and effective communication with whom, if once in France, I should be entirely debarred. As to remaining at Cahergillagh in solitude, and for aught I knew, exposed to hidden dangers, it appeared to me scarcely less objectionable than the former proposition; and yet I feared that with one or other I must comply, unless I was prepared to come to an actual breach with Lord Glenfallen; full of these unpleasing doubts and perplexities, I retired to rest. I was wakened, after having slept uneasily for some hours, by some person shaking me rudely by the shoulder; a small lamp burned in my room, and by its light, to my horror and amazement, I discovered that my visitant was the self-same blind, old lady who had so terrified me a few weeks before. I started up in the bed, with a view to ring the bell, and alarm the domestics, but she instantly anticipated me by saying, "Do not be frightened, silly girl; if I had wished to harm you I could have done it while you were sleeping, I need not have wakened you; listen to me, now, attentively and fearlessly; for what I have to say, interests you to the full as much as it does me; tell me, here, in the presence of God, did Lord Glenfallen marry you, *actually marry* you?—speak the truth, woman."

"As surely as I live and speak," I replied, "did Lord Glenfallen marry me in presence of more than a hundred witnesses."

"Well," continued she, "he should have told you *then*, before you married him, that he had a wife living, which wife I am; I feel you tremble—tush! do not be frightened. I do not mean to harm you—mark me now—you are *not* his wife. When I make my story known you will be so, neither in the eye of God nor of man; you must leave this house upon to-morrow; let the world know that your husband has another wife living; go, you, into retirement, and leave him to justice, which will surely overtake him. If you remain in this house after to-morrow you will reap the bitter fruits of your sin," so saying, she quitted the room, leaving me very little disposed to sleep.

Here was food for my very worst and most terrible suspicions; still there was not enough to remove all doubt. I had no proof of the truth of this woman's statement. Taken by itself there was nothing to induce me to attach weight to it; but when I viewed it in connection with the extraordinary mystery of some of Lord Glenfallen's proceedings, his strange anxiety to exclude me from certain portions of the mansion, doubtless, lest I should encounter this person—the strong influence, nay, command, which she possessed over him, a circumstance clearly established by the very fact of her residing in the very place, where of all others, he should least have desired to find her—her thus acting, and continuing to act in direct contradiction to his wishes; when, I say, I viewed her disclosure in connection with all these circumstances, I could not help feeling that there was at least a fearful veri-similitude in the allegations which she had made. Still I was not satisfied, nor nearly so; young minds have a reluctance almost insurmountable to believing upon any thing short of unquestionable proof, the existence of premeditated guilt in any one whom they have ever trusted; and in support of this feeling I was assured that if the assertion of Lord Glenfallen, which nothing in this woman's manner had led me to disbelieve, were true, namely, that her mind was unsound, the whole fabric of my doubts and fears must fall to the ground. I determined to state to Lord Glenfallen freely and accurately the substance of the communication which I had just heard, and in his words and looks to seek for its proof or refutation;

full of these thoughts I remained wakeful and excited all night, every moment fancying that I heard the step, or saw the figure of my recent visitor towards whom I felt a species of horror and dread which I can hardly describe. There was something in her face, though her features had evidently been handsome, and were not, at first sight, unpleasing, which, upon a nearer inspection, seemed to indicate the habitual prevalence and indulgence of evil passions, and a power of expressing mere animal anger, with an intenseness that I have seldom seen equalled, and to which an almost unearthly effect was given by the convulsive quivering of the sightless eyes. You may easily suppose that it was no very pleasing reflection to me to consider, that whenever caprice might induce her to return, I was within the reach of this violent, and, for aught I knew, insane woman, who had, upon that very night, spoken to me in a tone of menace, of which her mere words, divested of the manner and look with which she uttered them, can convey but a faint idea. Will you believe me when I tell you that I was actually afraid to leave my bed in order to secure the door, lest I should again encounter the dreadful object lurking in some corner or peeping from behind the window curtains, so very a child was I in my fears.

The morning came, and with it Lord Glenfallen. I knew not, and indeed I cared not, where he might have been; my thoughts were·wholly engrossed by the terrible fears and suspicions which my last night's conference had suggested to me; he was, as usual, gloomy and abstracted, and I feared in no very fitting mood to hear what I had to say with patience, whether the charges were true or false. I was, however, determined not to suffer the opportunity to pass, or Lord Glenfallen to leave the room, until, at all hazards, I had unburdened my mind.

"My Lord," said I, after a long silence, summoning up all my firmness, "my lord, I wish to say a few words to you upon a matter of very great importance, of very deep concernment to you and to me." I fixed my eyes upon him to discern, if possible, whether the announcement caused him any uneasiness, but no symptom of any such feeling was perceptible.

"Well, my dear," said he, "this is, no doubt, a very grave preface, and portends, I have no doubt, something extraordinary—pray let us have it without more ado."

He took a chair, and seated himself nearly opposite to me.

"My lord," said I, "I have seen the person who alarmed me so much a short time since, the blind lady, again, upon last night"; his face, upon which my eyes were fixed, turned pale, he hesitated for a moment, and then said—

"And did you, pray madam, so totally forget or spurn my express command, as to enter that portion of the house from which your promise, I might say, your oath, excluded you—answer me that?" he added, fiercely.

"My lord," said I, "I have neither forgotten your *commands*, since such they were, nor disobeyed them. I was, last night, wakened from my sleep, as I lay in my own chamber, and accosted by the person whom I have mentioned—how she found access to the room I cannot pretend to say."

"Ha! this must be looked to," said he, half reflectively; "and pray," added he, quickly, while in turn he fixed his eyes upon me, "what did this person say, since some comment upon her communication forms, no doubt, the sequel to your preface."

"Your lordship is not mistaken," said I, "her statement was so extraordinary that I could not think of withholding it from you; she told me, my lord, that you had a wife living at the time you married me, and that she was that wife."

Lord Glenfallen became ashy pale, almost livid; he made two or three efforts to clear his voice to speak, but in vain, and turning suddenly from me, he walked to the window; the horror and dismay, which, in the olden time, overwhelmed the woman of Endor, when her spells unexpectedly conjured the dead into her presence, were but types of what I felt, when thus presented with what appeared to be almost unequivocal evidence of the guilt, whose existence I had before so strongly doubted. There was a silence of some moments, during which it were hard to conjecture whether I or my companion suffered most. Lord Glenfallen soon recovered his self command; he returned to the table, again sat down and said—

"What you have told me has so astonished me, has unfolded such a tissue of motiveless guilt, and in a quarter from which I had so little reason to look for ingratitude or treachery, that your announcement almost deprived me of speech; the person in question, however, has one excuse, her mind is, as I told you before, unsettled. You should have remembered that, and hesitated to receive as unexceptionable evidence against the honour of your husband, the ravings of a lunatic. I now tell you that this is the last time I shall speak to you upon this subject, and, in the presence of the God who is to judge me, and as I hope for mercy in the day of judgment, I swear that the charge thus brought against me, is utterly false, unfounded, and ridiculous; I defy the world in any point to taint my honour; and, as I have never taken the opinion of madmen touching your character or morals, I think it but fair to require that you will evince a like tenderness for me; and now, once for all, never again dare to repeat to me your insulting suspicions, or the clumsy and infamous calumnies of fools. I shall instantly let the worthy lady who contrived this somewhat original device, understand fully my opinion upon the matter—good morning"; and with these words he left me again in doubt, and involved in all horrors of the most agonizing suspense. I had reason to think that Lord Glenfallen wreaked his vengeance upon the author of the strange story which I had heard, with a violence which was not satisfied with mere words, for old Martha, with whom I was a great favourite, while attending me in my room, told me that she feared her master had ill used the poor, blind, Dutch woman, for that she had heard her scream as if the very life were leaving her, but added a request that I should not speak of what she had told me to any one, particularly to the master.

"How do you know that she is a Dutch woman?" inquired I, anxious to learn anything whatever that might throw a light upon the history of this person, who seemed to have resolved to mix herself up in my fortunes.

"Why, my lady," answered Martha, "the master often calls her the Dutch hag, and other names you would not like to hear, and I am sure she is neither English nor Irish; for, whenever they talk together, they speak some queer foreign lingo, and fast enough, I'll be bound; but I ought not to talk about her at all; it might be as much as my place is worth to mention her—only you saw her first yourself, so there can be no great harm in speaking of her now."

"How long has this lady been here?" continued I.

"She came early on the morning after your ladyship's arrival," answered she; "but do not ask me any more, for the master would think nothing of turning me out of doors for daring to speak of her at all, much less to *you*, my lady."

I did not like to press the poor woman further; for her reluctance to speak on this topic was evident and strong. You will readily believe that upon the very slight grounds which my information afforded, contradicted as it was by the solemn oath of my husband, and derived from what was, at best, a very questionable source, I could not take any very decisive measure whatever; and as to the menace of the strange woman who had thus unaccountably twice intruded herself into my chamber, although, at the moment, it occasioned me some uneasiness, it was not, even in my eyes, sufficiently formidable to induce my departure from Cahergillagh.

A few nights after the scene which I have just mentioned, Lord Glenfallen having, as usual, early retired to his study, I was left alone in the parlour to amuse myself as best I might. It was not strange that my thoughts should often recur to the agitating scenes in which I had recently taken a part; the subject of my reflections, the solitude, the silence, and the lateness of the hour, as also the depression of spirits to which I had of late been a constant prey, tended to produce that nervous excitement which places us wholly at the mercy of the imagination. In order to calm my spirits, I was endeavouring to direct my thoughts into some more pleasing channel, when I heard, or thought I heard, uttered, within a few yards of me, in an odd half-sneering tone, the words, "There is blood upon your ladyship's throat." So vivid was the impression, that I started to my feet, and involuntarily placed my hand upon my neck. I looked around the room for the speaker, but in vain. I went then to the room-door, which I opened, and peered into the passage, nearly faint with horror, lest some leering, shapeless thing should greet me upon the threshold. When I had gazed long enough to assure myself that no strange object was within sight.

"I have been too much of a rake, lately; I am racking out my nerves," said I, speaking aloud, with a view to re-assure myself. I rang the bell, and, attended by old Martha, I retired to settle for the night. While the servant was, as was her custom, arranging the lamp which I have

already stated always burned during the night in my chamber, I was
employed in undressing, and, in doing so, I had recourse to a large
looking-glass which occupied a considerable portion of the wall in
which it was fixed, rising from the ground to a height of about six feet;
this mirror filled the space of a large pannel in the wainscoting opposite
the foot of the bed. I had hardly been before it for the lapse of a minute,
when something like a black pall was slowly waved between me and it.

"Oh, God! there it is," I exclaimed wildly. "I have seen it again,
Martha—the black cloth."

"God be merciful to us, then!" answered she, tremulously crossing
herself. "Some misfortune is over us."

"No, no, Martha," said I, almost instantly recovering my collectedness; for, although of a nervous temperament, I had never been
superstitious. "I do not believe in omens. You know, I saw, or fancied I
saw, this thing before, and nothing followed."

"The Dutch lady came the next morning," replied she.

"Methinks, such an occurrence scarcely deserved a supernatural announcement," I replied.

"She is a strange woman, my lady," said Martha, "and she is not
gone yet—mark my words."

"Well, well, Martha," said I, "I have not wit enough to change your
opinions, nor inclination to alter mine; so I will talk no more of the
matter. Good night," and so I was left to my reflections. After lying for
about an hour awake, I at length fell into a kind of doze; but my imagination was still busy, for I was startled from this unrefreshing sleep
by fancying that I heard a voice close to my face exclaim as before,
"There is blood upon your ladyship's throat." The words were instantly followed by a loud burst of laughter. Quaking with horror, I awakened, and heard my husband enter the room. Even this was a relief.
Scared as I was, however, by the tricks which my imagination had
played me, I preferred remaining silent, and pretending to sleep, to
attempting to engage my husband in conversation, for I well knew that
his mood was such, that his words would not, in all probability, convey
anything that had not better be unsaid and unheard. Lord Glenfallen
went into his dressing-room, which lay upon the right-hand side of the
bed. The door lying open, I could see him by himself, at full length
upon a sofa, and, in about half an hour, I became aware, by his deep
and regularly drawn respiration, that he was fast asleep. When slumber
refuses to visit one, there is something peculiarly irritating, not to the
temper, but to the nerves, in the consciousness that some one is in your
immediate presence, actually enjoying the boon which you are seeking
in vain; at least, I have always found it so, and never more than upon
the present occasion. A thousand annoying imaginations harassed and
excited me, every object which I looked upon, though ever so familiar,
seemed to have acquired a strange phantom-like character, the varying
shadows thrown by the flickering of the lamp-light, seemed shaping
themselves into grotesque and unearthly forms, and whenever my eyes

wandered to the sleeping figure of my husband, his features appeared to undergo the strangest and most demoniacal contortions. Hour after hour was told by the old clock, and each succeeding one found me, if possible, less inclined to sleep than its predecessor. It was now considerably past three; my eyes, in their involuntary wanderings, happened to alight upon the large mirror which was, as I have said, fixed in the wall opposite the foot of the bed. A view of it was commanded from where I lay, through the curtains, as I gazed fixedly upon it, I thought I perceived the broad sheet of glass shifting its position in relation to the bed; I rivetted my eyes upon it with intense scrutiny; it was no deception, the mirror, as if acting of its own impulse moved slowly aside, and disclosed a dark aperture in the wall, nearly as large as an ordinary door; a figure evidently stood in this; but the light was too dim to define it accurately. It stepped cautiously into the chamber, and with so little noise, that had I not actually seen it, I do not think I should have been aware of its presence. It was arrayed in a kind of woollen night-dress, and a white handkerchief or cloth was bound tightly about the head; I had no difficulty spite of the strangeness of the attire in recognising the blind woman whom I so much dreaded. She stooped down, bringing her head nearly to the ground, and in that attitude she remained motionless for some moments, no doubt in order to ascertain if any suspicious sound were stirring. She was apparently satisfied by her observations, for she immediately recommenced her silent progress towards a ponderous mahogany dressing table of my husband's; when she had reached it, she paused again, and appeared to listen attentively for some minutes; she then noiselessly opened one of the drawers from which, having groped for some time, she took something which I soon perceived to be a case of razors; she opened it and tried the edge of each of the two instruments upon the skin of her hand; she quickly selected one, which she fixed firmly in her grasp; she now stooped down as.before, and having listened for a time, she, with the hand that was disengaged, groped her way into the dressing room where Lord Glenfallen lay fast asleep. I was fixed as if in the tremendous spell of a night mare. I could not stir even a finger; I could not lift my voice; I could not even breathe, and though I expected every moment to see the sleeping man murdered, I could not even close my eyes to shut out the horrible spectacle, which I had not the power to avert. I saw the woman approach the sleeping figure, she laid the unoccupied hand lightly along his clothes, and having thus ascertained his identity, she, after a brief interval, turned back and again entered my chamber; here she bent down again to listen. I had now not a doubt but that the razor was intended for my throat; yet the terrific fascination which had locked all my powers so long, still continued to bind me fast. I felt that my life depended upon the slightest ordinary exertion, and yet I could not stir one joint from the position in which I lay, nor even make noise enough to waken Lord Glenfallen. The murderous woman now, with long, silent steps, approached the bed; my very heart seemed turning to ice; her left hand, that which was disengaged, was upon the pillow; she gradually slid it forward towards my head, and in an instant, with the speed of lightning, it was clutched in my hair, while, with the other hand, she dashed the razor at my throat. A slight inaccuracy saved me from instant death; the blow fell short, the point of the razor grazing my throat; in a moment I know not how, I found myself at the other side of the bed uttering shriek after shriek; the wretch was, however, determined if possible to murder me; scrambling along by the curtains, she rushed round the bed towards me; I seized the handle of the door to make my escape; it was, however, fastened; at all events I could not open it, from the mere instinct of recoiling terror, I shrunk back into a corner—she was now within a yard of me—her hand was upon my face —I closed my eyes fast, expecting never to open them again, when a blow, inflicted from behind by a strong arm, stretched the monster senseless at my feet; at the same moment the door opened, and several domestics, alarmed by my cries, entered the apartment. I do not recollect what followed, for I fainted. One swoon succeeded another so long and death-like, that my life was considered very doubtful. At about ten o'clock, however, I sunk into a deep and refreshing sleep, from which I was awakened at about two, that I might swear my deposition before a magistrate, who attended for that purpose. I, accordingly, did so, as did also Lord Glenfallen; and the woman was fully committed to stand her trial at the ensuing assizes. I shall never forget the scene which the examination of the blind woman and of the other parties afforded. She was brought into the room in the custody of two servants; she wore a kind of flannel wrapper which had not been changed since the night before; it was torn and soiled, and here and there smeared with blood, which had flowed in large quantities from a wound in her head; the white handkerchief had fallen off in the scuffle; and her grizzled hair fell in masses about her wild and deadly pale countenance. She appeared perfectly composed, however, and the only regret she expressed throughout, was at not having succeeded in her attempt, the object of which she did not pretend to conceal. On being asked her name, she called herself the Countess Glenfallen, and refused to give any other title.

"The woman's name is Flora Van-Kemp," said Lord Glenfallen.

"It *was*, it *was*, you perjured traitor and cheat," screamed the woman; and then there followed a volley of words in some foreign language. "Is there a magistrate here?" she resumed; "I am Lord Glenfallen's wife—I'll prove it—write down my words. I am willing to be hanged or burned, so *he* meets his deserts. I did try to kill that doll of his; but it was he who put it into my head to do it—two wives were too many—I was to murder her, or she was to hang me—listen to all I have to say."

Here Lord Glenfallen interrupted.

"I think, sir," said he, addressing the magistrate, "that we had better proceed to business, this unhappy woman's furious recriminations but waste our time; if she refuses to answer your questions, you had better, I presume, take my depositions."

"And are you going to swear away my life, you black perjured murderer?" shrieked the woman. "Sir, sir, sir, you must hear me," she continued, addressing the magistrate, "I can convict him—he bid me murder that girl, and then when I failed, he came behind me, and struck me down, and now he wants to swear away my life—take down all I say."

"If it is your intention," said the magistrate, "to confess the crime with which you stand charged, you may, upon producing sufficient evidence, criminate whom you please."

"Evidence!—I have no evidence but myself," said the woman. "I will swear it all—write down my testimony—write it down, I say—we shall hang side by side, my brave Lord—all your own handy-work, my gentle husband." This was followed by a low, insolent, and sneering laugh, which, from one in her situation, was sufficiently horrible.

"I will not at present hear anything," replied he, "but distinct answers to the questions which I shall put to you upon this matter."

"Then you shall hear nothing," replied she sullenly, and no inducement or intimidation could bring her to speak again.

Lord Glenfallen's deposition and mine were then given, as also those of the servants who had entered the room at the moment of my rescue; the magistrate then intimated that she was committed, and must proceed directly to gaol, whither she was brought in a carriage of Lord Glenfallen's, for his lordship was naturally by no means indifferent to the effect which her vehement accusations against himself might produce, if uttered before every chance hearer whom she might meet with between Cahergillagh and the place of confinement whither she was dispatched.

During the time which intervened between the committal and the trial of the prisoner, Lord Glenfallen seemed to suffer agonies of mind which baffle all description, he hardly ever slept, and when he did, his slumbers seemed but the instruments of new tortures, and his waking hours were, if possible, exceeded in intensity of terrors by the dreams which disturbed his sleep. Lord Glenfallen rested, if to lie in the mere attitude of repose were to do so, in his dressing-room, and thus I had an opportunity of witnessing, far oftener than I wished it, the fearful workings of his mind; his agony often broke out into such fearful paroxysms that delirium and total loss of reason appeared to be impending; he frequently spoke of flying from the country, and bringing with him all the witnesses of the appalling scene upon which the prosecution was founded; then again he would fiercely lament that the blow which he had inflicted had not ended all.

The assizes arrived, however, and upon the day appointed, Lord Glenfallen and I attended in order to give our evidence. The cause was called on, and the prisoner appeared at the bar. Great curiosity and interest were felt respecting the trial, so that the court was crowded to excess. The prisoner, however, without appearing to take the trouble of listening to the indictment, pleaded guilty, and no representations on the part of the court availed to induce her to retract her plea. After much time had been wasted in a fruitless attempt to prevail upon her to reconsider her words, the court proceeded according to the usual form, to pass sentence. This having been done, the prisoner was about to be removed, when she said in a low, distinct voice.—

"A word—a word, my Lord:—is Lord Glenfallen here in the court?" On being told that he was, she raised her voice to a tone of loud menace, and continued—

"Hardress, Earl of Glenfallen, I accuse you here in this court of justice of two crimes—first, that you married a second wife, while the first was living, and again, that you prompted me to the murder, for attempting which I am to die—secure him—chain him—bring him here."

There was a laugh through the court at these words, which were naturally treated by the judge as a violent extemporary recrimination, and the woman was desired to be silent.

"You won't take him, then," she said, "you won't try him? You'll let him go free?"

It was intimated by the court that he would certainly be allowed "to go free," and she was ordered again to be removed. Before, however, the mandate was executed, she threw her arms wildly into the air, and uttered one piercing shriek so full of preternatural rage and despair, that it might fitly have ushered a soul into those realms where hope can come no more. The sound still rang in my ears, months after the voice that had uttered it was for ever silent. The wretched woman was executed in accordance with the sentence which had been pronounced.

For some time after this event, Lord Glenfallen appeared, if possible, to suffer more than he had done before, and altogether, his language, which often amounted to half confessions of the guilt imputed to him, and all the circumstances connected with the late occurrences, formed a mass of evidence so convincing that I wrote to my father, detailing the grounds of my fears, and imploring him to come to Cahergillagh without delay, in order to remove me from my husband's control, previously to taking legal steps for a final separation. Circumstanced as I was, my existence was little short of intolerable, for, besides the fearful suspicions which attached to my husband, I plainly perceived that if Lord Glenfallen were not relieved, and that speedily, insanity must supervene. I therefore expected my father's arrival, or at least a letter to announce it, with indescribable impatience.

About a week after the execution had taken place, Lord Glenfallen one morning met me with an unusually sprightly air—

"Fanny," said he, "I have it now for the first time, in my power to explain to your satisfaction every thing which has hitherto appeared suspicious or mysterious in my conduct. After breakfast come with me to my study, and I shall, I hope, make all things clear."

This invitation afforded me more real pleasure than I had experienced for months; something had certainly occurred to tranquillize my husband's mind, in no ordinary degree, and I thought it by no means impossible that he would, in the proposed interview, prove himself the most injured and innocent of men. Full of this hope I repaired to his study at the appointed hour; he was writing busily when I entered the room, and just raising his eyes, he requested me to be seated. I took a chair as he desired, and remained silently awaiting his leisure, while he finished, folded, directed, and sealed his letter; laying it then upon the table, with the address downward, he said—

"My dearest Fanny, I know I must have appeared very strange to you and very unkind—often even cruel; before the end of this week I will show you the necessity of my conduct; how impossible it was that I should have seemed otherwise. I am conscious that many acts of mine must have inevitably given rise to painful suspicions—suspicions, which indeed, upon one occasion you very properly communicated to me. I have gotten two letters from a quarter which commands respect, containing information as to the course by which I may be enabled to prove the negative of all the crimes which even the most credulous suspicion could lay to my charge. I expected a third by this morning's post, containing documents which will set the matter for ever at rest, but owing, no doubt, to some neglect, or, perhaps, to some difficulty in collecting the papers, some inevitable delay, it has not come to hand this morning, according to my expectation. I was finishing one to the very same quarter when you came in, and if a sound rousing be worth anything, I think I shall have a special messenger before two days have passed. I have been thinking over the matter within myself, whether I had better imperfectly clear up your doubts by submitting to your inspection the two letters which I have already received, or wait till I can triumphantly vindicate myself by the production of the documents which I have already mentioned, and I have, I think, not unnaturally decided upon the latter course; however, there is a person in the next room, whose testimony is not without its value—excuse me for one moment."

So saying, he arose and went to the door of a closet which opened from the study, this he unlocked, and half opening the door, he said, "It is only I," and then slipped into the room, and carefully closed and locked the door behind him. I immediately heard his voice in animated conversation; my curiosity upon the subject of the letter was naturally great, so smothering any little scruples which I might have felt, I resolved to look at the address of the letter which lay as my husband had left it, with its face upon the table. I accordingly drew it over to me, and turned up the direction. For two or three moments I could scarce believe my eyes, but there could be no mistake—in large characters were traced the words, "To the Archangel Gabriel in heaven." I had scarcely returned the letter to its original position, and in some degree recovered the shock which this unequivocal proof of insanity produced, when the closet door was unlocked, and Lord Glenfallen re-entered the study, carefully closing and locking the door again upon the outside.

"Whom have you there?" inquired I, making a strong effort to appear calm.

"Perhaps," said he musingly, "you might have some objection to seeing her, at least for a time."

"Who is it?" repeated I.

"Why," said he, "I see no use in hiding it—the blind Dutchwoman; I have been with her the whole morning. She is very anxious to get out of that closet, but you know she is odd, she is scarcely to be trusted."

A heavy gust of wind shook the door at this moment with a sound as if something more substantial were pushing against it.

"Ha, ha, ha!—do you hear her," said he, with an obstreperous burst of laughter. The wind died away in a long howl, and Lord Glenfallen, suddenly checking his merriment, shrugged his shoulders, and muttered—

"Poor devil, she has been hardly used."

"We had better not tease her at present with questions," said I, in as unconcerned a tone as I could assume, although I felt every moment as if I should faint.

"Humph! may be so," said he, "well, come back in an hour or two, or when you please, and you will find us here."

He again unlocked the door, and entered with the same precautions which he had adopted before, locking the door upon the inside, and as I hurried from the room, I heard his voice again exerted as if in eager parley. I can hardly describe my emotions; my hopes had been raised to the highest, and now in an instant, all was gone—the dreadful consummation was accomplished—the fearful retribution had fallen upon the guilty man—the mind was destroyed—the power to repent was gone. The agony of the hours which followed what I would still call my *awful* interview with Lord Glenfallen, I cannot describe; my solitude was, however, broken in upon by Martha, who came to inform me of the arrival of a gentleman, who expected me in the parlour. I accordingly descended, and to my great joy, found my father seated by the fire. This expedition, upon his part, was easily accounted for: my communications had touched the honour of the family. I speedily informed him of the dreadful malady which had fallen upon the wretched man. My father suggested the necessity of placing some person to watch him, to prevent his injuring himself or others. I rang the bell, and desired that one Edward Cooke, an attached servant of the family, should be sent to me. I told him distinctly and briefly, the nature of the service required of him, and, attended by him, my father and I proceeded at once to the study; the door of the inner room was still closed, and everything in the outer chamber remained in the same order in which I had left it. We then advanced to the closet door, at which we knocked, but without receiving any answer. We next tried to open the door, but in vain—it was locked upon the inside; we knocked more loudly, but in vain. Seriously alarmed, I desired the servant to force the door, which was, after several violent efforts, accomplished, and we entered the closet. Lord Glenfallen was lying on his face upon a sofa.

"Hush," said I, "he is asleep"; we paused for a moment.

"He is too still for that," said my father; we all of us felt a strong reluctance to approach the figure.

"Edward," said I, "try whether your master sleeps."

The servant approached the sofa where Lord Glenfallen lay; he leant his ear towards the head of the recumbent figure, to ascertain whether the sound of breathing was audible; he turned towards us, and said—

"My lady, you had better not wait here, I am sure he is dead!"

"Let me see the face," said I, terribly agitated, "you *may* be mistaken."

The man then, in obedience to my command, turned the body round, and, gracious God! what a sight met my view—he was, indeed, perfectly dead. The whole breast of the shirt, with its lace frill, was drenched with gore, as was the couch underneath the spot where he lay. The head hung back, as it seemed almost severed from the body by a frightful gash, which yawned across the throat. The instrument which had inflicted it, was found under his body. All, then, was over; I was never to learn the history in whose termination I had been so deeply and so tragically involved.

The severe discipline which my mind had undergone was not bestowed in vain. I directed my thoughts and my hopes to that place where there is no more sin, nor danger, nor sorrow.

Thus ends a brief tale, whose prominent incidents many will recognize as having marked the history of a distinguished family, and though it refers to a somewhat distant date, we shall be found not to have taken, upon that account, any liberties with the facts, but in our statement of all the incidents, to have rigorously and faithfully adhered to the truth.

THE MURDERED COUSIN

"And they lay wait for their own blood: they lurk privily for their own lives.

"So are the ways of every one that is greedy of gain; which taketh away the life of the owner thereof."

This story of the Irish peerage is written, as nearly as possible, in the very words in which it was related by its "heroine," the late Countess D——, and is therefore told in the first person.

My mother died when I was an infant, and of her I have no recollection, even the faintest. By her death my education was left solely to the direction of my surviving parent. He entered upon his task with a stern appreciation of the responsibility thus cast upon him. My religious instruction was prosecuted with an almost exaggerated anxiety; and I had, of course, the best masters to perfect me in all those accomplishments which my station and wealth might seem to require. My father was what is called an oddity, and his treatment of me, though uniformly kind, was governed less by affection and tenderness, than by a high and unbending sense of duty. Indeed I seldom saw or spoke to him except at meal-times, and then, though gentle, he was usually reserved and gloomy. His leisure hours, which were many, were passed either in his study or in solitary walks; in short, he seemed to take no further interest in my happiness or improvement, than a conscientious regard to the discharge of his own duty would seem to impose.

Shortly before my birth an event occurred which had contributed much to induce and to confirm my father's unsocial habits; it was the fact that a suspicion of *murder* had fallen upon his younger brother, though not sufficiently definite to lead to any public proceedings, yet strong enough to ruin him in public opinion. This disgraceful and dreadful doubt cast upon the family name, my father felt deeply and bitterly, and not the less so that he himself was thoroughly convinced of his brother's innocence. The sincerity and strength of this conviction he shortly afterwards proved in a manner which produced the catastrophe of my story.

Before, however, I enter upon my immediate adventures, I ought to relate the circumstances which had awakened that suspicion to which I have referred, inasmuch as they are in themselves somewhat curious, and in their effects most intimately connected with my own after-history.

My uncle, Sir Arthur Tyrrell, was a gay and extravagant man, and, among other vices, was ruinously addicted to gaming. This unfortunate propensity, even after his fortune had suffered so severely as to render retrenchment imperative, nevertheless continued to engross him, nearly to the exclusion of every other pursuit. He was, however, a proud, or rather a vain man, and could not bear to make the diminution of his income a matter of triumph to those with whom he had hitherto competed; and the consequence was, that he frequented no longer the expensive haunts of his dissipation, and retired from the gay world, leaving his coterie to discover his reasons as best they might. He did not, however, forego his favourite vice, for though he could not worship his great divinity in those costly temples where he was formerly wont to take his place, yet he found it very possible to bring about him a sufficient number of the votaries of chance to answer all his ends. The consequence was, that Carrickleigh, which was the name of my uncle's residence, was never without one or more of such visiters as I have described. It happened that upon one occasion he was visited by one Hugh Tisdall, a gentleman of loose, and, indeed, low habits, but of considerable wealth, and who had, in early youth, travelled with my uncle upon the Continent. The period of this visit was winter, and, consequently, the house was nearly deserted excepting by its ordinary inmates; it was, therefore, highly acceptable, particularly as my uncle was aware that his visiter's tastes accorded exactly with his own.

Both parties seemed determined to avail themselves of their mutual suitability during the brief stay which Mr. Tisdall had promised; the consequence was, that they shut themselves up in Sir Arthur's private room for nearly all the day and the greater part of the night, during the space of almost a week, at the end of which the servant having one morning, as usual, knocked at Mr. Tisdall's bed-room door repeatedly, received no answer, and, upon attempting to enter, found that it was locked. This appeared suspicious, and the inmates of the house having been alarmed, the door was forced open, and, on proceeding to the bed, they found the body of its occupant perfectly lifeless, and hanging halfway out, the head downwards, and near the floor. One deep wound had been inflicted upon the temple, apparently with some blunt instrument, which had penetrated the brain, and another blow, less effective

—probably the first aimed—had grazed his head, removing some of the scalp. The door had been double locked upon the *inside*, in evidence of which the key still lay where it had been placed in the lock. The window, though not secured on the interior, was closed; a circumstance not a little puzzling, as it afforded the only other mode of escape from the room. It looked out, too, upon a kind of court-yard, round which the old buildings stood, formerly accessible by a narrow doorway and passage lying in the oldest side of the quadrangle, but which had since been built up, so as to preclude all ingress or egress; the room was also upon the second story, and the height of the window considerable; in addition to all which the stone window-sill was much too narrow to allow of any one's standing upon it when the window was closed. Near the bed were found a pair of razors belonging to the murdered man, one of them upon the ground, and both of them open. The weapon which inflicted the mortal wound was not to be found in the room, nor were any footsteps or other traces of the murderer discoverable. At the suggestion of Sir Arthur himself, the coroner was instantly summoned to attend, and an inquest was held. Nothing, however, in any degree conclusive was elicited. The walls, ceiling, and floor of the room were carefully examined, in order to ascertain whether they contained a trap-door or other concealed mode of entrance, but no such thing appeared. Such was the minuteness of investigation employed, that, although the grate had contained a large fire during the night, they proceeded to examine even the very chimney, in order to discover whether escape by it were possible. But this attempt, too, was fruitless, for the chimney, built in the old fashion, rose in a perfectly perpendicular line from the hearth, to a height of nearly fourteen feet above the roof, affording in its interior scarcely the possibility of ascent, the flue being smoothly plastered, and sloping towards the top like an inverted funnel; promising, too, even if the summit were attained, owing to its great height, but a precarious descent upon the sharp and steep-ridged roof; the ashes, too, which lay in the grate, and the soot, as far as it could be seen, were undisturbed, a circumstance almost conclusive upon the point.

Sir Arthur was of course examined. His evidence was given with clearness and unreserve, which seemed calculated to silence all suspicion. He stated that, up to the day and night immediately preceding the catastrophe, he had lost to a heavy amount, but that, at their last sitting, he had not only won back his original loss, but upwards of £4,000 in addition; in evidence of which he produced an acknowledgment of debt to that amount in the handwriting of the deceased, bearing date the night of the catastrophe. He had mentioned the circumstance to Lady Tyrrell, and in presence of some of his domestics; which statement was supported by *their* respective evidence. One of the jury shrewdly observed, that the circumstance of Mr. Tisdall's having sustained so heavy a loss might have suggested to some ill-minded persons, accidentally hearing it, the plan of robbing him, after having murdered him in such a manner as might make it appear that he had committed suicide; a supposition which was strongly supported by the razors having been found thus displaced and removed from their case. Two persons had probably been engaged in the attempt, one watching by the sleeping man, and ready to strike him in case of his awakening suddenly, while the other was procuring the razors and employed in inflicting the fatal gash, so as to make it appear to have been the act of the murdered man himself. It was said that while the juror was making this suggestion Sir Arthur changed colour. There was nothing, however, like legal evidence to implicate him, and the consequence was that the verdict was found against a person or persons unknown, and for some time the matter was suffered to rest, until, after about five months, my father received a letter from a person signing himself Andrew Collis, and representing himself to be the cousin of the deceased. This letter stated that his brother, Sir Arthur, was likely to incur not merely suspicion but personal risk, unless he could account for certain circumstances connected with the recent murder, and contained a copy of a letter written by the deceased, and dated the very day upon the night of which the murder had been perpetrated. Tisdall's letter contained, among a great deal of other matter, the passages which follow:—

"I have had sharp work with Sir Arthur: he tried some of his stale tricks, but soon found that _I_ was Yorkshire, too; it would not do—you understand me. We went to the work like good ones, head, heart, and soul; and in fact, since I came here, I have lost no time. I am rather fagged, but I am sure to be well paid for my hardship; I never want sleep so long as I can have the music of a dice-box, and wherewithal to pay the piper. As I told you, he tried some of his queer turns, but I foiled him like a man, and, in return, gave him more than he could relish of the genuine _dead knowledge_. In short, I have plucked the old baronet as never baronet was plucked before; I have scarce left him the stump of a quill. I have got promissory notes in his hand to the amount of ——; if you like round numbers, say five-and-twenty thousand pounds, safely deposited in my portable strong box, alias, double-clasped pocket-book. I leave this ruinous old rat-hole early on to-morrow, for two reasons: first, I do not want to play with Sir Arthur deeper than I think his security would warrant; and, secondly, because I am safer a hundred miles away from Sir Arthur than in the house with him. Look you, my worthy, I tell you this between ourselves—I may be wrong—but, by ——, I am sure as that I am now living, that Sir A—— attempted to poison me last night. So much for old friendship on both sides. When I won the last stake, a heavy one enough, my friend leant his forehead upon his hands, and you'll laugh when I tell you that his head literally smoked like a hot dumpling. I do not know whether his agitation was produced by the plan which he had against me, or by his having lost so heavily; though it must be allowed that he had reason to be a little funked, whichever way his thoughts went; but he pulled the bell, and ordered two bottles of Champagne. While the fellow was bringing them, he wrote a promissory note to the full amount, which he signed, and, as the man came in with the bottles and glasses, he desired him to be off. He filled a glass for me, and, while he thought my eyes were off, for I was putting up his note at the time, he dropped something slyly into it, no doubt to sweeten it; but I saw it all, and, when he handed it to me, I said, with an emphasis which he might easily understand, 'There is some sediment in it, I'll not drink it.' 'Is there?' said he, and at the same time snatched it from my hand and threw it into the fire. What do you think of that? Have I not a tender bird in hand? Win or lose, I will not play beyond five thousand to-night, and to-morrow sees me safe out of the reach of Sir Arthur's Champagne."

Of the authenticity of this document, I never heard my father express a doubt; and I am satisfied that, owing to his strong conviction in favour of his brother, he would not have admitted it without sufficient inquiry, inasmuch as it tended to confirm the suspicions which already existed to his prejudice. Now, the only point in this letter which made strongly against my uncle, was the mention of the "double-clasped pocket-book," as the receptacle of the papers likely to involve him, for this pocket-book was not forthcoming, nor anywhere to be found, nor had any papers referring to his gaming transactions been discovered upon the dead man.

But whatever might have been the original intention of this man, Collis, neither my uncle nor my father ever heard more of him; he published the letter, however, in Faulkner's newspaper, which was shortly afterwards made the vehicle of a much more mysterious attack. The passage in that journal to which I allude, appeared about four years afterwards, and while the fatal occurence was still fresh in public recollection. It commenced by a rambling preface, stating that "a *certain person* whom *certain* persons thought to be dead, was not so, but living, and in full possession of his memory, and moreover, ready and able to make *great* delinquents tremble": it then went on to describe the murder, without, however, mentioning names; and in doing so, it entered into minute and circumstantial particulars of which none but an *eye-witness* could have been possessed, and by implications almost too unequivocal to be regarded in the light of insinuation, to involve the *"titled gambler"* in the guilt of the transaction.

My father at once urged Sir Arthur to proceed against the paper in an action of libel, but he would not hear of it, nor consent to my father's taking any legal steps whatever in the matter. My father, however, wrote in a threatening tone to Faulkner, demanding a surrender of the author of the obnoxious article; the answer to this application is still in my possession, and is penned in an apologetic tone: it states that the manuscript had been handed in, paid for, and inserted as an advertisement, without sufficient inquiry, or any knowledge as to whom it referred. No step, however, was taken to clear my uncle's character in the judgment of the public; and, as he immediately sold a small property, the application of the proceeds of which were known to none, he was said to have disposed of it to enable himself to buy off the threatened information; however the truth might have been, it is certain that no charges respecting the mysterious murder were afterwards publicly made against my uncle, and, as far as external disturbances were concerned, he enjoyed henceforward perfect security and quiet.

A deep and lasting impression, however, had been made upon the public mind, and Sir Arthur Tyrrell was no longer visited or noticed by the gentry of the county, whose attentions he had hitherto received. He accordingly affected to despise those courtesies which he no longer enjoyed, and shunned even that society which he might have commanded. This is all that I need recapitulate of my uncle's history, and I now recur to my own.

Although my father had never, within my recollection, visited, or been visited by my uncle, each being of unsocial, procrastinating, and indolent habits, and their respective residences being very far apart— the one lying in the county of Galway, the other in that of Cork—he was strongly attached to his brother, and evinced his affection by an active correspondence, and by deeply and proudly resenting that neglect which had branded Sir Arthur as unfit to mix in society.

When I was about eighteen years of age, my father, whose health had been gradually declining, died, leaving me in heart wretched and desolate, and, owing to his habitual seclusion, with few acquaintances, and almost no friends. The provisions of his will were curious, and when I was sufficiently come to myself to listen to, or comprehend them, surprised me not a little: all his vast property was left to me, and to the heirs of my body, for ever; and, in default of such heirs, it was to go after my death to my uncle, Sir Arthur, without any entail. At the same time, the will appointed him my guardian, desiring that I might be received within his house, and reside with his family, and under his care, during the term of my minority; and in consideration of the increased expense consequent upon such an arrangement, a handsome allowance was allotted to him during the term of my proposed residence. The object of this last provision I at once understood; my father desired, by making it the direct apparent interest of Sir Arthur that I should die without issue, while at the same time he placed my person wholly in his power, to prove to the world how great and unshaken was his confidence in his brother's innocence and honour. It was a strange, perhaps an idle scheme, but as I had been always brought up in the habit of considering my uncle as a deeply injured man, and had been taught, almost as a part of my religion, to regard him as the very soul of honour, I felt no further uneasiness respecting the arrangement than that likely to affect a shy and timid girl at the immediate prospect of taking up her abode for the first time in her life among strangers. Previous to leaving my home, which I felt I should do with a heavy heart, I received a most tender and affectionate letter from my uncle, calculated, if anything could do so, to remove the bitterness of parting from scenes familiar and dear from my earliest childhood, and in some degree to reconcile me to the measure. It was upon a fine autumn day that I approached the old domain of Carrickleigh. I shall not soon forget the impression of sadness and of gloom which all that I saw produced upon my mind; the sunbeams were falling with a rich and melancholy lustre upon the fine old trees, which stood in lordly groups, casting their long sweeping shadows over rock and sward; there was an air of neglect and decay about the spot, which amounted almost to desolation, and mournfully increased as we approached the building itself, near which the ground had been originally more artificially and carefully cultivated than elsewhere, and where consequently neglect more immediately and strikingly betrayed itself.

As we proceeded, the road wound near the beds of what had been formerly two fish-ponds, which were now nothing more than stagnant swamps, overgrown with rank weeds, and here and there encroached upon by the straggling underwood; the avenue itself was much broken; and in many places the stones were almost concealed by grass and nettles; the loose stone walls which had here and there intersected the broad park, were, in many places, broken down, so as no longer to answer their original purpose as fences; piers were now and then to be seen, but the gates were gone; and to add to the general air of dilapidation, some huge trunks were lying scattered through the venerable old trees, either the work of the winter storms, or perhaps the victims of some extensive but desultory scheme of denudation, which the projector had not capital or perseverance to carry into full effect.

After the carriage had travelled a full mile of this avenue, we reached the summit of a rather abrupt eminence, one of the many which added to the picturesqueness, if not to the convenience of this rude approach; from the top of this ridge the grey walls of Carrickleigh were visible, rising at a small distance in front, and darkened by the hoary wood which crowded around them; it was a quadrangular building of considerable extent, and the front, where the great entrance was placed, lay towards us, and bore unequivocal marks of antiquity; the time-worn, solemn aspect of the old building, the ruinous and deserted appearance of the whole place, and the associations which connected it with a dark page in the history of my family, combined to depress spirits already predisposed for the reception of sombre and dejecting impressions. When the carriage drew up in the grass-grown court-yard before the hall-door, two lazy-looking men, whose appearance well accorded with that of the place which they tenanted, alarmed by the obstreperous barking of a great chained dog, ran out from some half-ruinous out-houses, and took charge of the horses; the hall-door stood open, and I entered a gloomy and imperfectly-lighted apartment, and found no one within it. However, I had not long to wait in this awkward predicament, for before my luggage had been deposited in the house, indeed before I had well removed my cloak and other muffles, so as to enable me to look around, a young girl ran lightly into the hall, and kissing me heartily and somewhat boisterously exclaimed, "My dear cousin, my dear Margaret—I am so delighted—so out of breath, we did not expect you till ten o'clock; my father is somewhere about the place, he must be close at hand. James—Corney—run out and tell your master; my brother is seldom at home, at least at any reasonable hour; you must be so tired—so fatigued—let me show you to your room; see that Lady Margaret's luggage is all brought up; you must lie down and rest yourself. Deborah, bring some coffee—up these stairs; we are so delighted to see you—you cannot think how lonely I have been; how steep these stairs are, are not they? I am so glad you are come—I could hardly bring myself to believe that you were really coming; how good of you, dear Lady Margaret." There was real good nature and delight in my cousin's greeting, and a kind of constitutional confidence of manner which placed me at once at ease, and made me feel immediately upon terms of intimacy with her. The room into which she ushered me, although partaking in the general air of decay which pervaded the mansion and all about it, had, nevertheless, been fitted up with evident attention to comfort, and even with some dingy attempt at luxury; but what pleased me most was that it opened, by a second door, upon a lobby which communicated with my fair cousin's apartment; a circumstance which divested the room, in my eyes, of the air of solitude and sadness which would otherwise have characterised it, to a degree almost painful to one so depressed and agitated as I was.

After such arrangements as I found necessary were completed, we both went down to the parlour, a large wainscotted room, hung round with grim old portraits, and, as I was not sorry to see, containing, in its ample grate, a large and cheerful fire. Here my cousin had leisure to talk more at her ease; and from her I learned something of the manners and the habits of the two remaining members of her family, whom I had not yet seen. On my arrival I had known nothing of the family among whom I was come to reside, except that it consisted of three individuals, my uncle, and his son and daughter, Lady Tyrrell having been long dead; in addition to this very scanty stock of information, I shortly learned from my communicative companion, that my uncle was, as I had suspected, completely retired in his habits, and besides that, having been, so far back as she could well recollect, always rather strict, as reformed rakes frequently become, he had latterly been growing more gloomily and sternly religious than heretofore. Her account of her brother was far less favourable, though she did not say anything directly to his disadvantage. From all that I could gather from her, I was led to suppose that he was a specimen of the idle, coarse-mannered, profligate "squirearchy"—a result which might naturally have followed from the circumstance of his being, as it were, outlawed from society, and driven for companionship to grades below his own—enjoying, too, the dangerous prerogative of spending a good deal of money. However, you may easily suppose that I found nothing in my cousin's communication fully to bear me out in so very decided a conclusion.

I awaited the arrival of my uncle, which was every moment to be expected, with feelings half of alarm, half of curiosity—a sensation which
I have often since experienced, though to a less degree, when upon the
point of standing for the first time in the presence of one of whom I have
long been in the habit of hearing or thinking with interest. It was,
therefore, with some little perturbation that I heard, first a slight bustle
at the outer door, then a slow step traverse the hall, and finally
witnessed the door open, and my uncle enter the room. He was a striking looking man; from peculiarities both of person and of dress, the
whole effect of his appearance amounted to extreme singularity. He
was tall, and when young his figure must have been strikingly elegant;
as it was, however, its effect was marred by a very decided stoop; his
dress was of a sober colour, and in fashion anterior to any thing which I
could remember. It was, however, handsome, and by no means
carelessly put on; but what completed the singularity of his appearance
was his uncut, white hair, which hung in long, but not at all neglected
curls, even so far as his shoulders, and which combined with his
regularly classic features, and fine dark eyes, to bestow upon him an air
of venerable dignity and pride, which I have seldom seen equalled
elsewhere. I rose as he entered, and met him about the middle of the
room; he kissed my cheek and both my hands, saying—

"You are most welcome, dear child, as welcome as the command of
this poor place and all that it contains can make you. I am rejoiced to
see you—truly rejoiced. I trust that you are not much fatigued; pray be
seated again." He led me to my chair, and continued, "I am glad to
perceive you have made acquaintance with Emily already; I see, in your
being thus brought together, the foundation of a lasting friendship. You
are both innocent, and both young. God bless you—God bless you, and
make you all that I could wish."

He raised his eyes, and remained for a few moments silent, as if in
secret prayer. I felt that it was impossible that this man, with feelings
manifestly so tender, could be the wretch that public opinion had
represented him to be. I was more than ever convinced of his innocence.
His manners were, or appeared to me, most fascinating. I know not
how the lights of experience might have altered this estimate. But I was
then very young, and I beheld in him a perfect mingling of the courtesy
of polished life with the gentlest and most genial virtues of the heart. A
feeling of affection and respect towards him began to spring up within
me, the more earnest that I remembered how sorely he had suffered in
fortune and how cruelly in fame. My uncle having given me fully to understand that I was most welcome, and might command whatever was
his own, pressed me to take some supper; and on my refusing, he
observed that, before bidding me good night, he had one duty further to
perform, one in which he was convinced I would cheerfully acquiesce.
He then proceeded to read a chapter from the Bible; after which he took
his leave with the same affectionate kindness with which he had greeted
me, having repeated his desire that I should consider every thing in his

house as altogether at my disposal. It is needless to say how much I was
pleased with my uncle—it was impossible to avoid being so; and I could
not help saying to myself, if such a man as this is not safe from the
assaults of slander, who is? I felt much happier than I had done since
my 'father's death, and enjoyed that night the first refreshing sleep
which had visited me since that calamity. My curiosity respecting my
male cousin did not long remain unsatisfied; he appeared upon the next
day at dinner. His manners, though not so coarse as I had expected,
were exceedingly disagreeable; there was an assurance and a
forwardness for which I was not prepared; there was less of the vulgari-
ty of manner, and almost more of that of the mind, than I had anticipated. I felt quite uncomfortable in his presence; there was just that
confidence in his look and tone, which would read encouragement even
in mere toleration; and I felt more disgusted and annoyed at the coarse
and extravagant compliments which he was pleased from time to time
to pay me, than perhaps the extent of the atrocity might fully have
warranted. It was, however, one consolation that he did not often
appear, being much engrossed by pursuits about which I neither knew
nor cared anything; but when he did, his attentions, either with a view
to his amusement, or to some more serious object, were so obviously
and perseveringly directed to me, that young and inexperienced as I
was, even *I* could not be ignorant of their significance. I felt more
provoked by this odious persecution than I can express, and dis-
couraged him with so much vigour, that I did not stop even at rudeness
to convince him that his assiduities were unwelcome; but all in vain.

This had gone on for nearly a twelvemonth, to my infinite annoyance, when one day, as I was sitting at some needlework with my
companion, Emily, as was my habit, in the parlour, the door opened,
and my cousin Edward entered the room. There was something, I
thought, odd in his manner, a kind of struggle between shame and im-
pudence, a kind of flurry and ambiguity, which made him appear, if
possible, more than ordinarily disagreeable.

"Your servant, ladies," he said, seating himself at the same time;
"sorry to spoil your *tête-à-tête;* but never mind, I'll only take Emily's
place for a minute or two, and then we part for a while, fair cousin.
Emily, my father wants you in the corner turret; no shilly, shally, he's
in a hurry." She hesitated. "Be off—tramp, march, I say," he exclaimed, in a tone which the poor girl dared not disobey.

She left the room, and Edward followed her to the door. He stood
there for a minute or two, as if reflecting what he should say, perhaps
satisfying himself that no one was within hearing in the hall. At length
he turned about, having closed the door, as if carelessly, with his foot,
and advancing slowly, in deep thought, he took his seat at the side of
the table opposite to mine. There was a brief interval of silence, after
which he said:—

"I imagine that you have a shrewd suspicion of the object of my early
visit; but I suppose I must go into particulars. Must I?"

"I have no conception," I replied, "what your object may be."

"Well, well," said he becoming more at his ease as he proceeded, "it may be told in a few words. You know that it is totally impossible, quite out of the question, that an off-hand young fellow like me, and a good-looking girl like yourself, could meet continually as you and I have done, without an attachment—a liking growing up on one side or other; in short, I think I have let you know as plainly as if I spoke it, that I have been in love with you, almost from the first time I saw you." He paused, but I was too much horrified to speak. He interpreted my silence favourably. "I can tell you," he continued, "I'm reckoned rather hard to please, and very hard to *hit*. I can't say when I was taken with a girl before, so you see fortune reserved me ——."

Here the odious wretch actually put his arm round my waist: the action at once restored me to utterance, and with the most indignant vehemence I released myself from his hold, and at the same time said:—

"I *have*, sir, of course, perceived your most disagreeable attentions; they have long been a source of great annoyance to me; and you must be aware that I have marked my disapprobation, my disgust, as unequivocally as I possibly could, without actual indelicacy."

I paused, almost out of breath from the rapidity with which I had spoken; and without giving him time to renew the conversation, I hastily quitted the room, leaving him in a paroxysm of rage and mortification. As I ascended the stairs, I heard him open the parlour-door with violence, and take two or three rapid strides in the direction in which I was moving. I was now much frightened, and ran the whole way until I reached my room, and having locked the door, I listened breathlessly, but heard no sound. This relieved me for the present; but so much had I been overcome by the agitation and annoyance attendant upon the scene which I had just passed through, that when my cousin Emily knocked at the door, I was weeping in great agitation. You will readily conceive my distress, when you reflect upon my strong dislike to my cousin Edward, combined with my youth and extreme inexperience. Any proposal of such a nature must have agitated me; but that it should come from the man whom, of all others, I instinctively most loathed and abhorred, and to whom I had, as clearly as manner could do it, expressed the state of my feelings, was almost too annoying to be borne; it was a calamity, too, in which I could not claim the sympathy of my cousin Emily, which had always been extended to me in my minor grievances. Still I hoped that it might not be unattended with good; for I thought that one inevitable and most welcome consequence would result from this painful *éclaircissement,* in the discontinuance of my cousin's odious persecution.

When I arose next morning, it was with the fervent hope that I might never again behold his face, or even hear his name; but such a consummation, though devoutly to be wished, was hardly likely to occur. The painful impressions of yesterday were too vivid to be at once erased; and I could not help feeling some dim foreboding of coming annoyance and evil. To expect on my cousin's part anything like delicacy or consideration for me, was out of the question. I saw that he had set his heart upon my property, and that he was not likely easily to forego such a prize, possessing what might have been considered opportunities and facilities almost to compel my compliance. I now keenly felt the unreasonableness of my father's conduct in placing me to reside with a family, with all the members of which, with one exception, he was wholly unacquainted, and I bitterly felt the helplessness of my situation. I determined, however, in the event of my cousin's persevering in his addresses, to lay all the particulars before my uncle, although he had never, in kindness or intimacy, gone a step beyond our first interview, and to throw myself upon his hospitality and his sense of honour for protection against a repetition of such annoyances.

My cousin's conduct may appear to have been an inadequate cause for such serious uneasiness; but my alarm was awakened neither by his acts nor by words, but entirely by his manner, which was strange and even intimidating. At the beginning of our yesterday's interview, there was a sort of bullying swagger in his air, which, towards the end, gave place to something bordering upon the brutal vehemence of an undisguised ruffian, a transition which had tempted me into a belief that he might seek, even forcibly, to extort from me a consent to his wishes, or by means still more horrible, of which I scarcely dared to trust myself to think, to possess himself of my property.

I was early next day summoned to attend my uncle in his private room, which lay in a corner turret of the old building; and thither I accordingly went, wondering all the way what this unusual measure might prelude. When I entered the room, he did not rise in his usual courteous way to greet me, but simply pointed to a chair opposite to his own; this boded nothing agreeable. I sat down, however, silently waiting until he should open the conversation.

"Lady Margaret," at length he said, in a tone of greater sternness than I thought him capable of using, "I have hitherto spoken to you as a friend, but I have not forgotten that I am also your guardian, and that my authority as such gives me a right to controul your conduct. I shall put a question to you, and I expect and will demand a plain, direct answer. Have I rightly been informed that you have contemptuously rejected the suit and hand of my son Edward?"

I stammered forth with a good deal of trepidation:—

"I believe, that is, I have, sir, rejected my cousin's proposals; and my coldness and discouragement might have convinced him that I had determined to do so."

"Madame," replied he, with suppressed, but, as it appeared to me, intense anger, "I have lived long enough to know that *coldness and discouragement*, and such terms, form the common cant of a worthless coquette. You know to the full, as well as I, that *coldness and discouragement* may be so exhibited as to convince their object that he is neither distasteful nor indifferent to the person who wears that manner. You know, too, none better, that an affected neglect, when skillfully managed, is amongst the most formidable of the allurements which artful beauty can employ. I tell you, madame, that having, without one word spoken in discouragement, permitted my son's most marked attentions for a twelvemonth or more, you have no *right* to dismiss him with no further explanation than demurely telling him that you had always looked coldly upon him, and neither your wealth nor *your ladyship* (there was an emphasis of scorn on the word which would have become Sir Giles Overreach himself) can warrant you in treating with contempt the affectionate regard of an honest heart."

I was too much shocked at this undisguised attempt to bully me into an acquiescence in the interested and unprincipled plan for their own aggrandisement, which I now perceived my uncle and his son had deliberately formed, at once to find strength or collectedness to frame an answer to what he had said. At length I replied, with a firmness that surprised myself:—

"In all that you have just now said, sir, you have grossly misstated my conduct and motives. Your information must have been most incorrect, as far as it regards my conduct towards my cousin; my manner towards him could have conveyed nothing but dislike; and if anything could have added to the strong aversion which I have long felt towards him, it would be his attempting thus to frighten me into a marriage which he knows to be revolting to me, and which is sought by him only as a means for securing to himself whatever property is mine."

As I said this, I fixed my eyes upon those of my uncle, but he was too old in the world's ways to falter beneath the gaze of more searching eyes than mine; he simply said—

"Are you acquainted with the provisions of your father's will?"

I answered in the affirmative; and he continued:—"Then you must be aware that if my son Edward were, which God forbid, the unprincipled, reckless man, the ruffian you pretend to think him"—(here he spoke very slowly, as if he intended that every word which escaped him should be registered in my memory, while at the same time the expression of his countenance underwent a gradual but horrible change, and the eyes which he fixed upon me became so darkly vivid, that I almost lost sight of everything else)—"if he were what you have described him, do you think, child, he would have found no shorter way than marriage to gain his ends? A single blow, an outrage not a degree worse than you insinuate, would transfer your property to us!!"

I stood staring at him for many minutes after he had ceased to speak, fascinated by the terrible, serpent-like gaze, until he continued with a welcome change of countenance:—

"I will not speak again to you, upon this topic, until one month has passed. You shall have time to consider the relative advantages of the two courses which are open to you. I should be sorry to hurry you to a decision. I am satisfied with having stated my feelings upon the subject, and pointed out to you the path of duty. Remember this day month; not one word sooner."

He then rose, and I left the room, much agitated and exhausted.

This interview, all the circumstances attending it, but most particularly the formidable expression of my uncle's countenance while he talked, though hypothetically, of *murder,* combined to arouse all my worst suspicions of him. I dreaded to look upon the face that had so recently worn the appalling livery of guilt and malignity. I regarded it with the mingled fear and loathing with which one looks upon an object which has tortured them in a night-mare.

In a few days after the interview, the particulars of which I have just detailed, I found a note upon my toilet-table, and on opening it I read as follows:—

"My Dear Lady Margaret,
You will be, perhaps, surprised to see a strange face in your room to-day. I have dismissed your Irish maid, and secured a French one to wait upon you; a step rendered necessary by my proposing shortly to visit the Continent with all my family.
Your faithful guardian,
"ARTHUR TYRELL."

On inquiry, I found that my faithful attendant was actually gone, and far on her way to the town of Galway; and in her stead there appeared a tall, raw-boned, ill-looking, elderly Frenchwoman, whose sullen and presuming manners seemed to imply that her vocation had never before been that of a lady's-maid. I could not help regarding her as a creature of my uncle's, and therefore to be dreaded, even had she been in no other way suspicious.

Days and weeks passed away without any, even a momentary doubt upon my part, as to the course to be pursued by me. The allotted period had at length elapsed; the day arrived upon which I was to communicate my decision to my uncle. Although my resolution had never for a moment wavered, I could not shake off the dread of the approaching colloquy; and my heart sank within me as I heard the expected summons. I had not seen my cousin Edward since the occurrence of the grand *éclaircissement;* he must have studiously avoided me; I suppose from policy, it could not have been from delicacy. I was prepared for a terrific burst of fury from my uncle, as soon as I should make known my determination; and I not unreasonably feared that some act of violence or of intimidation would next be resorted to. Filled with these dreary forebodings, I fearfully opened the study door, and the next minute I stood in my uncle's presence. He received me with a courtesy which I dreaded, as arguing a favourable anticipation respecting the answer which I was to give; and after some slight delay he began by saying—

"It will be a relief to both of us, I believe, to bring this conversation as soon as possible to an issue. You will excuse me, then, my dear niece, for speaking with a bluntness which, under other circumstances, would be unpardonable. You have, I am certain, given the subject of our last interview fair and serious consideration; and I trust that you are now prepared with candour to lay your answer before me. A few words will suffice; we perfectly understand one another."

He paused; and I, though feeling that I stood upon a mine which might in an instant explode, nevertheless answered with perfect composure: "I must now, sir, make the same reply which I did upon the last occasion, and I reiterate the declaration which I then made, that I never can nor will, while life and reason remain, consent to a union with my cousin Edward."

This announcement wrought no apparent change in Sir Arthur, except that he became deadly, almost lividly pale. He seemed lost in dark thought for a minute, and then, with a slight effort, said, "You have answered me honestly and directly; and you say your resolution is unchangeable; well, would it had been otherwise—would it had been otherwise—but be it as it is; I am satisfied."

He gave me his hand—it was cold and damp as death; under an assumed calmness, it was evident that he was fearfully agitated. He continued to hold my hand with an almost painful pressure, while, as if unconsciously, seeming to forget my presence, he muttered, "Strange, strange, strange, indeed! fatuity, helpless fatuity!" there was here a long pause. "Madness *indeed* to strain a cable that is rotten to the very heart; it must break—and then—all goes." There was again a pause of some minutes, after which, suddenly changing his voice and manner to one of wakeful alacrity, he exclaimed,

"Margaret, my son Edward shall plague you no more. He leaves this country to-morrow for France; he shall speak no more upon this subject —never, never more; whatever events depended upon your answer must now take their own course; but as for this fruitless proposal, it has been tried enough; it can be repeated no more."

At these words he coldly suffered my hand to drop, as if to express his total abandonment of all his projected schemes of alliance; and certainly the action, with the accompanying words, produced upon my mind a more solemn and depressing effect than I believed possible to have been caused by the course which I had determined to pursue; it struck upon my heart with an awe and heaviness which *will* accompany the accomplishment of an important and irrevocable act, even though no doubt or scruple remains to make it possible that the agent should wish it undone.

"Well," said my uncle, after a little time, "we now cease to speak upon this topic, never to resume it again. Remember you shall have no farther uneasiness from Edward; he leaves Ireland for France to-morrow; this will be a relief to you; may I depend upon your *honour* that no word touching the subject of this interview shall ever escape you?" I gave him the desired assurance; he said, "It is well; I am satisfied; we have nothing more, I believe, to say upon either side, and my presence must be a restraint upon you, I shall therefore bid you farewell." I then left the apartment, scarcely knowing what to think of the strange interview which had just taken place.

On the next day my uncle took occasion to tell me that Edward had actually sailed, if his intention had not been prevented by adverse winds or weather; and two days after he actually produced a letter from his son, written, as it said, *on board*, and despatched while the ship was getting under weigh. This was a great satisfaction to me, and as being likely to prove so, it was no doubt communicated to me by Sir Arthur.

During all this trying period I had found infinite consolation in the society and sympathy of my dear cousin Emily. I never, in after-life, formed a friendship so close, so fervent, and upon which, in all its progress, I could look back with feelings of such unalloyed pleasure, upon whose termination I must ever dwell with so deep, so yet unembittered a sorrow. In cheerful converse with her I soon recovered my spirits considerably, and passed my time agreeably enough, although still in the utmost seclusion. Matters went on smoothly enough, although I could not help sometimes feeling a momentary, but horrible uncertainty respecting my uncle's character; which was not altogether unwarranted by the circumstances of the two trying interviews, the particulars of which I have just detailed. The unpleasant impression which these conferences were calculated to leave upon my mind was fast wearing away, when there occurred a circumstance, slight indeed in itself, but calculated irrepressibly to awaken all my worst suspicions, and to overwhelm me again with anxiety and terror.

I had one day left the house with my cousin Emily, in order to take a ramble of considerable length, for the purpose of sketching some favourite views, and we had walked about half a mile when I perceived that we had forgotten our drawing materials, the absence of which would have defeated the object of our walk. Laughing at our own thoughtlessness, we returned to the house, and leaving Emily outside, I ran up stairs to procure the drawing-books and pencils which lay in my bed-room. As I ran up the stairs, I was met by the tall, ill-looking Frenchwoman, evidently a good deal flurried; "Que veut Madame?" said she, with a more decided effort to be polite, than I had ever known her make before. "No, no—no matter," said I, hastily running by her in the direction of my room. "Madame," cried she, in a high key, "restez ici s'il vous plaît, votre chambre n'est pas faite." I continued to move on without heeding her. She was some way behind me, and feeling that she could not otherwise prevent my entrance, for I was now upon the very lobby, she made a desperate attempt to seize hold of my person; she succeeded in grasping the end of my shawl, which she drew from my shoulders, but slipping at the same time upon the polished oak floor, she fell at full length upon the boards. A little frightened as well as angry at the rudeness of this strange woman, I hastily pushed open the door of my room, at which I now stood, in order to escape from her; but great was my amazement on entering to find the apartment preoccupied. The window was open, and beside it stood two male figures; they appeared to be examining the fastenings of the casement, and their backs were turned towards the door. One of them was my uncle; they both had turned on my entrance, as if startled; the stranger was booted and cloaked, and wore a heavy, broad-leafed hat over his brows; he turned but for a moment, and averted his face; but I had seen enough to convince me that he was no other than my cousin Edward. My uncle had some iron instrument in his hand, which he hastily concealed behind his back; and coming towards me, said something as if in an explanatory tone; but I was too much shocked and confounded to understand what it might be. He said something about "*repairs*—windowframes—cold, and safety." I did not wait, however, to ask or to receive explanations, but hastily left the room. As I went down stairs I thought I heard the voice of the Frenchwoman in all the shrill volubility of excuse, and others uttering suppressed but vehement imprecations, or what seemed to me to be such.

I joined my cousin Emily quite out of breath. I need not say that my head was too full of other things to think much of drawing for that day. I imparted to her frankly the cause of my alarms, but, at the same time, as gently as I could; and with tears she promised vigilance, devotion, and love. I never had reason for a moment to repent the unreserved confidence which I then reposed in her. She was no less surprised than I at the unexpected appearance of Edward, whose departure for France neither of us had for a moment doubted, but which was now proved by his actual presence to be nothing more than an imposture practised, I feared, for no good end. The situation in which I had found my uncle had very nearly removed all my doubts as to his designs; I magnified suspicions into certainties, and dreaded night after night that I should be murdered in my bed. The nervousness produced by sleepless nights and days of anxious fears increased the horrors of my situation to such a degree, that I at length wrote a letter to a Mr. Jefferies, an old and faithful friend of my father's, and perfectly acquainted with all his affairs, praying him, for God's sake, to relieve me from my present terrible situation, and communicating without reserve the nature and grounds of my suspicions. This letter I kept sealed and directed for two or three days always about my person, for discovery would have been ruinous, in expectation of an opportunity, which might be safely trusted, of having it placed in the post-office; as neither Emily nor I were permitted to pass beyond the precincts of the demesne itself, which was surrounded by high walls formed of dry stone, the difficulty of procuring such an opportunity was greatly enhanced.

At this time Emily had a short conversation with her father, which she reported to me instantly. After some indifferent matter, he had asked her whether she and I were upon good terms, and whether I was unreserved in my disposition. She answered in the affirmative; and he then inquired whether I had been much surprised to find him in my chamber on the other day. She answered that I had been both surprised and amused. "And what did she think of George Wilson's appearance?" "Who?" inquired she. "Oh! the architect," he answered, "who is to contract for the repairs of the house; he is accounted a handsome fellow." "She could not see his face," said Emily, "and she was in such a hurry to escape that she scarcely observed him." Sir Arthur appeared satisfied, and the conversation ended.

This slight conversation, repeated accurately to me by Emily, had the effect of confirming, if indeed any thing was required to do so, all that I had before believed as to Edward's actual presence; and I naturally became, if possible, more anxious than ever to despatch the letter to Mr. Jefferies. An opportunity at length occurred. As Emily and I were walking one day near the gate of the demesne, a lad from the village happened to be passing down the avenue from the house; the spot was secluded, and as this person was not connected by service with those whose observation I dreaded, I committed the letter to his keeping, with strict injunctions that he should put it, without delay, into the receiver of the town post-office; at the same time I added a suitable gratuity, and the man having made many protestations of punctuality, was soon out of sight. He was hardly gone when I began to doubt my discretion in having trusted him; but I had no better or safer means of despatching the letter, and I was not warranted in suspecting him of such wanton dishonesty as a disposition to tamper with it; but I could not be quite satisfied of its safety until I had received an answer, which could not arrive for a few days. Before I did, however, an event occurred which a little surprised me. I was sitting in my bed-room early in the day, reading by myself, when I heard a knock at the door. "Come in," said I, and my uncle entered the room. "Will you excuse me," said he, "I sought you in the parlour, and thence I have come here. I desired to say a word to you. I trust that you have hitherto found my conduct to you such as that of a guardian towards his ward should be." I dared not withhold my assent. "And," he continued, "I trust that you have not found me harsh or unjust, and that you have perceived, my dear niece, that I have sought to make this poor place as agreeable to you as may be?" I assented again; and he put his hand in his pocket, whence he drew a folded paper, and dashing it upon the table with startling emphasis he said, "Did you write that letter?" The sudden and fearful alteration of his voice, manner, and face, but more than all, the unexpected production of my letter to Mr. Jefferies, which I at once recognised, so confounded and terrified me, that I felt almost choking. I could not utter a word. "Did you write that letter?" he repeated, with slow and intense emphasis. "You did, liar and hypocrite. You dared to write that foul and infamous libel; but it shall be your last. Men will universally believe you mad, if I choose to call for an inquiry. I can make you appear so. The suspicions expressed in this letter are the hallucinations and alarms of a moping lunatic. I have defeated your first attempt, madam; and by the holy God, if ever you make another, chains, darkness, and the keeper's whip shall be your portion." With these astounding words he left the room, leaving me almost fainting.

I was now almost reduced to despair; my last cast had failed; I had no course left but that of escaping secretly from the castle, and placing myself under the protection of the nearest magistrate. I felt if this were not done, and speedily, that I should be *murdered*. No one, from mere description, can have an idea of the unmitigated horror of my situation; a helpless, weak, inexperienced girl, placed under the power, and wholly at the mercy of evil men, and feeling that I had it not in my power to escape for one moment from the malignant influences under which I was probably doomed to fall; with a consciousness, too, that if violence, if murder were designed, no human being would be near to aid me; my dying shriek would be lost in void space.

I had seen Edward but once during his visit, and as I did not meet him again, I began to think that he must have taken his departure; a conviction which was to a certain degree satisfactory, as I regarded his absence as indicating the removal of immediate danger. Emily also arrived circuitously at the same conclusion, and not without good grounds, for she managed indirectly to learn that Edward's black horse had actually been for a day and part of a night in the castle stables, just at the time of her brother's supposed visit. The horse had gone, and as she argued, the rider must have departed with it.

This point being so far settled, I felt a little less uncomfortable; when being one day alone in my bed-room, I happened to look out from the window, and to my unutterable horror, I beheld peering through an opposite casement, my cousin Edward's face. Had I seen the evil one himself in bodily shape, I could not have experienced a more sickening revulsion. I was too much appalled to move at once from the window, but I did so soon enough to avoid his eye. He was looking fixedly down into the narrow quadrangle upon which the window opened. I shrunk back unperceived, to pass the rest of the day in terror and despair. I went to my room early that night, but I was too miserable to sleep.

At about twelve o'clock, feeling very nervous, I determined to call my cousin Emily, who slept, you will remember, in the next room, which communicated with mine by a second door. By this private entrance I found my way into her chamber, and without difficulty persuaded her to return to my room and sleep with me. We accordingly lay down together, she undressed, and I with my clothes on, for I was every moment walking up and down the room, and felt too nervous and miserable to think of rest or comfort. Emily was soon fast asleep, and I lay awake, fervently longing for the first pale gleam of morning, and reckoning every stroke of the old clock with an impatience which made every hour appear like six.

It must have been about one o'clock when I thought I heard a slight noise at the partition door between Emily's room and mine, as if caused by somebody's turning the key in the lock. I held my breath, and the same sound was repeated at the second door of my room, that which opened upon the lobby; the sound was here distinctly caused by the revolution of the bolt in the lock, and it was followed by a slight pressure upon the door itself, as if to ascertain the security of the lock. The person, whoever it might be, was probably satisfied, for I heard the old boards of the lobby creak and strain, as if under the weight of somebody moving cautiously over them. My sense of hearing became unnaturally, almost painfully acute. I suppose the imagination added distinctness to sounds vague in themselves. I thought that I could actually hear the breathing of the person who was slowly returning along the lobby.

At the head of the stair-case there appeared to occur a pause; and I could distinctly hear two or three sentences hastily whispered; the steps then descended the stairs with apparently less caution. I ventured to walk quickly and lightly to the lobby door, and attempted to open it; it was indeed fast locked upon the outside, as was also the other. I now felt that the dreadful hour was come; but one desperate expedient remained—it was to awaken Emily, and by our united strength, to attempt to force the partition door, which was slighter than the other, and through this to pass to the lower part of the house, whence it might be possible to escape to the grounds, and so to the village. I returned to the bed-side, and shook Emily, but in vain; nothing that I could do availed to produce from her more than a few incoherent words; it was a death-like sleep. She had certainly drunk of some narcotic, as, probably, had I also, in spite of all the caution with which I had examined every thing presented to us to eat or drink. I now attempted, with as little noise as possible, to force first one door, then the other; but all in vain. I believe no strength could have affected my object, for both doors opened inwards. I therefore collected whatever moveables I could carry thither, and piled them against the doors, so as to assist me in whatever attempts I should make to resist the entrance of those without. I then returned to the bed and endeavoured again, but fruitlessly, to awaken my cousin. It was not sleep, it was torpor, lethargy, death. I knelt down and prayed with an agony of earnestness; and then seating myself upon the bed, I awaited my fate with a kind of terrible tranquillity.

I heard a faint clanking sound from the narrow court which I have already mentioned, as if caused by the scraping of some iron instrument against stones or rubbish. I at first determined not to disturb the calmness which I now experienced, by uselessly watching the proceedings of those who sought my life; but as the sounds continued, the horrible curiosity which I felt overcame every other emotion, and I determined, at all hazards, to gratify it. I, therefore, crawled upon my knees to the window, so as to let the smallest possible portion of my head appear above the sill.

The moon was shining with an uncertain radiance upon the antique grey buildings, and obliquely upon the narrow court beneath; one side of it was therefore clearly illuminated, while the other was lost in obscurity, the sharp outlines of the old gables, with their nodding clusters of ivy, being at first alone visible. Whoever or whatever occasioned the noise which had excited my curiosity, was concealed under the shadow of the dark side of the quadrangle. I placed my hand over my eyes to shade them from the moonlight, which was so bright as to be almost dazzling, and, peering into the darkness, I first dimly, but afterwards gradually, almost with full distinctness, beheld the form of a man engaged in digging what appeared to be a rude hole close under the wall. Some implements, probably a shovel and pickaxe, lay beside him, and to these he every now and then applied himself as the nature of the ground required. He pursued his task rapidly, and with as little noise as possible. "So," thought I, as shovelful after shovelful, the dislodged rubbish mounted into a heap, "they are digging the grave in which, before two hours pass, I must lie, a cold, mangled corpse. I am *theirs*—I cannot escape." I felt as if my reason was leaving me. I started to my feet, and in mere despair I applied myself again to each of the two doors alternately. I strained every nerve and sinew, but I might as well have attempted, with my single strength, to force the building itself from its foundations. I threw myself madly upon the ground, and clasped my hands over my eyes as if to shut out the horrible images which crowded upon me.

The paroxysm passed away. I prayed once more with the bitter, agonised fervour of one who feels that the hour of death is present and inevitable. When I arose, I went once more to the window and looked out, just in time to see a shadowy figure glide stealthily along the wall. The task was finished. The catastrophe of the tragedy must soon be accomplished. I determined now to defend my life to the last; and that I might be able to do so with some effect, I searched the room for something which might serve as a weapon; but either through accident, or else in anticipation of such a possibility, every thing which might have been made available for such a purpose had been removed.

I must then die tamely and without an effort to defend myself. A thought suddenly struck me; might it not be possible to escape through the door, which the assassin must open in order to enter the room? I resolved to make the attempt. I felt assured that the door through which ingress to the room would be effected was that which opened upon the lobby. It was the more direct way, besides being, for obvious reasons, less liable to interruption than the other. I resolved, then, to place myself behind a projection of the wall, the shadow would serve fully to conceal me, and when the door should be opened, and before they should have discovered the identity of the occupant of the bed, to creep noiselessly from the room, and then to trust to Providence for escape. In order to facilitate this scheme, I removed all the lumber which I had heaped against the door; and I had nearly completed my arrangements, when I perceived the room suddenly darkened, by the close approach of some shadowy object to the window. On turning my eyes in that direction, I observed at the top of the casement, as if suspended from above, first the feet, then the legs, then the body, and at length the whole figure

of a man present itself. It was Edward Tyrrell. He appeared to be
guiding his descent so as to bring his feet upon the centre of the stone
block which occupied the lower part of the window; and having secured
his footing upon this, he kneeled down and began to gaze into the room.
As the moon was gleaming into the chamber, and the bed-curtains were
drawn, he was able to distinguish the bed itself and its contents. He
appeared satisfied with his scrutiny, for he looked up and made a sign
with his hand. He then applied his hands to the window-frame, which
must have been ingeniously contrived for the purpose, for with apparently no resistance the whole frame, containing casement and all,
slipped from its position in the wall, and was by him lowered into the
room. The cold night wind waved the bed-curtains, and he paused for a
moment; all was still again, and he stepped in upon the floor of the
room. He held in his hand what appeared to be a steel instrument,
shaped something like a long hammer. This he held rather behind him,
while, with three long, *tip-toe* strides, he brought himself to the bedside.
I felt that the discovery must now be made, and held my breath in
momentary expectation of the execration in which he would vent his
surprise and disappointment. I closed my eyes; there was a pause, but
it was a short one. I heard two dull blows, given in rapid succession; a
quivering sigh, and the long-drawn, heavy breathing of the sleeper was
for ever suspended. I unclosed my eyes, and saw the murderer fling the
quilt across the head of his victim; he then, with the instrument of death
still in his hand, proceeded to the lobby-door, upon which he tapped
sharply twice or thrice. A quick step was then heard approaching, and
a voice whispered something from without. Edward answered, with a
kind of shuddering chuckle, "Her ladyship is past complaining; unlock
the door, in the devil's name, unless you're afraid to come in, and help
me to lift her out of the window." The key was turned in the lock, the
door opened, and my uncle entered the room. I have told you already
that I had placed myself under the shade of a projection of the wall,
close to the door. I had instinctively shrunk down cowering towards the
ground on the entrance of Edward through the window. When my
uncle entered the room, he and his son both stood so very close to me
that his hand was every moment upon the point of touching my face. I
held my breath, and remained motionless as death.

"You had no interruption from the next room?" said my uncle.

"No," was the brief reply.

"Secure the jewels, Ned; the French harpy must not lay her claws
upon them. You're a steady hand, by G—d; not much blood—eh?"

"Not twenty drops," replied his son, "and those on the quilt."

"I'm glad it's over," whispered my uncle again; "we must lift the—
the *thing* through the window, and lay the rubbish over it."

They then turned to the bedside, and, winding the bed-clothes round
the body, carried it between them slowly to the window, and exchang-
ing a few brief words with some one below, they shoved it over the
window-sill, and I heard it fall heavily on the ground underneath.

"I'll take the jewels," said my uncle; "there are two caskets in the lower drawer."

He proceeded, with an accuracy which, had I been more at ease, would have furnished me with matter of astonishment, to lay his hand upon the very spot where my jewels lay; and having possessed himself of them, he called to his son:—

"Is the rope made fast above?"

"I'm no fool; to be sure it is," replied he.

They then lowered themselves from the window; and I rose lightly and cautiously, scarcely daring to breathe, from my place of concealment, and was creeping towards the door, when I heard my uncle's voice, in a sharp whisper, exclaim, "Get up again; G—d d—n you, you've forgot to lock the room door"; and I perceived, by the straining of the rope which hung from above, that the mandate was instantly obeyed. Not a second was to be lost. I passed through the door, which was only closed, and moved as rapidly as I could, consistently with stillness, along the lobby. Before I had gone many yards, I heard the door through which I had just passed roughly locked on the inside. I glided down the stairs in terror, lest, at every corner, I should meet the murderer or one of his accomplices. I reached the hall, and listened, for a moment, to ascertain whether all was silent around. No sound was audible; the parlour windows opened on the park, and through one of them I might, I thought, easily effect my escape. Accordingly, I hastily entered; but, to my consternation, a candle was burning in the room, and by its light I saw a figure seated at the dinner-table, upon which lay glasses, bottles, and the other accompaniments of a drinking party. Two or three chairs were placed about the table, irregularly, as if hastily abandoned by their occupants. A single glance satisfied me that the figure was that of my French attendant. She was fast asleep, having, probably, drank deeply. There was something malignant and ghastly in the calmness of this bad woman's features, dimly illuminated as they were by the flickering blaze of the candle. A knife lay upon the table, and the terrible thought struck me—"Should I kill this sleeping accomplice in the guilt of the murderer, and thus secure my retreat?" Nothing could be easier; it was but to draw the blade across her throat, the work of a second.

An instant's pause, however, corrected me. "No," thought I, "the God who has conducted me thus far through the valley of the shadow of death, will not abandon me now. I will fall into their hands, or I will escape hence, but it shall be free from the stain of blood; His will be done." I felt a confidence arising from this reflection, an assurance of protection which I cannot describe. There were no other means of escape, so I advanced, with a firm step and collected mind, to the window. I noiselessly withdrew the bars, and unclosed the shutters; I pushed open the casement, and without waiting to look behind me, I ran with my utmost speed, scarcely feeling the ground beneath me, down the avenue, taking care to keep upon the grass which bordered it.

I did not for a moment slacken my speed, and I had now gained the central point between the park-gate and the mansion-house. Here the avenue made a wider circuit, and in order to avoid delay, I directed my way across the smooth sward round which the carriageway wound, intending, at the opposite side of the level, at a point which I distinguished by a group of old birch trees, to enter again upon the beaten track, which was from thence tolerably direct to the gate. I had, with my utmost speed, got about half way across this broad flat, when the rapid tramp of a horse's hoofs struck upon my ear. My heart swelled in my bosom, as though I would smother. The clattering of galloping hoofs approached; I was pursued; they were now upon the sward on which I was running; there was not a bush or a bramble to shelter me; and, as if to render escape altogether desperate, the moon, which had hitherto been obscured, at this moment shone forth with a broad, clear light, which made every object distinctly visible. The sounds were now close behind me. I felt my knees bending under me, with the sensation which unnerves one in a dream. I reeled, I stumbled, I fell; and at the same instant the cause of my alarm wheeled past me at full gallop. It was one of the young fillies which pastured loose about the park, whose frolics had thus all but maddened me with terror. I scrambled to my feet, and rushed on with weak but rapid steps, my sportive companion still galloping round and round me with many a frisk and fling, until, at length, more dead than alive, I reached the avenue-gate, and crossed the stile, I scarce knew how. I ran through the village, in which all was silent as the grave, until my progress was arrested by the hoarse voice of a sentinel, who cried "Who goes there?" I felt that I was now safe. I turned in the direction of the voice, and fell fainting at the soldier's feet. When I came to myself, I was sitting in a miserable hovel, surrounded by strange faces, all bespeaking curiosity and compassion. Many soldiers were in it also; indeed, as I afterwards found, it was employed as a guard-room by a detachment of troops quartered for that night in the town. In a few words I informed their officer of the circumstances which had occurred, describing also the appearance of the persons engaged in the murder; and he, without further loss of time than was necessary to procure the attendance of a magistrate, proceeded to the mansion-house of Carrickleigh, taking with him a party of his men. But the villains had discovered their mistake, and had effected their escape before the arrival of the military.

The Frenchwoman was, however, arrested in the neighbourhood upon the next day. She was tried and condemned at the ensuing assizes; and previous to her execution confessed that *"she had a hand in making Hugh Tisdall's bed."* She had been a housekeeper in the castle at the time, and a *chère amie* of my uncle's. She was, in reality, able to speak English like a native, but had exclusively used the French language, I suppose to facilitate her designs. She died the same hardened wretch she had lived, confessing her crimes only, as she alleged, that her doing so might involve Sir Arthur Tyrrell, the great author of her guilt and misery, and whom she now regarded with unmitigated detestation.

With the particulars of Sir Arthur's and his son's escape, as far as they are known, you are acquainted. You are also in possession of their after fate; the terrible, the tremendous retribution which, after long delays of many years, finally overtook and crushed them. Wonderful and inscrutable are the dealings of God with his creatures!

Deep and fervent as must always be my gratitude to heaven for my deliverance, effected by a chain of providential occurrences, the failing of a single link of which must have ensured my destruction, it was long before I could look back upon it with other feelings than those of bitterness, almost of agony. The only being that had ever really loved me, my nearest and dearest friend, ever ready to sympathise, to counsel, and to assist; the gayest, the gentlest, the warmest heart; the only creature on earth that cared for me; *her* life had been the price of my deliverance; and I then uttered the wish, which no event of my long and sorrowful life has taught me to recall, that she had been spared, and that, in her stead, *I* were mouldering in the grave, forgotten, and at rest.

THE EVIL GUEST

"When Lust hath conceived, it bringeth forth Sin: and Sin, when it is finished, bringeth forth Death."

About sixty years ago, and somewhat more than twenty miles from the ancient town of Chester, in a southward direction, there stood a large, and, even then, an old-fashioned mansion-house. It lay in the midst of a demesne of considerable extent, and richly wooded with venerable timber; but, apart from the sombre majesty of these giant groups, and the varieties of the undulating ground on which they stood, there was little that could be deemed attractive in the place. A certain air of neglect and decay, and an indescribable gloom and melancholy, hung over it. In darkness, it seemed darker than any other tract; when the moonlight fell upon its glades and hollows, they looked spectral and awful, with a sort of churchyard loneliness; and even when the blush of the morning kissed its broad woodlands, there was a melancholy in the salute which saddened rather than cheered the heart of the beholder.

This antique, melancholy, and neglected place, we shall call, for distinctness sake, Gray Forest. It was then the property of the younger son of a nobleman, once celebrated for his ability and his daring, but who had long since passed to that land where human wisdom and courage avail nought. The representative of this noble house resided at the family mansion in Sussex, and the cadet, whose fortunes we mean to sketch in these pages, lived upon the narrow margin of an encumbered income, in a reserved and unsocial discontent, deep among the solemn shadows of the old woods of Gray Forest.

The Hon. Richard Marston was now somewhere between forty and fifty years of age—perhaps nearer the latter; he still, however, retained, in an eminent degree, the traits of manly beauty, not the less remarkable for its unquestionably haughty and passionate character. He had married a beautiful girl, of good family, but without much money, somewhere about eighteen years before; and two children, a son and a daughter, had been the fruit of this union. The boy, Harry Marston, was at this time at Cambridge; and his sister, scarcely fifteen, was at home with her parents, and under the training of an accomplished governess, who had been recommended to them by a noble relative of Mrs. Marston. She was a native of France, but thoroughly mistress of the English language, and, except for a foreign accent, which gave a certain prettiness to all she said, she spoke it as perfectly as any native Englishwoman. This young Frenchwoman was eminently handsome and attractive. Expressive, dark eyes, a clear olive complexion, small even teeth, and a beautifully-dimpling smile, more perhaps than a strictly classic regularity of features, were the secrets of her unquestionable influence, at first sight, upon the fancy of every man of taste who beheld her.

Mr. Marston's fortune, never very large, had been shattered by early dissipation. Naturally of a proud and somewhat exacting temper, he acutely felt the mortifying consequences of his poverty. The want of what he felt ought to have been his position and influence in the county in which he resided, fretted and galled him; and he cherished a resentful and bitter sense of every slight, imaginary or real, to which the same fruitful source of annoyance and humiliation had exposed him. He held, therefore, but little intercourse with the surrounding gentry, and that little not of the pleasantest possible kind; for, not being himself in a condition to entertain, in that style which accorded with his own ideas of his station, he declined, as far as was compatible with good breeding, all the proffered hospitalities of the neighbourhood; and, from his wild and neglected park, looked out upon the surrounding world in a spirit of moroseness and defiance, very unlike, indeed, to that of neighbourly good-will.

In the midst, however, of many of the annoyances attendant upon crippled means, he enjoyed a few of those shadowy indications of hereditary importance, which are all the more dearly prized, as the substantial accessories of wealth have disappeared. The mansion in which he dwelt was, though old-fashioned, imposing in its aspect, and upon a scale unequivocally aristocratic; its walls were hung with ancestral portraits, and he managed to maintain about him a large and tolerably respectable staff of servants. In addition to these, he had his extensive demesne, his deer-park, and his unrivalled timber, wherewith to console himself; and, in the consciousness of these possessions, he found some imperfect assuagement of those bitter feelings of suppressed scorn and resentment, which a sense of lost station and slighted importance engendered. Mr. Marston's early habits had, unhappily, been of a kind to aggravate, rather than alleviate, the annoyances incidental to reduced means. He had been a gay man, a voluptuary, and a gambler. His vicious tastes had survived the means of their gratification. His love for his wife had been nothing more than one of those vehement and headstrong fancies, which, in self-indulgent men, sometimes result in marriage, and which seldom outlive the first few months of that life-long connexion. Mrs. Marston was a gentle, noble-minded woman. After agonies of disappointment, which none ever suspected, she had at length learned to submit, in sad and gentle acquiescence, to her fate. Those feelings, which had been the charm of her young days, were gone, and, as she bitterly felt, for ever. For them there was no recall—they could not return; and, without complaint or reproach, she yielded to what she felt was inevitable. It was impossible to look at Mrs. Marston, and not to discern, at a glance, the ruin of a surpassingly beautiful woman; a good deal wasted, pale, and chastened with a deep, untold sorrow, but still possessing the outlines, both in face and form, of that noble beauty and matchless grace, which had made her, in happier days, the admired of all observers. But equally impossible was it to converse with her, for even a minute, without hearing, in the gentle and melancholy music of her voice, the sad echoes of those griefs to which her early beauty had been sacrificed, an undying sense of lost love, and happiness departed, never to come again.

One morning, Mr. Marston had walked, as was his custom when he expected the messenger who brought from the neighbouring post-office his letters, some way down the broad, straight avenue, with its double rows of lofty trees at each side, when he encountered the nimble emissary on his return. He took the letter-bag in silence. It contained but two letters—one addressed to "Mademoiselle de Barras, chez M. Marston," and the other to himself. He took them both, dismissed the messenger, and opening that addressed to himself, read as follows, while he slowly retraced his steps towards the house:—

"Dear Richard,

"I am a whimsical fellow, as you doubtless remember, and have lately grown, they tell me, rather hippish besides. I do not know to which infirmity I am to attribute a sudden fancy which urges me to pay you a visit, if you will admit me. To say truth, my dear Dick, I wish to see a little of your part of the world, and, I will confess it, *en passant*, to see a little of *you* too. I really wish to make acquaintance with your family; and though they tell me my health is very much shaken, I must say, in self-defence, I am not a troublesome inmate. I can perfectly take care of myself, and need no nursing or caudling whatever. Will you present this, my petition, to Mrs. Marston, and report her decision thereon to me. Seriously, I know that your house may be full, or some other *contretemps* may make it impracticable for me just now to invade you. If it be so, tell me, my dear Richard, frankly, as my movements are perfectly free, and my time all my own, so that I can arrange my visit to suit your convenience.—Yours, &c.,

"*WYNSTON E. BERKLEY.*

"P. S.—Direct to me at —— Hotel, in Chester, as I shall probably be there by the time this reaches you."

"Ill-bred and pushing as ever," quoth Mr. Marston, angrily, as he thrust the unwelcome letter into his pocket. "This fellow, wallowing in wealth, without one nearer relative on earth than I, and associated more nearly still with me the—psha! not affection—the *recollections* of early and intimate companionship, leaves me unaided, for years of desertion and suffering, to the buffetings of the world, and the troubles of all but overwhelming pecuniary difficulties, and now, with the cool confidence of one entitled to respect and welcome, invites himself to my house. Coming here," he continued, after a gloomy pause, and still pacing slowly towards the house, "to collect amusing materials for next season's gossip—stories about the married Benedick—the bankrupt beau—the outcast tenant of a Cheshire wilderness"; and, as he said this, he looked at the neglected prospect before him with an eye almost of hatred. "Ay, to see the nakedness of the land is he coming, but he shall be disappointed. His money may buy him a cordial welcome at an inn, but curse me if it shall purchase him a reception here."

He again opened and glanced through the letter.

"Ay, purposely put in such a way thàt I can't decline it without affronting him," he continued doggedly. "Well, then, he has no one to blame but himself—affronted he shall be; I shall effectually put an end ot this humorous excursion. Egad, it is rather hard if a man cannot keep his poverty to himself."

Sir Wynston Berkley was a baronet of large fortune—a selfish, fashionable man, and an inveterate bachelor. He and Marston had been schoolfellows, and the violent and implacable temper of the latter had as little impressed his companion with feelings of regard, as the frivolity and selfishness of the baronet had won the esteem of his relative. As boys, they had little in common upon which to rest the basis of a friendship, or even a mutual liking. Berkley was gay, cold, and satirical; his cousin—for cousins they were—was jealous, haughty, and relentless. Their negative disinclination to one another's society, not unnaturally engendered by uncongenial and unamiable dispositions, had for a time given place to actual hostility, while the two young men were at Oxford. In some intrigue, Marston discovered in his cousin a too-successful rival; the consequence was, a bitter and furious quarrel, which, but for the prompt and peremptory interference of friends, Marston would undoubtedly have pushed to a bloody issue. Time had, however, healed this rupture, and the young men came to regard one another with the same feelings, and eventually to re-establish the same sort of cold and indifferent intimacy which had subsisted between them before their angry collision.

Under these circumstances, whatever suspicion Marston might have felt on the receipt of the unexpected, and indeed accountable proposal, which had just reached him, he certainly had little reason to complain of any violation of early friendship in the neglect with which Sir Wynston had hitherto treated him. In deciding to decline his proposed visit, however, Marston had not consulted the impulses of spite or anger. He knew the baronet well; he knew that he cherished no good-will towards him, and that in the project which he had thus unexpectedly broached, whatever indirect or selfish schemes might possibly be at the bottom of it, no friendly feeling had ever mingled. He was therefore resolved to avoid the trouble and the expense of a visit in all respects distasteful to him, and in a gentlemanlike way, but, at the same time, as the reader may suppose, with very little anxiety as to whether or not his gay correspondent should take offence at his reply, to decline, once for all, the proposed distinction.

With this resolution, he entered the spacious and somewhat dilapidated mansion which called him master; and entering a sitting-room, appropriated to his daughter's use, he found her there, in company with her beautiful French governess. He kissed his child, and saluted her young preceptress with formal courtesy.

"Mademoiselle," said he, "I have got a letter for you; and, Rhoda," he continued, addressing his pretty daughter, "bring this to your mother, and say, I request her to read it."

He gave her the letter he himself had just received, and the girl tripped lightly away upon her mission.

Had he narrowly scrutinised the countenance of the fair Frenchwoman, as she glanced at the direction of that which he had just placed in *her* hand, he might have seen certain transient, but very unmistakeable evidences of excitement and agitation. She quickly concealed the letter, however, and with a sigh, the momentary flush which it had called to her cheek subsided, and she was tranquil as usual.

Mr. Marston remained for some minutes—five, eight, or ten, we cannot say precisely—pretty much where he had stood on first entering the chamber, doubtless awaiting the return of his messenger, or the appearance of his wife. At length, however, he left the room himself to seek her; but, during his brief stay, his previous resolution had been removed. By what influence we cannot say; but removed completely it unquestionably was, and a final determination that Sir Wynston Berkley should become his guest had fixedly taken its place.

As Marston walked along the passages which led from this room, he encountered Mrs. Marston and his daughter.

"Well," said he, "you have read Wynston's letter?"

"Yes," she replied, returning it to him; "and what answer, Richard, do you purpose giving him?"

She was about to hazard a conjecture, but checked herself, remembering that even so faint an evidence of a disposition to advise might possibly be resented by her cold and imperious lord.

"I have considered it, and decided to receive him," he replied.

"Ah! I am afraid—that is, I hope—he may find our housekeeping such as he can enjoy," she said, with an involuntary expression of surprise; for she had scarcely had a doubt that her husband would have preferred evading the visit of his fine friend, under his gloomy circumstances.

"If our modest fare does not suit him," said Marston, with sullen bitterness, "he can depart as easily as he came. We, poor gentlemen, can but do our best. I have thought it over, and made up my mind."

"And how soon, my dear Richard, do you intend fixing his arrival?" she inquired, with the natural uneasiness of one upon whom, in an establishment whose pretensions considerably exceeded its resources, the perplexing cares of housekeeping devolved.

"Why, as soon as he pleases," replied he. "I suppose you can easily have his room prepared by to-morrow or next day. I shall write by this mail, and tell him to come down at once."

Having said this in a cold, decisive way, he turned and left her, as it seemed, not caring to be teased with further questions. He took his solitary way to a distant part of his wild park, where, far from the likelihood of disturbance or intrusion, he was often wont to amuse himself for the live-long day, in the sedentary sport of shooting rabbits. And there we leave him for the present, signifying to the distant inmates of his house the industrious pursuit of his unsocial occupation, by the dropping fire which sullenly, from hour to hour, echoed from the remote woods.

Mrs. Marston issued her orders; and having set on foot all the necessary preparations for so unwonted an event as a stranger's visit of some duration, she betook herself to her little boudoir—the scene of many an hour of patient but bitter suffering, unseen by human eye, and unknown, except to the just Searcher of hearts, to whom belongs mercy and VENGEANCE.

Mrs. Marston had but two friends to whom she had ever spoken upon the subject nearest her heart—the estrangement of her husband, a sorrow to which even time had failed to reconcile her. From her children this grief was carefully concealed. To them she never uttered the semblance of a complaint. Anything that could by possibility have reflected blame or dishonour upon their father, she would have perished rather than have allowed them so much as to suspect. The two friends who did understand her feelings, though in different degrees, were, one, a good and venerable clergyman, the Rev. Doctor Danvers, a frequent visiter and occasional guest at Gray Forest, where his simple manners and unaffected benignity and tenderness of heart had won the love of all, with the exception of its master, and commanded even his respect. The second was no other than the young French governess, Mademoiselle de Barras, in whose ready sympathy and consolatory counsels she found no small happiness. The society of this young lady had indeed become, next to that of her daughter, her greatest comfort and pleasure.

Mademoiselle de Barras was of a noble though ruined French family, and a certain nameless elegance and dignity attested, spite of her fallen condition, the purity of her descent. She was accomplished—possessed of that fine perception and sensitiveness, and that ready power of self-adaptation to the peculiarities and moods of others, which we term tact —and was, moreover, gifted with a certain natural grace, and manners the most winning imaginable. In short, she was a fascinating companion; and when the melancholy circumstances of her own situation, and the sad history of her once rich and noble family, were taken into account, with her striking attractions of person and air, the combination of all these associations and impressions rendered her one of the most interesting persons that could well be imagined. The circumstances of Mademoiselle de Barras's history and descent seemed to warrant, on Mrs. Marston's part, a closer intimacy and confidence than usually subsists between parties mutually occupying such a relation.

Mrs. Marston had hardly established herself in this little apartment, when a light foot approached, a gentle tap was given at the door, and Mademoiselle de Barras entered.

"Ah, mademoiselle, so kind—such pretty flowers. Pray sit down," said the lady, with a sweet and grateful smile, as she took from the tapered fingers of the foreigner the little bouquet which she had been at the pains to gather.

Mademoiselle sat down, and gently took the lady's hand and kissed it. A small matter will overflow a heart charged with sorrow—a chance word, a look, some little office of kindness—and so it was with mademoiselle's bouquet and gentle kiss. Mrs. Marston's heart was touched; her eyes filled with bright tears; she smiled gratefully upon her fair and humble companion, and as she smiled, her tears overflowed, and she wept in silence for some minutes.

"My poor mademoiselle," she said, at last, "you are so very, very kind."

Mademoiselle said nothing; she lowered her eyes, and pressed the poor lady's hand.

Apparently to interrupt an embarrassing silence, and to give a more cheerful tone to their little interview, the governess, in a gay tone, on a sudden said—

"And so, madame, we are to have a visiter, Miss Rhoda tells me—a baronet, is he not?"

"Yes, indeed, mademoiselle—Sir Wynston Berkley, a gay London gentleman, and a cousin of Mr. Marston's," she replied.

"Ha—a cousin!" exclaimed the young lady, with a little more surprise in her tone than seemed altogether called for—"a cousin? oh, then, that is the reason of his visit. Do, pray, madame, tell me all about him; I am so much afraid of strangers, and what you call men of the world. Oh, dear Mrs. Marston, I am not worthy to be here, and he will see all that in a moment; indeed, indeed, I am afraid. Pray tell me all about him."

She said this with a simplicity which made the elder lady smile, and while mademoiselle re-adjusted the tiny flowers which formed the bouquet she had just presented to her, Mrs. Marston good-naturedly recounted to her all she knew of Sir Wynston Berkley, which, in substance, amounted to no more than we have already stated. When she concluded, the young Frenchwoman continued for some time silent, still busy with her flowers. But, suddenly, she heaved a deep sigh, and shook her head.

"You seem disquieted, mademoiselle," said Mrs. Marston, in a tone of kindness.

"I am thinking, madame," she said, still looking upon the flowers which she was adjusting, and again sighing profoundly, "I am thinking of what you said to me a week ago; alas!"

"I do not remember what it was, my good mademoiselle—nothing, I am sure, that ought to grieve you—at least nothing that was intended to have that effect," replied the lady, in a tone of gentle encouragement.

"No, not intended, madame," said the young Frenchwoman, sorrowfully.

"Well, what was it? Perhaps you misunderstood; perhaps I can explain what I said," replied Mrs. Marston, affectionately.

"Ah, madame, you think—you think I am *unlucky*," answered the young lady, slowly and faintly.

"Unlucky! Dear mademoiselle, you surprise me," rejoined her companion.

"I mean—what I mean is this, madame; you date unhappiness—if not its beginning, at least its great aggravation and increase," she answered, dejectedly, "from the time of my coming here, madame; and though I know you are too good to dislike me on that account, yet I must, in your eyes, be ever connected with calamity, and look like an ominous thing."

"Dear mademoiselle, allow no such thought to enter your mind. You do me great wrong, indeed you do," said Mrs. Marston, laying her hand upon the young lady's, kindly.

There was a silence for a little time, and the elder lady resumed:—

"I remember now what you allude to, dear mademoiselle—the increased estrangement, the widening separation which severs me from one unutterably dear to me—the first and bitter disappointment of my life, which seems to grow more hopelessly incurable day by day."

Mrs. Marston paused, and, after a brief silence, the governess said:—

"I am very superstitious myself, dear madame, and I thought I must have seemed to you an inauspicious inmate—in short, *unlucky*—as I have said; and the thought made me very unhappy—so unhappy, that I was going to leave you, madame—I may now tell you frankly—going away; but you have set my doubts at rest, and I am quite happy again."

"Dear mademoiselle!" cried the lady, tenderly, and rising, as she spake, to kiss the cheek of her humble friend; "never—never speak of this again. God knows I have too few friends on earth, to spare the kindest and tenderest among them all. No, no. You little think what comfort I have found in your warm-hearted and ready sympathy, and how dearly I prize your affection, my poor mademoiselle."

The young Frenchwoman rose, with downcast eyes, and a dimpling, happy smile; and, as Mrs. Marston drew her affectionately toward her, and kissed her, she timidly returned the embrace of her kind patroness. For a moment her graceful arms encircled her, and she whispered to her, "Dear madame, how happy—how very happy you make me."

Had Ithuriel touched with his spear the beautiful young woman, thus for a moment, as it seemed, lost in a trance of gratitude and love, would that angelic form have stood the test unscathed? A spectator, marking the scene, might have observed a strange gleam in her eyes—a strange expression in her face—an influence for a moment *not* angelic, like a shadow of some passing spirit, cross her visibly, as she leaned over the gentle lady's neck, and murmured, "Dear madame, how happy—how very happy you make me." Such a spectator, as he looked at that gentle lady, might have seen, for one dreamy moment, a lithe and painted serpent, coiled round and round, and hissing in her ear.

A few minutes more, and mademoiselle was in the solitude of her own apartment. She shut and bolted the door, and taking from her desk the letter which she had that morning received, threw herself into an arm-chair, and studied the document profoundly. Her actual revision and scrutiny of the letter itself was interrupted by long intervals of profound abstraction; and, after a full hour thus spent, she locked it carefully up again, and with a clear brow, and a gay smile, rejoined her pretty pupil for a walk.

We must now pass over an interval of a few days, and come at once to the arrival of Sir Wynston Berkley, which duly occurred upon the evening of the day appointed. The baronet descended from his chaise but a short time before the hour at which the little party, which formed the family at Gray Forest were wont to assemble for the social meal of supper. A few minutes devoted to the mysteries of the toilet, with the aid of an accomplished valet, enabled him to appear, as he conceived, without disadvantage at this domestic re-union.

Sir Wynston Berkley was a particularly gentlemanlike person. He was rather tall, and elegantly made, with gay, easy manners, and something indefinably aristocratic in his face, which, however, was a little more worn than his years would have strictly accounted for. But Sir Wynston had been a *roué*, and, spite of the cleverest possible making up, the ravages of excess were very traceable in the lively beau of fifty. Perfectly well dressed, and with a manner that was ease and gaiety itself, he was at home from the moment he entered the room. Of course, anything like genuine cordiality was out of the question; but Mr. Marston embraced his relative with perfect good breeding, and the baronet appeared determined to like everybody, and be pleased with everything.

He had not been five minutes in the parlour, chatting gaily with Mr. and Mrs. Marston and their pretty daughter, when Mademoiselle de Barras entered the room As she moved towards Mrs. Marston, Sir Wynston rose, and, observing her with evident admiration, said in an under-tone, inquiringly, to Marston, who was beside him—

"And *this?*"

"That is Mademoiselle de Barras, my daughter's governess, and Mrs. Marston's companion," said Marston, drily.

"Ha!" said Sir Wynston; "I *thought* you were but three at home just now, and I was right. Your son is at Cambridge; I heard so from our old friend, Jack Manbury. Jack has his boy there too. Egad, Dick, it seems but last week that you and I were there together."

"Yes," said Marston, looking gloomily into the fire, as if he saw, in its smoke and flicker, the phantoms of murdered time and opportunity; "but I hate looking back, Wynston. The past is to me but a medley of ill-luck and worse management."

"Why what an ungrateful dog you are!" returned Sir Wynston, gaily, turning his back upon the fire, and glancing round the spacious and handsome, though somewhat faded apartment. "I was on the point of congratulating you on the possession of the finest park and noblest demesne in Cheshire, when you begin to *grumble*. Egad, Dick, all I can say to your complaint is, that *I* don't pity you, and there are dozens who may honestly *envy* you—that is all."

In spite of this cheering assurance, Marston remained sullenly silent. Supper, however, had now been served, and the little party assumed their places at the table.

"I am sorry, Wynston, I have no sport of any kind to offer you here," said Marston, "except, indeed, some good trout-fishing, if you like it. I have three miles of excellent fishing at your command."

"My dear fellow, I am a mere cockney," rejoined Sir Wynston; "I am not a sportsman; I never tried it, and should not like to begin now. No, Dick, what I much prefer is, abundance of your fresh air, and the enjoyment of your scenery. When I was at Rouen three years ago ——."

"Ha!—Rouen? Mademoiselle will feel an interest in that; it is her birth-place," interrupted Marston, glancing at the Frenchwoman.

"Yes—Rouen—ah—yes!" said mademoiselle, with very evident embarrassment.

Sir Wynston appeared for a moment a little disconcerted too, but rallied speedily, and pursued his detail of his doings at that fair town of Normandy.

Marston knew Sir Wynston well; and he rightly calculated that whatever effect his experience of the world might have had in intensifying his selfishness or hardening his heart, it certainly could have had none in improving a character originally worthless and unfeeling. He knew, moreover, that his wealthy cousin was gifted with a great deal of that small cunning which is available for masking the little scheming of frivolous and worldly men; and that Sir Wynston never took trouble of any kind without a sufficient purpose, having its centre in his own personal gratification.

This visit greatly puzzled Marston; it gave him even a vague sense of uneasiness. Could there exist any flaw in his own title to the estate of Gray Forest? He had an unpleasant, doubtful sort of remembrance of some apprehensions of this kind, when he was but a child, having been whispered in the family. Could this really be so, and could the baronet have been led to make this unexpected visit merely for the purpose of personally examining into the condition of a property of which he was about to become the legal invader? The nature of this suspicion affords, at all events, a fair gauge of Marston's estimate of his cousin's character. And as he revolved these doubts from time to time, and as he thought of Mademoiselle de Barras's transient, but unaccountable embarrassment at the mention of Rouen by Sir Wynston—an embarrassment which the baronet himself appeared for a moment to reciprocate —undefined, glimmering suspicions of another kind flickered through the darkness of his mind. He was effectually puzzled; his surmises and conjectures baffled; and he more than half repented that he had acceded to his cousin's proposal, and admitted him as an inmate of his house.

Although Sir Wynston comported himself as if he were conscious of being the very most welcome visiter who could possibly have established himself at Gray Forest, he was, doubtless, fully aware of the real feelings with which he was regarded by his host. If he had in reality an object in prolonging his stay, and wished to make the postponement of his departure the direct interest of his entertainer, he unquestionably took effectual measures for that purpose.

The little party broke up every evening at about ten o'clock, and Sir Wynston retired to his chamber at the same hour. He found little difficulty in inducing Marston to amuse him there with a quiet game of picquet. In his own room, therefore, in the luxurious ease of dressing-gown and slippers he sat at cards with his host, often until an hour or two past midnight. Sir Wynston was exorbitantly wealthy, and very reckless in expenditure. The stakes for which they played, although they gradually became in reality pretty heavy, were in his eyes a very unimportant consideration. Marston, on the other hand, was poor, and played with the eye of a lynx and the appetite of a shark. The ease and perfect good-humour with which Sir Wynston lost were not unimproved by his entertainer, who, as may readily be supposed, was not sorry to reap this golden harvest, provided without the slightest sacrifice, on his part, of pride or independence. If, indeed, he sometimes suspected that his guest was a little more anxious to lose than to win, he was also quite resolved not to perceive it, but calmly persisted in, night after night, giving Sir Wynston, as he termed it, his revenge; or, in other words, treating him to a repetition of his losses. All this was very agreeable to Marston, who began to treat his visiter with, at all events, more external cordiality and distinction than at first.

An incident, however, occurred, which disturbed these amicable relations in an unexpected way. It becomes necessary here to mention that Mademoiselle de Barras's sleeping apartment opened from a long corridor. It was *en suite* with two dressing-rooms, each opening also upon the corridor, but wholly unused and unfurnished. Some five or six other apartments also opened at either side, upon the same passage. These little local details being premised, it so happened that one day Marston, who had gone out with the intention of angling in the trout-stream which flowed through his park, though at a considerable distance from the house, having unexpectedly returned to procure some tackle which he had forgotten, was walking briskly through the corridor in question to his own apartment, when, to his surprise, the door of one of the deserted dressing-rooms, of which we have spoken, was cautiously pushed open, and Sir Wynston Berkley issued from it. Marston was almost beside him as he did so, and Sir Wynston made a motion as if about instinctively to draw back again, and at the same time the keen ear of his host distinctly caught the sound of rustling silks and a tip-toe tread hastily withdrawing from the deserted chamber. Sir Wynston looked nearly as much confused as a man of the world can look. Marston stopped short, and scanned his visiter for a moment with a very peculiar expression.

"You have caught me peeping, Dick. I am an inveterate explorer," said the baronet, with an effectual effort to shake off his embarrassment. "An open door in a fine old house is a temptation which ——"

"That door is usually closed, and ought to be kept so," interrupted Marston, drily; "there is nothing whatever to be seen in the room but dust and cobwebs."

"Pardon me," said Sir Wynston, more easily, "you forget the view from the window."

"Ay, the view, to be sure; there *is* a good view from it," said Marston, with as much of his usual manner as he could resume so soon; and, at the same time, carelessly opening the door again, he walked in, accompanied by Sir Wynston, and both stood at the window together, looking out in silence upon a prospect which neither of them saw.

"Yes, I do think it is a good view," said Marston; and as he turned carelessly away, he darted a swift glance round the chamber. The door opening toward the French lady's apartment was closed, but not actually shut. This was enough; and as they left the room, Marston repeated his invitation to his guest to accompany him; but in a tone which showed that he scarcely followed the meaning of what he himself was saying.

He walked undecidedly toward his own room, then turned and went down stairs. In the hall he met his pretty child.

"Ha! Rhoda," said he, "you have not been out to-day?"

"No, papa; but it is so very fine, I think I shall go now."

"Yes; go, and mademoiselle can accompany you. Do you hear, Rhoda, mademoiselle goes with you, and you had better go at once."

A few minutes more, and Marston, from the parlour-window, beheld Rhoda and the elegant French girl walking together towards the woodlands. He watched them gloomily, himself unseen, until the crowding underwood concealed their receding figures. Then, with a sigh, he turned, and reascended the great stair case.

"I shall sift this mystery to the bottom," thought he. "I shall foil the conspirators, if so they be, with their own weapons; art with art; chicane with chicane; duplicity with duplicity."

He was now in the long passage which we have just spoken of, and glancing back and before him, to ascertain that no chance eye discerned him, he boldly entered mademoiselle's chamber. Her writing-desk lay upon the table. It was locked; and coolly taking it in his hands, Marston carried it into his own room, bolted his chamber-door, and taking two or three bunches of keys, he carefully tried nearly a dozen in succession, and when almost despairing of success, at last found one which fitted the lock, turned, and opened the desk.

Sustained throughout his dishonourable task by some strong and angry passion, the sight of the open escritoire checked and startled him for a moment. Violated privilege, invaded secrecy, base, perfidious espionage upbraided and stigmatised him, as the intricacies of the outraged sanctuary opened upon his intrusive gaze. He felt for a moment shocked and humbled. He was impelled to lock and replace the desk where he had originally found it, without having effected his meditated treason; but this hesitation was transient; the fiery and reckless impulse which had urged him to the act returned to enforce its consummation. With a guilty eye and eager hands, he searched the contents of this tiny repository of the fair Norman's written secrets.

"Ha! the very thing," he muttered, as he detected the identical letter which he himself had handed to Mademoiselle de Barras but a few days before. "The handwriting struck me, ill-disguised; I thought I knew it; we shall see."

He had opened the letter; it contained but a few lines: he held his breath while he read it. First he grew pale, then a shadow came over his face, and then another, and another, darker and darker, shade upon shade, as if an exhalation from the pit was momentarily blackening the air about him. He said nothing; there was but one long, gentle sigh, and in his face a mortal sternness, as he folded the letter again, replaced it, and locked the desk.

Of course, when Mademoiselle de Barras returned from her accustomed walk, she found everything in her room, to all appearance, undisturbed, and just as when she left it. While this young lady was making her toilet for the evening, and while Sir Wynston Berkley was worrying himself with conjectures as to whether Marston's evil looks, when he encountered him that morning in the passage, existed only in his own fancy, or were, in good truth, very grim and significant realities, Marston himself was striding alone through the wildest and darkest solitudes of his park, haunted by his own unholy thoughts, and, it may be, by those other evil and unearthly influences which wander, as we know, "in desert places." Darkness overtook him, and the chill of night, in these lonely tracts. In his *solitary* walk, what fearful *company* had he been keeping! As the shades of night deepened round him, the sense of the neighbourhood of ill, the consciousness of the foul fancies of which, where he was now treading, he had been for hours the sport, oppressed him with a vague and unknown terror; a certain horror of the thoughts which had been his comrades through the day, which he could not now shake off, and which haunted him with a ghastly and defiant pertinacity, scared, while they half-enraged him. He stalked swiftly homewards, like a guilty man pursued.

Marston was not perfectly satisfied, though very nearly, with the evidence now in his possession. The letter, the stolen perusal of which had so agitated him that day, bore no signature; but, independently of the handwriting, which seemed, spite of the constraint of an attempted disguise, to be familiar to his eye, there existed, in the matter of the letter, short as it was, certain internal evidences, which, although not actually conclusive, raised, in conjunction with all the other circumstances, a powerful presumption in aid of his suspicions. He resolved, however, to sift the matter further, and to bide his time. Meanwhile his manner must indicate no trace of his dark surmises and bitter thoughts. Deception, in its two great branches, simulation and *dis*simulation, was easy to him. His habitual reserve and gloom would divest any accidental and momentary disclosure of his inward trouble of everything suspicious or unaccountable, which would have characterized such displays and eccentricities in another man.

His rapid and reckless ramble, a kind of physical vent for the paroxysm which had so agitated him throughout the greater part of the day, had soiled and disordered his dress, and thus had helped to give to his whole appearance a certain air of haggard wildness, which, in the privacy of his chamber, he hastened carefully and entirely to remove.

At supper, Marston was apparently in unusually good spirits. Sir Wynston and he chatted gaily and fluently upon many subjects, grave and gay. Among them the inexhaustible topic of popular superstition happened to turn up, and especially the subject of strange prophecies of the fates and fortunes of individuals, singularly fulfilled in the events of their after-life.

"By-the-by, Dick, this is rather a nervous topic for me to discuss," said Sir Wynston.

"How so?" asked his host.

"Why, don't you remember?" urged the baronet.

"No, I don't recollect what you allude to," replied Marston, in all sincerity.

"Why, don't you remember Eton?" pursued Sir Wynston.

"Yes, to be sure," said Marston.

"*Well?*" continued his visiter.

"Well, I really don't recollect the prophecy," replied Marston.

"What! do you forget the gipsy who predicted that you were to murder *me*, Dick—eh?"

"Ah—ha, ha!" laughed Marston, with a start.

"Don't you remember it now?" urged his companion.

"Ah, why yes, I believe I do," said Marston; "but another prophecy was running in my mind; a gipsy prediction, too. At Ascot, do you recollect the girl told me I was to be lord chancellor of England, and a duke besides?"

"Well, Dick," rejoined Sir Wynston, merrily, "if both are to be fulfilled, or neither, I trust you may never sit upon the woolsack of England."

The party soon after broke up: Sir Wynston and his host, as usual, to pass some hours at picquet; and Mrs. Marston, as was her wont, to spend some time in her own boudoir, over notes and accounts, and the worrying details of housekeeping.

While thus engaged, she was disturbed by a respectful tap at her door, and an elderly servant, who had been for many years in the employment of Mr. Marston, presented himself.

"Well, Merton, do you want anything?" asked the lady.

"Yes, ma'am, please, I want to give warning; I wish to leave the service, ma'am;" replied he, respectfully, but doggedly.

"To leave us, Merton!" echoed his mistress, both surprised and sorry for the man had been long her servant, and had been much liked and trusted.

"Yes, ma'am," he repeated.

"And why do you wish to do so, Merton? has anything occurred to make the place unpleasant to you?" urged the lady.

"No, ma'am—no, indeed," said he, earnestly, "I have nothing to complain of—nothing, indeed, ma'am."

"Perhaps, you think you can do better, if you leave us?" suggested his mistress.

"No, indeed, ma'am, I have no such thought," he said, and seemed on the point of bursting into tears; "but— but, somehow—ma'am, there is something come over me, lately, and I can't help, but think, if I stay here, ma'am—some—some—*misfortune* will happen us all— and that is the truth, ma'am."

"This is very foolish, Merton— a mere childish fancy," replied Mrs. Marston; "you like your place, and have no better prospect before you; and now, for a mere superstitious fancy, you propose giving it up, and leaving us. No, no, Merton, you had better think the matter over—and if you still, upon reflection, prefer going away, you can then speak to your master."

"Thank you ma'am—God bless you," said the man, withdrawing.

Mrs. Marston rang the bell for her maid, and retired to her room.

"Has anything occurred lately," she asked, "to annoy Merton?"

"No, ma'am, I don't know of anything; but he is very changed, indeed, of late," replied the maid.

"He has not been quarrelling?" inquired she.

"Oh, no, ma'am, he never quarrels; he is very quiet, and keeps to himself always; he thinks a wonderful deal of himself," replied the servant.

"But, you said that he is much changed—did you not?" continued the lady; for there was something strangely excited and unpleasant in the man's manner, in this little interview, which struck Mrs. Marston, and alarmed her curiosity. He had seemed like one charged with some horrible secret—intolerable, and which he yet dared not reveal.

"What," proceeded Mrs. Marston, "is the nature of the change of which you speak?"

"Why, ma'am, he is like one frightened, and in sorrow," she replied; "he will sit silent, and now and then shaking his head, as if he wanted to get rid of something that is teasing him, for an hour together."

"Poor man!" said she.

"And, then, when we are at meals, he will, all on a sudden, get up, and leave the table; and Jem Boulter, that sleeps in the next room to him, says, that, almost as often as he looks through the little window between the two rooms, no matter what hour in the night, he sees Mr. Merton on his knees by the bedside, praying or crying, he don't know which; but, any way, he is not happy—poor man!— and that is plain enough."

"It is very strange," said the lady, after a pause; "but, I think, and hope, after all, it will prove to have been no more than a little nervousness."

"Well, ma'am, I do hope it is not his conscience that is coming against him, now," said the maid.

"We have no reason to suspect anything of the kind," said Mrs. Marston, gravely; "quite the reverse; he has been always a particularly proper man."

"Oh, indeed," responded the attendant, "goodness forbid I should say or think anything against him; but I could not help telling you my mind, ma'am, meaning no harm."

"And, how long is it since you observed this sad change in poor Merton?" persisted the lady.

"Not, indeed, to say very long, ma'am," replied the girl; "somewhere about a week, or very little more—at least, as we remarked, ma'am."

Mrs. Marston pursued her inquiries no further that night. But, although she affected to treat the matter thus lightly, it had, somehow, taken a painful hold upon her imagination, and left in her mind those undefinable and ominous sensations, which, in certain mental temperaments, seem to foreshadow the approach of unknown misfortune.

For two or three days, everything went on smoothly, and pretty much as usual. At the end of this brief interval, however, the attention of Mrs. Marston was recalled to the subject of her servant's mysterious anxiety to leave, and give up his situation. Merton again stood before her, and repeated the intimation he had already given.

"Really, Merton, this is very odd," said the lady. "You like your situation, and yet you persist in desiring to leave it. What am I to think?"

"Oh, ma'am," said he, "I am unhappy; I am tormented, ma'am. I can't tell you, ma'am; I can't indeed ma'am!"

"If anything weighs upon your mind, Merton, I would advise you to consult our good clergyman, Dr. Danvers," urged the lady.

The servant hung his head, and mused for a time gloomily; and then said decisively—

"No, ma'am; no use."

"And pray, Merton, how long is it since you first entertained this desire?" asked Mrs. Marston.

"Since Sir Wynston Berkley came, ma'am," answered he.

"Has Sir Wynston annoyed you in any way?" continued she.

"Far from it, ma'am," he replied; "he is a very kind gentleman."

"Well, his *man*, then; is *he* a respectable, inoffensive person?" she inquired.

"I never met one more so," said the man, promptly, and raising his head.

"What I wish to know is, whether your desire to go is connected with Sir Wynston and his servant?" said Mrs. Marston.

The man hesitated, and shifted his position uneasily.

"You need not answer, Merton, if you don't wish it," she said kindly.

"Why, ma'am, yes, it *has* something to say to them both," he replied, with some agitation.

"I really cannot understand this," said she.

Merton hesitated for some time, and appeared much troubled.

"It was something, ma'am—something that Sir Wynston's man said to me; and there it is out," he said at last, with an effort.

"Well, Merton," said she, "I won't press you further; but I must say, that as this communication, whatever it may be, has caused *you*, unquestionably, very great uneasiness, it seems to me but probable that it affects the safety or the interests of some person—I cannot say of whom; and, if so, there can be no doubt that it is your duty to acquaint those who are so involved in the disclosure, with its purport."

"No, ma'am, there is nothing in what I heard that could touch anybody but myself. It was nothing but what others heard, without remarking it, or thinking about it. I can't tell you any more, ma'am; but I am very unhappy, and uneasy in my mind."

As the man said this, he began to weep bitterly.

The idea that his mind was affected now seriously occurred to Mrs. Marston, and she resolved to convey her suspicions to her husband, and to leave him to deal with the case as to him should seem good.

"Don't agitate yourself so, Merton; I shall speak to your master upon what you have said; and you may rely upon it, that no surmise to the prejudice of your character has entered my mind," said Mrs. Marston, very kindly.

"Oh, ma'am, you are too good," sobbed the poor man, vehemently. "You don't know me, ma'am; I never knew myself till lately. I am a miserable man. I am frightened at myself, ma'am—frightened terribly. Christ knows, it would be well for me I was dead this minute."

"I am very sorry for your unhappiness, Merton," said Mrs. Marston; "and, especially, that I can do nothing to alleviate it; I can but speak, as I have said, to your master, and he will give you your discharge, and arrange whatever else remains to be done."

"God bless you, ma'am," said the servant, still much agitated, and left her.

Mr. Marston usually passed the early part of the day in active exercise, and she, supposing that he was, in all probability, at that moment far from home, went to "mademoiselle's" chamber, which was at the other end of the spacious house, to confer with her in the interval upon the strange application thus urged by poor Merton.

Just as she reached the door of Mademoiselle de Barras's chamber, she heard voices within exerted in evident excitement. She stopped in amazement. They were those of her husband and mademoiselle. Startled, confounded, and amazed, she pushed open the door, and entered. Her husband was sitting, one hand clutched upon the arm of the chair he occupied, and the other extended, and clenched, as it seemed, with the emphasis of rage, upon the desk which stood upon the table. His face was darkened with the stormiest passions, and his gaze was fixed upon the Frenchwoman, who was standing with a look half-guilty, half-imploring, at a little distance.

There was something, to Mrs. Marston, so utterly unexpected, and even so shocking, in this *tableau*, that she stood for some seconds pale and breathless, and gazing with a vacant stare of fear and horror from her husband to the French girl, and from her to her husband again. The three figures in this strange group remained fixed, silent, and aghast, for several seconds. Mrs. Marston endeavoured to speak; but, though her lips moved, no sound escaped her; and, from very weakness, she sank, half-fainting, into a chair.

Marston rose, throwing, as he did so, a guilty and furious glance at the young Frenchwoman, and walked a step or two toward the door; he hesitated, however, and turned, just as mademoiselle, bursting into tears, threw her arms round Mrs. Marston's neck, and passionately exclaimed—

"Protect me, madame, I implore, from the insults and suspicions of your husband."

Marston stood a little behind his wife, and he and the governess exchanged a glance of keen significance, as the latter sank, sobbing, like an injured child into its mother's embrace, upon the poor lady's tortured bosom.

"Madame, madame! he says—Mr. Marston says—I have presumed to give you advice, and to meddle, and to interfere; that I am endeavouring to make you despise his authority. Madame, speak for me. Say, madame, have I ever done so?—say, madame, am I the cause of bitterness and contumacy? Ah, *mon Dieu! c'est trop*— it is too much, madame. I shall go—I must go, madame. Why, ah! why, did I stay for this?"

As she thus spoke, mademoiselle again burst into a paroxysm of weeping, and again the same significant glance was interchanged.

"Go; yes, you shall go," said Marston, striding toward the window. "I will have no whispering or conspiring in my house: I have heard of your confidences and consultations. Mrs. Marston, I meant to have done this quietly," he continued, addressing his wife; "I meant to have given Mademoiselle de Barras my opinion and her dismissal without your assistance; but it seems you wish to interpose. You are sworn friends, and never fail one another, of course, at a pinch. I take it for granted that I owe your presence at our interview which I am resolved shall be, as respects mademoiselle, a final one, to a message from that intriguing young lady—eh?"

"I have had no message, Richard," said Mrs. Marston; "I don't know—do tell me, for God's sake, what is all this about?" And as the poor lady thus spoke, her overwrought feelings found vent in a violent flood of tears.

"Yes, madame, that is the question. I have asked him frequently what is all this anger, all these reproaches about; what have I done?" interposed mademoiselle, with indignant vehemence, standing erect, and viewing Marston with a flashing eye and a flushed cheek. "Yes, I am called conspirator, meddler, *intrigante*. Ah, madame, it is intolerable."

"But what have I done, Richard?" urged the poor lady, stunned and bewildered; "how have I offended you?"

"Yes, yes," continued the Frenchwoman, with angry volubility, "what has she done that you call contumacy and disrespect? Yes, dear madame, *there* is the question; and if he cannot answer, is it not most cruel to call me conspirator, and spy, and *intrigante*, because I talk to my dear madame, who is my only friend in this place?"

"Mademoiselle de Barras, I need no declamation from you; and, pardon me, Mrs. Marston, nor from you either," retorted he; "I have my information from one on whom I can rely; let that suffice. Of course you are both agreed in a story. I dare say you are ready to swear you never so much as canvassed my conduct, and my *coldness* and *estrangement*—eh? These are the words, are not they?"

"I have done you no wrong, sir; madame can tell you. I am no mischief-maker; no, I never was such a thing. Was I, madame?" persisted the governess—"bear witness for me?"

"I have told you my mind, Mademoiselle de Barras," interrupted Marston; "I will have no altercation, if you please. I think, Mrs. Marston, we have had enough of this; may I accompany you hence?"

So saying, he took the poor lady's passive hand, and led her from the room. Mademoiselle stood in the centre of the apartment, alone, erect, with heaving breast and burning cheek—beautiful, thoughtful, guilty— the very type of the fallen angelic. There for a time, her heart all confusion, her mind darkened, we must leave her; various courses before her, and as yet without resolution to choose among them; a lost spirit, borne on the eddies of the storm; fearless and self-reliant, but with no star to guide her on her dark, malign, and forlorn way.

Mrs. Marston, in her own room, reviewed the agitating scene through which she had just been so unexpectedly carried. The tremendous suspicion which, at the first disclosure of the *tableau* we have described, smote the heart and brain of the poor lady with the stun of a thunderbolt, had been, indeed, subsequently disturbed, and afterwards contradicted; but the shock of her first impression remained still upon her mind and heart. She felt still through every nerve the vibrations of that maddening terror and despair which had overcome her senses for a moment. The surprise, the shock, the horror, outlived the obliterating influence of what followed. She was in this agitation when Mademoiselle de Barras entered her chamber, resolved with all her art to second and support the success of her prompt measures in the recent critical emergency. She had come, she said, to bid her dear madame farewell, for she was resolved to go. Her own room had been invaded, that insult and reproach might be heaped upon her; how utterly unmerited Mrs. Marston knew. She had been called by every foul name which applied to the spy and the maligner; she could not bear it. Some one had evidently been endeavouring to procure her removal, and had but too effectually succeeded. Mademoiselle was determined to go early the next morning; nothing should prevent or retard her departure; her resolution was taken. In this strain did mademoiselle run on, but in a subdued and melancholy tone, and weeping profusely.

The wild and ghastly suspicions which had for a moment flashed terribly upon the mind of Mrs. Marston, had faded away under the influences of reason and reflection, although, indeed, much painful excitement still remained, before Mademoiselle de Barras had visited her room. Marston's temper she knew but too well; it was violent, bitter, and impetuous; and though he cared little, if at all, for her, she had ever perceived that he was angrily jealous of the slightest intimacy or confidence by which any other than himself might establish an influence over her mind. That he had learned the subject of some of her most interesting conversations with mademoiselle she could not doubt, for he had violently upbraided that young lady in her presence with having discussed it, and here now was mademoiselle herself taking refuge with her from galling affront and unjust reproach, incensed, wounded, and weeping. The whole thing was consistent; all the circumstances bore plainly in the same direction; the evidence was conclusive; and Mrs. Marston's thoughts and feelings respecting her fair young confidante quickly found their old level, and flowed on tranquilly and sadly in their accustomed channel.

While Mademoiselle de Barras was thus, with the persevering industry of the spider, repairing the meshes which a chance breath had shattered, she would, perhaps, have been in her turn shocked and startled, could she have glanced into Marston's mind, and seen, in what was passing there, the real extent of her danger.

Marston was walking, as usual, alone, and in the most solitary region of his lonely park. One hand grasped his walking-stick, not to lean upon it, but as if it were the handle of a battle-axe; the other was buried in his bosom; his dark face looked upon the ground, and he strode onward with a slow but energetic step, which had the air of deep resolution. He found himself at last in a little churchyard, lying far among the wild forest of his demesne, and in the midst of which, covered with ivy and tufted plants, now ruddy with autumnal tints, stood the ruined walls of a little chapel. In the dilapidated vault close by lay buried many of his ancestors, and under the little wavy hillocks of fern and nettles, slept many an humble villager. He sat down upon a worn tombstone in this lowly ruin, and with his eyes fixed upon the ground, he surrendered his spirit to the stormy and evil thoughts which he had invited. Long and motionless he sat there, while his foul fancies and schemes began to assume shape and order. The wind rushing through the ivy roused him for a moment, and as he raised his gloomy eye it alighted accidentally upon a skull, which some wanton hand had fixed in a crevice of the wall. He averted his glance quickly, but almost as quickly refixed his gaze upon the impassive symbol of death, with an expression lowering and contemptuous, and with an angry gesture struck it down among the weeds with his stick. He left the place, and wandered on through the woods.

"Men can't control the thoughts that flit across their minds," he muttered, as he went along, "any more than they can direct the shadows of the clouds that sail above them. They come and pass, and leave no stain behind. What, then, of omens, and that wretched effigy of death? Stuff—psha! *Murder*, indeed! I'm incapable of murder. I have drawn my sword upon a man in fair duel; but *murder!* Out upon the thought, out upon it."

He stamped upon the ground with a pang at once of fury and horror. He walked on a little, stopped again, and folding his arms, leaned against an ancient tree.

"Mademoiselle de Barras, vous êtes une traîtresse, and you shall go. Yes, go you shall; you have deceived me, and we must part."

He said this with melancholy bitterness; and, after a pause, continued:—

"I will have no other revenge. No; though, I dare say, she will care but little for this; very little, if at all."

"And then, as to the other person," he resumed, after a pause, "it is not the first time he has acted like a trickster. He has crossed me before, and I will choose an opportunity to tell him my mind. I won't mince matters with him either, and will not spare him one insulting syllable that he deserves. He wears a sword, and so do I; if he pleases, he may draw it; he shall have the opportunity; but, at all events, I will make it impossible for him to prolong his disgraceful visit at my house."

On reaching home and his own study, the servant, Merton, presented himself, and his master, too deeply excited to hear him then, appointed the next day for the purpose. There was no contending against Marston's peremptory will, and the man reluctantly withdrew. Here was, apparently, a matter of no imaginable moment; whether this menial should be discharged on that day, or on the morrow; and yet mighty things were involved in the alternative.

There was a deeper gloom than usual over the house. The servants seemed to know that something had gone wrong, and looked grave and mysterious. Marston was more than ever dark and moody. Mrs. Marston's dimmed and swollen eyes showed that she had been weeping. Mademoiselle absented herself from supper, on the plea of a bad headache. Rhoda saw that something, she knew not what, had occurred to agitate her elders, and was depressed and anxious. The old clergyman, whom we have already mentioned, had called, and stayed to supper. Dr. Danvers was a man of considerable learning, strong sense, and remarkable simplicity of character. His thoughtful blue eye, and well-marked countenance, were full of gentleness and benevolence, and elevated by a certain natural dignity, of which purity and goodness, without one debasing shade of self-esteem and arrogance, were the animating spirit. Mrs. Marston loved and respected this good minister of God; and many a time had sought and found, in his gentle and earnest counsels, and in the overflowing tenderness of his sympathy, much comfort and support in the progress of her sore and protracted earthly trial. Most especially at one critical period in her history had he endeared himself to her, by interposing, and successfully, to prevent a formal separation which (as ending for ever the one hope that cheered her on, even in the front of despair) she would probably not long have survived.

With Mr. Marston, however, he was far from being a favourite. There was that in his lofty and simple purity which abashed and silently reproached the sensual, bitter, disappointed man of the world. The angry pride of the scornful man felt its own meanness in the grand presence of a simple and humble Christian minister. And the very fact that all his habits had led him to hold such a character in contempt, made him but the more unreasonably resent the involuntary homage which its exhibition in Dr. Danvers's person invariably extorted from him. He felt in this good man's presence under a kind of irritating restraint; that he was in the presence of one with whom he had, and could have, no sympathy whatever, and yet one whom he could not help both admiring and respecting; and in these conflicting feelings were involved certain gloomy and humbling inferences about himself, which he hated, and almost feared to contemplate.

It was well, however, for the indulgence of Sir Wynston's conversational propensities, that Dr. Danvers had happened to drop in; for Marston was doggedly silent and sullen, and Mrs. Marston was herself scarcely more disposed than he to maintain her part in a conversation; so that, had it not been for the opportune arrival of the good clergyman, the supper must have been despatched with a very awkward and unsocial taciturnity.

Marston thought, and, perhaps, not erroneously, that Sir Wynston suspected something of the real state of affairs, and he was, therefore, incensed to perceive, as he thought, in his manner, very evident indications of his being in unusually good spirits. Thus disposed, the party sat down to supper.

"One of our number is missing," said Sir Wynston, affecting a slight surprise, which, perhaps, he did not feel.

"Mademoiselle de Barras—I trust she is well?" said Doctor Danvers, looking towards Marston.

"I suppose she is; I don't know," said Marston, drily.

"Why, how should *he* know," said the baronet, gaily, but with something almost imperceptibly sarcastic in his tone. "Our friend, Marston, is privileged to be as ungallant as he pleases, except where he has the happy privilege to owe allegiance; but I, a gay young bachelor of fifty, am naturally curious. I really do trust that our charming French friend is not unwell."

He addressed his inquiry to Mrs. Marston, who, with some slight confusion, replied:—

"No; nothing, at least, serious; merely a slight headache. I am sure she will be quite well enough to come down to breakfast."

"She is, indeed, a very charming and interesting young person," said Doctor Danvers. "There is a certain simplicity about her which argues a good and kind heart, and an open nature."

"Very true, indeed, doctor," observed Berkley, with the same faint, but, to Marston, exquisitely provoking approximation to sarcasm. "There is, as you say, a very charming simplicity. Don't you think so, Marston?"

Marston looked at him for a moment, but continued silent.

"Poor mademoiselle!—she is, indeed, a most affectionate creature," said Mrs. Marston, who felt called upon to say something.

"Come, Marston, will you contribute nothing to the general fund of approbation?" said Sir Wynston, who was gifted by nature with an amiable talent for teasing, which he was fond of exercising in a quiet way. "We have all, but you, said something handsome of our absent young friend."

"I never praise anybody, Wynston; not even *you*," said Marston, with an obvious sneer.

"Well, well, I must comfort myself with the belief that your silence covers a great deal of good-will, and, perhaps, a little admiration, too," answered his cousin, significantly.

"Comfort yourself in any *honest* way you will, my dear Wynston," retorted Marston, with a degree of asperity, which, to all but the baronet himself, was unaccountable. "You may be right, you may be wrong; on a subject so unimportant it matters very little which; you are at perfect liberty to practise delusions, if you will, upon *yourself*."

"By-the-bye, Mr. Marston, is not your son about to come down here?" asked Doctor Danvers, who perceived that the altercation was becoming, on Marston's part, somewhat testy, if not positively rude.

"Yes; I expect him in a few days," replied he, with a sudden gloom.

"You have not seen him, Sir Wynston?" asked the clergyman.

"I have that pleasure yet to come," said the baronet.

"A pleasure it is, I do assure you," said Doctor Danvers, heartily. "He is a handsome lad, with the heart of a hero—a fine, frank, generous lad, and as merry as a lark."

"Yes, yes," interrupted Marston; "he is well enough, and has done pretty well at Cambridge. Doctor Danvers, take some wine."

It was strange, but yet mournfully true, that the praises which the good Doctor Danvers thus bestowed upon his son were bitter to the soul of the unhappy Marston. They jarred upon his ear, and stung his heart; for his conscience converted them into so many latent insults and humiliations to himself.

"Your wine is very good, Marston. I think your clarets are many degrees better than any I can get," said Sir Wynston, sipping a glass of his favourite wine. "You country gentlemen are sad selfish dogs; and, with all your grumbling, manage to collect the best of whatever is worth having about you."

"We sometimes succeed in collecting a pleasant party," retorted Marston, with ironical courtesy, "though we do not always command the means of entertaining them quite as we would wish."

It was the habit of Doctor Danvers, without respect of persons or places, to propose, before taking his departure from whatever domestic party he chanced to be thrown among for the evening, to read some verses from that holy Book, on which his own hopes and peace were founded, and to offer up a prayer for all to the throne of grace. Marston, although he usually absented himself from such exercises, did not otherwise discourage them; but upon the present occasion, starting from his gloomy reverie, he himself was the first to remind the clergyman of his customary observance. Evil thoughts loomed upon the mind of Marston, like measureless black mists upon a cold, smooth sea. They rested, grew, and darkened there; and no heaven-sent breath came silently to steal them away. Under this dread shadow his mind lay waiting, like the DEEP, before the Spirit of God moved upon its waters, passive and awful. Why for the first time now did religion interest him? The unseen, intangible, was even now at work within him. A dreadful power shook his very heart and soul. There was some strange, ghastly wrestling going on in his own immortal spirit, a struggle which made him faint, which he had no power to determine. He looked upon the holy influence of the good man's prayer—a prayer in which he could not join—with a dull, superstitious hope that the words, inviting better influence, though uttered by another, and with other objects, would, like a spell, chase away the foul fiend that was busy with his soul. Marston sate, looking into the fire, with a countenance of stern gloom, upon which the wayward lights of the flickering hearth sported fitfully; while at a distant table Doctor Danvers sate down, and, taking his well-worn Bible from his pocket, turned over its leaves, and began, in gentle but impressive tones, to read.

Sir Wynston was much too well-bred to evince the slightest disposition to aught but the most proper and profound attention. The faintest imaginable gleam of ridicule might, perhaps, have been discerned in his features, as he leaned back in his chair, and, closing his eyes, composed himself to at least an attitude of attention. No man could submit with more cheerfulness to an inevitable bore.

In these things, then, thou hast no concern; the judgment troubles thee not; thou hast no fear of *death*, Sir Wynston Berkley; yet there is a heart beating near thee, the mysteries of which, could they glide out and stand before thy face, would perchance appal thee, cold, easy man of the world. Ay, couldst thou but see with those cunning eyes of thine, but twelve brief hours into futurity, each syllable that falls from that good man's lips unheeded would peal through thy heart and brain like maddening thunder. Hearken, hearken, Sir Wynston Berkley, perchance these are the farewell words of thy better angel—the last pleadings of despised mercy!

The party broke up. Doctor Danvers took his leave, and rode homeward, down the broad avenue, between the gigantic ranks of elm that closed it in. The full moon was rising above the distant hills; the mists lay like sleeping lakes in the laps of the hollows; and the broad demesne looked tranquil and sad under this chastened and silvery glory. The good old clergyman thought, as he pursued his way, that here at least, in a spot so beautiful and sequestered, the stormy passions and fell contentions of the outer world could scarcely penetrate. Yet, in that calm secluded spot, and under the cold, pure light which fell so holily, what a hell was weltering and glaring!—what a spectacle was that moon to go down upon!

As Sir Wynston was leaving the parlour for his own room, Marston accompanied him to the hall, and said—

"I shan't play to-night, Sir Wynston."

"Ah, ha! very particularly engaged?" suggested the baronet, with a faint, mocking smile. "Well, my dear fellow, we must endeavour to make up for it to-morrow—eh?"

"I don't know *that*," said Marston, "and—— In a word, there is no use, sir, in our masquerading with one another. Each knows the other; each *understands* the other. I wish to have a word or two with you in your room to-night, when we shan't be interrupted."

Marston spoke in a fierce and grating whisper, and his countenance, more even than his accents, betrayed the intensity of his bridled fury. Sir Wynston, however, smiled upon his cousin as if his voice had been melody, and his looks all sunshine.

"Very good, Marston, just as you please," he said; "only don't be later than one, as I shall be getting into bed about that hour."

"Perhaps, upon second thoughts, it is as well to defer what I have to say," said Marston, musingly. "Tomorrow will do as well; so, *perhaps*, Sir Wynston, I may not trouble you to-night."

"Just as suits you best, my dear Marston," replied the baronet, with a tranquil smile; "only don't come after the hour I have stipulated."

So saying, the baronet mounted the stairs, and made his way to his chamber. He was in excellent spirits, and in high good-humour with himself: the object of his visit to Gray Forest had been, as he now flattered himself, attained. He had conducted an affair requiring the profoundest mystery in its prosecution, and the nicest tactique in its management, almost to a triumphant issue. He had perfectly masked his design, and completely outwitted Marston; and to a person who piqued himself upon his clever diplomacy, and vaunted that he had never yet sustained a defeat in any object which he had seriously proposed to himself, such a combination of successes was for the moment quite intoxicating.

Sir Wynston not only enjoyed his own superiority with all the vanity of a selfish nature, but he no less enjoyed, with a keen and malicious relish, the intense mortification which, he was well assured, Marston must experience; and all the more acutely, because of the utter impossibility, circumstanced as he was, of his taking any steps to manifest his vexation, without compromising himself in a most unpleasant way.

Animated by these amiable feelings, Sir Wynston Berkley sate down, and wrote the following short letter, addressed to Mrs. Gray, Wynston Hall:—

"*Mrs. Gray,*

"On receipt of this have the sitting-rooms and several bed-rooms put in order, and thoroughly aired. Prepare for my use the suite of three rooms over the library and drawing-room; and have the two great wardrobes, and the cabinet in the *state* bed-room, removed into the large dressing-room which opens upon the bed-room I have named. Make everything as comfortable as possible. If anything is wanted in the way of furniture, drapery, ornament, &c., you need only write to John Skelton, Esq., Spring-garden, London, stating what is required, and he will order and send them down. You must be expeditious, as I shall probably go down to Wynston, with two or three friends, at the beginning of next month.

"*WYNSTON BERKLEY.*

"P.S.—I have written to direct Arkins and two or three of the other servants to go down at once. Set them all to work immediately."

He then applied himself to another letter of considerably greater length, and from which, therefore, we shall only offer a few extracts. It was addressed to John Skelton, Esq., and began as follows:—

"*My dear Skelton,*

"You are, doubtless, surprised at my long silence, but I have had nothing very particular to say. My visit to this dull and uncomfortable place was (as you rightly surmise) not without its object—a little bit of wicked romance; the pretty demoiselle of Rouen, whom I mentioned to you more than once—la belle de Barras—was, in truth, the attraction that drew me hither; and I *think* (for, as yet, she affects hesitation), I shall have no further trouble with her. She is a fine creature, and you will admit, when you have seen her, well worth taking some trouble about. She is, however, a very knowing little minx, and evidently suspects me of being a sad, fickle dog—and, as I surmise, has some plans, moreover, respecting my morose cousin, Marston, a kind of wicked Penruddock, who has carried all his London tastes into his savage retreat, a paradise of bogs and bushes. There is, I am very confident, a *liaison* in that quarter. The young lady is evidently a good deal afraid of him, and insists upon such precautions in our interviews, that they have been very few, and far between, indeed. To-day, there has been a *fracas* of some kind. I have no doubt that Marston, poor devil, is jealous. His situation is really pitiably comic—with an intriguing mistress, a saintly wife, and a devil of a jealous temper of his own. I shall meet Mary on reaching town. Has Clavering (shabby dog!) paid his I.O.U. yet? Tell the little opera woman she had better be quiet. She ought to know me by this time; I shall do what is right, but won't submit to be bullied. If she is troublesome, snap your fingers at her, on my behalf, and leave her to her remedy. I have written to Gray, to get things at Wynston in order. She will draw upon you for what money she requires. Send down two or three of the servants, if they have not already gone. The place is very dusty and dingy, and needs a great deal of brushing and scouring. I shall see you in town very soon. By the way, has the claret I ordered from the Dublin house arrived yet? it is consigned to you, and goes by the 'Lizard'; pay the freightage, and get Edwards to pack it; ten dozen or so may as well go down to Wynston, and send other wines in proportion. I leave details to you." . . .

Some further directions upon other subjects followed; and having subscribed the despatch, and addressed it to the gentlemanlike scoundrel who filled the onerous office of factotum to this profligate and exacting man of the world, Sir Wynston Berkley rang his bell, and gave the two letters into the hand of his man, with special directions to carry them *himself*, in person, to the post-office in the neighbouring village, early next morning. These little matters completed, Sir Wynston stirred his fire, leaned back in his easy chair, and smiled blandly over the sunny prospect of his imaginary triumphs.

It here becomes necessary to describe, in a few words, some of the local relations of Sir Wynston's apartments. The bedchamber which he occupied opened from the long passage of which we have already spoken—and there were two other smaller apartments opening from it in train. In the further of these, which was entered from a lobby, communicating by a back stair with the kitchen and servants' apartments, lay Sir Wynston's valet, and the intermediate chamber was fitted up as a dressing-room for the baronet himself. These circumstances it is necessary to mention, that what follows may be clearly intelligible.

While the baronet was penning these records of vicious schemes—dire waste of wealth and time—irrevocable time!—Marston paced his study in a very different frame of mind. There were a gloom and disorder in the room accordant with those of his own mind. Shelves of ancient tomes, darkened by time, and upon which the dust of years lay sleeping—dark oaken cabinets, filled with piles of deeds and papers, among which the nimble spiders were crawling—and, from the dusky walls, several stark, pale ancestors, looking down coldly from their tarnished frames. An hour, and another hour passed—and still Marston paced this melancholy chamber, a prey to his own fell passions and dark thoughts. He was not a superstitious man, but, in the visions which haunted him, perhaps, was something which made him unusually excitable—for, he experienced a chill of absolute horror, as, standing at the farther end of the room, with his face turned towards the entrance, he beheld the door noiselessly and slowly pushed open, by a pale, thin hand, and a figure dressed in a loose white robe, glide softly in. He stood for some seconds gazing upon this apparition, as it moved hesitatingly towards him from the dusky extremity of the large apartment, before he perceived that the form was that of Mrs. Marston.

"Hey, ha!—Mrs. Marston—what on earth has called you hither?" he asked, sternly. "You ought to have been at rest an hour ago; get to your chamber, and leave me, I have business to attend to."

"Now, dear Richard, you must forgive me," she said, drawing near, and looking up into his haggard face with a sweet and touching look of timidity and love; "I could not rest until I saw you again; your looks have been all this night so unlike yourself; so strange and terrible, that I am afraid some great misfortune threatens you, which you fear to tell me of."

"My looks! why, curse it, must I give an account of my looks?" replied Marston, at once disconcerted and wrathful. "Misfortune! what misfortune can befall us more? No, there is nothing, nothing, I say, but your own foolish fancy; go to your room—go to sleep—my looks, indeed; psha!"

"I came to tell you, dear Richard, that I will do, in all respects, just as you desire. If you continue to wish it, I will part with poor mademoiselle; though, indeed, Richard, I shall miss her more than you can imagine; and all your suspicions have wronged her deeply," said Mrs. Marston.

Her husband darted a sudden flashing glance of suspicious scrutiny upon her face; but its expression was frank, earnest, noble. He was disarmed; he hung his head gloomily upon his breast, and was silent for a time. She came nearer, and laid her hand upon his arm. He looked darkly into her upturned eyes, and a feeling which had not touched his heart for many a day—an emotion of pity, transient, indeed, but vivid, revisited him. He took her hand in his, and said, in gentler terms than she had heard him use for a long time—

"No, indeed, Gertrude, you have deceived yourself; no misfortune has happened, and if I *am* gloomy, the source of all my troubles is *within*. Leave me, Gertrude, for the present. As to the other matter, the departure of Mademoiselle de Barras, we can talk of that to-morrow—*now* I cannot; so let us part. Go to your room; good night."

She was withdrawing, and he added, in a subdued tone—

"Gertrude, I am very glad you came—*very* glad. Pray for me to-night."

He had followed her a few steps toward the door, and now stopped short, turned about, and walked dejectedly back again.

"I *am* right glad she came," he muttered, as soon as he was once more alone. "Wynston is provoking and fiery, too. Were I, in my present mood, to seek a *tête-à-tête* with him, who knows what might come of it? Blood; my own heart whispers—*blood!* I'll not trust myself."

He strode to the study door, locked it, and taking out the key, shut it in the drawer of one of the cabinets.

"Now it will need more than accident or impulse to lead me to him. I cannot go, at least, without reflection, without premeditation. Avaunt, fiend! I have baffled you."

He stood in the centre of the room, cowering and scowling as he said this, and looked round with a glance half-defiant, half-fearful, as if he expected to see some dreadful form in the dusky recesses of the desolate chamber. He sate himself by the smouldering fire, in sombre and agitated rumination. He was restless; he rose again, unbuckled his sword, which he had not loosed since evening, and threw it hastily into a corner. He looked at his watch, it was half-past twelve; he glanced at the door, and thence at the cabinet in which he had placed the key; then he turned hastily, and sate down again. He leaned his elbows on his knees, and his chin upon his clenched hand; still he was restless and excited. Once more he arose, and paced up and down. He consulted his watch again; it was now but a quarter to one.

Sir Wynston's man having received the letters, and his master's permission to retire to rest, got into his bed, and was soon beginning to dose. We have already mentioned that his and Sir Wynston's apartments were separated by a small dressing-room, so that any ordinary noise or conversation could be heard but imperfectly from one to the other. The servant, however, was startled by a sound of something falling on the floor of his master's apartment, and broken to pieces by the violence of the shock. He sate up in his bed, listened, and heard some sentences spoken vehemently, and gabbled very fast. He thought he distinguished the words "wretch" and "God"; and there was something so strange in the tone in which they were spoken, that the man got up and stole noiselessly through the dressing-room, and listened at the door.

He heard him, as he thought, walking in his slippers through the room, and making his customary arrangements previously to getting into bed. He knew that his master had a habit of speaking when alone, and concluded that the accidental breakage of some glass or chimney-ornament had elicited the volley of words he had heard. Well knowing that, except at the usual hours, or in obedience to Sir Wynston's bell, nothing more displeased his master than his presuming to enter his sleeping-apartment while he was there, the servant quietly retreated, and, perfectly satisfied that all was right, composed himself to slumber, and was soon beginning to dose again.

The adventures of the night, however, were not yet over. Waking, as men sometimes do, without any ascertainable cause; without a start or an uneasy sensation; without even a disturbance of the attitude of repose, he opened his eyes and beheld Merton, the servant of whom we have spoken, standing at a little distance from his bed. The moonlight fell in a clear flood upon this figure: the man was ghastly pale; there was a blotch of blood on his face; his hands were clasped upon something which they nearly concealed; and his eyes, fixed on the servant who had just awakened, shone in the cold light with a wild and lifeless glitter. This spectre drew close to the side of the bed, and stood for a few moments there with a look of agony and menace, which startled the newly-awakened man, who rose upright, and said—

"Mr. Merton, Mr. Merton—in God's name, what is the matter?"

Merton recoiled at the sound of his voice; and, as he did so, dropped something on the floor, which rolled away to a distance; and he stood gazing silently and horribly upon his interrogator.

"Mr. Merton, I say, what *is* it?" urged the man. "Are you hurt? your face is bloody."

Merton raised his hand to his face mechanically, and Sir Wynston's man observed that it, too, was covered with blood.

"Why, man," he said, vehemently, and actually freezing with horror "you are *all* bloody; hands and face; all over blood."

"My hand is cut to the bone," said Merton, in a harsh whisper; and speaking to himself, rather than addressing the servant—"I wish it was my neck; I wish to God I bled to death."

"You have hurt your hand, Mr. Merton," repeated the man, scarce knowing what he said.

"Ay," whispered Merton, wildly drawing toward the bedside again; "who told you I hurt my hand? It is cut to the bone, sure enough."

He stooped for a moment over the bed, and then cowered down toward the floor to search for what he had dropped.

"Why, Mr. Merton, what brings you here at this hour?" urged the man, after a pause of a few seconds. "It is drawing toward morning."

"Ay, ay," said Merton, doubtfully, and starting upright again, while he concealed in his bosom what he had been in search of. "Near morning, is it? Night and morning, it is all one to me. I believe I am going mad, by ——"

"But what do you want? what did you come here for at this hour?" persisted the man.

"*What!* ay, *that* is it; why, his boots and spurs, to be sure. I forgot them. His—his—Sir Wynston's boots and spurs; I forgot to take them, I say," said Merton, looking toward the dressing-room, as if about to enter it.

"Don't mind them to-night, I say; don't go in there," said the man, peremptorily, and getting out upon the floor. "I say, Mr. Merton, this is no hour to be going about searching in the dark for boots and spurs. You'll waken the master. I can't have it, I say; go down, and let it be for to-night."

Thus speaking, in a resolute and somewhat angry under-key, the valet stood between Merton and the entrance of the dressing-room; and, signing with his hand toward the other door of the apartment, continued—

"Go down, I say, Mr. Merton, go down; you may as well quietly, for, I tell you plainly, you shall neither go a step further, nor stay here a moment longer."

The man drew his shoulders up, and made a sort of shivering moan, and clasping his hands together, shook them, as it seemed, in great agony. He then turned abruptly, and hurried from the room by the door leading to the kitchen.

"By my faith," said the servant, "I am glad he is gone. The poor chap is turning crazy, as sure as I am a living man. I'll not have him prowling about here any more, however; that I am resolved on."

In pursuance of this determination, by no means an imprudent one, as it seemed, he fastened the door communicating with the lower apartments upon the inside. He had hardly done this, when he heard a step traversing the stable-yard, which lay under the window of his apartment. He looked out, and saw Merton walking hurriedly across, and into a stable at the farther end.

Feeling no very particular curiosity about his movements, the man hurried back to his bed. Merton's eccentric conduct of late had become so generally remarked and discussed among the servants, that Sir Wynston's man was by no means surprised at the oddity of the visit he had just had; nor, after the first few moments of doubt, before the appearance of blood had been accounted for, had he entertained any suspicions whatever connected with the man's unexpected presence in the room. Merton was in the habit of coming up every night to take down Sir Wynston's boots, whenever the baronet had ridden in the course of the day; and this attention had been civilly undertaken as a proof of good-will toward the valet, whose duty this somewhat soiling and ungentlemanlike process would otherwise have been. So far, the nature of the visit was explained; and the remembrance of the friendly feeling and good offices which had been mutually interchanged, as well as of the inoffensive habits for which Merton had earned a character for himself, speedily calmed the uneasiness, for a moment amounting to actual alarm, with which the servant had regarded his appearance.

We must now pass on to the morrow, and ask the reader's attention for a few moments to a different scene.

In contact with Gray Forest upon the northern side, and divided by a common boundary, lay a demesne, in many respects presenting a very striking contrast to its grander neighbour. It was a comparatively modern place. It could not boast the towering timber which enriched and overshadowed the vast and varied expanse of its aristocratic rival; but, if it was inferior in the advantages of antiquity, and, perhaps, also in some of those of nature, its superiority in other respects was striking and important. Gray Forest was not more remarkable for its wild and neglected condition, than was Newton Park for the care and elegance with which it was kept. No one could observe the contrast, without, at the same time, divining its cause. The proprietor of the one was a man of wealth, fully commensurate with the extent and pretensions of the residence he had chosen; the owner of the other was a man of broken fortunes.

Under a green shade, which nearly met above, a very young man, scarcely one-and-twenty, of a frank and sensible, rather than a strictly handsome countenance, was walking, followed by half a dozen dogs of as many breeds and sizes. This young man was George Mervyn, the only son of the present proprietor of the place. As he approached the great gate, the clank of a horses's hoofs in quick motion upon the sequestered road which ran outside it, reached him; and hardly had he heard these sounds, when a young gentleman rode briskly by, directing his look into the demesne as he passed. He had no sooner seen him, than wheeling his horse about, he rode up to the iron gate, and dismounting, threw it open, and let his horse in.

"Ha! Charles Marston, I protest!" said the young man, quickening his pace to meet his friend. "Marston, my dear fellow," he called aloud, "how glad I am to see you."

There was another entrance into Newton Park, opening from the same road, about half a mile further on; and Charles Marston made his way lie through this. Thus the young people walked on, talking of a hundred things as they proceeded, in the mirth of their hearts.

Between the fathers of the two young men, who thus walked so affectionately together, there subsisted unhappily no friendly feelings. There had been several slight disagreements between them, touching their proprietary rights, and one of these had ripened into a formal and somewhat expensive litigation, respecting a certain right of fishing claimed by each. This legal encounter had terminated in the defeat of Marston. Mervyn, however, promptly wrote to his opponent, offering him the free use of the waters for which they had thus sharply contested, and received a curt and scarcely civil reply, declining the proposed courtesy. This exhibition of resentment on Marston's part had been followed by some rather angry collisions, where chance or duty happened to throw them together. It is but justice to say that, upon all such occasions, Marston was the aggressor. But Mervyn was a somewhat testy old gentleman, and had a certain pride of his own, which was not to be trifled with. Thus, though near neighbours, the parents of the young friends were more than strangers to each other. On Mervyn's side, however, this estrangement was unalloyed with bitterness, and simply of that kind which the great moralist would have referred to "defensive pride." It did not include any member of

Marston's family, and Charles, as often as he desired it, which was, in truth, as often as his visits could escape the special notice of his father, was a welcome guest at Newton Park.

These details respecting the mutual relation in which the two families stood, it was necessary to state, for the purpose of making what follows perfectly clear. The young people had now reached the further gate, at which they were to part. Charles Marston, with a heart beating happily in the anticipation of many a pleasant meeting, bid him farewell for the present, and in a few minutes more was riding up the broad, straight avenue, towards the gloomy mansion which closed in the hazy and sombre perspective. As he moved onward, he passed a labourer, with whose face, from his childhood, he had been familiar.

"How do you do, Tom?" he cried.

"At your service, sir," replied the man, uncovering, "and welcome home, sir."

There was something dark and anxious in the man's looks, which ill-accorded with the welcome he spoke, and which suggested some undefined alarm.

"The master, and mistress, and Miss Rhoda—are all well?" he asked eagerly.

"All well, sir, thank God," replied the man.

Young Marston spurred on, filled with vague apprehensions, and observing the man still leaning upon his spade, and watching his progress with the same gloomy and curious eye.

At the hall-door he met with one of the servants, booted and spurred.

"Well, Daly," he said, as he dismounted, "how are all at home?"

This man, like the former, met his smile with a troubled countenance, and stammered—

"All, sir—that is, the master, and mistress, and Miss Rhoda—quite well, sir; but ——"

"Well, well," said Charles, eagerly, "speak on—what is it?"

"Bad work, sir," replied the man, lowering his voice. "I am going off this minute for ——"

"For what?" urged the young gentleman.

"Why, sir, for the coroner," replied he.

"The coroner—the coroner! Why, good God, what has happened?" cried Charles, aghast with horror.

"Sir Wynston," commenced the man, and hesitated.

"Well?" pursued Charles, pale and breathless.

"Sir Wynston—he—it is *he*," said the man.

"He? Sir Wynston? Is he dead, or *who* is?—who is dead?" demanded the young man, almost fiercely.

"Sir Wynston, sir; it is he that is dead. There is bad work, sir—very bad, I'm afraid," replied the man.

Charles did not wait to inquire further, but, with a feeling of mingled horror and curiosity, entered the house.

He hurried up the stairs, and entered his mother's sitting-room. She was there, perfectly alone, and so deadly pale, that she scarcely looked like a living being. In an instant they were locked in one another's arms.

"Mother—my dear mother, you are ill," said the young man, anxiously.

"Oh, no, no, dear Charles, but frightened, horrified"; and as she said this, the poor lady burst into tears.

"What *is* this horrible affair? something about Sir Wynston. He is dead, I know, but is it—is it suicide?" he asked.

"Oh, no, *not* suicide," said Mrs. Marston, greatly agitated.

"Good God! then he is murdered," whispered the young man, growing very pale.

"Yes, Charles—horrible—dreadful! I can scarcely believe it," replied she, shuddering while she wept.

"Where is my father?" inquired the young man, after a pause.

"Why, why, Charles, darling—why do you ask for him?" she said, wildly, grasping him by the arm, as she looked into his face with a terrified expression.

"Why—why, *he* could tell me the particulars of this horrible tragedy," answered he, meeting her agonized look with one of alarm and surprise, "as far as they have been as yet collected. How is he, mother—is he well?"

"Oh, yes, quite well, thank God," she answered, more collectedly—"quite well, but, of course, greatly, dreadfully shocked."

"I will go to him, mother; I will see him," said he, turning towards the door.

"He has been wretchedly depressed and excited for some days," said Mrs. Marston, dejectedly, "and this dreadful occurrence will, I fear, affect him most deplorably."

The young man kissed her tenderly and affectionately, and hurried down to the library, where his father usually sat when he desired to be alone, or was engaged in business. He opened the door softly. His father was standing at one of the windows, his face haggard as from a night's watching, unkempt and unshorn, and with his hands thrust into his pockets. At the sound of the revolving door he started, and seeing his son, first recoiled a little, with a strange, doubtful expression, and then rallying, walked quickly towards him with a smile, which had in it something still more painful.

"Charles, I am glad to see you," he said, shaking him with an agitated pressure by both hands, "Charles, this is a great calamity, and what makes it still worse, is that the murderer has escaped; it looks badly, you know."

He fixed his gaze for a few moments upon his son, turned abruptly, and walked a little way into the room then, in a disconcerted manner, he added, hastily turning back—

"Not that it signifies to *us,* of course—but I would fain have justice satisfied."

"And who is the wretch—the murderer?" inquired Charles.

"Who? Why, everyone knows!—that scoundrel, Merton," answered Marston, in an irritated tone—"Merton murdered him in his bed, and fled last night; he is gone—escaped—and I suspect Sir Wynston's man of being an accessory."

"Which was Sir Wynston's bed-room?" asked the young man.

"The room that old Lady Mostyn had—the room with the portrait of Grace Hamilton in it."

"I know—I know," said the young man, much excited. "I should wish to see it."

"Stay," said Marston; "the door from the passage is bolted on the in-side, and I have locked the other; here is the key, if you choose to go, but you must bring Hughes with you, and do not disturb anything; leave all as it is; the jury ought to see, and examine for themselves."

Charles took the key, and, accompanied by the awe-struck servant, he made his way by the back stairs to the door opening from the dressing-room, which, as we have said, intervened between the valet's chamber and Sir Wynston's. After a momentary hesitation, Charles turned the key in the door, and stood

"In the dark chamber of white death."

The shutters lay partly open, as the valet had left them some hours before, on making the astounding discovery, which the partially-admitted light revealed. The corpse lay in the silk-embroidered dressing-gown, and other habiliments, which Sir Wynston had worn, while taking his ease in his chamber, on the preceding night. The coverlet was partially dragged over it. The mouth was gaping, and filled with clotted blood; a wide gash was also visible in the neck, under the ear; and there was a thickening pool of blood at the bedside, and quantities of blood, doubtless from other wounds, had saturated the bedclothes under the body. There lay Sir Wynston, stiffened in the attitude in which the struggle of death had left him, with his stern, stony face, and dim, terrible gaze turned up.

Charles looked breathlessly for more than a minute upon this mute and unchanging spectacle, and then silently suffered the curtain to fall back again, and stepped, with the light tread of awe, again to the door. There he turned back, and pausing for a minute, said, in a whisper, to the attendant—

"And Merton did this?"

"Troth, I'm afeard he did, sir," answered the man, gloomily.

"And has made his escape?" continued Charles.

"Yes, sir; he stole away in the night-time," replied the servant, "after the murder was done" (and he glanced fearfully toward the bed); "God knows where he's gone.'"

"The villain!" muttered Charles; "but what was his motive? why did he do all this—what does it mean?"

"I don't know exactly, sir, but he was very queer for a week and more before it," replied the man; "there was something bad over him for a long time."

"It is a terrible thing," said Charles, with a profound sigh; "a terrible and shocking occurrence."

He hesitated again at the door, but his feelings had sustained a terrible revulsion at sight of the corpse, and he was no longer disposed to prosecute his purposed examination of the chamber and its contents, with a view to conjecturing the probable circumstances of the murder.

"Observe, Hughes, that I have moved nothing in the chamber from the place it occupied when we entered," he said to the servant, as they withdrew.

He locked the door, and as he passed through the hall, on his return, he encountered his father, and, restoring the key, said—

"I could not stay there; I am almost sorry I have seen it; I am overpowered; what a determined, ferocious murder it was; the place is all in a pool of gore; he must have received many wounds."

"I can't say; the particulars will be elicited soon enough; those details are for the inquest; as for me, I hate such spectacles," said Marston, gloomily; "go now, and see your sister; you will find her there."

He pointed to the small room where we have first seen her and her fair governess; Charles obeyed the direction, and Marston proceeded himself to his wife's sitting-room.

The young man, dispirited and horrified by the awful spectacle he had just contemplated, hurried to the little study occupied by his sister. Marston himself ascended, as we have said, the great staircase leading to his wife's private sitting-room.

"Mrs. Marston," he said, entering, "this is a hateful occurrence, a dreadful thing to have taken place here; I don't mean to affect *grief* which I don't feel; but the thing is very shocking, and particularly so, as having occurred under my roof; but that cannot now be helped. I have resolved to spare no exertions, and no influence, to bring the assassin to justice; and a coroner's jury will, within a few hours, sift the evidence which we have succeeded in collecting. But my purpose in seeking you now is, to recur to the conversation we yesterday had, respecting a member of this establishment."

"Mademoiselle de Barras?" suggested the lady.

"Yes, Mademoiselle de Barras," echoed Marston; "I wish to say, that, having reconsidered the circumstances affecting her, I am absolutely resolved that she shall not continue to be an inmate of this house."

He paused, and Mrs. Marston said—

"Well, Richard, I am sorry, very sorry for it; but your decision shall never be disputed by me."

"Of course," said Marston, drily; "and, therefore, the sooner you acquaint her with it, and let her know that she must go, the better."

Having said this, he left her, and went to his own chamber, where he proceeded to make his toilet with elaborate propriety, in preparation for the scene which was about to take place under his roof.

Mrs. Marston, meanwhile, suffered from a horrible uncertainty. She never harboured, it is true, one doubt as to her husband's perfect innocence of the ghastly crime which filled their house with fear and gloom; but at the same time that she thoroughly and indignantly scouted the possibility of his, under any circumstances, being accessory to such a crime, she experienced a nervous and agonising anxiety lest any one else should possibly suspect him, however obliquely and faintly, of any participation whatever in the foul deed. This vague fear tortured her; it had taken possession of her mind; and it was the more acutely painful, because it was of a kind which precluded the possibility of her dispelling it, as morbid fears so often are dispelled, by taking counsel upon its suggestions with a friend.

The day wore on, and strange faces began to fill the great parlour. The coroner, accompanied by a physician, had arrived. Several of the gentry in the immediate vicinity had been summoned as jurors, and now began to arrive in succession. Marston, in a handsome and sober suit, received these visiters with a stately and melancholy courtesy, befitting the occasion. Mervyn and his son had both been summoned, and, of course, were in attendance. There being now a sufficient number to form a jury, they were sworn, and immediately proceeded to the chamber where the body of the murdered man was lying.

Marston accompanied them, and with a pale and stern countenance, and in a clear and subdued tone, called their attention successively to every particular detail which he conceived important to be noted. Having thus employed some minutes, the jury again returned to the parlour, and the examination of the witnesses commenced.

Marston, at his own request, was first sworn and examined. He deposed merely to the circumstance of his parting, on the night previous, with Sir Wynston, and to the state in which he had seen the room and the body in the morning. He mentioned also the fact, that on hearing the alarm in the morning, he had hastened from his own chamber to Sir Wynston's, and found, on trying to enter, that the door opening upon the passage was secured on the inside. This circumstance showed that the murderer must have made his egress at least through the valet's chamber, and by the back-stairs. Marston's evidence went no further.

The next witness sworn was Edward Smith, the servant of the late Sir Wynston Berkley. His evidence was a narrative of the occurrences we have already stated. He described the sounds which he had overheard from his master's room, the subsequent appearance of Merton, and the conversation which had passed between them. He then proceeded to mention, that it was his master's custom to have himself called at seven o'clock, at which hour he usually took some medicine, which it was the valet's duty to bring to him; after which he either settled again to rest, or rose in a short time, if unable to sleep. Having measured and prepared the dose in the dressing-room, the servant went on to say, he had knocked at his master's door, and receiving no answer, had entered the room, and partly unclosed the shutters. He perceived the blood on the carpet, and on opening the curtains, saw his master lying with his mouth and eyes open, perfectly dead, and weltering in gore. He had stretched out his hand, and seized that of the dead man, which was quite stiff and cold; then, losing heart, he had run to the door communicating with the passage, but found it locked, and turned to the other entrance, and ran down the back-stairs, crying "murder." Mr. Hughes, the butler, and James Carney, another servant, came immediately, and they all three went back into the room. The key was in the outer door, upon the inside, but they did not unlock it until they had viewed the body. There was a great pool of blood in the bed, and in it was lying a red-handled caseknife, which was produced, and identified by the witness. Just then they heard Mr. Marston calling for admission, and they opened the door with some difficulty, for the lock was rusty. Mr. Marston had ordered them to leave the things as they were, and had used very stern language to the witness. They had then left the room, securing both doors.

This witness underwent a severe and searching examination, but his evidence was clear and consistent.

In conclusion, Marston produced a dagger, which was stained with blood, and asked the man whether he recognised it.

Smith at once stated this to have been the property of his late master, who, when travelling, carried it, together with his pistols, along with him. Since his arrival at Gray Forest, it had lain upon the chimney-piece in his bed-room, where he believed it to have been upon the previous night.

James Carney, one of Marston's servants, was next sworn and examined. He had, he said, observed a strange and unaccountable agitation and depression in Merton's manner for some days past; he had also been several times disturbed at night by his talking aloud to himself, and walking to and fro in his room. Their bed-rooms were separated by a thin partition, in which was a window, through which Carney had, on the night of the murder, observed a light in Merton's room, and, on looking in, had seen him dressing hastily. He also saw him twice take up, and again lay down, the red-hafted knife which had been found in the bed of the murdered man. He knew it by the handle being broken near the end. He had no suspicion of Merton having any mischievous intentions, and lay down again to rest. He afterwards heard him pass out of his room, and go slowly up the back-stairs leading to the upper story. Shortly after this he had fallen asleep, and did not hear or see him return. He then described, as Smith had already done, the scene which presented itself in the morning, on his accompanying him into Sir Wynston's bedchamber.

The next witness examined was a little Irish boy, who described himself as "a poor scholar." His testimony was somewhat singular. He deposed that he had come to the house on the preceding evening, and had been given some supper, and was afterwards permitted to sleep among the hay in one of the lofts. He had, however, discovered what he considered a snugger berth. This was an unused stable, in the further end of which lay a quantity of hay. Among this he had lain down, and gone to sleep. He was, however, awakened in the course of the night by the entrance of a man, whom he saw with perfect distinctness in the moonlight, and his description of his dress and appearance tallied exactly with those of Merton. This man occupied himself for some time in washing his hands and face in a stable bucket, which happened to stand by the door; and, during the whole of this process, he continued to moan and mutter, like one in woful perturbation. He said, distinctly, twice or thrice, "by——, I am done for"; and every now and then he muttered, "and nothing for it, after all." When he had done washing his hands, he took something from his coat-pocket, and looked at it, shaking his head; at this time he was standing with his back turned toward the boy, so that he could not see what this object might be. The man, however, put it into his breast, and then began to search hurriedly, as it seemed, for some hiding-place for it. After looking at the pavement, and poking at the chinks of the wall, he suddenly went to the window, and forced up the stone which formed the sill. Under this he threw the object which the boy had seen him examine with so much perplexity, and then he readjusted the stone, and removed the evidences of its having been recently stirred. The boy was a little frightened, but very curious about all that he saw; and when the man left the stable in which he lay, he got up, and following to the door, peeped after him. He saw him putting on an outside-coat and hat, near the yard gate; and then, with great caution, unbolt the wicket, constantly looking back towards the house, and so let himself out. The boy was uneasy, and sat in the hay, wide awake, until morning. He then told the servants what he had seen, and one of the men having raised the stone, which *he* had not strength to lift, they found the dagger, which Smith had identified as belonging to his master. This weapon was stained with blood; and some hair, which was found to correspond in colour with Sir Wynston's, was sticking in the crevice between the blade and the handle.

"It appears very strange that *one* man should have employed two distinct instruments of this kind," observed Mervyn, after a pause. A silence followed.

"Yes, strange; it *does* seem strange," said Marston, clearing his voice.

"Yet, it is clear," said another of the jury, "that the same hand *did* employ them. It is proved that the knife was in Merton's possession just as he left his chamber; and proved, also, that the dagger was secreted by him after he quitted the house."

"Yes," said Marston, with a grisly sort of smile, and glancing sarcastically at Mervyn, while he addressed the last speaker—"I thank you for recalling my attention to the facts. It cerainly is not a very plea-

sant suggestion, that there still remains within my household an undetected murderer."

Mervyn ruminated for a time, and said he should wish to put a few
more questions to Smith and Carney. They were accordingly recalled,
and examined in great detail, with a view to ascertain whether any in-
dication of the presence of a second person having visited the chamber
with Merton was discoverable. Nothing, however, appeared, except
that the valet mentioned the noise and the exclamations which he had
indistinctly heard.

"You did not mention that before, sir," said Marston, sharply.

"I did not think of it, sir," replied the man, "the gentlemen were asking me so many questions; but I told you, sir, about it in the morning."

"Oh, ah—yes, yes—I believe you did," said Marston; "but you then
said that Sir Wynston often talked when he was alone; eh, sir?"

"Yes, sir, and so he used, which was the reason I did not go into the
room when I heard it," replied the man.

"How long afterwards was it when you saw Merton in your own
room?" asked Mervyn.

"I could not say, sir," answered Smith; "I was soon asleep, and can't
say how long I slept before he came."

"Was it an hour?" pursued Mervyn.

"I can't say," said the man, doubtfully.

"Was it five hours?" asked Marston.

"No, sir; I am sure it was not five."

"Could you swear it was more than half-an-hour?" persisted
Marston.

"No, I could not swear that," answered he.

"I am afraid, Mr. Mervyn, you have found a mare's nest," said
Marston, contemptuously.

"I have done my duty, sir," retorted Mervyn, cynically; "which
plainly requires that I shall have no doubt, which the evidence of the
witness can clear up, unsifted and unsatisfied. I happened to think it of
some moment to ascertain, if possible, whether more persons than one
were engaged in this atrocious murder. You don't seem to think the
question so important a one; different men, sir, take different views."

"Views, sir, in matters of this sort, especially where they tend to multiply suspicions, and to implicate others, ought to be supported by
something more substantial than mere fancies," retorted Marston.

"I don't know what you call fancies," replied Mervyn, testily; "but
here are *two* deadly weapons, a knife and a dagger, each, it would seem
employed in doing this murder; if you see nothing odd in that, I can't
enable you to do so."

"Well, sir," said Marston, grimly, "the *whole* thing is, as you term it
odd; and I can see no object in your picking out this particular singularity for long-winded criticism, except to cast scandal upon my household
by leaving a hideous and vague imputation floating among the
members of it. Sir, sir, this is a foul way," he cried, sternly, "to gratify a
paltry spite."

"Mr. Marston," said Mervyn, rising, and thrusting his hands into his pockets, while he confronted him to the full as sternly, "the country knows in which of our hearts the spite, if any there be between us, is harboured. I owe you no friendship, but, sir, I cherish no malice, either; and against the worst enemy I have on earth I am incapable of perverting an opportunity like this, and inflicting pain, under the pretence of discharging a duty."

Marston was on the point of retorting, but the coroner interposed, and besought them to confine their attention strictly to the solemn inquiry which they were summoned together to prosecute.

There remained still to be examined the surgeon who had accompanied the coroner, for the purpose of reporting upon the extent and nature of the injuries discoverable upon the person of the deceased. He, accordingly, deposed, that having examined the body, he found no less than three deep wounds, inflicted with some sharp instrument; two of them had actually penetrated the heart, and were, of course, supposed to cause instant death. Besides these, there were two contusions, one upon the back of the head, the other upon the forehead, with a slight abrasion of the eyebrow. There was a large lock of hair torn out by the roots at the front of the head, and the palm and fingers of the right hand were cut. This evidence having been taken, the jury once more repaired to the chamber where the body lay, and proceeded with much minuteness to examine the room, with a view to ascertain, if possible, more particularly the exact circumstances of the murder.

The result of this elaborate scrutiny was as follows:—The deceased, they conjectured, had fallen asleep in his easy chair, and, while he was unconscious, the murderer had stolen into the room, and, before attacking his victim, had secured the bedroom-door upon the inside. This was argued from the non-discovery of blood upon the handle, or any other part of the door. It was supposed that he had then approached Sir Wynston, with the view either of robbing, or of murdering him while he slept, and that the deceased had awakened just after he had reached him; that a brief and desperate struggle had ensued, in which the assailant had struck his victim with his fist upon the forehead, and having stunned him, had hurriedly clutched him by the hair, and stabbed him with the dagger, which lay close by upon the chimney-piece, forcing his head violently against the back of the chair. This part of the conjecture was supported by the circumstance of there being discovered a lock of hair upon the ground at the spot, and a good deal of blood. The carpet, too, was tumbled, and a water-decanter, which had stood upon the table close by, was lying in fragments upon the floor. It was supposed that the murderer had then dragged the half-lifeless body to the bed, where, having substituted the knife, which he had probably brought to the room in the same pocket from which the boy afterwards saw him take the dagger, he despatched him; and either hearing some alarm—perhaps the movement of the valet in the adjoining room, or from some other cause—he dropped the knife in the bed, and was not able to find it again. The wounds upon the hand of the dead man in-

dicated his having caught and struggled to hold the blade of the weapon
with which he was assailed. The impression of a bloody hand thrust
under the bolster, where it was Sir Wynston's habit to place his purse
and watch, when making his arrangements for the night, supplied the
motive of this otherwise unaccountable atrocity.

After some brief consultation, the jury agreed upon a verdict of wilful
murder against John Merton, a finding of which the coroner expressed
his entire approbation.

Marston, as a justice of the peace, had informations, embodying the
principal part of the evidence given before the coroner, sworn against
Merton, and transmitted a copy of them to the Home Office. A reward
for the apprehension of the culprit was forthwith offered, but for some
months without effect.

Marston had, in the interval, written to several of Sir Wynston's
many relations, announcing the catastrophe, and requesting that steps
might immediately be taken to have the body removed. Meanwhile undertakers were busy in the chamber of death. The corpse was enclosed
in lead, and that again in cedar, and a great oak shell, covered with
crimson cloth and gold-headed nails, and with a gilt plate, recording
the age, title, &c. &c., of the deceased, was screwed down firmly over
all.

Nearly a fortnight elapsed before any reply to Marston's letters was
received. A short epistle at last arrived from Lord H——, the late Sir
Wynston's uncle, deeply regretting the "sad and inexplicable occurrence," and adding, that the will, which, on receipt of the "distressing intelligence," was immediately opened and read, contained no
direction whatever respecting the sepulture of the deceased, which had
therefore better be completed as modestly and expeditiously as possible, in the neighbourhood; and, in conclusion, he directed that the accounts of the undertakers, &c., employed upon the melancholy occasion, might be sent in to Mr. Skelton, who had kindly undertaken to
leave London without any delay, for the purpose of completing these
last arrangements, and who would, in any matter of business connected
with the deceased, represent him, Lord H——, as executor of the late
baronet.

This letter was followed, in a day or two, by the arrival of Skelton, a
well-dressed, languid, impertinent London tuft-hunter, a good deal
faded, with a somewhat sallow and puffy face, charged with a pleasant
combination at once of meanness, insolence, and sensuality—just such
a person as Sir Wynston's parasite might have been expected to prove.

However well disposed to impress the natives with high notions of his
extraordinary refinement and importance, he very soon discovered that,
in Marston, he had stumbled upon a man of the world, and one
thoroughly versed in the ways and characters of London life. After some
ineffectual attempts, therefore, to overawe and astonish his host, Mr.
Skelton became aware of the fruitlessness of the effort, and condescended to abate somewhat of his pretensions.

Marston could not avoid inviting this person to pass the night at his house, an invitation which was accepted, of course; and next morning, after a late breakfast, Mr. Skelton observed, with a yawn—

"And now, about this body—poor Berkley!—what do you propose to do with him?"

"I have no proposition to make," said Marston, drily. "It is no affair of mine, except that the body may be removed without more delay. I have no suggestion to offer."

"H——'s notion was to have him buried as near the spot as may be," said Skelton.

Marston nodded.

"There is a kind of vault, is not there, in the demesne, a family burial-place?" inquired the visiter.

"Yes, sir," replied Marston, curtly.

"Well?" drawled Skelton.

"Well, sir, what then?" responded Marston.

"Why, as the wish of the parties is to have him buried—poor fellow! —as quietly as possible, I think he might just as well be laid *there* as anywhere else!"

"Had I desired it, Mr. Skelton, I should myself have made the offer," said Marston, abruptly.

"Then you don't wish it?" said Skelton.

"No, sir; certainly not—most peremptorily not," answered Marston, with more sharpness than, in his early days, he would have thought quite consistent with politeness.

"Perhaps," replied Skelton, for want of something better to say, and with a callous sort of levity; "perhaps you hold the idea—some people *do*—that murdered men can't rest in their graves until their murderers have expiated their guilt?"

Marston made no reply, but shot two or three lurid glances from under his brow at the speaker.

"Well, then, at all events," continued Skelton, indolently resuming his theme, "if you decline your assistance, may I, at least, hope for your advice? Knowing nothing of this country, I would ask you whither you would recommend me to have the body conveyed?"

"I don't care to advise in the matter," said Marston; "but if I were directing, I should have the remains buried in Chester. It is not more than twenty miles from this; and if, at any future time, his family should desire to remove the body, it could be effected more easily from thence. But you can decide."

"Egad! I believe you are right," said Skelton, glad to be relieved of the trouble of thinking about the matter; "and I shall take your advice."

In accordance with this declaration the body was, within four-and-twenty hours, removed to Chester, and buried there, Mr. Skelton attending on behalf of Sir Wynston's numerous and afflicted friends and relatives.

There are certain heartaches for which time brings no healing; nay, which grow but the sorer and fiercer as days and years roll on. Of this kind, perhaps, were the stern and bitter feelings which now darkened the face of Marston with an almost perpetual gloom. His habits became even more unsocial than before. The society of his son he no longer seemed to enjoy. Long and solitary rambles in his wild and extensive demesne consumed the listless hours of his waking existence; and when the weather prevented this, he shut himself up, upon pretence of business, in his study.

He had not, since the occasion we have already mentioned, referred to the intended departure of Mademoiselle de Barras. Truth to say, his feelings with respect to that young lady were of a conflicting and mysterious kind; and as often as his dark thoughts wandered to her (which, indeed, was frequently enough), his muttered exclamation seemed to imply some painful and horrible suspicions respecting her.

"Yes," he would mutter, "I thought I heard your light foot upon the lobby, on that *accursed* night. *Fancy!* Well, it *may* have been, but assuredly a *strange* fancy. I cannot comprehend that woman. She baffles my scrutiny. I have looked into her face with an eye she might well understand, were it indeed as I sometimes suspect, and she has been calm and unmoved. I have watched and studied her; still—doubt, doubt, hideous doubt!—is she what she seems, or—a TIGRESS?"

Mrs. Marston, on the other hand, procrastinated from day to day the painful task of announcing to Mademoiselle de Barras the stern message with which she had been charged by her husband. And thus several weeks had passed, and she began to think that his silence upon the subject, notwithstanding his seeing the young French lady at breakfast every morning, amounted to a kind of tacit intimation that the sentence of banishment was not to be carried into immediate execution, but to be kept suspended over the unconscious offender.

It was now six or eight weeks since the hearse carrying away the remains of the ill-fated Sir Wynston Berkley had driven down the dusky avenue; the autumn was deepening into winter, and as Marston gloomily trod the woods of Gray Forest, the withered leaves whirled drearily along his pathway, and the gusts that swayed the mighty branches above him were rude and ungenial. It was a bleak and sombre day, and as he broke into a long and picturesque vista, deep among the most sequestered woods, he suddenly saw before him, and scarcely twenty paces from the spot on which he stood, an apparition, which for some moments absolutely froze him to the earth.

Travel-soiled, tattered, pale, and wasted, John Merton, the murderer, stood before him. He did not exhibit the smallest disposition to turn about and make his escape. On the contrary, he remained perfectly motionless, looking upon his former master with a wild and sorrowful gaze. Marston twice or thrice essayed to speak; his face was white as death, and had he beheld the spectre of the murdered baronet himself, he could not have met the sight with a countenance of ghastlier horror.

"Take me, sir" said Merton, doggedly.

Still Marston did not stir.

"Arrest me, sir, in God's name! here I am," he repeated, dropping his arms by his side; "I'll go with you wherever you tell me."

"Murderer!" cried Marston, with a sudden burst of furious horror, "murderer—assassin—miscreant!—take *that!*"

And, as he spoke, he discharged one of the pistols he always carried about him full at the wretched man. The shot did not take effect, and Merton made no other gesture but to clasp his hands together, with an agonized pressure, while his head sunk upon his breast.

"Shoot me; shoot me," he said hoarsely; "kill me like a dog: better for me to be dead than what I am."

The report of Marston's pistol had, however, reached another ear; and its ringing echoes had hardly ceased to vibrate among the trees, when a stern shout was heard not fifty yards away, and, breathless and amazed, Charles Marston sprang to the place. His father looked from Merton to him, and from him again to Merton, with a guilty and stupified scowl, still holding the smoking pistol in his hand.

"What—how! Good God—Merton!" ejaculated Charles.

"Ay, sir, Merton; ready to go to gaol, or wherever you will," said the man, recklessly.

"A murderer; a madman; don't believe him," muttered Marston, scarce audibly, with lips as white as wax.

"Do you surrender yourself, Merton?" demanded the young man, sternly, advancing toward him.

"Yes, sir; I desire nothing more; God knows I wish to die," responded he, despairingly, and advancing slowly to meet Charles.·

"Come, then," said young Marston, seizing him by the collar, "come quietly to the house. Guilty and unhappy man, you are now my prisoner, and, depend upon it, I shall not let you go."

"I don't want to go, I tell you, sir. I have travelled fifteen miles to-day, to come here and give myself up to the master."

"Accursed madman!" said Marston unconsciously, gazing at the prisoner; and then suddenly rousing himself, he said, "Well, miscreant, you wish to die, and, by——, you are in a fair way to *have* your wish."

"So best," said the man, doggedly. "I don't want to live; I wish I was in my grave; I wish I was dead a year ago."

Some fifteen minutes afterwards, Merton, accompanied by Marston and his son Charles, entered the hall of the mansion which, not ten weeks before, he had quitted under circumstances so guilty and terrible. When they reached the house, Merton seemed much agitated, and wept bitterly on seeing two or three of his former fellow-servants, who looked on him in silence as they passed, with a gloomy and fearful curiosity. These, too, were succeeded by others, peeping and whispering, and upon one pretence or another crossing and re-crossing the hall, and stealing hurried glances at the criminal. Merton sate with his face buried in his hands, sobbing, and taking no note of the humiliating scrutiny of which he was the subject. Meanwhile Marston, pale and agitated, made out his committal, and having sworn in several of his labourers and servants as special constables, despatched the prisoner in their charge to the county gaol, where, under lock and key, we leave him in safe custody for the present.

After this event Marston became excited and restless. He scarcely ate or slept, and his health seemed now as much shattered as his spirits had been before. One day he glided into the room in which, as we have said, it was Mrs. Marston's habit frequently to sit alone. His wife was there, and, as he entered, she uttered an exclamation of doubtful joy and surprise. He sate down near her in silence, and for some time looked gloomily on the ground. She did not care to question him, and anxiously waited until he should open the conversation. At length he raised his eyes, and, looking full at her, asked abruptly—

"Well, what about mademoiselle?"

Mrs. Marston was embarrassed, and hesitated.

"I told you what I wished with respect to that young lady some time ago, and commissioned you to acquaint her with my pleasure; and yet I find her still here, and apparently as much established as ever."

Again Mrs. Marston hesitated. She scarcely knew how to confess to him that she had not conveyed his message.

"Don't suppose, Gertrude, that I wish to find fault. I merely wanted to know whether you had told Mademoiselle de Barras that we were agreed as to the necessity or expediency, or what you please, of dispensing henceforward with her services. I perceive by your manner that you have not done so. I have no doubt your motive was a kind one, but my decision remains unaltered; and I now assure you again that I wish you to speak to her; I wish you explicitly to let her know my wishes and yours."

"Not *mine*, Richard," she answered faintly.

"Well, *mine*, then," he replied, roughly; "we shan't quarrel about that."

"And when—how soon—do you wish me to speak to her on this, to both of us, most painful subject?" asked she, with a sigh.

"To-day—this hour—this minute, if you can; in short the sooner the better," he replied, rising. "I see no reason for holding it back any longer. I am sorry my wishes were not complied with immediately. Pray, let there be no further hesitation or delay. I shall expect to learn this evening that all is arranged."

Marston having thus spoken, left her abruptly, went down to his study with a swift step, shut himself in, and throwing himself into a great chair, gave a loose to his agitation, which was extreme.

Meanwhile Mrs. Marston had sent for Mademoiselle de Barras, anxious to get through her painful task as speedily as possible. The fair French girl quickly presented herself.

"Sit down, mademoiselle," said Mrs. Marston, taking her hand kindly, and drawing her to the priedieu chair beside herself.

Mademoiselle de Barras sate down, and, as she did so, read the countenance of her patroness with one rapid glance of her flashing eyes. These eyes, however, when Mrs. Marston looked at her the next moment, were sunk softly and sadly upon the floor. There was a heightened colour, however, in her cheek, and a quicker heaving of her bosom, which indicated the excitement of an anticipated and painful disclosure. The outward contrast of the two women, whose hands were so lovingly locked together, was almost as striking as the moral contrast of their hearts. The one, so chastened, sad, and gentle; the other, so capable of pride and passion; so darkly exciteable, and yet so mysteriously beautiful. The one, like a Niobe seen in the softest moonshine; the other, a Venus, lighted in the glare of distant conflagration.

"Mademoiselle, dear mademoiselle, I am so much grieved at what I have to say, that I hardly know how to speak to you," said poor Mrs. Marston, pressing her hand; "but Mr. Marston has twice desired me to tell you, what you will hear with far less pain than it costs me to say it."

Mademoiselle de Barras stole another flashing glance at her companion, but did not speak.

"Mr. Marston still persists, mademoiselle, in desiring that we shall part."

"*Est-il possible?*" cried the Frenchwoman, with a genuine start.

"Indeed, mademoiselle, you may well be surprised," said Mrs. Marston, encountering her full and dilated gaze, which, however, dropped again in a moment to the ground. "You may, indeed, naturally be surprised and shocked at this, to me, most severe decision."

"When did he speak last of it?" said she, rapidly.

"But a few moments since," answered Mrs. Marston.

"Ha!" said mademoiselle, and remained silent and motionless for more than a minute.

"Madame," she cried at last, mournfully, "I suppose, then, I must go; but it tears my heart to leave you and dear Miss Rhoda. I would be very happy if, before departing, you would permit me, dear madame, once more to assure Mr. Marston of my innocence, and, in his presence, to call heaven to witness how unjust are all his suspicions."

"Do so, mademoiselle, and I will add my earnest assurances again; though, heaven knows," she said, despondingly, "I anticipate little success; but it is well to leave no chance untried."

Marston was sitting, as we have said, in his library. His agitation had given place to a listless gloom, and he leaned back in his chair, his head supported by his hand, and undisturbed, except by the occasional fall of the embers upon the hearth. There was a knock at the chamber door. His back was towards it, and, without turning or moving, he called to the applicant to enter. The door opened—closed again: a light tread was audible—a tall shadow darkened the wall: Marston looked round, and Mademoiselle de Barras was standing before him. Without knowing how or why, he rose, and stood gazing upon her in silence.

"Mademoiselle de Barras!" he said, at last, in a tone of cold surprise.

"Yes, poor Mademoiselle de Barras," replied the sweet voice of the young Frenchwoman, while her lips hardly moved as the melancholy tones passed them.

"Well, mademoiselle, what do you desire?" he asked, in the same cold accents, and averting his eyes.

"Ah, monsieur, do you ask?—can you pretend to be ignorant? Have you not sent me a message, a cruel, cruel message?"

She spoke so low and gently, that a person at the other end of the room could hardly have heard her words.

"Yes, Mademoiselle de Barras, I *did* send you a message," he replied, doggedly. "A cruel one you will scarcely presume to call it, when you reflect upon your own conduct, and the circumstances which have provoked the measures I have taken."

"What have I done, Monsieur?—what circumstances do you mean?" asked she, plaintively.

"What have you done! A pretty question, truly. Ha, ha!" he repeated, bitterly, and then added, with suppressed vehemence, "ask your own heart, mademoiselle."

"I have asked, I do ask, and my heart answers—*nothing*," she replied, raising her fine melancholy eyes for a moment to his face.

"It lies, then," he retorted, with a fierce scoff.

"Monsieur, before heaven I swear, you wrong me foully," she said, earnestly, clasping her hands together.

"Did ever woman say she was accused *rightly*, mademoiselle?" retorted Marston, with a sneer.

"I don't know—I don't care. I only know that *I* am innocent," continued she, piteously. "I call heaven to witness you have wronged me."

"Wronged you!—why, after all, with what have I charged you?" said he, scoffingly; "but let that pass. I have formed my opinions, arrived at my conclusions. If I have not named them broadly, you at least seem to understand their nature thoroughly. I know the world. I am no novice in the arts of women, mademoiselle. Reserve your vows and attestations for schoolboys and simpletons; they are sadly thrown away upon me."

Marston paced to and fro, with his hands thrust into his pockets, as he thus spoke.

"Then you don't, or rather you will not believe what I tell you?" said she, imploringly.

"No," he answered, drily and slowly, as he passed her. "I don't, and I won't (as you say) believe one word of it; so, pray spare yourself further trouble about the matter."

She raised her head, and darted after him a glance that seemed absolutely to blaze, and at the same time smote her little hand fast clenched upon her breast. The words, however, that trembled on her pale lips were not uttered; her eyes were again cast down, and her fingers played with the little locket that hung round her neck.

"I must make, before I go," she said, with a deep sigh and a melancholy voice, "one confidence—one last confidence: judge me by it. You cannot choose but believe me now: it is a secret, and it must even here be *whispered, whispered, whispered!*"

As she spoke, the colour fled from her face, and her tones became so strange and resolute, that Marston turned short upon his heel, and stopped before her. She looked in his face; he frowned, but lowered his eyes. She drew nearer, laid her hand upon his shoulder, and whispered for a few moments in his ear. He raised his face suddenly: its features were sharp and fixed; its hue was changed; it was livid and moveless, like a face cut in gray stone. He staggered back a little and a little more, and then a little more, and fell backward. Fortunately, the chair in which he had been sitting received him, and he lay there insensible as a corpse. When at last his eyes opened, there was no gleam of triumph, no shade of anger, nothing perceptible of guilt or menace, in the young woman's countenance. The flush had returned to her cheeks; her dimpled chin had sunk upon her full white throat; sorrow, shame, and pride seemed struggling in her handsome face: and she stood before him like a beautiful penitent, who has just made a strange and humbling shrift to her father confessor.

Next day, Marston was mounting his horse for a solitary ride through his park, when Doctor Danvers rode abruptly into the court-yard from the back entrance. Marston touched his hat, and said—

"I don't stand on forms with you, doctor, and you, I know, will waive ceremony with me. You will find Mrs. Marston at home."

"Nay, my dear sir," interrupted the clergyman, sitting firm in his saddle, "my business lies with *you* today."

"The devil it does!" said Marston, with discontented surprise.

"Truly it does, sir," repeated he, with a look of gentle reproof, for the profanity of Marston's ejaculation, far more than the rudeness of his manner, offended him; "and I grieve that your surprise should have somewhat carried you away ——"

"Well, then, Doctor Danvers," interrupted Marston, drily, and without heeding his concluding remark, "if you really *have* business with me, it is, at all events, of no very pressing kind, and may be as well told after supper as now. So, pray, go into the house and rest yourself: we can talk together in the evening."

"My horse is not tired," said the clergyman, patting his steed's neck; "and if you do not object, I will ride by your side for a short time, and as we go, I can say out what I have to tell."

"Well, well, be it so," said Marston, with surpressed impatience, and without more ceremony, he rode slowly along the avenue, and turned off upon the soft sward in the direction of the wildest portion of his wooded demesne, the clergyman keeping close beside him. They proceeded some little way at a walk before Doctor Danvers spoke.

"I have been twice or thrice with that unhappy man," at length he said.

"*What* unhappy man? Unhappiness is no distinguishing singularity, is it?" said Marston, sharply.

"No, truly, you have well said," replied Doctor Danvers. "True it is that man is born unto trouble as the sparks fly upward. I speak, however, of your servant, Merton—a *most* unhappy wretch."

"Ha! you have been with *him*, you say?" replied Marston, with evident interest and anxiety.

"Yes, several times, and conversed with him long and gravely," continued the clergyman.

"Humph! I thought that had been the chaplain's business, not yours, my good friend," observed Marston.

"He has been unwell," replied Dr. Danvers; "and thus, for a day or two, I took his duty, and this poor man, Merton, having known something of me, preferred seeing me rather than a stranger; and so, at the chaplain's desire and his, I continued my visits."

"Well, and you have taught him to pray and sing psalms, I suppose; and what has come of it all?" demanded Marston, testily.

"He does pray, indeed, poor man! and I trust his prayers are heard with mercy at the throne of grace," said his companion, in his earnestness disregarding the sneering tone of his companion. "He is full of compunction, and admits his guilt."

"Ho! that is well—well for *himself*—well for his *soul*, at least; you are sure of it; he confesses; confesses his guilt?"

Marston put his question so rapidly and excitedly, that the clergyman looked with a slight expression of surprise; and recovering himself, he added, in an unconcerned tone—

"Well, well—it was just as well he did so; the evidence is too clear for doubt or mystification; he knew he had no chance, and has taken the seemliest course; and, doubtless, the best for his hopes hereafter."

"I did not question him upon the subject," said Doctor Danvers; "I even declined to hear him speak upon it at first; but he told me he was resolved to offer no defence, and that he saw the finger of God in the fate which had overtaken him"

"He will plead guilty, then, I suppose?" suggested Marston, watching the countenance of his companion with an anxious and somewhat sinister eye.

"His words seem to imply so much," answered he; "and having thus frankly owned his guilt, and avowed his resolution to let the law take its due course in his case, without obstruction or evasion, I urged him to complete the grand work he had begun, and to confess to you, or to some other magistrate fully, and in detail, every circumstance connected with the perpetration of the dreadful deed."

Marston knit his brows, and rode on for some minutes in silence. At length he said, abruptly—

"In *this*, it seems to me, sir, you a little exceeded your commission."

"How so, my dear sir?" asked the clergyman.

"Why, sir," answered Marston, "the man may possibly change his mind before the day of trial, and it is the hangman's office, not yours, my good sir, to fasten the halter about his neck. You will pardon my freedom; but, were this deposition made as you suggest, it would undoubtedly hang him."

"God forbid, Mr. Marston," rejoined Danvers, "that *I* should induce the unhappy man to forfeit his last chances of escape, and to shut the door of human mercy against himself, but on this he seems already resolved; he says so; he has solemnly declared his resolution to me; and even against my warning, again and again reiterated the same declaration."

"*That* I should have thought quite enough, were *I* in your place, without inviting a detailed description of the whole process by which this detestable butchery was consummated. What more than the simple knowledge of the man's guilt does any mortal desire; guilty, or not guilty, is the plain question which the law asks, and no more; take my advice, sir, as a poor Protestant layman, and leave the arts of the confessional and inquisition to Popish priests."

"Nay, Mr. Marston, you greatly misconceive me; as matters stand, there exists among the coroner's jury, and thus among the public, some faint and unfounded suspicion of the possibility of Merton's having had an accessory or accomplice in the perpetration of this foul murder."

"It is a lie, sir—a malignant, d—d lie—the jury believe no such thing, nor the public neither," said Marston, starting in his saddle, and speaking in a voice of thunder; "you have been crammed with lies, sir; malicious, unmeaning, vindictive lies; lies invented to asperse my family, and torture my feelings; suggested in my presence by that scoundrel Mervyn, and scouted by the common sense of the jury."

"I do assure you," replied Doctor Danvers, in a voice which seemed scarcely audible, after the stunning and passionate explosion of Marston's wrath, "I did not imagine that you could feel thus sorely upon the point; nay, I thought that you yourself were not without such painful doubts."

"Again, I tell you, sir," said Marston, in a tone somewhat calmer, but no less stern, "such doubts as you describe have *no* existence; your unsuspecting ear has been alarmed by a vindictive wretch, an old scoundrel who has scarce a passion left but spite towards me; few such there are, thank God; few such villains as would, from a man's very calamities, distil poison to kill the peace and character of his family."

"I am sorry, Mr. Marston," said the clergyman, "you have formed so ill an opinion of a neighbour, and I am very sure that Mr. Mervyn meant *you* no ill in frankly expressing whatever doubts still rested on his mind, after the evidence was taken."

"He did—the scoundrel!" said Marston, furiously striking his hand, in which his whip was clutched, upon his thigh; "he *did* mean to wound and torture me; and with the same object he persists in circulating what he calls his doubts. Meant me no ill, forsooth! why, my great God, sir, could any man be so stupid as not to perceive that the suggestion of such suspicions—absurd, contradictory, incredible as they were—was precisely the thing to exasperate feelings sufficiently troubled already; and not content with raising the question, where it was scouted, as I said, as soon as named, the vindictive slanderer proceeds to propagate and publish his pretended surmises— d—n him!"

"Mr. Marston, you will pardon me when I say that, as a Christian minister, I cannot suffer a spirit so ill as that you manifest, and language so unseemly as that you have just uttered, to pass unreproved," said Danvers, solemnly. "If you will cherish those bitter and unchristian feelings, at least for the brief space that I am with you, command your fierce, unbecoming words."

Marston was about to make a sneering retort, but restrained himself, and turned his head away.

"The wretched man himself appears now very anxious to make some further disclosures," resumed Doctor Danvers, after a pause, "and I recommended him to make them to *you*, Mr. Marston, as the most natural depository of such a statement."

"Well, Mr. Danvers, to cut the matter short, as it appears that a confession of some sort is to be made, be it so. I will attend and receive it. The judges will not be here for eight or ten weeks to come, so there is no great hurry about it. I shall ride down to the town, and see him in the jail some time in the next week."

With this assurance Marston parted from the old clergyman, and rode on alone through the furze and fern of his wild and sombre park.

After supper that evening Marston found himself alone in the parlour with his wife. Mrs. Marston availed herself of the opportunity to redeem her pledge to Mademoiselle de Barras. She was not aware of the strange interview which had taken place between him and the lady for whom she pleaded. The result of her renewed entreaties perhaps the reader has anticipated. Marston listened, doubted—listened, hesitated again—put questions, pondered the answers; debated the matter inwardly, and at last gruffly consented to give the young lady another trial, and permit her to remain some time longer. Poor Mrs. Marston, little suspecting the dreadful future, overwhelmed her husband with gratitude for granting to her entreaties (as he had predetermined to do) this fatal boon. Not caring to protract this scene—either from a disinclination to listen to expressions of affection, which had long lost their charm for him, and had become even positively distasteful, or perhaps from some instinctive recoil from the warm expression of gratitude from lips which, were the truth revealed, might justly have trembled with execration and reproach—he abruptly left the room, and Mrs. Marston, full of her good news, hastened, in the kindness of her heart, to communicate the fancied result of her advocacy to Mademoiselle de Barras.

It was about a week after this, that Marston was one evening surprised in his study by the receipt of the following letter from Dr. Danvers:—

"My dear Sir,

You will be shocked to hear that Merton is most dangerously ill, and at this moment in imminent peril. He is thoroughly conscious of his situation, and himself regards it as a merciful interposition of Providence to spare him the disgrace and terror of the dreadful fate which he anticipated. The unhappy man has twice repeated his anxious desire, this day, to state some facts connected with the murder of the late Sir Wynston Berkley, which, he says, it is of the utmost moment that you should hear. He says that he could not leave the world in peace without having made this disclosure, which he especially desires to make to yourself, and entreats that you will come to receive his communication as early as you can in the morning. This is indeed needful, as the physician says that he is fast sinking. I offer no apology for adding my earnest solicitations to those of the dying man; and am, dear sir, your very obedient servant,

"J. DANVERS."

"He regards it as a merciful interposition of Providence," muttered Marston, as he closed the letter, with a sneer. "Well, some men have odd notions of mercy and providence, to be sure; but if it pleases *him*, certainly *I* shall not complain for one."

Marston was all this evening in better spirits than he had enjoyed for months, or even years. A mountain seemed to have been lifted from his heart. He joined in the conversation during and after supper, listened with apparent interest, talked with animation, and even laughed and jested. It is needless to say all this flowed not from the healthy cheer of a heart at ease, but from the excited and almost feverish sense of sudden relief.

Next morning, Marston rode into the old-fashioned town, at the further end of which the dingy and grated front of the jail looked warningly out upon the rustic passengers. He passed the sentries, and made his inquiries of the official at the hatch. He was relieved from the necessity of pushing these into detail, however, by the appearance of the physician, who at that moment passed from the interior of the prison.

"Dr. Danvers told me he expected to see you here this morning," said the medical man, after the customary salutation had been interchanged. "Your call, I believe, is connected with the prisoner, John Merton?"

"Yes, sir, so it is," said Marston. "Is he in a condition, pray, to make a statement of considerable length?"

"Far from it, Mr. Marston; he has but a few hours to live," answered the physician, "and is now insensible; but I believe he last night saw Dr. Danvers, and told him whatever was weighing upon his mind."

"Ha!—and can you say where Dr. Danvers now is?" inquired Marston, anxiously and hurriedly. "Not *here*, is he?"

"No; but I saw him, as I came here, not ten minutes since, ride into the town. It is market-day, and you will probably find him somewhere in the high street for an hour or two to come," answered he.

Marston thanked him, and, lost in abstraction, rode down to the little inn, entered a sitting-room, and wrote a hurried line to Dr. Danvers, entreating his attendance *there*, as a place where they might converse less interruptedly than in the street; and committing this note to the waiter, with the injunction to deliver it at once, and an intimation of where Dr. Danvers was probably to be found, he awaited, with intense and agitating anxiety, the arrival of the clergyman.

It was not for nearly ten minutes, however, which his impatience magnified into an eternity, that the well-known voice of Dr. Danvers reached him from the little hall. It was in vain that Marston strove to curb his violent agitation: his heart swelled as if it would smother him; he felt, as it were, the chill of death pervade his frame, and he could scarcely see the door through which he momentarily expected the entrance of the clergyman.

A few minutes more, and Dr. Danvers entered the little apartment.

"My dear sir," said he, gravely and earnestly, as he grasped the cold hand of Marston, "I am rejoiced to see you. I have matters of great moment and the strangest mystery to lay before you."

"I dare say—I was sure—that is, I suspected so much," answered Marston, breathing fast, and looking very pale. "I heard at the prison that the murderer, Merton, was fast dying, and now is in an unconscious state; and from the physician, that you had seen him, at his urgent entreaty, last night. My mind misgives me, sir. I fear I know not what. I long, yet dread, to hear the wretched man's confession. For God's sake tell me, does it implicate anybody else in the guilt?"

"No; no one specifically; but it has thrown a hideous additional mystery over the occurrence. Listen to me, my dear sir, and the whole narrative, as he stated it to me, shall be related now to you," said Dr. Danvers.

Marston had closed the door carefully, and they sate down together at the further end of the apartment. Marston, breathless and ghastly pale; his lips compressed—his brows knit—and his dark, dilated gaze fixed immoveably upon the speaker. Dr. Danvers, on the other hand, tranquil and solemn, and with, perhaps, some shade of awe overcasting the habitual sweetness of his countenance.

"His confession was a strange one," renewed Dr. Danvers, shaking his head gravely. "He said that the first idea of the crime was suggested by Sir Wynston's man accidentally mentioning, a few days after their arrival, that his master slept with his bank-notes, to the amount of some hundreds of pounds, in a pocket-book under his pillow. He declared that as the man mentioned this circumstance, something muttered the infernal suggestion in his ear, and from that moment he was the slave of that one idea; it was ever present with him. He contended against it in vain; he dreaded and abhorred it; but still it possessed him; he felt his power of resistance yielding. This horrible stranger which had stolen into his heart, waxed in power and importunity, and tormented him day and night. He resolved to fly from the house. He gave notice to you and Mrs. Marston of his intended departure; but accident protracted his stay until that fatal night which sealed his doom. The influence which had mastered him forced him to rise from his bed, and take the knife—the discovery of which afterwards helped to convict him—and led him to Sir Wynston's chamber; he entered; it was a moonlight night."

Here the clergyman, glancing round the room, lowered his voice, and advanced his lips so near to Marston, that their heads nearly touched. In this tone and attitude he continued his narrative for a few minutes. At the end of this brief space, Marston rose up slowly, and with a movement backward, every feature strung with horror, and saying, in a long whisper, the one word, "yes," which seemed like the hiss of a snake before he makes his last deadly spring. Both were silent for a time. At last Marston broke out with hoarse vehemence—

"Dreadful—horrible—oh, God! God!—my God! how frightful!"

And throwing himself into a chair, he clasped his hands across his eyes and forehead, while the sweat of agony literally poured down his pale face.

"Truly it is so," said the clergyman, scarcely above his breath; and, after a long interval—"horrible indeed!"

"Well," said Marston, rising suddenly to his feet, wiping the dews of horror from his face, and looking wildly round, like one newly awoke from a nightmare, "I must make the most of this momentous and startling disclosure. I shall spare no pains to come at the truth," said he, energetically. "Meanwhile, my dear sir, for the sake of justice and of mercy, observe secrecy. Leave me to sift this matter; give no note anywhere that we *suspect*. Observe this reserve and security, and with it detection will follow. Breathe but one word, and you arm the guilty with double caution, and turn licentious gossip loose upon the fame of an innocent and troubled family. Once more I entreat—I expect—I implore silence—silence, at least, for the present—*silence!*"

"I quite agree with you, my dear Mr. Marston," answered Dr. Danvers. "I have not divulged one syllable of that poor wretch's confession, save to yourself alone. You, as a magistrate, a relative of the murdered gentleman, and the head of that establishment among whom the guilt rests, are invested with an interest in detecting, and powers of sifting the truth in this matter, such as none other possesses. I clearly see, with you, too, the inexpediency and folly of talking, for talking's sake, of this affair. I mean to keep my counsel, and shall most assuredly, irrespectively even of your request—which should, however, of course, have weight with me— maintain a strict and cautious silence upon this subject."

Some little time longer they remained together, and Marston, buried in strange thoughts, took his leave, and rode slowly back to Gray Forest.

Months passed away—a year, and more—and though no new character appeared upon the stage, the relations which had subsisted among the old ones became, in some respects, very materially altered. A gradual and disagreeable change came over Mademoiselle de Barras's manner; her affectionate attentions to Mrs. Marston became less and less frequent; nor was the change merely confined to this growing coldness; there was something of a positive and still more unpleasant kind in the alteration we have noted. There was a certain independence and carelessness, conveyed in a hundred intangible but significant little incidents and looks—a something which, without being open to formal rebuke or remonstrance, yet bordered, in effect, upon impertinence, and even insolence. This indescribable and provoking self-assertion, implied in glances, tones, emphasis, and general bearing, surprised Mrs. Marston far more than it irritated her. As often as she experienced one of these studied slights or insinuated impertinences, she revolved in her own mind all the incidents of their past intercourse, in the vain endeavour to recollect some one among them which could possibly account for the offensive change so manifest in the conduct of the young Frenchwoman.

Mrs. Marston, although she sometimes rebuked these artful affronts by a grave look, a cold tone, or a distant manner, yet had too much dignity to engage in a petty warfare of annoyance, and had, in reality, no substantial and well-defined ground of complaint against her, such as would have warranted her either in taking the young lady herself to task, or in bringing her conduct under the censure of Marston.

One evening it happened that Mrs. Marston and Mademoiselle de Barras had been left alone together, after the supper-party had dispersed. They had been for a long time silent, and Mrs. Marston resolved to improve the *tête-à-tête*, for the purpose of eliciting from mademoiselle an explanation of her strange behaviour.

"Mademoiselle," said she, "I have lately observed a very marked change in your conduct to me."

"*Indeed!*" said the Frenchwoman.

"Yes, mademoiselle; you must be yourself perfectly aware of that change; it is a studied and intentional one," continued Mrs. Marston, in a gentle but dignified tone; "and although I have felt some doubt as to whether it were advisable, so long as you observe toward me the forms of external respect, and punctually discharge the duties you have undertaken, to open any discussion whatever upon the subject; yet I have thought it better to give you a fair opportunity of explaining frankly, should you desire to do so, the feelings and impressions under which you are acting."

"Ah, you are very obliging, madame," said she, coolly.

"It is quite clear, mademoiselle, that you have either misunderstood me, or that you are dissatisfied with your situation among us: your conduct cannot otherwise be accounted for," said Mrs. Marston, gravely.

"My conduct—*ma foi!* what conduct?" retorted the handsome

Frenchwoman, confidently, and with a disdainful glance.

"If you question the fact, mademoiselle," said the elder lady, "it is enough. Your ungracious manner and ungentle looks, I presume, arise from what appears to you a sufficient and well-defined cause, of which, however, I know nothing."

"I really was not aware," said Mademoiselle de Barras, with a supercilious smile, "that my looks and my manner were subjected to so strict a criticism, or that it was my duty to regulate both according to so nice and difficult a standard."

"Well, mademoiselle," continued Mrs. Marston, "it is plain that whatever may be the cause of your dissatisfaction, you are resolved against confiding it to me. I only wish to know frankly from your own lips, whether you have formed a wish to leave this situation: if so, I entreat you to declare it freely."

"You are very obliging, indeed, madame," said the pretty foreigner, drily; "but I have no such wish, at least at present."

"Very well, mademoiselle," replied Mrs. Marston, with gentle dignity; "I regret your want of candour, on your own account. You would, I am sure, be much happier, were you to deal frankly with me."

"May I now have your permission, madame, to retire to my room?" asked the French girl, rising, and making a low courtesy— "that is, if madame has nothing further to censure."

"Certainly, mademoiselle; I have nothing further to say," replied the elder lady.

The Frenchwoman made another and a deeper courtesy, and withdrew. Mrs. Marston, however, heard, as she was designed to do, the young lady tittering and whispering to herself, as she lighted her candle in the hall. This scene mortified and grieved poor Mrs. Marston inexpressibly. She was little, if at all, accessible to emotions of anger and certainly, none such mingled in the feelings with which she regarded Mademoiselle de Barras. But she had found in this girl a companion, and even a confidante in her melancholy solitude; she had believed her affectionate, sympathetic, tender, and the disappointment was as bitter as unimagined.

The annoyances which she was fated to receive from Mademoiselle de Barras were destined, however, to grow in number and in magnitude. The Frenchwoman sometimes took a fancy, for some unrevealed purpose, to talk a good deal to Mrs. Marston, and on such occasions would persist, notwithstanding that lady's marked reserve and discouragement, in chatting away, as if she were conscious that her conversation was the most welcome entertainment possible to her really unwilling auditor. No one of their interviews did she ever suffer to close without in some way or other suggesting or insinuating something mysterious and untold to the prejudice of Mr. Marston. Those vague and intangible hints, the meaning of which, for an instant legible and terrific, seemed in another moment to dissolve and disappear, tortured Mrs. Marston like the intrusion of a spectre; and this, along with the portentous change, rather *felt* than visible, in mademoiselle's conduct toward her, invested the beautiful Frenchwoman, in the eyes of her former friend and patroness, with an indefinable character that was not only repulsive but formidable.

Mrs. Marston's feelings with respect to this person were still further disturbed by the half-conveyed hints and inuendoes of her own maid, who never lost an opportunity of insinuating her intense dislike of the Frenchwoman, and appeared perpetually to be upon the very verge of making some explicit charges, or some shocking revelations, respecting her, which, however, she as invariably evaded; and even when Mrs. Marston once or twice insisted upon her explaining her meaning distinctly, she eluded her mistress's desire, and left her still in the same uneasy uncertainty.

Marston, on his part, however much his conduct might tend to confirm suspicion, certainly did nothing to dissipate the painful and undefined apprehension respecting himself, which Mademoiselle de Barras, with such malign and mysterious industry, laboured to raise. His spirits and temper were liable to strange fluctuations. In the midst of that excited gaiety, to which, until lately, he had been so long a stranger, would sometimes intervene paroxysms of the blackest despair, all the ghastlier for the contrast, and with a suddenness so abrupt and overwhelming, that one might have fancied him crossed by the shadow of some terrific apparition. Sometimes for a whole day, or even more, he would withdraw himself from the society of his family, and, in morose and moody solitude, take his meals alone in his library, and steal out unattended to wander among the thickets and glades of his park. Sometimes, again, he would sit for hours in the room which had been Sir Wynston's, and, with a kind of horrible resolution, often loiter there till after nightfall. In such hours, the servants would listen with curious awe, as they heard his step, pacing to and fro, in that deserted and inauspicious chamber, while his voice, in broken sentences, was also imperfectly audible, as if maintaining a muttered dialogue. These eccentric practices gradually invested him, in the eyes of his domestics, with a certain preternatural mystery, which enhanced the fear with which they habitually regarded him, and was subsequently confirmed by his giving orders to have the furniture taken out of the ominous suite of rooms, and the doors nailed up and secured. He gave no reason for this odd and abrupt measure, and gossip of course reported that the direction had originated in his having encountered the spectre of the murdered baronet, in one of these strange and unseasonable visits to the scene of the fearful catastrophe.

In addition to all this, Marston's conduct towards his wife became strangely capricious. He avoided her society more than ever; and when he did happen to exchange a few words with her, they were sometimes harsh and violent, and at others remorsefully gentle and sad, and this without any changes of conduct upon her part to warrant the wayward uncertainty of his treatment. Under all these circumstances, Mrs.

Marston's unhappiness and uneasiness greatly increased. Mademoiselle de Barras, too, upon several late occasions, had begun to assume a tone of authority and dictation, which justly offended the mistress of the establishment. Meanwhile Charles Marston had returned to Cambridge; and Rhoda, no longer enjoying happy walks with her brother, pursued her light and easy studies with Mademoiselle de Barras, and devoted her leisure hours to the loved society of her mother.

One day Mrs. Marston, sitting in her room with Rhoda, had happened to call her own maid, to take down and carefully dust some richly-bound volumes which filled a bookcase in the little chamber.

"You have been crying, Willett," said Mrs. Marston, observing that the young woman's eyes were red and swollen.

"Indeed, and I was, ma'am," she replied, reluctantly, "and I could not help it, so I could not."

"Why, what has happened to vex you? has any one ill-treated you?" said Mrs. Marston, who had an esteem for the poor girl. "Come, come, you must not fret about it; only tell me what has vexed you."

"Oh! ma'am, no one has ill-used *me*, ma'am; but I can't but be vexed sometimes, ma'am, and fretted to see how things is going on. I have one wish, just one wish, ma'am, and if I got *that*, I'd ask no more," said the girl.

"And what *is* it?" asked Mrs. Marston; "what do you wish for? speak plainly, Willett; what is it?"

"Ah! ma'am, if I said it, maybe you might not be pleased. Don't ask me, ma'am," said the girl dusting the books very hard, and tossing them down again with angry emphasis. "I don't desire anybody's harm, God knows; but, for all that, I wish what I wish, and that is the truth."

"Why, Willett, I really cannot account for your strange habit of lately hinting, and insinuating, and always speaking riddles, and refusing to explain your meaning. What *do* you mean? speak plainly. If there are any dishonest practices going on, it is your duty to say so distinctly."

"Oh! ma'am, it is just a wish I have. I wish ——; but it's no matter. If I could once see the house clear of that Frenchwoman——"

"If you mean Mademoiselle de Barras, she is *a lady*," interrupted Mrs. Marston.

"Well, ma'am, I beg pardon," continued the woman; "lady or no lady, it is all one to me; for I am very sure, ma'am, she'll never leave the house till there is something bad comes about; and—and ——. I can't bring myself to talk to you about her, ma'am. I can't say what I want to tell you: but—but ——. Oh, ma'am, for God's sake, try and get her out, any way, no matter how; try and get rid of her."

As she said this, the poor girl burst into a passionate agony of tears, and Mrs. Marston and Rhoda looked on in silent amazement, while she for some minutes continued to sob and weep.

The party were suddenly recalled from their various reveries by a knock at the chamber-door. It opened, and the subject of the girl's deprecatory entreaty entered. There was something unusually excited and assured in Mademoiselle de Barras's air and countenance; perhaps she had a suspicion that she had been the topic of their conversation. At all events, she looked round upon them with a smile, in which there was someting supercilious, and even defiant; and, without waiting to be invited, sate herself down, with a haughty air.

"I was about to ask you to sit down, mademoiselle, but you have anticipated me," said Mrs. Marston, gravely. "You have something to say to me, I suppose; I am quite at leisure, so pray let me hear it now."

"Thank you, thank you, madame," replied she, with a sharp, and even scornful glance; "I ought to have asked your permission to sit; I forgot; but you have condescended to give it without my doing so; that was very kind, very kind, indeed."

"But I wish to know, mademoiselle, whether you have anything very particular to say to me?" said Mrs. Marston.

"You wish to know!—and why, pray madame? asked Mademoiselle de Barras, sharply.

"Because, unless it is something very urgent, I should prefer your talking to me some other time; as, at present, I desire to be alone with my daughter."

"Oh, ho! I ought to ask pardon again," said mademoiselle, with the same glance, and the same smile. "I find I am *de trop*—quite in the way. *Hélas*! I am very unfortunate to-day."

Mademoiselle de Barras made not the slightest movement, and it was evident that she was resolved to prolong her stay, in sheer defiance of Mrs. Marston's wishes.

"Mademoiselle, I conclude from your silence that you have nothing very pressing to say, and, therefore, must request that you will have the goodness to leave me for the present," said Mrs. Marston, who felt that the spirit of the French girl's conduct was too apparent not to have been understood by Rhoda and the servant, and that it was of a kind, for example sake, impossible to be submitted to, or tolerated.

Mademoiselle de Barras darted a fiery and insolent glance at Mrs. Marston, and was, doubless, upon the point of precipitating the open quarrel which was impending, by setting her authority at defiance; but she checked herself, and changed her line of operations.

"We are *not* alone madame," she said, with a heightened colour, and a slight toss of the head. "I was about to speak of Mr. Marston. I had something, not much, I confess, to say; but before servants I shan't speak; nor, indeed, *now* at all. So, madame, as you desire it, I shall no further interrupt you. Come, Miss Rhoda, come to the music-room, if you please, and finish your practice for to-day."

"You forget, mademoiselle, that I wish to have my daughter with me at present," said Mrs. Marston.

"I am very sorry, madame," said the French lady, with the same heightened colour and unpleasant smile, and her finely-pencilled brows just discernibly knit, so as to give a novel and menacing expression to her beautiful face—"I am very sorry, madame, but she must, so long as

I remain accountable for her education, complete her allotted exercises at the appointed hours; and nothing shall, I assure you, with my consent, interfere with these duties. Come, Miss Rhoda, precede me, if you please, to the music-room. Come, come.''

"Stay where you are, Rhoda," said Mrs. Marston, firmly and gently, and betraying no symptom of excitement, except in a slight tremor of her voice, and a faint flush upon her cheek—"Stay where you are, my dear child. I am your *mother*, and, next to your father, have the first claim upon your obedience. Mademoiselle," she continued, addressing the Frenchwoman, calmly but firmly, "my daughter will remain here for some time longer, and you will have the goodness to withdraw. I insist upon it, Mademoiselle de Barras."

"I will not leave the room, I assure you, madame, without my pupil," retorted mademoiselle, with resolute insolence. "Your husband, madame, has invested me with this authority, and she *shall* obey me. Miss Rhoda, I say again, go down to the music-room."

"Remain where you are, Rhoda," said Mrs. Marston again. "Mademoiselle, you have long been acting as if your object were to provoke me to part with you. I find it impossible any longer to overlook this grossly disrespectful conduct; conduct of which I had, indeed, believed you absolutely incapable. Willett," she continued, addressing the maid, who was evidently bursting with rage at the scene she had just witnessed, "your master is, I believe, in the library; go down, and tell him that I entreat him to come here immediately."

The maid started on her mission with angry alacrity, darting a venomous glance at the handsome Frenchwoman as she passed.

Mademoiselle de Barras, meanwhile, sate, listless and defiant, in her chair, and tapping her little foot with angry excitement upon the floor. Rhoda sate close by her mother, holding her hand fast, and looking frightened, perplexed, and as if she were on the point of weeping. Mrs. Marston, though flushed and excited, yet maintained her dignified and grave demeanour. And thus, in silence, did they all three await the arrival of the arbiter to whom Mrs. Marston had so promptly appealed.

A few minutes more, and Marston entered the room. Mademoiselle's expression changed as he did so to one of dejected and sorrowful submission; and, as Marston's eye lighted upon her, his brow darkened and his face grew pale.

"Well, well—what is it?—what is all this?" he said, glancing with a troubled eye from one to the other. "Speak, some one. Mrs. Marston, *you* sent for me; what is it?"

"I want to know, Mr. Marston, from your own lips," said the lady, in reply, "whether Rhoda is to obey me or Mademoiselle de Barras?"

"Bah!—a question of women's prerogative," said Marston, with muttered vehemence.

"*Of a wife's* and *a mother's* prerogative, Richard," said Mrs Marston, with gentle emphasis. "A very simple question, and one I should have thought needing no deliberation to decide it."

"Well, child," said he, turning to Rhoda, with angry irony, "pray what is all this fuss about? You are a very ill-used young lady, I dare aver. Pray what cruelties does Mademoiselle de Barras propose inflicting upon you, that you need to appeal thus to your mother for protection?"

"You quite mistake me, Richard," interposed Mrs Marston; "Rhoda is perfectly passive in the matter. I simply wish to learn from you, in mademoiselle's presence, whether I or she is to command my daughter?"

"*Command!*" said Marston, evading the direct appeal; "and pray what is all this *commanding* about?—what do you want the girl to do?"

"*I* wish her to remain here with me for a little time, and mademoiselle, knowing this, desires her instantly to go to the music-room, and leave me. That is all," said Mrs. Marston.

"And pray, is there nothing to make her going to the music-room advisable or necessary? Has she no music to learn, or studies to pursue? Psha! Mrs. Marston, what needs all this noise about nothing? Go, miss," he added, sharply and peremptorily, addressing Rhoda, "go this moment to the music-room."

The girl glided from the room, and mademoiselle, as she followed, shot a glance at Mrs. Marston which wounded and humbled her in the dust.

"Oh! Richard, Richard, if you knew all, you would not have subjected me to this indignity," she said; and throwing her arms about his neck, she wept, for the first time for many a long year, upon his breast.

Marston was embarrassed and agitated. He disengaged her arms from his neck, and placed her gently in a chair. She sobbed on for some time in silence—a silence which Marston himself did not essay to break. He walked to the door, apparently with the intention of leaving her. He hesitated however, and returned; took a hurried turn through the room; hesitated again; sat down; then returned to the door, not to depart, but to close it carefully, and walked gloomily to the window, whence he looked forth, buried in agitating and absorbing thoughts.

"Richard, to you this seems a trifling thing; but, indeed, it is not so," said Mrs. Marston, sadly.

"You are very right, Gertrude," he said, quickly, and almost with a start; "it is very far from a trifling thing; it is very important."

"You don't blame me, Richard?" said she.

"I blame nobody," said he.

"Indeed, I never meant to offend you, Richard," she urged.

"Of course not; no, no; I never said so," he interrupted, sarcastically; "what could you gain by that?"

"Oh! Richard, better feelings have governed me," she said, in a melancholy and reproachful tone.

"Well, well, I suppose so," he said; and after an interval, he added abstractedly, "This cannot, however, go on; no, no—it *cannot*. Sooner or later it must have come; better at once—better *now*."

"What do you mean, Richard?" she said, greatly alarmed, she knew not why. "What are you resolving upon? Dear Richard, in mercy tell me. I implore of you, tell me."

"Why, Gertrude, you seem to me to fancy that, because I don't talk about what is passing, that I don't *see* it either. Now this is quite a mistake," said Marston, calmly and resolutely. "I have long observed your growing dislike of Mademoiselle de Barras. I have thought it over; this *fracas* of to-day has determined me; it is decisive. I suppose you now wish her to *go*, as earnestly as you once wished her to stay. You need not answer. I know it. I neither ask nor care to whose fault I am to attribute these changed feelings—female caprice accounts sufficiently for it; but whatever the cause, the effect is undeniable; and the only way to deal satisfactorily with *it* is, to dismiss mademoiselle at once. You need take no part in the matter; I take it upon myself. To-morrow morning she shall have left this house. I have said it, and am perfectly resolved."

As he thus spoke, as if to avoid the possibility of any further discussion, he turned abruptly from her, and left the room.

The extreme agitation which she had just undergone combined with her physical delicacy to bring on an hysterical attack; and poor Mrs. Marston, with an aching head and a heavy heart, lay down upon her bed. She had swallowed an opiate, and before ten o'clock upon that night, an eventful one as it proved, she had sunk into a profound slumber.

Some hours after this, she became in a confused way conscious of her husband's presence in the room. He was walking, with an agitated mien, up and down the chamber, and casting from time to time looks of great trouble toward the bed where she lay. Though the presence of her husband was a strange and long unwonted occurrence there, at such an hour, and though she felt the strangeness of the visit, the power of the opiate overwhelmed her so, that she could only see this apparition gliding slowly back and forward before her, with the passive wonder and curiosity with which one awaits the issue of an interesting dream.

For a time she lay once more in an uneasy sleep; but still, throughout even this, she was conscious of his presence; and when, a little while after, she again saw him, he was not walking to and fro before the foot of the bed, but sitting beside her, with one hand laid upon the pillow on which her head was resting, the other supporting his chin. He was looking steadfastly upon her, with a changed face, an expression of bitter sorrow, compunction, and tenderness. There was not one trace of sternness; all was softened. The look was what she fancied he might have turned upon her had she lain there dead, ere yet the love of their early and ill-fated union had grown cold in his heart. There was something in it which reminded her of days and feelings gone, never to return. And while she looked in his face with a sweet and mournful fascination, tears unconsciously wet the pillow on which her poor head was resting. Unable to speak, unable to move, she heard him say—

"It was not your fault, Gertrude—it was not yours, nor mine. There is a destiny in these things too strong for us. Past is past—what is done, is done for ever; and even were it all to do over again, what power have I to mend it? No, no; how could I contend against the combined power of passions, circumstances, influences—in a word, of FATE? You have been good and patient, while *I*——; but no matter. Your lot, Gertrude, is a happier one than mine."

Mrs. Marston heard him and saw him, but she had not the power, nor even the will, herself to speak or move. He appeared before her passive sense like the phantasm of a dream. He stood up at the bedside, and looked on her steadfastly, with the same melancholy expression. For a moment he stooped over her, as if about to kiss her face, but checked himself, stood erect again at the bedside, then suddenly turned; the curtain fell back into its place, and she saw him no more.

With a strange mixture of sweet and bitter feelings this vision rested upon the memory of Mrs. Marston, until, gradually, deep slumber again overcame her senses, and the incident and all its attendant circumstances faded into oblivion.

It was past eight o'clock when Mrs. Marston awoke next morning. The sun was shining richly and cheerily in at the windows; and as the remembrance of Marston's visit to her chamber, and the unwonted manifestations of tenderness and compunction which accompanied it, returned, she felt something like hope and happiness, to which she had long been a stranger, flutter her heart. The pleasing reverie to which she was yielding was, however, interrupted. The sound of stifled sobbing in the room reached her ear, and, pushing back the bed-curtains, and leaning forward to look, she saw her maid, Willett, sitting with her back to the wall, crying bitterly, and striving, as it seemed, to stifle her sobs with her apron, which was wrapped about her face.

"Willet, Willett, is it *you* who are sobbing? What is the matter with you, child?" said Mrs. Marston, anxiously.

The girl checked herself, dried her eyes hastily, and walking briskly to a little distance, as if engaged in arranging the chamber, she said, with an affectation of carelessness—

"Oh, ma'am, it is nothing; nothing at all, indeed, ma'am."

Mrs. Marston remained silent for a time, while all her vague apprehensions returned. Meantime the girl continued to shove the chairs hither and thither, and to arrange and disarrange everything in the room with a fidgety industry, intended to cover her agitation. A few minutes, however, served to weary her of this, for she abruptly stopped, stood by the bedside, and, looking at her mistress, burst into tears.

"Good God! what is it?" said Mrs. Marston, shocked and even terrified, while new alarms displaced her old ones. "Is Miss Rhoda—can it be—is she—is my darling well?"

"Oh, yes, ma'am," answered the maid, "very well, ma'am; she is up, and out walking and knows nothing of all this."

"All *what?*" urged Mrs. Marston. "Tell me, tell me, Willett, what has happened. What is it? Speak, child; say what it is?"

"Oh, ma'am! oh my poor dear mistress!" continued the girl, and stopped, almost stifled with sobs.

"Willett, you must speak; you must say what is the matter. I implore of you—I desire you!" urged the distracted lady. Still the girl, having made one or two ineffectual efforts to speak, continued to sob.

"Willett, you will drive me mad. For mercy's sake, for God's sake, speak—tell me what it is!" cried the unhappy lady.

"Oh, ma'am, it is—it is about the master," sobbed the girl.

"Why he can't—he has not—oh, merciful God! he has not hurt himself!" she almost screamed.

"No, ma'am, no; not *himself;* no, no, but——" and again she hesitated.

"But *what?* Speak out, Willett; dear Willett have mercy on me, and speak out," cried her wretched mistress.

"Oh, ma'am, don't be fretted; don't take it to heart, ma'am," said the maid, clasping her hands together in anguish.

"Anything, anything, Willett; only speak at once," she answered.

"Well, ma'am, it is soon said—it is easy told. The master, ma'am—the master is gone with the Frenchwoman; they went in the travelling coach last night, ma'am; he is gone away with her, ma'am; that is all."

Mrs. Marston looked at the girl with a gaze of stupified, stony terror; not a muscle of her face moved; not one heaving respiration showed that she was living. Motionless, with this fearful look fixed upon the girl, and her thin hands stretched towards her, she remained, second after second. At last her outstretched hands began to tremble more and more violently; and as if for the first time the knowledge of his calamity had reached her, with a cry, as though body and soul were parting, she fell back motionless in her bed.

Several hours had passed before Mrs. Marston was restored to consciousness. To this state of utter insensibility, one of silent, terrified stupor succeeded; and it was not until she saw her daughter Rhoda standing at her bedside, weeping, that she found voice and recollection to speak.

"My child; my darling, my poor child," she cried, sobbing piteously, as she drew her to her heart and looked in her face alternately—"my darling, my darling child!"

Rhoda could only weep, and return her poor mother's caresses in silence. Too young and inexperienced to understand the full extent and nature of this direful calamity, the strange occurrence, the general and apparent consternation of the whole household, and the spectacle of her mother's agony, had filled her with fear, perplexity, and anguish. Scared and stunned with a vague sense of danger, like a young bird that, for the first time, cowers under a thunder-storm, she nestled in her mother's bosom; there, with a sense of protection, and of boundless love and tenderness, she lay frightened, wondering, and weeping.

Two or three days passed, and Dr. Danvers came and sate for several hours with poor Mrs. Marston. To comfort and console were, of course, out of his power. The nature of the bereavement, far more terrible than death—its recent occurrence—the distracting consciousness of all its complicated consequences—rendered this a hopeless task. She bowed herself under the blow with the submission of a broken heart. The hope to which she had clung for years had vanished; the worst that ever her imagination feared had come in earnest.

One idea was now constantly present in her mind. She felt a sad, but immoveable assurance, that she should not live long, and the thought, "what will become of my darling when I am gone; who will guard and love my child when I am in my grave; to whom is she to look for tenderness and protection then?" perpetually haunted her, and superadded the pangs of a still wilder despair to the desolation of a broken heart.

It was not for more than a week after this event, that one day Willett, with a certain air of anxious mystery, entered the silent and darkened chamber where Mrs. Marston lay. She had a letter in her hand; the seal and hand-writing were Mr. Marston's. It was long before the injured wife was able to open it; when she did so, the following sentences met her eye:—

Gertrude,

"You can be ignorant neither of the nature nor of the consequences of the decisive step I have taken: I do not seek to excuse it. For the censure of the world, its meddling and mouthing hypocrisy, I care absolutely nothing; I have long set *it* at defiance. And you yourself, Gertrude, when you deliberately reconsider the circumstances of estrangement and coldness under which, though beneath the same roof, we have lived for years, without either sympathy or confidence, can scarcely, if at all, regret the rupture of a tie which had long ceased to be anything better than an irksome and galling formality. I do not desire to attribute to you the smallest blame. There was an incompatibility, not of temper but of feelings, which made us *strangers* though calling one another man and wife. Upon this fact I rest my own justification; our living together under these circumstances was, I dare say, equally undesired by us both. It was, in fact, but a deference to the formal hypocrisy of the world. At all events, the irrevocable act which separates us for ever is done, and I have now merely to state so much of my intentions as may relate in anywise to your future arrangements. I have written to your cousin, and former guardian, Mr. Lattimer, telling him how matters stand between us. You, I told him, shall have, without opposition from me, the whole of your own fortune to your own separate use, together with whatever shall be mutually agreed upon as reasonable, from my income, for your support and that of my daughter. It will be necessary to complete your arrangements with expedition, as I purpose returning to Gray Forest in about three weeks; and as, of course, a meeting between you and those by whom I shall be accompanied is wholly out of the question, you will see the expediency of losing no time in ad-justing everything for your's and my daughter's departure. In the details, of course, I shall not interfere. I think I have made myself clearly intelligible, and would recommend your communicating at once with Mr. Lattimer, with a view to completing temporary arrangements, until your final plans shall have been decided upon.

"RICHARD MARSTON"

The reader can easily conceive the feelings with which this letter was perused. We shall not attempt to describe them; nor shall we weary his patience by a detail of all the circumstances attending Mrs. Marston's departure. Suffice it to mention that, in less than a fortnight after the receipt of the letter which we have just copied, she had for ever left the mansion of Gray Forest.

In a small house, in a sequestered part of the rich county of Warwick, the residence of Mrs. Marston and her daughter was for the present fixed. And there, for a time, the heart-broken and desolate lady enjoyed, at least, the privilege of an immunity from the intrusions of all external trouble. But the blow, under which the feeble remains of her health and strength were gradually to sink, had struck too surely home; and, from month to month—almost from week to week—the progress of decay was perceptible.

Meanwhile, though grieved and humbled, and longing to comfort his unhappy mother, Charles Marston, for the present absolutely dependant upon his father, had no choice but to remain at Cambridge, and to pursue his studies there.

At Gray Forest Marston and the partner of his guilt continued to live. The old servants were all gradually dismissed, and new ones hired by Mademoiselle de Barras. There they dwelt, shunned by everybody, in a stricter and more desolate seclusion than ever. The novelty of the unrestraint and licence of their new mode of life speedily passed away, and with it the excited and guilty sense of relief which had for a time produced a false and hollow gaiety. The sense of security prompted in mademoiselle a hundred indulgences which, in her former precarious position, she would not have dreamed of. Outbreaks of temper, sharp and sometimes violent, began to manifest themselves on her part, and renewed disappointment and blacker remorse to darken the soul of Marston himself. Often, in the dead of the night, the servants would overhear their bitter and fierce altercations ringing through the melancholy mansion, and often the reckless use of terrible and mysterious epithets of crime. Their quarrels increased in violence and in frequency; and, before two years had passed, feelings of bitterness, hatred, and dread, alone seemed to subsist between them. Yet upon Marston she continued to exercise a powerful and mysterious influence. There was a dogged, apathetic submission on his part, and a growing insolence on hers, constantly more and more strikingly visible. Neglect, disorder, and decay, too, were more than ever apparent in the dreary air of the place.

Doctor Danvers, save by rumour and conjecture, knew nothing of

Marston and his abandoned companion. He had, more than once, felt a
strong disposition to visit Gray Forest, and expostulate, face to face,
with its guilty proprietor. This idea, however, he had, upon consideration, dismissed; not on account of any shrinking from the possible
repulses and affronts to which the attempt might subject him, but from
a thorough conviction that the endeavour would be utterly fruitless for
good, while it might, very obviously, expose him to painful misinter-
pretation and suspicion, and leave it to be imagined that he had been
influenced, if by no meaner motive, at least by the promptings of a
coarse curiosity.

Meanwhile he maintained a correspondence with Mrs. Marston, and
had even once or twice since her departure visited her. Latterly,
however, this correspondence had been a good deal interrupted, and its
intervals had been supplied occasionally by Rhoda, whose letters,
although she herself appeared unconscious of the mournful event the
approach of which they too plainly indicated, were painful records of
the rapid progress of mortal decay.

He had just received one of those ominous letters, at the little post-
office in the town we have already mentioned, and, full of the melancholy news it contained, Dr. Danvers was returning slowly towards his
home. As he rode into a lonely road, traversing an undulating tract of
some three miles in length, the singularity, it may be, of his costume attracted the eye of another passenger, who was, as it turned out, no other
than Marston himself. For two or three miles of this desolate road, their
ways happened to lie together. Marston's first impulse was to avoid the
clergyman; his second, which he obeyed, was to join company, and ride
along with him, at all events, for so long as would show that he shrank
from no encounter which fortune or accident presented. There was a
spirit of bitter defiance in this, which cost him a painful effort.

"How do you do, Parson Danvers?" said Marston, touching his hat
with the handle of his whip.

Danvers thought he had seldom seen a man so changed in so short a
time. His face had grown sallow and wasted, and his figure slightly
stooped, with an appearance almost of feebleness.

"Mr. Marston," said the clergyman, gravely, and almost sternly,
though with some embarrassment, "it is a long time since you and I
have seen one another, and many and painful events have passed in the
interval. I scarce know upon what terms we meet. I am prompted to
speak to you, and in a tone, perhaps, which you will hardly brook; and
yet, if we keep company, as it seems likely we may, I cannot, and I
ought not, to be silent."

"Well, Mr. Danvers, I accept the condition—speak what you will,"
said Marston, with a gloomy promptitude. "If you exceed your
privilege, and grow uncivil, I need but use my spurs, and leave you
behind me preaching to the winds."

"Ah! Mr. Marston," said Dr. Danvers, almost sadly, after a considerable pause, "when I saw you close beside me, my heart was
troubled within me."

"You looked on me as something from the nether world, and expected to see the cloven hoof," said Marston, bitterly, and raising his booted foot a little as he spoke; "but, after all, I am but a vulgar sinner of flesh and blood, without enough of the preternatural about me to frighten an old nurse, much less to agitate a pillar of the Church."

"Mr. Marston, you talk sarcastically; but you *feel* that recent circumstances, as well as old recollections, might well disturb and trouble me at sight of you," answered Dr. Danvers.

"Well—yes—perhaps it is so," said Marston, hastily and sullenly, and became silent for a while.

"My heart is full, Mr. Marston; charged with grief, when I think of the sad history of those with whom, in my mind, you must ever be associated," said Doctor Danvers.

"Ay, to be sure," said Marston, with stern impatience; "but, then, you have much to console you. You have got your comforts and your respectability; all the dearer, too, from the contrast of other people's misfortunes and degradations; then you have your religion moreover ——"

"Yes," interrupted Danvers, earnestly, and hastening to avoid a sneer upon this subject; "God be blessed, I am an humble follower of his gracious Son, our Redeemer; and though, I trust, I should bear with patient submission whatever chastisement in his wisdom and goodness he might see fit to inflict upon me, yet I do praise and bless him for the mercy which has hitherto spared me, and I do feel that mercy all the more profoundly, from the afflictions and troubles with which I daily see others overtaken."

"And in the matter of piety and decorum, doubtless, you bless God also," said Marston, sarcastically, "that you are not as other men are, nor even as this publican."

"Nay, Mr. Marston; God forbid I should harden my sinful heart with the wicked pride of the Pharisee. Evil and corrupt am I already—over much. Too well I know the vileness of my heart, to make myself righteous in my own eyes," replied Dr. Danvers, humbly. "But, sinner as I am, I am yet a messenger of God, whose mission is one of authority to his fellow-sinners; and woe is me if I speak not the truth at all seasons, and in all places where my words may be profitably heard."

"Well, Doctor Danvers, it seems you think it your duty to speak to me, of course, respecting my conduct and my spiritual state. I shall save you the pain and trouble of opening the subject; I shall state the case for you in two words," said Marston, almost fiercely. "I have put away my wife without just cause, and am living in sin with another woman. Come, what have you to say on this theme? Speak out. Deal with me as roughly as you will, I will hear it, and answer you again."

"Alas, Mr. Marston! and do not these things trouble you?" exclaimed Dr. Danvers, earnestly. "Do they not weigh heavy upon your conscience? Ah, sir, do you not remember that, slowly and surely, you are drawing towards the hour of death, and the day of judgement?"

"The hour of death! Yes, I know it is coming, and I await it with indifference. But, for the day of judgment, with its books and trumpets!

my dear doctor, pray don't expect to frighten me with that."

Marston spoke with an angry scorn, which had the effect of interrupting the conversation for some moments.

They rode on, side by side, for a long time, without speaking. At length, however, Marston unexpectedly broke the silence—

"Doctor Danvers," said he, "you asked me some time ago if I feared the hour of death, and the day of judgment. I answered you truly, I do *not* fear them; nay *death*, I think, I could meet with a happier and a quieter heart than any other chance that can befall me; but there are other fears; fears that *do* trouble me much."

Doctor Danvers looked inquiringly at him; but neither spoke for a time.

"You have not seen the catastrophe of the tragedy yet," said Marston, with a stern, stony look, made more horrible by a forced smile and something like a shudder. "I wish I could tell you—*you*, Doctor Danvers—for you are honourable and gentle-hearted. I wish I durst tell you what I fear; the only, *only* thing I really do fear. No mortal knows it but myself, and I see it coming upon me with slow, but unconquerable power. Oh, God—dreadful Spirit—spare me!"

Again they were silent, and again Marston resumed—

"Doctor Danvers, don't mistake me," he said, turning sharply, and fixing his eyes with a strange expression upon his companion. "I dread nothing *human*; I fear neither death, nor disgrace, nor eternity; I have no secrets to keep—no exposures to apprehend; but I dread—I dread——"

He paused, scowled darkly, as if stung with pain, turned away, muttering to himself, and gradually became much excited.

"I can't tell you now, sir, and I won't, " he said, abruptly and fiercely, and with a countenance darkened with a wild and appalling rage that was wholly unaccountable. "I see you searching me with your eyes. Suspect what you will, sir, you shan't inveigle me into admissions. Ay, pry—whisper—stare—question, conjecture, sir—I suppose I must endure the world's impertinence, but d—n me if I gratify it."

It would not be easy to describe Dr. Danvers' astonishment at this unaccountable explosion of fury. He was resolved, however, to bear his companion's violence with temper.

They rode on slowly for fully ten minutes in utter silence, except that Marston occasionally muttered to himself, as it seemed, in excited abstraction. Danvers had at first felt naturally offended at the violent and insulting tone in which he had been so unexpectedly and unprovokedly addressed; but this feeling of irritation was but transient, and some fearful suspicions as to Marston's sanity flitted through his mind. In a calmer and more dogged tone, his companion now addressed him:—

"There is little profit you see, doctor, in worrying me about your religion," said Marston. "it is but sowing the wind, and reaping the whirlwind; and, to say the truth, the longer you pursue it, the less I am in the mood to listen. If ever *you* are cursed and persecuted as I have been, you will understand how little tolerant of gratuitous vexations and contradictions a man may become. We have squabbled over religion long enough, and each holds his own faith still. Continue to sun yourself in your happy delusions, and leave me untroubled to tread the way of my own dark and cheerless destiny."

Thus saying, he made a sullen gesture of farewell, and spurring his horse, crossed the broken fence at the roadside, and so, at a listless pace, through gaps and by farm-roads, penetrated towards his melancholy and guilty home.

Two years had now passed since the decisive event which had for ever separated Marston from her who had loved him so devotedly and so fatally; two years to him of disappointment, abasement, and secret rage; two years to her of gentle and heart-broken submission to the chastening hand of heaven. At the end of this time she died. Marston read the letter that announced the event with a stern look, and silently, but the shock he felt was terrific. No man is so self-abandoned to despair and degradation, that at some casual moment thoughts of amendment—some gleams of hope, however faint and transient, from the distant future—will not visit him. With Marston, those thoughts had somehow ever been associated with vague ideas of a reconciliation with the being whom he had forsaken—good and pure, and looking at her from the darkness and distance of his own fallen state, almost angelic as she seemed. But she was now dead; he could make her no atonement; she could never smile forgiveness upon him. This long-familiar image—the last that had reflected for him one ray of the lost peace and love of happier times—had vanished, and henceforward there was before him nothing but storm and fear.

Marston's embarrassed fortunes made it to him an object to resume the portion of his income heretofore devoted to the separate maintenance of his wife and daughter. In order to effect this it became, of course, necessary to recall his daughter, Rhoda, and fix her residence once more at Gray Forest. No more dreadful penalty could have been inflicted upon the poor girl—no more agonising ordeal than that she was thus doomed to undergo. She had idolised her mother, and now adored her memory. She knew that Mademoiselle de Barras had betrayed and indirectly *murdered* the parent she had so devotedly loved; she knew that that woman had been the curse, the fate of her family, and she regarded her naturally with feelings of mingled terror and abhorrence, the intensity of which was indescribable.

The few scattered friends and relatives, whose sympathies had been moved by the melancholy fate of poor Mrs. Marston, were unanimously agreed that the intended removal of the young and innocent daughter to the polluted mansion of sin and shame, was too intolerably revolting to be permitted. But each of these virtuous individuals unhappily thought it the duty of the *others* to interpose; and with a running commentary of wonder and reprobation, and much virtuous criticism, events were suffered uninterruptedly to take their sinister and melancholy course.

It was about two months after the death of Mrs. Marston, and on a bleak and ominous night at the wintry end of autumn, that poor Rhoda, in deep mourning, and pale with grief and agitation, descended from a chaise at the well-known door of the mansion of Gray Forest. Whether from consideration for her feelings, or, as was more probable, from pure indifference, Rhoda was conducted, on her arrival, direct to her own chamber, and it was not until the next morning that she saw her father. He entered her room unexpectedly; he was very pale, and as she thought, greatly altered, but he seemed perfectly collected, and free from agitation. The marked and even shocking change in his appearance, and perhaps even the trifling though painful circumstance that he wore no mourning for the beloved being who was gone, caused her, after a moment's mute gazing in his face, to burst into an irrepressible flood of tears.

Marston waited stoically until the paroxysm had subsided, and then taking her hand, with a look in which a dogged sternness was contending with something like shame, he said:—

"There, there; you can weep when I am gone. I shan't say very much to you at present, Rhoda, and only wish you to attend to me for one minute. Listen, Rhoda; the lady whom you have been in the habit (here he slightly averted his eyes) of calling Mademoiselle de Barras, is no longer so; she is married; she is my wife, and consequently you will treat her with the respect due to"—he would have said "a mother," but could not, and supplied the phrase by adding, "to that relation."

Rhoda was unable to speak, but almost unconsciously bowed her head in token of attention and submission, and her father pressed her hand more kindly, as he continued:—

"I have always found you a dutiful and obedient child, Rhoda, and expected no other conduct from you. Mrs. Marston will treat you with proper kindness and consideration, and desires me to say that you can, whenever you please, keep strictly to yourself, and need not, unless you feel so disposed, attend the regular meals of the family. This privilege may suit your present depressed spirits, and you must not scruple to use it."

After a few words more, Marston withdrew, leaving his daughter to her reflections, and bleak and bitter enough they were.

Some weeks passed away, and perhaps we shall best consult our readers' ease by substituting for the formal precision of narrative, a few extracts from the letters which Rhoda wrote to her brother, still at Cambridge. These will convey her own impressions respecting the scenes and personages among whom she was now to move.

"The house and place are much neglected, and the former in some parts suffered almost to go to decay. The windows broken in the last storm, nearly eight months ago, they tell me, are still unmended, and the roof, too, unrepaired. The pretty garden, near the well, among the lime-trees, that our darling mother was so fond of, is all but obliterated with weeds and grass, and since my first visit I have not had heart to go near it again. All the old servants are gone; new faces everywhere.

"I have been obliged several times, through fear of offending my father, to join the party in the drawing-room. You may conceive what I felt at seeing mademoiselle in the place once filled by our dear mamma. I was so choked with sorrow, bitterness, and indignation, and my heart so palpitated, that I could not speak, and I believe they thought I was going to faint. Mademoiselle looked very angry, but my father pretending to show me, heaven knows what, from the window, led me to it, and the air revived me a little. Mademoiselle (for I cannot call her by her new name) is altered a good deal—more, however, in the character than in the contour of her face and figure. Certainly, however, she has grown a good deal fuller, and her colour is higher; and whether it is fancy or not, I cannot say, but certainly to me it seems that the expression of her face has acquired something habitually lowering and malicious, and which, I know not how, inspires me with an undefinable dread. She has, however, been tolerably civil to me, but seems contemptuous and rude to my father, and I am afraid he is very wretched. I have seen them exchange such looks, and overheard such intemperate and even appalling altercations between them, as indicate something worse and deeper than ordinary ill-will. This makes me additionally wretched, especially as I cannot help thinking that some mysterious cause enables her to frighten and tyrannise over my poor father. I sometimes think he absolutely detests her; yet, though fiery altercations ensue, he ultimately submits to this bad and cruel woman. Oh, my dear Charles, you have no idea of the shocking, or rather the terrifying, reproaches I have heard interchanged between them, as I accidently passed the room where they were sitting—such terms as have sent me to my room, feeling as if I were in a horrid dream, and made me cry and tremble for hours after I got there. . . . I see my father very seldom, and when I do, he takes but little notice of me. . . . Poor Willett, you know, returned with me. She accompanies me in my walks, and is constantly dropping hints about mademoiselle, from which I know not what to gather. . . .

"I often fear that my father has some secret and mortal ailment. He generally looks ill, and sometimes quite *wretchedly*. He came twice lately to my room, I think to speak to me on some matter of importance; but he said only a sentence or two, and even these broken and incoherent. He seemed unable to command spirits for the interview; and, indeed, he grew so agitated and strange, that I was alarmed, and felt greatly relieved when he left me. . . .

"I do not, you see, disguise my feelings, dear Charles; I do not conceal from you the melancholy and anguish of my present situation. How intensely I long for your promised arrival. I have not a creature to whom I can say one word in confidence, except poor Willett; who, though very good-natured, and really dear to me, is yet far from being a companion. I sometimes think my intense anxiety to see you here is almost selfish; for I know you will feel as acutely as I do, the terrible change observable everywhere. But I cannot help longing for your return, dear Charles, and counting the days and the very hours till you arrive. . . .

"Be cautious, in writing to me, not to say anything which you would not wish mademoiselle to see; for Willett tells me that she *knows* that she often examines, and even intercepts the letters that arrive; and, though Willett may be mistaken,and I hope she is, yet it is better that you should be upon your guard. Ever since I heard this, I have brought my letters to the post-office myself, instead of leaving them with the rest upon the hall table; and you know it is a long walk for me. . . .

"I go to church every Sunday, and take Willett along with me. No one from this seems to think of doing so but ourselves. I see the Mervyns there. Mrs. Mervyn is particularly kind; and I know that she wishes to offer me an asylum at Newton Park; and you cannot think with how much tenderness and delicacy she conveys the wish. But I dare not hint the subject to my father; and, earnestly as I desire it, I could not but feel that I should go there, not to visit, but to *reside*. And so even in this, in many respects, delightful project, is mingled the bitter aprehension of dependence—something so humiliating, that, kindly and delicately as the offer is made, I could not bring myself to embrace it. I have a great deal to say to you, and long to see you." . . .

These extracts will enable the reader to form a tolerably accurate idea of the general state of affairs at Gray Forest. Some particulars must, however, be added.

Marston continued to be the same gloomy and joyless being as heretofore. Sometimes moody and apathetic, sometimes wayward and even savage, but never for a moment at ease, never social—an isolated, disdainful, ruined man.

One day as Rhoda sate and read under the shade of some closely-interwoven evergreens, in a lonely and sheltered part of the neglected pleasure-grounds, with her honest maid Willett in attendance, she was surprised by the sudden appearance of her father, who stood unexpectedly before her. Though his attitude for some time was fixed, his countenance was troubled with anxiety and pain, and his sunken eyes rested upon her with a fiery and fretted gaze. He seemed lost in thought for a while, and then, touching Willett sharply on the shoulder, said abruptly—

"Go; I shall call you when you are wanted. Walk down that alley." And, as he spoke, he indicated with his walking-cane the course he desired her to take.

When the maid was sufficiently distant to be quite out of hearing, Marston sate down beside Rhoda upon the bench, and took her hand in silence. His grasp was cold, and alternately relaxed and contracted with an agitated uncertainty, while his eyes were fixed upon the ground, and he seemed meditating how to open the conversation. At last, as if suddenly awaking from a fearful reverie, he said—

"You correspond with Charles?"

"Yes, sir," she replied, with the respectful formality prescribed by the usages of the time, "we correspond regularly."

"Ay, ay; and, pray, when did you last hear from him?" he continued.

"About a month since, sir," she replied.

"Ha!—and—and—was there nothing strange—nothing—nothing mysterious and menacing in his letter? Come, come, you know what I speak of." He stopped abruptly, and stared in her face with an agitated gaze.

"No, indeed, sir; there was not anything of the kind," she replied.

"I have been greatly shocked, I may say incensed," said Marston excitedly, "by a passage in his last letter to me. Not that it says anything specific; but—but it amazes me—it enrages me."

He again checked himself, and Rhoda, much surprised, and even shocked, said, stammeringly—

"I am sure, sir, that dear Charles would not intentionally say or do anything that could offend you."

"Ah, as to that, I believe so, too. But it is not with *him* I am indignant; no, no. Poor Charles! I believe he *is*, as you say, disposed to conduct himself as a son ought to do, respectfully and obediently. Yes, yes, Charles is very well; but I fear he is leading a bad life, notwithstanding —a very bad life. He is becoming subject to *influences* which never visit or torment the good; believe me, he is."

Marston shook his head, and muttered to himself, with a look of almost craven anxiety, and then whispered to his daughter—

"Just read this, and then tell me is it not so. Read it, read it, and pronounce."

As he thus spoke, he placed in her hand the letter of which he had spoken, and with the passage to which he invited her attention folded down. It was to the following effect:—

"I cannot tell you how shocked I have been by a piece of scandal, as I must believe it, conveyed to me in an anonymous letter, and which is of so very delicate a nature, that without your special command I should hesitate to pain you by its recital. I trust it may be utterly false. Indeed I assume it to be so. It is enough to say that it is of a very distressing nature, and affects the lady (Mademoiselle de Barras) whom you have recently honoured with your hand."

"*Now* you see," cried Marston, with a shuddering fierceness, as she returned the letter with a blanched cheek and trembling hand—"now you see it all. Are you stupid?—the stamp of the cloven hoof—eh?"

Rhoda, unable to gather his meaning, but, at the same time, with a heart full and trembling very much, stammered a few frightened words, and became silent.

"It is *he*, I tell you, that does it all; and if Charles were not living an evil life, he could not have spread his nets for him," said Marston, vehemently. "He can't go near anything good; but, like a scoundrel, he knows where to find a congenial nature; and when he does, he has skill enough to practise upon it. I know him well, and his arts and his smiles; ay, and his scowls and his grins, too. He goes, like his master, up and down, and to and fro upon the earth, for ceaseless mischief. There is not a friend of mine he can get hold of, but he whispered in his ear some damned slander of me. He is drawing them all into a common understanding against me; and he takes an actual pleasure in telling me how the thing goes on—how, one after the other, he has converted my friends into conspirators and libellers, to blast my character, and take my life, and now the monster essays to lure my children into the hellish confederation."

"Who is he, father, who is he?" faltered Rhoda.

"You never saw him," retorted Marston, sternly.

"No, no; you can't have seen him, and you probably never will; but if he *does* come here again, don't listen to him. He is half-fiend and half-idiot, and no good comes of his mouthing and muttering. Avoid him, I warn you, avoid him. Let me see: how shall I describe him? Let me see. You remember—you remember Berkley—Sir Wynston Berkley. Well, he greatly resembles that dead villain: he has all the same grins, and shrugs, and monkey airs, and his face and figure are like. But *he* is a grimed, ragged, wasted piece of sin, little better than a beggar—a shrunken, malignant libel on the human shape. Avoid him, I tell you, avoid him: he is steeped in lies and poison, like the very serpent that betrayed us. Beware of him, I say; for if he once gains your ear, he will delude you, spite of all your vigilance; he will make you his accomplice, and thenceforth, inevitably, there is nothing but mortal and implacable hatred between us!"

Frightened at this wild language, Rhoda did not answer, but looked up in his face in silence. A fearful transformation was there—a scowl so livid and maniacal, that her very senses seemed leaving her with terror. Perhaps the sudden alteration observable in her countenance, as this spectacle so unexpectedly encountered her, recalled him to himself; for he added, hurriedly, and in a tone of gentler meaning—

"Rhoda, Rhoda, watch and pray. My daughter, my child! keep your heart pure, and nothing bad can approach you for ill. No, no; you are good, and the good need not fear!"

Suddenly Marston burst into tears, as he ended this sentence, and wept long and convulsively. She did not dare to speak, or even to move; but after a while he ceased, appeared uneasy, half ashamed and half angry; and looking with a horrified and bewildered glance into her face, he said—

"Rhoda, child, what—what have I said? My God! what have I been saying? Did I—*do* I look ill? Oh, Rhoda, Rhoda, may you never feel this!"

He turned away from her without awaiting her answer, and walked away with the appearance of intense agitation, as if to leave her. He turned again, however, and with a face pallid and sunken as death, approached her slowly—

"Rhoda," said he, "don't tell what I have said to any one—don't, I conjure you, even to Charles. I speak too much at random, and say more than I mean—a foolish, rambling habit: so do not repeat one word of it, not one word to any living mortal. You and I, Rhoda, must have our little secrets."

He ended with an attempt at a smile, so obviously painful and fear-striken that as he walked hurriedly away, the astounded girl burst into a bitter flood of tears. What was, what could be, the meaning of the shocking scene she had then been forced to witness? She dared not answer the question. Yet one ghastly doubt haunted her like her shadow—a suspicion that the malignant and hideous light of madness was already glaring upon his mind. As, leaning upon the arm of her astonished attendant, she retracted her steps, the trees, the flowers, the familiar hall-door, the echoing passages—every object that met her eye —seemed strange and unsubstantial, and she gliding on among them in a horrid dream.

Time passed on: there was no renewal of the painful scene which dwelt so sensibly in the affrighted imagination of Rhoda. Marston's manner was changed towards her; he seemed shy, cowed, and uneasy in her presence, and thenceforth she saw less than ever of him. Meanwhile the time approached which was to witness the long-expected, and, by Rhoda, the intensely prayed for arrival of her brother.

Some four or five days before this event, Mr. Marston, having, as he said, some business in Chester, and further designing to meet his son there, took his departure from Gray Forest, leaving poor Rhoda to the guardianship of her guilty stepmother; and although she had seen so little of her father, yet the very consciousness of his presence had given her a certain confidence and sense of security, which vanished at the moment of his departure. Fear-stricken and wretched as he had been, his removal, nevertheless, seemed to her to render the lonely and inauspicious mansion still more desolate and ominous than before.

She had, with a vague and instinctive antipathy, avoided all contact and intercourse with Mrs. Marston, or as, for distinctness sake, we shall continue to call her, "Mademoiselle," since her return; and she on her part had appeared to acquiesce with a sort of scornful nonchalance, in the tacit understanding that she and her former pupil should see and hear as little as might be of one another.

Meanwhile poor Willett, with her good-natured honesty and her inexhaustible gossip, endeavoured to amuse and re-assure her young mistress, and sometimes even with some partial success.

We must now follow Mr. Marston in his solitary expedition to Chester. When he took his place in the stage-coach he had the whole interior of the vehicle to himself, and thus continued to be its solitary occupant for several miles. The coach, however, was eventually hailed, brought to, and the door being opened, Dr. Danvers got in, and took his place opposite to the passenger already established there. The worthy man was so busied in directing the disposition of his luggage from the window, and in arranging the sundry small parcels with which he was charged, that he did not recognise his companion until they were in motion. When he did so it was with no very pleasurable feeling; and it is probable that Marston, too, would have gladly escaped the coincidence which thus reduced them once more to the temporary necessity of a *tête-à-tête*. Embarrassing as each felt the situation to be, there was, however, no avoiding it, and, after a recognition and a few forced attempts at conversation, they became, by mutual consent, silent and uncommunicative.

The journey, though in point of space a mere trifle, was, in those slow-coach days, a matter of fully five hours' duration; and before it was completed the sun had set, and darkness began to close. Whether it was that the descending twilight dispelled the painful constraint under which Marston had seemed to labour, or that some more purely spiritual and genial influence had gradually dissipated the repulsion and distrust with which, at first, he had shrunk from a renewal of intercourse with Dr. Danvers, he suddenly accosted him thus:—

"Dr. Danvers, I have been fifty times on the point of speaking to you —confidentially of course—while sitting here opposite to you, what I believe I could scarcely bring myself to hint to any other man living; yet I must tell it, and soon, too, or I fear it will have told itself."

Dr. Danvers intimated his readiness to hear and advise, if desired; and Marston resumed abruptly, after a pause—

"Pray, Doctor Danvers, have you heard any stories of an odd kind; any surmises—I don't mean of a *moral* sort, for *those* I hold very cheap— to my prejudice? Indeed I should hardly say to my *prejudice;* I mean—I ought to say—in short, have you heard people remark upon any fancied eccentricities, or that sort of thing, about me?"

He put the question with obvious difficulty, and at last seemed to overcome his own reluctance with a sort of angry and excited self-contempt and impatience. Doctor Danvers was a little puzzled by the interrogatory, and admitted, in reply, that he did not comprehend its drift.

"Doctor Danvers," he resumed, sternly and dejectedly, "I told you, in the chance interview we had some months ago, that I was haunted by a certain fear. I did not define it, nor do I think you suspect its nature. It is a fear of nothing mortal, but of the immortal tenant of this body. My *mind,* sir, is beginning to play me tricks; my guide mocks and terrifies me."

There was a perceptible tinge of horror in the look of astonishment with which Dr. Danvers listened.

"You are a gentleman, sir, and a Christian clergyman; what I have said and shall say is confided to your honour; to be held sacred as the

confession of misery, and hidden from the coarse gaze of the world. I
have become subject to a hideous delusion. It comes at intervals. I do
not think any mortal suspects it, except, maybe, my daughter Rhoda. It
comes and disappears, and comes again. I kept my pleasant secret for a
long time, but at last I let it slip, and committed myself, fortunately, to
but one person, and that my daughter; and, even so, I hardly think she
understood me. I recollected myself before I had disclosed the grotesque and infernal chimera that haunts me."

Marston paused. He was stooped forward, and looking upon the
floor of the vehicle, so that his companion could not see his
countenance. A silence ensued, which was interrupted by Marston,
who once more resumed.

"Sir," said he, "I know not *why*, but I have longed, intensely longed,
for some trustworthy ear into which to pour this horrid secret; why I
repeat, I cannot tell, for I expect no sympathy, and hate compassion. It
is, I suppose, the restless nature of the devil that is in me; but, be it
what it may, I will speak to you, but to *you* only; for the present, at least,
to you alone."

Doctor Danvers again assured him that he might repose the most entire confidence in his secrecy.

"The human mind, I take it, must have either comfort in the past or
hope in the future," he continued, "otherwise it is *in danger*. To me, sir,
the past is intolerably repulsive; one boundless, barren, and hideous
Golgotha of dead hopes and murdered opportunities; the future, still
blacker and more furious, peopled with dreadful features of horror and
menace, and losing itself in utter darkness. Sir, I do not exaggerate.
Between such a past and such a future I stand upon this miserable present; and the only comfort I still am capable of feeling is, that no human
being pities me; that I stand aloof from the insults of compassion and
the hypocrisies of sympathetic morality; and that I can safely defy all
the respectable scoundrels in Christendom to enhance, by one feather's
weight, the load which I myself have accumulated, and which I myself
hourly and unaided sustain."

Doctor Danvers here introduced a word or two in the direction of
their former conversation.

"No, sir, there is no comfort from that quarter either," said Marston,
bitterly; "you but cast your seeds, as the parable terms your teaching,
upon the barren sea, in wasting them on me. My fate, be it what it may,
is as irrevocably fixed, as though I were dead and judged a hundred
years ago."

"This cursed dream," he resumed abruptly, "that every day enslaves
me more and more, has reference to that—that *occurrence* about
Wynston Berkley—he is the hero of the hellish illusion. At certain
times, sir, it seems to me as if he, though dead, were still invested with a
sort of spurious life; going about unrecognised, except by me, in squalor
and contempt, and whispering away my fame and life; labouring with
the malignant industry of a fiend to involve me in the meshes of that

special perdition from which alone I shrink, and to which this emissary of hell seems to have predestined me. Sir, this is a monstrous and hideous extravagance, a delusion, but, after all, no more than a trick of the *imagination;* the reason, the judgment, is untouched. I cannot choose but *see* all the damned phantasmagoria, but I do not believe it real, and this is the difference between my case and—and—*madness!*"

They were now entering the suburbs of Chester, and Doctor Danvers, pained and shocked beyond measure by this unlooked-for disclosure, and not knowing what remark or comfort to offer, relieved his temporary embarrassment by looking from the window, as though attracted by the flash of the lamps, among which the vehicle was now moving. Marston, however, laid his hand upon his arm, and thus recalled him, for a moment, to a forced attention.

"It must seem strange to you, Doctor, that I should trust this cursed secret to your keeping," he said; "and, truth to say, it seems so to myself. I cannot account for the impulse, the irresistible power of which has forced me to disclose the hateful mystery to you, but the fact is this, beginning like a speck, this one idea has gradually darkened and dilated, until it has filled my entire mind. The solitary consciousness of the gigantic mastery it has established there had grown intolerable; I must have told it. The sense of solitude under this aggressive and tremendous delusion was agony, hourly death to my soul. That is the secret of my talkativeness; my sole excuse for plaguing you with the dreams of a wretched hypochondriac."

Doctor Danvers assured him that no apologies were needed, and was only restrained from adding the expression of that pity which he really felt, by the fear of irritating a temper so full of bitterness, pride and defiance. A few minutes more, and the coach having reached its destination, they bid one another farewell, and parted.

At that time there resided in a decent mansion about a mile from the town of Chester, a dapper little gentleman, whom we shall call Doctor Parkes. This gentleman was the proprietor and sole professional manager of a private asylum for the insane, and enjoyed a high reputation, and a proportionate amount of business, in his melancholy calling. It was about the second day after the conversation we have just sketched, that this little gentleman, having visited, according to his custom, all his domestic patients, was about to take his accustomed walk in his somewhat restricted pleasure-grounds, when his servant announced a visitor.

"A gentleman," he repeated; "you have seen him before—eh?"

"No, sir," replied the man; "he is in the study, sir."

"Ha!—a *professional* call. Well, we shall see."

So saying, the little gentleman summoned his gravest look, and hastened to the chamber of audience.

On entering he found a man dressed well, but gravely, having in his air and manner something of high breeding. In countenance striking, dark-featured, and stern, furrowed with the lines of pain or thought, rather than of age, although his dark hairs were largely mingled with white.

The physician bowed, and requested the stranger to take a chair; he, however, nodded slightly and impatiently, as if to intimate an intolerance of ceremony, and, advancing a step or two, said abruptly—

"My name, sir, is Marston; I have come to give you a patient."

The doctor bowed with a still deeper inclination, and paused for a continuance of the communication thus auspiciously commenced.

"You are Dr. Parkes, I take it for granted," said Marston, in the same tone.

"Your most obedient, humble servant, sir," replied he, with the polite formality of the day, and another grave bow.

"Doctor," demanded Marston, fixing his eye upon him sternly, and significantly tapping his own forehead, "can you stay execution?"

The physician looked puzzled, hesitated, and at last requested his visiter to be more explicit.

"Can you," said Marston, with the same slow and stern articulation, and after a considerable pause—"can you *prevent* the malady you profess to cure?— can you meet and defeat the enemy half-way?—can you scare away the spirit of madness *before* it takes actual possession, and while it is still only hovering about its threatened victim?"

"Sir," he replied, "in certain cases—in very many, indeed—the enemy, as you well call it, *may* thus be met, and effectually worsted at a distance. Timely interposition, in ninety cases out of a hundred, is *everything*; and, I assure you, I hear your question with much pleasure, inasmuch as I assume it to have reference to the case of the patient about whom you desire to consult me; and who is, therefore, I hope, as yet merely *menaced* with the misfortune from which you would save him."

"I, myself, am that patient, sir," said Marston, with an effort; "your surmise is right. I am not mad, but unequivocally menaced with madness; it is not to be mistaken. Sir, there is no misunderstanding the tremendous and tolerable signs that glare upon my mind."

"And pray, sir, have you consulted your friends or your family upon the course best to be pursued?" inquired Dr. Parkes, with grave interest.

"No, sir," he answered sharply, and almost fiercely; "I have no fancy to make myself the subject of a writ *de lunatico inquirendo;* I don't want to lose my liberty and my property at a blow. The course I mean to take has been advised by no one but myself—is *known* to no other. I now disclose it, and the causes of it, to you, a gentleman, and my professional adviser, in the expectation that you will guard with the strictest secrecy my spontaneous revelations; this you promise me?"

"Certainly, Mr. Marston; I have neither the disposition nor the right to withhold such a promise," answered the physician.

"Well, then, I will first tell you the arrangement I propose, with your permission, to make, and then I shall answer all your questions, respecting my own case," resumed Marston, gloomily. "I wish to place myself under your care, to live under your roof, reserving my full liberty of action. I must be free to come and to go as I will; and on the other hand, I undertake that you shall find me an amenable and docile patient enough. In addition, I stipulate that there shall be no attempt whatever made to communicate with those who are connected with me: these terms agreed upon, I place myself in your hands. You will find in me, as I said before, a deferential patient, and I trust not a troublesome one. I hope you will excuse my adding, that I shall myself pay the charge of my sojourn here from week to week, in advance."

The proposed arrangement was a strange one; and although Dr. Parkes dimly foresaw some of the embarrassments which might possibly arise from his accepting it, there was yet so much that was reasonable as well as advantageous in the proposal, that he could not bring himself to decline it.

The preliminary arrangement concluded, Dr. Parkes proceeded to his more strictly professional investigation. It is, of course, needless to recapitulate the details of Marston's tormenting fancies, with which the reader has indeed been already sufficiently acquainted. Doctor Parkes, having attentively listened to the narrative, and satisfied himself as to the physical health of his patient, was still sorely puzzled as to the probable issue of the awful struggle already but too obviously commenced between the mind and its destroyer in the strange case before him. One satisfactory symptom unquestionably was, the as yet transitory nature of the delusion, and the evident and energetic tenacity with which reason contended for her vital ascendancy. It was a case, however, which for many reasons sorely perplexed him, but of which, notwithstanding, he was disposed, whether rightly or wrongly the reader will speedily see, to take by no means a decidedly gloomy view.

Having disburthened his mind of this horrible secret, Marston felt for a time a sense of relief amounting almost to elation. With far less of apprehension and dismay than he had done so for months before, he that night repaired to his bedroom. There was nothing in his case, Doctor Parkes believed, to warrant his keeping any watch upon Marston's actions, and accordingly he bid him good-night, in the full confidence of meeting him, if not better, at least not worse, on the ensuing morning.

He miscalculated, however. Marston had probably himself been conscious of some coming crisis in his hideous malady, when he took the decisive step of placing himself under the care of Doctor Parkes. Certain it is, that upon that very night the disease broke forth in a new and appalling development. Doctor Parkes, whose bedroom was next to that occupied by Marston, was awakened in the dead of night by a howling, more like that of a beast than a human voice, and which gradually swelled into an absolute yell; then came some horrid laughter and entreaties, thick and frantic; then again the same unearthly howl. The practised ear of Doctor Parkes recognised but too surely the terrific import of those sounds. Springing from his bed, and seizing the candle

which always burned in his chamber, in anticipation of such sudden
and fearful emergencies, he hurried with a palpitating heart, and spite
of his long habituation to such scenes as he expected, with a certain
sense of horror, to the chamber of his aristocratic patient.

Late as it was, Marston had not yet gone to bed; his candle was still
burning, and he himself, half dressed, stood in the centre of the floor,
shaking and livid, his eyes burning with the preterhuman fires of insanity. As Doctor Parkes entered the chamber, another shout, or rather
yell, thundered from the lips of this demoniac effigy; and the mad-
doctor stood freezing with horror in the doorway, and yet exerting what
remained to him of presence of mind, in the vain endeavour, in the flaring light of the candle, to catch and fix with his own practised eye the
gaze of the maniac. Second after second, and minute after minute, he
stood confronting this frightful slave of Satan, in the momentary expectation that he would close with and destroy him. On a sudden,
however, this brief agony of suspense was terminated; a change like an
awakening consciousness of realities, or rather like the withdrawal of
some hideous and visible influence from within, passed over the tense
and darkened features of the wretched being; a look of horrified
perplexity, doubt, and inquiry, supervened, and he at last said, in a
subdued and sullen tone, to Doctor Parkes—

"Who are you, sir? What do you want here? Who are you, sir, I
say?"

"Who am I? Why, your physician, sir; Doctor Parkes, sir; the owner
of this house, sir," replied he, with all the sternness he could command,
and yet white as a spectre with agitation. "For shame, sir, for shame, to
give way thus. What do you mean by creating this causeless alarm, and
disturbing the whole household at so unseasonable an hour? For
shame, sir; go to your bed; undress yourself this moment; for shame."

Doctor Parkes, as he spoke, was reassured by the arrival of one of his
servants, alarmed by the unmistakeable sounds of violent frenzy; he
signed, however, to the man not to enter, feeling confident, as he did,
that the paroxysm had spent itself.

"Ay, ay," muttered Marston, looking almost sheepishly; "Doctor
Parkes, to be sure. What was I thinking of? how cursedly absurd! And
this," he continued, glancing at his sword, which he threw impatiently
upon a sofa as he spoke. "Folly—nonsense! A false alarm, as you say,
doctor. I beg your pardon."

As Marston spoke, he proceeded with much agitation slowly to undress himself. He had, however, but commenced the process, when,
turning abruptly to Doctor Parkes, he said, with a countenance of
horror, and in a whisper—

"By ——, doctor, it has been upon me worse than ever. I would have
sworn I had the villain with me for hours—*hours*, sir—torturing me with
his damned sneering threats; till, by ——, I could stand it no longer,
and took my sword. Oh, doctor, can't you save me? can nothing be
done for me?"

Pale, covered with the dews of horror, he uttered these last words in accents of such imploring despair, as might have borne across the dreadful gulf the prayer of Dives for that one drop of water which never was to cool his burning tongue.

When Rhoda learned that her father, on leaving Gray Forest, had fixed no definite period for his return, she began to feel her situation at home so painful and equivocal, that, having taken honest Willett to counsel, she came at last to the resolution of accepting the often conveyed invitation of Mrs. Mervyn and sojourning, at all events until her father's return, at Newton Park.

"My dear young friend," said the kind lady, as soon as she heard Rhoda's little speech to its close, "I can scarcely describe the gratification with which I see you here; the happiness with which I welcome you to Newton Park; nor, indeed, the anxiety with which I constantly contemplated your trying and painful position at Gray Forest. Indeed I ought to be angry with you for having refused me this happiness so long; but you have made amends at last; though, indeed, it was impossible to have deferred it longer. You must not fancy, however, that I will consent to lose you so soon as you seem to have intended. No, no; I have found it too hard to catch you, to let you take wing so easily; besides, I have others to consult as well as myself, and persons, too, who are just as anxious as I am to make a prisoner of you here."

The good Mrs. Mervyn accompanied these words with looks so sly, and emphasis so significant, that Rhoda was fain to look down, to hide her blushes; and compassionating the confusion she herself had caused, the kind old lady led her to the chamber which was henceforward, so long as she consented to remain, to be her own apartment.

How that day was passed, and how fleetly its hours sped away, it is needless to tell. Old Mervyn had his gentle as well as his grim aspect; and no welcome was ever more cordial and tender than that with which he greeted the unprotected child of his morose and repulsive neighbour. It would be impossible to convey any idea of the countless assiduities and the secret delight with which young Mervyn attended their rambles.

The party were assembled at supper. What a contrast did this cheerful, happy—unutterably happy—gathering, present, in the mind of Rhoda, to the dull, drear, fearful evenings which she had long been wont to pass at Gray Forest.

As they sate together in cheerful and happy intercourse, a chaise drove up to the hall-door, and the knocking had hardly ceased to reverberate, when a well-known voice was heard in the hall.

Young Mervyn started to his feet, and merrily ejaculating, "Charles Marston! this *is* delightful!" disappeared, and in an instant returned with Charles himself.

We pass over all the embraces of brother and sister; the tears and smiles of re-united affection. We omit the cordial shaking of hands; the kind looks; the questions and answers; all these, and all the little attentions of that good old-fashioned hospitality, which was never weary of demonstrating the cordiality of its welcome, we abandon to the imagination of the good-natured reader.

Charles Marston, with the advice of his friend, Mr. Mervyn, resolved to lose no time in proceeding to Chester, whither it was ascertained his father had gone, with the declared intention of meeting and accompanying him home. He arrived in that town in the evening; and having previously learned that Doctor Danvers had been for some time in Chester, he at once sought him at his usual lodgings, and found the worthy old gentleman at his solitary "dish" of tea.

"My dear Charles," said he, greeting his young friend with earnest warmth, "I am rejoiced beyond measure to see you. Your father *is* in town, as you supposed; and I have just had a note from him, which has, I confess, not a little agitated me, referring, as it does, to a subject of painful and horrible interest; one with which, I suppose, you are familiar, but upon which I myself have never yet spoken fully to any person, excepting your father only."

"And pray, my dear sir, what *is* this topic?" inquired Charles, with marked interest.

"Read this note," answered the clergyman, placing one at the same time in his young visiter's hand.

Charles read as follows:—

"My dear Sir,
I have a singular communication to make to you, but in the strictest privacy, with reference to a subject which, merely to name, is to awaken feelings of doubt and horror; I mean the confession of Merton, with respect to the murder of Wynston Berkley. I will call upon you this evening after dark; for I have certain reasons for not caring to meet old acquaintances about town; and if you can afford me half an hour, I promise to complete my intended disclosure within that time. Let us be strictly private; this is my only proviso.

Yours with much respect,
"RICHARD MARSTON."

"Your father has been sorely troubled in mind," said Doctor Danvers, as soon as the young man had read this communication; "he has told me as much; it may be that the discovery he has now made may possibly have relieved him from certain galling anxieties. The fear that unjust suspicion should light upon himself, or those connected with him, has, I dare say, tormented him sorely. God grant, that as the providential unfolding of all the details of this mysterious crime comes about, he may be brought to recognise, in the just and terrible process, the hand of heaven. God grant, that at last his heart may be softened, and his spirit illuminated by the blessed influence he has so long and so sternly rejected."

As the old man thus spake—as if in symbolic answering to his prayer

—a sudden glory from the setting sun streamed through the funereal pile of clouds which filled the western horizon, and flooded the chamber where they were.

After a silence, Charles Marston said, with some little embarrassment—"It may be a strange confession to make, though, indeed, hardly so to you—for you know but too well the gloomy reserve with which my father has uniformly treated me—that the exact nature of Merton's confession never reached my ears; and once or twice, when I approached the subject, in conversation with you, it seemed to me that the subject was one which, for some reason, it was painful to you to enter upon."

"And so it was, in truth, my young friend—so it was; for that confession left behind it many fearful doubts, proving, indeed, nothing but the one fact, that, *morally*, the wretched man was guilty of the murder."

Charles, urged by a feeling of the keenest interest, requested Dr. Danvers to detail to him the particulars of the dying man's narration.

"Willingly," answered Dr. Danvers, with a look of gloom, and heaving a profound sigh—"willingly, for you have now come to an age when you may safely be entrusted with secrets affecting your own family, and which, although, thank God, as I believe they in no respect involve the honour of any one of its members, yet might deeply involve its peace and its security against the assaults of vague and horrible slander. Here, then, is the narrative: Merton, when he was conscious of the approach of death, qualified, by a circumstantial and detailed statement, the absolute confession of guilt which he had at first sullenly made. In this he declared that the guilt of design and intention only was his— that in the act itself he had been *anticipated*. He stated, that from the moment when Sir Wynston's servant had casually mentioned the circumstance of his master's usually sleeping with his watch and pocketbook under his pillow, the idea of robbing him had taken possession of his mind. With the idea of robbing him (under the peculiar circumstances, his servant sleeping in the apartment close by, and the slightest alarm being, in all probability, sufficient to call him to the spot) the idea of anticipating resistance by murder had associated itself. He had contended against these haunting and growing solicitations of Satan, with an earnest agony. He had intended to leave his place, and fly from the mysterious temptation which he felt he wanted power to combat, but accident or fate prevented him. In a state of ghastly excitement he had, on the memorable night of Sir Wynston's murder, proceeded, as had afterwards appeared in evidence, by the back stair to the baronet's chamber; he had softly stolen into it, and gone to the bedside, with the weapon in his hand. He drew his breath for the decisive stroke, which was to bereave the (supposedly) sleeping man of life, and when stretching his left hand under the clothes, it rested upon a dull, cold corpse, and, at the same moment, his right hand was immersed in a pool of blood. He dropped the knife, recoiled a pace or so. With a painful effort, however, he again grasped with his hand to recover the weapon he had suffered to escape, and secured, as it afterwards turned out, not the knife with which he had meditated the commission of his crime, but the dagger which was afterwards found where he had concealed it. He was now fully alive to the horror of his situation; he was compromised as fully as if he had in very deed driven home the weapon. To be found under such circumstances, would convict him as surely as if fifty eyes had seen him strike the blow. He had nothing now for it but flight; and in order to guard himself against the contingency of being surprised from the door opening upon the corridor, he bolted it; then groped under the murdered man's pillow for the booty which had so fatally fascinated his imagination. Here he was disappointed. What further happened you already know."

Charles listened with breathless attention to this recital, and, after a painful interval, said:—

"Then the actual murderer is, after all, unascertained. This is, indeed, horrible; it was very natural that my father should have felt the danger to which such a disclosure would have exposed the reputation of our family, yet I should have preferred encountering it, were it ten times as great, to the equivocal prudence of suppressing the truth with respect to a murder committed under my own roof."

"He has, however, it would seem, arrived at some new conclusions," said Dr. Danvers, "and is now prepared to throw some unanticipated light upon the whole transaction."

Even as they were talking, a knocking was heard at the hall-door, and after a brief and hurried consultation, it was agreed, that, considering the strict condition of privacy attached to this visit by Mr. Marston himself, as well as his reserved and wayward temper, it might be better for Charles to avoid presenting himself to his father on this occasion. A few seconds afterwards the door opened, and Mr. Marston entered the apartment. It was now dark, and the servant, unbidden, placed candles upon the table. Without answering one word to Dr. Danvers' greeting, Marston sat down, as it seemed, in agitated abstraction. Removing his hat suddenly (for he had not even made this slight homage to the laws of courtesy), he looked round with a care-worn, fiery eye, and a pale countenance, and said—

"We are quite alone, Dr. Danvers—no one anywhere near?"

Dr. Danvers assured him that all was secure.

After a long and agitated pause, Marston said—

"You remember Merton's confession. He admitted his *intention* to kill Berkley, but denied that he was the actual murderer. He spoke truth— no one knew it better than I; for *I* am the murderer."

Dr. Danvers was so shocked and overwhelmed that he was utterly unable to speak.

"Ay, sir, in point of law and of morals, literally and honestly, the MURDERER of Wynston Berkley. I am resolved you shall know it all. Make what use of it you will—I care for nothing now, but to get rid of the d—d, unsustainable secret, and that is done. I did not intend to kill

the scoundrel when I went to his room; but with the just feelings of ex-
asperation with which I regarded him, it would have been wiser had I
avoided the interview; and I meant to have done so. But his candle was
burning; I saw the light through the door, and went in. It was his evil
fortune to indulge in his old strain of sardonic impertinence. He
provoked me; I struck him—he struck me again—and with his own
dagger I stabbed him three times. I did not know what I had done; I
could not believe it. I felt neither remorse nor sorrow—why should I?—
but the thing was horrible, astounding. There he sat in the corner of his
cushioned chair, with the old fiendish smile on still. Sir, I never thought
that any human shape could look so dreadful. I don't know how long I
stayed there, freezing with horror and detestation, and yet unable to
take my eyes from the face. Did you see it in the coffin? Sir, there was a
sneer of triumph on it that was diabolic and prophetic."

Marston was fearfully agitated as he spoke, and repeatedly wiped
from his face the cold sweat that gathered there.

"I could not leave the room by the back stairs," he resumed, "for the
valet slept in the intervening chamber. I felt such an appalled antipathy
to the body, that I could scarcely muster courage to pass it. But, sir, I
am not easily cowed—I mastered this repugnance in a few minutes—
or, rather, I acted in spite of it, I knew not how; but instinctively it
seemed to me that it was better to lay the body in the bed, than leave it
where it was, shewing, as its position might, that the thing occurred in
an altercation. So, sir, I raised it, and bore it softly across the room, and
laid it in the bed; and, while I was carrying it, it swayed forward, the
arms glided round my neck, and the head rested against my cheek—
that *was* a parody upon a brotherly embrace!

"I do not know at what moment it was, but some time when I was
carrying Wynston, or laying him in the bed," continued Marston, who
spoke rather like one pursuing a horrible reverie, than as a man relating
facts to a listener, "I heard a light tread, and soft breathing in the lobby. A thunder-clap would have stunned me less that minute. I moved
softly, holding my breath, to the door. I believe, in moments of strong
excitement, men hear more acutely than at other times; but I thought I
heard the rustling of a gown, going *from* the door again. I waited—it
ceased; I waited until all was quiet. I then extinguished the candle, and
groped my way to the door; there was a faint light in the corridor, and I
thought I saw a head projected from the chamber-door, next to the
Frenchwoman's—mademoiselle's. As I came on, it was softly
withdrawn, and the door not quite noiselessly closed. I could not be absolutely certain, but I learned all afterward. And now, sir, you have the
story of Sir Wynston's murder."

Dr. Danvers groaned in spirit, being wrung alike with fear and
sorrow. With hands clasped, and head bowed down, in an exceeding
bitter agony of soul, he murmured only the words of the Litany—
"Lord, have mercy upon us; Christ, have mercy upon us; Lord, have
mercy upon us."

Marston had recovered his usual lowering aspect and gloomy self-possession in a few moments, and was now standing erect and defiant before the humbled and afflicted minister of God. The contrast was terrible—almost sublime.

Doctor Danvers resolved to keep this dreadful secret, at least for a time, to himself. He could not make up his mind to inflict upon those whom he loved so well as Charles and Rhoda the shame and agony of such a disclosure; yet he was sorely troubled, for his was a conflict of duty and mercy, of love and justice.

He told Charles Marston, when urged with earnest inquiry, that what he had heard that evening was intended solely for his own ear, and gently but peremptorily declined telling, at least until some future time, the substance of his father's communication.

Charles now felt it necessary to see his father, for the purpose of letting him know the substance of the letter respecting "mademoiselle" and the late Sir Wynston which had reached him. Accordingly, he proceeded, accompanied by Doctor Danvers, on the next morning, to the hotel where Marston had intimated his intention of passing the night.

On their inquiring for him in the hall, the porter appeared much perplexed and disturbed, and as they pressed him with questions, his answers became conflicting and mysterious. Mr. Marston was there—he had slept there last night; he could not say whether or not he was then in the house; but he knew that no one could be admitted to see him. He would, if the gentlemen wished it, send their cards to (*not* Mr. Marston, but) the *proprietor*. And, finally, he concluded by begging that they would themselves see "the proprietor," and despatched a waiter to apprise him of the circumstances of the visit. There was something odd and even sinister in all this, which, along with the whispering and the curious glances of the waiters, who happened to hear the errand on which they came, inspired the two companions with vague misgivings, which they did not care mutually to disclose.

In a few moments they were shown into a small sitting-room up stairs, where the proprietor, a fussy little gentleman, and apparently very uneasy and frightened, received them.

"We have called here to see Mr. Marston," said Doctor Danvers, "and the porter has referred us to you."

"Yes, sir, exactly—precisely so," answered the little man, fidgeting excessively, and as it seemed, growing paler every instant; "but—but, in fact, sir, there is, there has been—in short, have you not heard of the —the *accident?*"

He wound up with a prodigious effort, and wiped his forehead when he had done.

"Pray, sir, be explicit: we are near friends of Mr. Marston; in fact, sir, this is his son," said Doctor Danvers, pointing to Charles Marston; "and we are both uneasy at the reserve with which our inquiries have been met. Do, I entreat of you, say what has happened?"

"Why—why," hesitated the man, "I really—I would not for five hundred pounds it had happened in my house. The—the unhappy gentleman has, in short ——" He glanced at Charles, as if afraid of the effect of the disclosure he was on the point of making, and then hurriedly said—"He is *dead*, sir; he was found dead in his room, this morning, at eight o'clock. I assure you I have not been myself ever since."

Charles Marston was so stunned by this sudden blow, that he was upon the point of fainting. Rallying, however, with a strong effort, he demanded to be conducted to the chamber where the body lay. The man assented, but hesitated on reaching the door, and whispered something in the ear of Doctor Danvers, who, as he heard it, raised his hands and eyes with a mute expression of horror, and turning to Charles, said—

"My dear young friend, remain where you are for a few moments. I will return to you immediately, and tell you whatever I have ascertained. You are in no condition for such a scene at present."

Charles, indeed, felt that the fact was so, and, sick and giddy, suffered Doctor Danvers, with gentle compulson, to force him into a seat.

In silence the venerable clergyman followed his conductor. With a palpitating heart he advanced to the bedside, and twice essayed to draw the curtain, and twice lost courage; but gathering resolution at last, he pulled the drapery aside, and beheld all he was to see again of Richard Marston.

The bedclothes were drawn so as nearly to cover the mouth.

"*There* is the wound, sir," whispered the man, as with coarse officiousness he drew back the bedclothes from the throat of the corpse, and exhibited a gash, as it seemed, nearly severing the head from the body. With sickening horror Doctor Danvers turned away from the awful spectacle. He covered his face in his hands, and it seemed to him as if a soft, solemn voice whispered in his ear the mystic words, "Whoso sheddeth man's blood, by man shall his blood be shed."

The hand which, but a few years before, had, unsuspected, consigned a fellow-mortal to the grave, had itself avenged the murder—Marston had perished by his own hand.

Naturally ambitious and intriguing, the perilous tendencies of such a spirit in Mademoiselle de Barras had never been schooled by the mighty and benignant principles of religion. Of her accidental acquaintance at Rouen with Sir Wynston Berkley, and her subsequent introduction, in an evil hour, into the family at Gray Forest, it is unnecessary to speak. The unhappy terms on which she found Marston living with his wife, suggested, in their mutual alienation, the idea of founding a double influence in the household; and to conceive the idea, and to act upon it, were, in her active mind, the same. Young, beautiful, fascinating, she well knew the power of her attractions, and determined, though probably without one thought of transgressing the limits of literal propriety, to bring them to bear upon the discontented, retired *roué*, for whom she cared absolutely nothing, except as the instrument, and in part the victim of her schemes. Thus yielding to the double instinct that swayed her, she gratified, at the same time, her love of intrigue and her love of power. At length, however, came the hour which demanded a sacrifice to the evil influence she had hitherto worshipped on such easy terms. She found that her power must now be secured by crime, and she fell. Then came the arrival of Sir Wynston—his murder —her elopement with Marston, and her guilty and joyless triumph. At last, however, came the blow, long suspended and terrific, which shattered all her hopes and schemes, and drove her once again upon the world. The catastrophe we have just described. After it she made her way to Paris. Arrived in the capital of France, she speedily dissipated whatever remained of the money and valuables which she had taken with her from Gray Forest; and Madame Marston, as she now styled herself, was glad to place herself once more as a governess in an aristocratic family. So far her good fortune had prevailed in averting the punishment but too well earned by her past life. But a day of reckoning was to come. A few years later France was involved in the uproar and conflagration of revolution. Noble families were scattered, beggared, decimated; and their dependants, often dragged along with them into the flaming abyss, in many instances suffered the last dire extremities of human ill. It was at this awful period that a retribution so frightful and extraordinary overtook Madame Marston, that we may hereafter venture to make it the subject of a separate narrative. Until then the reader will rest satisfied with what he already knows of her history; and meanwhile bid a long, and as it may possibly turn out, an eternal farewell to that beautiful embodiment of an evil and disastrous influence.

The concluding chapter in a novel is always brief, though seldom so short as the world would have it. In a tale like this, the "winding up" must be proportionately contracted. We have scarcely a claim to so many lines as the formal novelist may occupy pages, in the distribution of poetic justice, and the final grouping of his characters into that effective tableau upon which, at last, the curtain gracefully descends. We, too, may be all the briefer, inasmuch as the reader has doubtless anticipated the little we have to say. It amounts, then, to this:—Within two years after the fearful event which we have just recorded, an alliance had drawn together, in nearer and dearer union, the inmates of Gray Forest and Newton Park. Rhoda had given her hand to young Mervyn. Of ulterior consequences we say nothing—the nursery is above our province. And now, at length, after this Christmas journey through somewhat stern and gloomy scenery, in this long-deferred flood of golden sunshine we bid thee, gentle reader, a kind farewell.

THE MYSTERIOUS LODGER

PART I

About the year 1822 I resided in a comfortable and roomy old house, the exact locality of which I need not particularise, further than to say that it was not very far from Old Brompton, in the immediate neighbourhood, or rather continuity (as even my Connemara readers perfectly well know), of the renowned city of London.

Though this house was roomy and comfortable, as I have said, it was not, by any means, a handsome one. It was composed of dark red brick, with small windows, and thick white sashes; a porch, too—none of your flimsy trellis-work, but a solid projection of the same vermillion masonry—surmounted by a leaded balcony, with heavy, half-rotten balustrades, darkened the hall-door with a perennial gloom. The mansion itself stood in a walled enclosure, which had, perhaps, from the date of the erection itself, been devoted to shrubs and flowers. Some of the former had grown there almost to the dignity of trees; and two dark little yews stood at each side of the porch, like swart and inauspicious dwarfs, guarding the entrance of an enchanted castle. Not that my domicile in any respect deserved the comparison: it had no reputation as a haunted house; if it ever had any ghosts, nobody remembered them. Its history was not known to me: it may have witnessed plots, cabals, and forgeries, bloody suicides and cruel murders. It was certainly old enough to have become acquainted with iniquity; a small stone slab, under the balustrade, and over the arch of the porch I mentioned, had the date 1672, and a half-effaced coat of arms, which I might have deciphered any day, had I taken the trouble to get a ladder, but always put it off. All I can say for the house is, that it was well stricken in years, with a certain air of sombre comfort about it; contained a vast number of rooms and closets; and, what was of far greater importance, was got by me a dead bargain.

Its individuality attracted me. I grew fond of it for itself, and for its associations, until other associations of a hateful kind first disturbed, and then destroyed, their charm. I forgave its dull red brick, and pinched white windows, for the sake of the beloved and cheerful faces within: its ugliness was softened by its age; and its sombre evergreens, and moss-grown stone flower-pots, were relieved by the brilliant hues of a thousand gay and graceful flowers that peeped among them, or nodded over the grass.

Within that old house lay my life's treasure! I had a darling little girl of nine, and another little darling—a boy—just four years of age; and dearer, unspeakably, than either—a wife—the prettiest, gayest, best little wife in all London. When I tell you that our income was scarcely £380 a-year, you will perceive that our establishment cannot have been a magnificent one; yet, I do assure you, we were more comfortable than a great many lords, and happier, I dare say, than the whole peerage put together.

This happiness was not, however, what it ought to have been. The reader will understand at once, and save me a world of moralising circumlocution, when he learns, bluntly and nakedly, that, among all my comforts and blessings, I was an infidel.

I had not been without religious training; on the contrary, more than average pains had been bestowed upon my religious instruction from my earliest childhood. My father, a good, plain, country clergyman, had worked hard to make me as good as himself; and had succeeded, at least, in training me in godly habits. He died, however, when I was but twelve years of age; and fate had long before deprived me of the gentle care of a mother. A boarding-school, followed by a college life, where nobody having any very direct interest in realising in my behalf the ancient blessing, that in fulness of time I should "die a good old man," I was left very much to my own devices, which, in truth, were none of the best.

Among these were the study of Voltaire, Tom Paine, Hume, Shelley, and the whole school of infidels, poetical as well as prose. This pursuit, and the all but blasphemous vehemence with which I gave myself up to it, was, perhaps, partly reactionary. A somewhat injudicious austerity and precision had indissolubly associated in my childish days the ideas of restraint and gloom with religion. I bore it a grudge; and so, when I became thus early my own master, I set about paying off, after my own fashion, the old score I owed it. I was besides, like every other young infidel whom it has been my fate to meet, a conceited coxcomb. A smattering of literature, without any real knowledge, and a great assortment of all the cut-and-dry flippancies of the school I had embraced, constituted my intellectual stock in trade. I was, like most of my school of philosophy, very proud of being an unbeliever; and fancied myself, in the complacency of my wretched ignorance, at an immeasurable elevation above the church-going, Bible-reading herd, whom I treated with a good-humoured superciliousness which I thought vastly indulgent.

My wife was an excellent little creature and truly pious. She had married me in the full confidence that my levity was merely put on, and would at once give way before the influence she hoped to exert upon my mind. Poor little thing! she deceived herself. I allowed her, indeed, to do entirely as she pleased; but for myself, I carried my infidelity to the length of an absolute superstition. I made an ostentation of it. I would rather have been in a "hell" than in a church on Sunday; and though I did not prevent my wife's instilling her own principles into the minds of our children, I, in turn, took especial care to deliver mine upon all occasions in their hearing, by which means I trusted to sow the seeds of that unprejudiced scepticism in which I prided myself, at least as early as my good little partner dropped those of her own gentle "superstition" into their infant minds. Had I had my own absurd and impious will in this matter, my children should have had absolutely no religious education whatsoever, and been left wholly unshackled to choose for themselves among all existing systems, infidelity included, precisely as chance, fancy, or interest might hereafter determine.

It is not to be supposed that such a state of things did not afford her great uneasiness. Nevertheless, we were so very fond of one another, and in our humble way enjoyed so many blessings, that we were as entirely happy as any pair can be without the holy influence of religious sympathy.

But the even flow of prosperity which had for so long gladdened my little household was not destined to last for ever. It was ordained that I should experience the bitter truth of more than one of the wise man's proverbs, and first, especially, of that which declares that "he that hateth suretyship is sure." I found myself involved (as how many have been before) by a "d—d good-natured friend," for more than two hundred pounds. This agreeable intelligence was conveyed to me in an attorney's letter, which, to obviate unpleasant measures, considerately advised my paying the entire amount within just one week of the date of his pleasant epistle. Had I been called upon within that time to produce the Pitt diamond, or to make title to the Buckingham estates, the demand would have been just as easily complied with.

I have no wish to bore my reader further with this little worry—a very serious one to me, however—and it will be enough to mention, that the kindness of a friend extricated me from the clutches of the law by a timely advance, which, however, I was bound to replace within two years. To enable me to fulfill this engagement, my wife and I, after repeated consultations, resolved upon the course which resulted in the odd and unpleasant consequences which form the subject of this narrative.

We resolved to advertise for a lodger, with or without board, &c.; and by resolutely submitting, for a single year, to the economy we had

prescribed for ourselves, as well as to the annoyance of a stranger's intrusion, we calculated that at the end of that term we should have li-
quidated our debt.

Accordingly, without losing time, we composed an advertisement in
the most tempting phraseology we could devise, consistently with that
economic laconism which the cost per line in the columns of the *Times*
newspaper imposes upon the rhetoric of the advertising public.

Somehow we were unlucky; for although we repeated our public
notification three times in the course of a fortnight, we had but two
applications. The one was from a clergyman in ill health—a man of
great ability and zealous piety, whom we both knew by reputation, and
who has since been called to his rest. My good little wife was very anxious that we should close with his offer, which was very considerably
under what we had fixed upon; and I have no doubt that she was influenced by the hope that his talents and zeal might exert a happy influence upon my stubborn and unbelieving heart. For my part, his
religious character displeased me. I did not wish my children's heads to
be filled with mythic dogmas—for so I judged the doctrines of our holy
faith—and instinctively wished him away. I therefore declined his offer;
and I have often since thought not quite so graciously as I ought to have
done. The other offer—if so it can be called—was so very inadequate
that we could not entertain it.

I was now beginning to grow seriously uneasy—our little project, so
far from bringing in the gains on which we had calculated, had put me
considerably out of pocket; for, independently of the cost of the advertisement I have mentioned, there were sundry little expenses involved in
preparing for the meet reception of our expected inmate, which, under
ordinary circumstances, we should not have dreamed of. Matters were
in this posture, when an occurrence took place which immediately
revived my flagging hopes.

As we had no superfluity of servants, our children were early obliged
to acquire habits of independence; and my little girl, then just nine
years of age, was frequently consigned with no other care than that of
her own good sense, to the companionship of a little band of playmates,
pretty similarly circumstanced, with whom it was her wont to play.
Having one fine summer afternoon gone out as usual with these little
companions, she did not return quite so soon as we had expected her;
when she did so, she was out of breath, and excited.

"Oh, papa," she said, "I have seen such a nice old, kind gentleman,
and he told me to tell you that he has a particular friend who wants a
lodging in a quiet place, and that he thinks your house would suit him
exactly, and ever so much more; and, look here, he gave me this."

She opened her hand, and shewed me a sovereign.

"Well, this does look promisingly," I said, my wife and I having first
exchanged a smiling glance.

"And what kind of gentleman was he, dear?" inquired she. "Was he
well dressed—whom was he like?"

"He was not like any one that I know," she answered; "but he had very nice new clothes on, and he was one of the fattest men I ever saw; and I am sure he is sick, for he looks very pale, and he had a crutch beside him."

"Dear me, how strange!" exclaimed my wife; though, in truth there was nothing very wonderful in the matter. "Go on, child," I said; "let us hear it all out."

"Well, papa, he had such an immense yellow waistcoat!—I never did see such a waistcoat," she resumed; "and he was sitting or leaning, I can't say which, against the bank of the green lane; I suppose to rest himself, for he seems very weak, poor gentleman!"

"And how did you happen to speak to him?" asked my wife.

"When we were passing by, none of us saw him at all but I suppose he heard them talking to me, and saying my name; for he said, 'Fanny—little Fanny—so, that's your name—come here child, I have a question to ask you.'"

"And so you went to him?" I said.

"Yes," she continued, "he beckoned to me, and I did go over to him, but not very near, for I was greatly afraid of him at first."

"Afraid! dear, and why afraid?" asked I.

"I was afraid, because he looked very old, very frightful, and as if he would hurt me."

"What was there so old and frightful about him?" I asked.

She paused and reflected a little, and then said—

"His face was very large and pale, and it was looking upwards: it seemed very angry, I thought, but maybe it was angry from pain; and sometimes one side of it used to twitch and tremble for a minute, and then to grow quite still again; and all the time he was speaking to me, he never looked at me once, but always kept his face and eyes turned upwards; but his voice was very soft, and he called me little Fanny, and gave me this pound to buy toys with; so I was not so frightened in a little time, and then he sent a long message to you, papa, and told me if I forgot it he would beat me; but I knew he was only joking, so that did not frighten me either."

"And what was the message, my girl?" I asked, patting her pretty head with my hand.

"Now, let me remember it all," she said, reflectively; "for he told it to me twice. He asked me if there was a good bedroom at the top of the house, standing by itself—and you know there is, so I told him so; it was exactly the kind of room that he described. And then he said that his friend would pay two hundred pounds a-year for that bedroom, his board and attendance; and he told me to ask you, and have your answer when he should next meet me."

"Two hundred pounds!" ejaculated my poor little wife; "why that is nearly twice as much as we expected."

"But did he say that his friend was sick, or very old; or that he had any servant to be supported also?" I asked.

"Oh! no; he told me that he was quite able to take care of himself, and that he had, I think he called it, an asthma, but nothing else the matter; and that he would give no trouble at all, and that any friend who came to see him, he would see, not in the house, but only in the garden."

"In the garden!" I echoed, laughing in spite of myself.

"Yes, indeed he said so; and he told me to say that he would pay one hundred pounds when he came here, and the next hundred in six months, and so on," continued she.

"Oh, ho! half-yearly in advance—better and better," said I.

"And he bid me say, too, if you should ask about his character, that he is just as good as the master of the house himself," she added; "and when he said that, he laughed a little."

"Why, if he gives us a hundred pounds in advance," I answered, turning to my wife, "we are safe enough; for he will not find half that value in plate and jewels in the entire household, if he is disposed to rob us. So I see no reason against closing with the offer, should it be seriously meant—do you, dear?"

"Quite the contrary, love," said she. "I think it most desirable—indeed, most *providential*."

"Providential! my dear little bigot!" I repeated, with a smile. "Well, be it so. I call it *lucky* merely; but, perhaps, you are happier in your faith, than I in my philosophy. Yes, you are *grateful* for the chance that I only rejoice at. You receive it as a proof of a divine and tender love—I as an accident. Delusions are often more elevating than truth."

And so saying, I kissed away the saddened cloud that for a moment overcast her face.

"Papa, he bid me be sure to have an answer for him when we meet again," resumed the child. "What shall I say to him when he asks me?"

"Say that we agree to his proposal, my dear—or stay," I said, addressing my wife, "may it not be prudent to reduce what the child says to writing, and accept the offer so? This will prevent misunderstanding, as she may possibly have made some mistake."

My wife agreed, and I wrote a brief note, stating that I was willing to receive an inmate upon the terms recounted by little Fanny, and which I distinctly specified, so that no mistake could possibly arise owing to the vagueness of what lawyers term a parole agreement. This important memorandum I placed in the hands of my little girl, who was to deliver it whenever the old gentleman in the yellow waistcoat should chance to meet her. And all these arrangements completed, I awaited the issue of the affair with as much patience as I could affect. Meanwhile, my wife and I talked it over incessantly; and she, good little soul, almost wore herself to death in settling and unsettling the furniture and decorations of our expected inmate's apartments. Days passed away—days of hopes deferred, tedious and anxious. We were beginning to despond again, when one morning our little girl ran into the breakfast-parlour, more excited even than she had been before, and fresh from a new interview with the gentleman in the yellow waistcoat. She had encountered him suddenly, pretty nearly where she had met him before, and the result was, that he had read the little note I have mentioned, and desired the child to inform me that his friend, *Mr. Smith,* would take possession of the apartments I proposed setting, on the terms agreed between us, that very evening.

"This evening!" exclaimed my wife and I simultaneously—*I* full of the idea of making a first instalment on the day following; *she,* of the hundred-and-one preparations which still remained to be completed.

"And so Smith is his name! Well, that does not tell us much," said I; "but where did you meet your friend on this occasion, and how long is it since?"

"Near the corner of the wall-flower lane (so we indicated one which abounded in these fragrant plants); he was leaning with his back against the old tree you cut my name on, and his crutch was under his arm."

"But how long ago?" I urged.

"Only this moment; I ran home as fast as I could," she replied.

"Why, you little blockhead, you should have told me that at first," I cried, snatching up my hat, and darting away in pursuit of the yellow waistcoat, whose acquaintance I not unnaturally coveted, inasmuch as a man who, for the first time, admits a stranger into his house, on the footing of permanent residence, desires generally to know a little more about him than that his name is Smith.

The place indicated was only, as we say, a step away; and as yellow waistcoat was fat, and used a crutch, I calculated on easily overtaking him. I was, however, disappointed; crutch, waistcoat, and all had disappeared. I climbed to the top of the wall, and from this commanding point of view made a sweeping observation—but in vain. I returned home, cursing my ill-luck, the child's dulness, and the fat old fellow's activity.

I need hardly say that Mr. Smith, in all his aspects, moral, social, physical, and monetary, formed a fruitful and interesting topic of speculation during dinner. How many phantom Smiths, short and long, stout and lean, ill-tempered and well-tempered—rich, respectable, or highly dangerous merchants, spies, forgers, nabobs, swindlers danced before us, in the endless mazes of fanciful conjecture, during that anxious *tête-à-tête,* which was probably to be interrupted by the arrival of the gentleman himself.

My wife and I puzzled over the problem as people would over the possible *dénouement* of a French novel; and at last, by mutual consent, we came to the conclusion that Smith could, and would turn out to be no other than the good-natured valetudinarian in the yellow waistcoat himself, a humorist, as was evident enough, and a millionaire, as we unhesitatingly pronounced, who had no immediate relatives, and as I hoped, and my wife "was certain," taken a decided fancy to our little Fanny; I patted the child's head with something akin to pride, as I thought of the magnificent, though remote possibilities, in store for her.

Meanwhile, hour after hour stole away. It was a beautiful autumn evening, and the amber lustre of the declining sun fell softly upon the yews and flowers, and gave an air, half melancholy, half cheerful, to the dark-red brick piers surmounted with their cracked and grass-grown stone urns, and furnished with the light foliage of untended creeping plants. Down the short broad walk leading to this sombre entrance, my eye constantly wandered; but no impatient rattle on the latch, no battering at the gate, indicated the presence of a visiter, and the lazy bell hung dumbly among the honey-suckles.

"When will he come? Yellow waistcoat promised *this evening!* It has been evening a good hour and a half, and yet he is not here. When will he come? It will soon be dark—the evening will have passed—will he come at all?"

Such were the uneasy speculations which began to trouble us. Redder and duskier grew the light of the setting sun, till it saddened into the mists of night. Twilight came, and then darkness, and still no arrival, no summons at the gate. I would not admit even to my wife the excess of my own impatience. I could, however, stand it no longer; so I took my hat and walked to the gate, where I stood by the side of the public road, watching every vehicle and person that approached, in a fever of expectation. Even these, however, began to fail me, and the road grew comparatively quiet and deserted. Having kept guard like a sentinel for more than half an hour, I returned in no very good humour, with the punctuality of an expected inmate—ordered the servant to draw the curtains and secure the hall-door; and so my wife and I sate down to our disconsolate cup of tea. It must have been about ten o'clock, and we were both sitting silently—she working, I looking moodily into a paper—and neither of us any longer entertaining a hope that anything but disappointment would come of the matter, when a sudden tapping, very loud and sustained, upon the window pane, startled us both in an instant from our reveries.

I am not sure whether I mentioned before that the sitting-room we occupied was upon the ground-floor, and the sward came close under the window. I drew the curtains, and opened the shutters with a revived hope; and looking out, saw a very tall thin figure, a good deal wrapped up, standing about a yard before me, and motioning with head and hand impatiently towards the hall-door. Though the night was clear, there was no moon, and therefore I could see no more than the black outline, like that of an *ombre chinoise* figure, signing to me with mop and hoe. In a moment I was at the hall-door, candle in hand; the stranger stept in—his long fingers clutched in the handle of a valise, and a bag which trailed upon the ground behind him.

The light fell full upon him. He wore a long, ill-made, black surtout, buttoned across, and which wrinkled and bagged about his lank figure; his hat was none of the best, and rather broad in the brim; a sort of white woollen muffler enveloped the lower part of his face; a pair of

prominent green goggles, fenced round with leather, completely concealed his eyes; and nothing of the genuine man, but a little bit of
yellow forehead, and a small transverse segment of equally yellow cheek
and nose, encountered the curious gaze of your humble servant.

"You are—I suppose"—I began; for I really was a little doubtful
about my man.

"Mr. Smith—the same; be good enough to show me to my bed-
chamber," interrupted the stranger, brusquely, and in a tone which,
spite of the muffler that enveloped his mouth, was sharp and grating
enough.

"Ha!—Mr. Smith—so I supposed. I hope you may find everything as
comfortable as we desire to make it ——"

I was about making a speech, but was cut short by a slight bow, and
a decisive gesture of the hand in the direction of the staircase. It was
plain that the stranger hated ceremony.

Together, accordingly, we mounted the staircase; he still pulling his
luggage after him, and striding lightly up without articulating a word,
and on reaching his bedroom, he immediately removed his hat, showing a sinister, black scratch-wig underneath, and then began unrolling
the mighty woolen wrapping of his mouth and chin.

"Come," thought I, "we *shall* see something of your face after all."

This something, however, proved to be very little; for under his
muffler was a loose cravat, which stood up in front of his chin and upon
his mouth, he wore a respirator—an instrument which I had never seen
before, and of the use of which I was wholly ignorant.

There was something so excessively odd in the effect of this piece of
unknown mechanism upon his mouth, surmounted by the huge goggles
which encased his eyes, that I believe I should have laughed outright
were it not for a certain unpleasant and peculiar impressiveness in the
tout ensemble of the narrow-chested, long-limbed, and cadaverous figure
in black. As it was, we stood looking at one another in silence for several
seconds.

"Thank you, sir," at last he said, abruptly. "I shan't want anything
whatever to-night; if you can only spare me this candle."

I assented; and, becoming more communicative, he added—

"I am, though an invalid, an independent sort of fellow enough. I am
a bit of a philosopher; I am my own servant, and, I hope, my own
master, too. I rely upon myself in matters of the body and of the mind.
place valets and priests in the same category—fellows who live by our
laziness, intellectual or corporeal. I am a Voltaire, without his luxuries
—a Robinson Crusoe, without his Bible—an anchorite, without
superstition—in short, my indulgence is asceticism, and my faith in
fidelity. Therefore, I shan't disturb your servants much with my bell
nor yourselves with my psalmody. You have got a rational lodger, who
knows how to attend upon himself."

During this singular address he was drawing off his ill-fitting black
gloves, and when he had done so, a bank-note, which had been slipped
underneath for safety, remained in his hand.

"Punctuality, sir, is one of my poor pleasures," he said; "will you allow me to enjoy it now? To-morrow you may acknowledge this; I should not rest were you to decline it."

He extended his bony and discoloured fingers, and placed the note in my hand. Oh, Fortune and Plutus! It was a £100 bank-note.

"Pray, not one word, my dear sir," he continued, unbending still further; "it is simply done pursuant to agreement. We shall know one another better, I hope, in a little time; you will find me always equally punctual. At present pray give yourself no further trouble; I require nothing more. Good night."

I returned the valediction, closed his door, and groped my way down the stairs. It was not until I had nearly reached the hall, that I recollected that I had omitted to ask our new inmate at what hour he would desire to be called in the morning, and so I groped my way back again. As I reached the lobby on which his chamber opened, I perceived a long line of light issuing from the partially-opened door, within which stood Mr. Smith, the same odd figure I had just left; while along the boards was creeping towards him across the lobby, a great, big-headed, buff-coloured cat. I had never seen this ugly animal before; and it had reached the threshold of his door, arching its back, and rubbing itself on the post, before either appeared conscious of my approach, when, with an angry growl, it sprang into the stranger's room.

"What do you want?" he demanded, sharply, standing in the doorway.

I explained my errand.

"I shall call myself," was his sole reply; and he shut the door with a crash that indicated no very pleasurable emotions.

I cared very little about my lodger's temper. The stealthy rustle of his bank-note in my waistcoat pocket was music enough to sweeten the harshest tones of his voice, and to keep alive a cheerful good humour in my heart; and although there was, indisputably, something queer about him, I was, on the whole, very well pleased with my bargain.

The next day our new inmate did not ring his bell until noon. As soon as he had had some breakfast, of which he very sparingly partook, he told the servant that, for the future, he desired that a certain quantity of milk and bread might be left outside his door; and this being done, he would dispense with regular meals. He desired, too, that, on my return, I should be acquainted that he wished to see me in his own room at about nine o'clock; and, meanwhile, he directed that he should be left undisturbed. I found my little wife full of astonishment at Mr. Smith's strange frugality and seclusion, and very curious to learn the object of the interview he had desired with me. At nine o'clock I repaired to his room.

I found him in precisely the costume in which I had left him—the same green goggles—the same muffling of the mouth, except that being now no more than a broadly-folded black silk handkerchief, very loose, and covering even the lower part of the nose, it was obviously intended for the sole purpose of concealment. It was plain I was not to see more of his features than he had chosen to disclose at our first interview. The effect was as if the lower part of his face had some hideous wound or sore. He closed the door with his own hand on my entrance, nodded slightly, and took his seat. I expected him to begin, but he was so long silent that I was at last constrained to address him.

I said, for want of something more to the purpose, that I hoped he had not been tormented by the strange cat the night before.

"What cat?" he asked, abruptly; "what the plague do you mean?"

"Why, I certainly did see a cat go into your room last night," I resumed.

"Hey, and what if you did—though I fancy you dreamed it—I'm not afraid of a cat; are you?" he interrupted, tartly.

At this moment there came a low growling mew from the closet which opened from the room in which we sat.

"Talk of the devil," said I, pointing towards the closet. My companion, without any exact change of expression, looked, I thought, somehow still more sinister and lowering; and I felt for a moment a sort of superstitious misgiving, which made the rest of the sentence die away on my lips.

Perhaps Mr. Smith perceived this, for he said, in a tone calculated to reassure me—

"Well, sir, I think I am bound to tell you that I like my apartments very well; they suit me, and I shall probably be your tenant for much longer than at first you anticipated."

I expressed my gratification.

He then began to talk, something in the strain in which he had spoken of his own peculiarities of habit and thinking upon the previous evening. He disposed of all classes and denominations of superstition with an easy sarcastic slang, which for me was so captivating, that I soon lost all reserve, and found myself listening and suggesting by turns —acquiescent and pleased—sometimes hazarding dissent; but whenever I did, foiled and floored by a few pointed satirical sentences, whose sophistry, for such I must now believe it, confounded me with a rapidity which, were it not for the admiration with which he had insensibly inspired me, would have piqued and irritated my vanity not a little.

While this was going on, from time to time the mewing and growling of a cat within the closet became more and more audible. At last these sounds became so loud, accompanied by scratching at the door, that I paused in the midst of a sentence, and observed—

"There certainly is a cat shut up in the closet?"

"Is there?" he ejaculated, in a surprised tone; "nay, I do not hear it."

He rose abruptly and approached the door; his back was toward me, but I observed he raised the goggles which usually covered his eyes and looked steadfastly at the closet door. The angry sounds all died away into a low, protracted growl, which again subsided into silence. He continued in the same attitude for some moments, and then returned.

"I do not hear it," he said, as he resumed his place, and taking a book from his capacious pocket, asked me if I had seen it before? I never had, and this surprised me, for I had flattered myself that I knew, at least by name, every work published in England during the last fifty years in favour of that philosophy in which we both delighted. The book, moreover, was an odd one, as both its title and table of contents demonstrated.

While we were discoursing upon these subjects, I became more and more distinctly conscious of a new class of sounds proceeding from the same closet. I plainly heard a measured and heavy tread, accompanied by the tapping of some hard and heavy substance like the end of a staff, pass up and down the floor—first, as it seemed, stealthily, and then more and more unconcealedly. I began to feel very uncomfortable and suspicious. As the noise proceeded, and became more and more unequivocal, Mr. Smith abruptly rose, opened the closet door, just enough to admit his own lath-like person, and steal within the threshold for some seconds. What he did I could not see—I felt conscious he had an associate concealed there; and though my eyes remained fixed on the book, I could not avoid listening for some audible words, or signal of caution. I heard, however, nothing of the kind. Mr. Smith turned back —walked a step or two towards me, and said—

"I fancied I heard a sound from that closet, but there is nothing— nothing—nothing whatever; bring the candle, let us both look."

I obeyed with some little trepidation, for I fully anticipated that I should detect the intruder, of whose presence my own ears had given me, for nearly half an hour, the most unequivocal proofs. We entered the closet together; it contained but a few chairs and a small spider table. At the far end of the room there was a sort of grey woollen cloth upon the floor, and a bundle of something underneath it. I looked jealously at it, and half thought I could trace the outline of a human figure; but, if so, it was perfectly motionless.

"Some of my poor wardrobe," he muttered, as he pointed his lean finger in the direction. "It did not sound like a cat, did it—hey—did it?" he muttered; and without attending to my answer, he went about the apartment, clapping his hands, and crying, "Hish—hish—hish!"

The game, however, whatever it was, did not start. As I entered I had seen, however, a large crutch reposing against the wall in the corner opposite to the door. This was the only article in the room, except that I have mentioned, with which I was not familiar. With the exception of our two selves, there was not a living creature to be seen there; no shadow but ours upon the bare walls; no feet but our own upon the comfortless floor.

I had never before felt so strange and unpleasant a sensation. "There is nothing unusual in the room but that crutch," I said.

"What crutch, you dolt? I see no crutch," he ejaculated, in a tone of sudden but suppressed fury.

"Why, that crutch," I answered (for somehow I neither felt nor

resented his rudeness), turning and pointing to the spot where I had
seen it. It was gone!—it was neither there nor anywhere else. It must
have been an illusion—rather an odd one, to be sure. And yet I could at
this moment, with a safe conscience, *swear* that I never saw an object
more distinctly than I had seen it but a second before.

My companion was muttering fast to himself as we withdrew; his
presence rather scared than reassured me; and I felt something almost
amounting to horror, as, holding the candle above his cadaverous and
sable figure, he stood at his threshold, while I descended the stairs, and
said, in a sort of whisper—

"Why, but that I am, like yourself, a philosopher, I should say that
your house is—is—a—ha! ha! ha!—HAUNTED!"

"You look very pale, my love," said my wife, as I entered the
drawing-room, where she had been long awaiting my return. "Nothing
unpleasant has happened?"

"Nothing, nothing, I assure you. Pale!—*do* I look pale?" I answered.
"We are excellent friends, I assure you. So far from having had the
smallest disagreement, there is every prospect of our agreeing but too
well, as you will say; for I find that he holds all my opinions upon
speculative subjects. We have had a great deal of conversation this
evening, I assure you; and I never met, I think, so scholarlike and able a
man."

"I am sorry for it, dearest," she said, sadly. "The greater his talents
if such be his opinions, the more dangerous a companion is he."

We turned, however, to more cheerful topics, and it was late before
we retired to rest. I believe it was pride—perhaps only vanity—but, at
all events, some obstructive and stubborn instinct of my nature, which
could not overcome—that prevented my telling my wife the odd occurrences which had disturbed my visit to our guest. I was unable or
ashamed to confess that so slight a matter had disturbed me; and
above all, that any accident could possibly have clouded, even for a moment, the frosty clearness of my pure and lofty scepticism with the
shadows of superstition.

Almost every day seemed to develop some new eccentricity of our
strange guest. His dietary consisted, without any variety or relief, of the
monotonous bread and milk with which he started; his bed had not
been made for nearly a week; nobody had been admitted into his room
since my visit, just described; and he never ventured down stairs, or out
of doors, until after nightfall, when he used sometimes to glide swiftly
round our little enclosed shrubbery, and at others stand quite
motionless, composed, as if in an attitude of deep attention. After
employing about an hour in this way, he would return, and steal up
stairs to his room, when he would shut himself up, and not be seen
again until the next night—or, it might be, the night after that—when
perhaps, he would repeat his odd excursion.

Strange as his habits were, their eccentricity was all upon the side
least troublesome to us. He required literally no attendance; and as he

his occasional night ramble, even *it* caused not the slightest disturbance
of our routine hour for securing the house and locking up the hall-door
for the night, inasmuch as he had invariably retired before that hour
arrived.

All this stimulated curiosity, and, in no small degree, that of my wife,
who, notwithstanding her vigilance and her anxiety to see our strange
inmate, had been hitherto foiled by a series of cross accidents. We were
sitting together somewhere about ten o'clock at night, when there came
a tap at the room-door. We had just been discussing the unaccountable
Smith; and I felt a sheepish consciousness that he might be himself at
the door, and have possibly even overheard our speculations—some of
them anything but complimentary, respecting himself.

"Come in," cried, I, with an effort; and the tall form of our lodger
glided into the room. My wife was positively frightened, and stood looking at him, as he advanced, with a stare of manifest apprehension, and
even recoiled mechanically, and caught my hand.

Sensitiveness, however, was not his fault: he made a kind of stiff nod
as I mumbled an introduction; and seating himself unasked, began at
once to chat in that odd, off-hand, and sneering style, in which he ex-
celled, and which had, as he wielded it, a sort of fascination of which I
can pretend to convey no idea.

My wife's alarm subsided, and although she still manifestly felt some
sort of misgiving about our visitor, she yet listened to his conversation,
and, spite of herself, soon began to enjoy it. He stayed for nearly half an
hour. But although he glanced at a great variety of topics, he did not
approach the subject of religion. As soon as he was gone, my wife
delivered judgment upon him in form. She admitted he was agreeable;
but then he was such an unnatural, awful-looking object: there was,
besides, something indescribably frightful, she thought, in his manner
—the very tone of his voice was strange and hateful; and, on the whole,
she felt unutterably relieved at his departure.

A few days after, on my return, I found my poor little wife agitated
and dispirited. Mr. Smith had paid her a visit, and brought with him a
book, which he stated he had been reading, and which contained some
references to the Bible which he begged of her to explain in that
profounder and less obvious sense in which they had been cited. This
she had endeavoured to do; and affecting to be much gratified by her
satisfactory exposition, he had requested her to reconcile some dis-
crepancies which he said had often troubled him when reading the
Scriptures. Some of them were quite new to my good little wife; they
startled and even horrified her. He pursued this theme, still pretending
only to seek for information to quiet his own doubts, while in reality he
was sowing in her mind the seeds of the first perturbations that had ever
troubled the sources of her peace. He had been with her, she thought,
no more than a quarter of an hour; but he had contrived to leave her
abundant topics on which to ruminate for days. I found her shocked
and horrified at the doubts which this potent Magus had summoned

from the pit—doubts which she knew not how to combat, and from the torment of which she could not escape.

"He has made me very miserable with his deceitful questions. I never thought of them before; and, merciful Heaven! I cannot answer them! What am I to do? My serenity is gone; I shall never be happy again."

In truth, she was so very miserable, and, as it seemed to me, so disproportionately excited, that, inconsistent in me as the task would have been, I would gladly have explained away her difficulties, and restored to her mind its wonted confidence and serenity, had I possessed sufficient knowledge for the purpose. I really pitied her, and heartily wished Mr. Smith, for the nonce, at the devil.

I observed after this that my wife's spirits appeared permanently affected. There was a constantly-recurring anxiety, and I thought something was lying still more heavily at her heart than the uncertainties inspired by our lodger.

One evening, as we two were sitting together, after a long silence, she suddenly laid her hand upon my arm, and said—

"Oh, Richard, my darling! would to God you could pray for me!"

There was something so agitated, and even terrified, in her manner, that I was absolutely startled. I urged her to disclose whatever preyed upon her mind.

"You can't sympathise with me—you can't help me—you can scarcely compassionate me in my misery! Oh, dearest Richard! some evil influence has been gaining upon my heart, dulling and destroying my convictions, killing all my holy affections, and—and absolutely transforming me. I look inward upon myself with amazement, with terror—with—oh, God!—with actual despair!"

Saying this, she threw herself on her knees, and wept an agonised flood of tears, with her head reposing in my lap.

Poor little thing, my heart bled for her! But what could I do or say?

All I could suggest was what I really thought, that she was unwell—hysterical—and needed to take better care of her precious self; that her change of feeling was fancied, not real; and that a few days would restore her to her old health and former spirits and serenity.

"And sometimes," she resumed, after I had ended a consolatory discussion, which it was but too manifest had fallen unprofitably upon her ear, "such dreadful, impious thoughts come into my mind, whether I choose it or not; they come, and stay, and return, strive as I may; and I can't pray against them. They are forced upon me with the strength of an independent will; and oh!—horrible—frightful—they blaspheme the character of God himself. They upbraid the Almighty upon his throne, and I can't pray against them; there is something in me now that resists prayer."

There was such a real and fearful anguish in the agitation of my gentle companion, that it shook my very soul within me, even while I was affecting to make light of her confessions. I had never before witnessed a struggle at all like this, and I was awe-struck at the spectacle.

At length she became comparatively calm. I did gradually succeed, though very imperfectly, in reassuring her. She strove hard against her depression, and recovered a little of her wonted cheerfulness.

After a while, however, the cloud returned. She grew sad and earnest, though no longer excited; and entreated, or rather implored, of me to grant her one special favour, and this was, to avoid the society of our lodger.

"I never," she said, "could understand till now the instinctive dread with which poor Margaret, in *Faust*, shrinks from the hateful presence of Mephistopheles. I now feel it in myself. The dislike and suspicion I first felt for that man—Smith, or whatever else he may call himself—has grown into literal detestation and terror. I hate him—I am afraid of him—I never knew what anguish of mind was until he entered our doors; and would to God—would to God he were gone."

I reasoned with her—kissed her—laughed at her; but could not dissipate, in the least degree, the intense and preternatural horror with which she had grown to regard the poor philosophic invalid, who was probably, at that moment, poring over some metaphysical book in his solitary bed-chamber.

The circumstance I am about to mention will give you some notion of the extreme to which these excited feelings had worked upon her nerves. I was that night suddenly awakened by a piercing scream—I started upright in the bed, and saw my wife standing at the bedside, white as ashes with terror. It was some seconds, so startled was I, before I could find words to ask her the cause of her affright. She caught my wrist in her icy grasp, and climbed, trembling violently, into bed. Notwithstanding my repeated entreaties, she continued for a long time stupified and dumb. At length, however, she told me, that having lain awake for a long time, she felt, on a sudden, that she could pray, and lighting the candle, she had stolen from beside me, and kneeled down for the purpose. She had, however, scarcely assumed the attitude of prayer, when somebody, she said, clutched her arm violently near the wrist, and she heard, at the same instant, some blasphemous menace, the import of which escaped her the moment it was spoken, muttered close in her ear. This terrifying interruption was the cause of the scream which had awakened me; and the condition in which she continued during the remainder of the night confirmed me more than ever in the conviction, that she was suffering under some morbid action of the nervous system.

After this event, which *I* had no hesitation in attributing to fancy, she became literally afraid to pray, and her misery and despondency increased proportionately.

It was shortly after this that an unusual pressure of business called me into town one evening after office hours. I had left my dear little wife tolerably well, and little Fanny was to be her companion until I returned. She and her little companion occupied the same room in which we sat on the memorable evening which witnessed the arrival of our eccentric guest. Though usually a lively child, it most provokingly happened upon this night that Fanny was heavy and drowsy to excess. Her mamma would have sent her to bed, but that she now literally feared to be left alone; although, however, she could not so far overcome her horror of solitude as to do this, she yet would not persist in combating the poor child's sleepiness.

Accordingly, little Fanny was soon locked in a sound sleep, while her mamma quietly pursued her work beside her. They had been perhaps some ten minutes thus circumstanced, when my wife heard the window softly raised from without—a bony hand parted the curtains, and Mr. Smith leaned into the room.

She was so utterly overpowered at sight of this apparition, that even had it, as she expected, climbed into the room, she told me she could not have uttered a sound, or stirred from the spot where she sate transfixed and petrified.

"Ha, ha!" he said gently, "I hope you'll excuse this, I must admit, very odd intrusion; but I knew I should find you here, and could not resist the opportunity of raising the window just for a moment, to look in upon a little family picture, and say a word to yourself. I understand that you are troubled, because for some cause you cannot say your prayers—because what you call your 'faith' is, so to speak, dead and gone, and also because what *you* consider bad thoughts are constantly recurring to your mind. Now, all that is very silly. If it is really impossible for you to believe and to pray, what are you to infer from that? It is perfectly plain your Christian system can't be a true one—faith and *prayer* it everywhere represents as the conditions of grace, acceptance, and salvation; and yet your Creator will not *permit* you either to believe or pray. The Christian system is, forsooth, a *free* gift, and yet he who formed *you* and *it,* makes it absolutely impossible for you to accept it. *I.* it, I ask you, from your own experience—is it a free gift? And if your own experience, in which you can't be mistaken, gives its pretensions the lie, why, in the name of common sense, will you persist in believing it? I say it is downright blasphemy to think it has emanated from the Good Spirit—assuming that there is one. It tells you that you must be tormented hereafter in a way only to be made intelligible by the image of eternal fires—pretty strong, we must all allow—unless you comply with certain conditions, which it pretends are so easy that it is a positive pleasure to embrace and perform them; and yet, for the life of you, you can't—physically *can't*—do either. Is this truth and mercy?—or is it swindling and cruelty? Is it the part of the Redeemer, or that of the tyrant, deceiver, and tormentor?

Up to that moment, my wife had sate breathless and motionless listening, in the catalepsy of nightmare, to a sort of echo of the vile and impious reasoning which had haunted her for so long. At the last word of the sentence his voice became harsh and thrilling; and his whole manner bespoke a sort of crouching and terrific hatred, the like of which she could not have conceived.

Whatever may have been the cause, she was on a sudden dis-
enchanted. She started to her feet; and, freezing with horror though she
was, in a shrill cry of agony commanded him, in the name of God, to
depart from her. His whole frame seemed to darken; he drew back
silently; the curtains dropped into their places, the window was let
down again as stealthily as it had just been raised; and my wife found
herself alone in the chamber with our little child, who had been startled
from her sleep by her mother's cry of anguish, and with the fearful
words, "tempter," "destroyer," "devil," still ringing in her ears, was
weeping bitterly, and holding her terrified mother's hand.

There is nothing, I believe, more infectious than that species of nervousness which shows itself in superstitious fears. I began—although I
could not bring myself to admit anything the least like it—to partake
insensibly, but strongly of the peculiar feelings with which my wife, and
indeed my whole household, already regarded the lodger up stairs. The
fact was, beside, that the state of my poor wife's mind began to make
me seriously uneasy; and, although I was fully sensible of the pecuniary
and other advantages attendant upon his stay, they were yet far from
outweighing the constant gloom and frequent misery in which the
protracted sojourn was involving my once cheerful house. I resolved,
therefore, at whatever monetary sacrifice, to put an end to these com-
motions; and, after several debates with my wife, in which the subject
was, as usual, turned in all its possible and impossible bearings, we
agreed that, deducting a fair proportion for his five weeks' sojourn, I
should return the remainder of his £100, and request immediate
possession of his apartments. Like a man suddenly relieved of an in-
sufferable load, and breathing freely once more, I instantly prepared to
carry into effect the result of our deliberations.

In pursuance of this resolution, I waited upon Mr. Smith. This time
my call was made in the morning, somewhere about nine o'clock. He
received me at his door, standing as usual in the stealthy opening which
barely admitted his lank person. There he stood, fully equipped with
goggles and respirator, and swathed, rather than dressed, in his
puckered black garments.

As he did not seem disposed to invite me into his apartment,
although I had announced my visit as one of business, I was obliged to
open my errand where I stood; and after a great deal of fumbling and
muttering, I contrived to place before him distinctly the resolution to
which I had come.

"But I can't think of taking back any portion of the sum I have paid
you," said he, with a cool, dry emphasis.

"Your reluctance to do so, Mr. Smith, is most handsome, and I
assure you, appreciated," I replied. "It is very generous; but, at the
same time, it is quite impossible for me to accept what I have no right to
take, and I must beg of you not to mention that part of the subject
again."

"And why should *I* take it?" demanded Mr. Smith.

"Because you have paid this hundred pounds for six months, and you are leaving me with nearly five months of the term still unexpired," I replied. "I expect to receive fair play myself, and always give it."

"But who on earth said that I was going away so soon?" pursued Mr. Smith, in the same dry, sarcastic key. "*I* have not said so—because I really don't intend it; I mean to stay here to the last day of the six months for which I have paid you. I have no notion of vacating my hired lodgings, simply because you say, *go*. I shan't quarrel with you—I never quarrel with anybody. I'm as much your friend as ever; but, without the least wish to disoblige, I can't do this, positively I cannot. Is there anything else?"

I had not anticipated in the least the difficulty which thus encountered and upset our plans. I had so set my heart upon effecting the immediate retirement of our inauspicious inmate, that the disappointment literally stunned me for a moment. I, however, returned to the charge: I urged, and prayed, and almost besought him to give up his apartments, and to leave us. I offered to repay every farthing of the sum he had paid me—reserving nothing on account of the time he had already been with us. I suggested all the disadvantages of the house. I shifted my ground, and told him that my wife wanted the rooms; I pressed his gallantry—his good nature—his economy; in short, I assailed him upon every point—but in vain, he did not even take the trouble of repeating what he had said before—he neither relented, nor showed the least irritation, but simply said—

"I can't do this; here I am, and here I stay until the half-year has expired. You wanted a lodger, and you have got one—the quietest, least troublesome, least expensive person you could have; and though your house, servants, and furniture are none of the best, I don't care for that. I pursue my own poor business and enjoyments here entirely to my satisfaction."

Having thus spoken, he gave me a sort of nod, and closed the door.

So, instead of getting rid of him the next day, as we had hoped, we had nearly five months more of his company in expectancy; I hated, and my wife dreaded the prospect. She was literally miserable and panic-struck at her disappointment—and grew so nervous and wretched that I made up my mind to look out for lodgings for her and the children (subversive of all our schemes of retrenchment as such a step would be), and surrendering the house absolutely to Mr. Smith and the servants during the remainder of his term.

Circumstances, however, occurred to prevent our putting this plan in execution. My wife, meanwhile, was, if possible, more depressed and nervous every day. The servants seemed to sympathise in the dread and gloom which involved ourselves; the very children grew timid and spiritless, without knowing why—and the entire house was pervaded with an atmosphere of uncertainty and fear. A poorhouse or a dungeon would have been cheerful, compared with a dwelling haunted unceasingly with unearthly suspicions and alarms. I would have made any sacrifice short of ruin, to emancipate our household from the odious mental and moral thraldom which was invisibly established over us—overcasting us with strange anxieties and an undefined terror.

About this time my wife had a dream which troubled her much, although she could not explain its supposed significance satisfactorily by any of the ordinary rules of interpretation in such matters. The vision was as follows.

She dreamed that we were busily employed in carrying out our scheme of removal, and that I came into the parlour where she was making some arrangements, and, with rather an agitated manner, told her that the carriage had come for the children. She thought she went out to the hall, in consequence, holding little Fanny by one hand, and the boy—or, as we still called him, "baby,"—by the other, and feeling, as she did so, an unaccountable gloom, almost amounting to terror, steal over her. The children, too, seemed, she thought, frightened, and disposed to cry.

So close to the hall-door as to exclude the light, stood some kind of vehicle, of which she could see nothing but that its door was wide open, and the interior involved in total darkness. The children, she thought, shrunk back in great trepidation, and she addressed herself to induce them, by persuasion, to enter, telling them that they were only "going to their new home." So, in a while, little Fanny approached it; but, at the same instant, some person came swiftly up from behind, and, raising the little boy in his hands, said fiercely, "No, the baby first"; and placed him in the carriage. This person was our lodger, Mr. Smith, and was gone as soon as seen. My wife, even in her dream, could not act or speak; but as the child was lifted into the carriage-door, a man, whose face was full of beautiful tenderness and compassion, leaned forward from the carriage and received the little child, which, stretching his arms to the stranger, looked back with a strange smile upon his mother.

"He is safe with me, and I will deliver him to you when you come."

These words the man spoke, looking upon her, as he received him, and immediately the carriage-door shut, and the noise of its closing wakened my wife from her nightmare.

This dream troubled her very much, and even haunted my mind unpleasantly too. We agreed, however, not to speak of it to anybody, not to divulge any of our misgivings respecting the stranger. We were anxious that neither the children nor the servants should catch the contagion of those fears which had seized upon my poor little wife, and, if truth were spoken, upon myself in some degree also. But this precaution was, I believe, needless, for, as I said before, everybody under the same roof with Mr. Smith was, to a certain extent, affected with the same nervous gloom and apprehension.

And now commences a melancholy chapter in my life. My poor little Fanny was attacked with a cough which soon grew very violent, and after a time degenerated into a sharp attack of inflammation. We were seriously alarmed for her life, and nothing that care and medicine could effect was spared to save it. Her mother was indefatigable, and scarcely left her night or day; and, indeed, for some time, we all but despaired of her recovery.

One night, when she was at the worst, her poor mother, who had sat for many a melancholy hour listening, by her bedside, to those plaintive incoherences of delirium and moanings of fever, which have harrowed so many a fond heart, gained gradually from her very despair the courage which she had so long wanted, and knelt down at the side of her sick darling's bed to pray for her deliverance.

With clasped hands, in an agony of supplication, she prayed that God would, in his mercy, spare her little child—that, justly as she herself deserved the sorest chastisement his hand could inflict, he would yet deal patiently and tenderly with her in this one thing. She poured out her sorrows before the mercy-seat—she opened her heart, and declared her only hope to be in his pity; without which, she felt that her darling would only leave the bed where she was lying for her grave.

Exactly as she came to this part of her supplication, the child, who had grown, as it seemed, more and more restless, and moaned and muttered with increasing pain and irritation, on a sudden started upright in her bed, and, in a thrilling voice, cried—

"No! no!—the baby first."

The mysterious sentence which had secretly tormented her for so long, thus piercingly uttered by this delirious, and, perhaps, dying child, with what seemed a preternatural earnestness and strength, arrested her devotions, and froze her with a feeling akin to terror.

"Hush, hush, my darling!" said the poor mother, almost wildly, as she clasped the attenuated frame of the sick child in her arms; "hush, my darling; don't cry out so loudly—there—there—my own love."

The child did not appear to see or hear her, but sate up still with feverish cheeks, and bright unsteady eyes, while her dry lips were muttering inaudible words.

"Lie down, my sweet child—lie down, for your own mother," she said; "if you tire yourself, you can't grow well, and your poor mother will lose you."

At these words, the child suddenly cried out again, in precisely the same loud, strong voice—"No! no! the baby first, the baby first"—and immediately afterwards lay down, and fell, for the first time since her illness into a tranquil sleep.

My good little wife sate, crying bitterly by her bedside. The child was better—*that* was, indeed, delightful. But then there was an omen in the words, thus echoed from her dream, which she dared not trust herself to interpret, and which yet had seized, with a grasp of iron, upon every fibre of her brain.

"Oh, Richard," she cried, as she threw her arms about my neck, "I am terrified at this horrible menace from the unseen world. Oh! poor, darling little baby, I shall lose you—I am sure I shall lose you. Comfort me, darling, and say he is not to die."

And so I did; and tasked all my powers of argument and persuasion to convince her how unsubstantial was the ground of her anxiety. The little boy was perfectly well, and, even were he to die before his sister, that event might not occur for seventy years to come. I could not, however, conceal from myself that there was something odd and unpleasant in the coincidence; and my poor wife had grown so nervous and excitable, that a much less ominous conjecture would have sufficed to alarm her.

Meanwhile, the unaccountable terror which our lodger's presence inspired continued to increase. One of our maids gave us warning, solely from her dread of our queer inmate, and the strange accessories which haunted him. She said—and this was corroborated by her fellow-servant—that Mr. Smith seemed to have constantly a companion in his room; that although they never heard them speak, they continually and distinctly heard the tread of two persons walking up and down the room together, and described accurately the peculiar sound of a stick or crutch tapping upon the floor, which my own ears had heard. They also had seen the large, ill-conditioned cat I have mentioned, frequently steal in and out of the stranger's room; and observed that when our little girl was in greatest danger, the hateful animal was constantly writhing, fawning, and crawling about the door of the sick room after nightfall. They were thoroughly persuaded that this ill-omened beast was the foul fiend himself, and I confess I could not—sceptic as I was—bring myself absolutely to the belief that he was nothing more than a "harmless, necessary cat." These and similar reports—implicitly believed as they palpably were by those who made them—were certainly little calculated to allay the perturbation and alarm with which our household was filled.

The evenings had by this time shortened very much, and darkness often overtook us before we sate down to our early tea. It happened just at this period of which I have been speaking, after my little girl had begun decidedly to mend, that I was sitting in our dining-parlour, with my little boy fast asleep upon my knees, and thinking of I know not what, my wife having gone up stairs, as usual, to sit in the room with little Fanny. As I thus sate in what was to me, in effect, total solitude, darkness unperceived stole on us.

On a sudden, as I sate, with my elbow leaning upon the table, and my other arm round the sleeping child, I felt, as I thought, a cold current of air faintly blowing upon my forehead. I raised my head, and saw, as nearly as I could calculate, at the far end of the table on which my arm rested, two large green eyes confronting me. I could see no more, but instantly concluded they were those of the abominable cat. Yielding to an impulse of horror and abhorrence, I caught a water-croft that was close to my hand, and threw it full at it with all my force. I must have missed my object, for the shining eyes continued fixed for a second, and then glided still nearer to me, and then a little nearer still. The noise of the glass smashed with so much force upon the table called in the servant, who happened to be passing. She had a candle in her hand, and, perhaps, the light alarmed the odious beast, for as she came in it was gone.

I had had an undefined idea that its approach was somehow connected with a designed injury of some sort to the sleeping child. I could not be mistaken as to the fact that I had plainly seen the two broad, glaring, green eyes. Where the cursed animal had gone I had not observed: it might, indeed, easily have run out at the door as the servant opened it, but neither of us had seen it do so; and we were every one of us in such a state of nervous excitement, that even this incident was something in the catalogue of our ambiguous experiences.

It was a great happiness to see our darling little Fanny every day mending, and now quite out of danger: this was cheering and delightful. It was also something to know that more than two months of our lodger's term of occupation had already expired; and to realise, as we now could do, by anticipation, the unspeakable relief of his departure.

My wife strove hard to turn our dear child's recovery to good account for me; but the impressions of fear soon depart, and those of religious gratitude must be preceded by religious faith. All as yet was but as seed strewn upon the rock.

Little Fanny, though recovering rapidly, was still very weak, and her mother usually passed a considerable part of every evening in her bedroom—for the child was sometimes uneasy and restless at night. It happened at this period that, sitting as usual at Fanny's bedside, she witnessed an occurrence which agitated her not a little.

The child had been, as it seems, growing sleepy, and was lying listlessly, with eyes half open, apparently taking no note of what was passing. Suddenly, however, with an expression of the wildest terror, she drew up her limbs, and cowered in the bed's head, gazing at some object; which, judging from the motion of her eyes, must have been slowly advancing from the end of the room next the door.

The child made a low shuddering cry, as she grasped her mother's hand, and, with features white and tense with terror, slowly following with her eyes the noiseless course of some unseen spectre, shrinking more and more fearfully backward every moment.

"What is it? Where? What is it that frightens you, my darling?" asked the poor mother, who, thrilled with horror, looked in vain for the apparition which seemed to have all but bereft the child of reason.

"Stay with me—save me—keep it away—look, look at it—making signs to me—don't let it hurt me—it is angry—Oh! mamma, save me, save me!"

The child said this, all the time clinging to her with both her hands, in an ecstasy of panic.

"There—there, my darling," said my poor wife, "don't be afraid; there's nothing but me—your own mamma—and little baby in the room; nothing, my darling; nothing indeed."

"Mamma, mamma, don't move; don't go near him"; the child continued wildly. "It's only his back now; don't make him turn again; he's untying his handkerchief. Oh! baby, baby; he'll *kill* baby! and he's lifting up those green things from his eyes; don't you see him doing it? Mamma, mamma, why does he come here? Oh, mamma, poor baby— poor little baby!"

She was looking with a terrified gaze at the little boy's bed, which lay directly opposite to her own, and in which he was sleeping calmly.

"Hush, hush, my darling child," said my wife, with difficulty restraining an hysterical burst of tears; "for God's sake don't speak so wildly, my own precious love—there, there—don't be frightened— there, darling, there."

"Oh! poor baby—poor little darling baby," the child continued as before; "will no one save him—tell that wicked man to go away—oh— there—why, mamma—don't—oh, sure you won't let him—don't— don't—he'll take the child's life—will you let him lie down that way on the bed—save poor little baby—oh, baby, baby, waken—his head is on your face."

As she said this she raised her voice to a cry of despairing terror which made the whole room ring again.

This cry, or rather yell, reached my ears as I sate reading in the parlour by myself, and fearing I knew not what, I rushed to the apartment; before I reached it, the sound had subsided into low but violent sobbing; and, just as I arrived at the threshold I heard, close at my feet, a fierce protracted growl, and something rubbing along the surbase. I was in the dark, but, with a feeling of mingled terror and fury, I stamped and struck at the abhorred brute with my feet, but in vain. The next moment I was in the room, and heard little Fanny, through her sobs, cry—

"Oh, poor baby is killed—that wicked man has killed him—he uncovered his face, and put it on him, and lay upon the bed and killed poor baby. I knew he came to kill him. Ah, papa, papa, why did you not come up before he went?—he is gone, he went away as soon as he killed our poor little darling baby."

I could not conceal my agitation, quite, and I said to my wife—

"Has he, Smith, been here?"

"No."

"What is it, then?"

"The child has seen *some* one."

"Seen whom? Who ? Who has been here?"

"I did not see it; but—but I am sure the child saw—that is, *thought* she saw *him;*—the person you have named. Oh, God, in mercy deliver us! What shall I do—what shall I do!"

Thus saying, the dear little woman burst into tears, and crying, as if her heart would break, sobbed out an entreaty that I would look at baby; adding, that she herself had not courage to see whether her darling was sleeping or dead.

"Dead!" I exclaimed. "Tut, tut, my darling; you must not give way to such morbid fancies—he is very well, I see him breathing;" and so saying, I went over to the bed where our little boy was lying. He was slumbering; though it seemed to me very heavily, and his cheeks were flushed.

"Sleeping tranquilly, my darling—tranquilly, and deeply; and with a warm colour in his cheeks," I said, rearranging the coverlet, and retiring to my wife, who sate almost breathless whilst I was looking at our little boy.

"Thank God—thank God," she said quietly; and she wept again; and rising, came to his bedside.

"Yes, yes—alive; thank God; but it seems to me he is breathing very short, and with difficulty, and he looks—*does* he not look hot and feverish? Yes, he *is* very hot; feel his little hand—feel his neck; merciful heaven! he is burning."

It was, indeed, very true, that his skin was unnaturally dry and hot; his little pulse, too, was going at a fearful rate.

"I do think," said I —resolved to conceal the extent of my own apprehensions—"I do think that he is just a *little* feverish; but he has often been much more so; and will, I dare say, in the morning, be perfectly well again. I dare say, but for little Fanny's *dream*, we should not have observed it at all."

"Oh, my darling, my darling, my darling!" sobbed the poor little woman, leaning over the bed, with her hands locked together, and looking the very picture of despair. "Oh, my darling, what has happened to you? I put you into your bed, looking so well and beautiful, this evening, and here you are, stricken with sickness, my own little love. Oh, you will not—you cannot, leave your poor mother!"

It was quite plain that she despaired of the child from the moment we had ascertained that it was unwell. As it happened, her presentiment was but too truly prophetic. The apothecary said the child's ailment was "suppressed small-pox"; the physician pronounced it "typhus." The only certainty about it was the issue—the child died.

To me few things appear so beautiful as a very young child in its shroud. The little innocent face looks so sublimely simple and confiding amongst the cold terrors of death—crimeless, and fearless, that little mortal has passed alone under the shadow, and explored the mystery of dissolution. There is death in its sublimest and purest image—no hatred, no hypocrisy, no suspicion, no care for the morrow ever darkened that little face; death has come lovingly upon it; there is nothing cruel, or harsh, in his victory. The yearnings of love, indeed, cannot be stifled; for the prattle, and smiles, and all the little world of thoughts that were so delightful, are gone for ever. Awe, too, will overcast us in its presence—for we are looking on death; but we do not fear for the little, lonely voyager—for the child has gone, simple and trusting, into the presence of its all-wise Father; and of such, we know, is the kingdom of heaven.

And so we parted from poor little baby. I and his poor old nurse drove in a mourning carriage, in which lay the little coffin, early in the morning, to the churchyard of ——. Sore, indeed, was my heart, as I followed that little coffin to the grave! Another burial had just concluded as we entered the churchyard, and the mourners stood in clusters round the grave, into which the sexton was now shovelling the mould.

As I stood, with head uncovered, listening to the sublime and touching service which our ritual prescribes, I found that a gentleman had drawn near also, and was standing at my elbow. I did not turn to look at him until the earth had closed over my darling boy; I then walked a little way apart, that I might be alone, and drying my eyes, sat down upon a tombstone, to let the confusion of my mind subside.

While I was thus lost in a sorrowful reverie, the gentleman who had stood near me at the grave was once more at my side. The face of the stranger, though I could not call it handsome, was very remarkable; its expression was the purest and noblest I could conceive, and it was made very beautiful by a look of such compassion as I never saw before.

"Why do you sorrow as one without hope?" he said, gently.

"I *have* no hope," I answered.

"Nay, I think you have," he answered again; "and I am sure you will soon have more. That little child for which you grieve, has escaped the dangers and miseries of life; its body has perished; but he will receive in the end the crown of life. God has given him an early victory."

I know not what it was in him that rebuked my sullen pride, and humbled and saddened me, as I listened to this man. He was dressed in deep mourning, and looked more serene, noble, and sweet than any I had ever seen. He was young, too, as I have said, and his voice very clear and harmonious. He talked to me for a long time, and I listened to him with involuntary reverence. At last, however, he left me, saying he had often seen me walking into town, about the same hour that he used to go that way, and that if he saw me again he would walk with me, and so we might reason of these things together.

It was late when I returned to my home, now a house of mourning.

PART II

Our home was one of sorrow and of fear. The child's death had stricken us with terror no less than grief. Referring it, as we both tacitly did, to the mysterious and fiendish agency of the abhorred being whom, in an evil hour, we had admitted into our house, we both viewed him with a degree and species of fear for which I can find no name.

I felt that some further calamity was impending. I could not hope that we were to be delivered from the presence of the malignant agent who haunted, rather than inhabited our home, without some additional proofs alike of his malice and his power.

My poor wife's presentiments were still more terrible and overpowering, though not more defined, than my own. She was never tranquil while our little girl was out of her sight; always dreading and expecting some new revelation of the evil influence which, as we were indeed both persuaded, had bereft our darling little boy of life. Against an hostility so unearthly and intangible there was no guarding, and the sense of helplessness intensified the misery of our situation. Tormented with doubts of the very basis of her religion, and recoiling from the ordeal of prayer with the strange horror with which the victim of hydrophobia repels the pure water, she no longer found the consolation which, had sorrow reached her in any other shape, she would have drawn from the healing influence of religion. We were both of us unhappy, dismayed, DEMON-STRICKEN.

Meanwhile, our lodger's habits continued precisely the same. If, indeed, the sounds which came from his apartments were to be trusted, he and his agents were more on the alert than ever. I can convey to you, good reader, no notion, even the faintest, of the dreadful sensation always more or less present to my mind, and sometimes with a reality which thrilled me almost to frenzy—the apprehension that I had admitted into my house the incarnate spirit of the dead or damned, to torment me and my family.

It was some nights after the burial of our dear little baby; we had not gone to bed until late, and I had slept, I suppose, some hours, when I was awakened by my wife, who clung to me with the energy of terror. She said nothing, but grasped and shook me with more than her natural strength. She had crept close to me, and was cowering with her head under the bed-clothes.

The room was perfectly dark, as usual, for we burned no night-light; but from the side of the bed next her proceeded a voice as of one sitting there with his head within a foot of the curtains—and, merciful heavens! it was the voice of our lodger.

He was discoursing of the death of our baby, and inveighing, in the old mocking tone of hate and suppressed fury, against the justice, mercy, and goodness of God. He did this with a terrible plausibility of sophistry, and with a resolute emphasis and precision, which seemed to imply, "I have got something to tell you, and, whether you like it or like it not, I *will* say out my say."

To pretend that I felt anger at his intrusion, or emotion of any sort, save the one sense of palsied terror, would be to depart from the truth. I lay, cold and breathless, as if frozen to death—unable to move, unable to utter a cry—with the voice of that demon pouring, in the dark, his undisguised blasphemies and temptations close into my ears. At last the dreadful voice ceased—whether the speaker went or stayed I could not tell—the silence, which he might be improving for the purpose of some hellish strategem, was to me more tremendous even than his speech.

We both lay awake, not daring to move or speak, scarcely even breathing, but clasping one another fast, until at length the welcome light of day streamed into the room through the opening door, as the servant came in to call us. I need not say that our nocturnal visitant had left us.

The magnanimous reader will, perhaps, pronounce that I ought to have pulled on my boots and inexpressibles with all available despatch, run to my lodger's bedroom, and kicked him forthwith downstairs, and the entire way moreover out to the public road, as some compensation for the scandalous affront put upon me and my wife by his impertinent visit. Now, at that time, I had no scruples against what are termed the laws of honour, was by no means deficient in "pluck," and gifted, moreover, with a somewhat excitable temper. Yet, I will honestly avow that, so far from courting a collision with the dreaded stranger, I would have recoiled at his very sight, and given my eyes to avoid him, such was the ascendancy which he had acquired over me, as well as everybody else in my household, in his own quiet, irresistible, hellish way.

The shuddering antipathy which our guest inspired did not rob his infernal homily of its effect. It was not a new or strange thing which he presented to our minds. There was an awful subtlety in the train of his suggestions. All that he had said had floated through my own mind before, without order, indeed, or shew of logic. From my own rebellious heart the same evil thoughts had risen, like pale apparitions hovering and lost in the fumes of a necromancer's cauldron. His was like the summing up of all this—a reflection of my own feelings and fancies— but reduced to an awful order and definiteness, and clothed with a sophistical form of argument. The effect of it was powerful. It revived and exaggerated these bad emotions—it methodised and justified them —and gave to impulses and impressions, vague and desultory before, something of the compactness of a system.

My misfortune, therefore, did not soften, it exasperated me. I regarded the Great Disposer of events as a persecutor of the human race, who took delight in their miseries. I asked why my innocent child had been smitten down into the grave?—and why my darling wife, whose first object, I knew, had ever been to serve and glorify her Maker, should have been thus tortured and desolated by the cruelest calamity which the malignity of a demon could have devised? I railed and blasphemed, and even in my agony defied God with the impotent rage and desperation of a devil, in his everlasting torment.

In my bitterness, I could not forbear speaking these impenitent repetitions of the language of our nightly visitant, even in the presence of my wife. She heard me with agony, almost with terror. I pitied and loved her too much not to respect even her weaknesses—for so I characterised her humble submission to the chastisements of heaven. But even while I spared her reverential sensitiveness, the spectacle of her patience but enhanced my own gloomy and impenitent rage.

I was walking into town in this evil mood, when I was overtaken by the gentleman whom I had spoken with in the churchyard on the morning when my little boy was buried. I call him *gentleman*, but I could not say *what* was his rank—I never thought about it; there was a grace, a purity, a compassion, and a grandeur of intellect in his countenance, in his language, in his mien, that was beautiful and kinglike. I felt, in his company, a delightful awe, and an humbleness more gratifying than any elation of earthly pride.

He divined my state of feeling, but he said nothing harsh. He did not rebuke, but he reasoned with me—and oh! how mighty was that reasoning—without formality—without effort—as the flower grows and blossoms. Its process was in harmony with the successions of nature—gentle, spontaneous, irresistible.

At last he left me. I was grieved at his departure—I was wonderstricken. His discourse had made me cry tears at once sweet and bitter; it had sounded depths I knew not of, and my heart was disquieted within me. Yet my trouble was happier than the resentful and defiant calm that had reigned within me before.

When I came home, I told my wife of my having met the same good, wise man I had first seen by the grave of my child. I recounted to her his discourse, and, as I brought it again to mind, my tears flowed afresh, and I was happy while I wept.

I now see that the calamity which bore at first such evil fruit, was good for me. It fixed my mind, however rebelliously, upon God, and it stirred up all the passions of my heart. Levity, inattention, and self-complacency are obstacles harder to be overcome than the violence of evil passions—the transition from hate is easier than from indifference, to love. A mighty change was making on my mind.

I need not particularise the occasions upon which I again met my friend, for so I knew him to be, nor detail the train of reasoning and feeling which in such interviews he followed out; it is enough to say, that he assiduously cultivated the good seed he had sown, and that his benignant teachings took deep root, and flourished in my soul, heretofore so barren.

One evening, having enjoyed on the morning of the same day another of those delightful and convincing conversations, I was returning on foot homeward; and as darkness had nearly closed, and the night threatened cold and fog, the footpaths were nearly deserted.

As I walked on, deeply absorbed in the discourse I had heard on the same morning, a person overtook me, and continued to walk, without much increasing the interval between us, a little in advance of me. There came upon me, at the same moment, an indefinable sinking of the heart, a strange and unaccountable fear. The pleasing topics of my meditations melted away, and gave place to a sense of danger, all the more unpleasant that it was vague and objectless. I looked up. What was that which moved before me? I stared—I faltered; my heart fluttered as if it would choke me, and then stood still. It was the peculiar and unmistakeable form of our lodger.

Exactly as I looked at him, he turned his head, and looked at me over his shoulder. His face was muffled as usual. I cannot have seen its features with any completeness, yet I felt that his look was one of fury. The next instant he was at my side; and my heart quailed within me— my limbs all but refused their office; yet the very emotions of terror, which might have overcome me, acted as a stimulus, and I quickened my pace.

"Hey! what a pious person! So I suppose you have learned at last that 'evil communications corrupt good manners'; and you are ab- solutely afraid of the old infidel, the old blasphemer, hey?"

I made him no answer; I was indeed too much agitated to speak.

"You'll make a good Christian, no doubt," he continued; "the in- dependent man, who thinks for himself, reasons his way to his prin- ciples, and sticks fast to them, is sure to be true to whatever system he embraces. You have been so consistent a philosopher, that I am sure you will make a steady Christian. You're not the man to be led by the nose by a sophistical mumbler. *You* could never be made the prey of a grasping proselytism; *you* are not the sport of every whiff of doctrine, nor the facile slave of whatever superstition is last buzzed in your ear. No, no: you've got a masculine intellect, and think for yourself, hey?"

I was incapable of answering him. I quickened my pace to escape from his detested persecution; but he was close beside me still.

We walked on together thus for a time, during which I heard him muttering fast to himself, like a man under fierce and malignant excite- ment. We reached, at length, the gateway of my dwelling; and I turned the latch-key in the wicket, and entered the enclosure. As we stood together within, he turned full upon me, and confronting me with an aspect whose character I felt rather than saw, he said—

"And so you mean to be a Christian, after all! Now just reflect how very absurdly you are choosing. Leave the Bible to that class of fanatics who may hope to be saved under its system, and, in the name of com- mon sense, study the Koran, or some less ascetic tome. Don't be gulled by a plausible slave, who wants nothing more than to multiply *professors* of his theory. Why don't you *read* the Bible, you miserable, puling poltroon, before you hug it as a treasure? Why don't you read it, and learn out of the mouth of the founder of Christianity, that there is one sin for which there is *no* forgiveness—blasphemy against the Holy Ghost, hey?—and that sin I myself have heard you commit by the hour —in my presence—in my room. I have heard you commit it in our free discussions a dozen times. The Bible seals against you the lips of mercy. If *it* be true, you are this moment as irrevocably damned as if you had died with those blasphemies on your lips."

Having thus spoken, he glided into the house. I followed slowly.

His words rang in my ears—I was stunned. What he had said I feared might be true. Giant despair felled me to the earth. He had recalled, and lighted up with a glare from the pit, remembrances with which I knew not how to cope. It was true I had spoken with daring im- piety of subjects whose sacredness I now began to appreciate. With trembling hands I opened the Bible. I read and re-read the mysterious doom recorded by the Redeemer himself against blasphemers of the Holy Ghost—monsters set apart from the human race, and damned and dead, even while they live and walk upon the earth. I groaned—I wept. Henceforward the Bible, I thought, must be to me a dreadful record of despair. I dared not read it.

I will not weary you with all my mental agonies. My dear little wife did something toward relieving my mind, but it was reserved for the friend, to whose heavenly society I owed so much, to tranquillise it once more. He talked this time to me longer, and even more earnestly than before. I soon encountered him again. He expounded to me the ways of Providence, and showed me how needful sorrow was for every servant of God. How mercy was disguised in tribulation, and our best happiness came to us, like our children, in tears and wailing. He showed me that trials were sent to call us up, with a voice of preternatural power, from the mortal apathy of sin and the world. And then, again, in our new and better state, to prove our patience and our faith—

"The more trouble befalls you, the nearer is God to you. He visits you in sorrow—and sorrow, as well as joy, is a sign of his presence. If, then, other griefs overtake you, remember this—be patient, be faithful; and bless the name of God."

I returned home comforted and happy, although I felt assured that some further and sadder trial was before me.

Still our household was overcast by the same insurmountable dread of our tenant. The same strange habits characterised him, and the same unaccountable sounds disquieted us—an atmosphere of death and malice hovered about his door, and we all hated and feared to pass it.

Let me now tell, as well and briefly as I may, the dreadful circumstances of my last great trial. One morning, my wife being about her household affairs, and I on the point of starting for town, I went into the parlour for some letters which I was to take with me. I cannot easily describe my consternation when, on entering the room, I saw our lodger seated near the window, with our darling little girl upon his knee.

His back was toward the door, but I could plainly perceive that the respirator had been removed from his mouth, and that the odious green goggles were raised. He was sitting, as it seemed, absolutely without motion, and his face was advanced close to that of the child.

I stood looking at this group in a state of stupor for some seconds. He was, I suppose, conscious of my presence, for although he did not turn his head, or otherwise take any note of my arrival, he readjusted the muffler which usually covered his mouth, and lowered the clumsy spectacles to their proper place.

The child was sitting upon his knee as motionless as he himself, with a countenance white and rigid as that of a corpse, and from which every trace of meaning, except some vague character of terror, had fled, and staring with a fixed and dilated gaze into his face.

As it seemed, she did not perceive my presence. Her eyes were transfixed and fascinated. She did not even seem to me to breathe. Horror and anguish at last overcame my stupefaction.

"What—what is it?" I cried; "what ails my child, my darling child?"

"I'd be glad to know, myself," he replied, coolly; "it is certainly something very queer."

"What is it, darling?" I repeated, frantically, addressing the child.

"What is it?" he reiterated. "Why it's pretty plain, I should suppose, that the child is ill."

"Oh merciful God!" I cried, half furious, half terrified—"You have injured her—you have terrified her. Give me my child—give her to me."

These words I absolutely shouted, and stamped upon the floor in my horrid excitement.

"Pooh, pooh!" he said, with a sort of ugly sneer; "the child is nervous —you'll make her more so—be quiet and she'll probably find her tongue presently. I have had her on my knee some minutes, but the sweet bird could not tell what ails her."

"Let the child go," I shouted in a voice of thunder; "let her go, I say —let her go."

He took the passive, death-like child, and placed her standing by the window, and rising, he simply said—

"As soon as you grow cool, you are welcome to ask me what questions you like. The child is plainly ill. I should not wonder if she had seen something that frightened her."

Having thus spoken, he passed from the room. I felt as if I spoke, saw, and walked in a horrid dream. I seized the darling child in my arms, and bore her away to her mother.

"What is it—for mercy's sake what is the matter?" she cried, growing in an instant as pale as the poor child herself.

"I found that—that *demon*—in the parlour with the child on his lap, staring in her face. She is manifestly terrified."

"Oh! gracious God! she is lost—she is killed," cried the poor mother, frantically looking into the white, apathetic, meaningless face of the child.

"Fanny, darling Fanny, tell us if you are ill," I cried, pressing the little girl in terror to my heart.

"Tell your own mother, my darling," echoed my poor little wife. "Oh! darling, darling child, speak to your poor mother."

It was all in vain. Still the same dilated, imploring gaze—the same pale face—wild and dumb. We brought her to the open window—we gave her cold water to drink—we sprinkled it in her face. We sent for the apothecary, who lived hard by, and he arrived in a few moments, with a parcel of tranquillising medicines. These, however, were equally unavailing.

Hour after hour passed away. The darling child looked upon us as if she would have given the world to speak to us, or to weep, but she uttered no sound. Now and then she drew a long breath as though preparing to say something, but still she was mute. She often put her hand to her throat, as if there was some pain or obstruction there.

I never can, while I live, lose one line of that mournful and terrible portrait—the face of my stricken child. As hour after hour passed away, without bringing the smallest change or amendment, we grew both alarmed, and at length absolutely terrified for her safety.

We called in a physician toward night, and told him that we had reason to suspect that the child had somehow been frightened, and that in no other way could we at all account for the extraordinary condition in which he found her.

This was a man, I may as well observe, though I do not name him, of the highest eminence in his profession, and one in whose skill, from past personal experience, I had the best possible reasons for implicitly confiding.

He asked a multiplicity of questions, the answers to which seemed to baffle his attempts to arrive at a satisfactory diagnosis. There was something undoubtedly anomalous in the case, and I saw plainly that there were features in it which puzzled and perplexed him not a little.

At length, however, he wrote his prescription, and promised to return at nine o'clock. I remember there was something to be rubbed along her spine, and some medicines beside.

But these remedies were as entirely unavailing as the others. In a state of dismay and distraction we watched by the bed in which, in accordance with the physician's direction, we had placed her. The absolute changelessness of her condition filled us with despair. The day which had elapsed had not witnessed even a transitory variation in the dreadful character of her seizure. Any change, even a change for the worse, would have been better than this sluggish, hopeless monotony of suffering.

At the appointed hour the physician returned. He appeared disappointed, almost shocked, at the failure of his prescriptions. On feeling her pulse he declared that she must have a little wine. There had been a wonderful prostration of all the vital powers since he had seen her before. He evidently thought the case a strange and precarious one.

She was made to swallow the wine, and her pulse rallied for a time, but soon subsided again. I and the physician were standing by the fire, talking in whispers of the darling child's symptoms, and likelihood of recovery, when we were arrested in our conversation by a cry of anguish from the poor mother, who had never left the bedside of her little child and this cry broke into bitter and convulsive weeping.

The poor little child had, on a sudden, stretched down her little hands and feet, and died. There is no mistaking the features of death the filmy eye and dropt jaw once seen, are recognised whenever we meet them again. Yet, spite of our belief, we cling to hope; and the distracted mother called on the physician, in accents which might have moved a statue, to say that her darling was not dead, not quite dead—that something might still be done—that it could not be all over. Silent ly he satisfied himself that no throb of life still fluttered in that little frame.

"It is, indeed, all over," he said, in tones scarce above a whisper; and pressing my hand kindly, he said, "comfort your poor wife"; and so, after a momentary pause, he left the room.

This blow had smitten me with stunning suddenness. I looked at the dead child, and from her to her poor mother. Grief and pity were both swallowed up in transports of fury and detestation with which the presence in my house of the wretch who had wrought all this destruction and misery filled my soul. My heart swelled with ungovernable rage; for a moment my habitual fear of him was neutralised by the vehemence of these passions. I seized a candle in silence, and mounted the stairs. The sight of the accursed cat, flitting across the lobby, and the loneliness of the hour, made me hesitate for an instant. I had, however, gone so far, that shame sustained me. Overcoming a momentary thrill of dismay, and determined to repel and defy the influence that had so long awed me, I knocked sharply at the door, and, almost at the same instant, pushed it open, and entered our lodger's chamber.

He had had no candle in the room, and it was lighted only by the "darkness visible" that entered through the window. The candle which I held very imperfectly illuminated the large apartment; but I saw his spectral form floating, rather than walking, back and forward in front of the windows.

At sight of him, though I hated him more than ever, my instinctive fear returned. He confronted me, and drew nearer and nearer, without speaking. There was something indefinably fearful in the silent attraction which seemed to be drawing him to me. I could not help recoiling, little by little, as he came toward me, and with an effort I said—

"You know why I have come: the child—she's dead!"

"Dead—ha!—*dead*—is she?" he said, in his odious, mocking tone.

"Yes—dead!" I cried, with an excitement which chilled my very narrow with horror; "and *you* have killed her, as you killed my other."

"How?—I killed her!—eh?—ha, ha!" he said, still edging nearer and nearer.

"Yes; I say you!" I shouted, trembling in every joint, but possessed by that unaccountable infatuation which has made men invoke, spite of themselves, their own destruction, and which I was powerless to resist —"deny it as you may, it is you who killed her—wretch!—FIEND!—no wonder she could not stand the breath and glare of HELL!"

"And you are one of those who believe that not a sparrow falls to the ground without your Creator's consent," he said, with icy sarcasm; and this is a specimen of Christian resignation—hey? You charge his act upon a poor fellow like me, simply that you may cheat the devil, and rave and rebel against the decrees of heaven, under pretence of abusing me. The breath and flare of hell!—eh? You mean that I removed this and these (touching the covering of his mouth and eyes successively) as I *shall* do now again, and show you there's no great harm in that."

There was a tone of menace in his concluding words not to be mistaken.

"Murderer and liar from the beginning, as you are, I defy you!" I shouted, in a frenzy of hate and horror, stamping furiously on the floor.

As I said this, it seemed to me that he darkened and dilated before my eyes. My senses, thoughts, consciousness, grew horribly confused, as if some powerful, extraneous will, were seizing upon the functions of my brain. Whether I were to be mastered by death, or madness, or possession, I knew not; but hideous destruction of some sort was impending: all hung upon the moment, and I cried aloud, in my agony, an adjuration in the name of the three persons of the Trinity, that he should not torment me.

Stunned, bewildered, like a man recovered from a drunken fall, I stood, freezing and breathless, in the same spot, looking into the room which wore, in my eyes, a strange, unearthly character. Mr. Smith was cowering darkly in the window, and, after a silence, spoke to me in a croaking, sulky tone, which was, however, unusually submissive.

"Don't it strike you as an odd procedure to break into a gentleman's apartment at such an hour, for the purpose of railing at him in the coarsest language? If you have any charge to make against me, do so; I invite inquiry and defy your worst. If you think you can bring home to me the smallest share of blame in this unlucky matter, call the coroner and let his inquest examine and cross-examine me, and sift the matter —if, indeed, there is anything to *be* sifted—to the bottom. Meanwhile go you about your business, and leave me to mine. But I see how the wind sits; you want to get rid of me, and so you make the place odious to me. But it won't do; and if you take to making criminal charge against me, you had better look to yourself; for two can play at that game."

There was a suppressed whine in all this, which strangely contrasted with the cool and threatening tone of his previous conversation.

Without answering a word I hurried from the room, and scarcely felt secure, even when once more in the melancholy chamber, where my poor wife was weeping.

Miserable, horrible was the night that followed. The loss of our child was a calamity which we had not dared to think of. It had come, and with a suddenness enough to bereave me of reason. It seemed all unreal, all fantastic. It needed an effort to convince me, minute after minute, that the dreadful truth was so; and the old accustomed feeling that she was still alive, still running from room to room, and the expectation that I should hear her step and her voice, and see her entering at the door, would return. But still the sense of dismay, of having received some stunning, irreparable blow, remained behind; and then came the horrible effort, like that with which one rouses himself from a haunted sleep, the question, "What disaster is this that has befallen?"— answered, alas! but too easily, too terribly! Amidst all this was perpetually rising before my fancy the obscure, dilated figure of our lodger, as he had confronted me in his malign power that night. I dismissed the image with a shudder as often as it recurred; and even now, at this distance of time, I have felt more than I could well describe in the mere effort to fix my recollection upon its hated traits, while writing the passages I have just concluded.

This hateful scene I did not recount to my poor wife. Its horrors were too fresh upon me. I had not courage to trust myself with the agitating narrative; and so I sate beside her, with her hand locked in mine: I had no comfort to offer but the dear love I bore her.

At last, like a child, she cried herself to sleep—the dull, heavy slumber of worn-out grief. As for me, the agitation of my soul was too fearful and profound for repose. My eye accidentally rested on the holy volume, which lay upon the table open, as I had left it in the morning; and the first words which met my eye were these—"For our light affliction, which is but for a moment, worketh for us a far more exceeding and eternal weight of glory." This blessed sentence riveted my attention, and shed a stream of solemn joy upon my heart; and so the greater part of that mournful night, I continued to draw comfort and heavenly wisdom from the same inspired source.

Next day brought the odious incident, the visit of the undertaker—the carpentery, upholstery, and millinery of death. Why has not civilisation abolished these repulsive and shocking formalities? What has the poor corpse to do with frills, and pillows, and napkins, and all the equipage in which it rides on its last journey? There is no intrusion so jarring to the decent grief of surviving affection, no conceivable mummery more derisive of mortality.

In the room which we had been so long used to call "the nursery," now desolate and mute, the unclosed coffin lay, with our darling shrouded in it. Before we went to our rest at night we visited it. In the morning the lid was to close over that sweet face, and I was to see the child laid by her little brother. We looked upon the well-known and loved features, purified in the sublime serenity of death, for a long time, whispering to one another, among our sobs, how sweet and beautiful we thought she looked; and at length, weeping bitterly, we tore ourselves away.

We talked and wept for many hours, and at last, in sheer exhaustion, dropt asleep. My little wife awaked me, and said—

"I think they have come—the—the undertakers."

It was still dark, so I could not consult my watch; but they were to have arrived early, and as it was winter, and the nights long, the hour of their visit might well have arrived.

"What, darling, is your reason for thinking so?" I asked.

"I am sure I have heard them for some time in the nursery," she answered. "Oh! dear, dear little Fanny! Don't allow them to close the coffin until I have seen my darling once more."

I got up, and threw some clothes hastily about me. I opened the door and listened. A sound like a muffled knocking reached me from the nursery.

"Yes, my darling!" I said, "I think they have come. I will go and desire them to wait until you have seen her again."

And, so saying, I hastened from the room.

Our bedchamber lay at the end of a short corridor, opening from the lobby, at the head of the stairs, and the nursery was situated nearly at the end of a corresponding passage, which opened from the same lobby at the opposite side As I hurried along I distinctly heard the same sounds. The light of dawn had not yet appeared, but there was a strong moonlight shining through the windows. I thought the morning could hardly be so far advanced as we had at first supposed; but still, strangely as it now seems to me, suspecting nothing amiss, I walked on in noiseless, slippered feet, to the nursery-door. It stood half open; some one had unquestionably visited it since we had been there. I stepped forward, and entered. At the threshold horror arrested my advance.

The coffin was placed upon tressles at the further extremity of the chamber, with the foot of it nearly towards the door, and a large window at the side of it admitted the cold lustre of the moon full upon the apparatus of mortality, and the objects immediately about it.

At the foot of the coffin stood the ungainly form of our lodger. He seemed to be intently watching the face of the corpse, and was stooped a little, while with his hands he tapped sharply, from time to time at the sides of the coffin, like one who designs to awaken a slumberer. Perched upon the body of the child, and nuzzling among the grave-clothes, with a strange kind of ecstasy, was the detested brute, the cat I have so often mentioned.

The group thus revealed, I looked upon but for one instant; in the next I shouted, in absolute terror—

"In God's name! what are you doing?"

Our lodger shuffled away abruptly, as if disconcerted; but the ill favoured cat, whisking round, stood like a demon sentinel upon the corpse growling and hissing, with arched back and glaring eyes.

The lodger, turning abruptly toward me, motioned me to one side Mechanically I obeyed his gesture, and he hurried hastily from the room.

Sick and dizzy, I returned to my own chamber. I confess I had no nerve to combat the infernal brute, which still held possession of the room, and so I left it undisturbed.

This incident I did not tell to my wife until some time afterwards and I mention it here because it was, and is, in my mind associated with a painful circumstance which very soon afterwards came to light.

That morning I witnessed the burial of my darling child. Sore and desolate was my heart; but with infinite gratitude to the great controller of all events, I recognised in it a change which nothing but the spirit of all good can effect. The love and fear of God had grown strong within me—in humbleness I bowed to his awful will—with a sincere trust I relied upon the goodness, the wisdom, and the mercy of him who had sent this great affliction. But a further incident connected with this very calamity was to test this trust and patience to the uttermost.

It was still early when I returned, having completed the last sad office. My wife, as I afterwards learned, still lay weeping upon her bed. But somebody awaited my return in the hall, and opened the door, anticipating my knock. This person was our lodger.

I was too much appalled by the sudden presentation of this abhorred spectre even to retreat, as my instinct would have directed, through the open door.

"I have been expecting your return," he said, "with the design of saying something which it might have profited you to learn, but now I apprehend it is too late. What a pity you are so violent and impatient; you would not have heard me, in all probability, this morning. You cannot think how cross-grained and intemperate you have grown since you became a saint—but that is your affair, not mine. You have buried your little daughter this morning. It requires a good deal of that new attribute of yours, *faith*, which judges all things by a rule of contraries, and can never see anything but kindness in the worst afflictions which malignity could devise, to discover benignity and mercy in the torturing calamity which has just punished you and your wife for *nothing!* But I fancy that it will be harder still when I tell you what I more than suspect—ha, ha. It would be really ridiculous, if it were not heart-rending; that your little girl has been actually buried *alive;* do you comprehend me?—alive. For, upon my life, I fancy she was not dead as she lay in her coffin."

I knew the wretch was exulting in the fresh anguish he had just inflicted. I know not how it was, but any announcement of *disaster* from his lips, seemed to me to be necessarily true. Half-stifled with the dreadful emotions he had raised, palpitating between hope and terror, I rushed frantically back again, the way I had just come, running as fast as my speed could carry me, toward the, alas! distant burial-ground where my darling lay.

I stopped a cab slowly returning to town, at the corner of the lane, sprang into it, directed the man to drive to the church of ——, and promised him anything and everything for despatch. The man seemed amazed; doubtful, perhaps, whether he carried a maniac or a malefactor. Still he took his chance for the promised reward, and galloped his horse, while I, tortured with suspense, yelled my frantic incentives to further speed.

At last, in a space immeasurably short, but which to me was protracted almost beyond endurance, we reached the spot. I hallooed to the sexton, who was now employed upon another grave, to follow me. I myself seized a mattock, and in obedience to my incoherent and agonised commands, he worked as he had never worked before. The rumbling mould flew swiftly to the upper soil—deeper and deeper, every moment, grew the narrow grave—at last I sobbed, "Thank God —thank God," as I saw the face of the coffin emerge; a few seconds more and it lay upon the sward beside me, and we both, with the edges of our spades, ripped up the lid.

There was the corpse—but not the tranquil statue I had seen it last. Its knees were both raised, and one of its little hands drawn up and clenched near its throat, as if in a feeble but agonised struggle to force up the superincumbent mass. The eyes, that I had last seen closed, were now open, and the face no longer serenely pale, but livid and distorted.

I had time to see all in an instant; the whole scene reeled and darkened before me, and I swooned away.

When I came to myself, I found that I had been removed to the vestry-room. The open coffin was in the aisle of the church, surrounded by a curious crowd. A medical gentleman had examined the body carefully, and had pronounced life totally extinct. The trepidation and horror I experienced were indescribable. I felt like the murderer of my own child. Desperate as I was of any chance of its life, I dispatched messengers for no less than three of the most eminent physicians then practising in London. All concurred—the child was now as dead as any other, the oldest tenant of the churchyard.

Notwithstanding which, I would not permit the body to be reinterred for several days, until the symptoms of decay became unequivocal, and the most fantastic imagination could no longer cherish a doubt. This, however, I mention only parenthetically, as I hasten to the conclusion of my narrative. The circumstance which I have last described found its way to the public, and caused no small sensation at the time.

I drove part of the way home, and then discharged the cab, and walked the remainder. On my way, with an emotion of ecstasy I cannot describe, I met the good being to whom I owed so much. I ran to meet him, and felt as if I could throw myself at his feet, and kiss the very ground before him. I knew by his heavenly countenance he was come to speak comfort and healing to my heart.

With humbleness and gratitude, I drank in his sage and holy discourse. I need not follow the gracious and delightful exposition of God' revealed will and character with which he cheered and confirmed my faltering spirit. A solemn joy, a peace and trust, streamed on my heart. The wreck and desolation there, lost their bleak and ghastly character, like ruins illuminated by the mellow beams of a solemn summer sunset.

In this conversation, I told him what I had never revealed to any one before—the absolute terror, in all its stupendous and maddening amplitude, with which I regarded our ill-omened lodger, and my agonised anxiety to rid my house of him. My companion answered me—

"I know the person of whom you speak—he designs no good for you or any other. He, too, knows me, and I have intimated to him that he must now leave you, and visit you no more. Be firm and bold, trusting in God, through his Son, like a good soldier, and you will win the vic tory from a greater and even worse than he—the *unseen* enemy of mankind. You need not see or speak with your evil tenant any more. Call to him from your hall, in the name of the Most Holy, to leave you bodily, with all that appertains to him, this evening. He knows that he must go, and will obey you. But leave the house as soon as may be yourself; you will scarce have peace in it. Your own remembrances will trouble you and *other minds have established associations within its walls and chambers too.*"

These words sounded mysteriously in my ears.

Let me say here, before I bring my reminiscences to a close, a word or two about the house in which these detested scenes occurred, and which I did not long continue to inhabit. What I afterwards learned of it, seemed to supply in part a dim explanation of these words.

In a country village there is no difficulty in accounting for the tenacity with which the sinister character of a haunted tenement cleaves to it. Thin neighbourhoods are favourable to scandal; and in such localities the reputation of a house, like that of a woman, once blown upon, never quite recovers. In huge London, however, it is quite another matter; and, therefore, it was with some surprise that, five years after I had vacated the house in which the occurrences I have described took place, I learned that a respectable family who had taken it were obliged to give it up, on account of annoyances, for which they could not account, and all proceeding from the apartments formerly occupied by our "lodger." Among the sounds described were footsteps restlessly traversing the floor of that room, accompanied by the peculiar tapping of the crutch.

I was so anxious about this occurrence, that I contrived to have strict inquiries made into the matter. The result, however, added little to what I had at first learned—except, indeed, that our old friend, the cat, bore a part in the transaction as I suspected; for the servant, who had been placed to sleep in the room, complained that something bounded on and off, and ran to-and-fro along the foot of the bed, in the dark. The same servant, while in the room, in the broad daylight, had heard the sound of walking, and even the rustling of clothes near him, as of people passing and repassing; and, although he had never seen anything, he yet became so terrified that he would not remain in the house, and ultimately, in a short time, left his situation.

These sounds, attention having been called to them, were now incessantly observed—the measured walking up and down the room, the opening and closing of the door, and the teazing tap of the crutch—all these sounds were continually repeated, until at last, worn out, frightened, and worried, its occupants resolved on abandoning the house.

About four years since, having had occasion to visit the capital, I resolved on a ramble by Old Brompton, just to see if the house were still inhabited. I searched for it, however, in vain, and at length, with difficulty, ascertained its site, upon which now stood two small, staring, bran-new brick houses, with each a gay enclosure of flowers. Every trace of our old mansion, and, let us hope, of our "mysterious lodger," had entirely vanished.

Let me, however, return to my narrative where I left it.

Discoursing upon heavenly matters, my good and gracious friend accompanied me even within the outer gate of my own house. I asked him to come in and rest himself, but he would not; and before he turned to depart, he lifted up his hand, and blessed me and my household.

Having done this, he went away. My eyes followed him till he disappeared, and I turned to the house. My darling wife was standing at the window of the parlour. There was a seraphic smile on her face—pale, pure, and beautiful as death. She was gazing with an humble heavenly earnestness on us. The parting blessing of the stranger shed a sweet and hallowed influence on my heart. I went into the parlour, to my darling: childless she was now; I had now need to be a tender companion to her.

She raised her arms in a sort of transport, with the same smile of gratitude and purity, and, throwing them round my neck, she said—

"I have seen him— it is he—the man that came with you to the door and blessed us as he went away—is the same I saw in my dream—the same who took little baby in his arms, and said he would take care of him, and give him safely to me again."

More than a quarter of a century has glided away since then; other children have been given us by the good God—children who have been from infancy to maturity, a pride and blessing to us. Sorrows and reverses, too, have occasionally visited us; yet, on the whole, we have been greatly blessed; prosperity has long since ended all the cares of the *res angusta domi*, and expanded our power of doing good to our fellow creatures. God has given it; and God, we trust, directs its dispensation. In our children, and—would you think it?—our *grand*-children, too, the same beneficent God has given us objects that elicit and return all the delightful affections, and exchange the sweet converse that makes home and family dearer than aught else, save that blessed home where the Christian family shall meet at last.

The dear companion of my early love and sorrows still lives, blessed be Heaven! The evening tints of life have fallen upon her; but the dear remembrance of a first love, that never grew cold, makes her beauty changeless for me. As for your humble servant, he is considerably her senior, and looks it: time has stolen away his raven locks, and given him a *chevelure* of snow instead. But, as I said before, I and my wife love, and, I believe, *admire* one another more than ever; and I have often seen our elder children smile archly at one another, when they thought we did not observe them, thinking, no doubt, how like a pair of lovers we two were.

A CATALOG OF SELECTED
DOVER BOOKS
IN ALL FIELDS OF INTEREST

A CATALOG OF SELECTED DOVER
BOOKS IN ALL FIELDS OF INTEREST

DRAWINGS OF REMBRANDT, edited by Seymour Slive. Updated Lippmann, Hofstede de Groot edition, with definitive scholarly apparatus. All portraits, biblical sketches, landscapes, nudes. Oriental figures, classical studies, together with selection of work by followers. 550 illustrations. Total of 630pp. 9⅛ × 12¼.
21485-0, 21486-9 Pa., Two-vol. set $25.00

GHOST AND HORROR STORIES OF AMBROSE BIERCE, Ambrose Bierce. 24 tales vividly imagined, strangely prophetic, and decades ahead of their time in technical skill: "The Damned Thing," "An Inhabitant of Carcosa," "The Eyes of the Panther," "Moxon's Master," and 20 more. 199pp. 5⅜ × 8½.   20767-6 Pa. $3.95

ETHICAL WRITINGS OF MAIMONIDES, Maimonides. Most significant ethical works of great medieval sage, newly translated for utmost precision, readability. Laws Concerning Character Traits, Eight Chapters, more. 192pp. 5⅜ × 8½.
24522-5 Pa. $4.50

THE EXPLORATION OF THE COLORADO RIVER AND ITS CANYONS, J. W. Powell. Full text of Powell's 1,000-mile expedition down the fabled Colorado in 1869. Superb account of terrain, geology, vegetation, Indians, famine, mutiny, treacherous rapids, mighty canyons, during exploration of last unknown part of continental U.S. 400pp. 5⅜ × 8½.   20094-9 Pa. $6.95

HISTORY OF PHILOSOPHY, Julián Marías. Clearest one-volume history on the market. Every major philosopher and dozens of others, to Existentialism and later. 505pp. 5⅜ × 8½.   21739-6 Pa. $9.95

ALL ABOUT LIGHTNING, Martin A. Uman. Highly readable non-technical survey of nature and causes of lightning, thunderstorms, ball lightning, St. Elmo's Fire, much more. Illustrated. 192pp. 5⅜ × 8½.   25237-X Pa. $5.95

SAILING ALONE AROUND THE WORLD, Captain Joshua Slocum. First man to sail around the world, alone, in small boat. One of great feats of seamanship told in delightful manner. 67 illustrations. 294pp. 5⅜ × 8½.   20326-3 Pa. $4.95

LETTERS AND NOTES ON THE MANNERS, CUSTOMS AND CONDI-TIONS OF THE NORTH AMERICAN INDIANS, George Catlin. Classic account of life among Plains Indians: ceremonies, hunt, warfare, etc. 312 plates. 572pp. of text. 6⅛ × 9¼.   22118-0, 22119-9 Pa. Two-vol. set $15.90

ALASKA: The Harriman Expedition, 1899, John Burroughs, John Muir, et al. Informative, engrossing accounts of two-month, 9,000-mile expedition. Native peoples, wildlife, forests, geography, salmon industry, glaciers, more. Profusely illustrated. 240 black-and-white line drawings. 124 black-and-white photographs. 3 maps. Index. 576pp. 5⅜ × 8½.   25109-8 Pa. $11.95

CATALOG OF DOVER BOOKS

THE BOOK OF BEASTS: Being a Translation from a Latin Bestiary of the Twelfth Century, T. H. White. Wonderful catalog real and fanciful beasts: manticore, griffin, phoenix, amphivius, jaculus, many more. White's witty erudite commentary on scientific, historical aspects. Fascinating glimpse of medieval mind. Illustrated. 296pp. 5⅜ × 8¼. (Available in U.S. only)   24609-4 Pa. $5.95

FRANK LLOYD WRIGHT: ARCHITECTURE AND NATURE With 160 Illustrations, Donald Hoffmann. Profusely illustrated study of influence of nature—especially prairie—on Wright's designs for Fallingwater, Robie House, Guggenheim Museum, other masterpieces. 96pp. 9¼ × 10¾.   25098-9 Pa. $7.95

FRANK LLOYD WRIGHT'S FALLINGWATER, Donald Hoffmann. Wright's famous waterfall house: planning and construction of organic idea. History of site, owners, Wright's personal involvement. Photographs of various stages of building. Preface by Edgar Kaufmann, Jr. 100 illustrations. 112pp. 9¼ × 10.
23671-4 Pa. $7.95

YEARS WITH FRANK LLOYD WRIGHT: Apprentice to Genius, Edgar Tafel. Insightful memoir by a former apprentice presents a revealing portrait of Wright the man, the inspired teacher, the greatest American architect. 372 black-and-white illustrations. Preface. Index. vi + 228pp. 8¼ × 11.   24801-1 Pa. $9.95

THE STORY OF KING ARTHUR AND HIS KNIGHTS, Howard Pyle. Enchanting version of King Arthur fable has delighted generations with imaginative narratives of exciting adventures and unforgettable illustrations by the author. 41 illustrations. xviii + 313pp. 6⅛ × 9¼.   21445-1 Pa. $6.50

THE GODS OF THE EGYPTIANS, E. A. Wallis Budge. Thorough coverage of numerous gods of ancient Egypt by foremost Egyptologist. Information on evolution of cults, rites and gods; the cult of Osiris; the Book of the Dead and its rites; the sacred animals and birds; Heaven and Hell; and more. 956pp. 6⅛ × 9¼.
22055-9, 22056-7 Pa., Two-vol. set $21.90

A THEOLOGICO-POLITICAL TREATISE, Benedict Spinoza. Also contains unfinished *Political Treatise*. Great classic on religious liberty, theory of government on common consent. R. Elwes translation. Total of 421pp. 5⅜ × 8½.
20249-6 Pa. $6.95

INCIDENTS OF TRAVEL IN CENTRAL AMERICA, CHIAPAS, AND YUCATAN, John L. Stephens. Almost single-handed discovery of Maya culture; exploration of ruined cities, monuments, temples; customs of Indians. 115 drawings. 892pp. 5⅜ × 8½.   22404-X, 22405-8 Pa., Two-vol. set $15.90

LOS CAPRICHOS, Francisco Goya. 80 plates of wild, grotesque monsters and caricatures. Prado manuscript included. 183pp. 6⅜ × 9⅜.   22384-1 Pa. $4.95

AUTOBIOGRAPHY: The Story of My Experiments with Truth, Mohandas K. Gandhi. Not hagiography, but Gandhi in his own words. Boyhood, legal studies, purification, the growth of the Satyagraha (nonviolent protest) movement. Critical, inspiring work of the man who freed India. 480pp. 5⅜ × 8½. (Available in U.S. only)
24593-4 Pa. $6.95

ILLUSTRATED DICTIONARY OF HISTORIC ARCHITECTURE, edited by Cyril M. Harris. Extraordinary compendium of clear, concise definitions for over 5,000 important architectural terms complemented by over 2,000 line drawings. Covers full spectrum of architecture from ancient ruins to 20th-century Modernism. Preface. 592pp. 7½ × 9⅜. 24444-X Pa. $15.95

THE NIGHT BEFORE CHRISTMAS, Clement Moore. Full text, and woodcuts from original 1848 book. Also critical, historical material. 19 illustrations. 40pp. 4⅝ × 6. 22797-9 Pa. $2.50

THE LESSON OF JAPANESE ARCHITECTURE: 165 Photographs, Jiro Harada. Memorable gallery of 165 photographs taken in the 1930's of exquisite Japanese homes of the well-to-do and historic buildings. 13 line diagrams. 192pp. 8⅜ × 11¼. 24778-3 Pa. $8.95

THE AUTOBIOGRAPHY OF CHARLES DARWIN AND SELECTED LETTERS, edited by Francis Darwin. The fascinating life of eccentric genius composed of an intimate memoir by Darwin (intended for his children); commentary by his son, Francis; hundreds of fragments from notebooks, journals, papers; and letters to and from Lyell, Hooker, Huxley, Wallace and Henslow. xi + 365pp. 5⅜ × 8. 20479-0 Pa. $6.95

WONDERS OF THE SKY: Observing Rainbows, Comets, Eclipses, the Stars and Other Phenomena, Fred Schaaf. Charming, easy-to-read poetic guide to all manner of celestial events visible to the naked eye. Mock suns, glories, Belt of Venus, more. Illustrated. 299pp. 5¼ × 8¼. 24402-4 Pa. $7.95

BURNHAM'S CELESTIAL HANDBOOK, Robert Burnham, Jr. Thorough guide to the stars beyond our solar system. Exhaustive treatment. Alphabetical by constellation: Andromeda to Cetus in Vol. 1; Chamaeleon to Orion in Vol. 2; and Pavo to Vulpecula in Vol. 3. Hundreds of illustrations. Index in Vol. 3. 2,000pp. 6⅛ × 9¼. 23567-X, 23568-8, 23673-0 Pa., Three-vol. set $38.85

STAR NAMES: Their Lore and Meaning, Richard Hinckley Allen. Fascinating history of names various cultures have given to constellations and literary and folkloristic uses that have been made of stars. Indexes to subjects. Arabic and Greek names. Biblical references. Bibliography. 563pp. 5⅜ × 8½. 21079-0 Pa. $7.95

THIRTY YEARS THAT SHOOK PHYSICS: The Story of Quantum Theory, George Gamow. Lucid, accessible introduction to influential theory of energy and matter. Careful explanations of Dirac's anti-particles, Bohr's model of the atom, much more. 12 plates. Numerous drawings. 240pp. 5⅜ × 8½. 24895-X Pa. $5.95

CHINESE DOMESTIC FURNITURE IN PHOTOGRAPHS AND MEASURED DRAWINGS, Gustav Ecke. A rare volume, now affordably priced for antique collectors, furniture buffs and art historians. Detailed review of styles ranging from early Shang to late Ming. Unabridged republication. 161 black-and-white drawings, photos. Total of 224pp. 8⅜ × 11¼. (Available in U.S. only) 25171-3 Pa. $12.95

VINCENT VAN GOGH: A Biography, Julius Meier-Graefe. Dynamic, penetrating study of artist's life, relationship with brother, Theo, painting techniques, travels, more. Readable, engrossing. 160pp. 5⅜ × 8½. (Available in U.S. only) 25253-1 Pa. $3.95

HOW TO WRITE, Gertrude Stein. Gertrude Stein claimed anyone could understand her unconventional writing—here are clues to help. Fascinating improvisations, language experiments, explanations illuminate Stein's craft and the art of writing. Total of 414pp. 4⅝ × 6⅝. 23144-5 Pa. $5.95

ADVENTURES AT SEA IN THE GREAT AGE OF SAIL: Five Firsthand Narratives, edited by Elliot Snow. Rare true accounts of exploration, whaling, shipwreck, fierce natives, trade, shipboard life, more. 33 illustrations. Introduction. 353pp. 5⅜ × 8½. 25177-2 Pa. $7.95

THE HERBAL OR GENERAL HISTORY OF PLANTS, John Gerard. Classic descriptions of about 2,850 plants—with over 2,700 illustrations—includes Latin and English names, physical descriptions, varieties, time and place of growth, more. 2,706 illustrations. xlv + 1,678pp. 8½ × 12¼. 23147-X Cloth. $75.00

DOROTHY AND THE WIZARD IN OZ, L. Frank Baum. Dorothy and the Wizard visit the center of the Earth, where people are vegetables, glass houses grow and Oz characters reappear. Classic sequel to *Wizard of Oz*. 256pp. 5⅜ × 8. 24714-7 Pa. $4.95

SONGS OF EXPERIENCE: Facsimile Reproduction with 26 Plates in Full Color, William Blake. This facsimile of Blake's original "Illuminated Book" reproduces 26 full-color plates from a rare 1826 edition. Includes "The Tyger," "London," "Holy Thursday," and other immortal poems. 26 color plates. Printed text of poems. 48pp. 5¼ × 7. 24636-1 Pa. $3.50

SONGS OF INNOCENCE, William Blake. The first and most popular of Blake's famous "Illuminated Books," in a facsimile edition reproducing all 31 brightly colored plates. Additional printed text of each poem. 64pp. 5¼ × 7. 22764-2 Pa. $3.50

PRECIOUS STONES, Max Bauer. Classic, thorough study of diamonds, rubies, emeralds, garnets, etc.: physical character, occurrence, properties, use, similar topics. 20 plates, 8 in color. 94 figures. 659pp. 6⅛ × 9¼. 21910-0, 21911-9 Pa., Two-vol. set $15.90

ENCYCLOPEDIA OF VICTORIAN NEEDLEWORK, S. F. A. Caulfeild and Blanche Saward. Full, precise descriptions of stitches, techniques for dozens of needlecrafts—most exhaustive reference of its kind. Over 800 figures. Total of 679pp. 8⅛ × 11. Two volumes. Vol. 1 22800-2 Pa. $11.95
Vol. 2 22801-0 Pa. $11.95

THE MARVELOUS LAND OF OZ, L. Frank Baum. Second Oz book, the Scarecrow and Tin Woodman are back with hero named Tip, Oz magic. 136 illustrations. 287pp. 5⅜ × 8½. 20692-0 Pa. $5.95

WILD FOWL DECOYS, Joel Barber. Basic book on the subject, by foremost authority and collector. Reveals history of decoy making and rigging, place in American culture, different kinds of decoys, how to make them, and how to use them. 140 plates. 156pp. 7⅞ × 10¾. 20011-6 Pa. $8.95

HISTORY OF LACE, Mrs. Bury Palliser. Definitive, profusely illustrated chronicle of lace from earliest times to late 19th century. Laces of Italy, Greece, England, France, Belgium, etc. Landmark of needlework scholarship. 266 illustrations. 672pp. 6⅛ × 9¼. 24742-2 Pa. $14.95

ILLUSTRATED GUIDE TO SHAKER FURNITURE, Robert Meader. All furniture and appurtenances, with much on unknown local styles. 235 photos. 146pp. 9 × 12. 22819-3 Pa. $7.95

WHALE SHIPS AND WHALING: A Pictorial Survey, George Francis Dow. Over 200 vintage engravings, drawings, photographs of barks, brigs, cutters, other vessels. Also harpoons, lances, whaling guns, many other artifacts. Comprehensive text by foremost authority. 207 black-and-white illustrations. 288pp. 6 × 9. 24808-9 Pa. $8.95

THE BERTRAMS, Anthony Trollope. Powerful portrayal of blind self-will and thwarted ambition includes one of Trollope's most heartrending love stories. 497pp. 5⅜ × 8½. 25119-5 Pa. $9.95

ADVENTURES WITH A HAND LENS, Richard Headstrom. Clearly written guide to observing and studying flowers and grasses, fish scales, moth and insect wings, egg cases, buds, feathers, seeds, leaf scars, moss, molds, ferns, common crystals, etc.—all with an ordinary, inexpensive magnifying glass. 209 exact line drawings aid in your discoveries. 220pp. 5⅜ × 8½. 23330-8 Pa. $4.95

RODIN ON ART AND ARTISTS, Auguste Rodin. Great sculptor's candid, wide-ranging comments on meaning of art; great artists; relation of sculpture to poetry, painting, music; philosophy of life, more. 76 superb black-and-white illustrations of Rodin's sculpture, drawings and prints. 119pp. 8⅜ × 11¼. 24487-3 Pa. $6.95

FIFTY CLASSIC FRENCH FILMS, 1912–1982: A Pictorial Record, Anthony Slide. Memorable stills from Grand Illusion, Beauty and the Beast, Hiroshima, Mon Amour, many more. Credits, plot synopses, reviews, etc. 160pp. 8¼ × 11. 25256-6 Pa. $11.95

THE PRINCIPLES OF PSYCHOLOGY, William James. Famous long course complete, unabridged. Stream of thought, time perception, memory, experimental methods; great work decades ahead of its time. 94 figures. 1,391pp. 5⅜ × 8½. 20381-6, 20382-4 Pa., Two-vol. set $23.90

BODIES IN A BOOKSHOP, R. T. Campbell. Challenging mystery of blackmail and murder with ingenious plot and superbly drawn characters. In the best tradition of British suspense fiction. 192pp. 5⅜ × 8½. 24720-1 Pa. $3.95

CALLAS: PORTRAIT OF A PRIMA DONNA, George Jellinek. Renowned commentator on the musical scene chronicles incredible career and life of the most controversial, fascinating, influential operatic personality of our time. 64 black-and-white photographs. 416pp. 5⅜ × 8¼. 25047-4 Pa. $8.95

GEOMETRY, RELATIVITY AND THE FOURTH DIMENSION, Rudolph Rucker. Exposition of fourth dimension, concepts of relativity as Flatland characters continue adventures. Popular, easily followed yet accurate, profound. 141 illustrations. 133pp. 5⅜ × 8½. 23400-2 Pa. $3.95

HOUSEHOLD STORIES BY THE BROTHERS GRIMM, with pictures by Walter Crane. 53 classic stories—Rumpelstiltskin, Rapunzel, Hansel and Gretel, the Fisherman and his Wife, Snow White, Tom Thumb, Sleeping Beauty, Cinderella, and so much more—lavishly illustrated with original 19th century drawings. 114 illustrations. x + 269pp. 5⅜ × 8½. 21080-4 Pa. $4.95

SUNDIALS, Albert Waugh. Far and away the best, most thorough coverage of ideas, mathematics concerned, types, construction, adjusting anywhere. Over 100 illustrations. 230pp. 5⅜ × 8½. 22947-5 Pa. $4.95

PICTURE HISTORY OF THE NORMANDIE: With 190 Illustrations, Frank O. Braynard. Full story of legendary French ocean liner: Art Deco interiors, design innovations, furnishings, celebrities, maiden voyage, tragic fire, much more. Extensive text. 144pp. 8⅞ × 11¾. 25257-4 Pa. $9.95

THE FIRST AMERICAN COOKBOOK: A Facsimile of "American Cookery," 1796, Amelia Simmons. Facsimile of the first American-written cookbook published in the United States contains authentic recipes for colonial favorites—pumpkin pudding, winter squash pudding, spruce beer, Indian slapjacks, and more. Introductory Essay and Glossary of colonial cooking terms. 80pp. 5⅜ × 8½. 24710-4 Pa. $3.50

101 PUZZLES IN THOUGHT AND LOGIC, C. R. Wylie, Jr. Solve murders and robberies, find out which fishermen are liars, how a blind man could possibly identify a color—purely by your own reasoning! 107pp. 5⅜ × 8½. 20367-0 Pa. $2.50

THE BOOK OF WORLD-FAMOUS MUSIC—CLASSICAL, POPULAR AND FOLK, James J. Fuld. Revised and enlarged republication of landmark work in musico-bibliography. Full information about nearly 1,000 songs and compositions including first lines of music and lyrics. New supplement. Index. 800pp. 5⅜ × 8¼. 24857-7 Pa. $14.95

ANTHROPOLOGY AND MODERN LIFE, Franz Boas. Great anthropologist's classic treatise on race and culture. Introduction by Ruth Bunzel. Only inexpensive paperback edition. 255pp. 5⅜ × 8½. 25245-0 Pa. $5.95

THE TALE OF PETER RABBIT, Beatrix Potter. The inimitable Peter's terrifying adventure in Mr. McGregor's garden, with all 27 wonderful, full-color Potter illustrations. 55pp. 4¼ × 5½. (Available in U.S. only) 22827-4 Pa. $1.75

THREE PROPHETIC SCIENCE FICTION NOVELS, H. G. Wells. *When the Sleeper Wakes, A Story of the Days to Come* and *The Time Machine* (full version). 335pp. 5⅜ × 8½. (Available in U.S. only) 20605-X Pa. $6.95

APICIUS COOKERY AND DINING IN IMPERIAL ROME, edited and translated by Joseph Dommers Vehling. Oldest known cookbook in existence offers readers a clear picture of what foods Romans ate, how they prepared them, etc. 49 illustrations. 301pp. 6⅛ × 9¼. 23563-7 Pa. $7.95

SHAKESPEARE LEXICON AND QUOTATION DICTIONARY, Alexander Schmidt. Full definitions, locations, shades of meaning of every word in plays and poems. More than 50,000 exact quotations. 1,485pp. 6½ × 9¼. 22726-X, 22727-8 Pa., Two-vol. set $29.90

THE WORLD'S GREAT SPEECHES, edited by Lewis Copeland and Lawrence W. Lamm. Vast collection of 278 speeches from Greeks to 1970. Powerful and effective models; unique look at history. 842pp. 5⅜ × 8½. 20468-5 Pa. $11.95

THE BLUE FAIRY BOOK, Andrew Lang. The first, most famous collection, with many familiar tales: Little Red Riding Hood, Aladdin and the Wonderful Lamp, Puss in Boots, Sleeping Beauty, Hansel and Gretel, Rumpelstiltskin; 37 in all. 138 illustrations. 390pp. 5⅜ × 8½. 21437-0 Pa. $6.95

THE STORY OF THE CHAMPIONS OF THE ROUND TABLE, Howard Pyle. Sir Launcelot, Sir Tristram and Sir Percival in spirited adventures of love and triumph retold in Pyle's inimitable style. 50 drawings, 31 full-page. xviii + 329pp. 6½ × 9¼. 21883-X Pa. $6.95

AUDUBON AND HIS JOURNALS, Maria Audubon. Unmatched two-volume portrait of the great artist, naturalist and author contains his journals, an excellent biography by his granddaughter, expert annotations by the noted ornithologist, Dr. Elliott Coues, and 37 superb illustrations. Total of 1,200pp. 5⅜ × 8.
Vol. I 25143-8 Pa. $8.95
Vol. II 25144-6 Pa. $8.95

GREAT DINOSAUR HUNTERS AND THEIR DISCOVERIES, Edwin H. Colbert. Fascinating, lavishly illustrated chronicle of dinosaur research, 1820's to 1960. Achievements of Cope, Marsh, Brown, Buckland, Mantell, Huxley, many others. 384pp. 5¼ × 8¼. 24701-5 Pa. $7.95

THE TASTEMAKERS, Russell Lynes. Informal, illustrated social history of American taste 1850's–1950's. First popularized categories Highbrow, Lowbrow, Middlebrow. 129 illustrations. New (1979) afterword. 384pp. 6 × 9.
23993-4 Pa. $8.95

DOUBLE CROSS PURPOSES, Ronald A. Knox. A treasure hunt in the Scottish Highlands, an old map, unidentified corpse, surprise discoveries keep reader guessing in this cleverly intricate tale of financial skullduggery. 2 black-and-white maps. 320pp. 5⅜ × 8½. (Available in U.S. only) 25032-6 Pa. $5.95

AUTHENTIC VICTORIAN DECORATION AND ORNAMENTATION IN FULL COLOR: 46 Plates from "Studies in Design," Christopher Dresser. Superb full-color lithographs reproduced from rare original portfolio of a major Victorian designer. 48pp. 9¼ × 12¼. 25083-0 Pa. $7.95

PRIMITIVE ART, Franz Boas. Remains the best text ever prepared on subject, thoroughly discussing Indian, African, Asian, Australian, and, especially, Northern American primitive art. Over 950 illustrations show ceramics, masks, totem poles, weapons, textiles, paintings, much more. 376pp. 5⅜ × 8. 20025-6 Pa. $6.95

SIDELIGHTS ON RELATIVITY, Albert Einstein. Unabridged republication of two lectures delivered by the great physicist in 1920–21. *Ether and Relativity* and *Geometry and Experience.* Elegant ideas in non-mathematical form, accessible to intelligent layman. vi + 56pp. 5⅜ × 8½. 24511-X Pa. $2.95

THE WIT AND HUMOR OF OSCAR WILDE, edited by Alvin Redman. More than 1,000 ripostes, paradoxes, wisecracks: Work is the curse of the drinking classes, I can resist everything except temptation, etc. 258pp. 5⅜ × 8½. 20602-5 Pa. $4.50

ADVENTURES WITH A MICROSCOPE, Richard Headstrom. 59 adventures with clothing fibers, protozoa, ferns and lichens, roots and leaves, much more. 142 illustrations. 232pp. 5⅜ × 8½. 23471-1 Pa. $3.95

PLANTS OF THE BIBLE, Harold N. Moldenke and Alma L. Moldenke. Standard reference to all 230 plants mentioned in Scriptures. Latin name, biblical reference, uses, modern identity, much more. Unsurpassed encyclopedic resource for scholars, botanists, nature lovers, students of Bible. Bibliography. Indexes. 123 black-and-white illustrations. 384pp. 6 × 9. 25069-5 Pa. $8.95

FAMOUS AMERICAN WOMEN: A Biographical Dictionary from Colonial Times to the Present, Robert McHenry, ed. From Pocahontas to Rosa Parks, 1,035 distinguished American women documented in separate biographical entries. Accurate, up-to-date data, numerous categories, spans 400 years. Indices. 493pp. 6½ × 9¼. 24523-3 Pa. $9.95

THE FABULOUS INTERIORS OF THE GREAT OCEAN LINERS IN HISTORIC PHOTOGRAPHS, William H. Miller, Jr. Some 200 superb photographs capture exquisite interiors of world's great "floating palaces"—1890's to 1980's: *Titanic, Ile de France, Queen Elizabeth, United States, Europa,* more. Approx. 200 black-and-white photographs. Captions. Text. Introduction. 160pp. 8⅞ × 11¾. 24756-2 Pa. $9.95

THE GREAT LUXURY LINERS, 1927–1954: A Photographic Record, William H. Miller, Jr. Nostalgic tribute to heyday of ocean liners. 186 photos of Ile de France, Normandie, Leviathan, Queen Elizabeth, United States, many others. Interior and exterior views. Introduction. Captions. 160pp. 9 × 12. 24056-8 Pa. $10.95

A NATURAL HISTORY OF THE DUCKS, John Charles Phillips. Great landmark of ornithology offers complete detailed coverage of nearly 200 species and subspecies of ducks: gadwall, sheldrake, merganser, pintail, many more. 74 full-color plates, 102 black-and-white. Bibliography. Total of 1,920pp. 8⅝ × 11¼. 25141-1, 25142-X Cloth. Two-vol. set $100.00

THE SEAWEED HANDBOOK: An Illustrated Guide to Seaweeds from North Carolina to Canada, Thomas F. Lee. Concise reference covers 78 species. Scientific and common names, habitat, distribution, more. Finding keys for easy identification. 224pp. 5⅜ × 8½. 25215-9 Pa. $5.95

THE TEN BOOKS OF ARCHITECTURE: The 1755 Leoni Edition, Leon Battista Alberti. Rare classic helped introduce the glories of ancient architecture to the Renaissance. 68 black-and-white plates. 336pp. 8⅜ × 11¼. 25239-6 Pa. $14.95

MISS MACKENZIE, Anthony Trollope. Minor masterpieces by Victorian master unmasks many truths about life in 19th-century England. First inexpensive edition in years. 392pp. 5⅜ × 8½. 25201-9 Pa. $7.95

THE RIME OF THE ANCIENT MARINER, Gustave Doré, Samuel Taylor Coleridge. Dramatic engravings considered by many to be his greatest work. The terrifying space of the open sea, the storms and whirlpools of an unknown ocean, the ice of Antarctica, more—all rendered in a powerful, chilling manner. Full text. 38 plates. 77pp. 9¼ × 12. 22305-1 Pa. $4.95

THE EXPEDITIONS OF ZEBULON MONTGOMERY PIKE, Zebulon Montgomery Pike. Fascinating first-hand accounts (1805–6) of exploration of Mississippi River, Indian wars, capture by Spanish dragoons, much more. 1,088pp. 5⅜ × 8½. 25254-X, 25255-8 Pa. Two-vol. set $23.90

A CONCISE HISTORY OF PHOTOGRAPHY: Third Revised Edition, Helmut Gernsheim. Best one-volume history—camera obscura, photochemistry, daguerreotypes, evolution of cameras, film, more. Also artistic aspects—landscape, portraits, fine art, etc. 281 black-and-white photographs. 26 in color. 176pp. 8⅜ × 11¼. 25128-4 Pa. $13.95

THE DORÉ BIBLE ILLUSTRATIONS, Gustave Doré. 241 detailed plates from the Bible: the Creation scenes, Adam and Eve, Flood, Babylon, battle sequences, life of Jesus, etc. Each plate is accompanied by the verses from the King James version of the Bible. 241pp. 9 × 12. 23004-X Pa. $8.95

HUGGER-MUGGER IN THE LOUVRE, Elliot Paul. Second Homer Evans mystery-comedy. Theft at the Louvre involves sleuth in hilarious, madcap caper. "A knockout."—Books. 336pp. 5⅜ × 8½. 25185-3 Pa. $5.95

FLATLAND, E. A. Abbott. Intriguing and enormously popular science-fiction classic explores the complexities of trying to survive as a two-dimensional being in a three-dimensional world. Amusingly illustrated by the author. 16 illustrations. 103pp. 5⅜ × 8½. 20001-9 Pa. $2.25

THE HISTORY OF THE LEWIS AND CLARK EXPEDITION, Meriwether Lewis and William Clark, edited by Elliott Coues. Classic edition of Lewis and Clark's day-by-day journals that later became the basis for U.S. claims to Oregon and the West. Accurate and invaluable geographical, botanical, biological, meteorological and anthropological material. Total of 1,508pp. 5⅜ × 8½. 21268-8, 21269-6, 21270-X Pa. Three-vol. set $26.85

LANGUAGE, TRUTH AND LOGIC, Alfred J. Ayer. Famous, clear introduction to Vienna, Cambridge schools of Logical Positivism. Role of philosophy, elimination of metaphysics, nature of analysis, etc. 160pp. 5⅜ × 8½. (Available in U.S. and Canada only) 20010-8 Pa. $2.95

MATHEMATICS FOR THE NONMATHEMATICIAN, Morris Kline. Detailed, college-level treatment of mathematics in cultural and historical context, with numerous exercises. For liberal arts students. Preface. Recommended Reading Lists. Tables. Index. Numerous black-and-white figures. xvi + 641pp. 5⅜ × 8½. 24823-2 Pa. $11.95

28 SCIENCE FICTION STORIES, H. G. Wells. Novels, *Star Begotten* and *Men Like Gods,* plus 26 short stories: "Empire of the Ants," "A Story of the Stone Age," "The Stolen Bacillus," "In the Abyss," etc. 915pp. 5⅜ × 8½. (Available in U.S. only) 20265-8 Cloth. $10.95

HANDBOOK OF PICTORIAL SYMBOLS, Rudolph Modley. 3,250 signs and symbols, many systems in full; official or heavy commercial use. Arranged by subject. Most in Pictorial Archive series. 143pp. 8⅛ × 11. 23357-X Pa. $6.95

INCIDENTS OF TRAVEL IN YUCATAN, John L. Stephens. Classic (1843) exploration of jungles of Yucatan, looking for evidences of Maya civilization. Travel adventures, Mexican and Indian culture, etc. Total of 669pp. 5⅜ × 8½. 20926-1, 20927-X Pa., Two-vol. set $9.90

DEGAS: An Intimate Portrait, Ambroise Vollard. Charming, anecdotal memoir by famous art dealer of one of the greatest 19th-century French painters. 14 black-and-white illustrations. Introduction by Harold L. Van Doren. 96pp. 5⅜ × 8½.
25131-4 Pa. $3.95

PERSONAL NARRATIVE OF A PILGRIMAGE TO ALMANDINAH AND MECCAH, Richard Burton. Great travel classic by remarkably colorful personality. Burton, disguised as a Moroccan, visited sacred shrines of Islam, narrowly escaping death. 47 illustrations. 959pp. 5⅜ × 8½.   21217-3, 21218-1 Pa., Two-vol. set $19.90

PHRASE AND WORD ORIGINS, A. H. Holt. Entertaining, reliable, modern study of more than 1,200 colorful words, phrases, origins and histories. Much unexpected information. 254pp. 5⅜ × 8½.   20758-7 Pa. $5.95

THE RED THUMB MARK, R. Austin Freeman. In this first Dr. Thorndyke case, the great scientific detective draws fascinating conclusions from the nature of a single fingerprint. Exciting story, authentic science. 320pp. 5⅜ × 8½. (Available in U.S. only)   25210-8 Pa. $5.95

AN EGYPTIAN HIEROGLYPHIC DICTIONARY, E. A. Wallis Budge. Monumental work containing about 25,000 words or terms that occur in texts ranging from 3000 B.C. to 600 A.D. Each entry consists of a transliteration of the word, the word in hieroglyphs, and the meaning in English. 1,314pp. 6⅜ × 10.
23615-3, 23616-1 Pa., Two-vol. set $31.90

THE COMPLEAT STRATEGYST: Being a Primer on the Theory of Games of Strategy, J. D. Williams. Highly entertaining classic describes, with many illustrated examples, how to select best strategies in conflict situations. Prefaces. Appendices. xvi + 268pp. 5⅜ × 8½.   25101-2 Pa. $5.95

THE ROAD TO OZ, L. Frank Baum. Dorothy meets the Shaggy Man, little Button-Bright and the Rainbow's beautiful daughter in this delightful trip to the magical Land of Oz. 272pp. 5⅜ × 8.   25208-6 Pa. $4.95

POINT AND LINE TO PLANE, Wassily Kandinsky. Seminal exposition of role of point, line, other elements in non-objective painting. Essential to understanding 20th-century art. 127 illustrations. 192pp. 6½ × 9¼.   23808-3 Pa. $4.95

LADY ANNA, Anthony Trollope. Moving chronicle of Countess Lovel's bitter struggle to win for herself and daughter Anna their rightful rank and fortune— perhaps at cost of sanity itself. 384pp. 5⅜ × 8½.   24669-8 Pa. $8.95

EGYPTIAN MAGIC, E. A. Wallis Budge. Sums up all that is known about magic in Ancient Egypt: the role of magic in controlling the gods, powerful amulets that warded off evil spirits, scarabs of immortality, use of wax images, formulas and spells, the secret name, much more. 253pp. 5⅜ × 8½.   22681-6 Pa. $4.50

THE DANCE OF SIVA, Ananda Coomaraswamy. Preeminent authority unfolds the vast metaphysic of India: the revelation of her art, conception of the universe, social organization, etc. 27 reproductions of art masterpieces. 192pp. 5⅜ × 8½.
24817-8 Pa. $5.95

CATALOG OF DOVER BOOKS

CHRISTMAS CUSTOMS AND TRADITIONS, Clement A. Miles. Origin, evolution, significance of religious, secular practices. Caroling, gifts, yule logs, much more. Full, scholarly yet fascinating; non-sectarian. 400pp. 5⅜ × 8½.
23354-5 Pa. $6.50

THE HUMAN FIGURE IN MOTION, Eadweard Muybridge. More than 4,500 stopped-action photos, in action series, showing undraped men, women, children jumping, lying down, throwing, sitting, wrestling, carrying, etc. 390pp. 7⅞ × 10⅝.
20204-6 Cloth. $21.95

THE MAN WHO WAS THURSDAY, Gilbert Keith Chesterton. Witty, fast-paced novel about a club of anarchists in turn-of-the-century London. Brilliant social, religious, philosophical speculations. 128pp. 5⅜ × 8½. 25121-7 Pa. $3.95

A CEZANNE SKETCHBOOK: Figures, Portraits, Landscapes and Still Lifes, Paul Cezanne. Great artist experiments with tonal effects, light, mass, other qualities in over 100 drawings. A revealing view of developing master painter, precursor of Cubism. 102 black-and-white illustrations. 144pp. 8¾ × 6⅜. 24790-2 Pa. $5.95

AN ENCYCLOPEDIA OF BATTLES: Accounts of Over 1,560 Battles from 1479 B.C. to the Present, David Eggenberger. Presents essential details of every major battle in recorded history, from the first battle of Megiddo in 1479 B.C. to Grenada in 1984. List of Battle Maps. New Appendix covering the years 1967–1984. Index. 99 illustrations. 544pp. 6½ × 9¼. 24913-1 Pa. $14.95

AN ETYMOLOGICAL DICTIONARY OF MODERN ENGLISH, Ernest Weekley. Richest, fullest work, by foremost British lexicographer. Detailed word histories. Inexhaustible. Total of 856pp. 6½ × 9¼.
21873-2, 21874-0 Pa., Two-vol. set $17.00

WEBSTER'S AMERICAN MILITARY BIOGRAPHIES, edited by Robert McHenry. Over 1,000 figures who shaped 3 centuries of American military history. Detailed biographies of Nathan Hale, Douglas MacArthur, Mary Hallaren, others. Chronologies of engagements, more. Introduction. Addenda. 1,033 entries in alphabetical order. xi + 548pp. 6½ × 9¼. (Available in U.S. only)
24758-9 Pa. $11.95

LIFE IN ANCIENT EGYPT, Adolf Erman. Detailed older account, with much not in more recent books: domestic life, religion, magic, medicine, commerce, and whatever else needed for complete picture. Many illustrations. 597pp. 5⅜ × 8½.
22632-8 Pa. $8.95

HISTORIC COSTUME IN PICTURES, Braun & Schneider. Over 1,450 costumed figures shown, covering a wide variety of peoples: kings, emperors, nobles, priests, servants, soldiers, scholars, townsfolk, peasants, merchants, courtiers, cavaliers, and more. 256pp. 8⅜ × 11¼. 23150-X Pa. $8.95

THE NOTEBOOKS OF LEONARDO DA VINCI, edited by J. P. Richter. Extracts from manuscripts reveal great genius; on painting, sculpture, anatomy, sciences, geography, etc. Both Italian and English. 186 ms. pages reproduced, plus 500 additional drawings, including studies for *Last Supper, Sforza* monument, etc. 860pp. 7⅞ × 10¾. (Available in U.S. only) 22572-0, 22573-9 Pa., Two-vol. set $29.90

THE ART NOUVEAU STYLE BOOK OF ALPHONSE MUCHA: All 72 Plates from "Documents Decoratifs" in Original Color, Alphonse Mucha. Rare copy-right-free design portfolio by high priest of Art Nouveau. Jewelry, wallpaper, stained glass, furniture, figure studies, plant and animal motifs, etc. Only complete one-volume edition. 80pp. 9⅜ × 12¼. 24044-4 Pa. $8.95

ANIMALS: 1,419 COPYRIGHT-FREE ILLUSTRATIONS OF MAMMALS, BIRDS, FISH, INSECTS, ETC., edited by Jim Harter. Clear wood engravings present, in extremely lifelike poses, over 1,000 species of animals. One of the most extensive pictorial sourcebooks of its kind. Captions. Index. 284pp. 9 × 12.
23766-4 Pa. $9.95

OBELISTS FLY HIGH, C. Daly King. Masterpiece of American detective fiction, long out of print, involves murder on a 1935 transcontinental flight—"a very thrilling story"—NY Times. Unabridged and unaltered republication of the edition published by William Collins Sons & Co. Ltd., London, 1935. 288pp. 5⅜ × 8½. (Available in U.S. only) 25036-9 Pa. $4.95

VICTORIAN AND EDWARDIAN FASHION: A Photographic Survey, Alison Gernsheim. First fashion history completely illustrated by contemporary photographs. Full text plus 235 photos, 1840–1914, in which many celebrities appear. 240pp. 6½ × 9¼. 24205-6 Pa. $6.95

THE ART OF THE FRENCH ILLUSTRATED BOOK, 1700–1914, Gordon N. Ray. Over 630 superb book illustrations by Fragonard, Delacroix, Daumier, Doré, Grandville, Manet, Mucha, Steinlen, Toulouse-Lautrec and many others. Preface. Introduction. 633 halftones. Indices of artists, authors & titles, binders and provenances. Appendices. Bibliography. 608pp. 8⅜ × 11¼. 25086-5 Pa. $24.95

THE WONDERFUL WIZARD OF OZ, L. Frank Baum. Facsimile in full color of America's finest children's classic. 143 illustrations by W. W. Denslow. 267pp. 5⅜ × 8½. 20691-2 Pa. $5.95

FRONTIERS OF MODERN PHYSICS: New Perspectives on Cosmology, Relativity, Black Holes and Extraterrestrial Intelligence, Tony Rothman, et al. For the intelligent layman. Subjects include: cosmological models of the universe; black holes; the neutrino; the search for extraterrestrial intelligence. Introduction. 46 black-and-white illustrations. 192pp. 5⅜ × 8½. 24587-X Pa. $6.95

THE FRIENDLY STARS, Martha Evans Martin & Donald Howard Menzel. Classic text marshals the stars together in an engaging, non-technical survey, presenting them as sources of beauty in night sky. 23 illustrations. Foreword. 2 star charts. Index. 147pp. 5⅜ × 8½. 21099-5 Pa. $3.50

FADS AND FALLACIES IN THE NAME OF SCIENCE, Martin Gardner. Fair, witty appraisal of cranks, quacks, and quackeries of science and pseudoscience: hollow earth, Velikovsky, orgone energy, Dianetics, flying saucers, Bridey Murphy, food and medical fads, etc. Revised, expanded In the Name of Science. "A very able and even-tempered presentation."—The New Yorker. 363pp. 5⅜ × 8.
20394-8 Pa. $6.50

ANCIENT EGYPT: ITS CULTURE AND HISTORY, J. E Manchip White. From pre-dynastics through Ptolemies: society, history, political structure, religion, daily life, literature, cultural heritage. 48 plates. 217pp. 5⅜ × 8½. 22548-8 Pa. $5.95

SIR HARRY HOTSPUR OF HUMBLETHWAITE, Anthony Trollope. Incisive, unconventional psychological study of a conflict between a wealthy baronet, his idealistic daughter, and their scapegrace cousin. The 1870 novel in its first inexpensive edition in years. 250pp. 5⅜ × 8½. 24953-0 Pa. $5.95

LASERS AND HOLOGRAPHY, Winston E. Kock. Sound introduction to burgeoning field, expanded (1981) for second edition. Wave patterns, coherence, lasers, diffraction, zone plates, properties of holograms, recent advances. 84 illustrations. 160pp. 5⅜ × 8¼. (Except in United Kingdom) 24041-X Pa. $3.50

INTRODUCTION TO ARTIFICIAL INTELLIGENCE: SECOND, EN-LARGED EDITION, Philip C. Jackson, Jr. Comprehensive survey of artificial intelligence—the study of how machines (computers) can be made to act intelligently. Includes introductory and advanced material. Extensive notes updating the main text. 132 black-and-white illustrations. 512pp. 5⅜ × 8½. 24864-X Pa. $8.95

HISTORY OF INDIAN AND INDONESIAN ART, Ananda K. Coomaraswamy. Over 400 illustrations illuminate classic study of Indian art from earliest Harappa finds to early 20th century. Provides philosophical, religious and social insights. 304pp. 6⅜ × 9⅜. 25005-9 Pa. $8.95

THE GOLEM, Gustav Meyrink. Most famous supernatural novel in modern European literature, set in Ghetto of Old Prague around 1890. Compelling story of mystical experiences, strange transformations, profound terror. 13 black-and-white illustrations. 224pp. 5⅜ × 8½. (Available in U.S. only) 25025-3 Pa. $6.95

ARMADALE, Wilkie Collins. Third great mystery novel by the author of *The Woman in White* and *The Moonstone*. Original magazine version with 40 illustrations. 597pp. 5⅜ × 8½. 23429-0 Pa. $9.95

PICTORIAL ENCYCLOPEDIA OF HISTORIC ARCHITECTURAL PLANS, DETAILS AND ELEMENTS: With 1,880 Line Drawings of Arches, Domes, Doorways, Facades, Gables, Windows, etc., John Theodore Haneman. Sourcebook of inspiration for architects, designers, others. Bibliography. Captions. 141pp. 9 × 12. 24605-1 Pa. $6.95

BENCHLEY LOST AND FOUND, Robert Benchley. Finest humor from early 30's, about pet peeves, child psychologists, post office and others. Mostly unavailable elsewhere. 73 illustrations by Peter Arno and others. 183pp. 5⅜ × 8½. 22410-4 Pa. $3.95

ERTÉ GRAPHICS, Erté. Collection of striking color graphics: *Seasons, Alphabet, Numerals, Aces* and *Precious Stones*. 50 plates, including 4 on covers. 48pp. 9⅜ × 12¼. 23580-7 Pa. $6.95

THE JOURNAL OF HENRY D. THOREAU, edited by Bradford Torrey, F. H. Allen. Complete reprinting of 14 volumes, 1837–61, over two million words; the sourcebooks for *Walden*, etc. Definitive. All original sketches, plus 75 photographs. 1,804pp. 8½ × 12¼. 20312-3, 20313-1 Cloth., Two-vol. set $80.00

CASTLES: THEIR CONSTRUCTION AND HISTORY, Sidney Toy. Traces castle development from ancient roots. Nearly 200 photographs and drawings illustrate moats, keeps, baileys, many other features. Caernarvon, Dover Castles, Hadrian's Wall, Tower of London, dozens more. 256pp. 5⅜ × 8¼. 24898-4 Pa. $5.95

CATALOG OF DOVER BOOKS

AMERICAN CLIPPER SHIPS: 1833–1858, Octavius T. Howe & Frederick C. Matthews. Fully-illustrated, encyclopedic review of 352 clipper ships from the period of America's greatest maritime supremacy. Introduction. 109 halftones. 5 black-and-white line illustrations. Index. Total of 928pp. 5⅜ × 8½.
25115-2, 25116-0 Pa., Two-vol. set $17.90

TOWARDS A NEW ARCHITECTURE, Le Corbusier. Pioneering manifesto by great architect, near legendary founder of "International School." Technical and aesthetic theories, views on industry, economics, relation of form to function, "mass-production spirit," much more. Profusely illustrated. Unabridged translation of 13th French edition. Introduction by Frederick Etchells. 320pp. 6⅛ × 9¼. (Available in U.S. only)
25023-7 Pa. $8.95

THE BOOK OF KELLS, edited by Blanche Cirker. Inexpensive collection of 32 full-color, full-page plates from the greatest illuminated manuscript of the Middle Ages, painstakingly reproduced from rare facsimile edition. Publisher's Note. Captions. 32pp. 9⅜ × 12¼.
24345-1 Pa. $4.95

BEST SCIENCE FICTION STORIES OF H. G. WELLS, H. G. Wells. Full novel *The Invisible Man,* plus 17 short stories: "The Crystal Egg," "Aepyornis Island," "The Strange Orchid," etc. 303pp. 5⅜ × 8½. (Available in U.S. only)
21531-8 Pa. $6.95

AMERICAN SAILING SHIPS: Their Plans and History, Charles G. Davis. Photos, construction details of schooners, frigates, clippers, other sailcraft of 18th to early 20th centuries—plus entertaining discourse on design, rigging, nautical lore, much more. 137 black-and-white illustrations. 240pp. 6⅛ × 9¼.
24658-2 Pa. $6.95

ENTERTAINING MATHEMATICAL PUZZLES, Martin Gardner. Selection of author's favorite conundrums involving arithmetic, money, speed, etc., with lively commentary. Complete solutions. 112pp. 5⅜ × 8½. 25211-6 Pa. $2.95

THE WILL TO BELIEVE, HUMAN IMMORTALITY, William James. Two books bound together. Effect of irrational on logical, and arguments for human immortality. 402pp. 5⅜ × 8½. 20291-7 Pa. $7.50

THE HAUNTED MONASTERY and THE CHINESE MAZE MURDERS, Robert Van Gulik. 2 full novels by Van Gulik continue adventures of Judge Dee and his companions. An evil Taoist monastery, seemingly supernatural events; overgrown topiary maze that hides strange crimes. Set in 7th-century China. 27 illustrations. 328pp. 5⅜ × 8½. 23502-5 Pa. $5.95

CELEBRATED CASES OF JUDGE DEE (DEE GOONG AN), translated by Robert Van Gulik. Authentic 18th-century Chinese detective novel; Dee and associates solve three interlocked cases. Led to Van Gulik's own stories with same characters. Extensive introduction. 9 illustrations. 237pp. 5⅜ × 8½.
23337-5 Pa. $4.95

Prices subject to change without notice.
Available at your book dealer or write for free catalog to Dept. GI, Dover Publications, Inc., 31 East 2nd St., Mineola, N.Y. 11501. Dover publishes more than 175 books each year on science, elementary and advanced mathematics, biology, music, art, literary history, social sciences and other areas.